Madge Swindel_____
land. As a teenag_____
where she studied archaeology and anthropology at
Cape Town University. Later, in England, she was
a Fleet Street journalist and the manager of her
own publishing company. Her earlier novels, *Summer
Harvest*, *Song of the Wind*, *Shadows on the Snow*,
The Corsican Woman and *Edelweiss* were international
bestsellers and have been translated into eight languages. Her most recent novel, *Harvesting the Past*, is
now available as a Little, Brown hardback. Madge
Swindells lives in South Africa.

MADGE SWINDELLS

The Sentinel

WARNER BOOKS

A *Warner* Book

First published in Great Britain in 1994
by Little, Brown and Company
This edition published by Warner Books in 1995

Copyright © Madge Swindells 1994

The moral right of the author has been asserted.

*All characters in this publication are fictitious
and any resemblance to real persons, living or dead,
is purely coincidental.*

A CIP catalogue record for this book
is available from the British Library.

ISBN 0 7515 1355 5

Printed in England by Clays Ltd, St Ives plc

Warner Books
A Division of
Little, Brown and Company (UK)
Brettenham House
Lancaster Place
London WC2E 7EN

To Peter de Beer

with love.

'But suppose a man deliberately murders his enemy in cold blood and then escapes ... the leaders of his own town are to send for him and hand him over ... so that he may be put to death. Show him no mercy. Rid Israel of this murderer, so that all will go well with you.'

Deuteronomy 19, 11–13

'For when a person dies, he is set free from the power of sin ... For sin pays its wage – death.'

Romans 6, 7 & 23

With thanks to Jenni Swindells and Peter de Beer for their immense editorial help and creative *'plotting'*. I would also like to thank Willem Steenkamp and Ivan Sokolsky for research assistance. I am indebted to Toivo Herman Ja Toivo whose brilliant and moving speech at his trial on September 25, 1968, provided me with much inspiration.

PART I

September 1982–December 1985

Chapter 1

She was barely into her teens, but under the hot African sun she had blossomed early and now, like the flame lilies that grew in red and yellow profusion over the bushveld, she was bursting into loveliness and lusting after life. Passionate and shy, she quivered at the force of her erotic longings, flushing often, as if for no reason, trying to conceal her hopes and dreams.

She leaned over the well, staring down at the water, but seeing Pieter. Remembering the way he had looked at her, she thrilled with joy and her hair shivered and shook over her shoulders like a caress, while goose pimples prickled.

'So strange,' she whispered. Lately, she saw a new intentness in his eyes. Sometimes she caught him staring at her breasts or her thighs and then he would flush and laugh, as he had this morning. 'You're really pretty, Liza,' he had said, his eyes shimmering with pride and lust.

He was the best – this man-boy of hers ... the best shot, the best hunter, the strongest, the bravest, and he was clever, too, but a rebel ... always in trouble at school. The girls hung around him like crazy even though he was poor, because of his size and his strength and his black curly hair, his green eyes and his sense of fun.

Liza's daydreams were interrupted by the donkeys who were thirsty, the poor things, restlessly jostling and pushing and watching her progress intently. Feeling guilty she heaved at the handle that wound up the heavy bucket swinging far below at the end of the chain. Oh, what a boring job. The wood chafed her palms and her arms ached. A cloud of tormenting flies appeared from nowhere and the sweat trickled into her eyes and stung madly. It took exactly thirty-five handle-turns to bring the heavy bucket swaying to the surface. Seven to go. Would it never end? If only Pieter were here to help her.

'Thirty-one, thirty-two,' she muttered. Peering over the edge, she strained into the darkness. The water was too far down. It had not rained for eight months and she knew that Gran was worried half to death in case the spring dried up. This precious water was their lifeline and they never wasted a drop. Its source was an underground river, draining the rocky hills on the de Vries' barren hectares adjoining their own farm, and flowing into the nearby Komati River.

She looked up, narrowing her eyes against the glare, searching for a cloud, but the sky was a merciless blue, for it was springtime, September, and there was little chance of rain for another month at least. Around lay the evidence of the long dry winter and last summer's semi-drought. The soil was crusted yellow, the grass almost translucent and the veld smelling strongly of toasted wild herbs. The pampas had turned brown and the apple mint that grew in a tangle by the door had wilted to a miserable heap. Gran's farm, measuring a mere twenty morgen, was situated on South Africa's borders. Beyond was a narrow strip of land forming part of the KaNgwane Homeland and four miles further east lay the Lebombo Mountains, which formed the border between the Eastern Transvaal and Mozambique.

Today would be another scorcher. It was only nine o'clock but already the sun was burning her back through her cotton blouse. The chickens were fanning their wings, the goats sweating and bleating and the donkeys were agitating to be let out of the kraal into the shade. The dry earth shifted sensuously between her toes as she pressed her bare feet down to lift the bucket over the rim. 'Careful,' she whispered. She tipped the brackish water into the trough and returned to the well. She felt she was rooted to the earth; strange vibrations rose up through her until her entire body was tingling.

An ant was crawling round the well's rim, huge red head lifted, twitching antennae, sensing the water. There was a sudden flash of yellow as a weaver bird streaked past, trailing pampas. She watched it weaving the frond into its nest in the acacia thorn tree, bright with yellow blossoms.

Sweating and tired, she was pouring the fourth load into the trough, when she heard the rumble of an approaching vehicle. Gran emerged from the cottage, wiping her hands on a cloth, her apron dazzling white in the sunlight.

'Did I hear a car, Liza?'

The girl stared towards the main road and frowned. 'Something's coming. Look there.' Above the farm track, the dust, as yellow as an adder, was snaking towards them.

'It's Monday. It can't be the priest.' Gran sounded uneasy and Liza automatically echoed Gran's anxiety. The unexpected usually meant bad news. She dropped the bucket into the depth and wound until her shoulders ached and her back was breaking. Pieter had promised to bring Gran something special for dinner. Would it be hare pie? Or braaied venison? Or her favourite, wild boar roasted slowly over the spit? No one could braai meat like Pieter. Funny how her thoughts went back to him every spare moment. Was this love?

The car negotiating their tricky farm track was covered in fine yellow dust. It skidded badly, obviously a city driver, and came to a halt only inches from the kraal's wall. With the windows covered in dust there was no way of telling who it was, but seconds later the door opened and a woman emerged and stood very still, staring at the brick wall. She looked pale.

Liza tried not to scan their visitor too obviously, for Gran had taught her never to stare. The stranger was short and plump, but smart-looking in her pale blue linen suit. She was kind of pretty with her deep blue eyes and bright red lips, but she looked so sad and Liza wondered why. If she had eyes like hers, she would never be sad. Liza's eyes were dark brown and she wished they were blue or green. Even grey would be better than brown.

'You must be Liza,' the woman said. 'Liza Frank. I've come

to see your Grannie, Mrs du Toit.'

She seemed to know a lot about them. Liza hung around
curiously. Grannie seemed to know the woman for she shook
hands and led her inside, glancing ever so briefly at Liza with
a look that said: 'Stay outside.'

What could this smart city woman want with them? Liza sat
on a rock, gazing at the closed door, wishing she had ears like
a baboon. Pieter said they could hear you stalking them from far
off.

Tense with anxiety, she watched the weaver bird quarrelling
with his mate as the female angrily unthreaded the nest. It
wasn't good enough and he would have to start all over again.
Poor bird!

But what did this strange woman want here? She could not
banish an unwelcome suspicion that they were talking about
her. Lately people were always whispering behind her back and
she did not know why. The girls at school talked and sniggered
and closed their mouths when she walked into a room. The boys
were not so friendly nowadays. The truth was, she no longer
enjoyed school. Yesterday Amy had taunted her ... 'I bet
you've never seen your real mother. You're old Mrs du Toit's
foster child. You don't even know who you are ...'

She had always ignored their silly taunts. So why did she feel
so anxious? She clasped her hands hard over her belly because
the twinges hurt. When Grannie had closed the door, she had
stared back at her with such a strange expression ... just as she
had looked when Pieter had to shoot Mavis, Gran's favourite
donkey, because its last tooth had fallen out and it couldn't chew
anymore ... *regretful and sad*. Why?

Bursting with anguished curiosity, Liza sped around the
house and crouched under the living-room window. Even with
her cheek pressed against the whitewashed bricks their words
came in snatches.

'...of course, the child loves to be in the sun ... burnt almost
black ...' Grannie's voice. 'I keep telling her ... children don't
listen!'

Was it a crime to be sunburnt? No one had told her. Gran kept begging her to wear a bonnet. No one moaned at Pieter and he was burned blacker than she.

'I'm sorry . . .' The stranger's voice was softer, harder to hear. '. . . found abandoned . . . we didn't know . . . this is painful for me, please understand.' She said that louder, more clearly. 'I don't believe in these terrible laws . . . but the truth is, she seems to be coloured, so she can't live in a white home.'

Coloured? But that was nonsense! Liza clenched her fists as a shaft of fear thrust through her bowels.

'. . . it's becoming more apparent. Impossible to ignore,' the soft voice, now hateful, went on mercilessly. 'Lately – well you've surely noticed . . . yet she's strangely beautiful. However, there have been complaints . . . too many . . . the school children . . . their parents . . . and, of course, the teachers . . .' They seemed to have moved closer to the window, for she could hear better.

'So what's to be done?'

Gan sounded on the verge of tears and Liza, too, began to quake with horror and shame. Wasn't Gran going to defend her?

'We have applied for Liza's reclassification. After that we'll take her away. I'll do my best for her, I promise you.'

'But what if she stayed here . . . ?' Gran's voice tailed off as if she realised the futility of such a suggestion.

'Oh, my dear Mrs du Toit. She cannot live in the same house as whites – you know the law. There are no facilities for coloureds in this town. Not even a school. She can't go to the cinema or a restaurant with you or with her friends. She would be an outcast.'

'She doesn't go to such places. We can't afford it . . .'

'She'll be happier with her own people.'

'She's a good girl. I'll say that for her.' Gran's voice was hoarse and she cleared her throat.

Liza clamped her hands over her ears. She couldn't bear to listen to these lies. The pain in her stomach was making her feel sick. Her mouth had dried, her hands were wet and slippery and her breath was coming in short sharp bursts as her heart hammered against her chest hard enough to crack the wall.

What did she mean . . . *happier with her own people*? Were they going to put her with the *Gammats*? [Gammat = half-breed] That was impossible! Insane! There was only one coloured family in Nelfontein and they squatted in an abandoned stable near the station. Their mother was always drunk. The children, snot-nosed and scabby, stinking worse than pigs, begged in the town, spraying lice wherever they went. They were to be moved out soon, teacher had told the class. 'Keep away from them,' she had said. 'There's no place for such people in Nelfontein.'

Oh God! What would become of her?

Liza began to feel dizzy. Everyone was telling such wicked lies behind her back. The whispers and sly taunts were now painfully clear . . . nothing could be lower than a coloured. Even the blacks despised them. Even God despised them. But of course it wasn't true. She wasn't a coloured. No, never! She was white. Crouching lower, she curled up like a hedgehog, longing to disappear into the earth, her body wracked with quivers of shame and fear.

Chapter 2

———◆———

Obsessed with the glory of the veld, Pieter hardly glanced at his friend Dan who was striding ahead. They had hunted together for years. Dan was like a part of himself, sensing his thoughts and moods and he was intuitive to Dan so that speech was seldom necessary. A flicker of a finger was enough warning to indicate a deadly rinkhals or a nod to show a monkey hiding in the branches overhead. Taking long, swinging strides, they hurried through plains of dried grass where daisies bloomed in patches of yellow and red, and clumps of sicklebush and thorny acacias, tall marulas and occasional groves of sycamore fig and fever trees. Squinting in the glare, their senses alert, sweating profusely and pausing occasionally to swill a mouthful from the watersacks slung over their shoulders, they kept moving eastwards. They were barefooted and dressed in khaki shorts and shirts. Water, Ma's rifle and hunting knives were all they ever carried, apart from a sack, rolled and fastened to their belts, to carry home the kill.

It was exceptionally hot for spring, each breath seared the lungs and parched the mouth, filling Pieter with joy. The bushveld was his deepest passion and he knew it intimately, its moods, its dangers and its haunting beauty.

Around noon they saw a herd of impala and a young grysbok standing motionless and poised for flight almost hidden amongst the tall grass. Overhead a scarlet-breasted roller hurtled to earth in its strange tumbling motion to perch on a branch of a nyala tree, largest and most beautiful of all the trees

9

around. Nearing a lake, they disturbed a colony of breeding queleas which rose into the air in their tens of thousands, twittering fit to bust their eardrums and darted eastwards like a long column of smoke.

When they reached the edge of a water hole, they sat in the shade and swilled some water from their watersacks, content to watch the game emerge silently from the thickets and move cautiously to the water's edge. Neither of them reached for their guns. They both knew that the bittersweet culmination of the hunt must always be delayed to the last possible moment and in the meantime every drop of joy must be wrung from the day. The eventual killing would be strictly and only for the pot. Never for pleasure.

Dan sat sliding his knife against a stone. It was as sharp as a razor, but never good enough for him. The two youths owed their hunting skills to Dan's maternal grandfather, who had been a famous tracker in his time. In turn, Pieter had taught Dan to shoot, but this was a luxury, for both of them could live off the land without rifles, if they had to.

Pieter stood up lazily and strolled over to the nearest tree where he pissed leisurely against the trunk. There was a sudden *whoosh* close to his ear, followed by a *thwack* as a knife struck the branch over his head. A tail lashed his cheek and looking up he saw the delicate but deadly green mamba impaled and thrashing. Flushing at his carelessness, he yanked the knife out of the wood, wiped it clean in the soil and handed it to Dan, mumbling his thanks. Dan clapped him on the shoulder.

When the first cumulus clouds appeared over the trees, they set off in a jogging trot. Pieter automatically moved behind because Dan was the better tracker. They were following the spoor of a family of warthogs and Dan was eager to get the first shot. He reached for the rifle, aimed and fired. The piglet stumbled and fell, but bounded to its feet a split second later and managed to reach the shelter of some dense brush skirting a watercourse. Pieter swore silently. 'Your baby,' he muttered, wishing that Dan had waited.

Dan went ahead, knife held ready for the final blow. Pieter watched him, sniffing the air, his skin prickling with unease. Dan was out of sight, but Pieter sensed danger. Suddenly he heard a mighty bellow of rage. The earth was shaking from pounding hooves, shrubs and branches were tossed aside, as Dan fled from the thicket towards the nearest tree.

A massive buffalo cow burst from the bush in a cloud of dust, snorting with temper, head lowered, tail in the air. She paused, thirty yards off, tossing her head, and beating her flanks with her tail. Then she charged.

Dan would never make the tree – there was no time. Pieter flung up his rifle, aimed and fired. He saw the bullet hit home, but the beast shook her head violently without slowing her charge. Pieter fired again and the cow stumbled, but only momentarily. She was gaining on Dan. Pieter rushed desperately towards the enraged beast, waving his arms and shouting. She turned her head, moving off-course slightly, angry eyes searching towards this new threat. Dan dived into some long grass and lay still and the cow paused, feeling confused. Unable to see Dan, she veered to the right and came straight at Pieter.

The pounding of her hooves was like thunder, he could hear her snorting breath, smell the scent of her and see her bloodshot eyes as two tons of savage temper bore down on him at forty miles an hour. His finger tightened on the trigger, but still he waited. Now the cow was only a few paces off and coming on fast. In that split second before she lowered her head to lunge her horns, Pieter shot a blast into the top of her chest. The infuriated beast changed course to the left and Pieter gave her a second blast close behind her shoulder. Now she was mortally wounded, but she managed to turn and rush back towards the cover of the thick brush.

Dan climbed out of the grass. 'Thanks,' he said, looking scared. He reached out and Pieter clasped his hand in their special thumbs-up manner.

'Two escapes. We don't need a third,' Pieter muttered.

Despite their fears, they knew they had to go into the brush and kill the wounded buffalo. After only a few moments hesitation they followed the trail of blood. Fighting their way through the track made by the beast, they were well aware that it might be circling them and creeping up from behind. They hadn't gone far before they found her lying dead. Her calf, only a day or two old, was standing by the carcase, blinking its huge eyes and bleating to its dead mother. Neither of them wanted to kill the calf, but they knew they must.

'It's my fault,' Dan said. 'I'll do it.' He took his knife and slit the calf's throat. While the blood was still running a jackal broke cover to make a dive at the carnage.

The killing of the calf had turned the day sour. It took hours to slice the buffalo meat and hang it high in the thorn tree to dry. They would retrieve it later. They worked in silence, slicing and packing the best of the meat to carry home. When they were about to leave, a pack of wild dogs burst on them unaware. Squealing with fear the dogs turned and ran for cover.

They saw the first vulture circling overhead as the blood-red sun sank behind the trees. The sky was deep crimson and the veld was transformed by the lovely, ephemeral twilight. As they left the scene, they heard hyenas and jackals moving in for the remains. There would be horns and perhaps a skull when they returned to collect the biltong hanging high and deep amongst the thorns, but little else.

It was almost dark when the boys reached Mrs du Toit's cottage. Pieter always felt sad that Liza's home was so poor. The walls were a foot thick and made of stones roughly set into compressed mud, the roof was of corrugated iron, and nothing was truly straight, but miraculously it had survived three centuries. When it was freshly whitewashed it didn't look too bad, but right now it could do with a new coat. Pieter decided to volunteer for the job. The small interior was roughly divided by stone walls with old wooden doors into three rooms, for their kitchen doubled as a living room.

They sorted the meat on a trestle table outside the backdoor and Pieter gave Gran a good share as well as the small warthog.

Where was Liza? he wondered. Gran looked depressed. 'Something wrong?' he asked.

Mrs du Toit clamped her toothless jaw together until her ridged nose almost met her pointed chin. There was a wart on her chin with a big hair growing out of it, and her skin looked as parched and transparent as grass before the rains; only the grass would recover, but she never would, Pieter thought.

He wondered how old she was. Maybe a hundred. Liza loved her and for that reason he loved her too, but he had to admit that a stranger would find her ugly. You had to search for the beauty that was hidden away, but it was there if you looked hard enough you could see it. Her deep brown eyes were sometimes alight like a girl's and most days they twinkled compassionately. She had thick white wavy hair, but she wore it scraped back into a bun. She had beautiful hands, too, and to see her arranging flowers was a delight, but it wasn't often that she had any.

Dan had cleaned the warthog. He laid it on the trestle table beside the back door and dawdled there for a moment until Pieter helped him to pack his share of the meat into a sack. Dan left with a wave and a quick grin.

'You spoil that kafir,' Grannie grumbled through the kitchen window.

Pieter scowled. His face became haughty as he glowered at Gran.

'Don't use that word. He's my friend,' he said hotly. My blood brother, he had wanted to say, for he and Dan had both been suckled by Dan's mother and they had been reared together and played together since his earliest memories. Later Sam had taught them both to track and survive in the bush. They had saved each other so often it was becoming a habit. Pieter had a sunny nature and his temper never lasted long. Moments later he was grinning at her, coaxing her to smile. 'Come on, Gran, we were hunting together. Half was his by right. Besides, he shares it out. Where's Liza?'

Grannie shook her head and looked uneasy. 'She's around somewhere,' she mumbled.

'I'll go look for her.'

Engrossed in her fear and anger, Liza did not hear Pieter's footsteps. She was gazing into the mirror that she had carried to the back of the kraal, fingering her straight black hair. *Gammats* had frizzy hair, didn't they? She jumped as a hand touched her shoulder and she looked up to see Pieter's well-loved face, round as an apple, peering down at her, his green eyes glinting with concern. For a moment she forgot her pain and blinked up lovingly.

'Oh, Pieter, you're so late,' she said. She stood up and flung her arms around his neck. He smelled good, a mixture of his own special musky sweat, tobacco and the tangy smell of veld herbs. She ran her hands over the black fuzz which had appeared recently on his cheeks and chin.

'Any guy would be pleased to have such a welcome.' He put his arms around her and grabbed the mirror. 'Don't you think I look divine, darling?' he said, in a falsetto voice, fluttering his eyelashes and smoothing his hair.

She laughed, but then her trauma hit home with a force that knocked the breath out of her. If she were coloured Pieter would be lost to her forever. But that was madness. It wasn't true. She was white!

'Oh, Pieter . . .' When she tried to tell him about her terrible plight she could not bring herself to voice such a disgraceful thing, even though it was a lie.

'Oh, oh, I wish I knew who I am,' she gasped, holding back her tears. 'I wish I knew my name. I long to find my real family.'

Pieter looked amused. 'One day I'll help you. Didn't I promise you? Come and see what I've brought . . . something special.'

He grinned and caught hold of her hand. Unwilling to face Gran, she pulled back. All at once they were tugging against each other – an old, familiar game. Today there was no fight in

Liza, she was squashed and demolished from the inside out. She allowed herself to be pulled to the kitchen where Gran was already frying liver over the wood stove. *Oh, Pieter, will you still love me when you hear the wicked lies they're saying about me?* She trapped her grief inside herself until her body shuddered and shook.

Gran shot a quick, piercing glance in her direction. *She knows I listened.* Liza looked away nervously. Everything looked the same and yet it was completely different, for now she felt alienated. She glanced at the familiar pictures hanging on the walls: the cabinet ministers looking grave and pompous in their thin black frames, the picture of Gran's bearded grandfather, a commando in the Boer War. Gran's father, pale and wan, wounded in Flanders in the First World War, and her husband who had died in Tobruk in World War II. Liza had adopted them all, for want of relatives of her own, but today their eyes seemed to say: 'What are you doing here, Liza? This is a proper white home.'

On the cement slab by the sink lay a warthog piglet of about four months, its mouth open in a silent scream, its eyes rolled back in ultimate despair. Liza, who had always thrilled to the sight of a suckling boar, shuddered with insecurity. The strangest feeling was surging through her mind, bringing her skin out in goose-pimples. She could be that pig. Since she had no idea who she was, she might as well be anything. Birth was accidental. She felt at one with all victims, for wasn't she a victim, too? Hours ago she had felt so secure. Poor they might be, but they were nature's aristocrats because they were white! And now they said she was a *gammat*? She looked round shamefully. Could they read her thoughts? Gran was stirring the sauce and Pieter was watching her. He looked hungry. If only Gran would say something.

Her head spinning with questions, Liza went into her room and put her mirror back on the cupboard, but she could not help gazing into it again. She saw a frightened girl, sallow-looking, with eyes like a startled antelope, hair as black and straight as a lion's mane, and nostrils only a hippo would be proud of. Her skin, she decided, examining it with loathing, was exactly the colour of Pieter's old army shirt, inherited from his late grandpa. Why had she thought she was pretty? Perhaps because so many of the boys at school had said so.

'This is me,' she whispered. 'You are me. But who am I really?' Her head began to throb alarmingly and she felt burning hot all over. Then Gran called her to the table.

Even the succulent liver, served with fried tomato and onion sauce, with thick wads of mealie pap, failed to revive her mood. She listened as Pieter described the day's hunt in detail. Her stomach was knotted and she could not swallow. She sat at the table gazing at her hands, turning them this way and that way to examine them better in the fading light. Why had she never noticed how sallow she was? Why didn't Gran reassure her? She hadn't said one word about the strange woman's visit. Eventually she said: 'Gran, who was that woman who came here today?'

'Mrs Frank from the Department of Social Welfare.'

Frank? But that was her name, too. 'What did she want?'

'Something to do with my pension.' Gran tried to smile, but it didn't work. Why was she lying?

Liza got up from the table and ran into her room, slamming the door behind her. After a while she heard Pieter knocking at the window.

'A guy can't sleep without his goodnight kiss,' he whispered through the crack.

'I'm tired,' she hissed.

He flattened his nose and lips against the glass and made his eyes go cross-eyed and gave a loud, sucking kiss. 'Aw! No kiss?' When there was no reply he frowned and looked puzzled. Then the cat jumped on the sill and he grabbed hold of it and waltzed it around the garden. 'Cattie loves me,' he called. 'Sleep tight.'

If only she could sleep, but the horrid reality of her plight kept her tossing and turning. She longed to remember her real family, but all she had was a dim memory of eyes as blue as the sky and hair the colour of wheat, and someone carrying her. She knew that she had been left in the police station at Nelfontein, and that the social welfare officer had placed her in Gran's care when she was four years old, because Gran had told her this, but the truth was, it seemed that she had been living in this tiny stone cottage with her Gran all her life.

Gran was paid for her keep. They often went together to the post office to collect the money. She was a ward of the State, she'd read that often enough, but did that mean they had a right to snatch her away from her home and put her with the *gammats*? She kept imagining how the girls at school would jeer when they found out. Tears came flooding out as she buried her head in her pillow to smother her sobs. Eventually she cried herself to sleep.

Chapter 3

———◆———

Darkness cloaked the bushveld under a brilliant starry sky, but in the east came a glimmer of grey. Under a lavender tree, on a rocky outcrop not far from Gran's cottage, a sack shuddered, shivered and writhed. From it, a shrill note, startlingly loud and of poignant clarity, pierced the air. As if in answer a francolin gave its kraa-kraa-kraa crow to herald the dawn. At once the birds began their morning chorus until the air reverberated with their noisy song. Grey turned to a crimson stain above the mountains, shedding a strange, mystical glow over the land.

The sack opened abruptly and Dan's head, black as night, emerged. A hornbill flew down and stared intently at the boy who was his friend. Dan grinned at the bird, white teeth glistening, then he leaned back against the silvery smooth tree trunk, dug in his pocket for his penny whistle and burst into a song of joy, for the glorious morning, for the birds who sang to him, for the hornbill whom he had tamed and for the wild melon warming at his feet. Hunger overcame joy. Thrusting the whistle into his pocket, he broke the melon, flung the seeds to the hornbill and thrust the bitter-sweet pulp into his mouth. The juice ran down his chin and on to his neck, tickling him.

He stood up, stretched and sauntered down towards the cottage where Liza lived. Mrs du Toit was up earlier than usual and that was a nuisance since he intended to steal an egg.

She called out: 'Morning, Dan. Bring up some wood from the shed. About two armfuls will do.'

Dan fetched the wood grudgingly, his face sullen with resentment.

'Here's some mealie pap left over from supper,' she said, slapping a large spoonful of grey cold stodge on to a tin plate, as if in payment for his chore.

'No thank you, Mrs du Toit, I'd rather not,' Dan said as politely as he could. Inside he was churning. He didn't work for her, so why did she give him jobs to do? Whites were all the same, every black was their servant, or so they thought. He left before she found another job for him.

Watching Dan saunter off towards the kraal, Aletta du Toit frowned and felt a surge of irritation, as she always did when Dan was around. It was something to do with his huge, glowing eyes that seemed to watch her critically, and his lips, which were usually twisted into a half smile. Even his hair rose up in a thick, wiry mass as if reaching for the stars. Just look at him, walking tall and proud as if he owned the world. And how dare he call her Mrs du Toit. 'Missus' was the traditional way to address her, but that boy was full of nonsense. Pap wasn't good enough for the likes of him. To Aletta, Dan's politeness was a veiled insult.

'You're just like your father,' she called after him. 'Too clever by half. And where have all those brains and superior ways got him?'

She broke off and turned back to the stove. A native was a native and as such she respected them. Any black could turn to her for help if in trouble, but when they started to ape whites she saw red. The trouble stemmed from that grandmother of his, Nosisi, the so-called *Sangoma* [witchdoctor/herbalist].

Arms akimbo, she watched Dan stroll past the donkeys, looking for all the world as if he did not know where the grey-speckled hen hid her eggs. She decided to speak to the de Vries family about Dan's bad attitude. Dismissing him from her mind, she turned her attention to the wood stove which was always temperamental in the morning. In next to no time she had the kettle boiling and the porridge simmering.

At the neighbouring farm, Pieter overslept. He woke to the smell of coffee and the sound of his mother working in the kitchen. Guilt sent him scrambling out of bed. He pulled on a T-shirt and shorts and went outside. It was going to be a glorious day. The sky was a delicate saffron tinged with pearl, the Lebombo mountain ridge was shining purple, the air had a sparkle that made each breath a pleasure, the spring flowers had laid a carpet of white and purple over the rocks and sandy earth and the *piet-my-vrou* cuckoo couldn't stop singing its head off with delight at the new day. Their whitewashed cottage seemed rose-coloured in the dawn glow and right behind it, masses of scarlet poinsettias swayed as the sunbirds dived in for nectar. Patches of blue lobelia, white pelargoniums and purple and white ericas were scattered around the grass and behind were clumps of brilliant yellow from the acacia thorn blossom where weaver birds were fighting out their noisy domestic dramas.

The donkeys brayed and Pieter trudged off to the shed. He tipped some feed into an old paraffin tin and lugged it to the kraal and stood there, loving the musky smell of the donkeys and the rough feel of their pelts as he rubbed his hand down their necks. Of the ten donkeys, Jacob and Lady were the oldest and so they were the leaders. Lady was getting too old. Her long brown teeth were chewed off and falling loose. If only she could be put out to graze, but there was no room for sentiment when you were poor and every mouthful had to be fought for. Life's a pain, he thought heavily. Just when they get well trained, you have to shoot them. Not for anything would he admit that he loved this old donkey.

They nuzzled and nudged and surged around him, knocking him off balance. He fell against the thorns, which was a painful experience. 'Ouch! One of these days I'll make a new kraal,' he muttered. Theirs was too dilapidated, one side was a broken brick wall and the other a wall of acacia thorn branches. But it worked, for the inch-long spikes were more than enough to confine ten wilful donkeys.

Their farm was large, a good nine hundred hectares, but it was mainly rock kopjes, gravel patches, and poor grazing. They had only two fertile fields on which they planted vegetables and tomatoes. This was not enough to make a living. His father was employed as farm foreman by the Cronjés, to supervise their huge sugar and tomato plantations. He had no time left to tend their place, but they had Sam, Dan's grandfather, and Pieter helped out before and after school. He heard his Ma calling from the kitchen.

'Coffee's ready, Pieter. Take a rusk,' she said when he went inside. 'I made them yesterday.'

She broke off and stood gazing at him, her eyes full of compassion. 'Listen, Pieter, I've got to tell you some bad news,' she began. 'It's best if you hear it from me and not someone else. Everyone's talking about it, so you're bound to find out. The girls at school, and their parents, have been complaining about Liza becoming so dark. You see, because she was found abandoned, no one ever knew who her parents were.'

She shot a quick glance at Pieter and saw how he was gazing impassively at the wall. He never showed his feelings, but she knew from experience that when his face blanked out like that he was suffering.

'At the time, the authorities assumed she was white. Now that she's growing up she's beginning to look as if she isn't. They say she's to be reclassified as a coloured. She'll be sent away to her own people. What a shame it is. I'm so sorry that it's me who has to tell you. I know how you'll miss her.' She put her hand on Pieter's shoulder.

Pieter shook off her arm and went outside. He stood in the kraal absentmindedly stroking a donkey, his ears ringing, a hollow pain inside his stomach. He'd been tossed into a state where nothing seemed real. Liza coloured? That was crazy. And Ma was talking as if it was an established fact. Did she believe that? Yes, he thought, she obviously did. And Liza was dark. The obvious had been staring him in the face for months and he'd never noticed. The shock came like a bolt from the blue. How could things like this happen? Gnawing at his fingernails he tried to get to grips with the bad news. Without thinking twice about it, he went to find Sam who was more like a friend than a labourer. When he reached the old man's shack he saw Sam hobble out, tucking his shirt in his trousers and blinking.

'What's the matter, Pieter?' Sam asked, noticing the boy's distress.

'Have you heard what they're saying about Liza?'

Watching Pieter's hurt, sadness surged. 'Of course I have, but no one knows for sure and that's the truth. They can only suspect. I'm sure they'll sort something out. Why don't you give me a hand, since it's too early for school,' Sam said, wishing he could say something constructive to help the boy.

They had to wait while the donkeys finished eating. Then they spanned-in, placing the donkeys in five rows of pairs as Pieter fitted the old leather harnesses over them. Only the two leaders had a bridle, the other eight would follow. By now the donkeys knew the business of raking and ploughing so well they could do it with their eyes closed, Sam reckoned. Whistling and clicking his tongue, Pieter pushed open the gate and led the donkeys to the plough which was lying in front of the de Vries's cottage. Fastening the donkeys to the drawline of the plough with chains, he grabbed the wooden handles and called to them. The donkeys laid back their ears, rolled their eyes and moved forward.

Usually the crisp snap of leather, the clip-clop of hooves, the donkeys' excitement and the waking veld brought a surge of happiness to Sam, but Pieter's hurt had ruined the morning. Sam loved the boy and he felt sorry for him. He was so proud and full of self-importance and bubbling over with hope, but his family had so little – they were practically poor whites. This town will destroy him, he thought, just as it did my Victor.

For a while he was lost in recollections of his only son, Victor, who had tried to buck the system. It was all his fault. Sam had been a schoolteacher and full of great ideas for change and freedom which he'd impressed on Victor. Now his son was serving a life sentence with hard labour on Robben Island. After his son's trial Sam had given up teaching and brought his son's wife and baby to the de Vries's farm where he had been born. He had moved into a shack and here he worked for a pittance, plus his food. Victor's wife had worked for Mrs de Vries, too, before she left for the city, abandoning her son, Dan. So Sam had taught the boys to hunt and survive in the bush and plough and a hundred other things boys needed to know. Once they had been inseparable, but lately social pressures were driving them apart.

He sighed. Nowadays he didn't often see Pieter.

As they began the long haul to rake the field, Sam was considering the whites and their curious, hard ways. Nelfontein was as pleasant a town as anyone could wish for, with flowers and trees along the pavements and grassy verges. Yes, when it came to beautifying the place, those people knew what they were doing, Sam thought bitterly. The Boer had an eye for beauty. The industrious farmers, with their genius for orderliness, had tamed their portion of Africa. Everything worked for them ... even the land, and whatever worked could stay, so they allowed the hippos to graze unrestricted in the river. And why ... ? Because the hippos kept the choking weeds down. Even the crocodiles, hiding in lucid pools amongst tall bulrushes and basking along sandy shores, had their place in the white man's system, so they could stay, too.

Blacks like him could stay if they had jobs, for their use lay in their labour. So they were documented, fingerprinted, issued with passes and permitted to work and sleep on white land when needed. For the rest, they were banished to their tribal trust homeland, *KaNgwane* where their families lived. In the white towns blacks and whites co-existed in a curious symbiotic relationship, masters and servants, the one coping for the needs of the other and the system worked if you let it be.

For a few moments Sam thought about Liza, wondering what he could say to comfort the boy? The town was buzzing with news of her predicament. She didn't stand much chance of staying in Nelfontein, Sam reckoned. The Boer was a tough, crafty, obstinate fellow, with his priorities firmly in order – first his God and his morals, then his family, closely followed by his land and his government. There was little compassion left for those outside their *laager* [a camp protected by a circle of wagons or armoured vehicles]. Gloomy thoughts kept smashing into Sam like a cloud of locusts as he trudged behind the plough hardly aware of what he was doing and with little heed of passing time.

The donkeys were well into their tracks for the day. 'Time for school,' he called to Pieter. 'Don't you take any insults from those white boys.' Wishing he were not so fond of Pieter, he watched him give Lady a smack on the rump, tickle her ear and produce a carrot from his pocket, before running back to get his schoolbag.

Chapter 4

Pieter saw Liza from a distance. She was sitting on a large stone at the side of the highway, her head in her hands, her schoolcase flung on the ground beside her. As he drew nearer he saw her white face and the shadows under her eyes. Liza's shame condemned her and why did she have to have that hang-dog expression? What was the matter with her? She was still his Liza, wasn't she? Blanking his mind to reality he decided to act as though everything was normal.

'Hi, Liza. Whose funeral is it?' he teased. She shuddered and stared at her feet, shoulders slumped, hair falling forward.

Perhaps joking wasn't the right approach. Crouching beside her, he put his arms round her and brushed the hair off her face.

'Please cheer up, Li. You can't let them see you like this. Where's your courage?'

Her head sunk lower until she was quite hidden by her hair.

'Who cares what *they* think? Sticks and stones can break your bones, but words can never harm you,' he chanted and then broke off short. That wasn't true. The girls at school had always been jealous of Liza, and now they had a weapon to wound and destroy her, to punish her for being beautiful.

'You're still the same Liza to everyone,' he said. But that wasn't true, either, not even with him. It wasn't that his feelings for her had *changed*. It was just that *she* was different ... different from what he had always imagined her to be, so he couldn't help looking at her in a *slightly* different light.

A lorry drew up. It was Mr Brits with his load of tomatoes en route to the station. Pieter climbed in to the front seat and gave Liza a hand up. Thankfully she didn't notice the look of scrutiny Mr Brits gave her. So the word had spread already . . .

Unaware of Pieter's confusion, Liza felt protected by their closeness. Gran had insisted that she wear her second-best dress, made of pretty blue floral cotton with a frill around the bottom. This was an unheard-of privilege. Liza's other dresses had been made by Gran from bleached mealie sacks and the girls always teased her. Her best dress was of pink muslin and it was only for church. Even on Sundays, as soon as they set foot in the house off came the precious garment and it was in the washtub before you could take a breath. From this simple act of kindness this morning, she knew Gran was with her in her ordeal.

Liza had no illusions of what faced her at school. She would be ostracised, teased, thwarted and verbally abused. So far she had borne their scorn stoically, knowing that right was on her side. But now . . . ? She no longer knew who or what she was.

'Just don't let me die of shame, dear God,' she whispered. Minutes later, her stomach churning with fear, Liza climbed down from the lorry and walked towards the school, forcing her legs to move forward.

'Hey, don't you say goodbye?' Pieter called after her. Then he remembered his history essay. It should have been handed in today, but they wouldn't be able to keep him late because school was closing early. There was to be a speech by old man Cronjé and a march past afterwards and a prize was to be awarded for pellet gun shooting. Pieter didn't have a pellet gun, so he couldn't compete. He was too young to get a licence for a rifle and shooting for the pot with Ma's archaic gun was strictly illegal, so he could hardly bring it to school.

The prize was a brand-new racing bicycle, which stood on the platform in front of the spectators' box beside the school playing field. Slender of line, but strong enough to take the roughest farm roads, it glittered tantalisingly in a blaze of chrome and metallic blue. It had nine speeds, the saddle was sprung leather, the bell chrome, and the lights at the back winked in the sunlight. Pieter went to examine it before prayers, knowing that it would never be his, but still he could not tear his eyes away. Unable to stop himself, he mounted the platform and ran his hands over the prize.

'You aiming to come first, Pieter?' a voice muttered just behind him. 'Let's see your gun. Going to show us how it's done?'

It was Tony, far and away the richest boy in the school, which was just as well, Pieter reckoned, since he was a skinny, white-faced runt. His pale blue eyes were glittering and his prim lips were drawn back into an ugly leer.

It was unfair that old Cronjé's farm, which neighboured his Ma's, was fertile, while theirs was stony and mainly barren, just like Mrs du Toit's. Besides his farm, Cronjé owned several other sugar plantations and a newspaper in Johannesburg. Add to that a few workshops making nuts and bolts in the KaNgwane African Homeland so Cronjé could claim generous tax benefits from the government, and a packaging factory somewhere on the Reef, and one could see why he was so pompous and his son so pampered. He was also the Independent Opposition Candidate for the district and that was why he was giving them a speech today. Strictly speaking he was supposed to be talking about environmental care, for no one was allowed to talk politics on school property, but Pieter knew he'd slip in a bit of propaganda here and there.

Pieter looked over his shoulder and glared at Tony who seemed to have more courage than usual, perhaps because his father was coming to the school. 'Have you hidden it in your mealie sack?' he taunted Pieter. Some of the boys joined in the laughter, for they knew he was proud and hated the fact that his shirts were homemade from bleached mealie sacks and they never fitted properly. Last week one of the boys had seen Pieter stun a hare with a stone from his catapult and this inspired a new gibe. 'Did you bring your catapult, Pieter? You gonna win with that?' 'Better ask your kafir friend to lend you his spear.'

Then a new gibe came out of the blue, unexpected and destructive, stunning Pieter with its cruelty: '*Your girlfriend's coloured. Everyone knows! She's gonna be reclassified.*'

'Sorry. Just say that again? I didn't hear you.' He wheeled round to see who had spoken. It was Johan, Tony's friend.

'Sure. I said that your girl—' He didn't get any further. A surge of white-hot anger gave Pieter speed and strength. Next minute they were rolling around on the ground, and the boys were chanting and urging them on: 'Fight, fight, fight . . .'

A blow in the stomach caught Pieter by surprise, winding him. Furious, he lashed out with his arms and legs. Punching and kicking. There was a sickening crunch and a howl of agony. Suddenly the boys stopped chanting.

'You broke my nose! You fucking broke my nose, you arsehole!' Johan cried, his hand held to his face. One look at the warm, red liquid dripping down his arm and he threw up.

'Don't pick on Liza if you know what's good for you.'

There were a few sniggers but no one wanted to take on Pieter. He always won.

He was late for prayers. As he slipped into the back row, his mind was agonising for Liza. Here in the Lowveld people were as quick to spot colour as an egret would a tick. She'd never be accepted, so what was the point of all her beauty?

It was two p.m. and hot as an oven. They'd been standing in the sun for over an hour listening to Cronjé drone on and on. All very well for him. He was in the shade of the overhanging roof of the pavilion, next to the gleaming bicycle. His voice came robot-like from the inferior microphone.

'Those of you who have passed through *KaNgwane* will have noticed the soil erosion and the litter and the over-grazing of their skinny cattle. Those people don't know how to care for the land. We Afrikaners have a sacred duty to God, we are God's emissaries, charged with nourishing the land. Those people take from the sacred soil. We give to God's soil.'

Cronjé seemed to notice the headmaster scowling at him and he passed on smoothly. 'That is why you must give your time to keep our land pure and free of litter.' One of the boys in the parade fainted and there was a pause while he was carried off by the school medic. The headmaster muttered in Cronjé's ear and he brought his talk to a rapid conclusion.

The shooting competition was about to be held against the grassy bank behind the rugby field. The boys had to shoot a target from fifteen metres. Not much of a challenge, Pieter thought contemptuously as they marched to the end of the field and listened to old Cronjé laying down the law. 'This is not a B.B. competition, any weapon . . .' he went on.

Pieter felt the adrenaline surging through his body, bringing him out in goose-pimples. Any weapon? Wasn't a catapult a weapon?

Looking as casual as he could he took up his position in the long line of boys. When they saw him take out his catapult there was an uproar of jeers and laughter. Tony was staggering around, bent double, holding his ribs, unable to get his breath. Pieter resisted an urge to fire a stone bang into his skinny rump, but he controlled himself.

'No talking. Get ready. Take your aim. Fire,' the games master yelled.

He was lucky. A fluke shot, he thought, as his stone shot deadly and true bang into the middle of the target.

The games master went from site to site, pushing stickers with No 1 pencilled on them over each hole.

'Get ready . . . aim . . . fire . . .'

All he had to do was imagine a fat guinea fowl eyeing him through the target, because the truth was he hadn't eaten that day and hunger always improved his aim. He pulled back his hand and flicked the stone dead centre once again.

Anyone could see that Pieter was winning. There were angry rumbles about not playing fair. The games master went to discuss this unexpected problem with Cronjé. Then Pieter was called to the side of the field. He went moodily, his heart heavy, knowing he was to be disqualified.

'Well, Pieter, my boy, you can show us a thing or two with your catapult. I never could get the hang of those darned things when I was a boy. Have you a pellet gun at home?'

Pieter shook his head. 'My mother has an ex-army .303 rifle, sir, but that's all. I'm too young for a licence, but my father wouldn't let me waste bullets for fun, sir. I only shoot for the pot.' He stopped, blushed and cleared his throat for he wasn't allowed to go hunting without a licence.

'Quite right, my boy. We're in a bit of a quandary here. You're winning, but maybe you have an unfair advantage. I don't know and that's the truth. So to even things up a bit I'm offering you the loan of my son's spare pellet gun and a few rounds. That way, everyone's going to be happy. Is that all right with you? We'll give you five minutes to get the hang of it.'

Pieter could hardly get his lips around his thanks. Was it all right? It was heaven!

'They're putting up a new target for you. Off you go, then. And good luck.'

Pieter felt ten inches taller as he walked back fingering the gun. What a beauty. A Daisy pellet, smooth and beautifully shaped, the barrel a joy to stroke.

Twenty minutes later, flushing with pride and joy, Pieter took possession of the gleaming miracle, stammering his thanks to Cronjé.

'I'll get you for using my Daisy,' Tony muttered as Pieter wheeled his new bicycle past him to the car park.

Tea was to be served in the striped tent erected on special days. Pieter could hardly tear himself away from his bicycle. He left it propped against the wall in the car park.

Liza had dreaded going to the loo, but she was now desperate. When she arrived her worst fears became reality. The girls saw her and bunched together to block the entrance. 'It's for whites only, Liza. Can't you read that sign up there? Go and use the cleaner's toilet.'

Liza's fears gave way to temper and she fought her way in, lashing out with her fists and feet. The girls parted, giggling madly. 'All Coloureds fight and swear and have lice and you'll be sent to live with them,' Amy Johnston cooed through the toilet door. She had always been bitchy because she hankered after Pieter. She'd never get Pieter. He couldn't stand her.

'Pieter thinks you look like a cow with big fat udders,' Liza called out and heard a long drawn-out gasp which was satisfying. She locked herself in until they had all gone. Eventually she crept out cautiously, but there was Gwen, a pimply, fat girl who had always been jealous of her, waiting silently by the door, a look of triumph on her face.

'My mum says you'll be put with the *gammats* squatting in the old ruined warehouse by the station. Have you seen them begging in the town?' She laughed contemptuously and ran outside.

Liza emerged and sat on the grassy verge, trying to keep a grip on herself. She wanted to scream and sob for help, but she dared not show weakness. If only she could disappear into the ground and never be seen again.

Pieter had been looking for her and eventually he saw her sitting under a tree, sadness surging out of her like an invisible cloud. She was all hunched over herself like a flower that closes its petals at night. Her shoulders were drooping, her long black hair fell veil-like over her face, her cardigan hid most of her arms and the sleeves were pulled down to conceal her hands, which were nervously plucking at the grass. She'd got hold of a pair of sunglasses from somewhere and he guessed that she was crying behind the frames.

'Come on, Liza,' he said, gripping her shoulder. 'Don't let them see they've got you down. Come and have tea. There's cake and biscuits.'

She grabbed his wrist and buried her face into the palm of his hand. 'I can't,' she whispered. 'I can't do it. Just now . . .' She broke off and took a deep shuddering sigh. 'I mustn't cry in front of them, but just now . . . they wouldn't let me in the toilet. Oh, Pieter. You don't know what's happened to me.'

'I do and I'm on your side,' he said. 'People are watching. Look there's Amy. She's got the hots for me. She trails behind me with her fanny bubbling on the pavement. Don't let her see you crying. I'll hold your hand. I don't care what they say. They suck – all of them.'

Now she was laughing and crying at the same time. Funny how she could always do that, even when she was a kid. She pulled a tissue from her pocket and dabbed her eyes and blew her nose. He hung on to her hand and led her to the striped tent.

Inside, the stuffy air was almost unendurable. Pieter gobbled some biscuits and shook hands with some of the masters. He managed to slip four more biscuits into his pocket for his mum and hurried off with Liza hard behind. He couldn't wait to get back to his wonderful prize. What a bicycle! He felt dizzy with happiness.

At the entrance to the car park he stopped short, swore under his breath and braced himself to keep his face from showing his concern. His bicycle lay mangled by the wall. Tony's gang stood around smirking and pretending not to watch as Pieter fumbled in the dust for the bell, the broken spokes and all the bits and pieces that had come loose. The handlebars were beyond hope, the nine speeds were dangling at the end of a long wire, the chain was hanging loose and both wheels were buckled. Pieter grovelled in the dust, retrieving all those precious pieces and shoving the small bits into his pockets. Never before had he known such a loss, for he had never owned anything worth having. Liza was on her knees trying to help him.

'Leave it,' he snarled. 'You're getting dirty.' Suddenly it was important that she look clean and close to perfect, but there were muddy streaks down her dress and her hands were grimy.

Looking up, he saw Tony laughing at them. A quick glance at Cronjé's larny bakkie told a bitter story. There were scratches on the front and the number plate was dangling.

Suddenly he was running towards Tony. All his aggression at the woes of the day went into one straight punch bang into Tony's stomach. Tony fell, doubled up, making a harsh grating noise in his chest. Pieter looked down in dismay as Tony croaked noisily, unable to draw breath. After what seemed a very long time he sucked in air, his knees pulled up to his chin, his face chalk white. He was going to be all right.

'Suck my arse, you bastard,' Pieter growled. He felt cheated. It was all over with one punch and he was bursting for a fight.

Marius Cronjé came puffing towards them, belly wobbling. His tie was askew, his shirt buttons had popped open and his face was deep purple.

'What the hell . . . what the hell . . . ?' he shouted.

He advanced menacingly towards Pieter while taking off his belt. Several teachers were running towards them from all directions.

'What happened? Get on your feet,' he said curtly to his son as he lurched towards Pieter.

'It's wrong to punish Pieter, sir,' Liza yelled, running between Pieter and Cronjé. 'Tony ran over his bicycle with your bakkie and flattened it. Look at it. It's not fair. And look at your bakkie, sir.'

'Oh, Liza,' Pieter whispered. 'Shut your mouth. Don't interfere.'

'Tony should pay for the bicycle,' she said, unmoved by Pieter's anger.

'No,' Pieter said. 'I'll mend it myself.' He picked up the mangled frame and wheeled it off, looking haughty and sulky.

Marius turned mottled purple and white as he bent over his son. 'Did you do that?'

Tony was still fighting to breathe and unable to stand. 'Yes,' he gasped stupidly. Bending the belt double, Cronjé began to beat his son, on his back, his legs, his shoulder and his head. His face became darker, his forehead broke out in a sweat with his anger and the unaccustomed exercise, and his breath was soon rasping in his throat. Tony tried to protect his face as he dragged himself under the bakkie. Seconds later he was out of sight, but they could all hear him sobbing.

'I'll punish him, you can be sure of that,' Cronjé told the teachers who had gathered round. 'He will buy a new bicycle with his own cash.'

Everyone was embarrassed for Tony blubbering under the bakkie and his father's awful exhibition of temper. They moved away without speaking. 'Come, sir,' one of the teachers said, taking Cronjé's arm.

Liza ran after Pieter and caught up with him on the road. 'Wait. Wait for me,' she called. She replayed Tony's humiliation, exaggerating the sobs and the beating to please Pieter, but he was not pleased.

'A man's got no right to humiliate his son,' Pieter said. 'It's times like this when I hate rich people. They're full of pent-up pride and it makes them cruel. I hit Tony. That was enough.'

Chapter 5

———◆———

'I have never seen anything as repulsive as your behaviour this afternoon.'

'Don't you ever look in the mirror?' Tony thought wearily. He stood in his father's impressive, oak-panelled office, watching him sip brandy. His father was straining to find words that would hurt the most. He was drunk – that was obvious from his cerise face, bloodshot eyes and puffy eyelids. An objectionable sight. Tony shivered. Without moving his head, he turned his eyes to the window. He could see the sun setting in a huge crimson globe behind the wild fig trees on his step-mother's ornamental lake. Safe on the island, the costly imported geese and swans were squabbling over their food. If I were a goose I'd be welcome here, Tony thought.

'You're a great disappointment to me, Tony. Bad blood from your mother's side. I've told you that enough times. She was a weakling, too.'

Tony quelled a vision of his mother's face after they found her gassed in her car. Father was working himself up into a temper and Tony looked to see what sort of a belt he was wearing. A thin snakeskin job that couldn't beat a kitten. His stomach relaxed with relief.

Father came closer. Brandy breath was mingled with another stranger odour that seemed to accompany his fits of rage. He was running out of control. Like an old bull he was mean, treacherous and brutal. Tony stood his ground trying to hide his fear, knowing that to cringe was to invite disaster. How he longed to thrust a knife into that bloated belly and see the bloody entrails spill out on to his disgusting Persian carpet. 'Olé,' he muttered under his breath.

'What's that?'

'Nothing.'

The door opened and his step-mother entered. She was thirty-four Tony knew, but she looked twenty-five with her long blonde hair, baby-blue eyes, and skinny figure like a boy's. He guessed she was beautiful in a way, with her starved look, her huge eyes and classical features, but her intentness scared him. She was wearing a tennis dress with a white towel bandana around her forehead. It showed off her tan.

'Marius,' she began. 'Leave him be. Dinner's ready. I'm hungry . . . and lonely. Please hurry.'

How could someone like her make love to someone like him? Tony thought, watching her as she moved towards Father. Her perfume wafted over him as she half turned towards him and gave an intimate, lilting smile leaving him somehow moved. He realised with a rush of blood to his cheeks that she was deliberately saving him.

His father blinked and shook his head as if he could not believe what he was hearing. 'Wait a bit,' he said, softening at once. 'I'm busy. This is important.' There wasn't much conviction in his voice. He tossed back another brandy with a funny twisted gesture and sat hunched over the glass, his blurred eyes gazing fondly at his young wife.

'My son . . . he's a failure. Takes after his mother,' he growled. 'This is my final word on the subject, Tony,' he said, still gazing at his wife. 'You can consider yourself lucky to get off so easily. You will make a friend of this Pieter de Vries. Be seen around with him. Go hunting with him. Learn to shoot. Maybe he'll turn you into a man. That's my decision. I've ordered another bicycle and you will deliver it and apologise.'

Tony's shoulders drooped disconsolately. He'd be the laughing-stock of his friends. 'But he's a poor white,' he began.

'Do as you're told.'

Tony went back to his room and locked himself in. He tried to read a book, but he was too angry to concentrate. God, how he hated Father. His hatred was like a living foetus to which his mind and his body played host. He was amazed when he heard a soft tap at his door around midnight. His step-mother stood there in a transparent nightdress and négligé. It was of blue and it shimmered in the glow from his desk lamp. He could see her bare flesh and the brown circles round her nipples pointing out of slightly plump protuberances. Hardly breasts, he thought. As she moved towards him he saw the dark triangle between her thighs. He felt his cheeks burning as if he'd fallen in a bed of nettles. His ears were singing and his mouth had dried. She was walking towards him like a vision. His penis throbbed, his hands were slippery wet, his mouth dried. 'I must be dreaming,' he thought. In her hands was a tray with a glass of milk and a plate of sandwiches.

'You poor boy,' she said. There was a shimmering sound of rustling nylon as she bent beside him and musky perfume seemed to envelope them in intimacy. Placing the tray on his desk, she ran her tongue over her lips. Was she nervous?

'Marius is a brute,' she whispered and amazingly her eyes filled with tears. Did she care about him? That was impossible. What was her angle? 'I'm on your side. I hate him. I'm sorry I couldn't get here before. I didn't dress for fear of waking him.'

As Tony stepped closer to her, the smell of the old goat came up from her nightdress, making him feel nauseous. She'd been lying next to him.

She smiled softly. 'Eat now. You've had no supper.' She perched on the edge of his bed, amongst the knives and pistols. 'What a marvellous collection. What's this for?'

She was fingering a Zulu knobkerrie. Tony moved towards her feeling light-headed, unable to pull his eyes from her stomach and thighs. He tried to talk, but had to clear his throat and suddenly he saw that she was laughing at him.

'How old are you now, seventeen . . . ?'

He nodded and licked his lips.

'There's something I want to tell you, Tony.' She caught hold of his hand and pressed her lips against his palm, sending a sword thrust of half-pleasure, half-pain through his groin. Momentarily she pressed his palm against her breast.

'I'm on your side. You and I need each other,' she whispered hoarsely. 'I hope we shall be friends.'

She stood watching him for a few seconds – then abruptly turned and left.

Long after she had left, Tony was still standing in the same spot, obsessed with the memory of her small, hard breast against his palm, the pink flesh seen through shimmering blue and the smell of her. He should have said something intelligent, or at last caught hold of her, but he had been in a state of shock. In bed later he relived the scene again and again while his swollen penis throbbed.

After the first rains the bushveld was simply lovely. Pieter and Dan were sitting on the ground in the doorway of the shed, working on the mangled bicycle. The sun shone on their black hair and their faces were glowing with health and happiness. Their feet were covered in earth, their fingers grimy and they were at one with each other as they worked silently. Around them, emerald green grass shoots were sprouting out of the brown hay not yet decayed. The ground was a multi-coloured carpet of wild flowers, birds were gathering in the trees chirping their joyful thanks for the gift of life and the pollen and berries that had miraculously appeared all over the place.

It was Saturday morning. Pieter had no farm work because Dad was back home attending to the place. At long last he had time to sit down and make a plan concerning his bicycle and Dan had arrived unexpectedly and offered his help. They had washed the mud off and reassembled part of it. One wheel had been bent back into shape and a friendly mechanic had soldered on the spokes for him. The nine speeds were connected, the brakes were working, the saddle was scuffed but usable, but the handlebars were hopelessly bent.

In a fit of recklessness, Ma had offered to sell a goose, to buy spare parts, but Pieter had scolded her. 'I'll fix it,' he had said tersely, but for the life of him he couldn't see how.

The two youths were polishing the spokes of one wheel when a bakkie approached along the farm road. When Pieter saw Cronjé's black tractor driver at the wheel, he caught his breath in annoyance. Tony the wimp, as he was known nowadays, emerged looking nervous. Shit! He's caught me cleaning the bike with Dan. Now he's got something to laugh about. Pieter longed to ignore him, but uppermost in his mind was his father's job. Tony was the boss's son, so he kept his gaze on the mangled handlebars, trying not to acknowledge defeat.

Tony felt his stomach lurch as he approached and gazed at that haughty face. 'I'm sorry,' he said, surprising himself. 'I hope you're big enough to accept an apology.'

Pieter scrambled to his feet in surprise. Tony was gazing up at him with an expression that reminded him of a begging dog. So what the hell did Tony want? A man shouldn't beg either. Pieter's black brows met in a ferocious scowl.

'What are you up to, Tony?' he said, gazing at a point over Tony's head.

As Tony moved closer, Pieter became aware of a disgusting smell coming from the creep: perfume, fancy soap, toothpaste and sweat. He saw him lick his lips and realised that Tony was afraid of him, which was odd since he was a full year older than him and in the power seat.

Tony smiled, eyes wide open in a guileless expression. Once again Pieter felt uneasy. Tie a ribbon round his neck and you would think he was a baby with his blond curls, light blue eyes and soft pink skin. The truth is, he's a real meanie and it pays to remember that.

'I've replaced your bicycle,' Tony said. 'It was the least I could do. Let's call it quits.' Here came the hand again.

Pieter frowned. 'Why, what have I done to you that we should call it quits?'

'You knocked the breath out of me.'

'Ah, come on, Tony, that was nothing much and you deserved it. I want to know what you have against me? I've never done you any harm.'

Tony stared pointedly at Dan, who took the hint and stood up. Picking up the wheel, Dan said: 'I'll clean the spokes at home and bring it back later.'

'Okay, talk,' Pieter said, when Dan had left.

Feeling intimidated, Tony found himself explaining in a halting manner. 'Father wants a winner for a son. He never lets up. I'd counted coming first this time. I'm a good shot, you see, but you're better. That's what the beating was really about. I didn't win. You did. Now Father insists that I become your friend. Perhaps he thinks some of your toughness will rub off on me. That's why I'm here. If it were up to me I'd tell you to go stuff yourself, but he holds all the power.'

Pieter laughed. 'So your dad's got you where he wants you. I'm glad I'm poor.'

'I hate him,' Tony said, and then swore under his breath at his stupidity. 'I wouldn't like . . .'

'I never gossip.' Pieter sat down again and began rubbing at the spokes with sandpaper.

'Let's go. The bicycle's at my place, we'll drive it back in the bakkie.'

Pieter felt torn in two. He longed for the bicycle, but he was too proud to accept.

'For God's sake take the damn thing or my life won't be worth living,' Tony urged him. 'Please, man.'

Pieter thought how hard Dan had worked on the bicycle to help him. If he got another, he could give this one to him. He shrugged and climbed into the back of the bakkie.

'I'll make sure your father changes his mind about me,' he promised Tony.

As they drove past Mrs du Toit's smallholding, Pieter saw Liza walking up from the dam looking sad. She had two turkey eggs in her hands. She flinched when she saw the bakkie and tried to dodge into the house.

'Come along with us, Liza,' Pieter called out. 'Please. I want you to come.'

'Yes, do, Liza,' Tony echoed. She shook her head, but Pieter went to fetch her.

'Leave her alone,' Gran said. She was bustling at the sink, as usual. Liza had gone into her room and closed the door.

'She can't hide away from this. She must face it and fight it,' he said. 'Come on, Liza.' After waiting a while the door opened and Liza came out, looking pale and swollen-eyed. He noticed she had changed into her blue floral dress, so obviously she was coming. To Pieter's surprise, Tony was friendly and kind to Liza. Perhaps he had some good in him after all. But then Pieter reasoned that Liza was probably the only person in the entire village to whom Tony didn't feel inferior.

Warmed by Tony's proffered friendship, Liza soon felt more relaxed and even managed to laugh a couple of times at his jokes. Tony had a wonderful sense of humour she realised. He'd never bothered to talk to her before.

Driving up to the homestead was an experience. There were five-barred gates, manned by guards in security uniforms who rushed out to wave and let them through. On either side were miles of rows of emerald green sugar spears. How could their sugar be so tall and green when it had only rained once this summer? She sighed with envy. It took ten minutes to reach the house and when she saw it in the distance she almost cried out with astonishment. There was a massive white gate, with a slave bell, and beyond it a fountain. But there was so much more . . . a pond full of Koi, a rose garden with hundreds of bushes, a house as big as a school, built in the shape of an E half enclosing the rose garden at one end and the fountain on the other.

She felt intimidated by the grandeur of it all as she followed Tony up the wide stone steps. Inside, the vast sitting room was filled with wonderful objects: paintings, pale blue shimmering silk curtains, Chinese carpets and antique tables with porcelain vases and ornaments on them. The floors were of inlaid mosaic tiles, intricate and costly. She oohed and aahed until Tony fetched a servant to show her round.

Liza followed the servant in a daze. Put all the rooms together and it probably covered close on half an acre, she reckoned, and there were two storeys. She tried not to look dazed. The kitchen alone was larger than Gran's whole cottage. Copper pots for show only hung around the walls under an oak-beamed ceiling with gleaming red quarry tiles underfoot. She followed her guide through three vast living rooms, a bar and a dining room with a table long enough to seat a regiment, then upstairs to the bedrooms and billiard room under the thatch, and back at last to the outdoor family room.

Gazing hesitantly through the door she saw the wide sweeping lawn sloping down to an ornamental lake, in the middle of which a man-made island had been created, so that Cronjé's imported geese and swans could sleep in perfect safety under wild fig and willow trees. Overlooking the lake was a wide patio where the Cronjés were entertaining guests. Liza lost her courage and asked the servant for the loo, where she locked herself in.

Where was Liza? She seemed to have vanished and Pieter couldn't help worrying what she was doing as he followed Tony along the enormous stoep to meet his folks.

Mrs Cronjé was a shock to Pieter. To start with she was so thin. He could see almost every bone, for she wasn't wearing much, just a blue halter top and the briefest black shorts. She was pretty, if you didn't look below her neck, and she was young. Her blue eyes seemed to burn out of a masklike face. He wondered why she was so tense. Her guests and her husband conformed exactly to Pieter's image of the very rich. Red-veined skin, flashy white teeth, bloated bellies, plenty of gold chains and eyes that seemed to say: 'Can I make a profit out of you, boy? No? Then get lost.'

There was a strange smell around: booze, garlic, expensive perfume, tobacco. Ugh! The way these people lived made him feel humble and angry at the same time. Couldn't his Ma just have one hundredth of what they had? But then maybe she'd land up looking and smelling like them.

'Ah-ha! Here's our champion with the catapult. Sit down, boys, pour the coke, Tony. Nice to see you, Pieter.' Cronjé turned to his guests. 'I must tell you the most delightful story . . .' He began to recount the story of the bicycle competition, omitting his son's role.

'Sit here, Pieter,' Mrs Cronjé purred, low-pitched and elegant. Strange how familiar her voice sounded. He puzzled about that as he sat and sipped his coke and tried to disguise his mounting annoyance. It appeared that he was there on show and would be performing like a circus animal any minute now. Marius Cronjé was gloating with pleasure as he recounted Pieter's victory. Watching him, Pieter felt puzzled. Why was he on his side instead of his son's? Then he realised that Cronjé liked to surround himself with winners. His wife had been a tennis champion, he remembered.

Mr Cronjé was getting to the point of his story. 'So it's like this, Pieter. My guests don't believe you can hit a target at twenty paces, so I've put up some tin cans there and we've made a small wager. Don't disappoint us, my boy. We're all dying to see if you can do it.'

'I didn't bring my catapult, sir.'

'Aha! I thought of that and I have one here.'

It was lying on the table. Pieter hadn't even noticed it – brand-new by the look of things. Picking it up, he examined it carefully. 'Mr Cronjé, I'm not a circus performer,' he said quietly.

Cronjé laughed. 'I'll give you half my winnings if you pull it off.'

He was still laughing as Pieter fired four stones, rattling the tin cans. The noise disturbed the geese and swans which rose from the dam in a flurry of wings and squawks to pass low overhead. A single shot on the head sent one spiralling down to land near Pieter, fluttering and dazed.

Pieter grabbed the rare goose and wrung its neck, flinging it over his shoulder. Mrs Cronjé's eyes were burning with temper, he noticed, and her face was even whiter than before.

'I won't take the cash,' he said. 'I don't believe in gambling, sir.' Then he farted long and loud.

'Don't ever bring him here again,' Cronjé said to Tony in a strangled voice. There was a low gurgle of amusement from his wife.

Now was the time for a perfect exit, Pieter reasoned, struggling to keep his face straight, but Liza was missing and that was a problem. Pieter walked over to the bakkie and saw the new bicycle lying in the back. Tony came racing after him, choking with laughter.

'You did it. You said you'd make him hate you and by God you did! I wish I had the courage to fart in his face.'

Pieter examined the bike carefully. It was the same brand, same colour, but somehow the magic had gone. Still, it would be useful. Now where the hell was Liza?

Liza had made the most of the loo. She had never before seen such soft and delicate pink tissues. There was some soap lotion that smelled divine and a soft fluffy pink towel and handcream in a cut-glass bowl, which she smoothed over her hands and knees. The talcum powder smelled of flowers. She took the large puff and dabbed the powder all over herself. What a toilet! The floor was of tiny checked black and white marble tiles, there was a miniature antique Bible with a silver lock lying near the loo, so you could get more holy as you did your business, but why bother since peeing in that loo was just like going to heaven. Taking some tissues from a box covered in muslin frills, she tiptoed outside and wandered around the front room, gasping with pleasure at the paintings.

She heard footsteps behind her, but she hardly noticed. She had fallen in love with the painting in front of her. It was a girl sitting on a swing, surrounded with flowers. 'Oh, how beautiful,' she sighed, envying the girl her big blue eyes and lovely dress. Then she turned and saw that Mrs Cronjé was staring at her in the strangest way. She looked as if she would scream.

Two bright spots of scarlet had appeared on either cheek.

'Who are you? What are you doing here?' she croaked, as if someone were strangling her.

'Please, ma'am, Mrs Cronjé, I'm Liza, Mrs du Toit's foster daughter, and I came here with Pieter.'

'Oh!' Mrs Cronjé looked horrified. Tears were starting up in her eyes, and her hands were clenched. 'Please go. Please . . . you shouldn't be here.'

Liza ran out of the beautiful house feeling loathsome and ugly. It was clear that this lovely woman had heard she was a *gammat*. She ran back to the bakkie and found Pieter clutching his new bike, a dead goose dangling from his belt.

'Oh, here you are,' he said, not noticing that she was crying with humiliation. 'Hop on to the saddle and hold my waist.'

'I'll drive you home,' Tony said, looking disappointed.

'Thanks, but we'll ride. Might as well try it out. See you.'

He stood up on the pedals and wobbling badly they headed for home.

Liza hung on to his waist tightly. She couldn't imagine what her life would be like without Pieter. She loved him dearly and she always would. He won't want to know me when I'm with the *gammats*, she thought. Her future was looming closer and more threatening, like the purple thunder clouds gathering low overhead right now. How dark it was.

Suddenly the rain came in a solid sheet of water. Like being under fifty thousand waterfalls, she thought, gasping for air. They were drenched within seconds. The road was a foot deep in muddy running water in next to no time. Soon they had to dismount and walk. Her blue dress was covered in mud and sticking to her. Gran would be angry.

The confrontation with Mrs Cronjé was the final straw that destroyed Liza's courage. She arrived home drenched and dismal and ran to Gran for comfort, blabbing out her meeting with the strange woman.

Gran had little comfort to offer. Instead she bustled around making Liza tea and even parted with one of their precious biscuits. Looking into Gran's eyes, Liza saw the bleakness of her future, for Gran was grieving and in her mind she had already said goodbye – that was as clear to her as the mole on Grannie's cheek. She searched for some way out.

'Perhaps I could be your maid,' Liza began. 'Perhaps I could stay here . . . what if I slept in the barn? Please don't send me away, Gran.'

Grannie pressed her lips together and busied herself at the stove, her back turned. Then she shook her head abruptly, as if shaking off a spider. 'I'm not your kin,' she said in a hard, flat voice. 'At this moment I wish I was. Then I would have some say over what's going to happen to you. When I took you on as a foster child, they made it quite clear to me that one day they would take you away. At the time they thought it might be when they found your parents. You are a ward of the courts and their word is law.'

'But the state won't care what happens to a *gammat*. No one cares about them, you know that.'

Impulsively, she pulled Grannie towards her in a strong hug, needing her approval. She respected her Gran. She was harsh, but just, old but strong, resigned to the harshness of their lives, but determined to hang on to her hope. Watching her, Liza thought uneasily about the shame she was bringing to their home. *Oh, Gran, one day you're going to be proud of me*, she thought in silent anguish. *You'll say I'm the best girl in the world. You will, you will.*

'Gran . . .' she faltered. 'Please, Gran. Let me stay.'

Gran looked down and flinched to see so much suffering. *If I'm kind to her it will be even harder for her to leave and leave she must. We are poor people. If I were rich I could send her to a private school, one of those English convents I've heard of where blacks and whites are learning together, the more's the pity, but even so it's out of the question. Besides, I have no control over her life. She's a ward of the court and I am only her foster mother.* She turned her attention back to the stove.

Liza sensed a shutting-off and shuddered. Lips compressed,

eyes red with unshed tears, Gran seemed engrossed with stirring mealie pap. 'Gran, I beg you.' She caught hold of her arm and shook her.

'Don't beg,' Gran said, steely-eyed. 'You'll be happier with your own kind.'

Wide-eyed with shock and rejection, Liza crawled into bed.

Chapter 6

———◆———

The tension was unbearable as Liza waited, fingers gripping the bedpost, every fibre in her body ready for flight as she forced herself to lie still. The slightest movement was enough to make her bedsprings squeal like a pig when Sam stuck his knife into its throat. If Grannie woke she was lost.

Through her open window, she could see scary black clouds racing past the moon. Each time it broke through, moonlight flooded her room. The lump in her throat was threatening to choke her as she gazed sadly at all those possessions, so achingly dear to her: the china rabbit Gran had bought, the wooden carving of a lynx Dan had made her, the fishing-tackle box Pieter had converted to hold her few pieces of jewellery. Would she ever see any of these precious things again?

She loved her room with the old oak cupboard Pieter had made her, the yellow-wood chair they had mended together, the patchwork quilt bedspread Gran had strained over for weeks. She gazed up at the picture of a white seal pup which she'd won by collecting the most cash in her class for the Animal Welfare Society. And there was her scrapbook of fashion drawings, her box of crayons and her many books. Dear God, how was she going to live without her books?

She loved her cat, too. Mimi slept on the chair, but tonight she was awake. She knew! Look how she was watching so intently. Her unblinking yellow eyes shone like the moon. They seemed to say: Liza, you are beneath contempt. Even a cat can live here in this humble cottage, but you cannot. Go and live with the *gammats* down by the stables.

This morning Grannie had brought back a registered envelope from the post office and hidden it in her drawer and Liza had seen her crying softly to herself. Gran's work had been put aside for the day, and she had taken all Liza's clothes and checked each garment for missing buttons and broken seams. She'd put a new collar on her best pink dress and mended the hem, before packing everything into their one canvas bag.

Liza could guess what was in the envelope – her amended birth certificate classifying her as coloured. She would never accept this. She was not coloured. She was *not*. She was white. But she couldn't stay here. She had to escape before Mrs Frank came to take her to the *gammats*. Where to go was a problem, but she would rather be dead than endure such shame. Uppermost was the thought of her school friends jeering as she joined the scruffy mob who daily begged around the streets, while her clothes became tattered and filthy and her hair hung lousy and unwashed.

Ah, Gran was snoring again. With a sudden rush of impatience Liza twisted her lithe body over the iron bedframe and landed face-down with a thump. The springs retracted, but the noise was not too bad. She lay on the floor listening, aware of the damp cold of the cement against her cheeks and the palm of her hands. Grannie's snores remained rhythmically reassuring. The cat leaped down beside her, hair erect, stiff-legged with tension, as if contaminated by her own fears. Liza kissed it goodbye. Then she grabbed the canvas bag, pushed up the sash window and slipped out.

She set off at a run, going behind the house, past Grannie's cactus garden, in order to make a wide detour past the kraal, for the donkeys would set up a commotion if they saw her. It was full moon and almost as bright as day, so she ran rapidly along the path, through the copse of jacaranda trees to reach the stony kopje between the river and her home. She paused there, lingering and regretful, close to tears and shivering because she was so scared. With a last sorrowful look back, she ran towards the road.

She had to walk a long way before she got a lift. It was almost dawn before the Cronjés' driver came past on his way to the station loaded with boxes of tomatoes. He looked shocked to see her.

'It's not safe for young girls to be out alone in the dark,' he lectured her. 'Whatever are you thinking of, Liza? Your Gran would have a fit? Hop up.'

'Gran's got the stomach ache and I'm going to get some medicine,' she lied.

'The chemist won't be open for hours.'

'I'm sure I'll have to call at his house,' she ad libbed.

'And the bag?'

'I'm delivering some sewing Gran did. We've been a bit short of cash lately,' she mumbled, quaking with fear. What if he took her back?

'I'll be coming back this way soon. If you want a lift be here before six.'

She gave a sharp sigh of relief. 'I should be home by then, thank you.'

I'll never see my home again, she thought, struggling to hold back her tears. I mustn't let him see I'm crying because he'd get suspicious and take me back to Gran. She had no idea where she was going, only the compulsion to run from this awful thing that she could not face. She had spent too long steeped in a culture that recognised 'whites' as the worthwhile beings. To be non-white was to be untouchable. As for coloureds, even the blacks despised them. She did not analyse her feelings for non-whites often, but if she touched one by mistake she would scrub her hands vigorously with soap as soon as she had the chance. She would never use the same cup any non-white had used and neither would anyone else. When Dan drank water out of their tin mug, kept specially for non-whites, they washed it in separate washing-up water. It would never do to put it in the basin with their crockery. Once, Pieter had given Dan a glass of water, and Gran had put that glass aside for his use only. She didn't understand why, but dark skins filled her with a compulsive abhorrence. So she was running just as hard and as fast as she could from her contaminated genes and the awful fate that awaited her.

The driver was humming to himself. Lisa felt a surge of envy and spite against him, and Pieter, and all those smug whites who were safe in their beds and closing their ranks against her. One day, she swore, she would come back here and teach them a lesson. She would be rich and famous and wear lovely clothes and have a better house than all of them and she would expose them for what they were – *liars*.

But meantime . . . where would she go? For a moment she had a wild desire to flee back to Gran and beg her to keep her, but she had tried that and failed. Then she remembered her teacher's words:

'Keep away from the *gammats* in the old warehouse by the station. They are going to be moved soon. There's no place for people like them in this town.'

And what had Mrs Frank said? 'She's clearly coloured. She'll be better off with her own people.' The memory set her teeth chattering. No, far better to leave this place.

She had planned to go straight to the station, but her feet took her the wrong way and she found herself creeping down the street to the abandoned warehouse. She had to see if 'they' were still there. Filled with dread, she crept closer. The ruined building looked deserted, so she hesitated and then, as if in a dream, crept through the gap of the half-broken door. The mingled stench of sweat, urine and wood smoke caught at her throat. She almost vomited as her stomach contracted with disgust. Perhaps they had gone, but then a heavy snore emerged from a pile of blankets by the wall.

Peering through the smoke-filled room, she saw two figures hard against each other: open mouths, decaying teeth, a smell of filth. She gagged, but watched fascinated as the woman reached up to scratch. Then she groaned and spoke.

Liza squealed with fright.

The man sat up and stared. His skin was dark brown, almost black, his eyes blood red, his face scraggy with a half-grey beard, his hair was straight and grey and as he scrambled to his feet, she saw that he was very tall and menacing.

'What the hell . . . ? Hey you? Who're you staring at?' he muttered, peering through the smoky gloom and rubbing his eyes. 'What are you doing here? D'you want a fuck?' He clutched his crotch, yanked his flies open and shook his penis at her. 'Come on then . . . come and get it . . .' His penis was purple and black and when he smiled his face seemed to mirror all the evil in the world.

She turned, sobbing and breathless, and fled back to the station. 'Dear God! Don't let Mrs Frank catch me and give me to the *gammats*. Please God.'

There was a train leaving at half past five . . . too soon for Gran to spread the word that she had run away. Besides, would she care? Wasn't Liza just an embarrassing problem she'd be better off without?

The porters were loading the railtrucks with crates of tomatoes. Another was full of cabbages. She sat on a bench waiting her chance and saw from the labels on the boxes that they were going to Johannesburg. Each time she heard footsteps approaching her heart leaped into her mouth.

It seemed hours before the porters went outside. This was her chance. Her heart pumping, her breath rasping in her chest, she scrambled up the side of the carriage, flung in her bag and fell over the top. There was a dusty canvas tarpaulin lying on the cabbages, so she scrambled under it. The dust rose up and filled her nose and her mouth and settled over her.

An eternity later, the train clanked forward in a series of lurches and the dust rose until she had only a fine yellow cloud of dust to breathe. Her nose itched, her eyes streamed, her mouth tasted as if she had licked the road clean. In no time she was so thirsty she thought she would die, but it would be a day or more before she reached Johannesburg. She should have brought water, but it was too late now.

By mid-morning she was nearly cooking under the tarpaulin, but when she scrambled on to it, the sun baked her and she knew she was turning blacker than a piece of charred toast, so she dived back under the suffocating canvas.

Tunnelling under the cabbages she pressed her hands over her face and tried to sleep. After a while she decided to pray. She screwed her eyes tightly shut and concentrated on her prayer, giving it all the passion of which she was capable.

'Let me stay white, dear God. I swear I'll never go in the sun again. I'll always be good and I'll say my prayers every night. Don't let anyone find out about me. Not ever!'

Midnight. Liza had succumbed to a delirious sleep where she dreamed she was as white as a lily in the veld. Reality hit her like a blow in the stomach as the train lurched to a halt. It was a nightmare, but it wouldn't go away. How could this have happened to her? Oh God, help me. She felt dirty and bruised, every limb ached from her pounding on the hard, knobbly, shifting cabbages. The dust and her thirst had turned her throat into a furnace. Her head ached abominably, and, worse still, she was homeless and terrified. Throwing back the tarpaulin she peered around. Neon lights lit the station and there was no one around, so she threw her bag to the platform and scrambled after it.

'Hey, you! Stop!'

Running feet pounded in her ears, a whistle blew, shouts echoed around her. Liza grabbed her bag and raced to the exit, pushing past the sleepy guard. Once outside, she kept running.

Liza was unprepared for the shock of the city. She had seen pictures of buildings of concrete and glass rearing up to thirty-six storeys, but she had thought that the city rose up from the veld, that she could walk beyond it to trees, and grass, and a river where she could drink and a tall bush she could sleep under. There was nothing at all like that here. The whole world seemed to be made up of tall buildings and straight, wide roads that went from north to south and east to west. Lights blazed from the buildings, shop windows of jewels and beautiful dresses and furs, glittered under harsh spotlights, behind plate glass and thick bars. She wandered in a daze from one street to the next, longing to find an open field or a clump of bushes, but nature was banished from this rich city and this frightened her. She began to run, heart and feet pounding together.

She slowed as exhaustion set in. Panting and sobbing for breath, she leaned against a pillar and looked around. She was halfway across the widest bridge she had seen. Water! She must have water. She peered over the parapet, but there was no sign of a river underneath, just railway tracks. Fighting back her disappointment and feeling light-headed, she hurried on. A group of people burst out of a doorway. She stood rooted in the shadows by a wastebin and watched them hurry past. The women were wearing shimmering gowns and jewels and they were laughing as they hurried towards a car. The car moved off swiftly and left her alone, and now she felt twice as lonely as before.

Trudging on, she came to an open square lit by street lights with flowering shrubs and fountains in circular cement ponds. Thrusting her head into the cool water she washed her face and hands. What a blessed relief it was to drink deeply. There was a bus shelter nearby. She sat on the bench, hugging her case and fell asleep. She woke to voices and a woman bending over her, shaking her arm.

'Don't you have a home to go to, dear? Where do you live?'

Liza looked up feeling puzzled and very cold. Where was she?

The woman's husband was frowning and tugging at his wife's arm. 'Leave her, Anne. She must be coloured. Don't interfere.'

'No, wait! I'm not sure. Who are you, little girl? Where do you come from. What's your name?'

'I tell you, she's coloured.'

Liza looked up into the woman's kind grey eyes and burst into tears. 'Oh, help me, please,' she sobbed. 'I'm lost. I have nowhere to sleep. I'm so tired and hungry.' The woman's expression of concern had brought home the terrors of her plight and now tears of self-pity brimmed over and ran down Liza's cheeks.

The woman straightened up. Her kind eyes seemed sterner. She hesitated and thrust a two-rand note into Liza's outstretched hands. 'You're probably right. I think she must be coloured. A beggar I suppose.' They hurried on and for a while, Liza trailed after them until the man turned and angrily told her to 'fuck off'.

She found a hotel blazing with lights and vibrating with the sound of jazz. A black man lay sprawled over the pavement outside. Was he hurt? Why didn't someone help him?

She tiptoed forward and caught a whiff of stale wine. The stench reminded her of the *gammats* in Nelfontein. He was drunk. As she moved back a hand shot out and caught her ankle. She screamed and kicked, but his hand was like a steel trap pulling her closer to her. She fell forward, grabbed the kerb and hung on while her screams reverberated around the building. A taxi drew up close by, some people stepped out. Unbelievably, they hurried into the hotel, leaving her screaming and clawing and kicking. 'Help me. Help me,' she yelled after them.

'You're wasting your time, little girl.' Unbelievably the black let go of her and sat up. 'No one helps no one in this hell city.' His hands latched on to her canvas bag.

'No! That's mine.' As she grabbed at it, his clenched fist shot up and she saw a knife gleaming. Yelling, she ran into the hotel. There was a man in braided uniform inside the revolving doors. 'Please, sir, there's a kafir with a knife outside and he's stolen my bag.'

'Get lost,' he grunted.

'Help me . . . please!'

'I'm not walking into any damned traps. Get out of here before I throw you out.'

A couple came hurrying through the foyer and she turned to them for help. 'Help me . . . please.'

The man fumbled in his pocket and flung two coins at her feet, while the woman hurried on without a backward glance.

'You'll lose your job if you let beggars in here, Smit.'

'I'm not a beggar,' she sobbed. 'A kafir stole my things . . . all I own.'

The porter's face was cold like stone – a graven image. He took hold of her arm and pushed her out through the swing doors. She fell heavily down the steps on to the pavement and for a moment she could hardly move from the numbing pain. Then she saw that the black tramp had gone and so had her bag and all her clothes, her bible, her hairbrush and toothbrush – everything she owned. She sat on the steps and cried.

Smit came out and thrust two rands into her hand. 'I'm warning you, I've called the police, so get lost,' he said.

The reality of being lost was more terrible than she had ever imagined. She could hardly breathe, her breath was coming in great gasps that hurt her chest. 'Oh . . . Oh . . . What shall I do?' she sobbed under her breath. 'Dear God . . . where can I go?'

Now it seemed as if her world had turned into a dream and she wandered on and on hardly aware of where she was going and not really caring. It was a strange world where the buildings became older and more dilapidated and tramps lay in doorways where the stench of stale wine and despair was all about them. Some of the tramps had white skins, but they were so ugly with faces like old gravel patches, with brown and purple blotches amongst the dirt and the warts. They were filthy and ragged. How could this be? She had never seen whites like this before.

At last she saw a park with thick shrubs and trees and real grass. She hurried towards it. Sitting on the grass, propped against a bench, was an old white lady. Her white hair was curly and streaked with yellow, her face a strange purple colour. She was wearing a black coat over a floral dress and lace-up brown shoes and her gnarled hands were clutching a brown paper bag.

Liza watched her with mounting pity. She was so old, so

beaten, so destroyed by this horrible city. 'I'll never get like her,' she whispered aloud. 'I'll wear beautiful clothes like those women I saw. One day I'll be so rich I'll have a new dress every day,' she solemnly promised herself. But right now she was tired and very scared. She backed into a clump of flowering shrubs until she was hidden, and gazed at the old woman. Had she ever been young? How did one get to look like her? Was it because she had no one to look after her? Perhaps she'd like a daughter, Liza wondered. Perhaps she won't care that I'm slightly dark. She looks so alone.

'Wake up . . . wake up quickly. Run. Come!'

Someone was shaking her. She stared at them. Who were they? Where was she? The moon had set and it was so dark. She was shivering with cold.

'Run . . . quickly.'

Two young coloured boys were gazing down at her. One of them pushed his hand over her mouth and peered over his shoulder, trembling with fright.

'Don't scream,' the other one whispered. 'Don't make a noise, or they'll kill you.'

'Let go of me.'

The boys fled towards an alleyway across the road leaving her alone. Peering around she saw tall black figures, dark as night, moving cautiously, black against black, the whites of their eyes glittering from the neon street lights. Something about them made her skin crawl. She dived out of the bushes and raced across the road to the doorway where the boys had run.

'They saw you. They're coming. Follow us . . . quietly.' They ran into a dark doorway and up a flight of stairs to the first floor, where one of them produced a key and unlocked the door to a women's toilet. They closed and locked it just in time as footsteps came running past.

One of them put his finger on his lips. 'Sh!' he whispered. 'We stole the key. They won't find us in here.'

Thrusting their heads through the open window, they pulled

Liza between them. She could feel them shivering violently.

They were overlooking the park and she could see the old woman propped against a tree near a street light, still clutching her paper bag. The youths circled around her, jostling each other, wary, searching the roads. They were like a pack of wild dogs in the bushveld, Liza thought shuddering. Their hair was teased up into weird straight peaks on their heads, their chests glittered with necklaces and beer tin fasteners glistened in their ears. They wore waistcoats over bare chests, wide belts, tattered jeans and running shoes. One of them prodded the old woman with his toe. He held up a bottle of coke and tipped the contents over her face. What for? What was he doing? Liza wondered.

The old woman woke, spluttering, cursing and struggling to her feet.

'Dance, whitey!' the boys shouted. 'Dance for us.'

Liza opened her mouth to scream, but a grubby hand was clutched hard over her face. All three of them began to shake convulsively as the match flared. The woman seemed to explode. All at once she was screaming horribly, clutching her face and staggering around in circles while the boys circled, jeering and laughing. Liza shut her eyes and tried not to listen but the weird, inhuman screams went on and on. Then came the wail of a police siren. Dazed and shocked, filled with a sense of unreality, too confused to think at all, Liza curled up into a foetal position in the corner of the toilet and stayed there until dawn.

Chapter 7

The white-tiled walls were becoming visible as the sky lightened. Liza gazed around, not understanding why she was there,
who she was, or what she was doing. She sort of knew, and yet
she didn't know. Her name was on the tip of her tongue, but she
could not quite remember what it was. Strange memories kept
flashing through her mind, like memories of events that had
only just occurred, a kaleidoscope of images: walking with a tall
boy with blue-black burnished hair while the sun beat down on
them. But who was he? Watching an old woman with brown
eyes and grey hair digging in a herb garden, winding up a bucket
from a well until her arms ached and her hands were blistered.
But then came that other horrible image of the old woman
screaming as she exploded into flames. But who was she?
Obsessed with the pictures flashing through her mind, Liza had
no interest in the present. She was only dimly aware of two
coloured urchins beside her.

Like creatures of the wild, the little scavengers yawned,
stretched, and prepared to set off for their day's hunt. Restless
and hungry, they paused in the doorway and stared at Liza
impatiently.

'Come,' one of them said. 'You can't stay here. The cleaners
are coming.'

She stared at them blankly, not understanding. 'Where can I
go?'

'What's your name?' one of them asked.

'I don't know.'

'Where do you come from?'

'I can't remember. Not right at this moment.' She began to shake violently.

'D'you want to come with us?' one of them asked more gently.

'She must have run away,' the other said. 'Like I did. She looks like my sister. I'm going to call her Angel, because she looks like an Angel.'

'Angels don't have black hair.'

'She does.'

Liza drank some water from the tap and looked at her reflection in the mirror. A strange face stared back, not one that she remembered, so she followed them meekly, since no alternative came to mind.

To Liza, the two boys were the only real people in her entire world. She was determined not to lose sight of them as they trotted westwards, a raggle-taggle, shivering threesome, to the car park of a shopping centre where the boys moved from spare lot to spare lot, waving in the morning cars and collecting the grudgingly given tips from the drivers.

'They have to pay us,' one of them told her solemnly, 'because they're scared we'll bust their windows if they don't.'

At eight a.m. the older tramps arrived and chased them away, so she sat on the bench with the younger of the two boys, while the other one went to buy bread at a supermarket. He returned looking triumphant with a loaf of bread and a coke, and three stolen chocolate bars which they shared. Liza felt better after eating.

Nico was the name of the taller boy, she learned. He was dark, with almond-shaped eyes and thick black brows that almost met across his forehead, and wiry hair. His face was mostly crinkled into a smile showing strong white teeth. Instinctively she trusted him. He claimed to be thirteen, but he looked younger. Between mouthfuls, she learned his story. Once he had lived with his mother in a corrugated-iron shack in a squatter settlement, but one day she had left for work and never returned. He'd been living on the streets for a year, but he still missed her a lot.

'Didn't you look for her?' Liza queried.

'What's the point? I guess she found some other man with a better place to live. He wouldn't want me.' He stared away obstinately. 'I like it here. I don't want to go back to her. I like being free.'

Ralph was ten and almost white, with milky-blue eyes and dark blond, kinky hair. He had a strangely adult-looking face, with a long bony nose and sharp cheekbones.

'My mother found a new man and got pregnant and my step-father kept beating me,' he said, in a hoarse, childish voice while looking very sad. 'I've been back three times over the past two years, but he always beats me until I leave.' He looked so wistful and she guessed that he, too, missed his mother and his home.

'There's hundreds of kids like us,' Nico told her. 'It's easy to stay alive on the streets if you know how.'

'You must be careful of the gang you saw last night. They're called the Jeppe Warriors. You must never be caught by them,' Ralph said. 'That's the worst thing that can happen to you. If you stay with us, we'll show you how to survive.'

They walked all morning, begging occasionally, stealing apples from a stall, cleaning windscreens at a car park, anything that came to mind. Liza followed them meekly, struggling to remember her name and to make sense out of the pictures in her mind's eye. By lunchtime she felt exhausted. Sitting on a bench by the parking lot, she fell asleep in the sun.

When she woke, she thought she was alone and panic sent her heart lurching. When she saw Ralph returning, her relief was so great that she burst into tears.

'Where's Nico?' she asked.

Ralph's angular face was twisted with anxiety. 'He got an offer from some guy. Maybe he'll be back some time.'

'An offer?'

'Yeah.' He looked embarrassed. 'It's easy. Ten rands a go.

Like I said – easy money. It doesn't hurt. Well, not much. I don't want you to do that, Angel.'

'What does he do?'

'Oh . . . well .. I don't want to talk about it. I don't like to do it. Listen. I'm worried about you, Angel. You see, it's easy to survive on the streets if you're a boy, but you're a girl, so it won't be the same for you. Couple of fellows have been following us.' He gazed around uneasily. 'You've got to look like a boy. It will be safer for you.'

They found an Indian woman who agreed to shave her scalp and pay for her hair. Then Liza found four rands in her pockets, although she couldn't imagine how the cash got there, and they bought a T-shirt, a windbreaker, and a pair of torn takkies, all of which had been discarded by the woman's son. With the rest of the cash they bought glue and Ralph took her to the corner of a park where the kids met and sniffed in safety. There were eight of them gathered around the fountain, skinny, noisy, anxious kids intent on sniffing away their troubles for a few hours.

She sniffed . . . and sniffed . . . but nothing seemed to happen. 'It doesn't work with me,' she exclaimed, flinging her arms up in abandon. 'Besides, I can't be bothered. I feel so happy.' This moment seemed to be engraved on her mind as being of special significance. She was here with her very good friends and she was at peace. 'Perhaps I'll try a little more,' she said.

She woke the next morning with a raging thirst, a splitting headache and her throat so dry she could hardly swallow. Worse still was the depression that had settled on her. Looking around she saw she was inside a wooden box, lying on a heap of straw. She crawled out and found herself on the roof of a tall block of flats. Around her were ugly rooftops with no sign of a tree or a blade of grass. She began to shake with fright. Her head was cold. Reaching up, her hands encountered bristly stubble. Where was she, what was happening? She had never felt so alone in her life. She crawled back into the box and spent a miserable hour quaking until Ralph returned with half a loaf of bread and a carton of milk which they shared. She grabbed her share and wolfed it down.

'I thought you'd gone forever,' she moaned.

'I would never leave you, Angel.'

'Then I, too, will never leave you. We shall stick together.' But Nico had gone. What if Ralph went, too? 'How can Nico find us?' she asked.

He shrugged. 'He'll be around. Let's get going.'

There was only one boy left on the rooftop. He was very young, maybe eight or nine years old. His eyelids were encrusted with sores, his clothes hung together in shreds. He stank and was so emaciated and weak, he could not stand up.

'Too much glue-sniffing. He's finished,' Ralph told her solemnly. 'A junkie! Leave him here. He's going to die anyway. The cops will pick him up one of these days.'

'No! Never!'

'He's not our problem,' Ralph said.

But he was and she knew that. In some subtle way, it was herself who was lying there untended. She had to save him to make her own world that much safer. 'If we look after each other, we'll be safer,' she argued. 'Go and get some bread and milk.'

Ralph was gone for a while. He returned breathless and triumphant. 'The pig saw me,' he gasped. 'But I gave him the slip.'

The milk strengthened the boy enough for him to shuffle down the pavement, leaning heavily on Liza, with Ralph leading the way, until they reached a long white building in Curzon Street. THE HOME SHELTER was written in black paint over the doorway.

'Anyone can come here,' Ralph told her, knocking on the door. 'They give you a bunk and three meals a day. They don't lock you in and it's free. They don't stop you from leaving, either.'

'Then why don't you stay here?' she asked, feeling puzzled.

'The older boys beat you up and they make you go to school and study. They tell you what to do and anyway, you can't stay here forever – only for a few days. They try to find your parents and send you home.

'He's been here enough times,' he grumbled, gesturing towards the boy who was still swaying on his feet. 'Help me push him inside. He won't stay. Next time he'll come looking for you because you fed him.'

Ralph was right, she discovered. A month later, the boy, whose name was Anton, found the three of them, for Nico was back. Later Johannes, a clever boy, half-Zulu, half-Indian, but crippled, and Hennie, a scraggy Cape Coloured of fourteen, who was wanted by the police, joined their gang. Now they were six, including Liza, and they were known as Angel's Gang.

At night they guarded parking lots and claimed tips from irate drivers. They stole what they could not afford, slept in toilets, underground parking lots, crates, disused sheds, the stairways of flats and anywhere else offering temporary shelter. Days and nights followed in a blur. Her gang members were inseparable and their loyalty to each other was deep and meaningful.

For Liza it was a strangely triumphant existence. She had learned to survive, she was healthy, amongst friends, and she had enough to eat. She had sipped the heady nectar of absolute freedom and she could fight her way out of a scrap if she had to. She had learned to be adept with a sharp knife she had stolen, and had become a skilled shoplifter.

She and her gang were both the hunters and the hunted, always on guard, taking risks, robbing, stealing and mugging the unwary, rifling cars and bags, counting on the dark to cover their tracks. She washed and drank when she pleased from the many fountains, keeping a wary eye out for police. Sometimes the gang went through garbage and sold the bottles and old clothes. From this they earned the grand total of fifty rand a month which they shared. She had learned to live on her wits and to survive in a tough city which she knew as intimately as if it were her own – and in a way, it was.

For the past six months, her memory had been restored to her in bits and pieces and at the strangest times. She would smell a flower and suddenly see her Gran's eyes smiling over her garden of flowers. One morning at the car park she saw a car skid badly, coming to rest near a wall, and suddenly she was propelled back in time to the traumatic visit of Mrs Frank, the social worker. A sudden downpour had her clinging to Pieter as they rode the new bicycle home. This brought on an explosion of grief that lasted for days. Despite her self-sufficiency, she was suffering. She could not see her wounds, but she sensed they were there, deep inside herself and they were festering.

Summertime in the Highveld. In Johannesburg at noon the tarmac melted, scorching their bare feet with patches of tar burned into flesh. Liza loved the sun, revelling in the warmth beating down on her and rising up from the pavement, fanning her legs. She gazed around contemptuously at the soft-skinned, pale-eyed whites scurrying like termites to their glass and concrete termitaries. She'd been inside them all, experienced the air-conditioned luxury, the deep pile carpets, larny furniture and paintings, bowls of fresh flowers, missing nothing as she zig-zagged down corridors, evading capture like a lost field mouse, until they pounced on her and flung her out.

She turned and ogled at herself in a shop window. She saw a tall, skinny boy-like figure, black hair crew cut, her skin burned dark by the sun, huge eyes glistening. She grinned triumphantly. She had been rejected, but she had survived. She was no longer Liza Frank, but Angel. She was part of the shifting, restless, predatory gangs of street kids who survived by their wits in the big cities.

One day she would take a giant spade and break down the walls of their termitaries, just as she used to do in the veld back home. She would watch the terrified creatures scurrying to safety and stamp her foot on them. Yes, she would, without mercy, for she despised them. Whites were no different to the ants. They, too, guarded their belongings and their power and their sense of superiority. 'I'll get you back for what you've done to me,' she muttered.

Maria de Vries watched her son and grieved for him. At some subtle level which she couldn't really reach, she knew he had been damaged by Liza's tragedy. At first he had been so rebellious, getting into brawls at school, threatening to run away, but there was nothing positive he could do and this had made him feel inadequate and helpless. She knew how he had longed to protect Liza, but he was prevented from doing so by the laws of the land. Six months had passed since Liza ran away, it was assumed to Johannesburg, and Pieter had kept his anguish locked inside himself, but Maria had noticed how he had become less sensitive to others. He'd had to harden himself, and squash his compassion, and this was affecting his entire world. That's what it's like for all of us, she thought. We all have to harden our hearts and we are all damaged.

And what about old Mrs du Toit, Liza's foster-mother. She had loved that girl, but nowadays she kept herself to herself and was seldom seen in the village. Maria had gone to visit her two days ago. She'd taken a dozen eggs and a jar of honey from her own hives, but Mrs du Toit had been remote.

'I don't want to talk about this thing,' she had said, looking flustered. 'I obey the letter of the law. I always have.' She had spent some time showing Maria the pictures of cabinet ministers that hung around her living-room walls. Maria sensed that Mrs du Toit had no capacity to bear something so intensely hurtful, so she had switched off. Liza was walled up somewhere deep down in the recesses of her heart.

I don't want Pieter to get like her, Maria thought. She decided to have it out with him, and chose Saturday morning as the best time, for he could help her in the garden.

*

As Pieter stood watching his mother busily plucking out weeds and disciplining her garden he thought that she was the most beautiful woman imaginable. Her deep blue eyes were narrowed with concentration, her face pale and freckled, her dark hair dragged back into a ponytail. She was slim, and lovely with a narrow waist and delicate hands and feet.

This was not Ma's first garden. Two years ago they had toiled together to dig up a patch of earth behind the kitchen door and they had planted wallflowers, poppies and roses.

'A woman must have a garden,' she had argued when he complained about the wasted effort. 'It's hard for a woman to remember what she is and to stay feminine in a place like this. She needs something that's creative and beautiful.'

After this he had toiled in silence.

In mid-summer, the small garden had bloomed into masses of colour. How she had loved those flowers, but the following summer brought drought conditions and when autumn came and they faced the long, dry winter, Ma let her flowers die. She had pressed her lips together and said: 'Folks like us can't have all the things we want. God takes care of our needs, not our wants. We have to save our water.'

Soon she had thought of a better idea and they had gone searching for beautiful rocks, borrowing Cronjé's lorry to transport them back to the garden where he had arranged and rearranged them under her direction down the side of the kopje. Then the tiny cacti and aloes had been collected from the bushveld and brought home to be planted in pockets of earth between the twisted rocks. Now the slope was a blaze of colour and, beyond the garden, weaver birds' nests swayed at the end of thorny branches.

The cicadas were chirping shrilly and the veld was noisy with the buzzing and twittering of millions of insects and birds. The heat from the sun seemed to vibrate right through you into the earth and back up again through the soles of your feet, yet there was Ma frowning away as she worked. Something was on her mind.

'I went to see Mrs du Toit this week,' she said. 'The poor old woman has taken it very hard. She can't seem to get to grips with her feelings. It would be better if she'd acknowledged her grief and let it all out. Instead she's bottling things up and that's bad for her.'

Sensing a coming lecture, Pieter felt defensive. 'It would have been better if they'd let Liza alone. She wasn't harming anyone,' he mumbled.

'Ag! Pieter, there was no alternative. After all, she's coloured,' she said.

'But what harm would it do if she were to stay here with her Gran? People are so cruel.'

'Whites can't live with non-whites, Pieter, you know that. It's not allowed. If she'd stayed with Mrs du Toit they'd both have been breaking the law. Whites can't marry non-whites and they can't even sit down and eat with whites, and we wouldn't want them to, so how could she stay there? She would have become so unhappy as she got older. You know that.'

'It's ridiculous,' he said petulantly, scowling as he dug a hole for a rock.

'It's not silly if you think about it properly,' she said. 'Those people are different from us. You heard that terrible programme on the radio last night, Pieter.'

Pieter shuddered at the memory. A black toddler of two years had been found lying in a ditch, his thumbs and sexual parts sliced off . . . and he'd survived. So the doctors were turning him into a girl with a series of operations and hormone pills. It was a common enough crime for the parts were needed for witchdoctors' muti. He did not want to think about it, so he pushed the unpleasant memory aside.

'Just you remember this, Pieter. If we can't make apartheid work we'll be swept under by a tide of millions of blacks. We'd be pushed out of our jobs, our homes, our schools and, worst of all, off our land. It's not easy to keep two groups of people entirely separate, but we want to live *our* way – not their way. There's only one way to do that and that's to keep the two groups quite apart – apartheid is the only way we can survive in Africa and we all have to make sacrifices.

'Besides, it's God's will that the *gammats* should be beneath us. "The sons of Noah that went forth out of the ark, were Shem, and Gam and Japhat . . . and of them was the whole earth overspread,"' Ma said, in her special singsong voice she kept for reciting what she could remember from the bible.

'"And Gam, who was the father of Canaan, saw the nakedness of his father, Noah, and told his two brethren without. And Noah awoke from his wine and knew what his younger son, Gam, had done unto him. And he said, 'Cursed be Canaan, a servant of servants shall he be unto his brethren. Blessed be the Lord God of Shem and Canaan shall be his servant.'" So you see the *Gammats* are the sons of *Gam* whom God made our servants.'

You couldn't argue against the Holy Book, Pieter decided, particularly with his mother, since it was the only book she'd ever read. Then he felt guilty for his disloyal thoughts. He sighed. No one ever seemed to understand him. 'For goodness sake. I was only talking about Liza,' he fumed.

'She's a borderline case. A victim of her parents' sin. There're thousands more like her. Let them into our white areas and there'd soon be more and more of them – like a crack in a dam, the whole wall would come tumbling down and we'd be drowned . . .'

'I know . . . in a black tide. . . really I don't want to talk about it, Ma.'

Maria felt that she had failed her son. She'd tried her best, but it was so difficult to get through to him nowadays. She would make a special milk tart for him. That would cheer him up.

In the afternoon, Pieter went off into the veld alone. He was supposed to be hunting, but he couldn't help worrying about Liza. How could she survive alone in a city as dangerous as Johannesburg, where no whites went walking out alone and unarmed at night for fear of robbing, murdering, mugging, torching or being paralysed by a bicycle spoke pushed through the spine? Just listening to Constable Willis Smit made your blood curdle. He was stationed in Nelfontein while he recovered from a nervous breakdown at what he had seen in the city. He'd told Pieter about youngsters killing old men for five cents, about feuds erupting between rival factions until every living thing was destroyed – homes, families, babes-in-arms, even the cats and dogs were put to death. How whole families were barricaded into their homes and burned.

No, Ma was right, they couldn't live with those people. In this savage continent, whites had to be strong to survive. But still, it wasn't *Liza*'s fault.

Chapter 8

————◆————

Tony was hiding in the shadows of a marula tree. The moon was rising above the Lebombo Mountains and casting an eerie glow that dimly lit the bushveld and made the black shadows of trees seem darker and more sinister. It was mid-summer and the earth was moist and heady with the scent of herbs and flowers, but Tony did not notice this. He was listening intently, but could hear little above the noisy din of cicadas and frogs and the cry of night birds. When he heard a hyena's morbid call and the jackals yelping, he shuddered. He loathed and feared the bushveld and he was afraid of the dark. Nothing but the promise of money would have brought him here at night.

Would they come? He was expecting a party of Mozambican refugees. Every day hundreds of families embarked on the dangerous trek to South Africa. Deprived of food, health-care, schools and jobs, their homes and families the prey of Frelimo or Renamo troops – whichever was occupying their tribal lands – they fled to an uncertain future over the border.

The fence itself was not particularly hazardous. It consisted of two strands of electrified wire, three rolls of razor wire, topped by two more electrified strands on the Mozambique side, all woefully inadequate to keep out starving refugees. It was the terrain that killed them – 35 kilometres of parched land where wild animals of every description roamed. Many attempted the journey, but only a few arrived.

If and when they made it, they had to pay the price for Tony's help, so they carried AK-47 Russian-made rifles, or rhino tusks, emeralds, aquamarines – anything of value. In return, he gave each one a parcel of food, a tin of coke and a lift into the interior – at least 50 kilometres from the border – to a farmer willing to employ illegal labour.

There was a sudden silence. Tony heard a twig snap. A guinea fowl screamed hysterically and set off a chorus of the noisy birds. Straining into the shadows, he saw figures materialising – shadow people, thin and insubstantial as the night, for they had starved for years.

He began to work on the fence and seconds later had the wires jacked apart. He leaned forward to help the first refugee step on to South African soil. The man's foot caught on the wire and for a moment the two were locked into a deathly embrace as the current raced through them. They fell on the ground, shocked and breathless. Tony got up, scowling.

'Be careful,' he snarled, his lips still caught back in a grimace of pain. The shadows moved lightly through the gap. Then Tony let the wire drop back and turned to check the loot.

They were only two kilometres from his farm. Ten minutes later they stumbled uncertain, shocked and exhausted into the abandoned sugar storage sheds near the river. Tony had transformed them into bunkrooms to cope with up to twenty-five refugees at a time. Here they would eat, drink and sleep until the following night. He checked the loot. There were two Russian-made rifles, one magnificent rhino horn, a few aquamarines – clear and deep blue – four small emeralds and a box full of garnets. He shrugged. Not bad. Amongst the 'gifts' was a piece of rock. He picked it up and almost dropped it, it was so amazingly heavy.

'What is it?' he asked the man who had brought it. He was tall and coal-black, only the whites of his eyes shone in the moonlight.

He shrugged. 'Heavy stone, baas. That's all.'

'Where do you lot come from?'

'Gelé, Baas, in the Zambesi Province.'

'Okay.' Tony pocketed the stone and led them to his lorry

which was hidden in a nearby glade. Before long, the loot was hidden in the hay store over the stables and the refugees were locked up. They had to eat, shower and sleep for the day before he could pass them off as prospective labour. He would deliver them the following evening.

His night's work completed, Tony went to bed.

He woke to the sound of shouting and the smell of fire and smoke. A woman began wailing in the distance. His stomach lurched as he realised the implications of these sensations. The refugees had accidentally set light to the stables. Now Father would find out.

Good God! What was he to do? He struggled into his clothes and raced outside, surprised to see the stain of red over the eastern mountain range. It must be almost five. He thought he'd only slept for a minute or so.

Their workers were tumbling out of the hostel and grabbing buckets. The fire was not serious, twenty minutes later the blaze was out, but it was too late to save him. Father stood there in his mohair tartan dressing-gown. The belt was tied so that he bulged above and below it. His eyes and cheeks were as swollen as his stomach, his mouth shouting obscenities at Tony who cringed.

'You cretinous vermin! You evil son of a bitch. You take after your crafty mother all right. Not an ounce of loyalty in you. So this is what you've been up to. You're like a jackal scrounging possessions from these pitiful people. If this gets out it will break me. Can you see the headlines? Politician's son smuggles refugees into SA. What do they pay you? This pathetic loot?

Father picked up the horn and hurled it into the rose garden. Tony made a mental note of where it had fallen. Someone had spied on him and shown Marius his store. Damn them!

'Why?' Father was demanding.

'To pay for my education since you won't,' Tony blurted out, instantly regretting his blunder.

'You're not going to university. You'll stay and run the

plantations. Someone has to. Believe me, my boy, if you try to dodge your responsibilities I'll report you to the police. You could get five years for this, plus dealing in rhino horns, that's tantamount to murder nowadays.'

He went on and on, beriding, accusing, insulting, until he had worked himself into a complete rage. Towering over Tony, he brought his sjambok [sjambok = heavy leather whip] crashing around his ears. Caught by surprise at this sudden violence, Tony backed off and grabbed an iron stave. He was panting and shaking. He took a deep breath and tried to pull himself together. He could see Father's hated face dimly through a haze of anger. His anger was so all-encompassing he could hardly move. He gasped for breath, but his throat had closed up.

'I'll get you,' he muttered, but Father turned abruptly and stamped off to the house. Tony felt something warm trickling down his neck. Putting his hand up, he was surprised to see blood and plenty of it. 'One day, you bastard ... You wait!' Voicing the idea seemed to make it more real. The thought was like soothing ointment on his wound. 'You won't look so pompous when your fat paunch is riddled with bullets,' he muttered.

An hour later, Tony sat at the window watching the swans on the lake. The sun was rising, the birds were singing, the whole world was happy, only he was plunged into new depths of misery. Why does it have to be like this? Why does he hate me so much? Why am I punished? Perhaps he should leave home and make his own way. Nothing could be worse than living like this – the pain, the grief, the self-loathing that he had to endure. No one cared about him. Shafts of sadness pierced him and he burst into sobs.

There was a light knock. The door opened and his step-mother came in, carrying a tray. She pushed the door to with her foot. Amazing strength, he thought, noting the heavy silver tray, the coffee pot with mugs and a plate of hot scones, butter, jam and cream. It comes from smashing at tennis balls six hours a day. She looks like a wraith, but there's steel under that delicate white skin.

'Do come in,' he said sarcastically as she sank on to his bed.

She laughed at him. 'Poor little Tony. What has he done to you this time? How can you bear it? When are you going to stand up to that monster?'

He felt humiliated, and he knew his face was wet with tears. He liked to show off to her when she visited him in his room, for lately it had become a habit. Sometimes they talked of his studies, or her tennis, or his dreams; anything except the subject that was uppermost in both their minds – their bond of hatred.

He walked into his bathroom and plunged his face into the basin, splashing it with cold water. When he straightened up he saw her behind him. She was smiling as she reached out and touched his cheek.

'I hope this won't scar.' She smoothed her forefinger over the cut on his neck.

'You're a strange boy. You never give in to your passions. You try to pretend that you don't have any. Learn to give way to your hatred and your lust. You do want to fuck me, don't you?'

He flushed despite his determination not to. He could feel his skin tingling and his eyes burning. He wanted to get back at her for laughing at him.

'Sit down. I'll put a plaster on this cut. What a disgusting brute he is, but it serves you right. You must stand up to him. Poor Tony! All your life you'll be poor Tony, because you can't grab what is your right.'

'Are you my right then? Is that what you're saying?' he said, with unaccustomed courage, fuelled by her contempt.

'Spoils of war, winner takes all. Here I am – the victor's prize.' She lay back on his bed and leaned on one hand while the other tossed her hair over one shoulder. What beautifully fine, ash-blonde hair she had. Her cool green eyes were mocking him.

'Perhaps you don't like girls, Tony,' she said. Now her eyes were narrowed into slits and her teeth were sparkling in a feline smile.

'Come on, Eleanor, don't start that again.' He turned away from her, deliberately switching his mind to other matters as he gazed out of the window.

Damn! Eleanor thought, watching Tony's shoulders quivering. His voice was deep and vibrant, but it emerged from a soft girl's mouth. He was a virgin and scared of his feelings. She longed to reveal the spunk in his balls and his mind. She had to turn him into a man. She needed him.

'Make love to me,' she whispered. 'Get your own back on Marius.' She watched his cheeks turn to burning scarlet. 'Imagine him watching us, trussed up like a Christmas turkey. He'd swell up and burst with bile.'

'Is that sexy image supposed to turn me on?'

'Can anything turn you on?' she taunted him.

He shrugged and looked away feeling furious.

'You're so content with losing,' she taunted him.

'Shut up, for goodness sake,' he muttered, grabbing her hair and thrusting his hand over her mouth.

She yanked his hand aside. 'You know something. You're so scared you make me puke.'

The hand on her mouth pressed harder until she felt the pain. His hand was fumbling with her blouse. He wrenched it open and pulled her bra up. Now he was fumbling with her breasts.

'Relax!' She pushed his hand aside, sat up and unzipped his trousers. Fumbling in his crotch, she gently massaged his penis. He began to groan and she saw the sweat on his forehead. 'Now, undress me slowly,' she murmured.

He was going to explode before he got anywhere, she could see that. 'Just this once, I'll do the work,' she said. 'Lie down.' She pushed off her shorts and climbed over him, swaying her hips forward and backward, twisting and reaching behind her to cup his balls in her hand. Such beautiful, downy soft, heavy balls. Moments later she felt him coming. To her surprise she responded with a surge of passion that left her crying softly on the shoulder of the skinny boy who had touched her heart.

Chapter 9

It was half-past four in the afternoon. The air was moist and there was the sense of relief that always came after a storm. Today had been a scorcher, the air particularly dense and oppressive. At noon, the storm clouds gathered on the horizon; purple and black they seemed to rise up a mile high, squashing the air on to the long-suffering earth. The storm and deluge that followed had been awe-inspiring and now the tension and dust and everyone's bad temper had been washed away, leaving a sense of peace and lightness.

In the hall of Dan's school you could smell the damp earth and the glorious fresh air that was billowing in from the windows set high up in the walls. The roof and the trees were still dripping and in sudden silences between the applause and the talking, you could hear it plainly. Was there any sound more satisfying than that, Dan wondered?

Dan was feeling light-headed, too; he seemed to be floating, but was this relief from the storm, or because of his hunger, or was he in a state of shock, he wondered? Perhaps a mixture of all three.

It was the end-of-year prize giving, and it seemed that he had spent more time on the platform than sitting in his chair. He was conscious of the whispers and admiring glances in his direction from the younger pupils, but that was because he'd scored eleven goals in the latest KaNgwane soccer match.

'Daniel Tweneni!' the headmaster called again. Dan stood up and once again made his way to the platform, this time to receive the coveted athletics trophy. Shaking hands, he turned to go, but the headmaster motioned that he should stay. Holding up one hand to quiet the applause the headmaster said:

'I've seldom handed out so many prizes to the same boy ... the English prize, the mathematics prize, top of the year prize, a bravery award, the soccer trophy which Dan here accepted on behalf of the school team, and now the athletics trophy. For my part I wish I had a prize to award, too, for it would be given to one of the most pleasant young men I've ever had to deal with, Dan Tweneni. Dan, I feel sure that many of the younger pupils sitting in the audience might wish to follow your lead. Perhaps you'd like to say a few words. Tell us how you did it, Dan.'

Dan smiled, feeling embarrassed. He had been given no warning and for a few shocked moments he stood dazed, without a thought in his head. Then thoughts zoomed in like flies at a slaughtered buck, humming with self-importance. Which to choose? He hesitated. He almost fobbed them off with a few meaningless words about trying your best, but was that the real truth?

He cleared his throat and mumbled 'good evening' into the microphone, which was too low for him. By the time it had been adjusted, he had gathered his wits together.

'I must thank my grandparents who mainly brought me up,' he began. 'My Grandmother on my father's side, Nosisi ... well, some of you might have heard of her ... she's kind of old fashioned. I don't believe in a lot of the stuff *she* believes in, but some of the things she taught me have stuck in my head. Mainly, she taught me about love ...' the hall erupted into giggles and he laughed, looking embarrassed. 'Don't get me wrong, not the romantic sort of love you read about, not even love for your parents and brothers, but love of every moment of every day and a passionate love for whatever you do, whether studying, playing a soccer match or sweeping out the boss's cowshed. Love the present moment, for love is energy. Use that energy and you can't lose.'

As the hall erupted in applause, Dan stepped down.

*

The applause still echoed in his ears a month later, but now he was trying to hang on to his own advice, and despair was creeping closer. The all-time high of the last term was over. What was left was a massive anti-climax. What next? That was the question that gripped him.

Were six honours and a couple of trophies in standard eight to be the pinnacle of his glory? Was there to be a slow regression into the despair of poverty from now on? What would his future be . . . a shack like Sam's and a labouring job? Marriage to a girl in the Homelands whom he visited occasionally? The slow erosion of his dreams and hopes? No, never, he told himself. But what were his alternatives?

The school Dan attended, the only black school in the district, took pupils to standard 8, which was two years before University entrance exams, but high enough to become apprenticed for a trade. Dan was hoping against hope that some miracle would occur, enabling him to continue with his schooling so that he could gain University entrance and study law. Meantime, he would have to get a labouring job. As he walked towards the headmaster's study, he had a sudden premonition that the summons he had received the previous evening was not going to result in good news.

His headmaster was talking to another teacher. The sunlight from the window behind him shone brilliantly on his frizzy white hair that framed his black face like a halo. He looked like a picture in one of Dan's school books, where all the saints were black-skinned, so pupils would learn that Christianity was also for them, even though life taught otherwise.

He caught sight of Dan, smiled and pointed towards a chair. The English teacher turned and said: 'Ah! Here's our young prodigy. Congratulations,' and shook Dan's hand before leaving.

The headmaster looked at Dan sadly. 'No luck, I'm afraid. The American sports bursaries are only for Standard Tens. There are very few multi-racial schools and because they do not receive government support they are extremely costly.

'Your best chance is to learn a trade, Dan. As you know, our people were barred from learning any trades until 1980 when the government relaxed the race laws. Since then almost twelve thousand blacks have become apprentices, but so far this is only allowed in the motor, building and furniture industries and there are no opportunities around these parts.

'As for getting your matric to enable you to go to University, I cannot obtain permission to take you beyond Standard Eight, which you have just passed so brilliantly.

'Things are changing, Dan, but not soon enough for you. Let's face it, a brainy kafir is a scary matter for whites.

'On the positive side, three private, catholic, multi-racial schools have accepted you and I am prepared to pay your fees. No ... no thanks, please ... I want to tell you that this is not for you, it's for our people. You're a fighter, Dan, and brainy, too. We need you.'

'Sir, I couldn't possibly . . .'

The headmaster held up his hand. 'Dan, listen to me. Most of our leaders, like your father, are in prison.

'Right now we need your sort of brains, and you need a proper education. Dan, over the years, I have tried hard to give you the extra knowledge which was never included in the curriculum. Bantu education fits our people to be labourers and nothing more. I pray to God that some day in the future there will be enough young men like you to fight for us.'

Dan stood up. The headmaster, whom he loved, was getting perilously close to tears. He hugged him hard and close.

'I can't accept ... I'll be in touch. I have other contacts.'

'Please, Dan, reconsider. It's not just for you. Your scoring in the tests shows a unique intellect. Your kind of brilliance must be used for the people. Not just to better your own lifestyle. Remember that.'

Like my father's, Dan thought with silent pain.

Dan sat in the dust outside his grandmother's house and

watched the long line of customers, clutching their five rand notes, shuffle slowly forward towards the back door. The passivity of drought was all around them. Everything was still. The beasts and birds conserved their movements hoarding their energy, the trees withdrew their sap and shed their leaves, grass and shrubs retained only that which was essential for future growth. The landscape looked bleak and matched the shuffling queue of people. They, too, were eviscerated by the drought of human compassion, Dan thought with pain.

Why did they come here and stand in the sun and pay through their noses for Nosisi's spells? Because they still had hope. Crazy people. In all the world, there couldn't be a better business than his grandmother's, Dan thought with a twisted smile. She was the most famous *Sangoma* around, both for her business spells and her clairvoyance. He watched the Indian traders, black mamas, fat and ugly. Tearful eyes and sullen expressions. Young girls, pretty and hopeful. Then he saw Vanessa. That was a laugh. She was the black mistress of Marius Cronjé. He'd set her up in a house that was splendid by local standards, and he fucked her twice a week, Wednesday afternoons and Friday evenings. Everyone knew that. Now why would she want a spell? Was she losing her grip on him? There were five black farmers with larger smallholdings, no doubt pleading for rain. All were shuffling towards the back door. They would pay approximately five rands for five minutes and if they wanted longer they paid much more. Nosisi had never had a bad debt.

Dan had mixed feelings about his father's mother. He gave her the respect and honour due to a grandmother on his father's side, but he didn't believe in witchcraft, or spells or throwing the bones, or any of the herbs she sold as so-called medicine, although he believed in her philosophy of life, yet all her preaching of love and *Ubuntu* couldn't persuade her to part with a cent. She was as rich as she was miserly and he had come to beg, which made him feel resentful.

He had been sitting in the yard for an hour. He knew better than to interfere with business. She knew he was here and she would see him when she was ready.

At one o'clock her scraggy, nervous maid fetched him inside. The room – lino floor, three-piece suite, small table and chairs – could have been any room if it weren't for the herbs and corpses of wild animals strung up from the ceiling.

Nosisi swept in, floral toga with leather skirt and court shoes peeping from under, gold rings and bangles rattling against her outstretched hands. Dan noticed that she was looking older and very sad. She sat down with quick, nervous movements and gazed at him inquiringly.

Dan pulled his wits together. For Nosisi, time was money and she didn't appreciate other people wasting it for her. That's why she had banished her husband, Sam. He made the usual traditional greetings with all speed, while she watched him with a curious half-smile lurking.

'That cost you, Dan, didn't it?' she said in her deep rasping voice that sounded for all the world like sawing wood. 'You don't believe in my gifts or my medicine so you can't have come for that; you haven't visited me out of filial respect for years, so it can't be that. Could it be the lack of money that has brought you here?'

'I need an education and I don't have the cash to pay for it.'

'I won't help you,' she said sadly. 'You've turned your back on our traditional ways. You want to be a white man with a black face. Not with my money, Dan. I'll not send you the way of your father. I listened to his father, Dan, to my cost. Now my son's days are a living death.'

'Things are changing and you shouldn't blame Grandpa for what happened to my father.'

She ignored his lecture. 'Things are changing, but for the worse. We shall have bloodshed . . . unless . . .' She shook like a dog shaking off water. 'The whites don't have a system that works. How can we ape them? Their ways are not our ways. Our systems worked in the old days.'

She was so appallingly ignorant. How could you have a discussion with someone who had learned practically nothing?

Once his people had roamed over Africa, herding their cattle, growing their corn, and when one patch of land became tired, they simply moved on. Now they were hemmed in, contained, imprisoned on their Homelands which had become overused almost to death. No one was learning how to feed the land. There is only one great sin that the white man must answer for, he thought with sudden fury, and that is withholding knowledge, for it wasn't their knowledge in the first place, it belonged to the human race. Yet they kept it for themselves. How to explain that to this ignorant, but talented and shrewd woman. He said: 'A stone-age culture can't survive . . .' but then broke off as she silenced him with a scowl.

'We must go back to our ways. *Ubuntu*, that is the seed of our future success,' she said. 'Without that you are nothing, Dan. You are as powerless as a termite adrift from the termitary.'

'We must live by the law – I want to be a lawyer.'

'*Their* ways. *Their* laws. But listen . . .' She seemed to want to reach out to him. 'I'll throw the bones for you.'

Dan stirred restlessly and then he thought: 'Maybe she'll see herself coughing up for my education.'

Trying not to show his distaste, he watched her go through the curious rigmarole of her trade: the candles, the prayers, the beseeching of ancestors, then the throwing of the bones.

'Oh, what a tortuous path you have chosen, Dan. You have to try out the white man's ways . . . all of them. You will get your education, I promise you. All you've dreamed of, but it comes to you with great sorrow. You will abandon it voluntarily – and find your way back again . . . back to our ways. Without *Ubuntu* you have lost your soul.'

She stared at him with her penetrating eyes. 'It will all come right. Remember that. Don't hate.'

'I don't hate.'

'Not yet.' She glanced meaningfully at her watch.

Dan stood up, fuming with temper. What a fucking waste of the morning. She was a miserable old miser. He'd endured her ravings for nothing.

As he backed off to the door, wishing her well, he thought about *Ubuntu*. How could he explain it to someone like Pieter? Togetherness with love, a bond of mutual help and caring. It was not a thought process, but a state of being. The bond was emotional and the tribe were as one, unquestionably and irrevocably joined in a common bond of sharing and caring, their individuality merged into the tribe. What a two-faced old miser his grandmother was. Why wouldn't she help her own flesh and blood? What the hell was the meaning of togetherness if her cash was kept apart and exclusively for her own use?

He would have liked to argue with her, but despite his dislike of black traditions, he could never overcome his inborn reverence for the aged and particularly his own grandmother, so he kept his retorts to himself and squashed his anger sufficiently to kiss her cheek when he left.

Chapter 10

Pieter was crouched on the floor in the barn, knees up to his chin, the bent axle shaft between his legs, panting with the effort of straightening it. His forehead was wrinkled, his eyes screwed up against the dust, yet his expression was gentle and his face incongruously boyish against his strong bony frame. His hair was growing longer and curling around his neck and a shock of black curls fell forward and almost hid his frown. His beard of two weeks was curling over his cheeks and neck and lately hair had sprouted on his chest.

It was so damned, suffocatingly hot. He grabbed his oil cloth and mopped his face, leaving black streaks on his cheek. He glanced through the doorway at the dark sky. It would rain soon and the evening would be lovely.

While he worked, his mind was occupied with his problems. What was he going to do for a career? He longed to be a farmer, but their land was barren. Perhaps he could get a local job during the daytime and run the farm evenings and weekends. Turn it into something. What about a poultry farm? That paid well. Or pigs? All those ventures would need capital and they had none.

He sighed. He could learn a trade or go to university, but that would means years of semi-dependence upon his parents, an impossible burden for them.

Young unskilled whites in Africa faced a precarious future. It wasn't that he minded working with Africans, he'd always done that, but their sheer numbers would force wages down to rock bottom. Right now there was a law preventing any black being in authority over a white. What if they scrapped that law? The thought was sickening.

He could enter any of the government services reserved for whites only, such as the railways, but what if their worst dreams came true and majority rule brought in a black government? Job reservation would be abolished and half the white workforce would be unemployed overnight.

Pressure from industrialists would soon force the government to open up one field after the next to non-whites. So what would be left for an unskilled white? Nothing!

Pieter could find no solution to his problems. His year's military service looked like a blessing in disguise. It would give him a year's grace to make up his mind. He knew they also taught them trades in the army. That might work out all right.

Meantime he had a more pressing problem. How could he take a girl to the matric dance when he had no car? Perhaps he could meet her there, but then, how to get her home?

Pieter did not have a regular girlfriend because that state would require both transport and cash and Pieter seldom had either. It wasn't that Pa was mean, it was just that all the vehicles he used belonged to the Cronjés. Pieter often drove into the village to fetch produce or food, but borrowing a van for social purposes was out of the question. Yet to miss the matric dance was to admit defeat. Besides, having come first in every academic subject and won the swimming and water polo cups, as well as captaining the rugby team, he felt he deserved a rousing send-off.

Amy Johnston had no partner which was social suicide for her, he learned the following morning at school. Watching her pinched lips and anxious eyes, her growing sense of resignation and despair, compassion surged. But she's ugly, he thought, but then chided himself. That was a cruel thought. No one was ugly, it's just that she wasn't at all pretty. Pieter had to search hard to find her redeeming features, but he found some eventually. She had fine, light brown hair with golden threads here and there, which she wore plaited around her fat pink face. He noticed this when she dried her hair after a swimming match. Then, when she took off her glasses he saw that she had large grey eyes. Under her chubby cheeks and double chin she had perfectly reasonable features, too.

He sprung his question casually just as they were passing each other in the corridor, five days before the event.

'How about you and I going to the matric dance? You on? Free are you?'

Her body stiffened with shock, her face turned an even deeper beetroot, while her watery eyes gazed in ecstasy as if she was seeing a holy vision. She couldn't talk, only swallow. Lizard-like, her pink tongue flicked between her lips. Then she nodded and sort of grunted.

Putting a brave face on his choice, he winked lasciviously, grabbed his pants at the crotch and yanked them up and down in a quick, suggestive gesture. 'You want to fuck later . . . after the dance? Orgasm guaranteed.' He winked again.

Amy gasped, turned white and fled down the passage. 'You disgusting beast,' she said.

Then he understood that she thought he was joking about the invitation. 'Ah, come on, Amy. Can't you be teased? What's wrong with a laugh? I mean it. Let's go to the dance.'

His voice had become very deep lately and it reverberated around the classrooms. Pupils crowded the doorways as Pieter burst into a raucous laugh. He was laughing so much he couldn't run after Amy, but she paused and glanced over her shoulder.

'You're a cruel tease,' she accused him.

'Ja – sorry. Pick you up at eight. Okay?'

She nodded and fled.

The donkeys had been scrubbed, groomed and dolled up with ribbons and flowers and little silver bells. They had never looked so good and they knew this. Alert and happy, muscles tensed with excitement and pride, they tossed their heads to make the bells jingle and rolled their eyes. Pieter smacked Daisy on the rump and laughed. 'Fancy yourself, don't you, Daisy. You're darn right, you look divine.' He kissed her on the nose.

Ma came outside and watched him. 'There's a tub of water boiling on the stove.'

'Now I'm cross with you.' He stood up and stretched, and walking towards her, put one arm around her shoulders, and pressed his lips on her hair. 'I've told you a million times not to do that. You'll tear a muscle or worse. Be more careful. Besides, I'm going to shower.'

They had a cold shower running from one of the rain water tanks on the shed's roof. He grinned at her and Maria felt a rush of poignant love and regret. He'd be gone soon and she would never get over her loss. Did everyone feel like she did at the loss of a son? Surely no one had a boy like hers. He was altogether special, standing well over six foot, with massive, bony shoulders, but gracefully shaped, his smooth limbs disguising his strength. He was beautiful, too, with his jet black curly hair, huge slanting light green eyes and his short, delicate nose – a girl's nose – and pointed chin.

'What are you dreaming about?' Pieter said, pinching her cheek with his rough fingers.

She caught hold of his hand and gazed at his nails. They were chewed to the quick, but dirty. What small hands he had. How could such small hands be so strong?

'You're going to be late. All that fuss over those stupid beasts and look at you, still filthy.'

'Stop fussing!'

Ten minutes later he stood at the door looking concerned and awkward. 'Are you sure, Ma?' he said. He gazed at the mirror in despair. His grandfather's army tunic fitted him like a glove. He looked so tailored, sort of aristocratic with the straight shoulders and fitted waist. 'All the others will be wearing suits.'

'They would long to have such a tunic. Your grandfather was a hero, you know.'

Of course he knew. Ma never tired of telling him how grandfather had been awarded the DSO for carrying his wounded comrade for days across the desert after their tank was gutted in the Sidi Rezegh campaign in World War II.

It would be rude to question her further, Pieter reasoned, and pointless, too, since he had no jacket other than his school windbreaker, which was old, torn and too small for him.

Amy lived in a small house near the sugar mill where her father worked. Pieter tied the lead donkeys to a tree and sauntered to her front door. When Amy swung it open, he gasped. She was wearing a terrible blue taffeta dress which fell tent-like to a final stiff frill touching the ground. It had a square neckline and puffed sleeves and she looked absurd. Like a bridesmaid in Ma's childhood. Was it her mother who had fattened and ill managed her daughter so cruelly and was it deliberate?

'Oh, hi, Amy. Nice dress,' he lied.

'D'you really think so?' How anxious she looked.

'Maybe a bit too smart for this affair. D'you have something shorter? Maybe a bit more grown-up?' Now she was close to tears and he relented. 'On second thoughts I like it, but your hair should be loose. Come on. Let's see what we can do with it.'

'You're late,' she grumbled, 'and why are you wearing that ridiculous army jacket. You should have worn a suit.'

'I wear this tunic for all important functions in honour of my grandfather who was a war hero.' He had rehearsed his speech earlier.

Overcoming her resistance, he fluffed out her hair which was crimpled from the plaits. It looked pretty hanging over her shoulders. Maybe the square neckline could be stretched a bit. He tugged at it and it nearly tore, but he managed to push it over her shoulders.

'Be careful.' She stepped back into the passage.

'Where's your folks?'

'Out.'

'Can I come in?'

'I suppose so.'

'Don't you have a necklace or something?'

'Just a cross on a chain.'

'So wear that. And make-up?'

'Mum's got some.'

'Can you borrow it?'

'S'pose so.'

'Hurry.'

She came back with a box of stuff he'd watched his mother use dozens of times when she went out with Pa. 'I notice the girls put blue on their eyelids, and here's some lipstick. Try it.'

'You're a strange guy. I never would have thought you'd be interested in women like this.'

'I just want you to look good.'

Surprisingly, she looked reasonable. He took off her glasses, plastered her red cheeks with powder, smeared her eyes with more blue and gazed at her approvingly. 'Can you see all right?'

'Not really. Everything's blurred.'

'Well, you don't have to see tonight. Let's go. You look lovely,' he lied. The truth was, her happiness was appealing . . . but not for long. When she saw the donkeys her lips folded into an ugly grimace.

'You can't expect me to sit in a horse-drawn cart. I'm not a *gammat*.'

'They're donkeys! Don't they look pretty in their Sunday best? This is Daisy and this is Whiplash. Say hi to the pretty lady.'

'They're disgusting! Donkeys! My God! They stink. A donkey's even worse than a horse. Don't you have a horse?'

'No.'

'Nor a car?'

'No!'

'Oh God. How awful.'

'Relax, Amy.' He put his arm around her shoulders. 'We're going to have a good time. That's the main thing, isn't it?'

'Not really.'

Pieter glanced at her face which was twisted into pain and embarrassment. This is a terrible mistake, he thought. In no time at all she was huck-huck-hucking about the wind spoiling her hair, and the cold breeze that brought her out in goose-bumps, and the damp that was taking the crisp out of her taffeta frock.

'I'd never have come if I'd known we were going in a donkey cart,' she cried out. 'Your folks must be poor whites. Don't you even have a motorbike?'

Years of practice with his Pa, who was always nagging about something, had taught Pieter to switch off. He thought about the hunt he was planning for tomorrow. They could do with some meat in the larder. At the back of his mind was a growing dislike of this awful girl. How could she insult him so badly when he'd rescued her from being the only uninvited girl? She'd called him a poor white. That was the second worst thing anyone could call him.

'I'm bruised,' she whined. 'The seat's so hard.'

He was thankful he'd remembered to bring plenty of cushions. 'There's a pile of cushions back there. Help yourself. But you shouldn't mind too much. After all, you're well padded.'

'How dare you,' she whispered.

'Listen!' He drew the donkeys to a halt. 'D'you want to go home? You want me to take you back? Shall we call the dance off?'

'No,' she mumbled.

'Then shut up. Stop hucking. Let's have some peace around here.'

The donkeys set off again with a clipclop of hooves pounding on the gravel road. The wheels rumbled on the uneven surface and their bodies were forced into a strange forward-backward swaying motion that was almost hypnotic. After a while she began to look dreamy and she even smiled once at a joke he cracked.

'You look pretty when you smile,' he said meaningfully. 'You should try it more often.'

When they reached the school, the caretaker's 'boy' was bribed to keep an eye on the donkeys which were left hidden amongst the bushes by the school playing field, to please Amy. There was some lush *Kikuyu* grass there and the 'boy' brought them some water in a bucket.

'How come you didn't tell me you can't dance?' she whined when the waltz began.'

'I thought it was easy.' He stumbled around her, red-faced and sweating, while the other girls giggled and she strove manfully to teach him.

'You're stupid. *Really stupid*,' she said, giving up.

That was the worst thing she could say to him. No one, but no one was allowed to call him stupid. Now she was in for it.

When the music changed to something sensible, without all those silly set steps that Ma used to dance, or was it his grandma? Pieter was in his element. Now he could sway his hips and his shoulders and move with the music without standing on her big feet. He began to enjoy himself. Amy began to relax, too. After a while he caught her close to him and let his hand slide up her back and down again, noting that her eyes were nearly popping out of her head she was so randy. When the lights dimmed, he nuzzled his mouth on her ear and slid his fingers to the nape of her neck. She was gasping and groping up with her lips, feeling for him like a mole, without her glasses almost blind in the dim light. The music became more sultry and Pieter felt his willie taking over, rearing up to double its size, bursting at the seams. He pressed her close against him and she colluded with his every move. She was sweaty and panting and he knew her thighs would be wet and juicy and ready ... more than ready.

'Let's get out of here,' he mumbled around eleven.

She seemed unable to say yes or no as she stood still looking lost and scared. He tugged her arm and led her out.

'I've just got to have a joint,' he said. 'You smoke?'

'No.'

'Not even pot?'

'No.'

'Want to try?'

'Definitely not.'

'You coming with me?'

'Yes,' she said breathlessly.

They went hand in hand across the grounds to the copse where he had hidden the donkeys. Pieter climbed into the cart and arranged the cushions on the floor to make a bed, but sat on them, leaning his back against the seat. After some hesitation, she sat beside him. He got out the dagga and rolled and compressed the dried grass on the seat, taking the seeds and flipping them into the grass. 'Reckon they'll have a good crop here one of these days,' he said, laughing. Then he took a cigarette paper and rolled himself a joint. He drew it deep into his lungs and held it there while he put his arm around Amy and placed his lips on hers, opening her mouth with his tongue. 'Now breathe in,' he said harshly and blew out the smoke into her mouth.

She spluttered and choked a bit. 'Ooh! It burns.'

'S'posed to. Come here.'

He did it again and again and she began to relax and pressed closer to him. 'More,' she whispered dreamily. He felt a surge of triumph as he bent over her and exhaled the dagga smoke into her lungs. Not long now, he thought.

'Oh God, Oh God,' she was murmuring over and over. 'I never knew it could be like this.' His finger was wet and sticky from rubbing her clits. She was ripe and ready, but he was not. Not yet. He wanted another smoke. It had to be superb and it was worth waiting for. While he shared the joint with her, he was pinching and kneading her nipples. Big ones, too. How'd they get that big? he wondered. He liked big breasts and that was one good thing about her, but her cunt seemed pretty big, too, and he knew another joint would be needed to improve his sensations. When he flipped the butt over his shoulder he unzipped his trousers and pushed them off. Willie was vibrating fit to take off. 'Kiss it,' he commanded, but she was awkward, with a mouth full of teeth and too much enthusiasm, so he pushed her back and rolled over her.

Somewhere, somehow, he never knew when, the donkeys decided to walk home. They moved quietly forward and Pieter, intent on squeezing the last drop of pleasure out of this act and making it last, did not notice. Amy had become a long, pulsating tunnel through which he was panting and digging and thrusting towards the pot of gold.

Clip–clop, clip–clop. He was aware of the sound, but it did not register. The cart swayed backwards and forwards and they heaved and thrust and rolled around and tried each position in turn, and somewhere around the region of the main street, she came, with a rip-roaring scream of ecstasy.

To Pieter's annoyance he responded, although he'd wanted to wait until she came two or three times, but he could not. Too many joints had heightened his pleasure to unbearable heights, so he groaned long and loud and gave himself up to letting go.

Their mingled cries brought a gang of giggling school mates running from the cafe. Pieter looked up into their grinning faces. Amy screamed again, this time from pure horror. Suddenly they were groping for their clothes, which somehow they'd shed without even noticing. In their panicky haste, they collided, bumping their heads, which caused more shrieks of mirth from the onlookers.

Amy was crying softly as he took her home. 'I'll never be able to hold up my head again. What will they say about me?' she sobbed.

'They'll say you shouldn't go out with a stupid, poor white,' he said. 'This is where you live. Goodbye.'

'Oh, oh,' she sobbed as she scrambled out of the cart.

'That was good stuff,' he called after her, but he knew she would forget the pleasure and remember only the pain.

Chapter 11

One of the hardest things Pieter had ever had to do was to say goodbye to his mother. How would she cope without him? Upset by her grief, he hardly noticed the time pass as he scrubbed himself under the shower and dressed in his Grandpa's tunic, his jeans, and T-shirt and his best antelope hide shoes. Suddenly there was no time left to sit and drink coffee with Ma as he had intended.

'Whatever I earn I'll send home,' he promised. 'Well, almost everything. Let the old place go until I return. Don't try to do a man's work. You have your chicken and goats, you grow a few vegetables for the kitchen, you can sell eggs and there's your turkeys at Christmas. Pa earns a living – enough for you two to get by. Promise me, now.'

Ma didn't bother to answer, but he could read her mind. Two fields was her meagre inheritance, and by God, they would work for her. How harsh and upright she could be sometimes. This morning she was sterner than usual as she stood by the doorway, hands clasped together in front of her apron, blue eyes glinting, making sure that no emotion showed. She was thirty-eight years old and still beautiful, but she was also a brave, loyal, patriotic and hardworking Boer woman. She deserved so much more than her hard days.

'Ma . . .' he faltered. 'It won't be forever.'

'Yes,' she said. 'It will. You will not come back here . . . not to live . . . not once you've had a taste of something better. Remember, when you marry one day, you must choose a woman from a right-wing home, a good Afrikaans girl, a patriot. You must forget about Liza.'

'Oh, come on, Ma.' His voice always cracked when emotion gripped him, one minute high and then husky low. 'Don't behave as if we're at a funeral.' The truth was, he still longed for Liza. One day he would find her, he had promised himself.

'Do your duty, that's all. Remember you're a Boer. Remember your history. Don't worry about hardship. It's part of our lives. God be with you, my boy. Remember . . .'

She broke off. Pa stood outside, his eyes glittering with anger. There was always a sense of rivalry between them. His father was a short man, suntanned and lined, and years older than Ma. His main characteristic was his short, explosive temper. That's all he is really, Pieter thought sadly, a bag of temper. Once Pa used to lather into him with his belt, but that had stopped the day Pieter had lost his cool and fought back. Now there was mutual respect, like two male lions that kept their distance, unwilling either to fight or to bury the hatchet.

'If you want a lift to the station move your arse. I've been sitting in the lorry for the past ten minutes.'

'Sorry, Pa.'

Pieter stepped back and kissed his mother, smoothing her hair with his hands. 'Hold tight. I'll be back soon. You'll hardly notice I've been gone. You know I love you.' As her eyes filled with tears, she turned away abruptly. He'd miss his mother and his home so much. Wiping his face with the back of his hand he sprinted to the truck and climbed in next to Pa.

The drive to the station was fraught with embarrassment.

'Listen here, Piet,' Pa said. 'You and I don't get around to talking much, but I want you to know that I'll be thinking of you. Now do as you're told and don't you get into any trouble.'

'Sure thing. Thanks, Pa,' Pieter said.

'I fear for you, my boy. You've been brought up soft. Your mother cossetted you. You've been too protected. I used to get cross with her, it's not good to molly-coddle a boy. Now you'll find the going tough – the more's the pity – but don't be a coward. When the time comes that you have to take your punishment, then just take it in silence.'

Pieter looked at his father in surprise. Had Pa never heard of the fights he'd had? 'Yes, Pa,' he said.

'Now, you're growing up, my boy. Sooner or later you're going to find yourself in bed with a woman ... well, let's hope it's later. If that should happen remember to be careful. There's too many diseases going around nowadays. Things you've never even heard of.'

Now Pieter was openly amazed, but Pa didn't seem to notice. Eyes gazing straight ahead, ears burning scarlet, he ploughed on. 'There's these things called condoms, Piet. You sort of slip them over your willie if you find yourself in this situation. If you haven't got a condom with you, then just go home.'

'You mean these things, Pa?' Pieter produced one from his pocket. Pa's eyes nearly bolted out of his head and the lorry veered straight towards the ditch. Pieter caught hold of the wheel and wrenched it over.

'I think I know how to fight, Pa, and I reckon I'll look after myself. You just look after Ma. Okay? Perhaps you could take her out from time to time. She has a boring life.'

After that they drove in silence. The station seemed twice as far away this morning. When at last the lorry drew into the kerb, Pieter got out and grabbed his haversack. He stood there waiting, but Pa didn't get out. He gave a sort of half-wave and drove away looking relieved.

Funny sort of goodbye, Pieter thought as he turned away and walked towards the platform, but that was Pa for you. He hated anything emotional.

Thinking about his Dad always made Pieter angry. Why had he never loved him? One day he'd confront him with his hurt and anger. Thinking about it made him feel depressed, so he forced himself to think forward. This was going to be one hell of an adventure.

It was a perfect March evening. Pieter was sitting outside the bunkhouse, smoking a cigarette and watching the dusk spread over the veld behind the camp fence. Behind him one of the boys was playing a Beatles song on his mouth organ, the soft, sad strains matched the scene. Dusk was different here in the Cape. Here was no long, lingering light to transform the land into something magically beautiful, as they had in the Transvaal. Instead a blue dusk spread up as if from the earth itself, like a purple shroud to cloak the night that came on so fast. If only he could capture the twilight and hold it fast in his memory: the faint mauve glow around the distant mountain range, the soft ochre of the hills nearer the camp, the oak trees standing guard around the gate, tall and sombre and so still, but already it was darkening. Then someone switched on the bunkhouse lights and the feeling was altogether lost.

'Stow your fucking music,' one of the recruits growled, but the playing continued.

'Hey you – this isn't one of your Portuguese shops. Shut up or I'll ram that noisy bit of tin up your arse.'

'Leave him be.' Pieter recognised Andy Huntley's voice, a man whom Pieter particularly disliked. He was tall, blond, blue-eyed and arrogant-looking with an uppercrust English accent that jarred. He and Andy beat the others in everything, but held each other in deep contempt.

The squabble went on, spoiling the night which was a pity. Pieter wanted to think about this new life of his. So far the army camp seemed to him more like a luxury hotel. They had good bunks and blankets, and they ate meat twice a day. They had a liberal supply of water for showers which gushed out just as hot as you wanted, simply by turning on the taps. He had the company of some good guys. They trained together, ate together, slept together and suffered together. They were building up a sense of camaraderie which Pieter had never enjoyed at school. The work was easy for him. He was superbly fit and he could march and drill for hours. Sleeping out in the bush on short rations was no problem, since he'd spent most of his life doing just that.

*

For two months Pieter had drilled, jogged, and exercised and learned the basics of shooting, which he already knew, living off the land, at which he was an expert, radio communications, which they had on Cronjé's farm and navigation by the stars, which he'd known since he was a kid.

As each day rolled into the next, he became increasingly bored. Last week, for instance, they had been flown into the bush and told to find their own way home. Pieter had a clear idea where they were and he led the squad back without mishap, arriving well in time for supper. If it weren't for the tough meat, he might think he was in a holiday camp. They had siphoned off the dog handlers and the cooks who'd been sent to special training camps, then the medics and accountant-types and eventually everyone had been selected except for parabats and reconnaissance units. Their bunkhouse was down to twenty guys – a tough, quarrelsome crew of ten Afrikaners, with whom he felt more at home, three Portuguese from the Cape and seven English-speaking South Africans, whom Pieter despised. The English were so damned clannish and superior, forever complaining about the food, the sergeant, the drilling, and the lack of leave.

Pieter glanced over his shoulder and frowned. He saw Henri, a bull of an Afrikaner, with shoulders as thick as his brains, grab the Portuguese playing the mouth organ, whose name was Koos, and throw him over the table. Clearly he was trying to ram the offending instrument up his butt, but Koos was fighting furiously. Eventually, two others came to Henri's assistance to hold Koos down. It was then that Andy Huntley moved in fast with a couple of good karate kicks which knocked them all flying. Henri let go of Koos and grabbed Huntley, smashed his fist into his face and sent him skidding out of the door. He flew past Pieter and landed with his face in the dust. He must have had his mouth open because he sat up spitting out dust and blood and a tooth.

'Shit! It was capped. I lost the original in a rugby match.'

Pieter recovered the tooth and examined it. There was a screw protruding from it. 'You don't look so larny now,' he told Huntley, handing it back.

'Stuff off!' Huntley stood up, shook himself like a dog and moved towards the door. Pieter watched without much interest, yet felt his blood stirring for a good fight. Still, it wasn't his business. It wasn't Huntley's business either.

What a racket in there. Looking inside he saw the three Portuguese fighting furiously against the Afrikaners. 'You puss,' Koos was yelling. One of them pulled out a knife and after that there was chaos. Huntley ran up the stairs, but Pieter reached back and grabbed his foot.

'Hey! Why d'you want to tangle with Henri? He's a boxing champion and two of his buddies are wrestlers.'

'As an Afrikaner you could never possibly understand,' Huntley panted. He kicked Pieter off and plunged into the fight.

'Fuck you,' Pieter growled. He stood up reluctantly and walked inside. Two of the dagoes and one of the rooineks [rooineks = derogatory name for English referring to their sunburnt necks] were knocked out. Koos, bare-arsed, was spread over the table, but he was wriggling and kicking despite his pinned arms. Four Afrikaners had Huntley cornered and he was trying to fight his way out of them.

'Hey, come on, Henri, don't mess with the kids. Let's keep this amongst the men,' Pieter growled. He took hold of Henri's arm and flung him back.

'Get lost, Piet.'

'Says who?' With a quick kick he knocked Henri's feet from under him so that he staggered and fell sideways against the wall.

'Why you . . .' Henri scrambled to his feet looking murderous.

'Suck my arse, you overgrown turd,' Pieter said, kicking him back again.

Henri was up in a flash, quick as a bolt of lightning, Pieter noticed. Pieter's skin was prickling, his temper rising.

'Hey, Piet, you're a Boer, one of us. Keep out of this,' another called out.

'I thought I'd show you pansies how to fight,' Pieter snarled. He swung up a chair and brought it crashing full into Henri's face, and heard his nose crunch. Wrenching a leg off the chair he swiped Henri's arm as he fell back and knew from the crunch that he was out of the fight. Fast as a cobra he went in for the kill at the only other oke he felt could match him, smashing his fingers hard. As he doubled with pain, Pieter knocked him out with a blow on the back of the head.

There was a sudden silence. The two boys let Koos go and he hauled up his pants. 'Thanks, pal,' Huntley said to Pieter.

'I'm not your pal, you disgust me. What were you saying about my not understanding?'

'You guys don't know much about fair play. Seven against three is simply not on, old boy.'

Old boy, Pieter mused. 'Listen, man. If you want to fight, go in fast and damage your opponent so bad he can't fight back – otherwise you're lost. Like this . . .'

He dropped the table leg and dived at Huntley, but found himself sailing through the air from a quick twist of Huntley's body, propelled by his own momentum. He landed head on against the wall.

He woke to find himself in a cell together with Huntley and Koos. He shook himself and staggered to his feet. 'Jesus! I'm thirsty. My head feels like it's been cracked open. Hey, Andy. How the hell did you manage that?'

'I'll show you one of these days,' Andy said.

'Where're the others?'

'In hospital.'

'Hey, Koos, how's your mouth organ? Still in your pocket?'

'The captain wants to see us as soon as you recover,' Andy told him when they had stopped laughing. 'We're in big shit.'

Shortly afterwards they were marched into the CO's office.

Captain Scheepers was a shrewd-looking man tough and sinewy as ostrich biltong, withered before his time from the dry heat. He stared at them long and hard while they stood to attention. Pieter tried to keep his head on his shoulder. It felt as if it was about to roll off.

'Unbelievable as it may seem,' their Captain began, 'you three cretins came top in everything. Strange how you got together like that. Your sergeant saw some of the fight. Quite impressive, he told me. How would you like to volunteer for a holiday camp in Natal? Better pay, better prospects altogether, but it's not for losers. You'll be training for recé. You probably won't make it. Only sixteen out of every hundred do.'

They volunteered without hesitation and half an hour later they were being driven to the airport.

'This should relieve the boredom a bit,' Andy said to Pieter, when they had buckled up inside the belly of an old Dakota.

'Sure thing,' Pieter said, grinning. He shot a hard glance towards Koos. He'd never thought of a dago as having brains, let alone guts, but it seemed Koos was a South African at heart. He grinned at him.

Chapter 12

Six youthful criminals were huddled into a corner of the cell looking both defiant and very scared. They tried to pretend that they weren't listening as the constable explained patiently to Jean Arlington that she and the Home Shelter had better make sure the kids didn't pitch up in the cells again. Next time it would be prison, he warned.

Jean Arlington was a temporary assistant at the home and being a newly hatched PhD from London University, she was very green around the ears. The streetwise kids had picked this up from her sympathetic expression and they were wondering how to exploit the situation as they were led out of the cell.

The policeman explained that Angel was the leader of this raggle-taggle bunch of snot-nosed kids known as 'The Angels'. 'A misnomer if ever there was one,' he warned her. They'd been caught for begging and vagrancy a few times, but this was the first time they'd been arrested for breaking and entering.

'They said they needed medicine because they're ill. I bet they feel a damn sight sicker now,' the constable went on in his ponderous manner. 'You see, they were put in a cell with seven other older youths who beat them up in the night. When I came on duty at midnight I separated them. Regular little spitfires, all of them and fiercely protective of each other,' he told her.

Angel had fared the worst. He had two black eyes and several cuts and bruises. He was a fierce, angry boy, skinny, introverted – and very beautiful. Jean gazed at him in astonishment. She had never seen such perfect features. Despite his inch-long stubble of hair, he stood out from the others as someone altogether special. How proud and disdainful he looked, as he stalked out of the cell. His eyes stared intently at her without a flicker of nervousness, she noticed. His hair was blue-black, his eyes huge and amber-coloured, his nose was delicate and his features regular. He was dressed in ragged jeans and a leather jacket several sizes too big for him, which he kept buttoned up. Watching him Jean felt a shaft of fierce maternal caring surge through her.

'I'm taking you to the Home Shelter,' she told them. 'Have you been there before?'

Nico and Ralph shook their heads, but Angel continued to gaze at her without speaking, his expression a mixture of contempt and defiance. Something about his eyes twisted her heartstrings as the police ushered them into her car. She sensed his vulnerability.

'Keep your bag out of their reach,' the constable hissed in her ear.

'Missus,' the youngest moaned. 'I'm passing out with hunger, Missus. Me and my mates haven't eaten for three days. There's a Wimpy Bar, Missus. They sell take-aways. I've been lying in the cell all night longing for some bread and meat – anything.'

Surely it wouldn't do much harm if she were to buy them something, she thought? Poor little children. They would thrive with love and care. She parked the car and told them to wait while she bought the hamburgers. She was hardly in the queue before she heard the crash. The kids had wired the car and raced off, only to smash into the back of another car. 'Oh God!' she groaned.

The car still operated, so she gave her address to the other driver and swore that she'd forgotten to put her car in gear. The handbrake must have failed, she told him, and the kids had grabbed the wheel to try and steer it. Since she was parked on a hill he believed her story.

As she drove sombrely back to the Shelter she could not help trembling slightly, remembering her first meeting with Archie. If he found out, she'd be sacked.

She had done brilliantly at university and been commissioned by the United Nations Children's Organisation, to complete an investigation on the effects of apartheid on the nation's youth. She badly needed this appointment at the Shelter, to help her research. She had expected to be welcomed with open arms, but when she offered her services, to her annoyance she had been turned down. She had stood her ground and insisted she was given a chance.

Archie Bagnall, manager of the home, was an MCP de-luxe. He had stared at her accusingly as if her sudden appearance might prejudice his standards and undo months of patient groundwork.

'Female do-gooders are not suitable for the Shelter,' he'd growled. 'It might help if you think of our inmates as wild animals, Ms Arlington. A pack of wild dogs, if you like. Not an ounce of compassion amongst them. They're not children any more. They're shrewd, manipulative and cunning . . . and do you know why? Because they have to survive in one of the world's harshest environments, the downtown streets of Johannesburg. This city has the highest murder rate in the world, the highest rape statistics, highest muggings, robbery with violence.'

'I'm up to here in facts and figures.' Jean had tapped her forehead. 'I want to be with children, not statistics. That's why I came here. Otherwise I could have done my research with books.'

'You frighten me.' Archie's fierce brown eyes locked with hers and for a moment she could not look away. 'There's a do-gooder in you,' he said softly. 'It's hidden away under all that book learning and all those degrees of yours, but I sense it, I smell it and I fear it.'

Jean had made an effort to control her temper, reminding herself that Archie's training was mainly experience. Lacking a formal university degree he was bound to snipe at her, she'd decided.

'Some of them can never be tamed, but for every ten who grad-
uate into the criminal classes, there's that one soul waiting to be
helped. That's what this place is all about, Ms Arlington. Make no
mistake, they all sniff glue, they all prostitute themselves, they all
steal and mug and beat up defenceless old people. Sometimes they
set light to them. They'll run back on to the streets if you try to
impose an ounce of discipline before they're ready. Show kindness and you're targeted as their next victim. If I give you a try for
a few days, you'd better watch yourself.'

Jean had endured the lecture with mounting impatience.
Archie was the living image of Popeye's enemy, Brutus. He
stood six foot tall; his olive skin glistened; his neck and throat
were like a redwood tree; his eyes were huge, lustrous and
blazing with fierceness, and his thick black eyebrows were
knitted in a ferocious scowl.

'A fanatic,' she had thought, watching the strange light
glowing from behind his eyes. Was he Coloured? She wasn't
sure. Coming from England, she found it hard to tell. 'The kids
must be brave to come here. Either that or desperate.' She had
tried to imagine what it must feel like to be small and helpless
and caught in that implacable gaze.

'Are you listening to me, Ms Arlington?'

Archie had explained again to her about the six youthful
criminals waiting at Hillbrow police station whom she must
collect and bring to the Shelter.

'Sometimes the police break a few rules and hand the
youngsters over to us. They're not the hard-hearted bastards
portrayed in your English press. You people get everything
wrong. I bet you expected to see lions walking around the
streets.' He laughed heartily at his own foolish gibe. 'In fact, so
many of our police are English. They've come down the chute,
Kenya, Zambia, Zimbabwe and now South Africa. I wonder
what they think about the archetypal Nazi image you people try
to pin on them?

'Now – these six broke into a pharmacy and stole – would you
believe it – cough medicine and sore-throat sweets, plus a few

packets of aspirin. They're first-offenders and the proprietor has been persuaded by me not to press charges, so they're going to be set free, under our surveillance. Go and get them, Ms Arlington.'

'They've been here before,' Archie said. 'They pitch when the pickings are bad and they're desperate for food. Pathetic aren't they? Embryonic murderers and criminals. In ten years time they'll be finished – hooked on drugs, brutalized, wracked with disease. It makes me sick.'

'No,' Jean thought, surprising herself with her surge of passion. 'That must never happen – not to them, they're too young.' She had already forgiven them for trying to steal the car for they had explained how scared they were, not knowing where they were being taken. To hide her feelings she said, 'I'll get them some food and make up their bunks.'

'No. That would take away their freedom and their independence. The point of this place is that the kids must feel that they are totally free. Try to restrict them or pamper them in any way and we'll lose them,' he said. 'They help themselves at the canteen, which is out the back, they wash their plates and they get issued with a blanket for their bunks. That's our biggest loss item, by the way, although we try to keep an eye on them. They help keep the place clean, too.'

The 'Angels' were in time for breakfast, which was mealie pap with milk and sugar, plus bread and jam and coffee. Despite the hamburgers they had wolfed down, the gang scuttled to the wooden benches and ate as if they were starving, and they probably were, she decided. As she watched them, one of the older boys reached over and grabbed Angel's bread. In a flash he lunged out with a knife and caught the boy across the back of his hand. As blood spilled on to the table, Angel stuffed the bread into his mouth.

Jean stood stockstill with her mouth open. She almost screamed. 'Give me your knife,' she said to Angel.

'If I give it to you,' Angel whispered, looking fearfully

towards Archie, 'then I'll be beaten up by every bigger boy, because that fucking puss here will tell them you got my knife. Honest, miss,' he whined. 'I only use it when I'm threatened.'

'Give me your knife,' she hissed.

'D'you want me to tell Mr Bagnall about the hamburgers, Miss? You'd be sacked for sure.'

Jean backed away, realising that she was an alien here. Let Archie sort it out, she thought, waiting for the stabbed boy to complain, but he kept quiet about his wound and later she fixed it with some disinfectant and a plaster.

'Okay, Ms Arlington, they're all yours,' Archie told her after breakfast. 'Get hold of their parents or nearest relative and send them home. You'll find some of the addresses in the files, but they're probably out of date. You'll have to slog over it. Explain the facts of life to them. They've been handed to us by the police, which means that they had better keep off the streets for a while. We'd prefer to get them reconciled with their parents. Otherwise, second-best is a coloured orphanage. To get there they have to attend local school for a few weeks and show some signs of being tamed.'

Jean began her research by questioning the children. It was going to be a long, heart-breaking job, she realised an hour later. They seemed to have no idea where their mothers were and some of them were unsure of their race or their age. Clearly the kids were coloured, but that term covered a vast spectrum of shades of mixed blood, ranging from half-Chinese to near black or near white. Nico was close to black with very little mixed blood in him. Ralph, on the other hand, was almost white with his milky blue eyes, his dark blond kinky hair and light brown skin. He was freckled and frail and pathetically grateful for any attention.

Angel was altogether different and unusual. He had a sallow Mediterranean-type skin and a wide mouth, but otherwise perfect Grecian features and glossy, straight black hair. He might be part-Indian, or possibly Portuguese or Spanish. She longed to know his story, but the boy stuck obstinately to his claim of being white and of Afrikaans parentage. He said his name was Angel de Beer, and that he came from Johannesburg, but no such child had ever been registered. Despite her patient questioning over the next three weeks, Angel would not divulge any details of his childhood or parentage.

Three weeks later, Jean handed in her report. Five of the gang had been returned to their mothers, who had promised not to let them be abused in future. Only Angel's home could not be traced, so she battled to find a place for him at the local coloured orphanage. The boy had behaved erratically, leaving frequently, returning only to see his friends or cadge a meal, unexpectedly bursting into a rage when the last boy, Ralph, was sent home.

On that morning Angel came to her office and stood there looking sad and lonely. Jean hardened her heart. She had already decided that to trust Angel was to invite disaster.

'What is it?' she asked briskly.

'Please, Missus, I'll probably never see you again. I want to thank you for the hamburgers. I also want you to know that we were all sorry we used your weaknesses to get the better of you. And we're sorry about your car. Hope it didn't cost too much.'

She gaped at him, never believing that he could say all this, let alone think it up. 'And what exactly are my weaknesses?'

'You got lots of them, Missus. The worst one is wanting us . . .' He broke off. 'You think we can be good . . . like ordinary children, if you try hard enough.'

'And can't you be?'

'No.'

'I see. Well, Angel, I'm going to tell you something I want you to remember. You can be any damn thing you want to be. All you have to do is to will it to happen. You can be as successful as any child from a good home. Maybe more so, because you'll try harder.'

'Please, Missus, give me the addresses of my friends, so I can keep an eye on them?'

'No, certainly not. The Shelter will look after them with regular visits.'

'No, they won't. How could they? I must see them sometimes.'

'No,' she said firmly.

'Go suck yourself, Miss do-gooder,' Angel sneered. Later that day he ran away.

For days Jean checked the likely begging spots, but she could not find him. She felt absurdly rejected by this stubborn urchin who had got through to her.

A month later, she was leaving the Shelter to go home on a Friday afternoon, when a skinny figure blocked her path.

'Please, Missus! Help me, Missus.' She felt thrilled to see Angel, but irritated to hear that beggar's whine coming from such a lovely child. She felt angry and disappointed in him.

'Why did you run away, Angel?'

'That place sucks,' he said, pointing towards the Shelter. 'Besides, it's supposed to be open and free. We can do what we like? Isn't that so?'

His voice was soft and light, a girl's voice. Was he perhaps a hermaphrodite? Today he seemed so girlish and defenceless. Something had softened him and when she saw the tears in his eyes her heart went out to him again. She reached out and took his hand and, amazingly, he allowed her to touch him briefly before pulling away.

'Let's go inside,' she said gently, resigning herself to cancelling her trip to a game park. 'It's suppertime. Are you hungry? Come.'

'I can't go in there, Missus. Help me ... please. I'm sick, missus. Where can I go? What can I do?'

'I'll call a doctor.'

'No!' He sounded agonised. Then he turned away and she saw his shoulders shaking under his thick leather jacket.

Strange, she mused. She'd seen him fighting mercilessly, but now he was crying like a lost girl.

'I'll take you home,' she blurted out, knowing that she was breaking the rules. 'But you can't stay with me for long. Only until you're better. D'you understand?' She glanced nervously over her shoulder. Archie would have something to say about this. He'd be right, too. She sighed and straightened her shoulders. For the past month she had been wondering if she had chosen the right vocation, for she was unable to distance herself from the children's suffering. Lately she hardly slept.

When Angel leaned his head wearily against the seat she realised she would have to have it fumigated. Of course she would catch lice, but did it matter? Nevertheless, she was starting to itch. Once a month the staff deloused their hair.

Where would he sleep? She had rented a delightful one-bedroomed apartment in Killarney, but there was a divan bed pushed into the corner of her L-shaped livingroom. He could sleep there. She would buy him some clothes. Perhaps she could persuade St Patrick's, the local catholic boys' home, to take him. She would call her house doctor to see Angel, then Archie would never find out that she had taken the boy to her flat.

Her thoughts rushed on while she parked in the underground park and hurried to her front door, conscious of Angel's bare feet and rustling jacket behind her. She wondered why she felt such a surge of joy at bringing the small waif home. For the first time she accepted that she was lonely.

There! She closed the door. What next? 'All right, young Angel,' she said briskly. 'First things first. How about supper? Then I'll call the doctor.'

'I don't feel so sick no more. Perhaps I'm just hungry,' he whined unconvincingly.

To Jean the evening was a mass of confused impressions and pathetic revelations: Angel scrubbing his hands with the nail-brush before helping her peel potatoes, and then moving with deft, practised movements; the way he cleared up so carefully. He must have worked for someone for he even knew how to cook, but he had never seen an electric stove before, or an air extractor, or a dishwasher and he was intrigued and interested.

Strange! Why would he not take off his jacket? Her apartment had underfloor heating and, let's face it, she'd overdone the heat. She glanced sidelong at Angel, who was shaking the water from the lettuce he had washed so carefully. Stranger and stranger. When they sat at the table Angel mumbled grace into his delicate hands and put the napkin on his knees and knew how to use a knife and fork and once again she wondered.

'Who are you, Angel? Where do you come from?'

A shrug, eyes glittering with tears, and then all she saw was the top of his glossy blue-black head as he bent his face over his plate.

'Would you like a bath?' she asked after supper.

His face lit up and he grinned with delight.

'Do you need a doctor? You don't seem sick to me.' Yet he was pale and listless and there were deep shadows under his eyes. 'Tell me what's wrong. Maybe we can get something from the chemist. Or I can call the doctor if you prefer that.'

'I seem to be bleeding to death,' Angel whispered. 'It's coming from deep inside me. Pouring out . . . for days. I don't know what to do.'

'Oh!' The truth hit Jean so forcefully she wanted to cry out at her own stupidity. It had been staring her in the face this past month. 'Enjoy your bath, Angel. I'll find you a pair of my pyjamas. You won't mind girls' pyjamas, will you? I'll call a woman doctor. I'm sure you'll feel easier with her. Oh, and please don't worry. This is perfectly normal for girls. Let's see now, you're smaller than me, but you're tall and I'm sure some of my clothes will fit you.'

Ten minutes later, when she knocked and walked into the bathroom carrying a bundle of clothes and a nightdress, she found Angel gazing into the mirror as if enraptured, experimenting with the perfume, talcum and make-up.

'Have fun,' she whispered. She could hardly talk for the lump in her throat.

'You let a girl run loose on the streets?' The doctor was saying incredulously, while Jean stood in a daze listening. She was remembering a fight she had witnessed when Angel had floored a large boy with a well-aimed blow on the nose.

'He ... she ... seldom stayed the night. I'm beginning to understand why.'

'She's a virgin. Yes, unbelievable, isn't it?'

'Not really. Not if she pretended to be a boy. It was for protection, you see. That's what she told me. Quite clever really.'

'Her pretending days are over. She's fourteen years old. Rather late for puberty, but she's suffering so badly from malnutrition and trauma, her body has hardly developed. Her breasts are coming along, and you'll find that she'll change her entire personality now she has at last reached puberty. You'd better tell her the facts of life, buy her the necessary things. Here's a prescription for some pills to regulate the flow. You must explain what will happen to her if she tries to live on the streets – these coloured runaways don't stand a chance. She'll be forced into prostitution by persuasion or by other methods. Can you get her into a coloured orphanage?'

'Yes. I'm sure I can.'

'She can't stay here. I suppose you realise that. It's breaking the law.'

'I'll talk to her.'

Jean had no chance to explain. She put it off for three days, until she found a place for Angel at the girls' orphanage. When she woke next morning Angel had left. There was a note on the neatly made bed.

'Thank you for everything you've done, Dr Jean. Fancy you being a doctor. I read it on your letters. Thank you also for the clothes and the cash you gave me. I must leave. I'm not a *gammat. I'm white*, and I'm not going to be pushed into a coloured orphanage.'

She never saw Angel again.

Chapter 13

The grass was dry and brown for it had rained only once during winter, but all life was thrilling to the call of spring, for it was September and the promise of rain was only a month away. Since January, Daniel had raked the Cronjés' earth, up and down, east to west, his mind in a vacuum, trying to keep despair at bay, for it seemed that his dream of becoming a lawyer was to remain in the realms of vain hopes. Only his soccer kept him sane, for it was one area where he could excel.

But with spring came strange urgings and longings and his new dream centred on Jeanetta. She was young, luscious and ripe for picking and all the local youths had tried to date her, but without success. Dan was no exception, but she was pretty and clever, so he persevered.

On Sunday morning he tried to walk to church beside her, but she objected, so he trailed behind, noting for the first time how exactly she aped the whites with her cast-off tennis dress and peaked cap, her sunglasses, white gloves and high-heeled sandals a size too small for her, all of which had once been worn by Eleanor Cronjé – but not together. Didn't the silly girl know that? Oh, my, how she wobbled and limped. He felt sorry for her. But her buttocks swayed provocatively, and her waist was small enough for two hands to span, her features were fine, her eyes huge and black and full of fun most times, although this morning she was scowling ferociously. She had an unusually long neck, and beautiful hands, Dan noticed, and she was so fresh-looking. Perfume and the scent of soap and the crackle of nylon formed an aura around her.

He followed her, throwing compliments like corn to a greedy chick. She gobbled them up eagerly, and preened herself, but wouldn't throw him a kind word in return. Dan followed her until she lost her temper.

'There's no ways I'm going to be seen around with some dirty, stinking kafir. I'm keeping myself for a white man . . . one day,' she added wistfully.

Dan was shocked into silence.

'But you are black, Jeanetta, just like me. What whitey is going to marry you, and why would you want one?'

There was a silence for a while. 'You boys are full of nonsense, unreliable and shifty.' She recited what she had clearly picked up from the family.

'The truth is, you're darker than I am,' he said, catching up with her and laughing as he thrust out an arm.

She shrugged. Her huge black eyes shimmered with tears, she tossed her head, and tried to hurry, but she couldn't outwalk him. 'I've been brought up white,' she said eventually. 'That makes me just the same as them.'

'Some of my best friends are white,' he chortled.

'Oh, Dan, leave me be. Get lost!' she called, breaking into a run.

Dan winced as her foot wobbled over. She gasped and stood on one foot glowering at him. 'Fuck off, kafir-boy,' she said.

Dan lost his temper. 'I'm going. Who wants a dark-skinned girl like you?'

Then he felt so sorry, for there she was, sitting in despair on a rock, hugging her ankle. 'I'm sorry.' There was a hibiscus flower blooming in the hedge. He picked it and gave it to her. 'I didn't mean that. I, for one, would want a dark-skinned girl like you. Your skin is beautiful and so are you.' He gave her the flower and examined her ankle which was swollen. 'It's not very bad. I'll fetch the farm lorry and drive you to church. How's that?' He left at a run, but when he returned she was nowhere in sight.

*

'So what's her problem?' Dan asked Sam that night. They were sitting in the yard on a fallen log, watching the fire flaring from a pile of wood. Beside the fire, a braai-grid waited, filled with sausages and offal, and when the wood became dull embers they would start to grill. They were both hungry, so they poked at the fire with sticks, trying to hasten the process. Beside the fire was a big, round cast iron pot, filled with cooked mealie pap, covered in tomato and onion sauce.

This meal was Sam's favourite which he didn't often get. Sam was wearing old khaki trousers and shirt, his hair was white and his features still handsome. He never really looked the part of a farm labourer, Dan thought. He'd often wondered why Sam had crumpled so badly when father was imprisoned, but he'd never dared to ask.

'Jeanetta's like a *Hansi* [hand-reared pet lamb] taken from the flock and reared by hand, that can nevermore relate to sheep, but thinks it's some kind of a dog,' Sam was explaining to him. 'She was brought into the house and reared with the Cronjé children – Tony and his sister – to be a cross between a companion and a playmate. She never really knew who or what she was. I suppose they didn't know what else to do with her, for she was found abandoned in the stable when she was two years old. They're not cruel people. In fact, I liked the former Mrs Cronjé, but she didn't understand what it would be like for Jeanetta to be banished to the kitchen when the young daughter died in a car accident.

'She has a good job,' Dan said. 'She's the assistant to the Cronjés' cook. She has a room with TV and a shower of her own, food and prospects. After all, she's learning a skill.'

'But you can see the anguish in her eyes. Don't set your cap at her,' Sam muttered. 'You won't stay here forever and Jeanetta will always hate herself. She won't mix with her own people. She thinks "white" but they won't mix with her. She can't relate to blacks. So where does that leave Jeanetta?'

'Stuffing herself with whites-only food and listening to the radio by herself every night,' Dan said. 'You should see those trays of cream cakes. It's amazing she's still slender.'

'You're a bit like her in some ways, Dan. Could that be because you and Pieter played together for so many years and now he's shrugged you off?'

'It's not his fault,' Dan muttered. 'We still have the same bond when we're hunting or in the bush.'

'Maybe. You're brainy, Dan. That can be very lonely in a place like this. It's hard to adjust and relate to others. You don't believe what they believe, you don't think what they think. I doubt your brains will do you any good. A brainy black is worse than a kafir dog to the whites.'

'To hell with the whites!' Dan exploded. 'What's made you like this? What caused you to give in? You were right at the top of your profession.'

His grandfather shrugged and poked at the embers. He lifted the grid and placed it over the stones around the fire. Soon the smell of sizzling fat increased their hunger.

'I know it's true. My headmaster told me.'

'Perhaps I didn't want to send any more young men to their deaths, or to exile, or to a penal settlement. Perhaps you're happier sitting on a tractor . . .'

'Decaying . . .' Unwilling to fight, Dan closed his mouth firmly.

'I had a letter from Father last month,' Dan said after a while. It had been a sad, poignant letter from a father to a son who could not remember him. He was ill, he wrote, and uncertain about whether he'd live to reach the end of his sentence.

No words could describe their mutual anguish so they sat in silence for a while. Sam turned the grid. 'Just about ready,' he said, poking the embers to get more heat and smoothing them out. 'Dan, I know you blame me for giving up teaching and you blame Nosisi for refusing to pay for your education in the city away from home, but our lives have been hell, knowing each moment that your father, Victor, is on Robben Island, breaking rocks, or alone in his cell, year after year. I couldn't go through that again with you.'

'I understand,' Dan said, and suddenly, for the first time, he truly did. In a moment of rare emotion he clasped the old man's hand and held it tightly against his cheek.

Dan left after supper. He didn't feel like sleeping. The night was warm, the cicadas were chirping, frogs croaking, the owl's haunting cries echoed overhead. He felt so restless.

He walked along the river bank remembering how he and Pieter had made a dugout canoe and kept it hidden in the bulrushes. Perhaps it was still here. And old Caesar, the massive crocodile, who often frightened them half to death, used to lurk here.

One of his earliest horror memories was of this place, too. The night of 25 April 1974 was engraved on his mind. He had been just a boy. Pieter and he had stood together watching the pitiful Mozambique refugees fleeing across the river. Farmers and their workers had driven their bulldozers to the shore and waded shoulder-deep into the river with ropes to haul the people across. He and Pieter had helped to distribute blankets and coffee.

One woman had knocked the coffee from his hand and screamed with terror when she looked at him. They'd taken her to hospital in an ambulance shortly afterwards.

'Why?' he had asked Pieter. 'Why me?'

'They've seen their people stabbed, burned, raped and kicked to death by blacks. I expect she thought you were one of them. After all, you're black.'

It was the first time he had thought about the difference between their colour of skin. Since then he'd hardly ever thought of anything else. Deep inside him a gigantic inferiority complex had grown and spread until it had contaminated every part of him: his intellect, his emotions, his drive, his self-love. Was that why he was still a virgin at eighteen? He reckoned that it was.

His thoughts turned back to Jeanetta, a fellow sufferer. Self-condemned to be second-class. It was so wrong. He had to help her, and, at the same time, himself.

He went there thoughtfully, choosing his words. He had so much to tell her, but the crux of his message was – we are black and therefore special. He picked several of Mrs Cronjé's roses on the way. Somehow he knew that he would spend the night in Jeanetta's bed.

Chapter 14

———◆———

They had marched all night and at dawn they swam across a small channel dividing an island from the mainland, carrying their kit in bundles, their rifles wrapped in polythene and strapped on their heads. Despite their exhaustion and hunger, they squatted obediently in front of the sergeant for the next lesson, knowing that nothing could save them if they were caught dozing. They learned their skills under the same conditions they'd be working in. If they weren't going to make it, now was the time to find out. There were fifteen of them, all that was left from fifty eager boys who had begun the course. Now they were deeply tired from the physical and mental abuse, yet they were all on edge, never relaxing, wary of traps the army set for them, scared of the punishment dished out for next to nothing, safeguarding themselves as best they could, knowing they were fully dispensable.

They had lived, drilled, trained and slept in the bush, in pouring rain, in hot sun, drenched by the sea, hungry or tired – it made no difference to anyone. They were discovering that they could survive almost anything, but they weren't sure that it mattered any more.

Nine months in the army, six of which had been in the Special Services camp, had changed Pieter. He was taller, broader and very thin. His hair was thicker and his cheeks and neck were covered in a thick, curly black beard. He was wearing camouflage overalls that were covered in mud and he knew that he stank. Twice a month they were taken back to base for the two S's, and as far as he was concerned it couldn't be too soon. He hated to be filthy.

In some indefinable way, he had changed from a boy to a man. He had learned to live on iron rations, haphazardly distributed, supplemented with occasional raw fish if they found themselves by the sea; when they were desperate enough even scorpions and locusts supplemented their diet. Trapped birds were the occasional rare luxury. Starved of the basic necessities of life, they survived somehow. They'd been told the score enough times: the camp was designed to test their mental stamina to the uttermost. The army wasn't looking for Rambos, they were trying to weed out those who might break mentally in any situation.

Pieter was sitting cross-legged on the ground, on a lagoon island near the Natal coast, and the smell of the ozone was all about him. The warm sea mist had dampened his skin and his clothes and it seemed to calm his aching guts and limbs, and soothe his hunger and exhaustion. Jesus, he was tired. For a second his gaze moved from the sergeant to the far horizon. Thinking of all those fish down there made him feel twice as hungry.

'If I'm boring you, de Vries, why don't you take over?' Sergeant Smit said.

'Sorry, sir.'

'Come up here. We'll wake you up.' Pieter stepped forward unwillingly. 'For your benefit, I was saying that there are two types of interrogation: primary or in-depth. Primary interrogation is the sort of thing you men are going to have to do a lot of, if you ever make it through this course. It means you need to get the info quickly and relay it to the nearest headquarters, perhaps to save your buddies' lives, perhaps to save your battalion, or other people's families.

'In-depth interrogation is usually conducted back at base when there's enough time to do things properly, but you lot will have to learn to improvise.

'Now! Take a look at this bush telephone. Everytime you

twist the handle you send a powerful electric shock through the wire. Come here, de Vries. You're our victim.' He smiled at Pieter, but there was no friendship in his eyes. 'There's various places where you can wind the cable. You might think the testicles would be the most sensitive. Well, you'd be wrong. Round the ears or round the knees are the places most likely to make your prisoner talk. Sit down, private.'

'Sir, I'll tell you anything you want to know. You want to know where the best-looking tart in Durban hangs out? Or if it's little boys . . .'

The squad erupted into laughter and the sergeant managed a painful grin. 'Let's see how your famous sense of humour copes with this,' he said. 'Now, remember, guys, we do try to keep up appearances and you will make sure that you have some K.Y. jelly around.' He took out a jar and passed it round. 'This jelly forms a sort of cushion between the wires and the captive's skin, and prevents burn marks. Might be handy if he tries to escape. This fucker might get himself photographed by Amnesty International, or use his burns to campaign for funds for the African National Congress in the States. So we're not going to oblige him with burns or scars or any other damn thing. You got that?' He plastered Pieter's skin with the jelly.

Gritting his teeth, Pieter kept his cool by imagining exactly what he'd do to the sergeant if he ever caught him alone with no witnesses.

'Okay, let's pretend your name's Mgongo, shall we? You've just been taken from a village that's suspected of harbouring Swapo terrorists. Pick up the receiver. We're going to play a little game, Mgongo. It's called ET phones home. Say "Hello, Mama."'

'Hello, Mama. How are you keeping?' Pieter said, imitating a classic black accent, to more laughter from the squad.

'Tell Mama where the Swapo terrorists are hiding out. Okay?'

As the sergeant wound the handle, the pain hit Pieter in the head and ear until he thought he would explode. He hung on and then let out a roar. Miraculously, the pain stopped.

'Mama! You've got to catch this fucking son of a bitch and put out his light for me,' Pieter stuttered into the phone.

'Had enough, have you? One second of it has you screaming.'

One second? It had seemed like a minute at least. 'All right,' the sergeant's hand dropped away from the handle and Pieter relaxed. 'Unwind. Tell them what it's like,' he said, gesturing towards the class squatting on the ground.

Pieter glowered at the sergeant. 'Bad enough to make you long to kill whoever does it to you,' he muttered.

Smit threw back his head and laughed. 'Want to have a try?' The laugh stopped abruptly. 'Let's get on with it. Every one of you will have access to a bush telephone, so let that be a source of inspiration to you.

'Take another instance. You've blundered into a minefield – they're all around you, yet the locals are walking safely through the area. Why? Because they know where the mines are. So you get one of them and tie him on to the front of your vehicle. Drive forward slowly and it won't be long before you know exactly where the mines are. If you're lucky enough to find someone with a wounded leg or arm, it's that much quicker, because you must use that weakness to get info fast. Remember, this is war and you're fighting against vermin. Those commie bastards don't have a soul. Wipe them out and the world is that much better off. You got that?'

Pieter's ears were still ringing and he felt dizzy. He tried to pull himself together. 'One of these days we'll get that fucking puss,' Koos murmured.

After the four-hour lesson, they began the long march back to base. Perhaps they'd get a meal. Pieter began to dream of stew, braaied mutton chops, boerewors, fried eggs ... God, he was hungry.

A mile from the island the sergeant stopped and let out a roar of rage. One long brown turd was lying on the ground beside a bush, near where they'd eaten their rations the previous evening.

'You careless bunch of fuckers! For once and for all you're gonna learn to bury your waste. I'm gonna teach you a lesson you won't forget in a hurry. All of you. You're gonna eat that fucking turd. That's all that's needed to show Swapo exactly where you are.'

Pieter stood still feeling disgusted. Their training here had taught them to obey without thought or rebellion, a breach of discipline meant goodbye to Special Services. Pieter had set his heart on getting into the Service, but he wouldn't eat shit. The sergeant looked into his eyes and saw his rebellion. He was smiling sarcastically as he pushed a portion towards Pieter with a stick. 'Smells real good,' he said.

He knows damn well I can't eat it. He looked up towards Koos standing to the side of the sergeant and yelled: 'Look out, Koos.' The sergeant jumped and turned. 'Boomslang, sir. It went into the bush.' The sergeant let off a couple of shots and then realised he'd been taken. He snapped back, but too late, all the portions of turd had disappeared. Pieter was munching with a look of ecstasy on his face. 'Gosh, I was so hungry, sergeant. Thanks. Tastes better than the rations you give us.'

Sergeant Smit knew when he was beaten. 'Let's go,' he said briefly. 'We have to trek back to camp. Tonight we're going to the movies.'

They dined splendidly in the canteen at headquarters – pork cutlets, sweet potatoes, pumpkin, gravy, beans . . . what a feast! They seldom had a proper meal or a roof over their heads. Later, feeling dazed with happiness, they filed into the lecture room.

The documentary began with shots of South Africa, the beautiful vineyards of the Cape, the magnificent Cederberg Mountains, sugar plantations in Natal, the Knysna forests, the gold mines, mile after mile of wheat and dairy farmlands, the forests of the Eastern Transvaal, bikini girls lying on Clifton beach, which brought a chorus of frustrated wolf whistles from the boys.

'There are two types of human beings,' the narrator was saying, 'those who rape the land and those who protect the land.' Then followed scenes of the arid soil erosion of northern countries where once tobacco and maize flourished.

The point made, the narrator introduced Captain Anton Joubert, captured by the Angolans and held for five years. In a quiet, unassuming voice that stuttered often, he told them exactly what had been done to him, when he could remember what he was talking about, and he had to be prompted often for he lacked concentration. Before his capture he had been decorated for bravery, now he was a shambling six-foot shell.

They saw smuggled shots of African prisons and the prisoners, starving to death, manacled to the wall, lying in their own filth, then the charred bodies of people burned in cars, necklaced, beaten, mutilated. They saw animals chained and starving and burned to death for carrying evil spirits. Lastly came shots from the Mozambique revolution, a kaleidoscope of blood and death as Portuguese settlers, fleeing to the borders, were raped, beaten, burned, shot and tortured to death.

'Okay, fellows,' the Captain said around midnight as the lights were switched on. 'Pleasant dreams!' A chorus of groans drowned his words. He waited a moment. 'I expect you're wondering why we showed you this sort of filth. It's a reminder of what could happen to our own people, our own land, if we're not prepared to protect it. All the shots you were shown came from neighbouring states. Think about that.

'You've just seen why this force was created. You are the elite of the South African Defence Force. Your job is to make sure that those commie bastards never get across our borders. Furthermore, the commie rot must be rooted out and destroyed in our own land. It's a great responsibility and that's why you have to be the best ... and why your training is so tough, because you have a rough job ahead of you. A pint of sweat saves a gallon of blood. Many of your buddies haven't made it. They've been sent back to the regular force. Each of you who remain will have cost a packet by the time you qualify. Think about that, too. You might not feel so hot right now, but, I assure you, you're valuable property.'

He waited for the whistles and catcalls to die down.

'You're being trained to make sure that our beautiful land and the people who are dear to us never fall prey to what we've seen tonight,' he said quietly. 'We're placing our faith in you. *You will be our sentinels*. Goodnight, fellows.'

Chapter 15

Dan was sitting in Jeanetta's room waiting for her to return from her duties. The Cronjés were having a dinner party and she was likely to be late. Nowadays they were lovers and more than that, they were friends, too. He was giving her nightly lessons in English and bookkeeping for she hoped to own a restaurant one day.

'What's the point of dreaming?' he had said when she first told him about her ambition. 'You can't open a business in a white area and the blacks don't earn enough for your fancy cooking in the homelands or the ghettos.'

'Oh, you faithless one,' she had chided him. 'You get more like your grandfather every day.'

She was a lovely girl. Pretty, clean, a devout Christian, hardworking and loyal. He knew she hoped to marry him one day when they were older, but that was out of the question. He had a long way to go. He didn't know how or when, but he knew he was going. Lately a great lassitude had him in its grip and he seemed to be rooted, but not trapped.

He was feeling hungry as he leafed through a catalogue of recipes and listened to the radio with half an ear. It was news time. Nine o'clock. Would Jeanetta remember to bring him something special from the leftovers?

Then he heard the news announcer say: 'Victor Tweneni, sentenced to twenty years' hard labour for an act of terrorism on November 22, 1968, died today in his cell in the maximum security prison of Robben Island. The report states that

Tweneni died of cancer of the lungs, for which he had been receiving treatment. He was accused of heading an unlawful terrorist group and bombing a state department's premises, resulting in the death of three people.'

Dan sat up shaking badly and buried his face in his hands, overwhelmed with a grief that he had never before experienced. His father had died alone in his cell, within a few years of his release. What a lonely, sad life.

'Oh God! Oh God!' He broke into harsh sobs, giving himself up to his grief. Later he became aware of children clustered in the doorway watching him, so he stood up and walked outside, feeling numb with anger.

He was not sure what happened for the rest of the night, only that he found himself back in Sam's shack at dawn. Sam had heard the news. He was sitting in silence outside his home, his head in his hands.

They looked at each other, but did not speak. Dan rifled his tin trunk and found the precious folder containing his father's speech which he had made to the court just before he was sentenced. He knew it by heart, but he read it again, the tears rolling down his cheeks.

'My Lord. I find myself here in Johannesburg, convicted under laws made by a minority group for the sole purpose of safeguarding their unlawful privileges. I do not recognise your right to try me for demonstrating against laws made by a government which has no legal right to rule and which binds my fellow blacks in a web of restrictive legislation designed to keep them in a state of virtual slavery.

'I have been detained without a trial for four hundred days. Finally I was brought to trial under the ugly name of terrorism. Yet we call ourselves patriots or freedom fighters, because it is our ambition to overthrow the yoke of slavery that you have placed upon our people by virtue of your superior arms and army.

'I will not try to convince you of the severity of the laws that control every black's life because I know that your function and your intention is not to uphold justice, but to safeguard white minority interests.

'Every man has the right to an education, to be able to live with his family, to have access to the law, to be free to work for the person of his choice, to have freedom of movement within his own country and, finally, to be ruled by the people that he wants to be ruled by, and not those who rule him because they have more guns than he has.

'It was only after years of passive resistance that I decided to take up arms against our white rulers. My first target was an explicit act of war against the issuing of passes that document each black as if he were merely a unit of slave labour.

'I call upon all black South Africans who have an education to devote their lives to the betterment of their brothers, and I call upon right-thinking, white South Africans to help us black people in our struggle. Only when whites come to accept our rights as human beings will we be able to live in peace together.

'The outside world is with us in our struggle. You cannot oppose the entire world forever. But we know that the world will not hand us our freedom on a plate. We must struggle and it is for this struggle that I am being sentenced today. I say to you now, you can put me away for all of my life, or hang me, but you cannot stop the process of change. You will maintain your rule only for as long as your power is greater than ours.'

Dan sat on the floor, the tears streaming down his cheeks. 'Oh God, why didn't you help him? Dearest Father! To suffer so much and then to die without even regaining your freedom.'

Dan knew in his heart that his father was a great and brave warrior. He hardly remembered him for he had been only three years old when his father was arrested. Now he would never meet him and he had waited for so long.

Maria de Vries was thinking about Sam and his grief as she searched over the veld at sunset. She looked a pretty picture in her blue floral dress and the high leather boots she always wore outside to protect her from snakes. She had been searching for turkey eggs and she had found fifteen which she would put under her broody hens. With luck she could have fifty turkeys ready for Christmas. That could bring her a thousand rands, enough to buy her husband Davie, and Pieter everything they longed for.

She hurried home, planning how to spend her cash. As she neared the cottage, she noticed that the donkeys looked tense. Ears back, they were rolling their eyes as they jostled each other and circled the kraal. She had a moment of misgiving. Could there be a snake in their camp? She'd better fetch the gun. But then she thought Davie would be back in an hour's time, so perhaps she would wait for him to investigate. Ignoring the whinny of fear from Daisy, she walked into the cottage.

One step over the doorway sent her senses reeling. There was a pungent stench of unwashed bodies and dagga. Spilt coffee was sizzling on the stove. The kist had been ransacked.

Kafirs!

Thoughts of escape flashed through her mind. Where was the rifle? A quick glance at the rack showed that it was gone. As she stepped back, a sharp push sent her stumbling over the kitchen floor. She sprang towards the bathroom. If she locked the door in time she might escape through the window.

A sudden violent blow on her shoulder sent her crashing to the ground. The pain was agonising. She pushed herself up on to her knees and hung on to the table, praying quietly, too scared to look up. '*Our Father, which art in heaven ...*' she began.

Another blow hit her shoulder. She fell heavily on to her back. Eyes wide, she saw six youths looking down at her. They began to laugh cruelly.

She screamed and began to fight with every ounce of strength she possessed, but she knew she was doomed. Sam was in the village and no one could hear her screams. She was no match for six big men. They punched her into the ground, but she would not submit, so they hammered her almost senseless, until she could no longer see through her swollen eyes, and they raped her brutally, as if beating her. She fainted when they bit off her nipples, but she recovered when they threw a bucket of cold water over her.

'Beg us for your life,' they told her much later as she lay on the floor drifting in and out of consciousness. 'Beg us, you white trash.' One of them prodded her with his foot.

What fool would beg a kafir? she wondered. Everyone knew they were merciless.

Then they were leaving. Thank God, she thought through mists of semi-consciousness. One of them was holding a large rock over his head. It seemed to be falling in slow motion. She saw all this as if detached from the scene, as if watching her own death from a distance. This couldn't be happening. Not to her. There was a blinding flash, a massive sense of impact, and her world exploded.

Chapter 16

———◆———

Clad in camouflage overalls, his face plastered with mud and wearing a hat poked full of leafy twigs, Pieter stumbled towards the clearing that was their base camp, and collapsed on the sand. He was aching in every limb and weak from hunger and exhaustion. They had spent two nights and one day in mock bush warfare. Now it was dawn. The eastern sky was turning rose, the birds were twittering and with luck they'd get some time off to catch up on sleeping. He was exhausted, but they were to be briefed before they could sleep, the sergeant told them.

'For two days,' the sergeant said when they had assembled, 'we've studied tracking, the art of being invisible, and ways to outmanoeuvre the enemy. Now it's time to start practical lessons. Here's the maps.' He handed round some rough pencilled drawings with only rudimentary markings. The bridge is marked with an X. See it? Each stick is going to take turns in trying to blow up the bridge, while the rest of us defend it against you. Needless to say, you silly fuckers will use fireworks and flare pistols. It's not the shooting that counts, it's the ability to be right there on the spot past our defences without being detected. Once you start shooting, you're dead anyway. If you manage to set off a flare within five metres of the bridge you've won.

'The bulk of the squad will proceed to the bridge by lorry at dusk. The chosen stick will find their own way there. Now de Vries, Huntley and Spiro will be first. You will try to penetrate

133

our defences during the night. You'll have a moonless sky to your advantage. Our job is to make sure you don't make it. Once we see you close enough to identify you, you can take it that you're dead. There's a box of flares, fuse wire and matches in the truck which we'll hand out at dusk. Try not to blow each other up. In the meantime, get some sleep. We start at nineteen hundred hours.'

Pieter, Koos and Andy comprised a fighting unit, known as a stick. They were far and away the most efficient unit in the battalion. They knew this and they were proud of their reputation and proud of their successes in outwitting the sergeant's traps.

The guys spread themselves around and fell asleep and the sergeant crawled into the back of the lorry.

'We don't stand a hope in hell,' Koos grumbled. 'That fucker intends to hold us up to ridicule.'

'We don't have the element of surprise which is essential in this sort of operation,' Andy added in his larny accent.

'Fuck him! I owe him one,' Pieter grumbled. 'If we can lure him out of the truck, we could steal the flares now, get over there, lay the fuses and be back here by dusk. When he hands out the ammo we'll have to fix it so he doesn't know it's already gone.'

'Another day without sleep will just finish me off,' Andy said.

'If we sleep, we lose,' Koos argued. 'We could sleep later during the night.'

'The problem is, how to get him out of the truck?'

'I know how,' Pieter said. 'I've been waiting for a chance to get him back since the ET phone home business. I've got a super strong laxative in my kit. Regular dynamite.'

The two stared at him, their lips flickering into smiles.

'We could make him a cup of coffee.'

'He'd be suspicious.'

'What if we got Johnson to take it to him. He's such an arsehole creeper, Sarge wouldn't suspect him?'

'And Johnson? Won't he suspect?'

Koos was already lighting the fire. 'We'll make everyone coffee. That way no one will notice. We'll suggest to Johnson that the sarge might like a cup – it's up to you to lace the right one, Pieter.'

The plan worked. When the squad was out for the count and the sergeant was groaning and farting in the bushes, they stole the ammo under cover of darkness and set off at a run, spreading the load between them. By dusk the following day they were back.

'You three look like shit,' the sergeant said, yawning. 'Didn't you sleep?'

'You should know, sarge. You don't look too hot yourself, sir. Are you all right? You look sort of eviscerated, *sir*,' Andy said.

'Evisc . . . What the hell is that?'

'Empty,' Koos said, grinning until Pieter trod on his foot.

'Okay, let's get the ammo.' The sergeant groaned and staggered as he moved. 'I seem to have caught a bug.'

'We'll do it, sir,' Huntley said.

By the time they reached the bridge, the sergeant had his defences so well deployed they wouldn't have stood a chance to lay the fuses or the flares. They had previously chosen a clump of bushes at the mouth of a cave, overlooking the ravine, as their vantage point and base and they settled in to wait.

'It's not a contest, it's ridiculous,' Huntley moaned. 'Just look at them spread out round that bridge.'

'The bastard just wanted to take the piss out of us.' Pieter sat down and dug for his bar of chocolate.

'I think they should stay awake all night. Near dawn, just when they think they've won, we'll let off the charges. We'd better take turns in keeping watch while two of us sleep.'

It was midnight when they heard a vehicle approaching. Searchlights blared and the lieutenant hailed the sarge by loudspeaker.

'Something's wrong,' Andy said. 'We'd better make it now

while we have the chance.' Koos set off the charges.

Shortly afterwards a massive release of distress rockets and flares lit the sky.

'Better than a Guy Fawkes show,' Andy chuckled.

'Right up their arses,' Pieter growled.

The guys below were running round like startled ants, the sergeant was roaring instructions, then Johnson fell off the bridge. His howls drowned the sirens. He had broken something, it seemed, for the sergeant plunged into the river and dragged him out. Shortly afterwards he was strapped on a stretcher. The sergeant, grim-faced and wet through, bellowed for Pieter.

'You're to go back to base with the lieutenant,' he shouted.

'For a corpse you sure make a lot of noise,' Pieter retorted.

For once the sergeant let it ride and this worried Pieter on the drive back to base.

Twelve hours later Pieter stepped off the military aircraft on to the airstrip at Nelfontein where Lieutenant Myers was waiting for him. Pieter was mainly aware of big feet and ears and the immense height of the man. Myers said very little as he drove him to the police station.

Pieter was fighting down his grief. He could not think of anything except how to keep a grip on himself. As they walked into the station, he felt like a puppet when the strings had fallen loose, nothing seemed to hang together. He wanted to lie on the floor and never get up again. Horror images of their weekly propaganda movies were confused in his mind with the many images he had of his mother's last minutes of life. He couldn't get rid of these terrible pictures in his mind's eye.

He looked to Myers for reassurance. 'Did she suffer badly?'

Myers cleared his throat and looked away, avoiding his gaze. 'Yes,' he said. 'You see, she surprised them. I'm very sorry, Pieter.'

'Where are they?' Pieter's voice was so hoarse he could hardly get the words out. 'Did you catch them?'

'They went back across the river into KaNgwane. We assume they reached Mozambique. There's too many terrorist camps over there. Of course they were moving fast. We think they were part of a small gang trying to infiltrate South Africa for terrorist purposes. Dogs and trackers couldn't catch up with them, they ran like hell back to base. We can expect many more like them.' He sighed heavily.

'I'm afraid you'll have to identify the body and take the death certificate to the undertakers. They'll collect the corpse from us and . . .'

It's not a corpse, it's my Ma, he wanted to blurt out, but he wasn't a kid anymore.

Myers seemed to understand. 'Are you a religious person, de Vries?' he asked gently.

'Yes, I was brought up religious, but lately I don't think much about it.'

'It helps to think that your mother's somewhere up there. What you're going to see is only her corpse.'

'Thanks . . . why didn't Pa?' It was the first time he'd remembered his father. Strange that he didn't meet the plane.

'Your father went after the terrorists and he won't come back – not yet. He's hired a tracker and a couple of good dogs and he's somewhere in the bush, near the border last seen. He may be in shock. We can't find him. Doing something probably helps.'

Pieter's mind was racing into the past. He could see his Ma as clearly as if she was standing there in the doorway, the sunlight playing on her blonde hair, her eyes deep blue like the sea, a young girl's eyes, and they had gazed at him with so much love. Whatever he'd done, however wrong he'd been, there was that love beaming out at him, even if she were crying. He'd grown to manhood in the security of Ma's unconditional love. Suddenly he could hardly swallow for the lump in his throat.

He kept silent because he couldn't trust himself to speak as they drove to the mortuary. They were shown into a room filled with artificial flowers, three easy chairs and some magazines on a table, religious writs with hand-painted flowers round them were hanging on the walls as well as quotations from the bible. It seemed a pretty nice place for a state mortuary, not at all the sort of thing you saw on the movies, and he felt comforted by the official care shown by these human touches. How many people had come here like him, suffering and bereaved?

They waited. Eventually the policeman in charge of the mortuary came in apologising for the delay and slid back a curtain along the wall. There was his Ma lying on a stretcher, wrapped in a white plastic shroud, lit by a harsh neon tube behind a sheet of plate glass. He could see that her features had been pushed back into place, but despite the efforts of the morgue doctor, he could see how she'd been horribly battered. Her mouth was quite smashed, her skin black and swollen, a large piece of plaster covered her forehead and one side of her head. 'This is the good side,' the policeman said. 'Sorry.'

The lights switched off, the curtain was drawn back and he heard the stretcher being rolled out mechanically.

'Can you identify the body of Mrs Maria Vanessa de Vries, your mother?' The policeman gabbled, knowing that it was only a formality.

Pieter nodded. Yet he knew that in some subtle way, it was not his mother, but merely the shell she had inhabited. He had the strangest feeling that she was standing right next to him, trying to tell him something. It occurred to him then that he must go and fetch Pa home.

Later at the funeral, after days and nights of grieving and watching his Pa broken and lost, Pieter decided to sign on to the permanent force. Others must never feel the grief and sorrow he was feeling. Other people's mothers must never be bludgeoned to death. From now on he was a man with a mission – a man who had learned to hate. The enemy must be found and destroyed before they crossed the borders. There was no place for vermin in South Africa.

Chapter 17

'Do you love me?'

The question jarred Tony's nerves, making him flinch. For a wild, heedless moment he wanted to hit out at Eleanor and he nearly did. Torture! What had begun as an exciting sideline was now a boring duty. Worse than boring, he thought, a punishment. It was not the sex that bothered him. He needed that like he needed breakfast and a good walk from time to time; it was her endless neurotic demands on him. Eighteen months ago when she seduced him, he had been an innocent youth. Since then he had enjoyed one-night stands with a few girls in the village and quite honestly he could do without Eleanor, he told himself. Unfortunately he was in a ridiculous position, for every time he tried to call it off, she threatened to confess to Father.

'Do you . . . ? Do you . . . ?'

'Most times,' he answered. 'Sometimes.'

'Well, is it sometimes or most times? Do you love me *now*?' She was petulant and close to tears.

'Shut up and screw,' Tony murmured.

'Oh, Tony, this is wonderful,' she whispered, as if remembering belatedly that she was supposed to be caught up in the moment. She pressed her nipples hard against him, writhed her hips under his, while her fingers kneaded his neck and her fluttering eyelashes fanned his cheeks. Tony was not fooled. He knew that it was some other reason that brought her to his bed night after night. Was it because of her craving for attention or some far more devious need?

He came and Eleanor closed her legs as he rolled to the side of the bed. Now he wanted to get out of that suffocating place, but months ago she had taught him the need for after-sex tenderness, reading from a book to prove her point, so now she snuggled up on his shoulder and her hair tickled his neck.

'Tell me something nice,' she whined. 'Say you love me.'

'I love you.'

'Forever?'

'Sh! I'm thinking.' The force of Eleanor's needs amazed Tony. Even more shocking was the dawning realisation that he was supposed to satisfy those needs. That was his function and it was called love, he was learning. She needed constant reassurance, that she was young and desirable, that he loved her now and would love her in the future and that their age difference would never be noticed. She needed a father-figure to lean on and to make all her decisions – what she wore, what she ate, who she befriended and how she used her time. She needed constant petting and approval, plus sex and still more sex. But was it really the act she craved and the culmination? Tony was sure that she had never been sexually frustrated. What she needed was the union, the brief ecstatic moment when she was no longer alone. She traded her body for her needs, so what did that make her?

'Where's Marius?' he asked.

'Giving a speech in Nelspruit.'

If Father had spent a quarter of the time he wasted on politics on their estates they would not be facing bankruptcy today, Tony thought moodily. Blinded with self-importance and a craving for power, Marius was leading them straight to disaster. He should have been certified long ago. If he weren't a politician what would he have been? Political parties provided a haven for the misfits of the nation . . . all those with delusions of grandeur and obsessions of sainthood.

Mental disorders were inherited, he'd read somewhere. Did he take after his father? Surely not? He was probably the only sane person in a world filled with emotional idiots. To Tony, only money and business mattered. He could see his future laid out like a game of chess, each move and its ramifications, and its endless variations of complicated opposition, and he could usually think up a solution to every move.

Right now the only way to save the estates and free him from his boring days of running the farms was to bury Marius. Perhaps he would drop dead with a heart attack. Father's political aspirations were draining the estates and their newspaper was losing massive sums on a monthly basis, the packaging plant was limping along, and the drought had hit the plantations. But surely he deserved better than being a mere farm foreman? Give him his head and he could make a fortune, he knew.

He was not an intellectual. He had no love of art or music and no so-called sense of beauty, or so Eleanor had told him and she was probably right, since he couldn't see the sense in drivelling over the sunset or flowers like she did. In fact, he couldn't see the sense in flowers. You couldn't eat them.

He had another talent, which was that of minding his own business. He was not concerned with other people or their affairs. He'd felt embarrassed for Pieter, openly crying at his mother's funeral. Pieter was a tough guy and had been his hero, but now he wondered. Perhaps it had all been put on for the benefit of the mourners. Eleanor kept talking about love, but he didn't understand her. Likewise, the way she felt about Marius, that glowing furnace of passionate hatred, was incomprehensible to him. He disliked his father and that was as far as it went – except when he beat him. If there was one thing in life he feared and hated, it was pain. There was only one thing he wanted, and that was wealth. To get it he needed an education, otherwise he'd be walking blindfolded through the hazardous jungle of private enterprise. Meantime his monotonous days succeeded one on another, days of unrelenting misery on the tractor, and if it weren't for his nightly studies, for he was getting a business degree by correspondence, he would have gone crazy. He had just passed his first year in business and economics with honours in every subject.

'What are you thinking?'

'I was thinking about my studies.' He pushed her off his shoulder and stood up.

She looked up at him, frowning. 'You've changed so much. Now you're a man, you've thickened up.' She touched his shoulders and prodded his ribs.

'It's the farm work. I hate it.'

She laughed. 'It's more than muscles. You've become handsome.'

He frowned. 'I can't think of anything more useless to me.'

'You may change your mind one day.' Her blue eyes narrowed until she glinted catlike at him.

He could sense another fight coming. 'It's absurd to be jealous of future improbabilities.'

She laughed nervously and pulled on her nightdress. She was never shy. He had to admit that she didn't have much in the way of feminine curves to be shy of.

'I've been doing some work for Marius, secretarial help. Things he doesn't want the staff to find out about,' she said, surprising him, for he had trained her not to talk drivel when she was with him.

'How dull.'

'Not really. You'd be amazed what I find out when I'm doing his personal filing.'

'Such as?'

'Marius is insured for two million rands. Enough to save the farm and get you an education. I can't help wishing that the terrorists had raided us instead of Mrs de Vries's place. Can you imagine . . . two million rands? Then there's the newspaper and the plastics factory, both of which go to you, and the plantations which we share, except that this house and farm belong to me.'

She propped herself up on one elbow, her fist under her chin. 'I'm scared. He's thinking of cancelling his insurance. Says he can't afford the premiums. If he died without insurance, there'd be no way we could hang on to the estate. Just think of the death duties. Poor Tony, all that work on the tractor for other people to take our land. You'll be a poor white, landless and without a proper education. He's taken our heritage and used it to prop up his failing political career. I've heard the party might replace him as their candidate, because of his drinking. And there's another problem . . .'

Her voice tailed off and suddenly she was sobbing into the pillow. 'He has a woman, a black woman whom he supports. Can you imagine, she's nineteen years old and he fucks her on Tuesdays and Fridays after the party meetings which he swore kept him out all night? That's where he is now. How could he? If I divorce him I might lose my home. When those accountants take stock they'll find there's nothing left to share.' She went on and on, the words tumbling out with her sobs. Her tears irritated Tony.

'If I were a man I would kill Marius. We'll be ruined!'

He looked at her in dismay. He had never wanted to hear her daydreams expressed so blatantly. They lived by allusions, hints, half-expressed feelings for a life without Marius. This blatant suggestion was like a blow below the belt. He got up and went to the shower and immersed himself in hot water. After a while he heard the door close quietly and knew that she had gone.

He crept out of the shower and stared wonderingly in the mirror. She was right, he looked different. How thick his arms had become and they were covered in long blond hair. There were hairs on the back of his shoulders and his neck had thickened. The white skinny kid had fled and in his place was a well-formed man with a long bony sun-tanned face and a shock of ash-blond hair on top.

Tony peered closer into those shrewd grey eyes. 'You may look tough,' he murmured, 'but you're still a scared youth who fears his father more than anything in the world.'

Chapter 18

———◆———

Liza wobbled across the paved courtyard of the Mayfair –
Johannesburg's newest and most luxurious five-star hotel – in
her ultra-high-heeled shoes. She tried to look sophisticated, but
she tripped on the deep pile of the carpet. 'Shit!' She squared
her shoulders, flicked her hair and tried harder. Her feet hurt
badly, but who cared? This was her first pair of grown-up shoes
and the only extravagance she had ever allowed herself. Six
months ago she had found a job as a char in this hotel, then
graduated to chambermaid, and later a part-time waitress, so
her tips were far more than her wages. She lived in, scrounged
her food from the kitchen, and saved her earnings. Until today,
when the sight of the black patent leather shoes with their
gleaming silver buckles had caught her eye. Overcome with a
longing to be grown-up, she had parted with some of her
precious savings.

As she crossed the foyer she saw Joe, the porter, staring. She
knew that the shoes made her look sexy. Her hair had grown
longer and she had tied it with a red chiffon scarf. She wore
large, looped wire earrings, a red cotton blouse and a short black
skirt. Joe was eyeing her legs, she noticed as she drew closer.

'Angel, you know you're not allowed to enter the foyer when
you come on duty. It's only for guests. Use the staff entrance.'
He said that every time, but she kept on breaking the rules.

'Listen, puss-face, I'm practising. I'll be a guest one of these
days,' she snarled. 'Just watch me.' She walked through the
snack bar and pushed open the swing doors to the kitchen area.

She had never forgotten what Dr Arlington had told her. 'You can be any damn thing you want to be. Just will it to happen.' So she was willing it with all the intentness of her fifteen years.

As the doors swung behind her, Joe pushed through. He caught hold of her wrist and squeezed hard.

'You're hurting me. Lay off, you silly fucker,' she said softly.

'Someone should teach you a lesson. I've half a mind to put you over my knees.'

I'd like to see you try, she thought, smiling inwardly. 'You've no right to say that to me, Joe,' she murmured. 'Go suck yourself.'

He shook her hard. 'Someone has to knock some sense into you. You gotta come down to earth, Angel. You gotta make do with what life has to offer you . . .'

'You mean yourself?' she queried.

'You're a lovely girl. You've got looks, brains and a good job. You and I could go places together, but you've got to get this silly nonsense out of your head that you're white and special.'

'You'll find out, Joe.'

'Aw! Come on, Angel. You look, walk, talk and act coloured, and you always will. Street-child is written all over you. Believe me.' He laughed at her shocked expression. 'I know your secret, yet you never even told me. And why? Because it shows. You aren't ever gonna be anything different from what you are.'

'D'you really mean that, Joe?' she asked sadly, blinking back her tears. 'Don't lie to me.'

'True as God, Angel. But that's no crime. I don't want you to waste your life.'

'I don't intend to waste my life,' she whispered. 'Specially not on you.'

Losing his cool, he pulled her hard against his chest.

Liza twisted her head away. 'Let me go, Joe. I don't want to hurt you.'

'You crazy idiot. How could you?' He pushed his mouth hard

over hers. A moment later he was retching on the floor from a hard kick in the testicles.

'Don't ever make me hurt you again, Joe,' she said. 'I'm fond of you, see? But not that way.'

The incident upset Liza, for Joe had always been kind to her. She wished she had not kicked him so hard. Rushing to the kitchen, she pulled on her overall and hurried to the breakfast restaurant to take orders. Ham and eggs, scrambled eggs, kippers and toast, coffee; she hardly ever wrote anything down, but this morning her head was spinning. She walked and talked coloured, Joe had said. Was she labelled for the rest of her life?

Obsessed with her woes, she made too many mistakes, but no one reported her. At ten o'clock she went to make sure that Joe was all right. 'I'm real sorry,' she told him. 'It's just that I see red when people try to box me into some situation I don't want to be in.' Joe looked pale and unhappy.

Back in the restaurant, a middle-aged couple and their spoiled teenager daughter were getting agitated because they'd had to wait five minutes.

How unfair life was. Liza ached with envy as she watched the girl, who seemed to have everything, act so spoiled. Her skin was several shades darker than her own, yet no one would think she was coloured. Why was that, Liza wondered? Was it her jewellery, or her expensive clothes, or the school blazer, or just her general air of being right on top of the heap? Her parents adored her, that was obvious, and Liza's self-pity reached an all-time frenzy as she stood waiting, admiring the brat's pearl necklace and matching earrings, the spangled white band around her dark hair, the gold belt and bracelets and lovely Omega watch. Oh, to be so spoiled and self-assured. The girl remained bent over the menu.

'Hurry up, Milly,' her father grumbled.

'Millicent, not Milly,' her mother said. 'Milly sounds too common for our daughter.'

The brat changed her mind about what she would have half

a dozen times, finally settling on orange juice, scrambled eggs, pancakes and maple syrup. Liza's eyes narrowed with temper as she endured the girl's rudeness.

Ten minutes later, when Liza brought fried eggs instead of scrambled, Milly flushed with temper.

'I hate fried eggs, you stupid girl. And you forgot my juice,' she whined. Turning to her father, she said: 'They should have white staff here, not dumb coloureds who ruin the tone of the place. I don't want to come here again. You should tell the manager, Daddy.'

Liza scowled at her.

'You don't have to be harsh, Milly,' her father said in a strong cockney accent. 'A little kindness does wonders.' Liza went to get the juice, her cheeks burning, her mind in a turmoil.

'Dammit, I said orange, not guava,' Milly shrieked when she returned. She banged the glass down so hard the juice slopped on the tablecloth.

'You don't do much for the tone of the place, either,' Liza whispered, leaning over the brat, feeling her temper rising. 'Pigs make less mess than you.'

'You bitch!' the girl shrieked.

'Milly!' Her father snapped. He waved his fork at her and his egg fell on the tablecloth. 'Mind your manners. It's not done to have a slanging match with the staff.'

'I warned you,' the mother snapped, turning on her husband. 'You shouldn't have sent her to that multi-racial convent. She's learned to treat non-whites like equals. Blame yourself.'

Liza felt her temper rising. They were cruel and she felt tainted.

'The girls at school are okay,' the brat explained in a cultured voice, so different from that of her parents.

Liza swabbed the mess, hoping against hope that the floor manager was not around.

'Listen here, Milly,' her father grumbled. 'All our lives we've been labelled. I want you to be luckier. I want you to marry into society. That's why I'm shedding banknotes to that school of yours faster than a bookmaker when the favourite wins. And why? Because all the jet-set girls go to St Augustine's. You've got the voice, the looks and the training, even if you ain't got the breeding. Yet you're still behaving like a tramp.'

'You can't make a silk purse from a pig's ear,' her mother added, her voice trembling with satisfaction.

'Shut up, Mother!' Brat hammered her fist on the table. 'Listen,' she said, turning to Liza. 'Get me an orange juice and cheese cake and quit listening in.'

Liza raced to the kitchen and gave the order and ran back to the public phone booth. Rifling through the pages she found that St Augustine's College for young ladies was in Parktown, only a bus ride away. She raced back to fetch the cake.

'We don't have plain cheese cake, but this is cheese cake covered in blueberry sauce and cream,' the chef said. Liza took it with a sinking feeling.

'Boy, you must be the thickest servant I've come across,' brat said, waving away the cake. 'That isn't what I ordered.'

'Have it anyway,' Liza said, tipping it over her head. The cream splashed down her face on to her lovely pearl necklace and lace blouse. The brat let out a wail that seemed to have no end. Moments later Liza was grabbed by Joe, as the manager and staff tried to pacify the screaming girl.

'Oh Lawd, Angel, what have you done?' he muttered.

'I quit, Joe, so don't try to sack me,' she said, twisting out of his grasp.

'You better get going fast,' Joe urged. 'I reckon the management will have it in for you.'

Rushing to her room, Liza thrust her clothes into a large paper bag. Then she rifled in it for something smarter to wear. It was hot, and she decided to douse herself with the cheap perfume Joe had given her. It was a bit strong, but better than smelling of sweat. She had a sequinned black blouse that one of the cleaners had grown out of and given her and she thought it would go well with her new shoes and short black mini skirt.

She swept her hair over her head and fastened it in place with a comb so that it fell back over her shoulders in a short pony tail. Glancing in the mirror she thought she looked a bit sallow so she poked some artificial flowers into the comb and added bright red lipstick and rouge to her face. That was much better, she hoped, for it was so dark in her room she could hardly see. A sudden brainwave provoked her into rubbing talcum powder over her cheeks and forehead which seemed to give her skin a satisfying translucent glow. Now she was ready.

Ignoring the catcalls and whistles as she wobbled across the courtyard, she made her way to the bus stop.

It was a real scorcher. Her feet began to swell in the tight shoes, the sweat was trickling into her eyes, and her clothes were damp and sticking to her by the time she reached St Augustine's College. For a few minutes she was overcome with the grandeur of the place and she cowered behind the gate. A long gravel driveway, edged with oaks, led to the gaunt old building with its many towers and windows. It must be as big as Buckingham Palace, she thought. Eventually she found the courage to walk up the driveway.

Mounting the wide marble steps, she knocked at a carved door, itself as wide as a room. No one answered. After a while she pushed the door open and walked inside. She found herself in a long, shabby room, the furniture too old, the carpets worn, but the flowers on the long polished tables were quite beautiful.

Wandering through the room, she found another door and walked through it. Now she was in a large courtyard with a crazy-paving circular pathway around a well of ferns and trees. Pretty, she thought. A strange woman came hurrying along; she was so tall, over six foot, a regular beanpole and dressed in the weirdest garb she'd ever seen ... a long black gown with a funny white bit like a man's collar stuck round her face. Liza gaped at her, and the woman gasped and stared back. Eventually the woman found her tongue. 'Who or what are you?' she asked.

Feeling slighted, Liza bridled with temper. 'I'm Angel and I wanna see the person in charge – the headmistress. You understand?' Her voice faltered, as her confidence began to seep away into the courtyard.

At that moment, some silly girls, dressed alike in blue and white, passed by in utter silence . . . until they saw Angel. Then the smirks and titters began.

The silly cunts! What were they laughing about? she wondered. Maybe her dress was a little low in the neckline. She yanked it up, but then her midriff was bared. Oh Heck! Who cares? I've got the cash. That's all that counts in this world. 'The silly wankers,' she said to their retreating figures.

'Come in here,' the tall woman said frigidly. 'I am Sister Agnes. Why exactly do you want to see the Mother Superior?'

So that's what she was called. 'I'm going to come here and learn to be larny, you see. I've got the cash . . . I've been saving . . .' Her voice tailed off. 'I'm sure it's enough,' she added, as her doubts settled in.

'Please wait here. It may be some time. She is busy right now. She only sees people by appointment, but I'll ask her to see you.'

'Well, I haven't got all day, you know. I can take my money somewhere else . . . if I want to,' she added fearfully.

As Liza waited the minutes passed ever more slowly and her confidence began to ebb. The place looks so old, she thought. They'll be glad of a bit more cash.

There was a large clock on one wall and the ticks were so loud they seemed to hammer inside her head. Each tick seemed to take longer than the one before. The room was full of dusty books and dust made her sneeze. 'Oh God, don't let me start sneezing now,' she prayed, but God wasn't listening this morning and her nose began to run, while her eyes began to swell up. 'Shit!' she whispered, taking out her tissue.

It was so humid that even the plastic flower in her hair began to sag. 'Whoever heard of a plastic flower wilting?' she said to herself. She reached up and touched it. Yes, it was definitely melting.

Another five minutes passed. What if she won't take me?

Perhaps she'll think I'm not good enough for her damned college and those puss-faced girls. I'll tell her what she can do with her convent if she tries to be stuck up with me. But it will be all right. It has to be! This is my big chance to gatecrash my world. My only chance, she thought desperately.

The next five minutes lasted so long she wondered if the clock had stopped. She'll probably try to refuse, but I won't take 'no' for an answer. I'm as good as any of those silly fuckers. Dumb and ugly – the lot of them.

By the time Sister Agnes returned, Angel was sure she was going to be flung out on her ear and she had worked herself up into a fury.

'What is your name?'

A frosty-faced bitch if ever there was one. 'Angel de Beer,' she said.

'Come this way please.'

Angel tossed her head, squared her shoulders and stalked like a caged leopard to face the woman who by now had become her enemy. The room brought another convulsion of shivers. It was so white and pure. There were high-vaulted ceilings, black and white marble tiles on the floor, lovely white walls with pictures of pastel-coloured saints and stained-glass windows. It was a big room and she had to walk half a mile to the desk where another nun, dressed in white, was writing in a book. Suddenly her own clothes seemed so tawdry. She felt as out of place as a beetle in a rice pudding.

The nun didn't look up immediately, obviously to show her that she was less than nothing.

'This place sucks,' Liza began fast and furious. 'I'm not sure it's good enough for me,' she snarled. 'It's a bit shoddy, but I'm prepared to give it a try.' She leaned over the desk and glowered at the Mother Superior. 'Here's my cash. I worked hard for it – three shifts a day most days.'

She flung her bag on the desk and tipped it upside down. The cash fell out, part notes, part silver. 'There's well over a thousand rands there. Go on . . . count it,' she said.

The woman made no effort to count the money. Instead, she looked up and – horror of horrors – Liza found herself staring into stern brown eyes that reminded her so forcibly of her Gran.

She's going to send me away, just like Gran did.

'You're not going to reject me,' Liza said furiously. 'I'm not going to let you. Not this time. You see I was young and stupid when they flung me out. They said I was a *gammat* and that was a lie. I felt so ashamed, so I didn't fight back. But this time I've learned a thing or two. I know how to stand up for myself. My cash is as good as anyone else's.'

There was no answer. Those old eyes kept staring at her as if she saw right into her mind. Liza felt obliged to fling out more words to soak up this terrible silence. 'This place looks like it could do with a bit of cash, so take it all. I want you to turn me into a . . .' She searched around for what it was she wanted, but she could only remember the words of the brat's father. 'Turn me into a lady,' she said finally.

Gran's eyes looked her up and down. Oh God! What would Gran have said at her sequinned blouse and her tight short skirt and her three-inch heels. Suddenly she saw herself as tawdry and common.

The Mother Superior seemed to be in shock.

'Maybe you think I'm not good enough,' Liza went on desperately. 'I've got news for you. I'll beat all those puss-faced girls you've got here. I was always top at everything. I saw the way those fucking kids laughed at me. You may not like my clothes, or my voice, or the way I walk – you may think – like Joe did – that I'm a *gammat*, but I'm white. I want to learn everything you can teach me, and more besides. You got that? You'll find I'm very quick on the uptake.'

'Sit down,' Mother Superior said eventually. 'You make me nervous towering over me like that.'

Liza collapsed on a chair, filled with envy of that soft, deep cultured voice.

'For starters, I want a voice like yours. I want to get my matric, I want . . .'

The silly flower chose that moment to give up the ghost, fall over her face and biff her in the eye. The whole morning seemed to be one huge mistake. Tears welled out of her eyes. That was the end for her, she knew. Liza had long since learned the consequences of showing a weakness. Perhaps it was Gran's eyes that had unnerved her. She hadn't thought much about Gran since the day she ran away. She'd blocked her off somewhere deep in her mind, but now she couldn't stave off the memories those eyes evoked.

'Once I was rejected. The truth is, they threw me out,' she whispered. 'They said I was coloured, but I'm not. I know my place in the world and it's not living on the streets and it's not cleaning floors at the Mayfair.'

'And what exactly is your right place?'

Liza's eyes took on a wistful glow. 'One day I'll be rich and famous,' she said. 'I'll sweep into the Mayfair as a guest and stay in the best suite. I'll have jewels and lovely clothes, but I'll make it all for myself. No one is ever going to do it for me. I don't want help from anybody.'

'Normally girls come to me with their parents,' the nun said. 'Do you have any parents or guardians? Where do you live?'

'Until this morning I had a room in the Mayfair's staff quarters.'

'And before . . . ?'

'I lived on the streets, but sometimes I went to the Home Shelter.' Oh God, why was she telling her this. The woman seemed to have a knack of breaking her defences. Now she was done for.

'Once you must have had a mother.'

'I had a foster-Gran. She didn't stand by me. I'd just passed Standard Five. Gran looked a lot like you, too. I'm never going to tell you who she is, so don't ask. I've put her behind me.'

'I see. Well now, Angel,' Mother Superior said briskly. 'This cash will cover your expenses until you leave the college, which might be two or three years depending on how quickly you catch up and how well you do. You will have to learn to obey orders here. If you are disobedient you will be expelled and I will have no more foul language. Do you understand me? There will be no second chances.'

'Yes,' Liza mumbled. A feeling of joy and relief was welling up inside her. There was a funny singing noise in her ears, her heart was pounding and leaping into her throat, and her dreaded tears were pouring down her cheeks and splashing all over the place. 'It feels like I'm raining,' she said, smiling at the same time. 'I don't know why.'

'Is there any sport you're good at, or any subject you once excelled at?'

'Once I was the school gym champion ... and I got the English prize.' She broke off. This woman had a habit of catching you out when your defences were down. She'd have to watch out.

'I'm going to go outside for a while. I want you to wait here. Try to stop crying, Angel.' She swept the money into a dish and left.

Money counts, Liza thought, watching her. You can buy anything if you have enough cash.

The Mother Superior swept into the bursar's office. 'Write out a receipt for this cash and start a file for Angel de Beer,' she said to the bursar. 'Get me Bishop Laval on the telephone.'

'Bishop Laval,' she said sweetly, five minutes later. 'I have accepted a young girl called Angel de Beer as your first bursary pupil. No, she didn't pass the exam, but I wish to take her on. She will require full support, clothes, boarding, books and holiday accommodation. Quite penniless. Yes, a very deserving candidate and she has no parents. I will vouch for her. I assume she's coloured, I'm not sure, but you, of all people, can't be racist, Bishop Laval. Yes, thank you. I just wanted to let you know.'

'She's your charge,' the Mother Superior told the horrified Sister Agnes shortly afterwards.

'I can't believe that you could waste that precious bursary on this ... wretched urchin,' Sister Agnes finished off lamely as words failed her.

'She has courage, stamina, brains and determination. She will make a beautiful nun one day. It's up to you. You have two to three years to tone down her vices and bring out her good qualities. Make her your vocation, Sister.'

Sister Agnes knew better than to argue, but for once she felt that their saintly Mother Superior had made a terrible mistake.

Chapter 19

———◆———

Tony tried to control himself, but Father's words seemed to come from far away. His father's face leered at him across the supper table, cheeks bloated with alcohol, eyes red veined, mouth set into an angry leer. Tony had just read him a report he'd seen in the weekly financial press. '*Marius Cronjé is unlikely to be able to finance his fatuous fantasies much longer and with luck we shall soon be spared his trite political editorials.*' What followed was a financial report proving that the family was virtually bankrupt: the drought had plunged the plantations heavily into debt, their sugar crop was well nigh nil, the tomato harvest less than half the average, their plastics plant was battling to survive and half the staff had been laid off, and the newspaper's circulation was falling daily. It was only a matter of months before it folded, the report read.

'Well, it's all true,' Father repeated for the second time.

Mouth dry with fear, Tony tried to get some facts and figures. 'Just how insolvent are we?' he gabbled. 'Can't we pull through?'

'Unlikely,' his father snapped back. In a jerky, impulsive movement, he knocked over his glass of red wine.

'You damned fool of a woman! How many times have I told you not to use this blasted lace tablecloth?' he shouted.

Eleanor sat still, face as pale as death. 'And my inheritance,' she asked eventually. 'Has that been used to fuel your disgusting ego trip?'

'We're almost bankrupt. It's not my fault. Blame the drought, the recession and the government's policies. All those things have knocked our holdings into a cocked hat.'

'Let me try to sort out something, Father,' Tony said, trying to sound respectful.

'You? Business is for men, not for boys. Besides, your mother was a fool and you're worse than her. That's one reason why I won't spend a penny on your education. You're a failure.'

'Then I must take after you,' Tony's voice rang out loud and clear.

Marius swore, picked up his glass and lurched off to his office.

The two of them sat in stunned silence listening to his door being locked and shortly afterwards his favourite music blaring out. After a long while they turned and looked desperately at each other. 'Stupid you,' Eleanor said. 'Why fight? That doesn't solve anything. He is destroying us. I can't leave him. This is my home ... my inheritance ... and he won't go ... at least, not voluntarily. I hope you find some courage before we are utterly destroyed,' she said.

The contempt in her cold eyes made him shudder.

What right did Eleanor have to be so contemptuous, Tony asked himself? He had returned to his room and flung himself on his bed. She was rushing him headfirst into a situation they hadn't thought out properly. At the same time he had to agree that their problems would be solved if Marius died. He stood up and paced about. He felt claustrophobic with the windows shut, but if he opened them the room would fill with mosquitoes and he'd be bitten all night.

Tony had a plan forming. He thought about it constantly, visualised it, perfected it to the smallest detail. It was Eleanor who had given him the idea. 'If only they had killed Marius instead of poor Mrs de Vries,' she had said. 'What harm did she ever do anyone?' And at the time he was drunk in the boma. He deserved to die.

Some years back they had built a shack overlooking the Komati River. It was circular in shape, made of mud walls with a thatched roof and a large, circular chimney in the centre. A third of one wall was open for bird watching, and it was called in turn, the birdwatch, the summerhouse and the boma – when they braaied. Marius kept some booze, binoculars and books on birds there. Lately Tony and Eleanor used it as a tryst, but Marius sometimes went there to watch birds or crocodiles, using his night-vision binoculars, another unnecessary extravagance, but then he was always spoiling himself.

Tony's plan was to shoot his father with a Russian-made, AK-47 rifle, let off a few more shots, throw the rifle in the river, and leave the servants to discover the body in the morning. He had concealed the rifle under the counter of the bar, but that was as far as he was ever likely to go. He lacked the courage and that was the truth, hence Eleanor's contempt, for he had told her of his plan.

They were meeting in the boma after supper. It seemed chilly tonight, although it was mid-summer, so he pulled on a sweat shirt and sauntered down towards the river. Perhaps he'd be able to study there while he waited.

The cicadas abruptly silenced their din, the guinea fowls screamed their warning cries into the night, the frogs waited in silence for the all-clear and there was a subtle splash as a crocodile took off into the water. He could smell honey-suckle and the sweet scent of newly cut grass. An African owl, perched on a branch over the river, let out its mournful cry. It was after the newly hatched Egyptian goslings.

He walked inside and took Father's binoculars. They were remarkable, he could see the owl, and the old croc creeping out of the river. He would have liked the boma and the night to himself. Lately Eleanor was so clinging and demanding. Sex was becoming a duty and, consequently, passion had fled. To Eleanor, sex was an act of war, not of love, he surmised. Each time she came it was a small triumph over Marius.

He suspects, Eleanor thought, gazing thoughtfully at Marius's reflection in the mirror. Tingles of fear crept up her skin from her fingertips to the back of her shoulders. So be it!

Her husband was crouched forward over his desk, head lowered, peering up from under his wide forehead, which was plastered with damp grey curls. There was bafflement and moody hatred in his bloodshot eyes. Good God! I've seen that look before – from a wounded buffalo when it stands at bay before its final deadly charge. He wants to kill me and he's drunk. Another shudder of fear shot up her spine. From the hidden depths of her mind came the thrilling thought – this is your chance. There'll never be a better time.

Marius wanted to make love. He stood up unsteadily and moved behind her, placing his red hands on her neck. She must not give in to him, although he was pinching her shoulders until she could scream. If she allowed him to come he would fall asleep until morning, snoring all the while. No, not tonight. She pushed him off roughly and saw surprise turn to temper.

'What the hell's got into you?' he growled.

'Jeanetta's sick. I have to see her. She's quite ill.'

'Who cares about the fucking maid?'

'You do ... according to those drivelling reports you publish.' She flinched at her own audacity. What was giving her this courage? Hope?

Menace and suspicion clouded his eyes. He was deliberately pulling himself together, trying to appear calm. 'Off you go then,' he said quietly.

'I'll be back soon. Go to sleep meanwhile.'

She pulled on her gown, grabbed a packet of pills. Showing them to him too obviously, she hurried outside. Now she was running barefooted over the grass to the steep slope down to the river. Branches flayed her, stones cut into her feet, but this was trivial compared to the overwhelming awareness of the moment. 'This is it,' she panted.

There was no moon. Balmy air wafted against her flesh. There was a scent of tobacco flowers and jasmine. What a night! She looked up briefly at the stars. How bright they were. 'Tonight or never. It must be done. Help me, help me,' she whispered.

Tony was sitting behind the bar, bent over his textbook. The light from the paraffin lamp hanging above had attracted a swarm of maybugs and he was swatting at them absentmindedly. There were deep shadows under his eyes, his face looked pinched and pale, his cheek bones too prominent, lips pursed into a thin straight line. It was a face she loved to distraction and her heart went out to him. It was more than a year since she had seduced the skinny youth who had explored her body so shyly. Since then she had learned to love the man who had emerged from the chrysalis of youth. His steel-like resolve had been forged in white-hot fires of hatred, but there was a flaw in the steel, his fear of his father. Tonight he must destroy what he feared, or they would be lost.

'Tony, I love you,' she gasped. She rushed to him and flung her arms around his neck. Then, placing her hands gently on his cheeks, she turned his face towards her, kissing his ears, his eyelids, the tip of his nose and his mouth. She would give him her courage if she could. She almost forgot her hatred in that glorious moment of melting her lips into his. Deftly she let her dress slip over her shoulders to fall to the floor. She was naked and smiling softly at Tony's expression. Some sixth sense seemed to warn him of Marius's approach.

'Oh my God, Tony!' she gasped. 'Is the gun loaded? I thought I saw someone move behind the hedge.'

She grabbed at Tony, but he pushed her away violently, looking scared. She saw his eyes widen with horror, as Marius's unmistakable bulky figure loomed outside the window. Moving her hips seductively, she pushed herself against Tony.

Tony swore quietly and stared at her in horror. Then he said: 'You bitch!' and this stunned her.

'Tony,' she whispered, trying to turn his anger from her to Marius. 'He tried to rape me. I ran away. He knows everything, he told me so. He's going to kill you . . . us.'

Tony seemed rooted to the ground, his mouth open, his expression frozen in horror.

A massive kick flung the door open. Marius, breathless,

purple-faced and in distress, was waving a sjambok. 'I'm going to take the skin off your hide,' he wheezed at Tony, 'and then I'm going to kill you.' He staggered across the room.

The first swipe of the whip caught Tony across his shoulder, cutting through his vest into his flesh. Tony clamped his hand on the wound and peered at the blood, frowning. His world seemed to be retreating into a dreamlike state as he watched his father advance. He couldn't be there. This couldn't be real. As if in a dream Tony went through the actions he had rehearsed in his mind so many times.

The sjambok was held high, poised to descend. 'Kill him,' Eleanor screamed.

Tony grabbed the rifle, aimed at his father's barrel chest, and then his trembling hands fell to his side. He stood staring at the weapon as the sjambok caught him across the shoulder.

Eleanor stooped, gathered up the rifle, swung up the barrel and pulled the trigger in a smooth, continuous movement.

Her husband's face changed from anger to shock. There was the sound of the report as she saw a small hole appear on his forehead. Marius flung up his arms as he crashed back against the wall. For a split second that seemed to last an eternity, he looked as if he was pinned against the wall. Then he fell with a crash and lay twitching.

How long had they stood there gazing at their crime? Tony recovered first as a bolt of fear tore through him.

How long? How long? Eleanor was still naked. Her mouth was moving, but no sound was coming. She seemed to be rooted to the ground. He ran to her and shook her. 'Pull yourself together!'

God! What was he to do? The shot had been so loud. Then he remembered that the servants were at a soccer match. But maybe one of them had stayed and if so, they would come to investigate. All this went through his mind in a split second. Moments later he was slapping Eleanor's cheek and pushing her arms into her gown.

'Go to your room, wash your feet – they're covered in earth and take a strong sleeping pill – the ones you've been giving to Marius. Stay there. You were never here. Do you understand what I'm saying?'

Her eyes filled with tears and she began to shake violently. 'I love you,' she murmured.

'Do what I say. When they wake you they'll tell you that Marius is dead. You must play the part of the mourning widow. You can do it.'

She was light-headed and almost fell. 'Thank you,' she whispered. Then she fled.

Tony removed his text book and glass and put out the light. Taking the sjambok and the rifle, he ran lightly down to the river. Then he remembered that there must be more shots and he crept back again. All was quiet and deserted. He let off a round in the Boma. Looking at his father's corpse he felt a surge of elation and confidence. The nightmare was over forever.

The second terrorist attack in one month set the town alight with rage. The police staged an armed search throughout the KaNgwane Homeland and over 200 suspects were arrested, 500 illegal Mozambicans were caught and deported, two caches of Russian-made arms were found and confiscated and six terrorists were shot dead while trying to escape. No real proof of the attack on the Cronjés' farm was uncovered. Marius was given a hero's funeral and the townsfolk and farmers updated their security.

'This is the price we have to pay,' the farmers told each other moodily. 'We are the country's unpaid frontier guards. All the public ever does is moan about our farming subsidies.'

Chapter 20

Dan was hunched forward on the tractor as if in a trance. Every two seconds he glanced back to check that the plough was straight in the last run's furrow, but it was so dark he could hardly see. The clouds lay heavy and purple overhead and he guessed that the storm would break soon. This was his life. He had turned into a robot, or so it seemed to him. His days were entirely automatic and he feared that he would go off his head if this job lasted much longer.

Each morning he tumbled out of the staff compound dazed with sleep, pulled on his trousers and shirt and staggered off to the shed where the tractors were kept. Five minutes later he roared out into the pitch-dark morning, steering by searchlight towards a distant field. By dawn he was ready to start ploughing, or raking, or cultivating, or harvesting. There were always more fields to work and his monotonous task had no end. Hour after hour, day after day, he drove a straight furrow, returning long after dark, to a brief interlude of happiness with Jeanetta. This was his life and he was drowning in despair.

Summer had started off with some good rains, each day much the same, the heat building up oppressively until noon when a mass of black clouds, stretching from the treetops up to heaven itself it seemed, rolled overhead. Forked lightning pierced the clouds and assaulted the earth, stabbing it time and again, sending birds and beasts scattering for cover. Then came the deluge. Red-hot iron roofs steamed and hissed, branches bowed under the battering, and hailstones as big as eggs pelted down.

A sudden fork of lighting hit the field and Dan looked up anxiously as thunder pounded his eardrums. Today the rains were holding off, but it was darker than at dusk and there was an oppressive heaviness, as if the air was squashed between the trembling earth and the frenzied clouds. Daniel took great gulping breaths, feeling claustrophobic as he tried to concentrate on keeping straight.

Should he dash for the open earth and wait there, he wondered? The tractor acted as a conductor for lightning. Not far away was a tree, but that was almost as dangerous in an electric storm. Around him a vast sea of mud stretched to the horizon. In the distance he could see the next driver bent over his wheel with dogged determination. It would be weeks before they finished preparing this plantation for the new sugar cane shoots.

Another stab of light made him gaze up anxiously. In a flickering blue-white flash he saw a woman hurrying along the river bank keeping to the bulrushes, her face hidden under an old wide-brimmed canvas hat. She was bare-footed, her clothes were of tattered black cloth and she was carrying a basket filled with herbs that she had gathered in the veld. He frowned and watched her guardedly. Despite her ragged appearance, he recognised his grandmother in her usual disguise. Now what did she want with him?

Nosisi mounted the river bank as light as an impala and stood at the side of the field flapping her arms like a vulture drying out in the sun. She was beckoning to him. Why? Had she changed her mind about paying for his education? Reason told him not. Reluctantly, Dan switched off the engine and walked over to her.

'You must get out of this place!' she said in her hoarse, melodramatic voice, as soon as he was within earshot. 'Leave Nelfontein. I see great danger for you. I'm afraid . . . !'

Dan stared at her wrinkled face with mounting frustration and temper. Her cunning, uneducated eyes made his hackles rise. Ignorance was gazing back at him, yet there was no denying her gift of second sight. Her worldly vision was limited, but she saw inwardly to some other plane of existence that he knew nothing about. Nor did he want to. He shuddered.

'Did the spirits tell you this?' he asked, half inclined to laugh, but still apprehensive.

'Never mock your ancestors, or our traditional ways,' she scolded. 'Leave this town, I'm begging you.'

'No ... never. Let me alone.' Dan kicked a stone into the river to release some of his exasperation. They were two strangers linked by blood, but aliens all the same.

Nosisi muttered something under her breath and turned away without saying goodbye. Dan went back to the tractor feeling depressed and scared.

An hour later he saw the police van negotiating the muddy farm track and he knew without any doubt that they were coming for him. He'd done no wrong. He was damned if he'd run. To hell with Nosisi and her stupid predictions.

After twenty-four hours of interrogation, Dan was almost finished. His body was a mass of bruises, his fingers squashed, his head covered in bumps where he'd been slammed against the wall time and again. He was suffering from lack of sleep, dehydration, hunger and shock. Every blow seemed to drive home Nosisi's words.

Momentarily, Dan seemed to be propelled back in time to his childhood when he lived with his grandmother. He was wandering behind Nosisi, listening to her interminable lectures, his memory so real it seemed to be happening now. 'You may excel in brains and sport,' she told him. 'You may bath six times a day, or play your penny whistle sweet as any bird, and ape the whites as clever as a monkey, but I'm telling now, you'll be a thick-headed, stinking kafir until you die.'

'So what's the answer? How do I get to be human?' he'd asked her then in a fit of heady courage.

'You don't. You die a kafir, Dan, but don't die a coward. Use your brains for our people and maybe your children might get to be humans.'

A bucket of ice-cold water flung over his head brought him back to his senses. At moments like this, Daniel thought, gazing round in despair, Nosisi seems to make a lot of sense.

The man confronting him was Corporal Strydom and clearly he was enjoying himself. Dan looked into Strydom's pale blue eyes and felt a bolt of fear run down his spine at the force of the hostility and contempt he saw there. Nothing he said or did would ever change the way those eyes looked, for they expressed pure racial hatred. Strydom was gazing at something he would rather not see. Eyes like that created gas ovens, Dan thought with a shudder.

As if reading his thoughts, Strydom said: 'I hate kafirs so much, Tweneni. Provoke me . . . why don't you? Let's have a bit of fun.' He was tall and powerful, but pot-bellied and he drank. You could tell that from his puffy eyes and bulbous nose. Dan knew he could beat him in a fair fight, but he was never likely to get that chance. He longed for the opportunity to squeeze his hands round Strydom's fat neck.

And what must I look like to him, Dan wondered? A punchbag, perhaps. No, I must look like a figure of fun, for Strydom was smiling most of the time and laughing some of the time. When he reopened Dan's split lip he smiled, when Dan winced with pain, he smiled, when Dan slipped and fell headlong on to the floor he laughed heartily, and now that Dan was crouched in the corner, trying to protect his head and his private parts from Strydom's hobnail boots he was giggling like a hyena scenting blood.

'Get up,' Strydom ordered. 'On your feet.' Dan tried. After a while he found the strength to hang on to the windowsill and drag himself up. He felt light-headed from hunger and thirst, his body was like an iron chain, too heavy to move. A dead weight! His arms were too feeble to tackle this task. His head was pounding and each nerve fibre was shrieking with pain. He was aware that he stank, that he had laid in his own faeces, urine and vomit for hours. Foremost was a thought that kept him silent: Strydom longs to kill me. Give him half a reason and he will. I must not give him that reason.

The door opened and another police officer walked in. He was tall and ungainly, with a big head and oversized ears that stuck out at right-angles. His brown eyes, bushy eyebrows, nose and chin were all too big for his face. Yet the overall effect was of mildness and sweetness. Dan had seen him before, but where? Then he remembered. He was Lieutenant Myers who often watched their football matches.

'You should have stuck to football, Dan, instead of murdering farmers.'

'I'm innocent,' Dan managed to croak again. 'You're making a terrible mistake.'

'Fetch his cell guard,' Myers called over his shoulder. He turned to Strydom. 'Lay off him. You're getting nowhere. They're all alike – they clam up under duress. We're not here to punish him, we're trying to find out what happened and where his accomplices are hiding out.'

The guard came in. 'Clean up this mess. Feed him. I want him back here in four hours smelling of roses and wide awake.'

Somehow Dan found the strength to stagger along the passage and keep on his feet under the ice-cold shower. He opened his mouth and took in great draughts of water, rejoicing as the filth was washed away. The cold water soothed his burns and bruises and he began to feel human again. He was pushed into a cell. A tin plate of mealie pap followed with a cup of black coffee laced with sugar and a clean prison uniform. He swallowed the food greedily, feeling the lifegiving sugar seeping into his veins, bringing him strength, and with it came the ability to think straight. He must prove his innocence to Myers, who was the only one who cared a damn about rights, he thought as he fell into a deep sleep.

Lieutenant Myers' big ears gave the impression of two antennae searching amongst the lies and deceit for the truth, while his soft brown eyes gave out a sense of confidence.

'Like I was saying, Dan . . .' His wide mouth was downturned into an expression of sympathy. 'It looks bad for you. Your father was an activist, your Gran has been suspected of liaising with terrorists any number of times. Your father died in his cell not long ago. You're bitter about that, aren't you?'

'Yes,' Dan said hoarsely. 'Of course.'

'So you locked up the dogs while the terrorists slipped in to murder Cronjé.'

'No, the dogs weren't locked up. And Cronjé had nothing to do with my father.'

'But he's white and he's a powerful man. Why didn't the dogs bark?'

Dan shrugged. 'They might have barked. I only said that I didn't hear them. Neither did Jeanetta.'

'We've questioned Jeanetta and it seems she's sweet on you, Tweneni, so she's not a reliable witness. We think you shot Cronjé yourself with an AK-47 rifle and threw it in the river.'

'No. I didn't,' Dan said wearily.

'Or perhaps you let the terrorists know which evening the servants and labourers would be off watching the soccer match. Strange that you weren't there, isn't it?'

'No. I don't think so.'

'You opted out of soccer – just like that. I questioned the team. You weren't sacked. You just threw in the towel. Why?'

'Why not?'

'That sort of attitude won't save you from the gallows, Dan.'

The gallows! Dan sat up with a start. So far he had only worried about how long the beating would last and how soon he would be released. Myers was his only hope.

'It's difficult to explain,' he began haltingly. 'My life is like an anti-climax. School went well, but all that studying . . . all that success . . . finally it was just shit. I'm driving a tractor and I might just as well never have gone to school. The same with soccer. All that acclaim . . . for what . . . ? Finally there'll be the inevitable anti-climax. I don't want another few months of hell like I've just been through. So I walked out.'

'Let's get back to the Cronjés. You were the only labourer

within earshot of the terrorist attack and you say you heard one shot. Then much later, another six. That was when you went to investigate. Strange. Am I supposed to believe a story like that?'

'Well, what's your explanation?' Dan asked, feeling puzzled.

'I think you shot Cronjé after a fight. Perhaps he caught you stealing his booze. He kept enough of it there. But as an afterthought you decided to make it look like a terrorist attack.'

'You don't think it was a terrorist attack? So who . . . ?'

'I'll ask the questions.'

'Maybe there were more shots in between,' Dan said slowly, 'but I didn't hear them, because I had the radio on loud.'

'Why? . . .'

Dan flushed. 'Because Jeanetta's a squealer, when the mood takes her.'

'I see. And you were listening to . . . ?'

'Radio 702. They have some pretty good music at that time of night.'

'You were in the school band, I hear. What did you play?'

'Whistle and flute . . .'

'It says in your file that you play in a band sometimes, so I guess you know popular music. Can you recall what they were playing? Or were you too busy screwing?'

Dan was surprised. Of course he could. Hope flooded through him. He had an alibi after all.

'Sure, I can,' he mumbled, hoarse with emotion, his eyes lighting with joy.

'Hang on . . . Yes . . . I remember . . . Around eleven o'clock they opened with Ella Fitzgerald singing "Digital III at Montreux", followed by Aretha Franklin's "Hold on, I'm comin'" – rather appropriate, I was thinking at the time – that's why I remember that one. Then . . . I think they got on to some other hits. I'm pretty certain one was Pat Benetar's "Fire and Ice", the other . . . I just can't remember – something new. There were a couple more, but . . . damn it . . . I just can't . . .

'Next thing I remember hearing was Count Basie and his orchestra. They were playing . . . er . . . "Warm Breeze". Yeh, that's it. And that was when the first shot came.'

'You were screwing all that time?'

'Yup.'

'Why didn't you go and investigate then? Surely that would have been the normal thing to do?'

'Old man Cronjé used to get a bit pissed in the boma, specially late at night. It usually meant he'd had a tiff with his wife. He'd often take a pot shot at a croc. I think it made him feel powerful. He never hit anything.'

'Carry on . . .'

'After the shot they opened the air for phone-ins. That was when some old fogey – the third caller, I think – requested Beethoven's trio in B flat . . . something like that. I don't follow classical much and it lasted about five minutes. Then something else classical. Sorry, I'd never heard of it. Then came a whole load of shots, one after the other, but this was a good ten minutes after the first shot. I told Jeanetta to wait there while I went to see what was going on.'

'Okay. We've been through that.' The Lieutenant was still scribbling in his notebook. 'Did you see Tony Cronjé or Mrs Cronjé?'

'I woke them . . . after I called the police.'

'Do you usually take your girl to the soccer when you play?'

'Sure.'

'So if you'd gone, no one would have been within earshot?'

'I guess so.'

'I'll check out the music.'

He was as good as his word, Dan realised, for he was released precisely one hour later.

'You must understand that by law I could detain you for an indefinite period for being suspected of being a party to the terrorist attack, but I don't think you were. Keep out of trouble, boy. You're free for now.'

'*Boy!*' It was only one step better than kafir, but he was free. He stumbled out feeling that he had looked death in the face and survived.

Chapter 21

———————◆———————

Tony moved back from the office window and willed himself to relax. He had been going through *poor father*'s papers. He had trained himself never to think of the old bastard as anything other than *poor father*. In an unguarded moment, an involuntary thought uttered aloud could cause trouble. The truth was, he was afraid of the newly promoted Captain Myers. Even a slight hesitation was enough to make him blink through his thick lenses and peer closer, his mouth slightly open, head on one side, for all the world like a secretary bird examining a strange, suspicious insect. To gobble or not to gobble?

What the hell's the matter with me? Tony rounded on himself with fury. He glanced in the mirror that Marius – no, *poor father* – kept hidden at the back of his liquor cabinet. He saw a face as white as chalk, staring, glacial blue eyes and a taut mouth. A dead give-away. He tried out a grin, but only managed a grimace.

The inquest had been held and the verdict was murder by person or persons unknown. Since then, Marius had been cremated, the will had been read, and the farm and factories would soon be the richer by two million rands' insurance payout.

The insurance company was prevaricating, claiming that the policies did not include political riot cover, and that since the murder weapon was a Russian AK-47 rifle, it stood to reason that the murder was politically motivated. *Dear father* had failed to take proper precautions with his insurance, which was typical.

Tony opened his balcony door and frowned as he saw the policeman gazing at the lake Marius had built for Eleanor. Why was that bastard here again? It was the fourth time this week. A swan was gliding ethereal and silent, the willow fronds trembled in a breeze he could not detect, there was a sudden call of a wild goose and when the plaintive cry died away, the morning seemed twice as quiet. Like church! Tony flinched with unease and his first twinge of guilt brought his skin out in goose-pimples. With it came a sudden understanding of what was wrong with Eleanor. Until now he had assumed she was cowed by fear. Now he knew it was guilt. But why? She'd got what she wanted.

'Would you like some coffee, Captain Myers?' he said, firmly but sadly, in a manner he'd been practising for days. 'Interested in birds are you – that was my father's hobby. He loved them so much, so he created this lake.'

Myers ignored Tony's question. 'We've had to let Daniel Tweneni go. He wasn't guilty, we're sure of that. Besides, some smart-arsed lawyer pitched from Johannesburg. God knows who paid him. We could have detained Tweneni for as long as we wished, but the boy's never been political. We're convinced he knows nothing.'

'Johnston, bring the coffee out here,' Tony called, trying not to look concerned with Myers' investigation. He screwed up his eyes and visualised the scene he had imagined down to the last detail, but Myers didn't ask him to repeat his statement. He was looking bored, yet he seemed to be waiting for something – or someone.

Then Eleanor walked on to the stoep and Tony could sense the charge of interest emanating from Myers. Eleanor's face was whiter than usual, bloodless lips were opening and closing, her hair had fallen awry over her shoulders, her pale green eyes were wide with fear.

She is the weak link, Tony realised, and it was she who kept Captain Myers wandering around the house like a dog after a bitch on heat. He had picked up a scent, fear perhaps, and he wouldn't give up. Eleanor was wearing a short black skirt, a black boob tube and a black bolero. If she thought that looked like mourning she was wrong, Tony thought critically. She had agreed to look like a mourning widow. The black skirt accentuated the whiteness of her smooth long legs, even her arms looked naked, and he could see the swelling of her small breasts through the stretch fabric. He wanted to fuck her right there and then. He wished Myers would go away.

Eleanor was smiling, but then she saw Myers. She jumped visibly, clasped her hands over her heart and bolted.

'She's going through hell,' Tony said with sudden inspiration as they watched her race towards the garage. 'You see, they had a fight – she and *poor father*. A terrible argument about something or other. I don't know what, but Father stomped off down to the bird watch, otherwise he might have been alive. He disturbed them . . . presumably. She feels so guilty.'

'Is that so? Well, that would give a reason for him going there at that time of night.'

There was a sudden squeal of tyres as Eleanor drove past them towards the gate. They sat silently watching as the air became thick with suspicion and dust.

'She's speeding,' Myers said.

Something would have to be done about Eleanor. Tony sat in silence, trying to put himself into Myers' shoes, thinking, planning, questioning. Without doubt, Eleanor was his best bet. He'd probably been hanging around waiting for her to come outside. She was verging on a nervous breakdown.

Moments later they heard the sound of a distant crash. As they raced side by side towards Myers' car, Tony was thinking: 'I hope to God she's knocked herself out. I'll have her locked up for a while. I'll find a place near Johannesburg where Myers can't find her. He's got no authority to badger her like this.'

Panting slightly, for he had been jogging for miles, Dan was on the way to his Gran. There was something he had to tell her –

she'd been right. All at once he became aware of a truck cruising alongside of him, keeping pace.

Gancing sidelong, Dan recognised Gert Basson, a small-time farmer. Gert was a bad egg, neglecting his land and blaming everyone but himself. He'd been arrested for assaulting workers many times, and nowadays he could only get illegal Mozambicans, no one else would have anything to do with him. As he drove, his pig eyes were fixed triumphantly on Dan and the van was lurching towards him. Dan searched desperately for some means of escape. He veered to the left and raced over the veld towards the river.

He heard the truck squeal to a standstill, running feet, at least six by the sound of things, but he knew he could outrun them. A whoosh of bullets past his ear warned him not to try. He held up his hands.

'You have no right to arrest me,' he told the six burly farmers advancing on him.

'Sure we do. You're guilty and since that kafir-lover, Myers, has let you out, it's up to us to beat the truth out of you.'

Fear made his legs weak as they tied his hands behind his back and marched him to the van. He was flung into the back. As the farmers climbed in, they kicked him in turn.

'You fucking puss. We'll fuck you up until your mother won't recognise you. We're gonna beat you to a pulp.' A foot lashed into his ribs and Dan cried out with pain.

They took him to Gert's place, which was on the mountainside, surrounded by miles of veld. Dan watched their preparations with dreadful fascination as they forced him to strip naked and lashed him to an old home-made ladder. When they brought out a sjambok from Gert's dilapidated house, his wife, a pale-faced, bedraggled wreck of a woman, began to argue in a high-pitched nasal whine. She trailed behind Gert, past their neglected vegetable patch, arguing all the while, until Gert silenced her with a threat. Then she heaved a long sobbing sigh and hurried indoors.

They manhandled the ladder until it was set against the wall of the barn at a 45 degree angle, his head hanging down.

'God help me,' he prayed. 'Get me out of this.'

Whack! came the hide whip on to his shoulders. The pain was excruciating. Dan's body shrank into itself, every nerve shrieking as he gritted his teeth not to scream. Taking turns, they lashed his head, his shoulders, the soles of his feet, his buttocks and his testicles. Beer tins in their hands, they stopped now and then for more refreshments, all the while arguing the pros and cons of Myers' infinite stupidity in setting him free.

The world was turning dark, mists swirled in front of his eyes, the pain was receding and Dan found himself floating above the scene, looking down on his bloody, twitching body spreadeagled over the ladder. He could hear what they were saying and he saw the sweat stains spreading over their shirts. They were overweight and the sun was hot. They had drunk too much and soon they would go to sleep.

'There's a rot spreading in high places,' Basson said.

'The rot starts at the top. We'll have to be careful. They've got most of the police with them. There're too many kafir-lovers in the force.'

'The more's the pity. Race is like a living organism. Once the rot sets in, the whole thing goes bad. It has to be cut out.'

'People like Myers are the biggest danger we have. Far worse than the blacks. Bloody commie . . .'

'There're plenty more like him.'

'One of these days we'll have to take over. Shoot the kafirs. Necklacing is too good for the likes of Myers.'

Eventually, they went off to eat and sleep, as Dan had predicted, leaving his body lying there. Dusk fell, the flies buzzed and fought over the feast, ants crawled up his legs, the sun sank and dusk lit the scene with a strange surreal light.

Dan, floating from his vantage point, watched as he was cut free and carried to the van, where they threw him in like a piece of carrion. Dimly he realised they were driving into the bush. Then he was thrown out of the moving vehicle into a clump of bushes. He didn't want to go back into that tortured body, but he knew he must. His Gran had been right. Someone had to fight the bastards and it might as well be him.

Tony glanced round at the lavish bouquets of flowers, the courteous expressions of the reception staff, the antiseptic corridors where prints of flower studies and birds enlivened the long corridors and he shuddered at the cost. Nevertheless, somehow the cash must be found, for Eleanor could not come home yet. He liked the power of running the estates and the homestead without any interference from his stepmother and he was about to tackle the newspaper.

Tony's image had undergone a metamorphosis in the past three months: dark business suit had replaced his jeans and T-shirt, his hair was longer and well styled, a bottle-green shirt, Paisley tie, soft suede shoes, and a small briefcase completed the image of the up-and-coming business tycoon. He knew he looked good because the nurses were giving him the eye.

He hurried towards Eleanor's private ward and walked swiftly inside, locking the door behind him. Eleanor was reading. She threw the book down and tried to leap out of bed, but her one plastered leg held her back. Eventually she limped towards him. 'Tony, Tony,' she gabbled, flinging her arms around his neck. 'Thank God! I've been so bored and so lonely. I can't stand another day of it. Take me home.'

'It's not safe yet,' he lied. 'I think Myers suspects us. You're far better off here. Just stick it out while I handle everything. D'you realise what you said when you hit your head on the steering wheel?'

She stepped away, wary, scared and sullen, only half believing him.

'You almost spilled out everything, but I managed to get my hand over your mouth. You're not as well as you think, Eleanor. You've had a breakdown. Now sit tight and wait.'

She flung herself on the bed and sat there glaring at him, lips compressed. She was wearing a white pyjama top over a white nightdress. Sprawled over her white bed, against the white wall, she looked like a photographic study designed to advertise a product where purity was essential. That was a laugh. She was evil. None of this bloody mess was his fault. She had lured *poor father* to the Boma and shot him.

She looked up. Noticing his expression, she forced a brave smile while trying to disguise her shudder.

'Why don't you call? I lie here hour after hour, not knowing . . . scared to death. For God's sake, Tony.'

'And if the phone's tapped? Sh!' He put one finger to his lips and stared around melodramatically. 'Walls have ears.'

The prospect of being spied on would probably keep her quiet for a while. 'The police are practically living at the house. Captain Myers has dug up half the area around the bird watch.'

'Oh my God . . . how awful.' Tears welled out of her eyes. She turned abruptly and pushed her face into the pillow, muffling her sobs.

The sound and sight of a woman in tears never failed to turn him on. He longed to inflict more hurt and searched for a way of doing so.

'Someone shot at your swans. One of them hid up in the trees and got gangrene. It died eventually.'

'Oh, no, no . . .' Her sobs intensified.

Poor Eleanor! He put his hand up her nightdress into her crotch and fumbled with the soft downy hair, parting a way for his fingers, stroking her clit until his fingers became moist and then wet and sticky.

'Stop it! Someone might come,' she hissed, snake-like. She writhed like a snake, with one leg stuck out stiff and ungainly.

'Mind my leg,' she moaned.

'You'll have to lie over the bed. I'll fuck you from behind.'

'No. You're mad . . .'

'Why, we've done it before.' He pushed her down roughly and saw her white buttocks gleaming as he flipped up her gown.

'You can't rape me,' she gasped.

'Why not? How old was I when you first seduced me. Seventeen, I think. D'you realise I could turn state evidence and put you away for life. The innocent, seduced boy, under the thumb of his wicked stepmother. They'd crucify you. Now, shut up and screw.' Eleanor's cunt was as tight as a rubber band. When she came she clenched and unclenched it like a fist, and she came often. He tried to hang on and make it last, but he never could with her. He'd tried a couple of girls in Johannesburg recently, but she beat them all. Fucking her was the best. He'd missed her cunt, but he could do without the rest of her.

'I must get going.' He zipped up his fly and Eleanor clambered back on the bed, just in time as the nurse tried the handle. Tony unlocked the door.

'We had some private business to see to,' he said, pointing at his briefcase. Lying successfully was something that thrilled him.

Tony took out some papers and pushed his pen towards her. 'I want you to sign power of attorney for me to handle your affairs.'

There was rebellion in her eyes as she frowned at him.

'I never really knew you, did I? You seemed so vulnerable . . . defenceless almost. I wanted to mother you.'

'Don't kid yourself. It was lust and incest. There's nothing motherly about either of those. Don't waste time, sign,' Tony argued.

She shook her head. Stupid bitch.

'Eleanor, listen to the facts of life. You own the farm and the homestead, and Marius left you the adjoining plantation, which strictly speaking belongs to me. It was Mother's, you see. I could fight you in court, but I won't, because the whole damn lot is insolvent. Without cash it will all go under. God knows what Marius thought he was going to do while he was strutting up and down those platforms.

'Then there's the major insurance policy they won't pay out because Marius never thought of adding political insurance. The life policy left to me was paid out – different company, different rules – so I control the only cash we have between us. I shall not spend my cash on your assets unless I have complete

power of attorney. Got it? Without my cash, your assets go bust.
Now trust me, Eleanor, we're together, aren't we? And sign
here. I'll make you rich. I promise. Okay?'

'Okay,' she murmured, looking anxious.

Five minutes later, Tony opened the door of his father's
Mercedes and set off towards Johannesburg, filled with nervous
excitement.

Situated in the financial end of the city, quite near to the Stock
Exchange, was an older, four-storey building almost lost
amongst the skyscrapers. It was called Cronjé's Press, and it
housed their newspaper, the *Morning News*, but Tony called it
The Black Hole. For the past decade it had gobbled up the fruits
of the farm and the plantations, the profits of the plastics factory
and the capital saved by three generations of thrifty farmers. It
had been Marius's dream which he had used to further his
political career and push forward his views, and it had kept them
poor for two decades.

Well, all that would change now, Tony thought, but would
he find a buyer for a newspaper that was heavily in debt and
pushing an unpopular laissez-faire viewpoint, with vague
leanings towards liberalism? If there was one thing he'd learned
from watching Marius, it was the absurdity of trying to hold
back change and sit on the fence. But as yet he had no better
plan.

Chapter 22

Dan's visitor came at midnight. He was an old, gnarled Tswana of noble features and unusual height, standing well over six foot three, so that he had to stoop to enter Nosisi's front door. His eyes were large and slanting and they seemed to burn from some hidden light behind. His teeth were yellow, his skin shrivelled to parchment, but there was a presence about him that caused Dan to scramble to his feet, despite the pain of his wounds.

'Isn't it time you joined us, Dan?' The old man, who was called Joshua Bene, said, when he had been settled in a comfortable chair with tea and biscuits. 'I was with your father from the very start of things.'

'I have never believed in terrorism,' Dan said. 'Even now . . .'

'You believe in being beaten instead?' There was more than a touch of contempt in the old man's voice.

'I believe in the brotherhood of man and an end to racialism.'

'We all believe in that, but some of us believe that the only way to get it is to fight for it.'

Dan sighed. Familiar arguments – he'd been listening to them all his life, it seemed. 'There are better ways to win our freedom. I am against violence. I always have been. Education is the key.'

'But the whites don't give our children the education we crave, we are restricted in learning technical skills. You know that. Will they give us these things on a plate?'

'We have to be organised . . .' Dan broke off. He had been

thinking a great deal about his rights while lying in agony on Nosisi's bed.

'That is why I am here, my friend. I am offering you a hard, full-time job recruiting members. There will be no pay.'

Dan smiled painfully. 'I might have known.'

'You must take to the roads, work where you can, recruit, teach, plan, keep yourself alive with manual labour. All we want are our democratic rights, those rights to which we are entitled, as laid down by the United Nations charter. That is what every man wants. Our methods differ, but our ambitions coincide. I shall come and teach you at night. After that it will be up to you. Do you accept?'

'A month ago I would have said no, but now I realise that the people have to be protected. The so-called law is not here for us.'

The old man joined his hands as if in prayer and smiled as he gazed at his fingertips. 'That ordeal prepared you for the way ahead. It had to be.'

Nosisi smoothed the last lingering touch of ointment on Dan's back, straightened up and sighed. She gazed at him, half triumphant, half sad.

'You are almost better and you must leave,' she told him. She was wearing a toga of handpainted green silk, her hair was wrapped in a yellow turban and she was carrying a basin filled with the remains of the white paste she had used. There were smudges of white on her toga and her cheek.

Dan rolled on to his back and winced with pain. The weals had healed but the bruises would take longer. His grandmother had saved his life, finding him, bringing him home, and healing him. He had never pieced together exactly how she had found him in the veld, concealed under a bush and close to death.

'Tell me again, how did you find me, Nosisi?' he asked, gasping as he got to his feet.

'They led me to you,' she said, with a vague gesture skywards. 'Just as they led me to this . . .' She reached into her wardrobe and brought out a long thin package wrapped in plastic sheets. 'This is the AK-47 rifle that killed Cronjé. I found it under the mud amongst the bulrushes below the family's boma. Even the white police must believe that no terrorist throws away his rifle. There are seven cartridges missing from thirty rounds. Do what you like with it. One day you may want it.'

Dan sat watching her, disbelieving all she said, yet knowing it was true. 'Keep it for me, please,' he said.

'Last night your father gave me a message for you. When you are facing danger, he will be there with you. You have a long life ahead of you. And you will get your education. He needs your love. He says you must think about him often. And he said . . .' She laughed . . . 'He was amazed to find he was indestructible after all.'

Dan turned away as his eyes filled with tears. It was two weeks since the beating and his fast recovery was remarkable. Nosisi's medicines were always effective. She was famous for her knowledge of herbs, quite apart from her clairvoyance.

She was a good woman, Dan decided, but obsessed with her vocation. In the past two weeks she had told him time and again the story of her calling. For once she had a captive audience and he had listened to how she had been paralysed at the age of twelve, bedridden for a year and even the white doctors could not cure her, until one night when she had heard a woman's voice calling to her. The voice had told her to stand up, beg her mother for money for her fare, and take the train to Mochudi, on the Botswana border, where she would be met.

Her family had been awed by her miraculous recovery and they had given the money for the train. At Mochudi she learned that she had been chosen to be the apprentice of a famous witchdoctor in the Kgatleng district, where she remained for the next six years. Her philosophy confused Dan, for it seemed to be laced with Christianity, his people's ancient creed, Buddhism and the occult.

'The white man's ways are destroying the earth,' she told him daily. 'The earth is sickening and the spirits are concerned. The white man is spiritually dying. He is destroying himself with his mania for growth, more possessions, more wastage, more pollution. He has lost the art of caring for others. I do not want you to ape the white man's ways. You must find something better. Something enduring. You must combine our two cultures. Show the people how to do this. One day you will have the power.'

Heady words. Eventually Dan half believed her, but now it was time to leave and thoughts of greatness seemed ludicrous. He'd be lucky to find a labouring job to give him food and shelter while he searched for recruits. He knew he must leave Nelfontein forever and move forward to seek his destiny.

Tony was thinking of survival, too, as he sat in the chairman's office of the *Morning News* and tried to smother his yawns. The man had made an appointment for eleven p.m., stating that pressure of work kept him at his desk all day, but when he had arrived, Tony had recognised him at once as Dr Johan Cloete, a backbencher and a member of an old, conservative family, an ex-professor of philosophy and a well-known naturalist to boot.

He was a funny-looking old guy of about sixty-five, with whiskers trimmed to a square to frame his rounded, fat face. His blue eyes twinkled from behind his gold-rimmed spectacles and his head was bald with a bluish sheen in the fluorescent lights.

Since his arrival he had rambled on until Tony began to wonder if he was senile. Cloete had tried to draw him out on politics, economics, foreign policy and the plight of Africa. Now it was two a.m. and Tony was bored.

Then Cloete said: 'I'm acting on behalf of the government's information department. We might be interested in going into partnership with you, undercover, of course. You'd be heavily subsidised, while you rebuild circulation.'

Suddenly Tony was wide awake.

'There's a good deal involved besides this newspaper,' Cloete said. 'I represent right-wing elements who are at present within the government. Who knows where we'll be in the future. We need an undercover man, but we'd have to be sure we have the right man. That could take time. You see, Tony, my boy, later we envisage buying into the overseas news and entertainment media, so we need a front man. This person would have a share of everything we jointly buy and his reputation as an up and coming whizz-kid would be made.'

Cloete had a strange habit of staring hard with his eyes focused on a point just behind Tony's head. It was disconcerting.

'Let me explain our problem,' he was saying. 'We need an English-language newspaper to offset the malicious propaganda of the English press.

'If we were to combine our resources, no one must ever learn about the connection between the government and this newspaper. That would be disastrous. We need to reach English readers and black readers. Another spin-off is that overseas newspapers frequently quote from the liberal English press – so we must be as liberal as they are – until that vital moment when we need to push home our point of view – in other words the truth.'

The truth – as you see it, Tony thought silently. Were they intending to buy his newspaper, go into partnership, or just pay him for his co-operation? Whatever! As long as it spelled money Tony was intrigued and excited. The plan was sheer genius. The English newspapers were liberal to the point of socialism, and they catered for the readership of English-speaking South Africans – a considerable voting power. Curbs on the press would result in massive overseas censure, which the government could not afford. Controlling their own English newspaper to push home their propaganda was the obvious answer, but if the English readers – who were traditionally opposed to Afrikaans politics – were to find out about the connection, they might as well close down. He would have to box clever, particularly since he intended to keep controlling interest of the *Morning News*. Politicians were notoriously changeable.

'Why me?' Tony asked.

'You are the only young man we know who combines certain qualities and owns a newspaper – furthermore one with a reputation for being doggedly independent against all financial dictates.'

'You can say that again,' Tony said bitterly.

'Well, then . . .' Cloete stood up. 'Shall we shake hands on our mutual interests?'

Tony stood up, not quite sure how to bring up his dire need for money. 'I might not be in business in a month's time. Father left an incredible mess . . . He was a drunk,' he said bitterly. 'He didn't even have the sense to take out riot insurance, so the insurance company are disputing the claim. They're winning.'

'Who insured you?' Cloete asked. Tony told him. 'Ah, we have influence in that company. We can get going faster if our cash injections can be legitimised. We'd better hold the next meeting tomorrow night. Are you interested in further discussions?'

I mustn't look too anxious, Tony thought. They need me as much as I need them. He said: 'Just as long as I can conduct my other business ambitions at the same time. This newspaper is only one of my many responsibilities. I'm also studying parttime for an economics degree.'

The old man's eyes were twinkling with amusement. He held out his hand and Tony grasped it without hesitation.

Ten days later, Tony sat at his desk gazing in wonder at a cheque for two million rands drawn on the insurance company which he held in his shaking hands.

It had all been so quick. In the past week, he had run two headline stories that had erupted into first-class scandals. Firstly, pictures of an opposition M.P. secretly meeting a banned communist. Then came the exposure of a multi-million-rand fraud perpetrated by the management of a British-owned, multi-national bank. The story led to the British shareholders pulling their assets out of South Africa. Their readership had shot up and so had his reputation.

The following morning, a well-known editor of an Afrikaans daily, who had been sacked for his aggressive opposition to the government, had applied for the post of editor of the *Morning News*. Cloete called and told him to hire the man. 'But don't let your editor know about our connection,' Cloete had warned him. 'Just brief him on how he should handle the news – your father's way, an independent, non-attached voice of moral common sense trying to unravel the truth from the mire of party dogma. When we have something important, we'll let you know. By the way, we are organising a private line with a scrambler for you.

'In a few months time you'll be able to go public,' Cloete went on. 'Offer only ten per cent to public subscription and change the name to *The Peoples' Morning News*. This will take time, but set it in motion, and write about it. Tell them you're on the people's side, cutting through political dogma. Brief your editor – and tell him to continue your father's policy of independence. We have some government leaks for you. Attack both sides with equal venom. Don't be afraid to attack us, my boy. We'll tell you when we need you.'

Tony gazed back at the cheque, musing on the implications of his part-time position as their man. Hadn't Cloete said that the newspaper was only part of their plan? For the first time in his life, his future was looking fantastic, but only if he could act the part.

An hour later, Tony was still sitting at his desk deep in thought. If only Father had left him a profitable gold mine instead of a newspaper. He sighed. He had a very clear insight into the present maelstrom of violence and rhetoric sweeping the country. It was something he would far rather not be involved in. 'I've got ten years,' he said aloud. 'If I don't have a fortune hidden overseas within ten years I'll be wiped out.' In the meantime, he had to carve an independent path through this minefield of conflicting interests and try to look sincere about it, too. If he failed he would go under.

Problems: he wrote on his desk pad. What exactly were the problems? First and foremost, a minority of four million whites were governing a country of more than twenty-two million blacks, coloureds and Indians. The non-whites were fighting for a democratically elected government on the basis of one-man one-vote. Overseas interests had backed their bid for universal suffrage by imposing sanctions which had hit the economy to such an extent that growth was down to 1.7 per cent. But the explosive black population was pushing millions more job-seekers on to the labour market each year. Already 45 per cent of blacks were unemployed; most were either unemployable or not sufficiently educated to receive artisan training. The position was not likely to improve in the next decade.

Local opposition to the white government was mainly a three-pronged attack. Education was a sore point. Blacks knew that while R1385 was spent on educating every white child, only R192 was spent per black child. In many areas their education system only prepared them for manual work, therefore, black schools had become a flashpoint for action against the apartheid system. Boycotts and riots were almost everyday occurrences.

The fighting arm of the African National Congress (ANC), called *Umkhonto we Sizwe* (Spear of the Nation), was intent on making South Africa ungovernable with a well-planned campaign. The Pan African Congress (PAC) had vast support amongst younger blacks and was also advocating violence against the government. The State President himself was virtually straitjacketed by the violently opposed wishes of his white electorate, ranging from liberals who backed the blacks' demands for one-man one-vote; middle-of-the-road do-gooders, who saw a gradual unfolding of rights leading to power sharing, and the rightwingers who had vowed never to accept a black majority government. They comprised around 45 per cent of the white electorate and included much of the army, airforce and police. So the whites were split down the middle.

Add to that the problem of tribalism, Tony thought

gloomily, and you have the very good recipe for a multi-faceted revolution.

Only a fool would try to pick a path of moral righteousness through this turbulent powerplay, but that was what he had been told to do.

Chapter 23

———◆———

Thoughts were whirling in Pieter's head as fast as the wheels of the bus racing towards Maputo. It was dark and he could not see where they were. Around him his mates, dressed in civilian clothes, were sweating in the hot night air. He could smell their sweat and their fear, but he could only see their dark shapes silhouetted against the faintest glow of the starlit night.

They had crossed the border into Mozambique four hours ago and they were travelling by passenger coach through enemy territory, with their Russian and Czech-made weapons thrust under seats and along the passageway. Their assignment was to destroy an enemy target – an ANC camp in a Maputo suburb. How could they get away with this? It was impossible, but it was happening.

Pieter shuddered. The shudder began in his ankles and raced up the back of his calves, set his entire body shaking and his teeth chattering. Then it swept down his arms, prickling the hairs and ended in his fingertips which were left sweaty and burning hot.

What's got into me? I'm not a coward. My life is not important. Didn't I make that decision at Ma's funeral? The cause is bigger than all of us, it's nothing less than the survival of the *Volk*. Big words, but he couldn't stop shaking. They passed a petrol station and the lights shone into the bus. Pieter glanced around and saw the pinched, white faces of his companions. Andy looked remote and anxious and Koos had withdrawn into a trance, it seemed. They were good guys and

189

they'd had the best training in the world. What was it sarge had said: 'A pint of sweat saves a gallon of blood.' They were sweating enough to save a regiment.

There were thirteen handpicked men on the bus, including a medic and a lieutenant. Then there was the '*stranger*', who would direct them to the house. He was the only unknown amongst them. A curious guy, Pieter thought, in his disguise as an out-of-date hippie, with beads, a floral headband, bermuda shorts and black vest. His nervous eyes were forever darting this way and that way, his long fingers playing with his beads. Pieter had first noticed him while they were waiting for the bus at Ressano Garcia, a small village just across the Mozambique border. He seemed to melt into corners and shadows. He never stood in a doorway, or against the light, or any place he'd make a good target. He spoke in monosyllables, and then said next to nothing. He was supposed to be a crazy, ex-Portuguese settler left behind in the exodus, but there was nothing crazy about his eyes, or his erect military bearing.

Pieter reckoned the guy was a highly trained operator, a recé scout of sorts, probably the same agent who had tipped them off about the squad of SA-born saboteurs, trained in Russia, who were hiding out in Maputo, prior to their infiltration into South Africa in order to to blow up Sasol, the country's vital, billion-dollar coal to oil installation.

They'd been briefed at length using photographs of the exterior and interior of the house where the terrorists were training. They even had a full description of the commies' weapons. These photographs and descriptions of the inmates of the house, plus a good map, had been the object of their studies for the past week in Swaziland.

Pieter glanced surreptitiously at the scruffy figure sitting beside the driver. They'd been told that an agent like that was worth well over a million rands. That was his replacement cost. If so, he would be fluent in Russian and Portuguese and perhaps Xhosa and Zulu. If he really was an operator, then he'd be too valuable to waste in a fight.

The bus was racing downhill now, past small villages and the occasional store. They'd been told that many of the inhabitants had been bribed to see nothing. Could they be trusted? Would there be a welcoming committee to ambush them in Maputo?

Faster now. His stomach did a somersault as a smudge of light showed in the distance. Soon they could distinguish pinpoints of light. Dear God protect me and my mates, he prayed.

We're okay, the best-trained recé force in the world, as good as the Israelis, he reminded himself. Recently he'd signed on for four years, but he knew it was forever. He was no longer suitable for society. Why? Because society was a bunch of double-dealing, hypocritical mother-fuckers. He and his squad were on the side of the angels.

O-three hundred hours. Dead on time, the bus drew up on the corner. The hippie got out and motioned them to join him. Hearts hammering they crept out of the bus and helped haul out the equipment. There was a new moon, a slight sea mist drifting around, and a sickening stench of rotting garbage, wood smoke and sewage. The scout was pointing to a house which he recognised at once. A light was burning from somewhere round the back. The rest of the windows were dark. It was a pleasant villa-type home, double-storeyed with a large balcony, trellises, and a half-acre of garden that had given up the ghost entirely. He could hear a frog croaking loudly from somewhere nearby. A skinny dog came running and whining. It must have been owned by whites once. *Goddamn it! It's not a house, it's a target.* But the target still looked like a graceful old house in sad need of repair.

Now they were running, faster, acting out a play they had rehearsed hundreds of times with a faithfully constructed replica of the building. He knew exactly which window he had to smash, the place where his grenade must fall, but they hadn't mentioned the frogs croaking, or the scent of jasmine, or the old dog fawning behind, or the sudden shrill wail of a baby from somewhere inside there. Oh God! What the hell was a baby doing there? His hands were shaking so badly he couldn't hold the grenade. His mouth was too dry to shout. The whirling in his ears was blotting out sound.

At the first crack of gunshot the dog fled. There was a strong smell of burning. Then he seemed to go into a trance as his training took over. The door had burst open from the blast of the mortars. Fire was raging inside, there were screams, shouts, some shots being fired at random. Their sarge burst open a door with a blast from his sub-machine gun and fired half a magazine off at chest level, the other half at ankle level. Andy and Koos raced in after him.

Inside there was too much smoke to see a damn thing except shapes running away. He heard the cough of bombs detonating, as he raced up the stairs. A black shape was coming down. He shot it and kicked it over the banisters. His job was to clear the rooms off the upstairs back passage. He blasted the first door which crashed open with a loud splintering of wood. There were two shapes under a blanket. He aimed, fired, and heard the obscene sound of bullets smashing into flesh. There was a dull groan, the scent of blood. Pulling back the blankets he saw a white arm, a woman's arm. Another tug revealed her naked, wounded body and that of the black man she'd been sleeping with, his hand on her bare breast. How could this be? The house was burning fast now. Hurry!

He tore down the passage, singed by the scorching flames. A target jumped out of the window of the next room screaming hideously, its clothes alight. He raked it with bullets as it fell. More targets were pouring out of the doors. They ran into a haze of bullets and fell. He had to race into the burning flames to check the last room which was empty.

His part was over. He raced to the stairs which were burning fast, plunged down them, hoping they'd hold, and fled into the night.

Looking up he saw a man half out of the window, pointing a rifle. He let off a round and the corpse hung there, caught on a jagged piece of glass. A shot rang out and he sprawled forward, wondering if he'd been hit. Near him lay a woman with a baby clutched to her breast. Both were dead.

He was only stunned, not wounded, he found as he lurched to his feet. Koos was waiting by the gate.

'Andy didn't come out,' he yelled.

Pieter tore back into the blazing inferno with Koos right behind him. 'Andy!' his voice roared. He knew he was being a fool and that he was silhouetted against the flames. Then he heard a shout in the direction of the kitchen.

'I'm coming,' he yelled. Andy was shot in the thigh and he was close to passing out from shock. 'Shit.' Pieter swore at the sight of him. He flung him over his shoulder and turned into an impenetrable wall of flames.

Koos was smashing out the back door. 'This way,' he yelled. Pieter kept running. Suddenly he remembered the long hours of jogging over the veld, his buddy flung over his shoulder. *So this is what it was all about.*

They were piling into the bus, leaving their weapons behind. The dog was running behind them, but it was soon lost to sight. That hippie was back in the bus, counting them, his clever brown eyes giving them the once over.

'Well done,' he said eventually. 'One bad wound here, three minor wounds, target totally destroyed. Very well done.' The lieutenant looked sick, but the medic was calm as he trussed up Andy and gave him a shot.

It was all over! The enormity of what they had done hit him like a blow to his solar-plexus. He'd been so cool, but suddenly he began to shake. He had to hide his face from the hippie who seemed to see everything.

'It's not over, yet,' the hippie said to him. 'Don't let go. Hang on. We have to pray we get out of here.'

They were approaching an open plot where a helicopter hovered. As they drove up fast it landed. Seconds later they were handing up the wounded and clambering in, to the sound of shots, sirens and vehicles in hot pursuit. To his horror the hippie waved briefly and ran for the trees.

What must it be like to stay behind in enemy territory after something like this? Pieter wondered.

It was all over and they were airborne, soaring home – away from the stench of putrid drains, broken sewers and uncollected garbage littering the streets, away from starving dogs and a country that was decaying. So why was he crying for the dead? The tears were coming fast and furious. He could no longer hide his terrible sobs. He had killed a white woman? The thought was obscene. She was better off dead than bedded with a black, he comforted himself, yet the sobs kept coming up as if from the depths of his soul.

'*Thou shalt not kill.*' Tonight he had offended against God and against nature. For the first time he realised the true cost of his vocation. He remained crouched over his knees, hiding the bitter, scalding tears that would not stop.

Chapter 24

———◆———

'Excuse me, porter. I want to phone home. Can you give me the right change?' Liza held out a five-rand note to Joe, the porter at the Mayfair and smiled beguilingly, but behind her self-assured exterior she was quaking. Would Joe recognise her? Had she shed her *gammat* skin successfully?

The porter was entranced by her manner. Despite her establishment school uniform and cultured voice, there was more than a touch of sensuality about this lovely young girl. Was she Italian perhaps, or Spanish? She was sixteen, he guessed, and she was going to be a rare beauty. He admired her thick black brows slanting up from either side of her shapely nose, her large brown eyes that were almond-shaped and glowing with warmth, and her full lips trembling as if bursting to laugh. Her jet black hair hung straight to just below her ears, revealing a long, shapely neck. The rich had prettier children, perhaps because they could afford lovelier wives, Joe decided. He counted out fifty- and twenty-cent coins, eyeing the young girl longingly. Something about her reminded him of someone he once knew. But who? He could not remember.

Liza let out her breath in a long sigh. Joe hadn't recognised her. She'd won, and she'd done it all on her own. 'Thank you,' she murmured, taking the change. It had all been worthwhile, the years of self-discipline, speech training, deportment, study-ing . . . all of it. Only she knew the efforts she had taken to keep out of the sun, the punishments she had endured for skipping tennis and hockey, the pocket money used exclusively for skin lightening cream, which she rubbed in obsessively every night. Triumph surged.

'The public box is just around the corner, madam.' He bowed slightly.

Liza clapped her hand over her mouth to hold back her giggles. Joe had called her 'madam'. So much for his predictions of doom. She could still hear his voice pronouncing her life sentence: '*You look, talk, walk and act coloured, Angel, and you always will.*' She grinned to herself as she dialled.

Now that she had finally found the courage and saved enough cash, the phone rang and rang. Eventually the operator came on the line. 'Sorry, Madam, this number has been disconnected.'

'Oh, but why?' Liza wailed. 'I'm calling from Johannesburg. The de Vries's are my friends. Can't you find their new number?' After all, she reasoned, it was a very small town.

'Mrs de Vries died. Her husband went to work in Nelspruit, I believe. Their son is in the army.'

Died . . . ? Liza replaced the receiver feeling numb with shock. Of course Pieter would be doing his military service, she should have remembered, but what had his poor mother died of? Her eyes brimming with tears she stumbled across the lounge, feeling cheated. She had held an image of Nelfontein close in her heart, unchanged and unchanging since the night when she ran away. It was strangely shocking to realise that everything might be different now. *She might never find Pieter.* All that she had done had been for Pieter. She had fought to stay white because she loved him.

Collapsing into a chair, she leaned back and closed her eyes. In her mind's eye, she saw Pieter looking down and smiling his own special smile, his eyes beaming affection, his lips curled in a mischievous smile. 'Oh, Pieter, I love you,' she whispered. 'One day we'll be together.'

'Can I get you something, madam? Is anything wrong?' It was the hotel manager.

She looked up, smiling tremulously. She had all the cash she'd been saving for the call. She might as well celebrate her triumph over Joe. 'I'll have a big icecream with cherries and strawberries, and perhaps a banana, with cream over it, and a coke.'

'Would that be a banana split, madam? Here's the menu. If you'd care to go into the restaurant, I'll find you a table.'

'I want to stay here. You see ...' she tried to think of a reasonable excuse, besides the truth, which was her longing to watch the very rich passing to and fro. 'I'm waiting for my parents.'

'Of course, madam. I see you're at St Augustine's College. My niece goes there. Perhaps you know her. Maria Dobson. I think she's in Standard Six.'

'Yes, I know her. She plays the piano beautifully.'

He beamed and spoke for a while about the college. For Liza each word was a tribute to her victory. He had absolutely no idea who she was. 'Of course you may eat it here,' he promised.

The icecream arrived and Liza sat feeling like a princess, despite her sad news. It was mid-summer and baking hot outside, but pleasantly cool inside the foyer. She felt soothed by the deep pile of the carpets, the heady scent of the massive bowls of fresh flowers, and that indefinable sense of well-being that comes from being soothed, flattered and surrounded with luxury.

A loud crash came from the restaurant, followed by shouts. Then a small boy fled through the swing doors, pursued by two waiters.

'Oh no!' she cried incredulously, jumping to her feet. It was Ralph. He hadn't changed a bit, and he'd hardly grown. How thin he looked. Trembling with fright, Liza watched him dodging around the settees clutching a loaf of bread. He was trying to reach the door. Glancing over his shoulder, he fell headlong over the carpet. They caught him at once. A waiter hauled him to his feet by his T-shirt, while the others began to pummel him with their fists.

'Don't! Don't do that,' Liza shouted.

A packet of cigarettes fell from under Ralph's jersey as the pounding continued. A blow caught him on his neck and he gasped with pain.

'Stop it!' she yelled. 'You're killing him.'

Joe, the porter, rushed to join the punishment squad.

'You fucking brutes!' she swore. Grabbing an antique chair she hit Joe full in the face. 'Go suck, Joe,' she hissed.

Liza flung herself into the fray, using the chair as a weapon, hitting out, kicking, and biting when one of them grabbed her hand. When the chair shattered, she grabbed a leg and used it as a cosh. The waiters retreated looking murderous.

'Run!' she yelled. Grabbing Ralph's hand she fled out of the hotel. They heard whistles, shouts and pounding feet close behind. Without a second thought they raced down the stairs into the underground arcade, along the passage to more steps up, back across the steet to an alleyway, where they clambered up the fire escape steps to the entrance to a shop's boiler room. This was an old escape route and many was the time they had sheltered here.

'Some things never change,' she said, when she'd recovered her breath.

How thin and ill Ralph looked, she noticed sadly. She had shot up and was towering over him but he was still the same skinny kid in his torn black vest and shredded pants. Only his eyes looked old. There was something wrong with his eyes, she noticed. The pupils were dilated and he seemed to be acting strangely.

'You've been sniffing glue again,' she said. 'I can see how hungry you are, but you must never steal. It's wrong.'

'It's not wrong to take from those who have plenty,' he said, quoting an old theme song of deprived blacks that they'd learned from Nico. 'Are you really Angel?' He gazed at her in awe. 'You seem so different . . . like one of them.'

'And did it seem like I was one of them when we were fighting back there?'

'No, Angel,' he said, giving her another hug. It was heart-breaking to feel his skinny ribs, and smell the curious scent of a street child which brought back poignant memories. Suddenly she was crying, for him, for herself, for all their old street friends.

While they waited for darkness, Ralph told her of his agony. The Shelter kept sending him home and his stepfather kept slinging him out. 'He beats my mother because of me,' he said sadly. 'So I can't stay there.'

When it was dark, Liza forced Ralph to go with her to the Home Shelter. For Liza, it was like returning to the past. When she stood before Archie Bagnall and gazed into his intimidating eyes, she began to tremble, just as she used to, but, as before, she would not show her fear.

Archie looked older and he was wearing glasses. He stared at them suspiciously.

'Mr Bagnall, you must help Ralph,' Liza pleaded. 'He wants another chance. It's no good sending him home. Far better to put him in the orphanage. You must stick it out, Ralph,' she told the shivering boy. 'I'll visit you when I can.'

'And who are you?' he said, glowering fiercely at her.

'I'm Angel,' she said simply. 'Don't you remember me?'

Archie's face turned very red. His eyes filled with tears and then he blinked several times. He tried to speak and finally cleared his throat. 'Angel?' he managed to croak eventually. 'Come into my office. I'm going to make some tea. I might even find a cake to celebrate. You can clean up in the shower. Did you know that your dress is torn?'

'Oh dear. I'll get into trouble,' she said.

'I want you to tell me what happened to you after you left here. Every last detail.'

She explained briefly over cake and tea. When she came to telling him about the cash she had slammed on the Mother Superior's desk, Archie laughed.

'Come on, Angel, who are you kidding? That place costs more than a thousand rands a term, plus uniforms, books, pocket money, laundry, etcetera. Six thousand rands a year is the minimum outlay for parents with a girl around your age. I suppose your Mother Superior saw something in you I never saw and accepted you as a bursary child. She was right – it's paid off.

'I want to tell you something, Angel,' he went on, watching Ralph tucking into the cake. 'For every hundred kids who come here, only one or two make it. The statistics are heart-breaking. Did you know this shelter is privately owned? I started it with my own cash. It was tough at first, but nowadays I get backing from church funds. This used to be my own house. I turned it into a shelter after a couple of eight-year olds threatened me with knives because they wanted some bread. Sometimes I feel I'm a fool to waste my life and my energy and resources. But then, out of the blue, something happens that makes me realise it's all worthwhile. This is one of those times, Angel.'

'Yes,' she said smiling softly. 'Thank you, Mr Bagnall. Miss Arlington helped me . . .' she tried to explain. 'It was something she told me. She said I can be any damned thing I want to be if I will it to happen. Where's she gone?'

'She went home. Now, Angel, you must go back to school. I'll take you in my car. It's very late. I'll look after Ralph for you, I promise.'

Liza managed to climb through an open window and reach her room without being seen. The following day, no one mentioned her absence at supper, perhaps because so many girls had been out late with their parents. She began to relax. She'd got away with it.

It was so scary to watch the silent world of the sisters early each morning. By the time the pupils hurried into the chapel for mass, the nuns were already in place, looking as if they were carved out of stone. Liza often wondered about the lives they led. Did they, too, have their secrets? Were they hiding from problems they could not face? Or had it taken superhuman courage to give up the world and all it offered?

She peered at them through her fingers. Would I be able to stand their terrible lives of endurance and discipline or would I crack? she wondered.

After prayers a frightening summons arrived via Sister Agnes, who looked grave. Liza was to see the Mother Superior at nine sharp, which meant missing maths. This had never happened before and Liza summoned all her courage, as she waited outside the nun's sanctuary.

Sharp at nine she was called in. Mother Superior's eyes were red from weeping. Because of me? Surely not.

'Well, Angel, do you have anything to tell me?' she asked. There was a long silence.

'No,' Liza said after a while.

The nun sighed. 'Angel, I want you to try to put yourself in my shoes. I want you to imagine that one day a certain young urchin girl arrives looking as if she's had no chance in life at all, she's alone and working for her living, yet she's only fifteen. She reminds you so much of your own deprived childhood. She's saved some cash and she wants desperately to buy herself out of the mess she's in. She seems to have courage, integrity and ambition and you remember how you were once helped and your heart is touched.

'You long to help her, but how? There is a waiting list of fifty girls to enter the college, all from rich homes who can afford to pay the high fees. Then you remember the special fund set up by the church for girls wishing to become nuns and clever enough to deserve the standard of education the college offers. Somehow you manage to get this precious bursary awarded to this girl.'

The Mother Superior took out her handkerchief and dabbed her eyes. 'You vouch for her,' she went on in the same soft voice, 'and then, after two years of patient training, and almost full-time coaching from one of your nuns, your protégée goes out one afternoon, and reverts to what she once was, a street urchin.

'She liaises with another former accomplice, hangs around in the lounge waiting to share the spoils, orders an icecream for which she does not pay, and when her accomplice is caught, she attacks the waiters with a chair, causing multiple injuries including a broken nose and a black eye. The two criminals flee and this impostor comes back here and pretends that nothing has happened.

'Unfortunately for her, she was wearing school uniform. The management have laid charges and the police are investigating. Now tell me, Liza, what would you do with this young girl?'

Liza gazed at her hands, filled with despair, her mind in a turmoil. Would she go to prison? If so, that would be the end of her.

'Speak, child,' the nun commanded sharply.

'I wouldn't believe all I heard,' Liza mumbled. 'I mean that bit about waiting for an accomplice – that's not true. It wasn't planned. All right, so Ralph stole, but he looked so hungry. I was amazed when I saw him racing out of the restaurant, clutching a loaf. Poor Ralph. I couldn't bear it when they beat him and he screamed.'

'Is that young boy your brother?'

Liza shook her head. 'Long ago Ralph saved my life. I didn't just learn book work here, Mother Superior,' she murmured. 'I learned about moral obligations. I learned that love is important. And that one must always pay one's debts.'

'Start right at the beginning, Angel,' the nun said sharply.

'My name's not Angel,' Liza began, feeling as if a massive weight was being lifted from her shoulders. 'My name is Liza Frank. All I can remember of my life began when I was five years old. I used to think I was so special and I lived with my foster-Gran in Nelfontein, on a small holding. We had chickens and donkeys and goats . . .'

As her tearful story poured out, the Mother Superior listened gravely. 'You see,' she finished her story an hour later, dry-mouthed with nervousness. 'I've turned my back on the streets, but not on my friends, so I took Ralph to the Home Shelter. I'm so sorry. I don't want to leave here, but I can't think what else I could have done.

'I learned another strange thing yesterday,' Liza went on, her cheeks wet with tears. 'Something that you have now confirmed. I thought I was paying my way. How naive of me. You gave me a bursary. Why is that? Did you hope that I would become a nun one day?'

'We have always hoped.'

'It is not what I had planned for myself, but I owe you so much. I'll try . . . but I can't promise.'

'As long as you live up to the standards we have taught you,' the nun said sharply, 'that will be enough for the time being. I'll persuade the hotel management not to lay charges and I'll speak to the bishop about this Ralph of yours. I'm sure they can accommodate him somewhere more permanent than the Shelter. You are forbidden to leave the school premises until the end of the year. Is that clear?'

Liza nodded gratefully.

'You may go.'

It was so hot in the cottage. November was always insufferable, but this time it was a scorcher. Grannie du Toit had left the door and the back window open all morning, hoping that a draught would cool the place, but the corrugated-iron roof seemed to attract the sun's heat. She was feeling anxious as she double-checked the cleanliness of the cottage and put on her best black church dress. She smoothed her hair back into a bun, washed her hands and busied herself with last-minute tidying.

When she heard a car coming along the farm track, she pushed the coffee percolator back on the hob. Pausing for a moment, she thought of the letter that had arrived two days ago. It had said that Sister Agnes from Johannesburg would be visiting her at 11 am the following Tuesday morning and she hoped that this would be convenient.

What about? she wondered. A charity collection? She had five rands to last her until the end of the month. How would she manage to spare. . . ?

A rustle and swish of starched fabrics brought her back to the present. Goodness, she's terribly tall for a woman, Gran thought as the nun stooped to pass through the doorway. She looked so stern, too. The cat jumped up, arched his back and fled through the window.

Sister Agnes thrust out her long white hand and smiled, but her eyes remained hard. Gran sensed her dislike immediately and this puzzled her.

'I'm Sister Agnes . . . and you must be Mrs du Toit.'

'Yes. Come in. I'm afraid you've had a dusty drive. Perhaps you'd like a cup of coffee? There's some brewing on the stove.'

'Thank you.' Sister Agnes looked around as if uncertain of where she should sit.

'Sit there,' Gran said. 'Then you'll have a good view through the doorway, which is better than looking at those old walls. Have you come to collect money for the Catholic church? If so, I'm afraid I can't help you. I have very little income. I live off my land, which is poor. Sometimes we have good rains, but even then . . .' She broke off, thinking that it was perfectly clear how poor she was. She busied herself pouring coffee and handing over a mug and saucer with a homemade rusk balanced on it.

'Oh, but it's not that at all.' Sister Agnes seemed bemused. 'I came to talk to you about Liza, your foster-child.'

'*Liza!* Where is she?'

Her mug clattered to the floor, sending coffee flying everywhere. She tried to clean up the mess as the nun bent over her. 'Please, calm yourself. Liza is very well. I was with her yesterday.'

'Oh!' Suddenly the dam burst, the dam behind which she had pushed all those horrible pictures of what might have happened to Liza, her grief and her guilt and her terrible anger; all of it came frothing out and she couldn't hold back a shuddering sob.

This won't do, she thought, as she rushed into the bedroom and slammed the door. Unable to see through her tears, she fumbled in a drawer for a handkerchief and blew her nose vigorously several times. When she felt she had herself under control, she returned, her handkerchief clenched in her fist just in case.

Sister Agnes had a cup of coffee ready for her. 'Look, Mrs du

Toit, I'm only asking you to let her come home for the long Christmas holidays. She has turned into a lovely young girl. I've grown very fond of her.'

Seeing the old woman's shocked expression, the nun began to explain: 'I know it's sometimes hard to accept, but times are changing fast. We're being tossed into a new South Africa. Petty apartheid is crumbling. It hasn't worked and we've become the world's lepers because of it. The laws which prevented Liza from being a part of your family will be done away with one day ... In the meantime, we have obtained special permission ...'

'Please, Sister,' Aletta interrupted anxiously. 'Tell me about Liza. Where has she been all this time?'

'I'll tell you her story, or as much as I know of it.'

Four cups of coffee later she concluded: 'So you see, Mrs du Toit, you would not be breaking the law by loving Liza.'

Aletta took a deep breath. 'It hasn't been easy for me. I've always obeyed the laws of our government.' She gestured towards the pictures of cabinet ministers on the wall. 'I always trusted the authorities. They gave me Liza to look after, but she was never really mine. She was a *foster* child. They emphasised that. So when they said Liza must go, I had to agree with them. And now? Must I have her back only to lose her again? My heart is not a punch bag to be knocked this way and that. And what about my views? These racist feelings are deep inside me, inside my people. I loved Liza as if she were mine, and yet knowing what she is now, to bring her into my home would be against everything I have ever felt. I am too old to change my ways. I have to keep forcing myself to overcome the fact that she has ... she is ... It's so confusing. All those years I raised her like my own child and now, *suddenly*, she is not the person I always thought she was. It's such a shock and I don't know how to accept it. How *could* we have overlooked something like that, something which was staring us in the face all those years?'

She paused and searched the nun's face, hoping for understanding and wondering if she was making sense.

'My little Liza ... she was such a pretty girl, and yet there was always something different about her. The other children, they knew, and they punished her for it. So you see, there's the whole town to think of. All this should never have happened.'

'It's not Liza's fault. She learned your prejudices and those of this society. Consequently, she can never accept her reclassification. Life will not be easy for Liza. At least if she had a home . . .'

'Very well. She may come. I'll try my best.'

'Thank you, Mrs du Toit. I know you'll never regret this.'

'I wonder,' Aletta said. 'It's not just me I'm thinking of.'

After Sister Agnes had left, Aletta took out her precious snapshots and gazed at them for a long time. In most of them, Liza was standing together with Pieter and the two of them looked so happy. She had a sudden premonition that she had made the wrong decision.

Chapter 25

Dan hitched a lift on a wool lorry and slept snug amongst the sacks, waking to find that the countryside was flat as far as the eye could see and white with frost. His breath was smoking in the frosty air.

'Six degrees below freezing, that's the Highveld for you,' the driver said as he dropped him off at dawn. 'There's Johannesburg – over there. I turn off here, so you'll have to hitch another ride.'

In the far distance Dan could see a misty silhouette of skyscrapers grouped together in a small enclave looking lost on the limitless horizon.

He set off at a jog to keep warm. After thirteen months on the road, he was as lean and fit as a man could be. He had tramped the length and breadth of South Africa talking, teaching, persuading and always recruiting, while working at any labouring job he could get. He'd made too many mistakes, he felt, but he'd been successful overall and the party was pleased with him. He'd been keeping the plum, the massive black suburb of Soweto, home to over a million people, until last, but lately he'd felt he could tackle this massive challenge.

Around noon he found himself in Sandton, amongst the graceful homes set in acres of well-kept gardens, pools, tennis courts and enough servants to maintain all this, yet it was not as easy to find a job as he had anticipated. The gates were guarded by fierce dogs and he could never get near the houseowners, because the gardeners, jealous of their territory, would wave him away.

Shortly afterwards he was bitten by a mean old bulldog with brown teeth. Its owner, an old lady with an uncanny resemblance to her pet, gave him a new pair of trousers, a meal and a half-day job. He had to cut her grass with an ancient lawnmower that was rusted and blunt. 'You can come here twice a month,' she said, smiling optimistically as he left.

That night he slept in an old disused tannery by the Liesbeck River. Despite the cold, he sat on the river bank smoking his pipe, watching an owl swooping over the river and listening to the gentle country sounds. It was rural and peaceful and the sight of the lovely homes with lights behind curtains, and the sound of music floating in the air made him lonely.

The following morning, the contrast was depressing, when he hitched to Alexander Township and for the first time experienced the full impact of a massive squatter settlement that had arisen accidentally and illegally in the midst of opulent white suburbs. Walking along narrow dusty alleys, he shuddered at the maze of ramshackle shacks constructed of old corrugated iron, rolled-out petrol drums, cardboard cartons and a few sticks. Rejected people and half-starved ragged children roamed aimlessly around.

One old man, whom he recruited in a queue outside the trading store, invited him to his home to drink coffee. He found the shack homely and clean. He and his wife had insulated the walls with cardboard cartons and on them they had pasted tin labels – hundreds of them, a montage of white prosperity – blackberry jam, cling peaches, Israeli olives, Feta cheese, marmalade, baked beans . . . All the colours of the rainbow made their shack glow and gave an impression of plenty. Yet they were like stick insects, they were so painfully thin.

After the squalor of Alexander Township, the spacious homes of Parktown with their old oak trees and lawns offended his sense of justice as he rolled through on the back of a pallet of logs destined for the gold mines. He was glad when they left the wealthy suburbs and reached poorer white areas. Fifteen kilometers south-west of Johannesburg, they reached his destination. He wondered at this strange suburb of identical square concrete homes, with identical patches of gravel-garden, wire fences, roofs, windows, front doors and streets. A tribute to whites' methodical minds, he thought, feeling murderous.

There was no winter in Soweto, only the cold. How could there be seasons, he reasoned, if there are no trees or grass or flowers. Nature had not been welcomed here. He'd heard the people's excuses in a hundred ghettos all over the country: 'This is not our real home. We were forced to live here. Why should we do anything to beautify these places? To do so would be giving in to the system.' Dan was not sure he agreed.

He walked all day, talking, arguing, persuading, signing up new members and handing out membership cards. By seven o'clock it was dark and Dan was feeling uneasy. His shoes or his trousers were adequate reasons to kill him, for these people were ferocious in their anger and deprivation. Any stranger was a likely victim. It seemed that there was nowhere to stay and no one invited him to share their houses.

An hour later he caught a whiff of food cooking and turned, swift as a jackal, towards the source. Rounding the corner, he saw lights flashing and heard the strains of a jazz band coming in snatches on the wind. Then he drew close enough to make out a double-storey building, decorated to look like an English tudor pub. The neon lights blazed: *Miriam's Tavern*.

As he opened the door, the noise, tobacco and dagga fumes, and the warmth caught him like an unexpected wave, and he stood breathless, blinking with happiness, blocking the doorway until someone asked him to move on. His hunger picked out the tempting aromas: sizzling steak, curry and rice, Eastern spices, fried onions . . . God, he was hungry. When had he last eaten?

The woman in the kiosk operating the till was watching him intently. He looked and smiled and shrugged, indicating his ragged clothes apologetically. Then he did a double-take. She was a most intriguing woman. Her skin was ebony, yet there was no sign of the broad flat cheek bones, the wide nose or thick lips that marked the Southern Africans. She could have been an

Ethiopian woman with her pinched sloping nose, her long bony face and her huge glittering eyes. As he walked towards her, admiring her, he thought that he had never before seen such expressive eyes.

He looked away as he threaded his way through the tables, but her image was impressed in his mind: those sensual, heavy-lidded eyes, flashing with humour and compassion, tiny breasts with a pearl pendant lying between two mounds of firm flesh, her hands delicate and manicured as she smoothed the papers on her desk, her eyes showing intrigue and curiosity. He liked the way her hair had been straightened and pulled into a bun with a blue chiffon scarf tied around it. She wore a full mauve and blue floral skirt and a black sweater with a deep V-neck which showed off the smooth skin of her throat. He smelled her heady perfume and he thought enviously that someone must love her very much. With that thought came a sudden swift shaft of envy. This was one very sensual woman, Dan thought, despite her age, for he guessed she was in her forties.

She was watching him inquiringly. 'I'm hungry, I wish to offer my services in return for a meal,' he blurted, regretting for the first time the poverty-stricken nature of his work. He was about to say, any labouring work, but the words stuck in his throat. He longed to look good in her eyes. 'I'm a musician from the north,' he blurted out. Adding, truthfully, 'I haven't played for over a year – any job will do.'

With eyes like hers, who needed to talk? They were brimful of compassion, but not patronising. She gestured to a small table behind the kiosk. 'Order whatever you like,' she said. Her voice was deep contralto and when she spoke her throat seemed to vibrate slightly. He couldn't tear his eyes away from her as she beckoned the waiter.

'What about the boss?' he asked, not wishing to make trouble for her.

'I have influence with the boss,' she said and once again a shaft of envy pierced his guts.

'What's your name?'

'Dan . . . Dan Tweneni.'

'A famous name for those with long memories,' she said.

'Victor Tweneni was my father,' he said hoarsely, feeling touched by her recollection.

The waiter brought a huge T-bone steak with sizzling fried potatoes, pumpkin, peas and mealie pap covered in onion and tomato gravy. Dan tried to eat slowly and not show her that he was starving.

Cele, the waiter, a surly fellow, brought an icecream, and thumped it down. He seemed to be annoyed at the free meal, but she leaned over the counter and called out: 'Enjoy.'

He mumbled his thanks, too embarrassed to explain that he hated desserts of all descriptions.

When the band reassembled and began to play, Dan tried not to listen to the notes drummed out like a herd of unruly donkeys. Could he do better? It had been so long. He looked at his hands, which had thickened and grown strong and gnarled with hard manual labour. Would they find their way around the notes, he wondered?

Suddenly the band hit a bad patch and there were a couple of boos from the youngsters clustered around the bar.

'What d'you play?' she called above the din.

'Flute . . . penny whistle . . .'

'We had a flautist, but he got stabbed three days ago. He's down in the mortuary while they try to find the next of kin to bury him.'

'Where's his flute?'

'Here, I suppose.' She frowned. 'Just how good are you? If it doesn't work you must get right down from there.'

She gestured towards the raised dais where the three hardworking youngsters, flushed and sweaty, were galloping on.

He wanted to reassure her. 'It's been a long time . . . I'll give it a try. If it doesn't work I'll wash dishes. Okay?'

Now she was smiling. 'Good. We keep a high standard here, boy.'

He noted the 'boy' with amusement. She was trying to keep him in his place. Was she the owner's wife? She wasn't wearing a ring and there was no mistaking the message that beamed out of her eyes.

'Thanks for the meal. I was ready to pass out.'

He strolled over to the band. The players were having another break, wiping their sweaty faces with dirty handkerchiefs and drinking their beer with noisy gulps.

Dan took the flute and blew three long shrill blasts, like a train whistle.

She turned, startled, mouth open with anger, but he winked and let fly into a peal of sound, soaring up and up with pleasure at his feeling of well-being, at the ripe beauty of Miriam, at his full stomach, at the joy of living and laughter and good friends. He remembered those heady mornings in the bushveld with the hornbill, and the birds waking.

He paused, trying to remember, suddenly noticing the awful silence in the tavern. Had he shocked them? Was his jazz too way out for this type of audience? He turned to the three startled youths. 'Can you improvise? Strum a background ... okay? This is a song I composed myself,' he told the surprised audience. 'It's called "Daybreak".'

He wooed her with care, caressing her with every note. His eyes never left her. He saw how she soaked in the music like the earth soaks in the rain. Her soul was yearning and pining and he sensed a deep sorrow. He wanted to mend her wounds with his music, bring her renewed life and joy and love, so he played only for her.

The last customers swayed off, full of booze, warmth and companionship around 3 o'clock. Miriam was looking as good as new as she checked the takings with flashing eyes and jingling bracelets. The kohl around her eyes was smudged which made her look more sexy and desirable.

She handed some notes to the band, but when she tried to pay him, he shook his head. 'I was playing for my supper.'

The lamp was glittering low, the mellow light flickering on her ebony skin. When she turned away, he saw her perfect profile. She was like Eve, the mother of all women and he wanted her more than anything he had ever experienced. His desire was like an open flame, white hot from an inexhaustible font of lust. Instinctively he knew that they would both be burned by it.

'Hey, Dan,' her soft voice whispered, sending shivers up and down his skin. 'You got a place to stay, Dan?'

'No.'

'Now you have.'

'Yes.'

Her short staccato sentence was offset by her expressive eyes. So many promises in those burning eyes under trembling eyelids.

'I have to move around a lot,' he said. 'But I'll always come home, like a bee to the hive, and I'll never let you down, not all the time you want me.'

'You're a smooth-tongued bastard. Your words are like your music. They sort of get deep inside to those vulnerable areas. I guess I really can't help myself. So . . . okay,' she said softly.

Miriam was a very straightforward lady, Dan discovered. He was given a shelf in the bathroom, hanging space in the wardrobe and the righthand side of the bed. His salary as a flautist was agreed upon there and then, and his duties were outlined to him. It included being the club's bouncer when necessary. She wanted him to work fulltime, but he explained that he had another commitment.

He took a shower and returned to find Miriam lying naked on the bed, smoking a cigarette.

'I didn't know you smoked.' Strangely, it annoyed him. None of my damn business, he told himself.

'It's a joint – improves sex.'

'You reckon I'm going to need some help?'

'Who knows?' She exploded into a girlish giggle. She was full of surprises tonight.

Dan felt nervous, for he was tossed headlong into a world he hardly knew. Screwing Jeanetta plus a few one-night stands were his total sexual experience. The scary thought came that he was on trial. He so desperately wanted to love her, not just for tonight but for years. He had the strangest sense that he would love her even when she was too old for him.

'How old are you?' he asked.

'Don't ask.'

'Forty-six?'

'Add a couple.'

And he was twenty-one. The reality of it was like a bucket of cold water. Twenty-seven years! When he was thirty, she'd be close on sixty, or forty to seventy. It was getting worse. *I'll live for the present. She's lovely and truly fuckable. Perhaps when she's old the relationship will change into something more enduring, like friendship.* Right now he was supposed to be showing her what he was made of.

'I wish I could fuck you with my flute,' he whispered nervously.

'You did. All night long. Come! Lie next to me. I'm so tired and I've been hankering for a big shoulder to lie on for oh so long.'

She was trying to reassure him, sensing his shyness. Dan felt tormented by conflicting emotions. She was too beautiful to be defiled by his monumental member which was embarrassing him despite the towel wrapped tightly around his waist. At the same time, he'd better perform.

Clumsily, he climbed over her and suddenly it was all right. He gave himself up to expressing his feelings and relieving his lust. Was it minutes later or hours later when he heard her groaning?

'Dan . . . Dan . . . Oh,' she groaned. 'Please . . . come . . . oh . . . come all over me . . . please . . .' Her voice tailed off in a groan.

All over her? That was a new idea. Was she kinky? Intent on satisfying every whim of his new love, Daniel wrenched himself out of that lovely home. There was no time for regrets or hesitation, he was poised on the very tip of explosion. Grabbing his swollen, throbbing penis firmly, he showered her breasts and stomach with his sperm. This took superhuman strength and willpower as he manoeuvred himself down the bed with the power of his knees and finally toppled off the end of it, mission completed and his own orgasm totally ruined.

A split-second later Miriam sat up and peered over the edge of the bed, her eyes glittering with annoyance. 'What the hell did you pull out for? What are you doing on the floor?'

He replied sulkily: 'I fell off the bed performing ridiculous feats at your weird command.'

'What!' she shrieked. 'I didn't command you to pull out and fall off the bed.'

'You said – I quote: "Come all over me."'

'A figure of speech.' She giggled softly.

'I was trying to please you,' he said sulkily.

'My God!' The giggles came loud and furious, until her body was caught in paroxysm of mirth. She shook so much she fell off the other side of the bed, choking as she tried to stop laughing. 'I'm impressed to see what lengths you're prepared to go to. D'you realise you hopped down the bed like a kangaroo, waving your dripping willie around?'

'I misunderstood you,' he said sulkily. 'Why don't you say what you mean?'

She burst into a fresh fit of giggles, choked, caught her breath and clutched her ribs. 'You looked ... shit ... you looked so ridiculous and I couldn't imagine ... Where're you going? Come back here.'

'Outside, until you pull yourself together.'

'Oh, Mister Sulky,' she said smiling and holding up her hand. He pulled her to her feet and eventually pulled her into his arms. She felt good standing naked against him.

'You're very young,' she said. 'Don't try too hard to please me. I'll fix you a drink. Would you like that?'

'No, I'd like some tea.'

'Tea it is.'

Later, when she was lying on his shoulder, Dan allowed himself a feeble laugh. 'You should remember that I'll always take you at your word,' he said.

'How sombre. I'm scared.'

'Why?'

'Because you mean much more to me than a one-night stand. I think I love you. I want you to stay here with me. You will, won't you? I can help you a lot.' She propped herself up on one elbow and ran her hand over his chest, her black eyes like dark pools glittering in moonlight. 'How beautiful you are,' she murmured. 'So young. Look at your skin, all dewy soft and unblemished. You're just a baby. I feel so guilty. I have a son your age. I feel as if I'm offending against nature.'

'Please, don't be negative. Age doesn't count, not to us. You are a sexy, beautiful woman and you fascinate me, even if you are damn rude. Let's have an understanding, Miriam. We're together on a bus for part of our journey through life. We'll stay together while it suits us, but when one of us wants to part, it will be as easy as stepping off a bus. Okay?'

She looked thoughtful and slightly sad. 'Okay, Dan. You're so young, but I must warn you, life has a habit of snaring you in your own traps.' She fell asleep on his shoulder, but Dan lay awake watching her. This night was too precious to waste in sleep.

Chapter 26

At the Cronjés' homestead Sunday morning brunch was traditionally held on the terrace overlooking the lake where several new acquisitions floated serenely around the island.

Eleanor was crunching her toast rather loudly, Tony thought fastidiously. He shot a couple of meaningful glances her way, but she was absorbed in the Sunday papers. She was wearing pale pink shorts and a T-shirt. Her ash–blonde hair fell loose over her white shoulders, but the baby-doll image was spoiled by the taut lines around her mouth, and her scraggy neck, Tony thought, watching her critically. He could see that she had taken care with her appearance from the gold earrings, eyelashes thick with mascara, rouge on her cheeks and bright pink lipstick. Right now her eyes were wide with startled amusement, for she had just read the headline of the business page.

'*South Africa's newest tycoon*, that's how they describe you. My God! They say you're destined to become one of the country's great newspapermen. You've increased the circulation by hundreds of thousands, taken the company from a loss to a profit situation, and uncovered some of the Government's best-kept secrets. Heavens, Tony. The truth is, you really are a genius – but only at pulling the wool over readers' eyes. I'm so proud of you.'

She sneered at him. There was no other word to describe that lop-sided, spiteful leer. She had spoiled the news entirely. A surge of dislike brought goose-pimples to his skin.

'I would have done it anyway, without the government's

help,' he said, wishing he'd never told her about Dr Cloete.

'Do you really think so? We have massive circulation support from practically every government department. You know as well as I do, that's the real reason for our increased readers, not your startling headlines, which were handed over on a plate. I really can't agree with you, Tony dear, but anyway, well done,' she flung at him as an afterthought.

As she bent forward over the table to fill his glass, her T-shirt fell forward revealing her breasts. Once this would have turned him on and she knew this. Tony turned his attention to the eggs their butler was placing in front of him. He was hungry. He'd already jogged around the farm, returning for a swim in the lake, followed by a Jacuzzi, finishing in time for a late breakfast. He felt good. Looking up, he saw her spiteful amusement. 'Okay, so I might have taken a little longer,' he admitted, 'but I'd have made it eventually.'

'Without the payoff from the insurance company, and the advertising from the various quasi-government institutions, and the leads they give you?'

He scowled at her, grabbed the newspaper and engrossed himself in the headlines: muggings, murders, rapes, necklacing. Nowadays a political murder was lucky to get a paragraph on page seven. People were bored with reading the same old thing day after day. Unrest had reached such a pitch that the government had to augment the police force with the army.

Flinging the paper aside, he turned his attention to his calculator, which nowadays was in permanent use, jotting up his debts, his hopes, and his fears of looming bankruptcy. In the packaging factory he was still facing mounting debt, strikes and probable disaster. The plastics factory was making heavy losses, too, and he'd laid off some of the staff. The drought had ruined the sugar and tomato crop and he was still paying off his father's political debts.

Eleanor minced across the tiles, pursing her lips, flicking her hair over her shoulder, her fingers fingering her neck, which showed she felt particularly nervous. She sat on the arm of his chair and smiled down coquettishly, but he could see that she did not feel like smiling. Her tongue flicked over her dry lips and her eyes were haggard as she ran her fingers round the back of his neck. 'What do you say to a little fuck?' She giggled. 'I know the answer to that one.'

'Hello, little fuck,' he said, trying to enter into her absurdly childish banter. He ran his slender hands through his hair.

As Eleanor crossed her legs, Tony tried not to look at her skinny crotch with the pale blonde hairs. Screwing Eleanor had become a boring duty, but she was so neurotic and he was scared to dump her. She might go to pieces and start blabbing her mouth off.

She said, 'It's been a long time, Tony. I've been longing for you. How about it?'

These words, which had once set every nerve vibrating long and loud to a thrilling note of lust, now made him cringe. 'I have to make a plan. So much isn't working for us. All this worry seems to have squashed my libido.'

His attention zoomed back to his anxieties. If only it would rain. The level of the river had fallen low and the corporation which supplied their electricity and controlled the dam up-river was shedding water into the river and charging farmers millions of rands to use it. You'd think it was their precious piss, not rain that fell from the sky. They'd been quick to let the public know how they were saving the wild life in the river, but who was paying for this generosity. Not them. They'd charge the bloody hippos if they thought they could squeeze anything out of them.

He heard a long sniff, followed by a sob, and looked up sharply, his face wreathed with annoyance and shock. Two big tears were rolling down Eleanor's cheeks, her mascara was smudged and the rouge was being washed away.

'Eleanor, we're in shit-street. Give me some peace to work this lot out. God knows there's enough medical bills you've run up.'

Eleanor wailed the same old cliché he'd heard a hundred times lately: 'You don't love me any more.' This time a new dimension crept in. 'I'm being punished. Marius's death has ruined our love. Sometimes I think I should confess everything and get it over with.'

At once he was on his feet, hand raised, longing to smash her to the ground. Then he forced a smile, knowing that she could destroy him. 'I've told you before, we're in it together.'

Nevertheless, he feared her. She was just the type to cut off her nose to spite her face. He'd have to do something about her. But what?

'I do love you,' he lied, 'but I'm worried, so I can't think about sex.'

'Be more creative. If you had any sense, you'd turn this place into a game park. It's ridiculous to pay so much for water. The rain never comes. You are a fool, Tony. This homestead would be ideal as a hotel. Turn the bloody plantations into a rich, private game farm and stock the place with game. We share a fence with the Kruger National Park, so some of the big cats might even crawl under it, particularly if you tempt them. Get a hunting concession. There's nothing the rich like more than killing everything they see. If you rope in old Mrs du Toit's place and the de Vries's, you'll have masses of space. As a matter of fact, the de Vries's farm is more suitable than ours. It's higher, giving lovely views over our plantations. You could put viewing sites up there. I begged Marius to do this for years.'

'Why didn't you tell me?'

'You never think long term.'

'What do you mean?' His indignation soared.

'How long do you think white rule will last? When the whites fall, so will our newspaper. Our massive circulation will crash even faster than you built it up.' She laughed spitefully. 'You have five years at the outside. Then those people will be nothing. What's more, if I don't get screwed, I'll have a nervous breakdown.'

He was left shivering and shaking with rage. Blatant blackmail. He'd have to lull her into a false sense of security until he made a plan.

*

The bitch was right, he thought as he serviced her, rising and falling out of habit, while his mind pondered on his problems. Even if he made a fortune, it was little better than Monopoly money. You couldn't get it out of the country. Exchange control let each emigrant take a laughable thirteen thousand pounds. Yet he knew plenty of businessmen stashing it away in Swiss banks and businesses owned by nominees. He must make a plan.

'Harder, faster,' she was panting.

Yes, she was right. The government's help was transitory. He must milk them for all they were worth, while they lasted. Somehow he had to float a company on the London Stock Exchange, and his newspaper wouldn't do.

Oh hell, he'd shrunk so much it was absurd to keep trying. He rolled off her.

Eleanor pushed her hair out of her eyes, and stared up at him. 'Are we fucking or are we fucking?'

'I don't know what to do,' he said, listing his problems. It was a relief to let it all out.

It was Eleanor who saved him at lunch. Cloete arrived, wearing a strangely old-fashioned suit with knickerbocker trousers and a carnation in his buttonhole, plus a huge bunch of them for Eleanor. She had wiped off her make-up and chosen a sombre black dress for a welcome change. Looking the part of the grief-stricken widow, she outlined to Cloete her husband's hopes and dreams, which she intended to put into practice, and all the while looked austere, remote and unattainable.

If only she knew how sexy she looks now, compared with that ridiculous baby pink outfit, he thought sourly.

'Everything we had was to be used for the benefit of the country,' she cooed to Dr Cloete. 'That was my husband's dream and since he died, I've been trying to carry on his work.'

Dr Cloete watched her cautiously.

'His wish was to turn our plantations into a private game

park, to bring more tourists to South Africa. He was a far-seeing man and he realised that overseas tourists need something more luxurious, allied to hunting. Could we count on the patronage of some of your influential friends?'

'Why naturally, my dear,' he assured her.

'And Marius wanted to do something for our black neighbours, too. He felt he could package their beer far more cheaply than the present arrangement. Of course our factory was geared up for this. We made a big investment and he took a gamble.' She laughed lightly. 'It would be a shame if the packaging plant brought Tony to his knees. His image is so important right now.'

'If you were to give a proper presentation and a competitive quote I think something might be arranged,' Dr Cloete said, giving her an intimate smile, as if they understood each other.

Over coffee, Eleanor disappeared and Cloete seemed more relaxed. 'We have a problem, Tony. All hell has been raised over the Maputo raid. Sanctions tightened, questions asked, demos, as you know. Let's face it, flak all round.

'I have a story here, which you will publish and we shall ban, in the interests of public security, but not before the story is circulated. Our idea is to start a witchhunt to find those responsible for arming South African blacks. Pursue this line of investigation with as much publicity as you can. Tie up the Maputo raid with the latest bomb attack at the white soccer match. The trouble with English liberals is they want to be good, but they want to be safe, too. They feel tainted by the Maputo killings, but they sure as hell don't want their families blown up.

'Go for it, Tony. Here's the statistics of the numbers of Russian-made rifles, sub-machine guns, hand-grenades and explosives picked up at the borders, and estimates of how much is stashed away within our borders. Those liberal sods lie safe in bed at night because our boys are dying out there. That's what I want you to tell them, Tony.'

Chapter 27

It was a minute before the game's end and silence had settled over the field as Dan dribbled the ball towards the goal post. The score was level and his team needed this one badly. The air was so tension-charged it seemed it would explode. He took a deep breath, momentarily steadied his balance and kicked. A split-second later the stadium erupted as six thousand voices roared in unison.

The game was over and Dan was chaired around the field. He lifted his arms in exhilaration, because they'd won, because he'd found a home here amongst the dispossessed, the workers and the unemployed, and because he was loved and respected by Miriam and that was a source of continual wonder to him.

She was waiting by the locker room, jumping up and down with excitement. She flung herself into his arms. 'I'm so proud of you,' she babbled with joy, eyes alight, small teeth glistening as she laughed, head thrown back and her throat pulsating.

Dan held her tightly. To hell with the gossip. He knew what everyone said, that this middle-aged, rich lady was making a fool of herself with a young buck half her age. Furthermore, she had fallen head over heels in love and was lavishing money on him. The truth was, he loved her, too, although with mixed feelings, one of which was anguish. He was aware that she filled so many needs, for the mother he'd never had, a home, a mistress – God knows he lusted over her – and a temporary haven from the storm of life, a bit of peace, sanity and a whole lot of love.

He got a good deal of open censure from the men in the team and those he worked with. They wanted to idolise him, but they couldn't. They didn't approve. His nickname was 'tavern toyboy'. To hell with all of them, one of these days he'd be able to keep her. At Miriam's insistence he was studying at an expensive cramming college and hoping to get his matric by the end of the year. He hated her paying for this, but she kept pointing out how much she had. 'You want to get to the top in politics, don't you? Well, you won't do it without an education, Dan.'

He was more than a little in awe of her, so he usually did what she said. Miriam was a rough, tough survivor who'd built herself up from a singer in a shack, to owning one of the most popular shebeens in Soweto. She had a good sense of humour that could wound and a quick tongue. People either loved her or hated her, he'd discovered.

Under Miriam's encouragement, he was studying days and recruiting nights, and improving his spoken English with expensive lessons which irritated the hell out of him, but she had a point. He'd never get powerful whites to take him seriously if he couldn't speak their language properly.

Saturday was their day. Mornings they went shopping together for the personal things they needed, stocking up the small fridge in the kitchenette in the attic flat where they lived, afternoons she watched him playing soccer and in the evenings he played in the band for a while. Today she seemed to be particularly excited and he wondered what was going on.

'I only scored once,' he said laughing at her. 'Calm down.'

She pushed the keys of her car towards him, but he avoided her hand. 'I'm bushed.'

'Get in then.' She drove badly, which always amazed him. How could she be so clever and yet so dumb – and all at the same time.

'Watch that corner. Jesus!' He whistled. 'That was a narrow shave.'

'You want to drive?'

'I want to live.'

'Oh, you!' She pinched his knee and left her hand lying on his thigh.

'Both hands on the wheel, please.'

'D'you know what day it is?' she said, removing her hand.

'No,' he lied, hoping she hadn't found out.

'Your birthday.'

He groaned. 'How the hell . . . ?'

She laughed. 'You left your ID lying around, so I have a surprise for you.'

'I don't want a surprise. Birthdays mean nothing to me.'

'That's tough because you're twenty-one today.' She began to hum the song happily under her breath.

The surprise was a Kawasaki motorbike, he learned. Reaching home, she led him into the garage, and there at the back where they stored sacks of maize was a gleaming monster. With such a bike, he could flit through traffic jams, give up the hour-long morning queue for transport, whizz out weekends with Miriam clinging at his back and turn life into a total pleasure. His anger at having to turn down such a gift was bitter.

'Miriam, look at me,' he stormed after he'd reduced her to tears. 'When I moved in here I had all my possessions in my backpack. I told you then, when I leave I'll take only what I can carry on my back, so don't waste your hard-earned cash on me. I won't accept this. Send it back.'

'If you're leaving me, get on with it!' she stormed. 'That's all I ever hear, when you leave.' Her tears were splashing on to her polished black shoes.

'I didn't mean it that way.'

'Well, that's the way it sounded. Damn you.' Her eyes mirrored her hurt; she was like a beaten dog, brimful of misery. 'Don't you love me even a little?'

'Don't ask stupid things like that. Just send the bike back.'

'It can stand there till it rusts for all I care. It's yours and if you want to be stuck-up, who cares? Do you love me?'

'I'm here, aren't I? If you wake up and find me on your pillow tomorrow morning, you'll know I love you.'

'Oh, Dan!' Laughter and tears together, that was Miriam's way. 'Take it because I love you. If you don't I'm going to be so hurt.'

It was days before he could bring himself to accept the motorbike; meantime it remained in the garage, but he used to creep down there and stare at it from time to time. All that wasted cash made him feel uneasy. Surely she was piling up retribution with her reckless spending. People around were starving. This bike was worth six cows and he told her so, but she just laughed at him.

'You're such a naive twit,' she said. 'I don't want six cows. Where would we put them?' She made him cross, so at bedtime he took out the motorbike and went roaring off into the night. When he returned, she was sitting inside the front door, hands clasped together, face taut, eyes wide. 'I thought you'd crashed,' she whispered, as her face relaxed in relief.

Each day Miriam fell ever more deeply in love with him. He had no idea of how this poignant affair would end, but often he was filled with a sense of dismay at what had happened to him and Miriam. The truth was, he did love her so desperately, but by day she looked what she was, a woman pushing fifty. Then he told himself to live for the present and stop worrying about the future. It was amazing. Miriam, the Soweto shebeen queen, survivor de-luxe and the toughest person he'd ever known, loved the silly boy that he was.

It was ten o'clock on a hot March night and inside the tavern you could hardly breathe, for it was packed to overflowing. Dan was playing the flute, letting rip, replete and happy, off-guard. There was a sudden crash. The door was flung open and bullets raked the ceiling. Chaos followed, as patrons screamed and flung themselves under the tables, chairs crashing over. Dan froze and glanced towards Miriam. She had closed the trellis bars that surrounded her kiosk. Fat lot of good that would do her, against sub-machine guns, he thought, shouting at her to get down on the floor.

Six armed men, faces masked, threaded their way through the tables, pointing their guns at everyone and everything. It was war by the look of things, but no one was dead yet, so perhaps there was hope.

'Okay, you lot, move outside.' Unbelievably, the leader of the gang was pointing his weapon at him. Why weren't they going for the cash takings? Dan put down his flute slowly, scared to make a hasty movement in case the trigger-happy jerk jumped to the wrong conclusion. The gunman jerked his thumb towards the door. 'Bring your flute and tell that lot to bring their instruments,' he said gesturing towards the band.

Dan was hardly able to hold back a peal of hysterical laughter as he realised they were hi-jacking the band, not robbing the till or shooting the patrons or kidnapping Miriam. He decided to go quietly. Our fame has spread, he whispered as he passed the till. He guessed she was clutching her revolver under the counter, her eyes glittering, mouth drawn back in a taut line. She seemed more angry than scared. He shook his head at her, motioning that she should keep quiet and still.

'Sorry to take your fancy boy, Miriam,' the lead gunman drawled. 'Guess you'll have to get along without him tonight. The boss says you can come along to him if you feel horny. If you want to hear a good band some future night you're always welcome.' He threw back his head and laughed at his own humour. Dan was tempted to go for him while he was off guard, but there were the five others and they were all heavily armed.

What was the point? he asked himself as he was herded into a new Combi. There didn't seem to be any danger. This overcrowded city of Soweto, lawless and uncontrollable, was policed by neighbourhood toughs. Each neighbourhood had their own so-called police, and ran their own kangaroo courts known as the People's Courts, where criminals were tried and punished there and then. What else could they do in this maze of underprivileged, over-crowded misery? All were prey to the gutter philosophy of the survival of the strong. Here a man could be stabbed to death for five cents. For two hundred rands you could hire a gang like this one to cripple your rival by pushing a bicycle spoke through his spine. Murder cost a little more, but not much. The very rich employed their own security gangs and this, no doubt, was Njoli's. Tonight it seemed he only wanted music.

It didn't take long to see where they were headed, right into Njoli's nightclub, which he'd heard of, but never seen. It was huge and glittering, like the ones you saw at the movies. Mike Njoli, ferocious as a grisly bear, met them at the door, his fake grin twinkling with three gold teeth, his fat hands holding a wad of notes which he was dealing out triumphantly, like a card-sharp slapping down aces. Fifty rands each!

'Miriam's been pinching my patrons,' he said in a gruff growl. 'Maybe because of you lot, who knows? We'll see. I hope for your sakes, you're on form tonight. I'm announcing you as a special guest appearance. Now ... you get fifty rands each for a two-hour performance. After that you're free to go, but I'm hoping you'll sign on with me at double your present salary. Okay? Now I've got some important people here tonight, so let's get going.'

They played brilliantly, the adrenaline surging through their veins bringing them to new and so far unattainable heights. Dan wasn't surprised when the rest decided to sign on with Njoli. It wasn't just the cash. They wanted to stay alive.

As he was the only one who refused to sign on, Dan found himself evicted without transport at 3 a.m., facing a five-mile walk home through the world's most dangerous streets. It was a dark night, which was just as well, he reckoned, and he kept to the shadows. Soweto was like the bushveld. Predators roamed at night and seized their prey.

He was not far from home when he picked up a gang of muggers. At first it was more of a feeling than a certainty, a footfall carelessly placed, a stone trickling, then a figure crossed the road ahead of him and as he turned the corner he found himself moving towards three more loitering youths. They were moving in for the kill.

Dan decided to run for it. He bolted, knocked one of them over with a flying tackle and sprinted forward. He reached the corner ahead of them and fell heavily over a trip wire strung across the alley. He had run into their trap.

They flung themselves on to him, beat him up and held him while they kicked him. Dan decided to save his strength until he could work out the odds. Then he was flung headlong through an open doorway. He crouched against the wall, trying to see something.

'Face the wall,' one of them called out. Then a match flared and someone lit a lantern.

'Okay, spread,' they said with pseudo–American accents.

They felt for weapons and took the cash he'd earned and his watch. Miriam had bought it for him and he'd always thought it too flashy, but he had worn it to please her.

'Don't turn round. Take off your jacket and hand it back. Now your trousers and your shoes.'

He turned, trousers in one hand, jacket in the other, and took in the room at a glance. There were six of them, five between him and the door, but he reckoned he'd make it. Not one of them was older than sixteen. He had little doubt they intended to kill him, otherwise they would never have let him see their faces.

All at once, the tallest of them swore. 'Fuck! It's DanTweneni. Quick – give him back his stuff.' He slapped the youngest boy on the ear. 'Why didn't you tell us who you are, man? Your last match was hot stuff. You shouldn't be out so late, Dan. Don't you know it's dangerous? There's bad types around. Real bad!'

'Put your jacket on.' One of them rushed to help him. Another was pushing on his shoes. 'You're not mad at us, are you? Just a joke! Hey, you're our hero, Dan. We made a dumb mistake.' Now they were grinning and clamouring for his autograph.

Dan felt as if he'd gone into shock. His body was overreacting with the tension he'd summoned for his fight. He had to hide his trembling hands. Right now he reckoned he had two chances – to be a hero or a corpse.

'I was just going to tackle you guys,' he said calmly. 'I'm glad I didn't have to. Wouldn't like you to get hurt. You guys shouldn't be doing this,' he said. 'Why don't you come down to the sports club and get in some practice. I train there three afternoons a week. After practice I could give you some tuition. Don't you have some better way to make a buck?'

They parted friends near Miriam's after offering their protection for the walk back. 'Bad neighbourhood, bad types around,' they assured him. 'They'd kill you just for your watch. Pretty nice watch.'

'Have it,' Dan said, handing it over. 'It's a gift for seeing me home safely. It's valuable, so don't sell it for next to nothing.'

'You mean that?'

'Sure. I never liked it. It's too larny for me. See you down the clubhouse.' He'd been intending to start a youth club down at the pitch. Now the time had come and Njoli would be their first patron, he decided, smiling to himself.

Once inside the door, he leaned against the wall and sighed with relief. Those poor dumb kids. They weren't all bad, only desperate and without any hope. They were the true victims of apartheid. They might have been artisans, or artists, or scholars, but their parents had been denied the right to learn a trade or live together with their wives and children, and these kids were the result, the debris of a crumbling system, and there were millions of them. The power edifice was collapsing, whites were giving in slowly and grudgingly, but these kids would never understand what was happening. They only knew that going to school was like giving in to the system, so they stayed away, and qualified in hate and violence. The nation's new workforce was emerging, unemployed and unemployable, to sabotage the future. That was the real crime whites would have to answer for, Dan decided there and then, withholding knowledge, for knowledge belonged to the world.

Miriam was asleep. He bent over her and caught the odour of dagga and booze. Her cheeks were salty with dried tears he found when he kissed her. She opened her eyes and reached up to catch hold of him, but not fast enough.

'No,' he said. 'I'm sleeping on the settee. You know the rules. I don't sleep with junkies or drunks.'

'I'm not drunk and I'm not stoned, you prissy bastard,' she shrieked. 'I didn't know where to start looking for you. I couldn't stand the tension.'

'Just the same, I'm sleeping on the settee. I don't like the smell of you.'

The end of a perfect evening, he thought wearily, trying unsuccessfully to make himself comfortable. He could hear her sobbing quietly on the bed and he was tempted to join her, but he resisted the urge. He'd almost cured her of her drug problem and the drinking. Giving up now might ruin everything. After a while she began to snore, as she always did when she'd smoked pot. She was out for the count, so he reckoned it was safe to creep back into bed without her knowing. At least he'd get a couple of hours decent sleep.

Chapter 28

———◆———

'I assure you,' the voice behind the face pack was murmuring through rigid lips. 'There is no danger involved. I am not a large-scale operator. Who could find me a threat? Little me – with my miserable three taxis. Besides, I am a woman and to tell the truth, Njoli has always fancied me.'

'But you insulted him by choosing a far younger man, so don't count on his support,' Dan said moodily.

It was Monday morning, Miriam's day off, and as usual she was sitting in her bedroom surrounded with basins of scented water, hot towels, lotions and paints – enough to stock a shop, he reckoned. She had just finished painting her toe-nails scarlet and the funny sponge fingers she'd stuck between her toes had splayed them like a gorilla's.

'You're crazy to take on Njoli. He's a powerful and unscrupulous man and that's being kind.'

He scowled at her, but she pulled a face at him and smiled to herself. If there was one fault Miriam had it was her desire to make more and more profits. She would never be anything more than the deprived child she once was. She never had enough – enough money, enough security, enough love. It was tragic.

'You're a millionaire,' he said sulkily.

'Oh, you small-time boy. You'll have to widen your horizons if you want to make your dreams come true. Having a million rands in assets means nothing. I could lose it overnight.'

'You could lose your life. Oh heck.' He sat on the edge of the bed and gazed at her in despair.

For the past six months he had threatened, pleaded and bullied her to give up this business. Miriam always pretended to agree, but the combis continued to do business and she continued to make profits with them.

When she bought a fourth taxi, Dan trembled with fear for her. Traditionally blacks had been deprived of owning any business in a white area, and since most areas were white, it effectively squashed blacks' entry into private enterprise. Trading stores in black townships were as far as they could hope to go, but with white-owned hypermarkets setting up virtually on their doorsteps, bringing down prices with mass buying, it was inevitable that the black trader was undercut and reduced to a small convenience store, functioning mainly after shop hours. Now the government had decided to allow Africans to own and run mini buses, which everyone called black taxis. Businessmen had been swift to grab the opportunity, but the prize was too high, for this was the only chance to get into business and make profits. Savage violence erupted virtually overnight, with rival taxi owners gunning each other down. Daily, pedestrians were strafed by bullets for taking a rival's taxi, or even for queueing at a rival's bus stop. Taxis and drivers were gunned down or set alight, bus drivers murdered, shot at, crippled, necklaced, or simply frightened half to death. Almost every taxi owner employed armed thugs to protect themselves and their property and intimidate the customers and their opposition. The entire business resembled bootleggers in the Chicago of the twenties.

Now Miriam had wandered into this maelstrom of violence, daring anyone to stop her. Dan wondered if he should run the new enterprise to deflect the violence from her. She was an amazing woman, naive and shrewd. She had the strange idea that she was inviolable. She would never accept that her friends and neighbours envied her money, her power, her success, her brains, her guts, her beauty and lately her youthful appearance, despite her years. The truth was, she was surrounded by malice and envy. Dan knew because he listened to the gossip. His own friends tried to warn him off her, criticising him for living with a woman old enough to be his mother. They thought he was after her wealth, but the truth was he loved her and they could never understand the depths of his feelings.

At first he'd tried to distance himself from her wealth, fighting each time a new garment appeared in his cupboard, but lately he'd given up trying to fend off her gifts. When his torn old shirt was replaced with a new pure cotton Italian-made one, he no longer objected. What was the point? He gave in eventually, because she never would. Only his shoes and jeans were his own because she had not succeeded in buying replacements that fitted properly. She'd tried. He smiled as he remembered the jeans she'd bought, with the crotch hanging around his knees. Then there was the powder-blue shirt he'd handed to the first unemployed bystander he saw, but these futile, childish gestures had not stopped Miriam. She took his criticism on the chin and kept doing what she wanted to do, and she wanted to buy him gifts.

Easy to guess what his friends thought when they saw him racing off each morning in his stylish leather jacket on his Kawasaki motorbike to the multi-racial cramming college where he was doing so well. He hadn't told Miriam, but he'd actually taken one of the British girls, with her creamy complexion and long flaxen hair, to lunch. She'd made a pass at him, which was amazing. He smiled to himself.

'What are you thinking?' Miriam had a hostile, suspicious look on her face. Times like this assured him that they had some ESP going between them. Or was it feminine intuition that warned her of competition?

'I was thinking about work,' he lied. Then he burst out laughing. She looked like an initiate in a tribal ceremony, her face a mass of white, her black eyes staring from holes, her hair wrapped in a white towel.

'You're a liar.' She smiled and the paste cracked and shattered. 'Shit!' She went to the bathroom, grabbed a face towel and wiped off the paste. 'I shouldn't have smiled, but you looked so guilty.'

'Why do you do this to yourself?'

'To look young – to look like someone you should be with.'

'But your eyes, your voice, your manner, your authority give your age away. Why bother? There's thousands of pretty young girls around. They don't have what you have.'

'I want you to desire me sexually.'

He stood up, unzipped his flies and moved towards the bed. 'Take a look. If this is what you can do to me with paste all over you, you don't have to worry. Have you any idea how desirable you are to a pimply gangly youth who seems to have fallen into paradise by accident?'

She laughed, took off her gown and sat naked, gazing at him warmly and affectionately while she dried her hair with her towel. He seldom saw her hair looking natural. She hated it. Once a week it was pulled straight at the hairdresser and screwed into a bun and it stayed like that, covered with a bright scarf. How slender she was. He loved the sight of her back, with those straight, brave shoulders sloping to the narrow waist. Her slenderness brought out all his protective instincts.

'I want you all the time,' she said. 'I don't understand myself. All my life, all my men complained that I was frigid. Now look at me. When I look at you I want you.'

He lay on the bed and pushed down his trousers. 'Hop on,' he said.

'No sooner said than done,' she whispered, straddling him.

He closed his eyes and gave himself up to the unbearable pleasure of Miriam's warm cunt and writhing hips.

'Why d'you always close your eyes?' she grumbled, still moving provocatively. 'Is it because I'm old? Or maybe you can't stand the sight of my hair.'

His manhood shrivelled to almost nothing. 'Oh heck. Your negativity really gets at me. One of these days you're going to ruin all that we have going for us.'

This made her angry, he could see her eyes widen with shock and disappointment. 'Maybe you were dreaming of that plump, insipid English girl you took to lunch on my cash.'

Desire crumpled utterly. He tried to sit up but she was heavy. 'Get off,' he said angrily.

'No.' She wriggled fast and furious, trying to recover his ardour.

Dan jerked his body upwards and sideways as if cracking a whip and she toppled sideways on to the bed.

'Oh fuck! I blew it.'

'You sure did. I am so sorry I wasted your hard-earned cash on someone's lunch. I should have realised that I've been bought, lock, stock and barrel, and that taking fellow pupils to lunch is totally forbidden. I should have known that someone as cunning as Miriam would have me tailed at all times. I'm truly sorry.'

'What are you sorry about?' she wailed.

'I'm sorry I'm here. I'm sorry I'm not a little puppy dog, which is clearly what you want and I'm sorry I'm penniless.' He stood up, pulled up his pants and went into the bathroom.

'Oh, Dan, what can I do to undo what I've said?'

'Nothing. Forget it. It's not important,' he called over his shoulder as he went downstairs.

But it was. He brooded all evening as he practised his sombre improvisations. How the hell had he got into this mess? Where he came from the men earned the cash and the women did as they were told. This strange reversal of roles was whittling away at his manhood. He'd land up a eunuch if he sank much lower. He was losing his pride and it all stemmed from accepting that damned motorbike for his birthday. After that it seemed paltry to moan about the new shirts, underpants, socks, watch, calculator, briefcase and all the other paraphernalia that kept appearing as if by accident in his cupboard. Yes, the motorbike had been the thin end of the wedge that had landed him in her debt. Shit!

After midnight, when he thought Miriam was asleep, Dan went upstairs and began to pack his backpack. What could he honestly take? All his clothes had been flung out. Was he entitled to replace them with this fancy imported stuff? He spent a long time trying to work out the morality of the situation. At the same time, he couldn't go naked. He rolled up what was left of his T-shirts. He didn't have to worry about the sunglasses and other gifts. They weren't his. They weren't even gifts. They were chains of bondage. Funny he hadn't recognised that in the first place.

As usual, he rolled his gear with precision so that it would be uncreased, stowing everything into its accustomed place, the heavy stuff at the bottom. He looked up into Miriam's eyes. She was sitting on the bed watching him, her face a mask of tragedy. Suddenly she looked her age. He tried not to look at her, not wanting to be overcome with compassion.

'I thought you loved me.'

'I do love you, but I don't want to be a *toyboy* any longer.'

'Don't say that! You never were. Please don't go,' she said. 'Please! Surely you know how much I love you?' Suddenly she was clawing, begging, wrapping her arms around his neck and then throwing his gear out of the backpack all over the room.

He sighed and began again. 'Stand clear,' he said. 'I don't want to hurt you.' At that moment they were strangers facing each other across an impenetrable gulf.

'If you leave me how will you get an education?'

'Who cares. What will be, will be. I was here because I love you. You can't buy people, Miriam.'

'If you love me, stay.' Her face was twisted with anguish.

'No, the price is too high. I can't lose my self-respect, even though I love you.'

'I'll do anything. Give this place to my son, live in a shack on your money. How's that? Is that what you want?'

He shook his head and she burst into tears. Dan wished she'd stayed asleep. He was tired of hurting her.

'All women get jealous,' she said, in a small tired voice. 'How come I'm not allowed to get jealous? Does my age and wealth prevent me from feeling like other women feel?'

'You're obsessed with age. I don't want to be spied on. I don't want your chains on me. You told me I earned my cash honestly playing the flute, so how come it's your cash when I take someone to lunch? How come you have me followed? I don't want to feel guilty if I ask someone to lunch and I don't want to put up with your endless negativity. If you don't like your age that's tough. Don't throw that burden on me.'

'Age never bothered me until I met you. And I didn't have you followed. We had a lunch appointment . . . remember? I was seeing my lawyer and I said I'd drop in. I couldn't resist following you.'

'Goddammit,' he whispered as he remembered. His guilt was now absolute. He couldn't live with it.

He walked out, shrugging into his windbreaker, his backpack slung over one shoulder. Half an hour later he remembered that he still had her front-door key, plus the keys to the motorbike and the upstairs apartment, so he trudged back.

He found Miriam unconscious on the bed. She was breathing heavily and there was a strong smell of vomit, for she had brought up some of the pills she'd swallowed. He caught hold of her arms and shook her, but her head fell back like a limp rag doll.

He swore under his breath as he picked her up and rammed his finger down her throat. Then he held her head over the bath until she threw up. He rushed into the kitchen and poured a glass of salt water. She choked and groaned as he forced some of it down her throat. Soon she began to vomit in earnest and he knew she'd be all right. An hour later, after walking her up and down the bedroom floor, he changed the sheets and tucked her in.

She sat up looking childlike and very sick. 'I'm sorry for this trouble,' she whispered. 'I didn't realise you'd come back. I just couldn't face losing you through my own stupidity.'

'I'm sorry. If I'm honest I'll admit that I resent your wealth and power. You pay for everything and I feel so damned inadequate. I'm just a bum, bumming off you.'

'Doesn't it help that you're your father's son? Or that you've recruited half of Soweto, or that you're the best striker in the Transvaal, or that your music packs my tavern?'

'It's not the music, I assure you. It's the soccer.'

'If I paid you what you're worth you'd be independent. You could pay off the bike yourself. Would that make you feel better?'

'Much better, as long as it's reasonable.'

'Will you stay?'

'Yes. I hated leaving.'

'Dan, I love you.'

'That goes without saying,' he said.

Something was wrong. But what? A nagging anxiety had been gnawing at Dan all morning, for no good reason that he could think of. His world was as near perfect as it was ever likely to be. He had just received his matric results, five As. Plus an assurance that he was accepted by Wits University, to start in January next year. He was scoring in his job, too. The recruitment drive was roaring ahead, although he guessed that his success had more to do with his soccer fame, than any political affiliations of his new members. Dan had everything in the world to be positive about, so why the strange sense of gloom? he wondered as he shook hands with the head master and his teacher and left the college.

He loitered in the car park, enjoying the view for the last time. It was late spring and the grass was turning green, for the first rains had fallen early this year. The trees were a mass of blossoms and Namaqualand Daisies bloomed over every grassy verge. I'm a country boy at heart, he thought. One day I'll make myself a garden like this one, perhaps in Mozambique with Miriam.

Adjusting the strap of his helmet, he mounted his bike and set off at a roar. The moment he parked his bike by the pavement outside the tavern he knew there was something wrong. The door lay open, the neighbours hurried inside and slammed their doors, some kids loitering eyed him triumphantly. Running inside, Dan shouted for Cele, their head waiter. Racing through the ground floor, he found him sitting on his bed, his head in his hands, crying as he rocked backwards and forwards.

'Where's everyone? Where's Miriam?'

There was no reply.

'For God's sake!' He shook the old man. 'Where is she?'

'They took her away,' he mumbled. Dan could smell the booze now. Goddammit, he was drunk.

'Who . . .? *Who* took her away? Damn you!' He caught hold of the old man and shook him violently, flinging him back on the bed. 'Who took her?'

'Njoli's men. They dragged her down to the People's Court. She's to be tried for crimes against the people – overcharging, cheating, short measures, a list as long as your arm . . . lies . . . all lies.'

'Where are they holding the court?'

'The clubhouse by the soccer field.'

Dan roared off, skidding in the mud and cursing at the crowds, for everyone seemed to be traipsing to the soccer field.

'Let me be in time. God let me be in time,' he prayed.

While he concentrated on speed, he was trying to make a plan. If he could get to Njoli in time he could offer a bribe . . . give him the taxis. If only he'd been tougher with Miriam. He should have forced her to sell out long ago. Would it help to plead her case? If he couldn't bribe Njoli in time the best plan would be a counter charge, to bring the taxi war into the open.

At that moment he skidded on to the field and roared across the grass to the edge of the crowd. He could see Njoli and his thugs gathered on the stoep of the clubhouse. There was no sign of Miriam, but there were hundreds of people milling around. Dumping his bike, he began pushing his way towards the so-called tribunal. Obsessed with his fears, he punched and clubbed his way through the throng.

'Miriam . . .! Hang on . . . I'm coming!' His voice, hoarse and desperate, rose above the clamour.

Heads turned. People laughed. A man flung him to the

ground, but he bounded back and fought past him. The shouting was louder now. People were clapping and cheering. Then came a long, high-pitched scream. 'No . . .!' drowned by the women's keening.

His fear gave him strength as he punched his way through an army of onlookers. 'They're going to necklace her,' someone shouted. The cry was taken up all round: 'Necklace, necklace, necklace!' A macabre cry, shouted in unison.

The women took up the chant in their shrill, piercing voices: 'Necklace her, necklace her!' The young girls hid their faces and yelped in horror and excitement. He could hear a shrill, high-pitched scream of agony from somewhere ahead.

There was a sudden lunge from the crowd, a tensing of excitement, and Dan was forced forward, his arms pinned by the crush, unable to fight, compelled to stagger with them. There was a whoosh. A roar. An inhuman scream. Dan kept pushing against the soft clammy human wall that engulfed him. He could hear himself screaming. A smell of burning rubber gave him desperate strength. Black smoke was rising above them. Now he could hear strange, inhuman noises and smell burning flesh. His arms came free, and for a moment he seemed to be swimming in a human tide. Then he won through to the front and bounded out, arms outstretched, propelled towards the flames.

Too late! He collapsed on the ground, cradling the charred remains, crying bitterly. Later would come time for vengeance, he knew, but now he could only grieve. All that he loved was destroyed.

The crowd was moving off, the platform emptying. Njoli's thugs shouldered their guns and left. The spectators, heads hanging, sauntered off, and Dan was left alone.

Chapter 29

———◆———

Sergeant Andy Huntley was just a bit mad. It was something to do with his Viking ancestry, he'd boasted to them often enough. 'The hot blood of warriors runs in my veins,' he was fond of saying. 'There's nothing I like more than a good old bush scrap.'

That might have been the reason why he had volunteered to temporarily join another stick and head up a party of bushman trackers on the trail of Swapo insurgents. The sergeant of this squad was down with malaria.

Or was it perhaps his curiosity, Pieter wondered? Andy had been longing for a chance to get inside Angola and lately their orders had changed. If the terrorists fled back across the line, they were permitted to go in after them.

Or maybe it was this growing conviction that he had to set the world right. They all suffered from it to a greater or lesser extent. To offset the unbearable trauma which had to be borne, the loneliness and the years of being set apart from normal society, they were bombarded with constant pep talks about the sacrifices they were making, the debt society owed them, and the extraordinary role they had assumed as the nation's sentinels. Lately, they were all playing host to embryonic megalomania.

Last week they'd come across a family of Ovambos who'd been carved up horribly by Swapo. It was the sequence of events, whispered by a dying woman into Andy's ear, that had switched on his wrath. First the terrorists had butchered the men and children and forced their women to watch. Then the women had been forced to cook, clean and service the men over the next ten days, yet before leaving the soldiers had mutilated them and left them to bleed to death, as most of them already had. It had been a shock to come across this horrible drama on a routine recé inspection of border villages.

Their Captain had tried to explain Swapo's actions to his sickened battalion while they stood swiping at flies, their handkerchiefs over their mouths and noses.

'The word "terrorist" implies terror,' he had said. 'Swapo must inspire terror in the locals. If they don't do this, the locals will not feed them, or help them, and they might even betray them to us. Traditionally, primitive people serve and support the masters they fear the most. That is their nature. So Swapo make sure they fear them more than they fear us. Got it? They either fear you, or they laugh at you.'

'Being an Ovambo is the worst,' Andy had muttered when they reached base. 'Either we recruit them, or Swapo recruit them. Or else they get caught in the crossfire. Whichever side they choose, they can't win and they can't stay neutral either.'

Two nights before, a party of Swapo had crossed the border into Namibia and murdered a German sheep farmer and his entire family. The previous day, a border guard on horseback had been blown to bits by a mine members of this same group had laid during the night. The horse and the corporal were killed, but the foetus of a young foal had died slowly under Andy's agonised eyes. Had Andy gone off on a personal vendetta?

It was stuffy and unbearably hot in the tent. Pieter was stretched on his bunk trying to concentrate on a book, but he couldn't get into the story. He was wearing an old T-shirt and khaki shorts. His beard and hair were long and curly. His chest and shoulders were covered with a thick black fuzz and he was burnt almost black by the sun. Finally he threw down the book in exasperation and sat up, wiping the sweat out of his eyes.

He couldn't seem to get any satisfaction out of being

off-duty. A nagging worry about Andy kept gnawing away at his mind. He fumbled for a coke and went outside, where it was much hotter, but not so unbearably stuffy. Twenty minutes later he was summoned to the captain.

'I'm afraid it's bad news, sergeant,' the captain said.

Pieter's stomach reacted with painful twinges. He could hardly control the surge of tension that raced through his body, but he showed no reaction as he stood to attention, his stern green eyes fixed on a point immediately above the captain's head.

'Our recé party out searching for the Swapo insurgents were surprised and shot. Two were taken prisoner. One of them was Huntley. The other one was Lieutenant Smith. I'm sorry, sergeant. You'll have to act fast, but we can't hold out any great hopes. Naturally we're sending a squad after them, but you know as well as I do how hard it is to find their camps. You're going ahead with Koos, pick three more scouts and a bushman tracker to help you find the trail. The squad will be right behind you, so keep close communications at all times. Stop at nothing, sergeant. Use any methods to find where they are – and make it fast. You get me? Both these men are in Spec' Services and they'll try to extract information. They might even fly them north, so this is an emergency. Good luck.'

Pieter stood sweating with heat and tension on the banks of the Luiana river, fifty kilometres north of Catehu, inside the Angolan border. The bush was sending him too many conflicting signals, so he paused, sniffing the air, listening, watching, keeping one eye on the bushman tracker and trying to sort out the various sounds. His senses were screaming 'danger ahead', and he reckoned it was about four hundred metres to the north of them. Across the river, the bushman was bent double as he ran, crouched over, from one track to the next. There was a village nearby and consequently, Pieter reckoned, their tracker was close to useless.

It was three p.m. and Andy had been captured at dawn. Nine

hours of hell – it didn't bear thinking about. Every second seemed to last an hour to Pieter as he tried to concentrate on the job and keep his fears for Andy's present state out of his mind.

He paused as he heard the sudden shrill scream of a monkey ahead. Since the last identifiable tracks of the terrorist group, they had been moving forward along the side of a dry river bed, keeping close to the tall buffalo grass which concealed them from the north but not the south side of the river. Half an hour ago, the bushman had picked up many footprints, probably from a nearby village, although one was not marked on Pieter's map. None of the maps were much good once you crossed over into Angola. They were wearing camouflage overalls, their faces plastered in 'cam-cream', leafy sticks in their caps, with mud all over them to disguise their scent. The bush was mainly denuded of wild life, but occasionally they disturbed a flock of red-headed quealas, or a family of egrets, who took off with loud cries of protest. As they progressed, the bush was silenced as the cicadas paused, pinpointing their position, and this worried Pieter more than anything else.

Now his skin was prickling with danger signals. It was some sort of intuitive sixth sense he'd picked up from living in the bush. He motioned to Koos to hide and waved the bushman back into the thicket. Breathless with tension, his mouth dry, eyes and ears straining, he backed into the grass and watched the riverbed. For five minutes they waited. Then an impala broke cover, trotted down the sandy plain and moved into a thicket. It stood there motionless, waiting. Koos wanted to move on, but the bushman knew better. Something was tracking the impala. Pieter sank lower into the bulrushes.

All at once, his eyes caught a movement behind some palms. Then he saw a tall, ragged man, with coal-black skin and watchful almond-shaped black eyes move cautiously towards them, keeping in the shade. When he was only a hundred metres away, he stood up, aiming his rifle at the thicket to their right. He was naked from the waist up, wearing only khaki shorts, but over his shoulder was the unmistakable grey line where his knapsack of landmines had been hanging for days.

Swapo!

Pieter felt his skin crawling with fear and anger. Shivers went up and down his back. How many were there? He could only see that one. If he captured him, would he talk? Pieter knew the answer to his question. He'd had many dealings with Swapo prisoners by now. They never talked.

With a sudden sharp movement, the terrorist swung his rifle to the right and pulled the trigger. There was a sharp report and simultaneously a thrashing sound from the bush. The impala buck burst from cover and raced off, only to collapse on its knees, fifty metres away.

The terrorist gave a long, high-pitched whistle and then moved off in long strides, leaving the buck thrashing on the ground. He was a good shot, Pieter acknowledged grudgingly.

Shortly afterwards, they heard excited voices shouting and singing in the distance. Then a long file of villagers appeared, brandishing their knives and spears.

They were so thin they seemed little more than bones held together by their skin. Tall stick insects with burning eyes and happy smiles. The women's breasts hung like empty sacks, their skin deeply wrinkled by the sun. The pot-bellied children were whooping with delight, brandishing imaginary rifles and reshooting the buck. Clearly they were in league with Swapo insurgents, sheltering and feeding them; in return the terrorist had shot them a buck.

It took a long time for the beast to be skinned, dismembered and packed into bundles. At sunset the villagers left in a long file, their precious burdens carried on the women's heads. Jackals appeared from the long grass where they had been hiding and squabbled over the entrails and skin, but Pieter and his stick remained in hiding. A lonely vulture arrived and sat in a tall tree, flapping its wings and swooping down impatiently, but there was nothing left.

At last Pieter reckoned it was safe to radio headquarters for instructions. The orders he received were simple: force the villagers to reveal the precise location of Swapo's headquarters and radio back fast so we can send in a fighting squad.

The village was small, fifteen huts around the kraal, and several men were hanging about the yard, presumably unemployed. What a miserable existence, Pieter thought. The mealies had almost died from the drought, a few cassava grew in clumps, but their scraggy goats had kept alive, and presumably they plus the cassava kept the village going.

Right now the villagers were laughing and singing, clapping their hands with glee as the offal sizzled over burning wood. The buck was slowly turning on a spit. It would be ready around three a.m. Pieter reckoned . . . and most probably that was when Swapo would return to join the feast.

When it was dark, Pieter and Koos moved in on the solitary youth guarding the spit, killing him. They dragged the men from their huts and pushed them into a long line in front of the spit where they sat on their haunches, heads on their knees while their hands were bound behind their backs. There were seven altogether.

The wailing women were pushed into the chief's hut and threatened with instant death if they didn't keep quiet. They were poor, undernourished, passive people who put up little resistance.

There was no time to be lost. Pieter went up to the first man in the line. He was their chief and he was old and white-haired. 'Tell us where Swapo have their headquarters? We must know now.'

'If I tell you,' the old man said, looking up fearfully, 'they will butcher all of us.'

'Tell us and we'll protect you.'

The chief laughed softly. 'You are strangers here and you cannot protect us. Why do you lie?'

'I shall count to ten,' Pieter said, putting his revolver against the old man's head. 'If you do not tell me I shall pull the trigger on the count of ten.'

On the count of ten he paused momentarily. The old man

looked up and smiled triumphantly and Pieter shot him at that moment. A wail rose from the Chief's hut as the women mourned. Now he had to work fast, for Swapo might have heard the shot. They could even be approaching now.

He moved to the next man in the line and shot him at the count of ten. He saw a youngster shaking visibly and pushed him to the end of the line. Then the third villager was shot.

Pieter felt shocked with horror. A sense of unreality took hold of him as he pulled the trigger again and again and each man fell forward like beasts in an abattoir.

Six men were lying in pools of blood. The last one left alive was still shaking. He looked about seventeen. A sensitive, effeminate boy wearing beaded necklaces, bracelets and anklets. Pieter had deliberately pushed him to the end so that he could talk without facing the contempt of his kin. He looked up like a trembling dog, his huge eyes weeping for his life and his dead comrades.

'You're next. Then I shoot the children,' Pieter told him, whlch was a lie. They were not allowed to wage war on women or children, but how could he know that?

He broke down and told them where Swapo's base camp was and almost everything else they wanted to know. 'They are not of our tribe,' he said repeatedly, as if to condone his weakness. 'They are strangers from Namibia. They take our food and boss us around.' Pieter was not listening. He was calling head-quarters on the radio. 'Ten miles northwest in a ruined farmhouse, formerly the Moreira's cotton plantation,' he said. 'The farm house is derelict, but about thirty Swapo are holed up there living and working in the underground cellars. The whole place is well guarded.'

It was exactly midnight when the helicopters dropped a squad of fifty commandos in the sheltering reeds of the dry river, five hundred metres from Swapo's base.

From a distance, the old homestead shone white in the moonlight, but from closer they could see that the place was half ruined.

'While you attack from the north, we'll enter and leave from the south,' Pieter briefed the commando chief. 'Draw their fire, but give us five minutes to get clear before you destroy the target. I'll send up a flare if and when we get clear.'

Pieter was praying as he scrambled through the overgrown shrubbery. 'Just let him be alive. Don't let him be mutilated. Please God we're in time.' As all hell broke loose up front, Pieter, Koos and his two scouts entered the house through the broken back door. The old kitchen was no longer used, for there was a large hole in the roof where the moon shone through, and the floor was jagged and broken. By now the entire house was reverberating with shots and grenades. A fire had started in a front room and it lit the passage with a red glow. Pieter swore loudly as the fire flared to the top storey. They would have to be quick or the men would be burned alive.

Swapo forces were running around like chicken when a fox gets in. They were leaping out of windows and rushing through the grounds to safety. The place was surrounded, so they wouldn't get far, Pieter reckoned. About ten of them had barricaded themselves into two front rooms and were trying to defend their base. Regardless of their own safety, the squad raced through the empty ground-floor rooms, looking for a way down to the cellars. Upstairs was only a ruin, but they checked out there, too, picking their way through fallen rafters.

Downstairs by the front door a terrorist was letting rip with a machine gun. Pieter crept towards him, silent as a cat, and grabbed the man round the neck, throttling him until he was half-unconscious. He dragged him to the kitchen, waving to the boys to keep guard. As the Swapo regained his senses, his eyes rolled around searching for a way to escape.

'Where are our men?' Pieter growled. 'Where's the entrance to the cellars?'

The terrorist spat at him and a moment later screamed as Pieter's gun butt smashed into his face. He was a mess, but he could still talk. Pieter brought his butt down hard on his arm, shattering it and he screamed again. 'Talk, bastard,' he muttered. A split-second later, Pieter took out his knife and dug the point into the man's neck. 'Talk. Where are they?' He had to hold fast to his rage. He wanted to squeeze the life out of the bastard, gouge out his eyes, hear him scream again and again. He stuck his knife in his ear and twisted it.

'Down there. . .' he gasped, retching with pain.

'Show me.'

Catching him by his hair, keeping him bent almost double, his arm shattered and useless, Pieter propelled his prisoner down the passage to the kitchen. There was a shed outside. The Ovambo pointed and Koos smashed the door open.

'You go ... first ...' The Ovambo was kicked down the stairs.

'I had nothing to do with this,' he muttered, but after flicking his torch around, Pieter killed him just the same.

The lieutenant was hanging from a rope tied around his shoulders. His testicles and penis were pushed into his mouth, his feet were charred and mainly burned away from a fire they'd lit below him, which had gone out. He was dead and he was the luckier of the two, Pieter reckoned staring at Andy, who was on the floor.

'I knew you'd make it,' Andy whispered. 'Now kill me.'

Pieter shouldered Andy and left the others to bring Smit's corpse. 'Set off the flare,' he told his shocked troops. 'Koos, get back to the commandos and tell them to destroy every last man. No prisoners. Tell them what they did.'

Ten minutes later, Andy died in the helicopter that was speeding them towards an army hospital, and Pieter thanked God.

Chapter 30

———◆———

The SADF plane put down at Nelfontein and discharged its solitary passenger. Stepping off, Pieter looked around hoping to see his father, but the airstrip was deserted. He'd sent a cable ahead, but maybe Pa hadn't received it.

The airport manager, Anton Pienaar, was having his tea in the operations hut. He stuck his head out of the window. 'Welcome home, stranger.'

'Oh. Hi, Anton,' Pieter called, striding over the tarmac. 'I was expecting Pa.'

Anton looked embarrassed. 'Your father's working in Nel-spruit,' he said. 'He sometimes comes back weekends.'

A ramshackle Volksie painted with pop art flowers came zooming from the gate. Anton's wife jumped out, followed by their young daughter. They had arranged to go shopping, but his replacement had not arrived.

'Heck, Anton. You still using that old jalopy? And it works?' he asked, fingering the fading flowers.

'Sure. Why not? Listen, Piet, I'd sure appreciate your hanging on here until Andries pitches. Your bus won't come by for another hour at least and I'm not expecting another arrival today.'

'Sure,' Pieter said. 'You go off.'

'Pieter,' Anton hesitated. 'Your father works in Nelspruit. He's getting married again, but of course you know that.' He drove off rapidly.

'I guess he knows he dropped a bombshell,' Pieter said aloud.

Why the hell hadn't Pa let him know? Anger vied with sadness and after a while a tremendous feeling of rejection surged through him until his throat was so swollen he could hardly swallow.

He forced his mind off his problems by thinking about Anton and his wife. Anton's wife was an anaemic blonde, pretty in a weak sort of way, and Anton wasn't much stronger. Their kid was around three, ash-blond hair like his parents, a sweet smile, but not much stamina by the look of things. They came from good settler stock. Anton's great-grandfather had trekked up from Natal and his feats were legendary, but generations of town-living had weakened the strain. There were too many like them. How could folks like that cope with the vermin gathering around their borders? Did they ever have sleepless nights wondering how many terrorists were slipping through? Did they have the slightest idea of what was going on out there? How could an *ouk* [young man] like Anton defend his family. The whites had gone weak with too much easy living. They had to be protected.

Pieter felt an enormous love for the Antons of this world, guys who did their job to the best of their ability, loved their wives, protected their children and worked hard to support decent homes. But out there was another world where lives were only pawns in an undercover struggle for the nation's superb infra-structure, fertile land and immense mineral wealth. He had a responsibility to look after people like Anton and his wife.

The replacement pitched up as the bus rumbled along the road. Piet stowed his backpack in the luggage compartment and stepped inside, but stopped at once, gaping in disgust. Sitting in the centre of the bus was a black man with a white woman. She was bare-shouldered and a black hand lay over her white skin like some obscene growth.

Pieter sat two seats ahead of them fighting for control. The so-called civilised world was a strange place where you couldn't pull a gun at your enemy. You smiled at them instead. Pieter was out of touch with civilised behaviour and he fought to control his mounting fury. Any minute now, he'd throw up at the disgusting conversation he couldn't help overhearing. His skin was prickling. In his mind's eye he relived the horror of that moment in Maputo when he had uncovered the bloody naked corpse of the white woman who had shared the terrorist's bed. But she was vermin, wasn't she? She was not human, just like the silly whore behind him.

His skin prickled as he heard the black call the woman Honey. She was American and she chattered on about the game park she'd been to and the animals she'd seen. Was she breaking the law at this moment, he wondered? She certainly wasn't allowed to have sex with that horny kafir, but Pieter wasn't sure about public necking and right now the two of them were about as close to sex as you could get in public.

Pieter's anger was reaching fever-pitch. It was this type of behaviour that led to innocent white girls being raped or attacked. How dare this foreign woman come here and break their laws. The black bastard had been quick enough to take advantage of her ignorance. He clenched his fists as the black switched on his massive portable radio, blasting his eardrums.

'Hey, turn it down, kafir,' he growled over his shoulder.

'You can't use that word, man. Not any more. Apologise,' he said, scrambling to his feet.

'Turn it down, kafir,' Pieter repeated.

'Fuck you, man.' The black pulled out a knife with a speed that warned Pieter to be quick, but for the moment he sat still gazing straight ahead.

'You gonna apologise?'

'Go suck yourself, kafir,' Pieter murmured with a sweet smile.

The knife lunged towards his neck, but in the same instant Pieter's hands shot up, grabbing the man's wrist and shoulder and swinging him over his head to smash headfirst through the window.

Chaos erupted from screaming passengers. Glass tinkled and tyres squealed as the driver slammed on the brakes. The

American woman began to pummel his back with her fists, yelling insults, so Pieter rammed the black out further, ignoring his screams.

The black driver came along, holding his hands up to quiet the noise. 'We don't want no more trouble here. What exactly is the problem?'

'He pulled a knife on me,' Pieter said, pointing at the knife with his foot.

'You bastard. You deliberately provoked him. I've heard of people like you,' the American woman screeched.

'Perhaps you've heard about our laws,' Pieter said. 'Keep them if you want to come to our country. You can whore around with blacks at home, but not here.'

She gasped and slapped his face hard. Pieter laughed at her. 'You better see to loverboy,' he said. 'He's about to bleed to death.'

The passengers lifted him back on to the floor of the bus and they drove on, drawing up in front of the police station. The driver went in to make a statement. Pieter and all the occupants of the bus followed.

The constable in the charge office was an old school mate of Pieter's called Jan. 'What the heck have you been up to?' he groaned. Ten minutes later, after the ambulance had taken away the wounded black, he waved the bus on.

'Looks like you've stumbled into a heap of shit,' Jan said. 'She's an American journalist returned from a fact-finding tour of KaNgwane refugee camp and he's her official interpreter.'

'She's a whore and he's a kafir and he had his arm around her.'

'Using the word "kafir" is a punishable offence nowadays. She wants to lay a charge on his behalf.'

'So charge me then.'

'Come on, Pieter, what's got into you? You get off home, but try to keep out of trouble.'

Pieter left and the constable watched him striding down the main highway. Those boys in Special Services were all the same,

Jan thought. Hyped up to save the country, feeling themselves to be an arm of the law and a law unto themselves. He'd noticed the missionary zeal shining out of Pieter's eyes as if lit from a spotlight somewhere inside his head. He'd seen it before. Psychiatrists called it megalomania. Give him a year or two and he'll be bush-fucked, the poor sod. Yet guys like him were keeping the country together. He solemnly tore up the charge. 'Stuff her,' he murmured.

Entering the bare cottage that had once been home was so painful Pieter almost fled straight back out of the place. There was a letter from his father on the old wood stove where once the coffee pot had stood. So Anton was right.

After his initial shock he lit the fire and burned the letter. Then he filled the percolator with water and coffee and put it on the hotplate. Give him a day or two and this place would be just like home.

He went outside. It was September, and hot for spring, the buds bursting into leaves, but the earth was dry and the dam was low, for the first rains had not yet come.

He trudged round the place, and popped in to say hello to Sam. Seeing his home with fresh eyes was a painful experience. He'd never realised how poor they were. Three years of drought had dried up the land. Even Sam's mealie patch was shrivelling. Only his goats were thriving.

Once upon a time he'd had such dreams, imagining Liza and himself in their little shack he'd intended to build beside his parents' cottage. He had planned to find a job in the village and spend his salary on building up a dairy farm. They would work hard and bring up their kids in much the same way he had been reared, in a safe and well-ordered world where sane and decent standards prevailed.

That dream would have been blasted even without Liza's reclassification. The sane world he had known was entirely missing. Two weeks on the border was enough to convince a man that he was fighting for the survival of all that was dear to him. Looking back, Liza's disaster seemed to be step one in a long and horrible walk to this present unhappy moment.

It was seven o'clock and he could not bear to spend the evening alone. He decided to walk over to the Cronjés'.

Life was full of shocks tonight. A gleaming Porsche stood at the front door of the homestead and inside wall-to-wall carpets covered the tiles. The place looked like something out of a movie set in Hollywood. Tony, playing the role of a wealthy whizz-kid extraordinarily well with his blue tinted glasses and manicured hands, showed him to the patio above the dam, but it was larger and covered over and resembled a Burmese jungle complete with creeping plants and tropical birds in an aviary.

'I hate to see birds cooped up,' Pieter said. 'I guess flying is the greatest gift life can offer. And then we take it away from them. Do we have the right . . .?'

'What, are you getting weird or something?' Tony said.

Eleanor was the next shock. She'd grown old and haggard. Just how old could she be, Pieter wondered? Not yet forty, but she looked fifty and her hands were shaking badly. She tossed back her drink as if she'd had plenty of practice and flushed with temper and shame when Tony refused to refill her glass. It seemed that her husband's murder had hit her badly.

'I assume you got my offer,' Tony said as soon as Pieter was sitting in a floppy leather chair with a beer in his hand.

'For the life of me, I can't imagine why you want my barren acres,' Pieter retorted. 'Even more unbelievable is your belief that I would hand them over to you in exchange for a few share certificates.'

'Not just pieces of paper, but a share of the land,' Eleanor began.

'For God's sake, he knows that, Eleanor,' Tony explained, as if humouring a child. 'Now leave this to the men.'

She flushed and stared down at her trembling hands.

'Don't you see what a wonderful offer this is? You get a ten per cent share of the total game reserve, including this homestead which will be converted to a guest house, plus the outbuildings and equipment. Don't forget my plantations are considerably more fertile than yours, and there's a fortune tied up in farm equipment.'

'Farm equipment gets obsolete. Land doesn't,' Pieter retorted. 'What good is fertile land if you don't want to farm it?'

'Good for pasture,' Tony retorted.

'I don't think I'm interested, Tony. You go ahead on your own if you're too damn lazy to farm your patch.'

'I'll make it fifteen per cent. The truth is, I can't go ahead unless you join me. Your farm is larger than mine. Not that you can do much with it, but we need the space.'

'And the hills,' Eleanor said dreamily. 'Such wonderful viewing sites from your hills. Our place is flat. I can just see the visitors up there . . .'

'Will you leave this to me, Eleanor,' Tony said flatly. He explained with surprising candour. 'We can turn this place into a real money-spinner and without too much effort, but we need yours to go ahead.'

'Why bother? You have enough without this. I read about you in the newspapers. They said everything you touch turns to gold. You're a millionaire, Tony. The country's youngest whizz-kid. Why don't you retire?'

'There's no such thing as enough. I have to show increased growth and profits every year just to survive.'

Pieter laughed. 'You seem to be on a treadmill.'

'You don't understand business, Pieter. You never did, but you always understood politics. Have you any idea what's been happening in the country while you've been up in Angola?'

Pieter leaned back and waited. He'd always been a good listener and he was keen to know how Tony knew where he'd been.

'South Africa has become the most violent country in the world,' Tony began. He got up to refill their glasses and sank down into a green leather beanbag almost hidden amongst the foliage. 'The government was forced to impose a state of emergency in July, this year. They said it was for a few weeks, but there's no sign of it being lifted. We've got our backs to the wall, Piet, make no mistake. The police have arrested five *thousand* black leaders. Last week thirty people died in the unrest. Right now hundreds of township shacks are burning. The rand is plunging, we've had to freeze our loan repayments, international relations are at an all-time low, France has announced a freeze on new investment in South Africa, the EEC nations have recalled their ambassadors for consultations, need I go on? Can't you see that it's time to look forward and work out what will replace apartheid?'

'And what's your guess?'

'A multi-racial democratic government – one-man one-vote.'

'We'd be voted out of the country. D'you expect us to hand over this beautiful nation on a plate, man? God forbid. When did you become a commie?'

Tony laughed. 'You blokes see a commie behind every tree. Listen to me, I don't have a point of view. I just try to out-guess the others and make something out of it. Put aside your political ideology for a minute and think about your own financial security. All you have is the farm. Right?'

Pieter nodded.

'What if a multi-racial government decided to dispossess white farmers? Can you be sure that you'll own this farm in twenty years time?'

'Yes, damn you,' Pieter growled.

'If you join me you'll stand a better chance. Once we have proclaimed these farms to be nature reserves, we get any number of tax benefits and a certain amount of protection. They won't grab the land because by then it won't be suitable for farming, but we could turn this whole area into a very profitable undertaking.'

Pieter narrowed his eyes as he gazed at Tony. He had the measure of the man now. All those clever brains were used for one purpose only, personal profits. He was absolutely indifferent to the welfare of the country or who governed it. Pieter sighed. He had to admit that the idea of a game park was a brilliant one. And since he'd embarked on an army career, it was a good way of utilising the land.

'Fifteen per cent is not enough,' he said. 'And I'd need certain assurances. There's Sam, for instance, and what about old Mrs Du Toit? She'd be holed up inside a game farm, too scared to go out at night. We'd have to talk to her.'

Tony beamed and looked delighted. 'I've got a plan for her, too. Something she can't say no to.'

For the next hour they sat and argued the toss, but the plan was sheer genius, Pieter could see. The more he thought about it, the more excited he became. It meant he'd have to go into partnership with the wimp, but Tony had business brains, you had to give him that.

At nine o'clock when Pieter stood up to leave, Tony insisted on lending him a car for the duration of his leave. 'It's Eleanor's. She never drives now,' he said, as if Eleanor were not present. 'She's had several bad accidents. It's her nerves. She's never recovered from Marius's death. I do what I can, but nowadays she spends more time inside the sanatorium than out of it.'

Half an hour later, Pieter parked outside the town's most popular bar and went in for a beer. Nothing much was going on, so after a while he strolled through to the Ladies' Bar and saw Amy Johnston sitting with a girlfriend. She'd changed. Her hair had bleached highlights which made her look blonder, her figure was trimmer, he could see she'd lost at least fifteen kilos, and her eyes were dazzling blue from contact lenses, but she couldn't do much with her mean, thin lips, he reckoned.

He sat with the girls, bought a couple of rounds and toyed with the idea of fucking Amy. He could see how much she wanted him to, her eyes were almost popping out of her head with lust, but then he remembered how rude and unkind she had been at the matric dance and she hadn't been much good in the sack either. At the same time, he'd been months without a girl.

After a couple more drinks, fucking Amy seemed like a good idea. Her nipples were sticking out hard against her cotton blouse and he knew just how sticky-wet she'd be.

'Hey, Amy,' he said, fixing her with a predatory stare, 'wanna take a spin? We'll go up the ridge, see the lights and come back again.'

'Sure,' she said, jumping up fast as if he might change his mind.

'You've lost weight,' he said, his arm around her waist as he manoeuvred the road with one hand. As she moved closer, he couldn't help thinking how sore it must be to have the gear lever thrust into the back of her leg. When they parked on the brow of the ridge between bushes, he thrust his hand into her crotch. She had the hots for him and no mistake. He opened his flies and pulled out his penis which reared up hopefully.

'Just like that,' she said incredulously. 'No foreplay, no sweet talk, you just haul it out?'

'You've seen it before, Amy. The fact is, just looking at this new you made me so randy I couldn't stand the pain of it stuck in my pants.'

'Ah,' she sighed and ran her finger over the tip of Willie, who was starting to drip.

'I can't stand this,' he said. 'I've got to get outside.' Lately, closed-in spaces made him claustrophobic. He lay on his back on the dry grass and looked up at the stars. He knew this spot well. How many times had he come up here as a youth? 'It's good to be home, Amy,' he said, and meant it.

'It's good to have you home, Pieter.' Amy, who had been hesitating by her car door, came over and sat beside him. 'I don't believe in one-night stands,' she said hesitatingly. 'I believe that sex is wrong unless you're going steady.'

'That so,' he said casually. 'Well, you're entitled to believe whatever you like.'

'And you?'

'I can't go steady. I'm in the army. God knows when I'll get another leave.'

'But we could write,' she suggested.

'You could. I doubt if I would.'

'Just how d'you feel about me? I mean, it's been a long time.'

'Aw, shut up, Amy. All this talk has put me off. D'you want to fuck or not?' He stood up, scowling and walked towards the car door.

'I want to,' he heard the sad, small voice behind him.

'Okay, if I still can, but please, keep your mouth shut, Amy. All that girl's talk pisses me off.'

At midnight the rain came and Pieter drove home through the deluge after dumping Amy. He parked outside the cottage and walked down the slope towards the dam. Lifting his face to the sky, he laughed with relief as the cool water splashed his face and drenched his hair, until he was saturated, supersaturated, gorged and bursting at the seams with joy and water. This was a glorious, life-giving reprieve for the land which would now soon be bursting with little shoots of grass and flowers. He walked up towards their spring and heard the water running down the kopje and bubbling into the dam. He could smell the sweetness of the damp earth and the sour dank scent of the water.

At that moment of peace he felt a soft hand on his shoulder. He could smell his mother's perfume and he clearly heard her voice whisper: 'I miss you, Pieter.' He had a sudden vivid image that was so real for a moment he imagined she was there beside him. Moments later he was crumpled on the wet earth, sobbing out his grief at the loss of his mother and his home.

Much later, when the rain stopped, Pieter returned to the cottage. He felt calm now, but guilty. He knew he'd been wrong to fuck Amy. The cruellest thing in the world was to give someone false hope. From now on he would avoid her, he decided.

Chapter 31

———◆———

They would never arrive, Liza raged. They were half an hour behind schedule, but the train still stopped at every level crossing and waited for ages at every station while they loaded crates of vegetables and milk churns and all the paraphernalia of country towns. She was sharing a 'whites only', third-class compartment with an English woman who oohed and aahed over the Krokodilespoort mountains and hung out of the compartment talking to the dirty *gammat* children who always hung around trains.

Liza did not approve and she said so.

By noon, the woman was suffering badly from the heat, so she lay on her bunk, a wet towel held over her forehead and that was a relief, but every ten minutes she begged Liza to wash out the towel.

Liza's fear increased as the train neared Nelfontein. She was only too glad to rush down the corridor once again with the wet flannel so she could gaze at herself in the toilet mirror. Her skin was pale, her hair black, her thick eyebrows almost met over the bridge of her nose and rose in huge arches, her nose was too big, her mouth too wide, her chin too pointed, her face too square, her teeth too big and there was a pimple starting up on her chin. It hurt. Did she look dark? Would anyone remember her? Would she be branded – *gammat*?

She groaned aloud, but pulled herself together when the water flooded over the basin and ran over her feet. She let the water out, wrung out the flannel and rushed back to the compartment.

Longing to get home, but scared, Liza sat nervously twisting her fingers. Would Gran be there to meet the train? A moment of blind panic brought bile rising into her mouth. She should never have come back. What madness had brought her here? She would not be accepted in this bastion of white supremacy.

Then she managed to dredge up some courage. Having got this far, she would go a lot further. Besides, she reasoned, had she ever been truly accepted? Hadn't she always felt alienated, perhaps because Gran was so poor, or because she was a foster child?

The whistle blew as the train drew into the station. Liza's heart lurched and she shook so much she could hardly lift down Sister Agnes's loaned suitcase. When she stepped on to the platform it was like stepping into the past.

The first thing she saw was Gran, dressed in the same Sunday black satin dress, with her black panama hat pulled down over her bun, and as always she was standing stiffly upright, her polished black boots shining like mirrors. The sight of that well-loved face came like a body blow into her solar plexus.

'Oh Gran, Gran,' she muttered, hoarse and furious with herself for she could feel those dreaded tears trickling down her cheeks. How small Gran was. How was that possible? Looking down over the top of her head, Liza saw how thin her white hair was getting. She was like a little bird.

'Heavens!' she began, but at that moment Gran said 'Heavens!' and they both laughed which broke the icy moment.

'You've grown, child,' Gran said briskly. 'Well, you're not a child now. Hurry, your train was delayed and we don't want to be late for church.'

Gran went on about the lazy riff-raff working for the railways, the dirt on the platform, the terrible coffee they served, while Liza bit back her tears, understanding all too clearly that Gran was anxious to keep their conversation to commonplace things. At the same time Liza felt stripped naked under Gran's searching glances. Intuitively she understood Gran's nervousness about having her back. I'm going to show her what an asset I'll be, Liza promised herself while Gran went on about the weather in Johannesburg, the comfort of the new train, and the journey. Had it been too hot? Plus dozens of trivialities which Liza sensed had been rehearsed beforehand. Gran, it's all right. Relax. I promise you it will be like it once was, she longed to say.

Outside the station was a surprise, for Gran led her towards an old Volkswagen and there was Sam sitting in the driver's seat. He turned and scowled at her.

'You came back?' was all he would say.

'Get in, Liza,' Gran said sharply. 'The Cronjés always lend me and Sam a car when I need to go somewhere, which is seldom enough. They took Sam on when Maria was murdered.'

They rattled and bumped over the roads while the farmers' expensive cars zoomed past them leaving trails of dust that seeped through the cracks around doors and windows and even up through the floor. By the time Sam drew up outside the church Liza was covered in dust while Gran's black satin dress looked yellowish. Brushing each other down with their hands, they walked inside the church, followed by Sam, who slipped silently into the back row, reserved for non-whites.

As they moved up the aisle first one head and then another turned towards them. Everyone was staring at them, mouths open. A congregation of simpletons, Liza thought, feeling exasperated. Whatever would Sister Agnes say at this breach of good manners. *I'll show them one day. I swear I will.*

Gran moved into a middle row and Liza was about to follow her when the verger tapped her on the shoulder and pointed to the back of the church. She recognised Hans Klopper who used to try to date her. He had always been arrogant.

'Non-whites sit back there,' he said in a stage whisper.

Head bent with shame, her legs turning to rubber, she quivered and shook. She longed to slap him, but how would that help? There was little point in claiming to be white in this town, she decided with a bitter little smile. Should she stalk out, or insist on sitting next to Gran which would cause a scene? Was she to fight the system single-handed? No! Not here . . . not now . . . but soon. One day she'd get her revenge on all of them. Oh, you idiot, Liza, she told herself. You had forgotten the pain of it. You thought the whole world was kind and fair like the convent. Well, more fool you.

Keeping her head high and her shoulders squared she strode to the back and sat next to Sam.

'It's a pleasure to sit with you, Liza,' Sam whispered. Three seats ahead, Amy tittered. She was still a bitch. Some things never changed.

Sam bent towards her and whispered in her ear: 'Dogs bark, but the caravan moves on. Hold on to that, Liza. Don't try to gatecrash their world because their values aren't worth having.'

'One day they'll be fawning all over me,' she whispered fiercely.

She remembered Sam's comforting words over the next few days as Gran kept her busy with one task after the next. They made tomato jam and chutney, and prickly-pear jam, spending hours removing the treacherous thorns from the fruit. They bottled the plums from the old tree by the dam, they made biltong from a small buck Sam shot and soap from its fat. They planted carrots, mended the gate, whitewashed the walls and slowly it dawned on Liza that Gran was deliberately keeping her busy at home. Why?

Nowadays Sam had time on his hands so he dug a new latrine for Gran and repaired the wall of the kraal with bricks made from the red clay that lay around the dam. How busy they were, and then one morning, from a careless word dropped by Gran, she realised why – *Pieter was home on leave*.

'You knew. Why didn't you tell me?' she demanded angrily.

The old woman's eyes looked bleak. 'I didn't want you to go over there. He's not for you. You'll get hurt again.'

'I am old enough to make that decision for myself,' she

retorted. 'I'm almost seventeen,' she said, trembling with rage.

'I don't want you to be rejected any more. I'm telling you now, don't go running after Pieter. Promise me.'

'No.' Liza stared at her feet obstinately. 'I won't promise you anything of the kind. Besides you have no right to ask me. No right at all; I'm old enough to make my own decisions.'

Gran's lips folded into a grim slash of disapproval.

'Oh, Gran, I'm so sorry,' Liza whispered, putting her arms around the old woman. 'You, more than anyone else in the world, know how much I love Pieter. Don't expect me to do something that is beyond me.'

Gran sighed. 'You should never have come back,' she whispered.

Hurt and anger made Liza's eyes sting. 'You didn't want me, did you?' she cried out. 'Sister Agnes made you take me back. She didn't understand how you feel about these things. You're ashamed of me. Don't deny it. You *never* loved me. If you had you would have protected me. We could have gone away together. Why didn't you fight them? You were like my real Gran. I never had anyone else to love, only you, but you washed your hands of me.'

All her pent-up anger came surging out and she couldn't stop. 'One day I'll make you proud of me and you'll feel so sorry for what you did,' she sobbed.

Then her guilt surged. Watching Gran flinch, Liza thought uneasily about the shame she was bringing on Gran who had always been kind to her. How sad she looked. If only she would say something.

Gran was feeling too confused to turn her muddled emotions into coherent words. Besides, it was not her custom to explain or apologise. She simply did not know how, but she worried about it as she busied herself in the kitchen.

Perhaps she should have abandoned her smallholding and taken Liza away, but how would they have lived? She would never have found a job at her age and what could she do? She wasn't trained to work. She could live off her land, but without it she would starve. Besides, how could she abandon this old place. It was all she had.

When she was younger, after her husband was killed in World War II, she had returned to this barren, abandoned farm, which was her only inheritance, and alone nursed her grief and her land. Without cash or equipment, she built the walls of the kraal and ploughed their small fields with a plough drawn by her donkeys. She had kept to herself and gone without when there was no cash, which was most times. She grew vegetables and made jam and pickles, took in sewing and owed no one a penny.

Then the police had asked her to take in a small child found abandoned outside the police station and she had agreed, although afterwards she had wondered if she'd made a mistake, for she was plagued with visits from social workers. Eventually the child was christened Liza Frank and she was given a pension so she could collect state maintenance from the post office each month.

Aletta had been grateful to have someone to care for and she had loved the child with all her heart. But later those same women had told her that Liza must leave because she was non-white. After weeks of soul-searching she had accepted their decision. Why? Partly because she had been too scared to leave her farm, and also because she had always obeyed the law. But now these same laws were changing, so just how right had the government been? She should have fought them. She was learning a bitter lesson far too late. She should have followed her heart and her instinct. Love was the only thing she should have guarded, not laws, not land. Her punishment was to lose the respect of her only kin, but she had no words to say all this to Liza, so she scowled and polished the kitchen stove.

Eventually she found the courage to say: 'I always loved you, but I was afraid. Oh, Liza, I never recovered from your leaving.' She waited for a minute, but there was no answer so she went outside and busied herself with the chicken.

*

For the next few days Liza fretted and yearned and longed to escape to see Pieter, but Gran was always watching her. She was obsessed with memories and doubts. Had he changed and did he remember her? Did he know that she was back home and if so why hadn't he come to see her? Pieter had loved her once, but did he now? Liza was tormented by her doubts and she began to look washed-out with big shadows under her eyes.

On Sunday morning Liza told Gran that she would not be coming to church. As Gran watched her put on her best dress, her lips folded into a taut line and she left without saying goodbye.

Free for once, Liza rushed out into the morning, her stomach as full of butterflies as the summer veld, her eyes bright with excitement.

She took off her shoes, pushed them into her bag and ran barefooted. What would she talk about? How could she impress him with her newfound sophistication. She could tell him about the play *Equus* the convent had taken them to see, and the exhibition of French impressionist art sent out from Paris, and the community centre where she worked some holidays – there was so much to tell him. When she came in sight of the small cottage, she paused, pushed her shoes over her muddy feet and tiptoed over the rough ground. The weeds were springing up amongst the cobbles. It looked as if Mrs de Vries's cactus garden was the only thing that had survived. It would probably last forever. Had Pieter left already?

Scanning the scene anxiously, she saw that the windows were open. She could hear banging coming from the shed. Someone was knocking a nail into the iron roof.

She was transfixed, unable to take a step forward or backwards; her desire to flee equalled her longing to walk inside. Her heart was colliding with her ribs, her eyes were burning, her hands sweating. What if he treated her like a *gammat*? That was the awful fear that gripped her.

A man came out of the shed. Surely he wasn't Pieter. He was so tall and so broad. But it was Pieter. She gasped. He looked so much older and so handsome. Her eyes took in the changes in a swift glance: he was burned dark by the sun, his black hair was long and curling round his neck and fell over his forehead in a shock of curls. He was wearing shorts and a T-shirt and he looked like a Voortrekker with his bushy tangled beard.

'Pieter,' she called out.

He looked shocked at first, then he smiled so sweetly, with so much compassion and caring, just as he used to. His hands were covered in grease. He held them up, wiggled them at her, shrugged and laughed. 'A man can't hug his girl with hands like this.'

His girl! Joy surged and she flung herself at him, winding her arms around his neck and stretching up on tiptoe to smother him with kisses. Then she stepped back frowning. 'Why didn't you come? You must have known I was back.'

There was a long and awkward silence while Liza fretted. Why had she forgotten her carefully rehearsed speech? She studied the expression in his eyes. Is that love or is that pity? I have to know.

'Come inside,' Pieter said. 'I've got some coffee percolating on the stove. First I must wash my hands. Then I can give you a hug without leaving marks all over you. I like the way you look,' he said carefully. 'Your new hairstyle suits you. And that's a nice dress.'

'You look so old,' she whispered, too overcome with the shock of meeting him to pull herself together.

'I feel old.'

'Pieter, I was so sorry to hear about your Ma.'

'Yes. Best not to talk about it,' he said.

'Where's your Pa?' she asked.

'In Nelspruit. This never was his place and he never really cared about it. It was my mother's, you see. Perhaps he felt he couldn't waste his time on it, or perhaps the memories were too painful for him. He found a job in Nelspruit. Now I hear he's to be married soon. That hurts a bit.'

'Oh, Pieter.' Liza watched as he lit the geyser, filled the basin with hot water and began to scrub his hands. She edged closer, until she was standing beside him, longing to touch him. The feeling was almost more than she could bear. There was an intolerable ache in her groin and her hands wanted to hold his. He must be the most handsome man ever created, she thought, admiring his back and the way he stood so erect and straight. His black curly hair was so long. He'd always kept it cut so short. She couldn't help admiring his taut buttocks and strong brown muscled legs.

'I remember . . .' she began, reaching out and touching the jagged tear in his T-shirt, '. . . when you tore this. We were searching round the dam for turkey eggs for Gran.'

He smiled at her. 'We're lucky we had those good times. There's some guys in the army who've never had good times.'

'Oh, Pieter . . . Oh dear . . .' She hung on to his hand and tried to stay calm, but the tears were trickling down her cheeks. 'All these years I've longed to be right here,' she sobbed. 'We were so close and then . . . Oh . . .'

Suddenly his arms were around her and her head was on his shoulder. 'I had so many smart things I was going to say to you. I rehearsed it all the way over. But there's one thing I must know. You must tell me. How do you see me now? As a . . .' However hard she tried, she could never say that word. Her mouth could not make the horrid sound. 'They made me sit at the back of the church,' she blurted out. 'I'll never go there again. Never!'

'I'm sorry. I shouldn't have said that.' She reached forward and took the nailbrush and began to scrub his fingernails. 'Remember how I always did this,' she said, but she was thinking, now I've ruined everything. I should have dazzled him with my worldliness. Foolish, foolish Liza.

'Liza, listen to me,' he began. 'When you ran away I wanted to find you, but there was no way of knowing where to start. I was miserable for months. I used to dream about how I would rescue you, and we would run away to some place where we could be together. Later, when my Ma was murdered, I realised what it's all about – all these laws. I came to accept that I am a Boer and there's no way I can ever be anything else. So where does that leave us? On opposite sides of a chasm that we can never cross. That's why I didn't come to see you, although I wanted to. But if you talk about love – well, then, yes, I do love you.'

He poured them coffee and they went outside and sat at a table on the stoep, as they often had in the distant past, and tried to bridge the years they'd been apart. Liza had always been a good listener and she sensed that Pieter needed to talk. The story of the Angolan village came pouring out as he told her of his horror at what he had done and his fear that he had lost his humanity. He tried to explain about the hatred that he carried inside him and the beast lurking under his skin and the horror and thrill of killing.

In the face of this massive trauma, her own problems seemed trivial, so she put them aside.

'You only obeyed orders – what else could you do since you're a soldier. Don't blame yourself.' She put her arms around his waist and laid her head on his bare neck and pressed her open lips on his throat, tasting his salty skin and loving the familiar smell of him. Feeling hot with longing, she pressed herself close against him, feeling his breath on her forehead, smelling the musky male scent of him while she studied the black hairs on his neck and chest that were so tantalisingly close to her lips.

Looking at Liza's black hair falling all over her shoulders, Pieter had the strangest sense of going back in time. He wanted nothing more than to make love to her. She was his Liza, she always had been, and all the rest was nonsense, but he resisted. Yet he could not bear to let her go home. Everytime she tried he hung on to her hand.

'Don't go, Liza. Stay with me,' he pleaded. 'Just a little while longer.'

Liza thrilled to his need, but thoughts of Gran's return kept her on edge.

'I must go,' she said at noon. 'Gran will come back from church and . . .'

Suddenly his arms were around her, crushing her against him, his lips were on hers and she felt herself melting away into his body. She was filled with an intense need to be joined with him. Only then could she shut out the pain and loneliness. Here was home. Not Gran's cottage, but here in Pieter's arms. 'Make love to me, Pieter,' she whispered.

Chapter 32

Pieter de Vries was a faithless, disloyal pig and he should be punished, Amy thought. Feeling anguished, she watched his tall, lithe figure outside the window of the butcher's shop where she now worked. He walked in, hunched a little, head turned away as if trying to avoid her glance.

'Hi, Pieter,' she called out and saw him flinch.

'Hi, Amy. How's it going?'

'Fine. How's yourself?'

Her new contact lenses were making her eyes sore, but she hoped he would not notice. 'How come I never see you?' she asked, trying to appear light-hearted.

'There's so much work back home. It's a mess.'

That's not the reason. Liar . . . You wicked liar. She sent her anger pushing towards him and saw him flush. Just look at him bent over the counter, smug and distant. A stranger! But how was that possible when he was her lover? How could he dump her after he'd fucked her. Since then she had yearned for him.

How carefully he prodded the meat. Two of this and two of that . . . and she knew why. He chose two pieces of rump steak as carefully as if he were buying a ring and approached her to pay. Amy fought back her tears, blinking hard as she totted up the takings of a customer.

Then she sneezed. Damn him! It was all his fault. She had been spying on him. Night after night she had waited in the bushes on a kopje overlooking Pieter's cottage. On Monday there had been a sudden downpour and she had sat out the night

273

in her sodden clothes, so now she had caught a cold.

Every evening Pieter made a wood fire in the stone braai behind his cottage and sat waiting until Liza came running from the next-door field. Remembering what happened after that sent sword-thrusts of jealousy through her stomach. They kissed, sat holding hands and talked for hours while the meat braaied. Sometimes, Pieter played music on his mother's old tape player. Then they held each other in tight embrace and stumbled around the yard, moving in time to the music. Did they think that was dancing? The stupid fools! Later they went inside and locked the door, and it was only hours later that Liza emerged with Pieter. Together they ran back to old Mrs du Toit's cottage.

Amy's hands shook as she took Pieter's money. She would give him one last chance. When she handed him the change she deliberately touched his fingers, but he pulled his hand back as if scalded. 'I'm having a party on Friday night. It's my birthday. Do come.'

'Sorry, Amy. I'll be gone by then,' he said. 'My leave's almost over.'

He rushed off before she could issue another invitation. Afterwards the shop seemed grey and empty. Cruel, cruel Pieter. She sneezed and cried into her tissue.

What they were doing was a wicked sin. The Immorality Act forbade sex across the colour bar and a minimum sentence of six months was imposed. Far worse than the sentence was the disgrace. Everyone would know that Pieter had screwed a *gammat*. As for Liza, she would be shamed out of town. Perhaps she'd be thrown out of her smart convent. That would serve her right. It was time she learned to leave white men alone.

Amy fumbled in her bag for another tissue and felt for her notebook which had carefully recorded details of six nights of sin.

Amy's story and zealous notes were not at all well received by Captain Myers. Anyone would think that she was the guilty party from the way he was glaring at her. She sat in his office and tried to stir his righteous indignation.

'They're breaking the law,' she repeated. 'You know that.' She tried to provoke his anger by revealing some more intimate details.

'Miss Johnston,' Myers said. 'You must understand that our boys up on the border areas deserve a little kindness. They have given up their freedom and they risk their lives daily so that we can sleep safely in our beds at night. If it weren't for boys like de Vries the communist terrorists would be flooding into South Africa. Our troops are slowly crippling the Russian economy. It costs them a fortune to hang onto their African gains. Surely the boys are entitled to some relaxation? God knows their lives are hell.'

'He's not entitled to break the law,' she said stubbornly.

Myers silenced her by calling in his assistant. 'Sergeant Laubscher, take a statement from Miss Johnston,' he said sternly. 'We'll keep an eye on the situation.'

For the next three nights Pieter continued to break the law, so Amy took a half-day off from work and travelled by train to Nelspruit where she spoke to Captain Myers's superior officer. She threatened to contact their local MP unless something was done about the filthy goings-on at the de Vries's farm.

Unaware of Amy's malice, Liza lay in Pieter's single bed, feeling drowsy and satisfied, her body tingling with the physical memory of their love, a sense of heaviness in her thighs. She was tight up against Pieter's body, his buttocks hard against her stomach. How wonderful it was to feel his bare skin against hers as she fell asleep.

She woke later when Pieter began to mutter and thrash. He flung his arm back, hitting her shoulder. Liza slipped out of bed and stayed crouched at the end of it, watching the man she loved endure his nightly torment. He began to count: 'Seven . . . six . . . five . . .' When he reached one, he screamed. It was a high-pitched scream of agony, culminating in deep, wracking sobs.

Liza shook his shoulders. 'Wake up, Pieter. It's only a nightmare. Wake up,' she repeated louder.

The instant he woke, he jerked like a spring and landed by the wall. Unbelievably, his gun was in his hand and it was pointing at her. He seemed wide awake.

'Good God! I nearly shot you.' He put down the gun and sat shaking on the bed, his head in his hands.

'What have they done to you, Pieter? Why do you scream night after night. Where did you learn Russian and Portuguese?'

'I don't speak Russian, or Portuguese,' he said gruffly. 'You've been dreaming.'

'No, not me. You. You've been having nightmares ... every night two or three ... you thrash around and mutter to yourself and sometimes you cry, or shout. But tonight was worse than usual. You were screaming. That's why I woke you. Why do you have such horrible dreams?'

He shrugged. 'All my life ... since childhood,' he said. 'Micky Mouse got me.'

'Don't lie. I'll make some coffee.'

She lit the primus and boiled the water, but her mind was on Pieter, this strange new tense Pieter of hers. Obviously he was in military intelligence. Why else would he learn Russian? She could only guess at the awful tension that caused those dreams. What had they done to him? And why pick on Pieter? A sweeter, kinder boy never lived. She felt so angry. They were turning him into a nervous wreck. 'Why were you counting?' she called out. 'Were you lighting a fuse?'

'Something like that, I guess. Don't ask because I can't tell you.'

She brought two mugs of coffee to the bed and they sat side by side. If only she could help him, she thought, watching him sidelong. He had stopped shaking, but his eyes were bloodshot. He had told her so little about the army, only that he spent months alone in the bush, and she only knew that because he'd told her of the wild life he'd studied. She knew that he'd had two close companions and one of them had died horribly. When she fished for information, he became angry.

Sighing, she climbed back into bed. 'Which side shall we lie on?'

'You turn that way. I'll snuggle behind you. Why were you sighing?'

'You don't trust me.'

'It's not that. It's classified info. I can't tell you about my work. Listen,' he murmured, half asleep already. 'You heard nothing. No Russian, no Portuguese, no screams. Nothing. You got that?'

'All right. I love you, Pieter.'

'I know you do, now go to sleep.'

'Do you love me?'

'What did I say when you asked me five days ago?'

'You said yes.'

'D'you think I change like the wind?'

Pieter lay awake for a while, pretending to be asleep, intending that Liza should drop off first. He felt so guilty. He had no right to fall asleep in the presence of civilians. He'd been warned enough times. But his real guilt concerned Liza. He was acting recklessly and selfishly. If they were caught they'd both be arrested. Liza was classified coloured, but she didn't seem coloured to him, she seemed a part of himself. The bond he had with her was deeper than lust, but what exactly was it. Liza was demanding love from him, but he had no idea what love was. Wasn't it something women read about in magazines? He hated to lie, but she kept putting him in a corner with her endless need for reassurance. He should not have made love to her. He was deeply fond of her and afraid that he might have harmed her. One-night stands were for other girls. Liza was special. Guilt surged through him and it was another hour before he managed to fall asleep.

*

He was in the bush, tracking a terrorist, all his senses alert. He heard twigs breaking and felt the approach of two terrorists. There was an ear-splitting crack, and he leapt sideways for cover, grabbing his handgun.

The door crashed open, the light came on and Pieter saw that he was back home. He was naked, that was strange. Then he recognised Dirk and Jan, who had been at school with him. They were police constables nowadays and they were wearing their uniforms.

'Jesus, I could have killed you guys, bursting in like that,' he said, putting his gun down. How pale and scared they looked. 'Don't worry, I won't,' he added. 'What the hell's going on?'

Dirk laughed nervously. 'Heck, Piet. You've got ultra-fast reactions,' he muttered.

Looking round, Pieter saw to his dismay that Liza was still there. She knelt up in the bed clutching at the sheet she had wrapped around herself. Her mouth was open, and her eyes were glittering with fear and embarrassment.

'Get the hell out of here!'

'Sorry, Piet. We've been ordered to bring you two in. You're both under arrest.'

Pieter felt himself flushing. He looked at Liza sadly. 'Just take me and let her go home,' he said.

'We can't do that, Pieter. You've both been breaking the law.'

'Can't you people ever let her alone,' he said. 'Who's to know who or what she is?'

'D'you want us to read you your rights, Piet?'

'No. Just go outside while she dresses.'

'We can't do that, either. You should know that. I'll take care of your gun, Piet.'

Pieter grabbed a blanket and held it in front of Liza. 'Get dressed quickly,' he muttered. 'I'm sorry, Liza. More sorry than you'll ever know.' He gazed into her tragic eyes. What had he done to her? His guilt was so strong he began to feel sick. This was all his fault. He should have known better, but how had they found out? Then he remembered Amy and the way she had looked in the butcher's shop. She must have been watching them.

'Are you all right, Liza?'

He couldn't bear to look at her face while they led her towards the police van. Pieter tried to follow her, but they stopped him and he felt too shocked to argue.

'That is the van for non-whites,' they said.

'You can't mean to leave her in the back with that lot?' he said incredulously, peering through the grid. 'I won't allow it.'

'Okay, she can go in the front with the driver. You're coming in the car with us. Weird taste you've got, Piet. I guess when you're out in the bush . . .'

'Shut up, Dirk,' Jan muttered. 'We don't want trouble.'

'We were badgered into this. Sorry, man,' Jan repeated back at headquarters half an hour later. He looked genuinely unhappy. 'We need fingerprints . . . mug shots. I'll be quick about it. Sit down – no, go over there.'

'You should know better than that,' Pieter said, wishing he could be with Liza as she went through this torment alone. 'Give me a pen.'

He scribbled a telephone number. 'Call headquarters. You can't take my photograph, nor my fingerprints. It's not allowed.'

So Pieter *was* one of them. Jan had often wondered. The constable's face registered respect bordering on hero-worship. Only the cream of the army went into Military Intelligence's Special Services and only a handful of exceptional men were chosen to be trained as agents. Once an agent was created, he could never be photographed, just in case the pictures fell into commie hands, which might enable the enemy to identify him if he should ever be captured.

Jan dialled the number and shortly afterwards put the call through to his superior, Captain Myers.

*

Five minutes later, Pieter was taken to Captain Myers's office.
A constable brought in two mugs of coffee on a tray. 'Have some
coffee,' Myers said. 'You look as if you could do with it. Nasty
business. I'd as soon have nothing to do with it, but we were
pressurised. You're going back to headquarters now,' the
Captain told him.

'Can't I say goodbye to my girl? What's going to happen to
her?'

'She'll be released with a small fine, and fast. We've been
ordered to squash the whole matter immediately. The Immorality Act is to be repealed this year. Nowadays the press blow up
every arrest and your superiors are anxious to keep you out of
it.'

'Whatever the fine is, I'll pay it,' Pieter said.

'You can reimburse me on your next leave,' Myers assured
him. 'Don't we have enough pretty girls in Nelfontein, de
Vries?'

'You know Liza's story as well as I do. I'll never believe she's
coloured until it's proved to me. No one knows who or what she
is,' Pieter said loyally.

Major Willis Groenewald was normally a good-humoured man.
He was six foot tall, with a complexion like a young girl's, snowy
white hair and beard and large twinkling blue eyes. It was hard
to tell his age, but Pieter guessed he was around forty-five. He
had always been a friend, as well as Pieter's superior officer.
Right now he was firing off faster than a Katharine Wheel while
Pieter stood to attention, gazing at a spot just above the major's
head. 'You're not the man I took you for,' he concluded.

There was no reaction from Pieter and the major felt
momentarily lost for words. 'Oh, for God's sake, sit down, man.
D'you want coffee?' He picked up his intercom and ordered
some.

'Listen to me, sergeant. Look how we stand today – a gallant,
God-fearing people surrounded by the forces of evil. International communism, malevolent multi-national business

cartels, black nationalism like a cancer in our guts, plus the rest of the hostile black African states gathered around our borders are threatening to engulf us. Our people need to stand together now more than ever before in our history. The Volk must brace themselves for the coming assault. As Boers we have always prized individual freedom, but there's one virtue we prize higher than that. D'you know what that is, de Vries?'

Pieter thought it wiser not to answer.

'Morality. Our adherence to our law, man. You, of all people, must obey the law. To date your training has cost the state a fortune. Did no one ever think to ask for your views on integration? This is the sort of thing you're trained to fight.'

'Sir ... can I speak?' At last Pieter was provoked into retaliating. 'Liza and I ... well, we were always friends until she was reclassified. At the time there was a lot of gossip, but no one really knew who or what she is. You see, she was found abandoned outside the Nelfontein police station not long after the Mozambique revolution. Our neighbour, old Mrs du Toit, took her into her home and became her legal foster-mother. She and I grew up together because we were neighbours. She's very lovely and she could be Portuguese, or Spanish, or any damn thing. I've never believed that she should have been labelled non-white.'

'Hm. Are you serious about her?'

'She pitched. I was randy. There's not much more to it than that.'

But that wasn't the whole truth, Pieter knew. There was a deep bond between them, but if he tried to express his feelings he wouldn't succeed, so what was the point in trying? He had not been thinking long term. How could he? In his job there was no such thing as a future.

'I want your word that you will never involve yourself in this kind of thing again.'

Pieter nodded.

'You've done exceptionally well, de Vries,' Groenewald muttered. 'I've a tough assignment for you. Consequently, you're going on a short officer's training course.'

'We don't need rank for what we do . . .'

The major lifted his hand and Pieter closed his mouth.

'In this case you do. We haven't yet decided what rank you'll need. You're going into northern Mozambique to liaise with Renamo rebel leaders. They give themselves all kinds of fancy titles and it's important that you outrank most of them. Your job will be to train their men and organise liaison with our troops if and when necessary. You'll also be responsible for supplying arms and medical equipment to them and helping them to organise their raids and guerilla campaigns. In other words, you're going to run military operations in the Zambesi Province as a sort of a backroom boy. You'll have two assistants – a Lieutenant Jan Mostert – he's just a kid, by the way – and a sergeant. Sergeant Koos Jeppe perhaps. You can call on more assistance, demolition experts for instance, when necessary.'

A hundred emotions were racing around in Pieter's mind, but uppermost was joy. What a glorious, exciting, mind-stopping chance.

'Poorest country in the world,' Groenewald was saying, 'and the most backward. Most of the youngsters in the north have never seen a white man, and those who have might wish they hadn't. You've no way of telling who are your friends and who are your enemies. Take it that they're all enemies and you might stay alive a bit longer than our last two commanders. Yes, we've lost both of them within twelve months. Okay, de Vries . . .' He stood up and shook hands. 'It's back to school for you. And take my advice. Forget that young woman.'

Ten minutes later Pieter was being driven towards the military airport. 'I won't ever forget you, Liza,' he murmured, 'but I'll never see you again.' He felt that he had damaged her badly. He knew, too, that he had broken the law and the Volk's Calvinistic moral code. Two and a half million Boers, with nothing but their beliefs to sustain them, dominated a huge nation. Why? Because of their unshakable moral faith in their mission. Maintaining the purity of the Afrikaner people, in their religion, their culture and their race, was the cornerstone of their strength. Guilt surged. For him love was over, Pieter vowed. From now on he would remain alone and be a sentinel for the nation.

Liza was still locked in a cell with a coloured prostitute and a black woman arrested for shoplifting. The smell was disgusting and she felt dazed and loathsome. She tried to hold on to her feeling of love, which had seemed so pure and meaningful, almost like going to church, she had thought, but now that love had been tainted by the unspoken contempt of the two policemen. She had seen their eyes and they had despised her and felt embarrassed for Pieter, their hero. Now that she was locked up with criminals she realised just how low she was. The time passed agonisingly slowly. She hardly slept on her hard bunk, but each time she did, she relived her horrible arrest. By noon she was feeling exhausted.

At two p.m. she was called to the charge office where the constable returned her watch and belt. 'All charges have been withdrawn,' he said, 'but Captain Myers wants to have a word with you.'

Liza tried to look dignified as she listened to Captain Myers explaining the facts of life to her.

'Your friend, Sergeant de Vries, was whisked back to headquarters smartly. They think very highly of him there, Liza, and if you have any feelings for him, keep away from him. Fortunately for you, this business is being hushed up because they need de Vries. Otherwise you'd get six months for sure and the non-white prison accommodation is not at all what you're used to.'

'Can I go now?' She wrapped her dignity around her like a ragged cloak and kept her head high as she walked outside and stumbled into Gran.

Suddenly flash bulbs were popping and a pimply young journalist was shouting questions at her. 'Where have you been living since you were reclassified, Liza? Is it true you've been reared in a convent? Who paid your fine, Liza? Why have they hushed up your crime?'

Gran hustled her into the Volkswagen. 'Well, they took long enough to release you. I've been waiting here half the day,' she said.

'Oh, Gran.' Lisa couldn't meet Gran's eyes. Instead she stared fixedly at her hands, her hair falling over her face like a veil.

'Well, Liza, fate dealt you a poor hand,' Gran said, 'but you don't have to play your cards so badly. This only makes it worse for you. Even with a bad start people can win. Your reckless and undisciplined behaviour makes me feel you've decided to be a loser. I hope that's not true.

'We'll drive straight to the station. I don't think anyone knows about your arrest, but of course, they'll find out soon enough when the newspaper comes out, but I shall deny it. You don't need me to tell you that I'm ashamed of you. You know that. I can read it in your eyes.

'Here we are. Out you get. Here's your suitcase. I packed your things. Go back to the convent, Liza, and stay there until you have learned decent behaviour. You may not be white, but you don't have to behave like a tramp. You were brought up white. That must count for something, Liza. You don't have to behave like a *gammat*.'

Liza burst into a flood of tears and stumbled along the platform behind Gran, feeling lower than the meanest cockroach crawling through refuse.

Gran did not kiss her goodbye, merely touched her hand with the briefest touch imaginable. Then, unbelievably, Gran began to cry and Liza was afraid to hug her in case she contaminated her. 'Oh, Gran, I'm so sorry,' she whispered.

'Even though you're coloured, I would still pray to be proud of you, Liza,' Gran said between her sobs.

Liza spun round and climbed into the carriage, slamming the door behind her. She wound up the window and buried her face in her hands.

'I'm not coloured. I'm not,' she stormed. 'I'm white. I despise you all – liars, all of you.' She burst into tears. 'I'll show you. You'll all see how wrong you are. Cruel, cruel, horrible people,' she stormed. Oh God, how she hated them all.

Later she managed to calm herself by remembering the Mother Superior and the peace of her convent days and the love she had received. She thought about dear Sister Agnes and how much the sisters wanted her to take orders. 'If I become a nun I will never have to face the world again,' she whispered. 'The convent will be my sanctuary and I will never ever be rejected. I will take orders. I'll tell the Mother Superior as soon as I return. There is no place for me in the outside world.'

PART II

November 1986–June 1991

Chapter 33

There were always more hungry, sick, disabled people waiting in a long queue outside the clinic in Alexander township where Liza had been working weekends for the past year as a student nurse. They would never finish today, Liza thought as she rushed from one chore to the next: 'Pass the swab ... Hold the bottle ... Clean the table ... Call the next one ...' And then back to the desk to fill in a card.

'Next!' She looked up and flinched.

The doctor noticed her shocked expression and frowned. A youth was bent over her and there was so much menace in his expression. His eyes echoed the hatred and distrust bred from a township childhood. All his aggression seemed to be pinpointed on the young student who looked scared.

The doctor thrust the child he was treating into Sister Agnes's arms and hurried to the door. That young Liza was more trouble than she was worth. She was too young and too vulnerable. He had complained to the Mother Superior several times. He did not want her here. The nun had fobbed him off with a sermon: 'We are all called to do God's work to the best of our ability. Liza is trying her best too. Have you any complaints about her work?'

'No,' he had muttered.

It was not that at all. How could he explain that she was too lovely. Look at her now – the light shining from the high window above brought a lustrous glow to her dark hair and her peach-like olive skin. Her full dark lips were parted in surprise, her eyes huge and glistening. She was exquisite. Madness to bring her here. But how could he expect a Mother Superior to recognise sex appeal when she saw it? Every part of her said '*Fuck me*'. She was to become a nun, he'd heard. What a crime to lock her in a convent. He'd tried to draw her out of her shell so many times, but she was trapped into some prison of her own making and there was a barrier he could not penetrate, yet she intrigued him.

'Oh God – trouble,' he muttered as he saw the African grab her arm. By the time he reached the door the youth had fled.

'Did he hurt you?'

'No, sir,' she said.

'Did he steal something?'

'No, sir.'

'Well,' he hesitated, sensing her evasiveness. 'That's all right then.' Why the hell couldn't he get through to her? Her hands were shaking, he noticed. She was not as self-possessed as she was pretending.

The sick child he'd been tending was suffering from malnutrition and all the ills that accompanied starvation. He could save it in the short-term, but there was no long-term cure. He went back to the examination.

Liza watched the doctor go and sighed with relief. She smoothed the crumpled note that had been thrust into her hand.

'*Angel, Bring penicillin, morphine, dressings and disinfectant to this address. Come soon . . .desperate.*'

Liza was feeling agonised as the hours passed. She had to steal the medicines, but how? She had to get out soon, but when? The queue shuffled forward towards them, the heat was unbearable, the air thick with their cloying scent, like a heady wreath to dead hopes. Oh God! Would it never end? She tried to fight back her nausea as she bent over an old woman. Sister Agnes was bathing her open cancerous wound. She offered the swab to Liza.

'I can't,' Liza murmured.

'You must. Look at her and see God,' the nun whispered.

'Then I would hate her,' she muttered.

The words, once spoken, could not be erased, but Sister Agnes was busy and she would forget, Liza hoped, grabbing the swab. She gritted her teeth and disinfected the wound.

Just before noon the doctor called a halt. By then she had managed to steal what she needed, but how to get it out of the clinic was puzzling her. A stabbing incident brought chaos to the clinic.

'Here we go again,' the doctor muttered. In the confusion Liza grabbed her parcel and slipped out.

Hostile eyes watched her from doorways and windows as she hurried through the narrow, muddy streets of the township. It was like a maze, and she had blundered into a cul-de-sac. She turned and found herself in another blind alley. The streets were only corridors here, the shacks like living creatures, squat and menacing, trying to trap her. Her heart leaped as she felt a sharp pain in her ankle. Startled, she spun round in time to see a kafir dog scurrying away. Whites were unwelcome here. She was vividly reminded of the old woman who was torched in the park. She could hear the voices ringing in her ears: '*Dance, Whitey – dance!*' It seemed hours before she reached the right place.

She pushed open the corrugated-iron door. 'Nico?' she called. Blinking from the bright sunlight she could dimly make out the figure of a man standing in the shadows.

'Nico! It is you, isn't it?' She looked away quickly. It was painful to see how the mischievous eyes of a street-wise kid had become so wary and distrustful. Bitterness and anger had etched deep lines on his face.

'Did you bring the stuff?' was his only greeting. 'I wouldn't have risked it if there had been any other way.' He motioned towards the floor. Liza looked down. Beside him on a straw mattress was a young boy. His back and buttocks were peppered with 'birdshot' wounds which had gone septic. She knelt beside him to feel his burning forehead and gasped in shock as he turned his face towards her. His features were distorted from the pain, but she recognised him immediately.

'Ralph! . . . Oh God! What happened?' She looked up at Nico for an explanation but saw only hatred there.

'The *pigs* did this,' he hissed. Suddenly she was afraid of him. Trying to hide her fear she began to clean the wounds. Who were they? PAC? Or the Azanian People's Liberation Movement? Or communists? Were they part of the group that had shot up a police van the previous day, killing all the occupants? Or had they been involved in a riot or a police bust?

Her voice came out sounding unnaturally high-pitched. 'All this shot . . . must be removed. I'm not a doctor. He needs an operation. I don't have any . . .'

'Don't panic,' Nico cut her off. 'We have someone. The problem is how to get him there. Fix him up for a five-hour journey: morphine . . . penicillin . . . Do what you can.'

I was never meant to be a nurse, she thought. Waves of nausea interspersed with dizziness made her feel faint as she cleaned Ralph's wounds with disinfectant. She had to get out of there. It was so hot and stuffy. Looking around she saw no windows, just an open door. The walls and roof of corrugated iron had turned the shack into an oven under the midday sun, and the air reeked of vomit, urine and sweat.

'Are you all right? You look greenish,' Nico said an hour later.

'Just hold this and keep quiet,' she snarled.

She gave the injections in Ralph's arm, his buttocks being too swollen. Smearing the wounds with an antibiotic ointment she covered him with dressings.

'That's the best I can do,' she said. 'Listen to me!' She caught hold of Nico's arm. 'Our doctor would help you. He's reliable. I know that. Please let me fetch him. He wouldn't report you to the police.'

'This is war, Angel!' he growled. 'You're on the wrong side. I've been watching you for the last couple of days. You trust the wrong people. What's happened to you?'

'That's not true,' she protested. 'I'm not on any side.'

His hatred was getting to her. She had to get out.

His bony fingers dug into her arm. 'Remember how we used to say the whites were like termites, Angel? Well, you may have changed but we haven't, and we'll never stop until they're driven out of *our* country ... One settler, one bullet. Haven't you heard?'

She was going to faint. No, not here, she urged herself. 'I have to get outside,' she whispered, 'I have to go back ... otherwise they will suspect me.'

At nine o'clock the following morning, Liza was summoned to the Mother Superior. A chill ran down her spine. They had found out what she had done. Perhaps they had seen her leave, or had Nico been arrested? She would be in terrible trouble. She smoothed her blue school skirt and hurried towards the room which she had always thought of as a sanctuary.

Over the years she had learned to trust the Mother Superior. It was here that she poured out her problems, her doubts, and her longings and she had returned here two years before after her humiliating arrest for immorality. Burning with shame and a sense of injustice she had pledged her life to the service of others and sworn to become a nun.

She had tried so hard, gained honours in each subject, learned typing and shorthand, and until yesterday she had confidently expected to be sent to college for a three-year nursing course. But now ...?

Swords of fear pierced her stomach as she knocked at the door. 'Enter,' she heard.

The Mother Superior was standing under the high window. The light from the stained-glass window above seemed to surround her with a saintly glow. A certain subtle exultation shone in her eyes and goodness hung all about her, heady as perfume from the stately white Arum lilies on her desk.

'Sit down, Liza.' The nun's voice was soft and calm.

'I want to congratulate you on your brilliant academic achievement. Your work at the township community centre has been praised by every doctor. We are proud of you. At prize-giving next week you will receive the English prize and another award for your selfless devotion to your duty.'

Liza mumbled her thanks and sighed with relief. Perhaps she was safe.

'It hasn't been easy for you, has it, Liza?'

Liza mumbled and shook her head. Just don't touch on that, she thought, or I'll flood this place with tears of self-pity. Would anyone ever understand the force of her rebellion? Would anyone care? Liza saw herself as a grubby interloper, her aura stained with nights of frustration and sexual urges, and spurts of rebellion against the vocation she had chosen. *Infinite regret* . . . What might have been was always in her mind and an image of Pieter was never far away. This morning she could add panic to her disordered mind. But she was committed and she would never deviate from her purpose.

'Liza, I heard something that disturbed me . . . Something Sister Agnes said. I must ask you a personal question and beg you to answer honestly.'

Liza looked up, startled as an antelope, quickly reinforcing her defences. This nun had a way of getting through to her as no one else could.

'Do you love God, Liza?'

'Oh, no.' She sighed. Then she smiled, feeling more confident. 'I do not believe in your God, or if there is a God he must be very cruel. Sister Agnes has her way of coping with the trauma of working at that place. She sees God in everyone, but I see mankind . . . hopeless, suffering, noble people. Were there a God, I would hate Him.'

'Do you love the people at the centre?'

'I feel sorry for them.'

'But when you become a nun you become a bride to Jesus. In your mind you must love Him more passionately than any lover.'

'A figure of speech, surely,' Liza argued.

'Why are you intent on becoming a nun, Liza?'

'Because . . .' The lectures she had been giving herself for so long shimmered away into the air. 'Because I feel safe here. Because I want to be like you. Pieter is lost to me and no one else wants me, and besides, this is my home.'

'The degree of selfless devotion and discipline that Christ demands of his brides could never be achieved without a deep love of Him.'

Liza sighed and sat staring at her hands.

'Liza , I have watched you for a long time, but I didn't want to talk to you until you had passed your exams. Your duty is to go out into the world and find yourself. I am quite sure that you were never meant to be a nun. Next month you must leave the convent, but rest assured we shall help you to find a job. The rest will be up to you. You will go with our blessing and God's blessing and in time you will find Him, too.'

Liza stumbled out of the sanctuary in a state of shock. She fled to her room and sat in the corner, her hands shaking, her head aching, her body in a turmoil that matched the confusion in her mind. After a while she began to sob, her whole body shaking with the force of her emotions. Only much later she realised that she was crying for joy. She would be free again.

Chapter 34

Her last morning at school passed in a daze of conflicting emotions as Liza said a tearful goodbye to her friends. The nuns had organised a farewell party in the games room, where Sister Agnes hovered like a black crow watching anxiously while Liza was given a new suitcase. Liza noticed that the nun's eyes were bloodshot. Could she still cry after all these years of self-denial? 'I shall miss you,' her harsh voice crackled.

'I shall miss you, too.' Suddenly she was in the nun's arms. She felt her iron back, limbs that were sinew and bone and the dry lips pressed against her cheek.

The Mother Superior clasped her hand and gave her the address of a coloured women's hostel. 'My dear,' she said, her eyes glowing with compassion, 'we tried to get you into the Young Woman's Christian Association, but despite our persistence, the government has not allowed non-whites in, so this was the best we could do for you. Here is the address of a supermarket where they are holding the job of filing clerk for you. If you work hard you could eventually become an accountant.' Her voice was crisp and decisive. 'Be thankful that the management of this food chain have opened their offices to non-whites. Go well, my dear. We'll be thinking of you.'

Liza mumbled her thanks. How could she explain that she would rather die than work in an office.

The bursar wanted to see her. She explained that the cash Liza had thrown on to the Mother Superior's desk four years before had been placed in a savings account. Liza trembled with shock. Interest had increased the original amount.

'For the past year, your friend, Pieter de Vries, has been sending a small sum each month to be saved for when you leave the convent,' the bursar went on. 'With interest it's amounted to quite a tidy sum. You have over three thousand rands, Liza. Here's your book,' she said. 'Don't waste the money.'

Pieter had sent her money. Oh glorious, wonderful fabulous day! Pieter still loved her. She raced to her room and flung herself on her bed, hugging her secret to herself.

It was time to go. How strange that she would never see this room again. It had been her refuge for four years. She tipped her clothes out of the bag Sister Agnes had lent her and packed them into her new suitcase. Then she raced downstairs, her heart singing. More hugs, more waves, more tears, and Liza found herself quite alone at the bus stop.

Life was one glorious adventure and it was starting now. She could not resist twirling around on the pavement and singing for joy.

An hour later, as she stood staring at The Christian hostel for coloured women, Liza's enthusiasm had deflated. This was not for her. She scowled at the board. A young Chinese girl looked out of the window. 'Are you Liza?' she called. 'We've been expecting you.'

'No!' Liza forced the words out of suffocated lungs. She had to get air. Almost running, she hurried away.

By noon she was exhausted and thirsty. The buildings shimmered in the heat, the pavement was melting, her shoes squelching into the tar. She would be burned brown, she remembered with sudden panic. Opening her suitcase, she found her battered school hat and thrust it on her head.

She had reached Hillbrow, a dense highrise suburb where she knew the hotels were cheap. The Europa took her fancy. It was newly painted in blue and white. There was a long balcony covered with a yellow awning and tubs of summer flowers stood amongst the tables. Pausing to put her hat back in her suitcase, she smoothed her hair and walked inside.

'I'd like a single room for a month. How much would that cost?' she asked.

The clerk was startled by her voice. It was low and cultured for such a young girl. He watched her carefully, trying to decide whether or not she was beautiful. Her black hair was pulled back into a thick bun which revealed the line of her long graceful neck and her throat which was smooth and lovely. Her eyes were huge, they seemed to stretch further than they should – soft and brown with more than a hint of sensuality. Her nose, lips, eyebrows and chin seemed too strong for real beauty, yet they all fitted together perfectly. There was something wrong, the clerk thought, but he could not put his finger on it. He studied her soft, pouting lips, her ivory skin ... Could she be coloured? She was a bit on the dark side.

'Do you have your ID?' he asked politely.

Those lovely eyes turned hostile and opaque and her lips trembled. 'No,' she said, feigning surprise. 'I didn't bring it.'

'We can't admit you without your ID. Or a passport.' The key which he had been pushing towards her was retrieved.

She hesitated, then she fumbled in her bag. 'Oh, here it is.' She waved it overcasually towards him.

'I must have the number.'

Now she was flushed and breathless with anger. He saw two red spots starting up on either cheek. She thrust it on the counter with an impatient gesture.

Opening it, he saw she was coloured. 'You can't stay here,' he said.

Her face fell. She looked angry rather than upset, and sullen-looking. 'Where can I go?'

He shrugged. 'This is a white area, so naturally there are no hotels for non-whites. You should know that. Where do you come from?'

She sighed.

'Listen,' he muttered. 'If I were to forge your number in my books it could cost me my job. I'd be willing to take a chance, but not for nothing. You understand?' His hand slid over the counter and grabbed her wrist. 'How about it?'

'Fuck off,' she hissed, jerking her hand away. Grabbing her suitcase, she fled.

Shoulders sagging, feet dragging, her self-image shattered, she did the rounds of the local boarding houses. There was no escape from her wretched ID number. Everyone asked to see it. Eventually she tried a small mean house, with a '*Rooms to Let*' sign in the bottom front window.

'Oh, no. Good heavens! Never! Why should you think that you could come here?' The blousy woman with dirty cuffs and collar, and streaky grey hair scanned her contemptuously. 'This is a respectable, clean home,' she said sternly.

But I am respectable and clean, Liza wanted to shout, but what was the point? There was nothing left for her but the hostel. She would never make it stamped second-class. Never! Whoever heard of a coloured woman becoming rich and famous? They didn't stand a chance.

Burning indignation brought a lump to her chest, and her throat constricted. For a moment she felt dizzy with suppressed anger. She leaned against a bus stop wondering what the future would hold for her. She was trapped by her wretched ID. Doomed! Pieter would be lost to her forever. They might as well have branded her forehead with a cattle-iron. Cold fury flooded through her.

A black minibus taxi drew up and the driver leaned out smiling sympathetically. 'You look bushed. Where're you going, friend? You can hop on. This taxi's for everyone – even whites.'

She put her chin up, squared her shoulders and stepped inside, choosing the seat beside the driver. He seemed somehow familiar.

'Where to?'

She sighed. 'I'm looking for a room.'

'Bit expensive here, is it?'

'No . . . it's my ID . . .' She sighed again.

The driver pulled up at the next stop and stared hard at her. 'You want to talk about it?' he asked.

What did it matter? She would never see him again. Her story poured out.

'Liza? Are you really Liza Frank? Don't you remember me? Dan! Dan Tweneni! Pieter and I—'

'Dan! But of course, I should have recognised you.' How could she have forgotten those huge almond-shaped eyes, and the way his hair stuck up from a widow's peak, or his massive, bony shoulders. But he had changed. There was so much sadness about him. Strange how much you can read in someone's eyes, she thought wonderingly. Anyone could see he was clever, but there was strength there, and sensitivity and so much warmth. Yet she sensed he could be sullen from his stormy black eyes.

Meeting a friend in this awful place broke down her defences. She flung her arms around him and burst into tears. The passengers began to clap and whistle.

'Dan . . . Oh, Dan. This is unreal – I mean bumping into you like this.'

'Not really,' he said. 'This is my beat. I do four hours a day to pay my way through University. I'm in second year law.' He broke off to brake by the kerb and take some new fares. 'I had to fight hard for this stretch of turf,' he went on. 'I know just the place for you to stay, Liza. If you sit tight until I've finished my run, I'll take you there.'

Liza was only too happy to sit tight. Her feet were throbbing, her head was aching, she was hungry and thirsty and feeling sorry for herself. 'You see, Dan,' she confided. 'I'm not coloured. I'm white. It's all a terrible mistake and it's so unfair. I aim to get a good job and get myself reclassified, but for that I need money to pay for a smart lawyer. Plus, I need to be accepted in white society.'

She recited from the research she had done at school. 'If

someone associates with whites, and lives in a white area, and has a white job, and is generally accepted as being white, then they can apply for reclassification.'

Dan shrugged. 'There are easier ways, Liza. I know a guy who forges IDs. I can get you one.'

Soon they were driving down the main street of Fordsburg with gaunt, grey warehouses on either side. Dan pulled into a backstreet amongst small coloured homes. This was not at all what she had in mind for herself. 'Dan, I'm not sure,' she murmured unhappily.

'Trust me, Liza. Martha will put you up for free until you find a job. She'll help you. She understands these things. I stay there myself.'

Oh God. He was taking her to a black home. Her stomach churned in revolt. 'Dan, I don't think . . .'

But it was too late. They were slowing beside a ten-foot-high wall with a solitary garage door set into it. She wouldn't get out of there in a hurry. Dan pressed a button on his remote controller and the doors slid open. Moments later they drove through into a dark garage and the doors closed behind them. Now they were in pitch darkness.

What a fool I am. What am I getting myself into?

The lights switched on and she saw she was in a garage. 'Okay, out you get,' Dan said, grabbing her suitcase.

Determined not to show her fear she stepped out of the taxi.

Chapter 35

Dan's firm grip was pushing her towards the door. It swung open revealing a large kitchen where a woman was standing with her back to them, bent over an ironing board. She turned and her face lit up. 'Dan. You're early. That's wonderful. We can have tea, I've just baked some scones.'

Liza was mesmerised by the woman's appearance. Her skin was amber brown, but her eyes were bright blue, which was odd. She resembled a chocolate-point Siamese cat. Liza had never seen a coloured woman with blue eyes. A shaft of envy jetted through her for those crystal clear blue eyes, so bright and compelling.

'Why, Dan,' the woman purred. 'Introduce me to your friend.' She smiled at Liza and held out her hand. 'I'm Martha,' she said.

There was so much warmth in the smile that Liza began to relax. She really liked her despite her unusual appearance. She was wearing tiger-striped pants, a low-cut black T-shirt and fluffy white slippers. She looked well past forty, but she was still pretty. Her long kinky hair was dyed red, and her figure was voluptuous, but there were deep shadows under her eyes. She looked as if she had been very tired for a long time.

'This is Liza,' Dan said. 'Liza, meet Martha – a colleague of mine.'

A colleague. What could that mean? 'Phew!' Liza said. 'It's cool in here. What a relief. I can't tell you how sorry I am to intrude.'

'What a lovely voice,' Martha said. 'You'll go a long way with that voice.'

'Can she stay here?' Dan asked. He seemed to take her answer for granted. 'She's had trouble finding accommodation. She's an old friend of mine and she has a problem. I've known her since she was five years old.'

'Have you really?' Liza asked. 'I don't remember that far back.'

'Put the kettle on, Dan,' Martha said. 'Come along, Liza. I can fit you into my sewing room. It's not much, but it's yours.'

For Liza it was love at first sight. The room was on the other side of a tiny enclosed yard, which Martha had turned into a jungle-like patio with tropical plants climbing over the walls, and Koi fish in a small pool. There was just room to fit a chair beside the pond.

'I never sew nowadays,' Martha was saying. 'We'll have to move a bed down from the attic, but we'll make it nice bit by bit, love.' It sounded as if she was expecting Liza to stay forever.

'Of course, I will pay you for my board,' Liza muttered.

'We'll talk about that when you get a job.'

'I can pay now. I have savings.'

'Well, you save them. That's the best thing to do with savings. I won't hear another word about it. Now you'd better know that this is an odd sort of house. It's actually two houses back to back, so we have two addresses, one in Swift Street – that's the white street that leads out into a white area, and one in Begonia Road – that's the coloured side, the one you came through. It's up to you which entrance you use.'

'Holy Shit!' was all Liza could say.

Had some guardian angel led her to Dan and Martha, Liza asked herself in the days that followed. Everyone was so kind, but secretive. Martha had four daughters and they seemed to live under a curious veil of secrecy. Everyone thought before they spoke and the word 'father' was used reverently, yet Father

was never around. Liza wondered if they belonged to some
secret religious sect.

Then, one morning, she came downstairs early to find
Martha in the kitchen with a white man. 'This is my husband,'
she told Liza smugly. His name was Reg Jessop, Liza learned,
and he was from Kent, in England, but so long ago, he'd almost
forgotten it, he told her. He had watery bulbous grey eyes, a pale
face, a long nose and a kind smile.

'So you're our little Liza, are you? I was wondering when I
was going to bump into you,' he said. 'Well, got to be off or I'll
be late. Bye for now.' She watched him leave through the 'white'
door.

There was a strange story here, Liza knew, but no one
volunteered any information and she didn't like to ask.

With Martha's help, she set about trying to land a job, but it
couldn't be just any job, Liza explained. It had to be special.
Something worthy of her talents. *Something to launch her to the
stars*.

'And what exactly are your talents, love?'

'Well, that's the problem. I really don't know yet. I don't like
nursing, or office work. I was only good at English at school. I
won the English prize each year and I have a strange feeling that
I ought to write, but I suppose I'm being ridiculous.'

'You must go by your instincts,' Martha said. 'A journalist is
just the job for you.' Once Martha decided something it was
very difficult to argue.

In the following weeks, it became clear to them all that
landing a job as a journalist was out of reach. You had to have
a degree and anyway there were no openings, so when an
advertisement appeared for a learner darkroom assistant to a
newspaper photographer – *whites only need apply* – Martha was
thrown into feverish activity. Liza must have paler make-up, her
hair must be highlighted . . . She rushed out there and then and
bought a kit from the corner chemist. 'We'll get rid of those
awful dark eyebrows of yours while we're at it,' she muttered.

The result shocked Liza. Her complexion looked muddy, and her eyes strangely luminous, but she had to admit she looked lighter. No one would suspect her secret.

Martha and her daughters were well satisfied. 'You look white. That's for sure,' they repeated. Everyone wanted to give her something, pearl earrings from one, a necklace from another, a powder blue suit from Martha.

The following morning, Liza had a last careful look in the mirror and, with gritty determination, left through the 'white' door.

She had an appointment at 11 a.m. with Barbara Newman, editor of the colour magazine section of the *Sunday Echo*, the largest Sunday weekly in Johannesburg. The building was situated in the eastern end of the city and it overlooked the park where, as a child, she had seen the old woman being torched. This unnerved her for a while, but she had plenty of time to pull herself together as she wandered along the corridors, trying to find the east wing of the sixth floor. Eventually she found the place and stood waiting nervously in front of the reception desk where a woman was trying to cope with a small switchboard.

'Yes,' she snapped irritably. How pretty she was. Liza couldn't help admiring her golden hair and large amber eyes.

'I have an appointment . . .'

'There's an emergency this morning. I don't think she'll see you. You'd better make another appointment.'

'Oh, but I can't do that. I'd rather wait,' she argued. Her disappointment banished her fear. She felt prepared to fight for the job if she had to. It was so right for her.

'She might be hours.'

'I'll wait,' she said firmly.

It's worse than the trauma clinic in Alexander Township, Liza thought, as she sat listening to the shouts and watching the agonised expressions on everyone's faces as they raced in and out of the boardroom.

'I'm Rose,' the receptionist told her after a while. 'I'm

supposed to be the editor's secretary, but the receptionist is sick so I'm expected to do everything. I have a migraine coming on. I don't know what I'm going to do. Would you like a cup of tea? I'd better make some. Sounds like they need it – and tranquillisers. We have an emergency. The *little man* has been here. He's not pleased with us.'

'Who's the little man?'

'God,' Rose said darkly.

She had to be content with that. Rose didn't stop grumbling once. She had to cope with the switchboard, do dictation, everyone expected her to do their typing, too. She had to deal with callers and do the filing. When a voice from the boardroom called for another round of tea she swore loudly, and Liza was amazed. She thought the word *fuck* belonged to street children. She began to smile to herself.

'I can't see straight,' Rose muttered. 'Can you help out here?' It did not take Liza long to get the hang of the small switchboard, which was just as well, she thought, as Rose collapsed on the settee in the adjoining office.

A blonde girl peered through the doorway. 'What's going on?' she asked.

'Rose is sick,' Liza said. 'She's lying down.'

'Lucky she found a "temp" at short notice. Barbara wants minutes of the meeting taken,' she said, pointing her thumb over her shoulder. 'Tell the main switchboard to take messages for an hour. Can you cope?'

Liza stood up decisively and picked up a notepad. 'My shorthand is good and I'm a fast typist. If you lend me a typewriter I'll have the minutes done right after the meeting.'

'Thanks. Let's hurry.'

It didn't take Liza long to fathom out who was who. The editor, Barbara Newman, was a small, intent woman with expressive brown eyes and a restless manner. She didn't notice as Liza walked in quietly and sat at the end of the table. Barbara was smoking nervously, stabbing at them with her cigarette and her hurtful taunts.

'The little man says our readership is slipping badly. We're being set up as the scapegoats for their fuck-ups. Listing our recent scoops and successes didn't help me at all. The little man wasn't interested. And why? Because it's past tense. You lot haven't produced a single scoop for a month. *What was . . . was.* Ancient history! It's today that counts. This load of claptrap can feed the shredder.'

Listening to Barbara Newman made Liza feel dizzy. Her voice went on and on in a breathless monotone. She flung some folders on the highly polished table and the five people gathered around the table cringed.

'As for you, Marge,' she said to the blonde girl on her right. 'You seem to be burned out. Is this supposed to be a fashion preview? Boring, boring, boring.'

'Well, fashion is in the doldrums,' Marge said softly, looking pained. 'There's nothing new. No one is making a statement.'

'Well, you make one for them. You're the fashion editor. Your job's at stake.

'Now, Enid, I haven't had a decent scandal out of you for weeks.'

'The back page took my last story.' Enid, with an English complexion that filled Liza with envy, sounded close to tears.

While Barbara worked herself into a worse fury, a tall, dark man sitting next to Liza drew quick sketches of Barbara caricatured as a cat terrifying the mice cowering round the table. He slid the cartoons slyly towards Liza and winked. They were so funny, she almost laughed out loud. She smiled at him, liking the look of his sorrowful spaniel eyes and his full, sensitive mouth. If he weren't so solemn-looking, he'd be handsome, she thought.

'As for you, Ed,' Barbara said, catching the movement. 'You're the laziest sod I ever met. Pull your finger out, lay off the booze and let's have something worthy of you. You haven't taken any worthwhile pix since God knows when. These cartoons stink. When did we last get a funny one?'

'Last week?' he suggested in a deep voice.

'Something like that,' she agreed. Then she leaned back and sighed. 'He's threatening to do away with us. What would the *Echo* be without its colour supplement?' Regaining her energy with a quick gulp of tea, she waved her hand, scattering cigarette ash over them. 'We need some sensational drivel. That's what God wants.'

Liza's eyes were nearly popping out of her head. So the tall dark man drawing funny pictures was Ed Segal, the man who had placed the ad. She shot a timid look at him and he passed her a picture of a mouse cowering under the desk.

'Your layouts stink, Valentine,' Barbara snarled turning to a freckled boy sitting next to Ed. Enid, who'd been playing footsie-footsie with him, burst into tears and fled from the room.

Barbara swore long and viciously. 'That's all I need,' she moaned. She leaned back and caught sight of Liza. 'Who the hell are you?'

'Miss Newman,' Liza said, jumping to her feet and squaring her shoulders. 'I'm Liza Frank. I had an appointment to see you at eleven. I want to be a journalist, but not having a degree, I applied for the job of darkroom assistant. I am qualified in shorthand and typing and I'll have these notes typed out in no time. I'll be ready whenever you wish to interview me. If I worked here, I could certainly help Rose with some of her workload,' she added hopefully. 'I'm sure I could think up a few scandals, too.'

'Oh God!' Barbara said, an expression of contempt on her face. 'She's all yours, Ed.' She gave a long-suffering sniff.

Ed looked up, grinning warmly. 'Do you eat garlic? Do your feet smell? These are important considerations for two people sharing a small, stuffy darkroom, I assure you. Are you hard-working? Will you work overtime without asking for extra pay – I can only teach you at night.'

'No, no, and yes, yes.' Her skin tingled as hope set in.

'Well, I guess you've already started,' he said. 'I'm serious about the night work. It's the only spare time I have.'

'My God! Can't you wait an hour before you soften her up?' Marge said laughing.

To Liza's surprise, Ed blushed and beads of moisture appeared on his forehead. She liked Ed, she decided.

'Our darkroom assistant just left to have a baby,' Ed explained, attempting to look very serious.

'Comes from all that night learning,' Valentine muttered.

'Oh for God's sake,' Ed exploded. 'It's hard enough to get someone to work long hours for next to no pay without you frightening the life out of her. You'll be quite safe, Liza, I assure you, but as a learner the pay is rotten and you'll work like a dog.'

'And put up with his temper,' Marge said.

'Please, I accept the job.' She gazed around at all of them, feeling a part of them already. In some strange way it seemed that she belonged here. 'Is that all right, Miss Newman?' she asked.

'I'm Barbara,' she said. 'And don't ask me, I have enough problems.'

Chapter 36

Riding their Rooikat armoured vehicle with the Commando M-4 mortar loaded on the back, Pieter and Koos, together with Jan, their raw recruit from Pretoria, drove slowly along the eroded gravel track towards Mopêia Velha. Ten miles to the north-east was their target, the major Caia bridge which linked the Zambezia and Sofala provinces. For some weeks Frelimo troops had been repairing the bridge prior to making a suspected assault into the Zambezia Province, which was mainly in Renamo hands. It was vital that the bridge be destroyed.

As they approached the outskirts of the town, Pieter cringed at the familiar ruins. He put his hand gently on Koos's shoulder and they braked. Pieter scanned his surroundings in silence, eyes narrowed to a permanent slit, his face lined and burnt black by the sun, all his senses alert. He quivered and sniffed the air, as much a part of the bush as any buck. The bitter-sweet, unbearable stench of death was all about him, but he knew without really thinking, that man was not here. Men had passed through two days before and the smoke curling in the morning breeze showed their latest destruction. Perhaps former inhabitants had tried to restore their homes. He felt sick in his stomach. The smell of death always did this to him, but he would hate his comrades to know this. 'Move,' he growled.

Soon they were driving down the main highway. On either side of the tree-lined route were the jagged, ruined shells of shops and offices. Windowless and roofless, the buildings had been stripped of all usable items. Every window broken, every door removed, each piece of furniture, even school desks and hospital beds and tables, had been looted or destroyed. Every hut on the outskirts of the town had been burned. It was part of the systematic policy of destruction that had taken place in towns and villages all over Mozambique. The communists must never be allowed to enjoy the fruits of their victory.

They moved on, but wherever they went, the destruction was absolute. Only the countryside was still lovely. As noon approached, clouds obscured the sun and the heat became bearable. They saw a small reedbuck in a dry river bed, which was unusual in these parts, as most of them had been eaten. Later they saw vervet monkeys squabbling in the trees and they almost ran over a spitting cobra, its olive brown body perfectly camouflaged on the gravel track. Koos braked violently and they waited, tense and watchful, while the snake moved across the road.

They were half a mile from the Caia bridge when the sound of gun fire, followed by mortars and grenades, halted them in their tracks. Pieter swore.

He knew from his intelligence that the bridge was guarded by a platoon of fifty heavily armed Frelimo troops. The plan had been to draw the troops away from the bridge by attacking the adjoining town, which would give the three of them a chance to lay their charges and blow up the repaired structure. The plan, so meticulously conceived and rehearsed, had one major drawback: it did not appeal to the locals. Presumably, Renamo soldiers had rushed in to demolish the enemy, heedless of personal safety or any thought of their ultimate objective. That was their style. To hell with plans! Just kill everything that moves. Pieter sighed.

He signalled to Koos to park their Rooikat in a nearby grove. 'Jan and I will go in ... You'll stay here. Let off the smokes every thirty seconds.'

Koos looked nervous. 'Why not wait? Our guys might pull a trick or two. Right now it's dicey.'

'We can't wait. They'll send up reinforcements. Start in thirty minutes. Got that?'

Koos gave the thumbs-up sign.

The smoke bomb, filled with a titanium tetrachloride charge, generated dense white smoke on contact with the water vapour in the air. Pieter preferred them to the usual white phosphorous bombs because of the fire hazard to the Mozambique bush.

The two moved forward to a vantage position on a ridge thick with buffalo grass. From here they could see that Frelimo had the advantage. They were holed into their prepared trenches and it would be difficult to winkle them out. As they watched through binoculars assault waves of Renamo troops were leaping into a hail of bullets and firing indiscriminately, sustaining huge losses. Pieter detoured around the ridge to a spot where the forest almost encroached on the river bed and here the two of them crept upstream into the tall grass.

From the screams coming from under the bridge he could tell that Renamo were scoring occasionally. Then he noticed one area of trenches, near the southern side of the foundations, was quiet, presumably destroyed. They would work from there. They moved up cautiously, took cover and waited.

Dead on time he heard the first zoom and saw the illuminated bomb parachute down on target, letting off a copious white smoke screen as it fell.

Pieter and Jan moved in fast. For Pieter it was a routine job he had done time and again. Heedless of danger he moved automatically, as if in a trance, clamping the limpet explosives to the understructure and the pillars of the bridge, and linking the wires. A few bullets splattered around them, but most of Frelimo's fire was still directed at the attacking troops.

Five minutes later it was all over. They returned to a safe distance in the bulrushes, let off the charges, and saw the bridge erupt in slow motion, while the valley rumbled with the thunderous blast, splattering bricks and stones all over the place.

'Mission accomplished,' he radioed happily.

'I'm surrounded, man. They're moving in,' he heard Koos's anguished whisper. 'About fifteen of them. Look out for yourselves. I love you, man.'

*

Pieter's guts knotted and rage seized him. There was no way to get to Koos in time. He should never have left him alone. What a fool he had been, but it was too late to think of that now. Koos didn't stand a chance, but he must make sure that he was dead. Koos would go down fighting. He was not a man to surrender tamely.

For a moment of blind grief, he could not bring himself to move. Then he shoved his emotions down ... way down into some deep bog at the bottom of his mind. Too many dead friends were down there. He'd seen too much suffering.

'We're gonna back out fast,' he whispered to Jan. 'Reckon we're surrounded. We'll go back up to the trees ... try and make cover there. Follow me and keep well down. If you lose me, hide up under the mud until dark, dig yourself in ... make your way down river five miles. By then you'll be in Renamo country. Get back to Chinde under cover of darkness and radio headquarters. You got that?'

Jan nodded. Poor kid! His eyes were almost popping out of his head.

They advanced slowly and cautiously, sending no ripples through the rushes. As they approached the trees a wild hope ran through him. There was just a one per cent chance that Frelimo had not yet attacked the Rooikat, but were waiting for him to return. He moved forward again, sensing that he was accompanied by an invisible brigade. He could smell them and hear them, but they did not know exactly where he was. He moved on, keeping well down amongst the ten-foot-tall grass, moving towards the trees, hoping against hope.

A few yards more ... He motioned to Jan. 'Hang on here, and hope like hell I get back to you,' Pieter whispered. 'Get into the mud.'

He sprang forward into the trees and paused, listening. He'd made it. Moving forward in lurches, he ran from one cover to the next until he reached the grove where they had left the Rooikat. It was gone. Disappointment almost turned his knees to rubber. 'Oh God, Koos. Where are you, man?'

He must go after him. Following the tracks, his skin crawling, every nerve shrieking 'danger' he forced himself to move forward until he reached the edge of the thicket. He climbed a waterberry tree, grateful for the dense foliage. Why weren't Frelimo waiting in the grove? Surely that was the best place to ambush him?

A second later he saw why. Their vehicle was parked in the middle of open veld, five hundred metres from the nearest cover. He studied it through his binoculars, but there was no sign of life. Had they mined the approach? Was he surrounded right now? Or were they waiting inside the Rooikat?

'Hey, you fucking Boer,' he heard on his radio. 'Your friend is waiting for you. He's got one arm left, but not much else. He might have trouble taking a pee.' Cackling laughter came over the Rooikat's radio. 'You want your pal back? Come and get him before we slice his last limb off.'

A brilliant light flashed like lightning out of the vehicle, and the noisy blast came a moment later. The Rooikat exploded and in that split-second the rest of their grenades went with it in one ear-splitting roar. Burning bodies were catapulted in all directions and pieces of flaming debris were scattered over the veld. Somehow Koos had got to the grenades. They should have cut off both of his arms, Pieter thought grimly, but how were they to know they had a bloody hero on their hands? By now the bush was burning hard enough for him to escape through the smoke.

The long low hotel at Chinde was built in colonial style, overlooking a once-pretty beach. It had seen better days. Lately troops and their whores were the only clientele, but somehow it had retained a certain grace and charm despite the ramshackle roof, the broken windows and doors, and the strong stench of urine and garbage that hung in the warm, moist air. It was here that they stored their spare kit and had their headquarters and where Pieter and Jan went for a self-awarded 48-hours' leave.

Despising the hotel's food, which was bound to lead to gut complications, and drinking only what came out of a tin, they locked themselves into their shared room, shook out the mattresses and moved them on to the wide balcony. They had DDT powder, a primus and they bought crayfish and vegetable cassava and together they boiled up a mushy, tasty soup which they knew was clean and wholesome. The water came dripping out of the shower, but at least it dripped. After food, a shower, a shave, and ten hours of sleep, they felt refreshed and clean enough to emerge. With the mud and dirt gone, Jan looked so young, hardly more than a kid with his pimpled skin and ash-blond hair falling all over the place.

'Is that really you, captain?' Jan asked, his eyes as round as pebbles. Pieter had shaved off his beard and he knew that he looked like a teenager. Perhaps he shouldn't have done that, but he was so sick of it and a rash had broken out on his chin.

'You need a crewcut, man,' Pieter snapped.

There was a nightclub of sorts downstairs. The girls, clad in next to nothing, were wiggling their navels and singing in perfect unison.

'Good God!' Jan said after a while. 'D'you know what they're singing? It's a Christmas carol. At least I think it is.'

'Silent Night in the local lingo,' Pieter said.

'Why?'

'It's Christmas Day tomorrow. Did you forget?'

'Ja! I guess so.'

'They're not short of rhythm and music,' Pieter said. 'It's about the only thing that's not in short supply round these parts.'

'Where did that come from?' Jan asked, noting the sudden addition of a wedding ring on Pieter's left hand.

'It saves a lot of insults. I don't fancy the local girls and this gives me the excuse to say "no". Otherwise they might get offended.'

They had arranged to get drunk in turn, the other keeping watch, but only in the safety of their own room. The plan was that in the public lounge they would stick to two tins of beer each.

'I want a girl bad,' Jan murmured, watching the gyrating thighs of the nubile dancers.

'You must be bush-fucked, man. You want a dose of *droopy-dick*? How many times must I tell you that most males over sixteen have a venereal disease. It's not called *droopy-dick* for nothing. There's no penicillin here. Every time I get back on leave I aim to bring some along, but what's the point? They've nothing to barter with and anyway they'd go right out and catch it again.'

A woman approached them tentatively. He knew her well. Her name was Miranda, and she was a particularly bright young woman who manned the local airport and spoke Portuguese, French, English and the local dialects, too. Once she had been a teacher and now, in her late twenties, she was destitute, but still quite lovely. Heck, Pieter thought to himself, when I start finding the local women lovely, it's time to go home. She was light-skinned, perhaps only slightly coloured, with huge black eyes, a pinched face, delicate nose, an impish smile and good teeth.

'Hi there, Captain Pieter,' she said with a catching laugh. 'D'you know what the girls are saying about you?'

'No. Nor do I care.'

'They say you are queer. Women frighten you, they say. Is that true?'

'Yes. Why not?' he said, listening with half an ear.

'They say you're a virgin.'

'Now you know my secret what are you going to do about it?'

'You are a very sexy man, Captain Pieter,' she said, perching on the arm of his chair. He could smell her sweat and the garlic on her breath and the musky scent of her need. 'And you are so young. You want to play jig–jig?'

'I promised my wife not to,' he said, tapping his ring.

She smiled. 'You're not fooling anyone, Pieter. We know you're gay.'

He sighed and shrugged. 'Want a drink?'

'Sure,' she said. 'Whisky.'

He called the waiter and ordered a double for her. To his annoyance, Jan decided to order the same.

'Ag! Come on, man,' Pieter whispered. 'You don't know what they've put in it. Keep to tins.'

'Are we off duty or what?'

'Yes, we are.'

'Then screw you, man,' Jan said.

Finally Pieter extricated himself from Miranda's embrace and went off to his balcony. He wanted to grieve for Koos and he had to be alone. Koos and he went back a long time.

He lay and thought about his mission here and softly, bit by bit, he allowed himself to think about Koos until he was groaning into his pillow. Koos was the last, the very last person he would ever allow himself to love. How many others had bought it over the past four years? They came and they died and to love them was to invite self-destruction. Why did Koos die? he asked himself.

Somehow the cliché to combat the spread of communism in Africa and protect the Volk's frontline was not enough. Their orders were straightforward. Make the territory ungovernable. He knew that he had been magnificently successful. Most of the village settlements were now empty. No one was trying to win a war, or win the people. It was a case of destruction, pure and simple – a policy of destabilisation, and they had done this in nine of the country's eleven provinces. They had destroyed economic targets and disrupted transport and communications. They had wrecked thousands of shops, hundreds of villages and vehicles, trains, sawmills, cotton gins and tea factories. Communal villages and their facilities such as health posts were regular targets. Crops were burned in the field and in peasant grain stores. The people were afraid to move from their villages, so they lived in a permanent state of siege. The people were the victims. People like Miranda. All she wanted was to earn her living and find some love and peace. That was all most of them wanted, Pieter knew. Eventually he fell asleep, still grieving.

It was three a.m. when he was woken by a loud knocking. Grabbing his gun, he swung the door open. Jan swayed there, his arms around Miranda.

'Let us in.' He slurched his words and nuzzled Miranda's ear. 'You take the balcony, man. We're having the room.'

'Oh no … no, you're not. Not while you're in my care, my boy.'

'You're not my bloody mother,' Jan swore.

He stepped forward, mouth open, in an aggressive stance, and Pieter felled him with a single right hook to his jaw. His mouth fell open, his head snapped back and he was unconscious before he landed. 'Heck, I hope I haven't broken something,' he muttered. 'Sorry, Miranda,' he said. 'Jan's got a girl back home. He's keeping himself for her.'

Her mouth was open, but no sounds were coming. Her eyes were saying enough, Pieter thought. He kept his cash in a drawer behind the door. Quickly he grabbed a handful of notes and thrust them at her. 'Buy yourself something pretty,' he told her.

She let rip with a string of curses in the local dialect. 'Fucking racist pig,' was her parting shot as she threw the cash on the floor and spat at him. Behind the anger he could sense her rejection and wistfulness. She'd never get out of Chinde. She'd work like a dog, but never escape from terrible poverty and later, in her old age, she would starve.

It was Christmas Day and Pieter was lonely. Jan had recovered, but he was surly and uncommunicative. Pieter had to get out of there. Besides, there was something he had to do. He borrowed a spade from the hotel, commandeered a truck and drove into the bush until he reached the Caia bridge. As he had thought, Frelimo troops had retreated in the night, leaving the locals to wander amongst the wreckage, looking for anything that might prove useful, an empty tin, a cigarette stub, anything.

He reached the spot where the Rooikat had blown up and saw the blackened veld stretching over a large area of grassland. He began to search around for human traces, scattering a pair of jackals, and throwing stones at the hovering vultures until they retreated to the surrounding tree tops.

He found an insignia and a tin mug, and a few bits and pieces that might have been Koos once and he dug a deep grave under an overhanging rock and scratched some words on a stone face. *Here lies a hero, Sergeant Koos Spiro, who sacrificed his life for others.*

He tried to weep for Koos, but no tears came. So he gave one last search around, and then threw the shovel into the truck. Then he sat in the sun, watching the bush trying to resurrect itself after the trauma of the battle and the fire.

After a while a bat-eared fox, emaciated, but alive, its silver mane glistening, loped past him. Then a small spotted genet crawled on its belly and began to fight off the egrets who were diving for roasted locusts and beetles, their favourite dish. A mongoose shining golden brown in the sun found a burned snake, ate it and hurried past.

And then Pieter noticed the half-burned silky plum tree, that had sprouted from a cleft in the rock. It was maimed by the blast, half of its branches torn and hanging, the sap pouring out of its wounds, its leaves shrivelling in the hot sun.

Just another casualty, but it touched a chord in Pieter. He had defiled nature. He wrapped his arms around the tree and sobbed out his grief for its wounds and its pain, and his own wounds and pain, for he too was maimed. 'I'm sorry,' he sobbed to the tree. 'Truly sorry. Forgive me for bringing this war to you. I never meant to harm you.'

He could not stop crying. Some deep primal need to be loved by God was nagging at him. Besides, he was lonely ... deeply lonely, imbued with a sense of bitter alienation from the human race.

He had been banished to be a sentinel of the Volk and he had turned into a beast. He had ripped back the thin veil of civilised behaviour and released the savage that lurked deep in his psyche. He had seen his men commit bestial acts against their enemies, but he doubted they were as guilty as he was, for they were raised in a philosophy of survival, whereas he had been brought up in a strict Calvinistic code. He had sinned against God, against man, against his Christian ethics and even more wounding, he had sinned against some deep atavistic adoration of nature. He had contaminated the font of love which should have bubbled out of him like the pure spring water welled from the rocks back home. He had soiled and crapped on his world, and his soul had dried up from sheer grief.

After a while, he dried his eyes and stood up and examined the tree. He reckoned it could be saved with a little judicious pruning and some tree glue. He could bind the trunk together with rope he had in the truck. He didn't have tree glue, but he could make up a hard paste by breaking off some of the clay from a nearby termitary. First he would need water. There was a river nearby, but how to transport it. Well, his hat would do. The sooner he got working, the better, for the leaves were wilting fast.

Three hours later he stood back and examined the tree critically. He could sense its gratitude and he knew it would survive.

He climbed into the truck and drove towards Chinde. At least he'd done one good thing during his years in Mozambique.

Chapter 37

'A man can crack up in many ways,' Major Groenewald was saying. 'He can crack up mentally, in which case he lands up in an asylum, or physically, so he ends being invalided out of the army, or emotionally, so he becomes maimed – an emotional cripple. I've never agreed with sending our boys behind enemy lines for such long periods.' He sighed, stood up and peered out of the window, his hands behind his back.

I wouldn't want his job, Pieter thought. The major looked worried and harassed.

'Now, you, Captain de Vries,' he went on after a long pause, 'have been operating outside the country's borders for over three years. You're at risk. We know that. You know that. But you're the best man for the job.'

He turned back to his desk, lit a cigarette and cleared his throat. 'The problem is, we're short of guys like you. Your country needs you, captain. That sounds a bit melodramatic, but it's the plain and simple truth. I expect you read about the farmer who was blown up yesterday. It's become a daily occurrence. Too many terrorists are getting through. It'll get worse unless . . .' He broke off scowling. 'What time is it?' The major glanced at his watch. 'Noon! Let's go and get ourselves a drink.'

Shortly afterwards, when they were sitting in the officers' mess, leaning over the bar, the major said: 'It's important that you understand what I'm saying, captain. Have you noticed any change in your behaviour or your feelings towards the peculiar circumstances we face today? In other words, you're the best person to know when you're in danger of getting bush-fucked, for want of a better word.'

What did it mean if you wanted to save a tree more than you wanted to save your own life, Pieter wondered? Was that bush-fucked? 'I'm fine, sir, I assure you.'

'I have a very important mission for you, captain. Today, as never before, we face . . .' He broke off, drained his glass and ordered another round. 'Perhaps I'll wait until you've checked out. As a matter of routine, you're to undergo check-ups. I want you to co-operate fully. That's an order, and while you're there I want you to improve your Portuguese.'

'I'm fluent in Portuguese, sir,' Pieter reminded him, trying to fight down his resentment.

'Yes, but I expect a bit of local dialect has crept in. You'll go back out there as a Portuguese ex-planter and you'll need the right accent. I'll see you at headquarters in a few weeks' time.'

Pieter didn't answer. He gazed at a spot over the major's head and thought about the bushveld. It was his way of controlling his temper. After what he'd endured he'd expected something better than a loony ward. To hell with him.

Having to put on striped pyjamas and climb into bed in a ward full of shell-shocked soldiers back from the border was a humiliating experience. Even worse was the patronising attitude of the pompous, but pretty young nurse, Jennifer Segger. She treated him exactly as she treated the two poor sods who'd been tortured by Swapo. As far as Pieter could see they'd be married to the ward until death did them part. He tried not to look at them, but endured his undeserved fate in icy silence.

'Now, Captain Pieter,' she said brightly. 'I'm going to take a blood sample, but you won't feel a thing, so close your eyes and count to ten, and it will be all over.'

She leaned towards him and grabbed his arm, feeling for the vein. As she plunged the needle in, he pressed his lips over her breast, straining through the thin fabric of her white overalls, and bit her nipple.

She yelped and pulled back, tearing his skin. His blood spurted over the sheets and her overall.

'Careless,' he said. 'You lied – it hurt. Never mind, you have nice tits.'

Tight-lipped, she manhandled his arm and drew off half his blood, or so it seemed to Pieter.

'Now it's time for your injection and this time it's definitely going to hurt, soldier,' she hissed at him.

Pieter gritted his teeth, wondering how to punish her. I'll screw the bitch, he decided. How many weeks was he going to be incarcerated in this hellhole? The major had said 'a few'. That could mean anything. I'll screw every woman who lays her hand on me. I swear I will. It's a question of honour.

When she'd finished puncturing his backside, he turned over. 'Sorry if it hurt,' she said smiling grimly. 'You're going to get a lot more injections. The doctor's put you on a course of Vitamin B. Whether or not they hurt depends on how you behave yourself. You get me?'

Screwing her wouldn't be too painful. 'Pain turns me on,' he said. 'Don't you have a whip? How about coming back later with a longer needle. We can have fun.'

'You filthy swine!' she snarled. Grabbing her equipment, she fled.

Doctor Friedland had a dry sense of humour and seemed sympathetic to his plight. 'The physical tests won't take more than a few days,' he said, 'but we want to build you up for your coming ordeal. Being interrogated by Major Odendaal is a gruelling experience, I assure you. Don't let on that I warned you.'

It was clear that he was being tested for every tropical fever in the books and more besides, plus *droopy dick* and a host of other venereal diseases.

At two sharp, a nurse told him that his Portuguese teacher had arrived. He was allowed to put on a dressing-gown and meet her in the gardens, for it was a cold, sunny afternoon.

'Thank God,' he murmured. The loonies in the ward were getting him down.

She was both voluptuous and pretty and it seemed as if the sun came out as he gazed at her. Her name was Miss Maria Lopes, and she was as juicy and succulent as a high-summer apricot. Her skin was velvety like a cling peach still on the tree, her black hair shone bluish like a ripe grape ready for wine-making. She would taste exquisite, he knew, and he longed to thrust his mouth against those soft, tremulous lips and strip away that awful black slack suit that tried in vain to disguise the soft plumpness of her body.

She excited him. This had something to do with her cool hand which lay overlong in his, and even more to do with her shy eyes under sweeping, flickering lashes. She was about thirty-two he reckoned, which made her considerably older than he was, but when she squeezed his arm she added her name to the list of women who had to be screwed.

It would be his pleasure, he decided, but how the hell could he seduce her on this square, antiseptic lawn in full view of bored nurses pushing their half-witted patients in wheelchairs? She was about to sit down at a table on the lawn when he saw a woodshed almost hidden amongst the shrubbery.

'I've got this terrible fear of open spaces, Miss Lopes,' he told her. 'After four years of bush war I only feel happy when I've got my back to a wall. It's ridiculous, I suppose . . .'

'Yes, ridiculous.' She breathed her words like a caress.

'D'you know what it's like to always be exposed? Never to know when a terrorist is creeping up behind you with a panga raised ready to . . .'

'Oh stop,' she cried out. She shuddered and rubbed her arms vigorously, and he guessed she had come out in goose-pimples.

Pieter glanced worriedly over his shoulder. 'That's why I'm in the nuthouse, Miss Lopes. Didn't they tell you?'

'It's not the nuthouse,' she chided him, smiling compassion-ately. 'It's a hospital. A very good one. You can feel safe here, you poor, poor boy.' She reached out and touched his hair, and for a moment her cool fingers lingered around the nape of his neck.

'I have to talk about the day I was surrounded,' he began.

'No . . . please don't . . . I couldn't bear it.'

'I can't feel safe, stuck out here.'

'Then let's go back to the ward at once.'

'I don't think you'll like it there. These guys that were tortured . . .'

'Stop . . . stop . . . please!' She was looking agonised.

'I think I might be able to concentrate in that log hut over there,' he said. 'Let's see if it's locked.'

He tried the handle. It wasn't. Excitement surged as she walked in without a tremor, as innocent and careless as a lamb to the slaughterhouse.

'Thank you, teacher. Shall we sit here?' he began, fumbling at his Portuguese and hoping his lessons would last forever.

'First things first,' she said, unbuttoning her blouse.

For a moment he was too shocked to speak. He sat there watching her, his eyes popping out of his head and his mouth open. What lovely breasts she had. He couldn't believe what was happening to him.

'Is this your first time?' she asked gently.

'Are you kidding?' He pulled himself together and pounced. She was every bit as tasty as he had imagined.

Apart from being sadistic, the day nurse, Jennifer Segger, was a virgin and proud of it. She presented an impossible challenge, but Pieter had time on his hands. She was like an impregnable fortress, for she was engaged to her second cousin, and both of them were confirmed baptists. She taught Sunday school at the local church and spent her spare time engaged in good works. She was rigidly disciplined, never late, and she humoured all her patients as if they were eight-year-olds.

On the second day, he discovered a crack in her fortress. It was hatred. It surged out of her every time the sister, Claire

Olivier, entered the ward. Claire was a honey-blonde, blue-eyed dream, slender, but voluptuous, with a happy smile, a freckled face and a good sense of humour and she was very popular with the patients. Perhaps that was why Jennifer hated her, but surely there must be a better reason.

Eventually he asked the night nurse, June. She told him that Claire had been discovered in bed with Doctor Friedland, with whom Jennifer had something going. Jennifer had become engaged to her second cousin on the rebound right after this.

'Hey, Jennifer,' Pieter called to her next morning. 'I don't know what to do. You know the sister, Claire . . . What's her name?'

'Olivier,' she snarled.

'I think she's fallen for me. I can't get rid of her. She keeps massaging my back and stroking my cheeks. She even came back last night during her off-time and held my hand. I think she fancies me, or does she do that with all the new intakes?'

'She's sex-mad,' Jennifer snarled.

Pieter was right. The chance of getting her own back on the sister was too strong to be resisted.

They did it in a shower cubicle. She stripped and backed against the cool tiles, uncertain of what to do next, so he lifted her with his hands under her buttocks and impaled her, pushing her gently backwards and forwards as she coiled her legs around his hips. She came in a noisy, clammy climax and he, caught unaware, had to hurry, before someone came to investigate the screams. It wasn't too good, but who cared. There was no shortage of cunts around this place.

By the fourth day, his medical tests were completed and his arm ached from the blood they'd taken. 'Is there any damn thing you haven't tested me for?' he asked Claire.

She smiled. 'You've kept yourself pretty aloof in the bush, soldier. You don't have a damn thing wrong with you.' She ran her fingers through his hair playfully.

'Sure have. D'you know why? I only fancy honey-blondes

with freckles and turned-up noses. It's a damn frustrating life because there aren't too many around.'

'Well, since your tests are all negative, I guess we ought to celebrate,' she said.

It was too easy. Damn it, Claire, he mourned silently as she pulled his curtains and stripped naked. A pretty girl like you should put up more resistance.

She was female. That was the first shock. The second shock was her strange appearance. Major Gertie Odendaal was tall and ultra-thin, with grey hair cut in a bob. Yet her moustache was much darker, which was odd, he mused. She might have been pretty once, it was hard to tell. Under her gravel-like skin were perfect features and her dark blue eyes were large and set wide apart. She was almost as tall as he was, and she looked him in the eyes man-to-man, and stretched out her hand.

'How do you do, Captain de Vries.' Her voice was deep and cultured, her nails manicured but without varnish, there was no frippery nor pandering to fashion, nor even a touch of lipstick to mar that stern exterior. She wore a plain khaki suit, a white blouse buttoned to the neck and a scarlet scarf tied raffishly round her neck. He eyed the scarf gloomily. Was there a hidden longing deep down in her dour psyche? Did she yearn for fun, or sex, or youth, or just to escape from the strict military discipline that dogged her days?

Her hand was still stretched out towards him.

He stepped back and saluted smartly, standing to attention and gazing at the wall above her head. 'Captain de Vries reporting, Ma'am,' he said.

She put her head on one side and gazed up at him sidelong, a curious look in her eyes.

'You don't have to be afraid of my rank, Captain,' she said. 'Let's do that again, shall we? How do you do, Pieter. You may call me Gertrude.' Out came the hand again. She wanted to touch him, but he was determined that she would not. He wasn't going to add this butch to his list.

'I thought it would be fitting if we shook hands,' she said, frowning at the slight.

'I'm sorry, I can't,' he stammered.

'Why ever not?' Now she was reaching for her notebook.

'I can't stand a woman's touch. It makes me feel sick deep in my soul. Please don't . . .' He backed away.

'Good heavens.' The pencil was flicking madly. 'I am sorry. Won't you lie on the couch over there.'

'Sure thing, Ma'am.' He lay down feeling awkward and vulnerable.

'Why do you think you feel this way? When did this trauma start? Can you remember? I want you to tell me about it.'

'I was raised in an orphanage in Nelfontein,' he ad-libbed.

'Wait a minute . . . your file says . . .'

'Okay, I had parents, but they weren't able to look after me, so . . . There was this matron . . .'

He jumped visibly as her hand touched his shoulder.

'Was that so bad?' she asked gently.

Not yet, but it's going to be. Goddammit. She had touched him. Now she was doomed and so was he. He looked up at her and sighed. 'You shouldn't have done that.'

'Done what?'

'Touched me.'

Pieter stared at the ceiling and tried to forget his boasting bluff made in a moment of extreme annoyance when Jennifer had clumsily torn his arm. But somehow or other he couldn't call it off. What was the point of vowing anything if you chickened out at the first sign of insurmountable odds? *Insurmountable*? Now why had he used that word? She was mountable. They all were, but just how bony and dried up was she?

'You've been out in the bush too long, Pieter,' she said. 'I've been pressurising the government to limit the time of a man's service behind enemy lines. In Britain I believe two years is the maximum time in the SAS. Then the boys go back to their brigades. Unfortunately I've been unsuccessful so far. I have your file here, Pieter. You've been decorated for bravery several times. You're highly thought of and you've seen a lot of action. Too many battles, too many deaths. I guess sometimes you feel you could set the whole country right with a couple of good men and a machine gun. Don't you?'

'No, ma'am,' he said. 'I'm not yet bush-fucked.'

'If you could go back to any action of the past four years and undo anything you regret, which event would you choose, Pieter?'

'Why four years?' he mumbled. 'I regret something that happened many years ago . . .' He broke off and covered his eyes with his hands. 'I can't talk about it.'

'I think you can.' She set about persuading him, and eventually Pieter allowed himself to give in.

'It was the orphanage matron,' he said, groping for inspiration. 'She was about thirty-eight and she looked remarkably like you. She had the most beautiful blue eyes and she was the only woman in my life who ever gave me love. I loved her, too. One day she took me into her office and she locked the door and hugged me and kissed me. I felt . . . Well, I can't describe what I felt, as if part of me was suffocating in my trousers, almost as if my ego had retreated from a spot behind my eyes and got down there, you know what I mean? I w-w-wanted to k-k-kiss her,' he stuttered. 'I h-h-had to know the meaning of love, but something inside me held me back and then, just when I was going to kiss her . . .'

'Yes . . .?' she asked.

'I threw up. You see, the fish they'd given us for lunch was off.'

'You're kidding!'

'That ruined everything. Now I know that if I hadn't eaten that fish . . . if I'd stayed there with her and let her do whatever she had in mind, I wouldn't have this awful trauma and I'd be able to get on with my life, and eat fish and fuck women.'

'You mean you're impotent?' She sort of exploded the word.

'Yes, ma'am.' Pieter was laughing so much he had to turn his back on her, but he knew she'd see his shoulders shaking. He was going to be in big shit any moment now. Then he heard her voice say: 'There's a box of tissues next to the couch, Pieter, but don't worry, crying is good for the soul, particularly after what you've been through.'

He grabbed a handful of tissues and rubbed his eyes hard enough to make them look red. Then he sat up. 'Sorry,' he said.

'I understand. That's what I'm here for. Clearing out the debris of the past is what I do.'

'I'd like to tell you more about her,' Pieter whispered hoarsely.

'Go ahead.'

'Well, her eyes were like yours. She had long legs like yours, they seemed to go on forever and I just knew that up the end of them was a secret wonderful place that was warm and soft and sensual, that would squirm if I ran my fingers through the silky hair. And I knew if I ran my hands softly over her white thighs, she'd shiver a bit and tremble. Then her lips would open slightly, just as yours are now, and her teeth would glisten, like yours, sort of moist and inviting, and her breasts would get all swollen up, her nipples pushing out of her blouse, like yours are.'

The major's eyes registered extreme suspicion. She stood up decisively.

Pieter grabbed his stomach. 'Oh God! Here I go again. Where's the bathroom?'

Speechless with amazement she pointed to a door behind him.

'Did you ever tell the army doctors of this ... well, this disability?' she asked him when he returned.

'No, why should I? You don't pull the trigger with your prick, do you?'

'I've decided to take you at face value. I think I can cure you, but it will take some months.'

'I only have a couple of weeks,' Pieter told her, which was the first truthful thing he'd said that morning. 'We'll have to work fast.'

'I can work fast if I have to.' She walked up to him and clutched his crotch. 'Feeling sick, soldier?' she asked, massaging his penis.

'I think I can bear it.' Amazingly his dick rose up like a mammoth mushroom.

'Young man, you intrigue me,' she said as she undid his dressing-gown cord.

'Ma'am, I've got the hots for you,' he replied as gallantly as he could.

It was all over bar the panting.

'Dawn!' Pieter surfaced from a nightmare, shuddered and looked around. He was not in the bush, he was in hospital and that was worse. He cowered under the bedclothes and pulled the pillow over his head, but there was no mercy for him. June, the night nurse, was about to go off and she had to have her screw before she left.

He heard the curtains being drawn and felt someone clambering into his bed.

'I've got a headache,' he groaned.

'Then we'll make it a quickie,' she whispered. 'Hurry! The day staff are arriving any minute.' He groaned aloud and performed the best he could. June seemed happy. She slid out of bed and pulled on her clothes just in time. Pieter tried to get back to sleep, but there was no place to hide.

Claire bent over him and woke him with a kiss. 'I couldn't sleep for longing,' she whispered. She didn't bother to ask, but just pulled down his pants and clambered over him. 'Come on,' she said impatiently. 'Come on, love. Get it up.'

He groaned. 'I think I have malaria.'

'What a lot of nonsense. Here we go. Hmmn . . . This is good stuff. I love you,' she murmured.

She probably did. She proved it too in so many ways, bringing him books and chocolates and little gifts and yesterday she had proposed. Fortunately, he had a ready answer. 'I'm married to my platoon, Claire,' he had explained softly. 'Besides my life expectancy is just about nil – statistically speaking,' which was true enough. Amazing vigour, he thought glumly as she bounced up and down, came twice and leaped out of bed.

Jennifer was in love, too, she'd said. She had broken her engagement to her second cousin and she spent hours reading to him every day. She'd tried to convert him to her faith. As he'd suspected, she was lurking in the bathroom when he stumbled in for his morning shower.

'I feel out of sorts,' he groaned to her. Fucked out would describe his feelings adequately, he thought ruefully.

'Fuck me,' she said coyly, pulling down her pants and leaning over the bath to run his water.

'I don't want a bath, I want a shower,' he grumbled.

'Then we'll make it in the shower.'

He didn't perform too well in the wooden hut that afternoon, but his Portuguese was almost perfect. A variety of sensual words in Portuguese were cluttering his huge stock of useless knowledge.

When Major Odendaal sent a message that she had a cancellation and could see him in the morning as well as the afternoon, he went racing to Claire for pep pills. She stole them for him in return for certain favours. Running her hands around his balls, she mistook his groans for passion and redoubled her efforts.

Oh God! Get me out of here, he prayed.

The end came swiftly. He was screwing Rose at six a.m. the following morning when Major Odendaal arrived to see why he had missed his afternoon session. She flung herself on to Rose, screaming like a she-devil, beating both of them. Claire, who had come on duty specially early, added her venom to the fray. Jennifer heard the fracas and came running. Understanding at a glance, she tipped a bedpan over his head. Doctor Friedland and a male nurse came to his rescue.

'Major Odendaal needs psychiatric treatment,' Pieter gasped as he crawled out from under the heap of screaming women. 'And for the rest of them I prescribe one screw a day, or you might have a riot on your hands.'

'The doctor reckons you're still sane,' his commanding officer told him the following morning when Pieter arrived, following an urgent summons. 'I won't tell you what Major Odendaal said. She's resigned, by the way.'

'Oh hell, I'm sorry.'

'You're going back on duty as soon as we can get you there. You'll be safer over the border. Now listen carefully. From now on, you're on your own. You're to replace Major Robert Rousseau. Remember him? He was the hippie who led the bus to Maputo when you boys did that night attack.'

Suddenly Pieter remembered how alone the hippie had looked when they took off by helicopter leaving him standing in the field. He'd lasted a long time after that, but Pieter had heard that six months ago he'd been arrested for spying in Angola, sentenced to life, and later died.

Pieter squared his shoulders and looked the major in the eye. 'I don't think I'd like your job much,' he said.

'I don't like it much myself,' the major said. 'You will be operating as Tomäs, an expatriate Portuguese who, as the teenage son of a rich planter, had been too drunk to join the general exodus at the time of the revolution. Tomäs is about your age and this is his photograph. He's slightly crazed and he's been doing manual labour around Maputo, mainly in the docks, in order to keep alive. After the revolution he was pretty badly treated, from what we can make out. Nowadays he's a junkie and a drunk. Think you can pull it off?'

'I guess so, but I'd like to meet Tomäs.'

'You will. We're holding him at our base in Saldahna Bay. A change of air might be safer for you. Spend a couple of weeks with him.'

'Yes, sir.'

'You'll be operating completely alone and if you're caught we shall deny all official knowledge of you, naturally. Your task is to sniff out the expatriate South African blacks who've been overseas for terrorist training. They wait up in Maputo for the signal to cross the borders. You will destroy all enemy headquarters, supplies and personnel, either yourself, or by calling for commandos. You'll evaluate the risks you can personally take remembering that you're too valuable to be killed. You got that?'

'Yes, sir.'

'Be careful, de Vries. Goodbye and good luck.'

Chapter 38

———◆———

Everyone agreed that Ed was a lazy bugger, but for Liza he took infinite pains to teach her the craft of becoming a good news photographer. The hours they spent locked in the darkroom together were happy ones for Liza. It was like being in a cocoon, warmed and soothed by the dim red light, working silently, words unnecessary as he guided her through the intricate business of developing, enlarging and printing. She loved the job. Some days she worked a straight 12-hour shift. She didn't mind. She felt happy to be learning a trade. Besides, while other people were getting tanned in the sun, she was becoming ever more pallid.

Sometimes Ed would amuse her with scathing stories of the hierarchy at the newspaper. He loathed Barbara. 'She's butch,' he confided to Liza.

'Oh, Ed! That's not fair. She's not. It's cruel to say that. Just because she's tough on you, doesn't mean she's butch.'

'There's a butch in every woman,' he said darkly.

He worked silently for a while. Then he switched off the enlarger, opened the darkroom door and beckoned to her. Unlocking the cupboards, he showed her scrapbooks of female celebrities. Caught off-guard they looked ferocious, greedy, fearful and pathetic in turn, but they were all funny. There was one of Barbara swotting a fly, distorted by a close-up lens, murder gleaming in her eyes. Liza choked with laughter.

'If she saw this she'd kill you,' she giggled.

'I've plenty more where that one came from,' he said.

'If you hate women,' she asked pointedly, 'why do you have so many photographs of them?'

He stared around the walls looking puzzled. Liza had always disliked Ed's workroom for wherever you looked some glamorous woman leered back from her niche on the walls or ceilings.

'I knew them all well,' he said. 'Unlikely and unworthy custodians of incredible beauty,' he said. 'Under their skins lurk real live monsters.'

Liza studied Ed curiously, sensing another side of him that she had not encountered. He was a loyal friend, a talented writer and photographer and loads of fun. This 'hating Ed' was a stranger to her.

'If you hate women, how come you're so kind to me?' she asked.

'Perhaps because you're vulnerable. I sense a deep hurt. That makes us fellow sufferers.'

'There's no point in blaming the entire female world for the one bad hurt you've obviously had,' Liza argued. 'In life, you have to learn to take it on the chin.'

His face changed. It was as if he had completely withdrawn.

'Okay, I'm sorry,' she muttered, but it was too late. Ed grabbed his jacket and left. 'See you,' he snarled.

He did not return that day, but at six p.m. he phoned in. Liza took the call in the darkroom where she was developing some pictures.

'The bitch will be screaming for her pages. Find something, do something, anything! What the hell does it matter anyway?' His words were slurred and she could hear that he was drunk.

Liza got on with her work hoping Ed would soon recover.

She had heard the gossip about him. His wife had run off with another man taking their small son, whom he adored, with her. Later, when he sued for custody, she had proved by medical tests that the boy was not his. It was a bad break, but not worth throwing away the rest of your life, Liza thought as she worked.

*

The following morning, Liza was called to Barbara's office.

'Where's Ed?' she snapped.

'I don't know. He was around, but he's not here now,' Liza stammered, trying to cover up.

'Find him. He's late with two pages of pictures and captions plus a thousand words on some scandal or other. Any bloody thing will do at this late stage. Final deadline is really midday today, but I'll give him until four. After that it's too late. We'd have to use syndicated stuff and that's exactly what the little man doesn't want.' She looked truly worried.

'Liza, you're new here,' she said in a conciliatory voice. 'Ed seems to have given up. He drinks, but he likes you, so try to find him and talk him back to earth. Tell him from me that if his work isn't in by four, he's fired. You got that?'

'Yes, of course.'

Liza searched his favourite watering holes, but no one had seen Ed around. He was not at home, either.

Feeling angry, Liza went back to their workroom. Rifling through the cupboards she found his absurd shots of famous women. Some of them looked obscene. Could she use them? Ed might slaughter her. Choosing the nine best she arranged them on a double-page spread. *A misogynist's view . . .* she wrote across the top. There was a revealing picture of the lusty singer, Deborah Dore, whose latest album had just flopped. Liza wrote underneath: *Succeed or bust, is Deb's motto. It seems she chose the latter.* Next, she found a picture of the well-known socialite, Myra Dee, whose seven-figure divorce settlement had just made the headlines. She was pictured laughing, her hand at her mouth, at the dinner table. Liza wrote: *Pardon! I gobbled my mate too fast.* 'Now . . . what next?' she muttered, searching anxiously through the scrapbooks.

Half an hour later she had finished the pages, but would this pass as Ed's work? The photos were his, so perhaps it would be all right, but what on earth could she do about the thousand-word scandal? It was past noon she noticed with a jolt of fear.

Feeling panicky she searched his files for ideas or some

half-written piece, but there was nothing usable. She would have to have a shot at it. It would probably be awful, but what was the alternative? Ed would be sacked.

What about street children? she pondered half an hour later, when nothing much had come to mind. She knew that subject well enough. A scandal, Barbara had said. Were they scandalous enough? Remembering how some of the kids had earned their cash, she thought — why not? She sat at the typewriter and began to write.

It is seven p.m. A skinny child lurks in a squalid alley between two smart highrise apartment blocks. This is his beat. Tonight he is very hungry and impatient to eat. He is hoping that a client will come. A Mercedes draws up at the kerb. Hope dawns, but the car moves off again. Then he hears footsteps approaching. The man looks rich. He is wearing a mohair suit, imported German shoes, a gold watch and a silk shirt. He looks at the shivering boy and says: 'Twenty rands.'

'Forty,' the boy says. They compromise and the deal is settled. The boy climbs on a wooden box, turns his back to the wall and grits his teeth. Minutes later, the business-man has gone and the cash feels good clamped in the boy's hand. He feels happy because he and his friends will eat. How is he to know that he has taken a road which he can never quit.

This is just one incident in a growing trade of child abuse where the very rich are the worst culprits. Who is the well-dressed businessman? He could be your boss, or your husband, or your father, for hundreds of well-heeled and so-called respectable businessmen frequent Hillbrow's alleyways in search of child prostitutes. Hundreds of street boys and girls of six years upwards live on immoral earnings. By twelve they are too old . . .

Liza wrote on, hardly noticing how the time was passing,

remembering Nico and the shame they had felt on his behalf.

Later she stopped, sighed and stretched. She was trembling all over with the force of her passion. The story was too long, but she had no idea what to cut. Oh, goodness, it was almost four. Was it rubbish? Of course it was. She flung it in the waste bin, but then took it out again and smoothed out the pages. Now it was crumpled and grimy, but she could put it through the photocopier. At last, trembling with nervousness, she carried the work through to Barbara's office.

'Ed left this . . . He had to rush off on a story,' she said, in a high-pitched voice. 'He told me to cut it down, but I can't see how to.'

'Typical,' Barbara said, grabbing the pages. 'How could you be expected to do that? Thank you, Liza. When he comes back, tell him to come here. I want to see him. Shit! This is a bit close to the bone,' she muttered.

Liza hung around, unable to stop trembling, wondering if she had lost Ed his job. She had to know if her work was good enough. Dare she ask? Barbara looked up. 'You don't have to stay. By the way, there's some mistake with your ID. Go and sort it out with the pay clerk, please. His name is Cleo and he's doing wages.'

'Oh, no.'

Her stomach lurched in panic. Her worst fears had materialised. Her ID was forged and now they had caught her out. She might go to prison. At the very best she would be sacked. Oh God, help me, she prayed. Was this the end?

She almost collapsed in the lift. 'Cheer up,' a stranger said. 'Nothing can be that bad.' But he was wrong. It was that bad. Her mouth was dry, her hands wet, her whole body trembling as she stumbled towards the accounts wing. In the month she had worked at the *Echo*, she felt she had found her niche. She loved the excitement, the deadline fever, the hyped-up meetings when ideas flew wild and crazy like bats in a tree, and everyone's adrenaline flowed and the atmosphere was so charged with ideas it almost crackled. Now they would throw her out. 'Someone up there hates me,' she murmured, brimming over with self pity.

She walked into the pay department, asked for Cleo and found herself facing a tall, thin black man with bulging, clever eyes.

'There seems to be something wrong here, Miss Frank,' he said. 'This number doesn't seem to exist on any records. It seems you don't exist, although you look perfectly real to me. I'm sure you have a reasonable explanation. No?' He laughed at her open mouth and shocked eyes. 'Then I'll tell you . . .'

He was mocking her and undressing her with his eyes. He fingered her ID as if he were holding a wad of bank notes. 'Miss Frank, do you know that the editorial staff of this newspaper is all-white as a matter of policy. Your ID is forged and you can't get away with it. You're very young, Miss Frank. You probably don't realise that the Boer has a genius for administration. There are twenty-six million documented blacks in this country. Each one of them is irrevocably tied to his ID number or passport, which shows where he was born, where he lives, every facet of his life, every job, every crime, and even the state of his health. If he has TB he will never get a job. They can't escape from their IDs and neither can you.

'Luckily for you, I am the only one who knows you are coloured and I can save you. If I were you, I would be very nice to me. Your job is at stake.'

'Your life will be at stake if you blackmail me,' she said, trying to sound confident. 'I have a lot of dangerous friends, like the people who forged my ID. If you get me fired, you won't last long.'

He laughed. 'I think I'll call you Liza. If I die I'll be replaced. The next man would discover your roots from your number on the paysheet. You see, I had to get your real number from Pretoria. How else could you join the tax scheme or the unemployment insurance. Trust me, Liza.'

I'd sooner trust a python, Liza thought. She scowled and left feeling crushed.

*

'There's no way Ed wrote this,' Barbara said to Simon, her sub-editor, flicking the sheets towards him. 'I know his style. It's good, but different ... rough around the edges – written with passion even though it's crude. I love it.' Maybe Liza? she wondered.

Ten minutes later, when Barbara was dictating letters to Rose, the PRO of the Johannesburg hospital called to tell her that Ed Segal had been admitted to hospital on the previous Friday, suffering from concussion and a broken rib, sustained in a car smash. He would be hospitalised for another three days.

Barbara called Simon back. 'I was right. Ed is hospitalised. Someone's been trying to help him.'

'It's raw, natural talent without any training. Didn't Liza say she longed to write? You don't usually have a burning desire to do something you're no good at.'

'I long to be a rich and pampered wife.'

He ignored her. 'Liza might have been helped by the others. Call her in and tell her Ed promised another story – I'll think of something – and that you want it soon. Keep the others busy so they can't get involved. Let's see what she comes up with.'

'Good thinking,' Barbara said.

Lunchtime in Hillbrow – a high-density suburb of highrise apartment blocks situated on a hill overlooking Johannesburg. It had always been a bohemian quarter, attracting immigrants from all over the world. Lately it had become a strangely mixed area where non-whites were moving in, encouraged by lenient landlords anxious to avoid empty apartments.

Liza arrived at noon wearing a tight, split skirt, a sequinned blouse and high black patent leather shoes. Ed's smallest camera was hidden in her bag. She felt dizzy with excitement, for she was out on a job. Admittedly it was Ed's job, but that was a trivial consideration compared with the amazing thrill of having an assignment. She had to cover the lunchtime prostitution racket and she intended to get some good pictures.

She stood on a street corner, looking provocatively at the

passing traffic, taking sly shots of the pretty girls climbing into smart cars. She hardly noticed two girls moving up on her.

'Hey, you,' one of them snarled, pinching her arm. 'This is our pavement. Get the hell off it. Try further down.' Liza gasped with pain and brought her heel down on the girl's foot, enjoying her squeal.

'I'm borrowing it just this once,' she said. 'Don't start a fight. You'll only lose. You see this?' She grabbed her camera and took their pictures. 'I'm writing a story about the lunchtime trade. Want to tell me why you're in it?'

They did. Annette was blonde and in her late twenties, while Lynn was a redhead of twenty-two. Both were housewives needing extra cash. They maintained a two-roomed flat between them, but most of the businessmen had their own pads, they told her. 'Why don't you try,' they said. 'Bet you don't earn much on a newspaper.'

A car drew up beside them. 'Hey! Are you girls looking for fun?' a middle-aged man asked.

'Sure are,' Lynn said

'A hundred rands,' Liza added. He looked up at her.

'For you?' he asked scathingly. 'You're too dark for me. I like mine blonde.'

Liza was so angry she took his picture as Annette climbed into his car. Then she photographed his number plate.

By half past one she had dozens of pictures and enough material for a series of stories. She was dazed by the brazenness of everyone involved. No one seemed to care that they were breaking the law.

Dare I get into a car? she wondered. I could always run away at the other end. Maybe the guy would talk to me. Maybe he'd even let me use his story. The girls have.

A mild-looking man in his late forties, with glasses and very white hands, drew up next to her.

'Want to come along with me, little lady?' he asked.

Her heart pumping, her mouth so dry she couldn't talk, she opened the door and got in.

'How much?'

'Fifty,' she croaked, remembering her last encounter.

'Only fifty? You got something wrong with you?'

'No,' she blurted out. 'I'm a beginner.'

'I can see that.' He chuckled. 'I want you to understand that I'm doing this on doctor's orders,' he explained, 'so I maintain a very cosy pad. My wife's an invalid, you see.'

Liza pressed her lips firmly together and tried not to giggle as he led her to a smart apartment block near a park. When he drew up in an underground parking lot she felt scared, but the thought that she might get to photograph his apartment was too tempting to be missed.

The 'cosy pad' was expensively furnished with leather furniture, antiques and Persian carpets. He was obviously well off. He poured her a stiff drink and said: 'Make yourself comfortable. There's a dressing-gown in the bathroom.' He gestured behind her. 'I like my girls to wear it, and nothing else. Okay? I'll be back in a few minutes.' He was slobbering with excitement.

Liza took a few shots of the lounge and photographed the black plastic 'dressing-gown' in the bathroom. Then she stood poised by the door, her camera ready, the door ajar.

Moments later the bedroom door opened, and her client emerged naked. Her flash bulb flared and she fled down the passage, hearing his angry shouts right behind her.

The door to the staircase was locked. Panic surged when she realised she was trapped. She fled back to the lift, but he blocked her way. 'I knew there was something fishy about you,' he panted, wrestling for her camera. His fist shot out and caught her in the face and for a few seconds she could only see yellow bicycle wheels revolving round. She hung on to the camera and kneed him in the groin. As he doubled over, she brought her fist down on his neck. The lift arrived and it was empty. Moments later she was racing down the pavement towards the taxi rank.

Barbara was delighted. She called in Simon and together they arranged to meet the *Echo*'s lawyer in the managing editor's office. 'We have a brilliant exposé of the bustling lunchtime prostitution racket,' Barbara told the 'little man'. 'Most of it takes place in flats owned by businessmen precisely for this purpose. We have two in-depth interviews with married whores discussing their regulars and their reasons for turning to prostitution. Listen to this: "He owns a chain store, but he's afraid of his wife so he hires a detective to make sure she doesn't have him tailed. He always leaves his shoes on for a quick getaway." And this from a middle-aged client: "I'm doing this on doctor's orders."

'Now, how much can we use?' She spread the pictures over the desk. 'This shot, for instance, shows a car number. We'll have to blank that out. It's over to you, Cyril. By the way, this was written by Liza Frank, our newest recruit. I think she deserves a by-line, don't you? It's hilarious. Of course we'll have to blank out their faces, little black squares.'

'Why not red hearts?' Simon said.

'Why not indeed!'

'Send her into me,' the little man said. 'I'd like to meet her.'

'Well, it's a bit complicated,' Barbara said, not wanting to explain that Liza still thought she was writing for Ed. 'The girl has a swollen black eye. Next week might be better.'

'Who are the flowers for, Rose?' Liza asked as she hurried through the foyer.

'For Ed. Didn't they tell you? He's in hospital. He crashed his car. You've both been in the wars.'

Liza gasped. 'Is he hurt badly?'

'I don't think so. He was concussed and he cracked a rib. He was unconscious. That's why no one let us know.'

'So when did he crash?'

'Three days ago.'

'I'll tell Barbara.'

'Oh, but she already knows.'

'That's impossible.' Liza felt very hot all of a sudden.

'Oh, by the way, congratulations on your story.'

'What?'

'The Hillbrow hookers . . .'

'Miss Newman,' Liza said, stalking into her office unan-
nounced. 'I want you to know that you are a total bitch. You
used me. You said you didn't know where Ed was, and I've been
worried sick about him. He never had to write about the
lunchtime prostitution racket, did he?'

'No, dear. That was your assignment. Well done.'

'You had no right . . . Besides, I should have visited Ed. You
are heartless.'

'So I've been told.'

'Well then,' Liza said. 'Believe it!'

She stalked out and heard Barbara's voice calling behind her:
'You're getting a by-line, Liza. The "little man" is very pleased
with you.'

Suddenly Liza was walking on air.

Chapter 39

———◆———

Dan had given countless speeches to groups of students at University, but this was his first appearance before masses of people and he felt scared to death. His mouth was dry and his hands were shaking so much he would never be able to hold his notes. He was sitting on the platform at the Orlando soccer stadium and the crowds were flocking to the stands although there was an hour to go before he began. His supporters were spread out around the stadium, barricading the approaching streets to make sure no pigs gatecrashed the party.

Dan had been recently appointed regional chief of the ANC Youth League, for whom he had been recruiting this past two years. He felt he was badly qualified for the job. They had chosen him because of his dedication and his soccer fame which could draw the crowds. What had soccer to do with politics? Being the fastest 'striker' did not qualify him to be an organiser or a public speaker, although it obviously brought the crowds flocking to the stadium. By six p.m. close on ten thousand people were waiting to see him make a fool of himself. Some of his assistants were checking the loudspeakers around the stadium. What would it sound like if they shouted him down? He grinned wryly to himself, knowing that he had prepared a highly contentious statement.

Dan was a communist first and foremost, and his membership and allegiance to the ANC came a close second. The two creeds often clashed. Dan had a vital brief from the communists,

346

which was to smooth away tribal differences and swing the black groups together.

After an interminable wait, his assistant signalled that it was time. Butterflies took flight in his stomach and his mouth dried. He couldn't spit, let alone talk. What was he to do? In a moment of inspiration he began to sing the ANC's anthem and in no time the crowd was singing with him. '*God bless Africa, Let the voice of the people be heard, God bless our people.*' If there was one thing guaranteed to please the people and pull them together it was a song. Dan began to lose his nervousness.

'Comrades,' he began. 'When those white settlers came here three hundred years ago they said: "Here is a plentiful source of cheap labour. We must make sure these kafirs never find out what civilisation is all about. How can we hold them back, so they will stay just as they are forever?"'

He paused and wondered if he had the crowd with him. The stadium was silent.

'Then one of them had a clever idea,' he went on, speaking slowly and using simple words because not everyone was fluent in English. 'Let us make them proud of their traditions. . . so proud that they will never want to abandon them. Their traditions hold them to the past. They can never progress if they only do what their forefathers did. Let us segregate these black people into their different tribes and keep them *apart* from each other, and *apart* from us, and teach them in their traditional stone-age languages. How can they unite against us settlers if they can't even understand each other? The mass of potential black power will be safely split so that it cannot harm us.

'And so that's what they did, my friends. Their plan worked. Our children are still taught in traditional languages. We have no words for television, electricity, motorways, tractors or explosives. Or psychoanalysis, or radar, or ophthalmics, or molecular structure. Why should we want these words? We do not understand what they mean. We can never learn these skills. We have been kept in the Dark Ages by a deliberate white power strategy called *apartheid* – or keeping people apart. And we, comrades, have played into their hands, by feeling like Zulus, Tswanas and Xhosas and forgetting our brotherhood. Comrades, by being proud of our differences we are playing into the white man's hands and supporting his policies.'

A murmur of discontent, almost like a rumble of thunder, ran through the twenty thousand listeners.

'I tell you this now, you are South Africans, and you are human beings and you live in the twentieth century. But who would believe this, when they see our children run barefooted and hungry after our skinny cows? And who would believe it when they see our wives daubed with white clay, grinding corn with a stone quern? Or when they see old women hoeing the soil with handmade stone hoes, or cutting off their children's fourth fingers to stave off evil spirits? We have become the white man's zombies.'

Now the roar from the crowd was ominous.

After another half an hour of taunts the crowd was yelling for his blood, although he reckoned he had about half of them on his side. He could hardly make himself heard over the angry shouts and supporting cheers. Scuffles were breaking out amongst the spectators.

'We must join forces comrades. We have enormous black power – *if we unite*. This is what the whites fear more than anything else. So now I reach out to you, my Zulu comrades, and I say to you, we are one people. We must unite and love one another and let go of our tribal differences, let them go to a museum where they belong!'

Strong words! Heady days! Dan stood down feeling exhausted, knowing that he was shaking like a leaf and needing a drink of water very badly. Someone handed him one, and he drained the glass.

At that precise moment, a Zulu in national costume leaped on to the platform, raised his spear and brought it smashing down on Dan's head. Dan ducked and swerved, and the spear, sharp as a razor, sliced his arm. It was all over in a second. His supporters had the Zulu warrior pinned to the ground and shortly afterwards they carried him away. Dan tried to staunch the blood, but it kept pouring down.

'Is there a doctor in the audience?' one of his men roared into the loudspeaker.

A pretty young woman climbed on to the platform, carrying her bag. 'I'm a doctor. Lay him down here. Please keep still,' she snapped. 'Don't move. You're losing a lot of blood. I need blankets,' she called into the loudspeaker. She had an American accent, but to Dan she looked a lot like a younger version of Miriam.

It seemed poetic justice that Dan found himself wrapped in piles of traditional Zulu blankets in next to no time.

'That was some speech,' she said. 'They tell me you're also a soccer champion and a local hero,' she said in her soft, lilting voice. 'Well, let's see just how tough you really are. I don't have any local anaesthetic and this wound must be disinfected and stitched.'

'Go ahead,' Dan said, feeling dazed and shocked. 'I don't believe you're real, so how can I feel pain? Someone as beautiful as you couldn't be a doctor, could they? Besides, you're too young.'

'Just keep quiet,' she snapped. 'You've said quite enough for one afternoon. Don't you think so?'

'I haven't finished,' Dan said.

'I'm telling you now, you've finished for the day,' she retorted.

Dan lay still while she stitched his arm. The pain was truly something, but he wanted her to admire him, so he sweated it out in silence. 'How about dinner?' he managed to say when she'd finished.

'My God! What are you? Superman?' She took a long, hard look at the people's hero lying on the floor pretending not to feel anything and she began to understand their adulation. Shit! He was good-looking and sexy, too. What a body! Yet he was so unaware of his appeal. She was due back in the States in six months and she'd promised herself not to get involved here.

*

Her name was Judy Turner. She was twenty-eight years old and came from Los Angeles. She had come to the meeting simply to try to understand what was going on. She seemed to be homesick for she spent half of dinner telling him about her family and her home. Over coffee, she caught up with the present and the reasons for her visit to South Africa, which was to learn.

'It's so confusing,' she said. 'So many groups of people are against each other and yet at the hospital where I work, no one is against anyone else. Even the whites seem to have a wonderful relationship with their black colleagues and nurses. I can't begin to get to grips with this country. There's rigid racialism without the hatred. It's group hatred rather than individual and so much of it is blacks against blacks.'

'Hence my speech,' Dan said. 'But it seemed to annoy a lot of people. Communism is the natural extension of our traditions here if we can let go of the old ways.'

'You're way behind the times,' she snarled.

Sensing their differences, Dan switched to music. 'Take jazz,' he said. 'It began here and d'you know why? A tribe shares everything, even the music. In the village the musician will play and sing a theme, but every person within hearing will add their own music and story, synchronising with the main theme, but doing their own thing, singing, dancing and making up stories. We don't have a separate word for song and dance, and that's because for us they can't be separated.'

At last he'd found something they could talk about. Jazz was her scene and they talked until midnight. Then she glanced at her watch and jumped up. 'Can you believe the time!' she gasped. 'I'm on duty at five o'clock. It was good to meet you, Dan. Hope I see you again.'

There was an imperceptible pause. Dan nodded, not quite sure what to say. She was a great kid, but compared with Miriam she was just that – a kid, and his heart was still firmly booked. It would take a long time to mourn Miriam, he knew.

After Judy had left he ordered another coffee and sat hunched over it, longing for Miriam picturing her, remembering her. After a while it almost seemed as if he could feel her beside him. A deep grief began to smother him. He felt his throat constricting and his eyes pricking. He stood up, paid his bill, and left his coffee unfinished. It was almost as if his blinding need for Miriam brought her to him. That happened often enough and then their mutual grief mingled and became overpowering until he almost drowned in it. Right now he had to be alone. He went home, creeping up the stairs, so that he wouldn't have to talk to Liza or Martha. It would be wrong of him to encourage Judy, he decided. He would never get over Miriam and never stop longing for her.

The telegram from Sam arrived the following morning. It read: 'Nosisi's smallholding has been confiscated by the state and she is to be evicted on Friday. Come home and help us.'

Dan left at once and drove directly to Nelfontein, stopping only to refill. He parked at the gate of her smallholding, for there was no driveway, and walked along the narrow path to the top of the hill overlooking her land. With an ache in his guts he saw at a glance that he was too late.

Today was Thursday, but that made no difference to the government officials, who clustered together looking awkward. The bulldozer was advancing towards Nosisi's home, the iron jaws gaping wide.

Standing still, as if rooted in the land, Nosisi blocked its path. She was so defenceless and so alone. Her hands were held high as if for protection, and for the first time Dan saw how vulnerable his grandmother really was. She had always intimidated him but now he saw her frailty and he loved her.

Surely they would stop? Time had switched to slow motion. Fear surged through him as he raced downhill, waving and yelling loudly. 'Get out of the way, Nosisi! Move aside.'

Could she hear him? The bulldozer was almost on top of her when the driver braked violently. The wheels squealed and turned, splaying her with mud. She turned towards the sound of Dan's voice and slipped in the mud.

Dan hauled her up and carried her out of the way. He felt her heart beating wildly and heard her muttered curses as the bulldozer smashed into her bungalow time and again until it was razed to the ground.

He tried to calm her. 'We'll get lawyers. We'll sue for compensation,' he promised. Then he realised that a government official was bending over them.

'I'll see you in court,' Dan muttered, feeling scared to look at the man, he longed to kill him so much. 'This is freehold land. D'you hear me? She holds the titles.' His voice cracked. 'For God's sake, this is theft! Her grandfather bought this land legally.'

'It is the land of my fathers. The graves of my ancestors are here,' Nosisi mumbled. 'And this is my home. I will not leave.'

The house that now lay in a jumbled heap of masonry and roofing tiles had cost Nosisi more than five thousand pounds to build. Dan knew this for she never tired of telling him that she was leaving it to him. It was not the cost of the house she was crying about, he knew, but the loss of her home and everything she possessed.

'You should have left before,' the official said sternly. 'This land was proclaimed white in 1953. My goodness, we've been very lenient. She's been living here on borrowed time. She can't live in a white area and she knows that as well as I do. You people make me sick, always whining and wailing. You've got your own Homeland.' He pointed eastwards towards Ka-Ngwane. 'And we've come all this way just to move you. Don't ever say we don't help you people.' He gestured towards the truck which they had driven over the land.

'You people must hurry up to carry your things to the lorry. Take whatever you like,' he said grandly.

'Or whatever one man with an arm in a sling and one old woman can lift,' Dan said.

'Don't be cheeky, boy. You people know you're not wanted

here. What did her grandfather want to go buying land in a white area for? It's against the law.' The official frowned and looked perplexed. 'Law's law and this is a white area. That's all there is to it, so get moving.'

Dan was speechless for once. The official was an oaf, a cretin, and there was no point in arguing with him.

It was then that they saw Sam plodding towards them sitting in the ramshackle donkey cart. 'They said Friday,' he muttered, his face contorted with frustrated rage. 'I came to help you move,' he added gently to Nosisi.

'I will not move. These men are robbers and they are trespassing and they have destroyed my property.' The tears were running down her face as she gazed at the wreckage.

'For the last time, do you want to make use of the lorry to move your possessions?' The official waited in silence. Then he shrugged. 'If you are not gone off this land by tomorrow you will be arrested and sentenced for vagrancy and trespassing.'

They drove off looking grave and burdened by the weight of their responsibilities.

Dan and Sam hired a lorry and moved every last item piece by piece to the plot she had been allocated in KaNgwane. The ground was stony and they broke six pickaxes before the foundations were completed, but within a week a shack of sorts had been erected and her possessions moved into it. Nosisi wandered around with a pathetic, childish expression, seeming agitated and bewildered, conducting rambling conversations with her ancestors and doing very little that was helpful. Then she broke down.

At first they did not know what had happened. One Sunday morning she sat on the floor in the corner of the shack with her arms around her knees and remained there staring at the wall. Around bedtime, when she had not moved or eaten, they realised something must be done. The doctor was called and she was put to bed where she remained passively staring at the ceiling for several days while her maid nursed her haphazardly and Sam watched over her and fetched the water from the nearest pump a kilometre away.

Dan stayed with her, sleeping on the couch, washing from a bucket, and buying their food from the cash he earned running an irregular bus service from KaNgwane to Nelfontein and all the time he was worrying himself sick about his studies.

On the second Sunday night, when the maid was off and Sam was out, Dan found himself alone with Nosisi. This worried him, but she fell asleep early so he sat reading the newspaper by candlelight. Then he seemed to hear knocking. It was strange, almost as if someone was inside, knocking to go out. The candle flickered and hissed and the room became cold. Dan folded the paper and sat listening intently. The knocking came again and he distinctly smelt Miriam's perfume. 'I'm going nuts,' he whispered.

Nosisi began to toss restlessly and mutter in her sleep. Dan got up and bent over her. She's old, he thought, feeling touched and protective. Now that she was not eating, her face was skeletal and her skin was loose and dull. She was so hot and sweaty. He took a cloth, soaked it in the precious water and wrung it out before wiping her face and hands.

She looked into his eyes and said: 'Miriam is here. She wants me to tell you that she loves you. Why are you so sad, she asks? You have forgotten joy and that makes her sad. She says you were right. She should never have bought the taxis. She regrets it so much. But you must not be bitter and you must play your flute for her. She longs to hear you play. She is happy and with friends and she comes often to see you. She says, "Do you remember when we met, something so funny happened. I laughed and laughed so much I fell out of bed."'

'I remember,' Dan said hoarsely. 'Tell her I love her.'

'She knows that,' Nosisi said. 'She has to go.'

Nosisi sat up and shivered. 'I'm hungry. Go and see what there is to eat,' she said.

'Do you remember what you just said?' Dan asked urgently. 'You gave me a message. Is Miriam still here?'

'Why should you care? You don't believe in these things,' Nosisi said, her shrewd eyes scanning his face. 'One day you will learn not to mock our old ways. I don't remember what I said. I was in a trance.'

The next morning Nosisi was back to normal. Dan packed his bag and returned to Johannesburg.

Chapter 40

———◆———

Liza was soon drawn into the tense world of newspaper reporting, where you are only as good as your last story and the trauma of deadline looms every week.

They all had their own way of coping. Marge would scream and shout, Barbara became more bitchy, Simon would get a migraine, Ed would go off and get drunk. Enid simply cried.

Liza was working like a dog, completing her seven-hour stint as a darkroom assistant and then writing her stories after hours, never letting up, intent on building up an image of the superb woman she would like to be, successful, popular and right in the swing of things.

Yet the more successful she became, the more her colleagues seemed to draw away from her. She felt isolated, almost an untouchable. Sometimes it seemed that she had been dropped on earth from outer space. She didn't belong anywhere. She was a fraud, a pretender, a no-good *gammat* who had gate-crashed the white world. But these thoughts belonged to the dark hours of the night. By day she hung on to her ambition and remained aloof. Sometimes, in moments of extreme loneliness, she made excuses for herself. How could she make a friend? In next to no time they would find out she was classified coloured, and that would be tickets for her.

So she laboured on alone and lately she even snubbed Ed and his friendly overtures, for he, too, might find out the truth about her. She knew that this had hurt Ed, and she noticed that he now avoided her. Who cares? she thought. She didn't need anyone's friendship. They were whites and therefore treacherous. They would reject her out of hand if they found out who and what she was.

For solace she turned to her work. She was making far more than just her low wages. Because she was employed as a darkroom assistant, the *Echo* management paid her free-lance rates for every article they used and Liza made sure her stories were sensational, so they could not refuse them.

She developed the habit of writing at night when her photographic work was done. Because there was no transport she often worked right through, snatching a few hours' sleep in the darkroom, and dumping a pile of articles in the editor's tray around 8 a.m. Early risers would find her working away in her cubicle-office, glossy head bent over her typewriter, eyes downcast, unaware of the time.

One winter evening she found a caricature of herself depicted as a porcupine, pinned on the wall behind her desk, with the caption: Species: *Lizavericious Porcupine*. Habits: Nocturnal, solitary, quick to shoot poisonous barbs into the unwary, dangerous and mainly feeds on friends. Has never been known to mate. In danger of extinction.

Ed, obviously, she thought without laughing. She screwed it up and threw it in the wastebin. Who cares? *Dogs bark but the caravan moves on.* That was her motto nowadays.

She was about to go home when a call came from the 'little man'. In her six months at the *Echo*, Liza had never set eyes on Cyril Watson, the managing editor, and she felt scared. Perhaps Cleo had reported her. Lately his threats had become more compelling. Had he told the editor she was a *gammat*? She'd be sacked, disgraced and ruined.

She was aware of curious looks as she walked through the open-plan offices. Even Ed looked the other way as she passed his workroom. Their aloofness reminded her of school. Was this the end? Once again she felt like that vulnerable young child of the past. Stomach churning, eyes burning, she forced her feet to move forward. Step by painful step she made her way to the opulently carpeted first floor where the head office was situated.

She had to wait. An eternity of anxiety kept her hands sweating and her mouth dry. As fear sank in deeper she could not get enough breath. *I mustn't pant. The Beagle is watching me.* The MD's secretary, Miss Hunt, was nicknamed for her doglike devotion to her master. So what, if he sacks me? I'll start again. Who needs the *Echo*? Oh God, I don't want to lose my job.

When she was called in, she realised why the managing editor was called the little man, for he barely came up to her shoulder. He was dark and stocky, with a Latin look about him and the longest curly eyelashes she had ever seen. They swept over his cheeks and half concealed his shrewd brown eyes. He looked grave as he shook her hand and asked her to sit down. By now she was shaking so much she had to sit on her hands to keep them still.

'Miss Frank, you are very young,' he said, flipping through her file.

Here it comes. Hold fast, Liza.

'I see you're making a very good thing out of working for the *Echo*. You are paid free-lance rates for the work you submit and consequently you're earning more than most editors. This won't do, my dear.'

'But what have I done wrong?' she asked. 'I don't force you to use them.'

'Relax, Liza. Can I call you Liza?'

She nodded, hanging on to her composure.

'I have never before offered someone as young as you the chance of their own column, but you seem to have exactly the right style we need. You poke fun at the establishment. How would you like to write your own column each week?'

Liza tried to say something, but could not. She was in shock.

'It would give you the opportunity to become one of the country's best-known journalists. Of course,' he added hastily, 'you would have to write much more than you are doing now.'

She could not talk. Her mouth opened, but no sound emerged. Then she managed to croak: 'Thank you, Mr Watson.

If you think I can do it.' She sounded so servile.

'Do *you* think you can do it?'

'Yes . . . Oh yes. I want to do it!' Now she was shouting. She took a deep breath and tried to calm herself.

Cyril Watson pressed his intercom. 'Coffee for two, please, Miss Hunt.' The Beagle returned with a tray, panting slightly, her eyes gleaming.

For the next half an hour Liza listened in a daze. The nitty-gritty was a considerable loss of income for writing a great deal more, plus a vast increase in prestige. She would have her own weekly column to be called *Liza Talks Frankly*. She could write whatever she pleased just as long as she checked it out with the managing editor every Monday. In addition, she must write one piece for the magazine after consultation with Barbara, and a story for the newspaper of women's interest and a scandalous exposé for the back page. For this she would get the modest salary of one thousand rands a month. Anything else she wrote must be submitted for the *Echo's* first refusal. If they did not use the story within three weeks she was free to sell it elsewhere. They would find a replacement for the darkroom.

Cyril Watson stood up and shook her hand. 'I feel sure you have a brilliant future ahead of you, Miss Frank,' he said.

Her own column! It was too good to be true. Now she had a weapon of her own to hit back at society. A sense of power surged through her. It felt tremendous. But she had to get something written by tomorrow.

Everyone stared curiously through their glass cubicles as she rushed back to her little compartment. Liza hardly noticed. She sat slumped at her desk, her head in her hands, which was how she created best. Something was there . . . something almost in her grasp, something she'd read. Ah! Now she had it. A minister had been quoted as saying in Parliament: 'When I talk about a black I mean a black, but when I say "somebody" I mean a white, naturally.' He had opened himself to ridicule. Moments later her fingers were racing over the keyboard.

Enid leaned over her, touching her shoulder. 'What is it, Liza? What's wrong?'

'Here, love,' Rose said, putting a cup of coffee on her desk. 'You look like you need it. What can we do to help?'

'Nothing's wrong,' Liza snarled. 'Were you hoping I'd be sacked? Sorry to disappoint you all.'

'Ouch!' Enid said, disappearing.

Rose watched her with a troubled smile. 'What's bugging you, Liza?' Rose said. 'We were only trying to help.'

'When I need help – I'll ask. I'm busy. Thanks for the coffee.'

She gritted her teeth and plunged into her story, enjoying the daggers she was thrusting into the government minister. She wanted to hit and barb and wound time and again. Boy, would they squirm. She couldn't wait for Sunday.

When she had finished she felt better. She looked round, and was surprised to see the editorial staff gathered round the reception desk. They were all drinking – even Barbara. Strange! She walked past them hesitantly.

'Hi, Liza!' Ed called, thrusting a glass into her hand. 'We're celebrating.'

'Whatever for?' She took a gulp and then flushed as she noticed a life-sized photograph of herself pinned on the wall. She was sitting at her desk, gazing over her shoulder into the camera, a look of amused spite on her face, her fingers out of focus as they flew over the keys. The caption read: *We hatched her so we love her as only a mother could*. There were ten signatures scrawled on the photograph.

'Barbara wants a photo for your column,' Ed said, flushing heavily.

'You love me?' she queried stupidly. 'And you all signed it?'

Oh God! She could feel the tears bubbling up and flowing down her cheeks. Then she burst into tears. What a disgrace! 'I have so many defences,' she said hoarsely, pulling herself together with an effort. 'I built them up over the years, but I never had to defend myself against kindness before. Please excuse me.' Then she fled.

*

There was no shortage of material to write about, for the South African mood was grim. Overseas sanctions were ruining the economy and had caused a foreign exchange loss of a staggering R40 billion. Forty-eight American companies, including IBM, Coca-Cola and General Electric, had disinvested or closed shop. Jobs were going down like ninepins, and unemployment had reached an all-time high for both whites and blacks. To make matters worse, millions of black school leavers were joining the labour market each year, but there were no jobs for them. Riots and strikes were causing unbearable tension for everyone. Trade Unions had stepped up their demands and hundreds of union leaders had been imprisoned during the year, leading to more protest strikes across the country.

Reform and placate was the government's answer. The central business districts of all major cities were opened to trading by all races. Hotels and restaurants were unexpectedly told they could serve everyone.

Whites were experiencing the first painful shock of change. Public facilities, such as parks and swimming pools, became overrun by blacks, beggars crowded every corner, squatter settlements appeared overnight, rapes and burglaries became commonplace. The whites' security and existence were threatened and they reacted with a swing to the far right. But the government doggedly continued with their reform programme and their efforts to reach agreement on some kind of power sharing with the black majority.

For the under-privileged, hope appeared with the repeal of the Influx Control Act. This meant that millions of blacks who had been restricted to their Homelands had freedom of movement for the first time in thirty years. They flooded to the cities by train, by bus, in black taxis and dilapidated cars, in donkey carts, or on foot – a never-ending tide of hopeful, homeless, jobless, hungry people. Leaving their drought-ridden arid acres, starvation and deprivation, they swelled the squatter camps, building homes of cardboard boxes or rolled-out drum sheets and began the heartbreaking task of searching for non-existent jobs.

For Liza it was manna from heaven. Wherever she looked another story was waiting to be written.

Chapter 41

A prayer for peace, the poster outside St Cyprian's church had announced. The peace-loving, liberal-minded people who lived in the rural, rambling country suburb of Honeydew, north of Johannesburg, had arrived at their church on Friday evening well in time for this unusual 7 p.m. service.

Against a backdrop of escalating violence and murder, the young vicar from England hoped to set a fashion for nationwide prayers for peace. Not that Honeydew had seen much unrest. Life rambled on comfortably from flower show to tennis party, but privately, in the sacred precincts of the golf club, business-men might be heard to confide that they couldn't see the *munts* [Zimbabwean colonial slang for blacks] making a worse job of running the state departments than the Boers, and that the sooner the 'New South Africa' was ushered in, the sooner they'd get the economy moving again.

Amongst the middle-class congregation was Pat Ingleton, from Kent, who had once played at Wimbledon, and who had just married off her last daughter in this very church. She was tall and athletic and she coached tennis at the local sports club. Her husband Bob, about to retire from forty years as a bank manager, had the misfortune to be as handsome as a Hollywood star with his friendly blue eyes, rugged features and wavy brown hair. After a scandalous affair last year, he and his wife now slept in separate rooms.

Biddy, who had run a dried-flower business since being widowed, had recently inherited a small fortune and was superbly dressed in a turquoise woollen suit from Paris with a matching felt hat with a white ribbon round it.

Rosemary Johnston, a well-known artist specialising in landscape paintings was with her eldest son, Jeremiah, a computer boffin. Emily and David Ireland, who co-owned an import business were about to leave for a six-month summer tour of Britain and Europe and they were excited and holding hands. Brian Jefferies, teacher and football coach at a local school, was there because he loved the aloof young physiotherapist, Joyce, who lived in a small, but lovely English-style cottage near the church. She was looking delightful in a cream jersey and skirt, with black hat, shoes and gloves. Each time she smiled at him his heart leaped for joy.

As the sermon began, most of the congregation tried to drag their minds from earthly preoccupations to think about peace and how lovely it had been in this beautiful country a decade back and how absolutely divine it would be if the bloody blacks and Boers would come to terms with each other and let everyone get on with their lives. The sermon was laboured. Kind though their new vicar was, he hadn't an ounce of creative talent in him. 'His heart's in the right place,' David whispered to Emily, smothering a yawn.

Brian didn't hear a word. Another smile from Joyce had sent his imagination soaring to a shared cottage near the school, convenient for their brood of kids, the boys like him, the girls pretty miniature clones of Joyce. Who could want more?

Rosemary glanced anxiously at Jeremiah. He was bored. He had always been brainy, but restless. Every minute spent with him was precious because he seldom came home nowadays. Home was boring. She sighed inwardly.

Biddy was mentally spending her fortune. She could do with a new bathroom, a few loads of compost would improve the garden enormously, and she could now afford a pool ... she broke off and blinked.

Out of the corner of her eye she had seen movement – some blacks arriving late. There were four of them and they were all carrying raincoats over their arms like London businessmen, but it was so hot. Strange! She turned to smile a welcome for she always patronised blacks unless they were drunk. Then she saw something that was impossible – a gun – and it was pointed at her, but this warning of deadly danger could not reach to her legs in time. Wide-eyed with shock she stood rooted to the spot and watched the black finger tighten on the trigger. She felt herself propelled backwards ...

In a split-second of utter incredulity, Brian had seen the four blacks produce guns from under their folded coats, and as the first shots rang out, he yelled to the congregation: 'Get down ... down ...! He threw down those close to him, but he was hemmed in. How could he get to Joyce? A hand-grenade soared in her direction. There would be no second chance. He leaped up, he could almost hear the schoolboys cheering as he made a perfect catch, pushed it into his stomach and fell face down over the grenade, hoping that his body would contain most of the blast. At that moment only one thing counted, her safety.

Jeremiah's reactions were fast. He flung his mother down and fell over her.

The nightmare had become reality. The vaulted ceiling echoed the screams of fear and pain, the rattle of sub-machine guns and the horrible explosion of the first grenade. The sounds and the smell of blood and smoke and tremors of fear assaulted their senses. Everyone was crouching over the flagged floor, but the guns kept raking their bodies.

Jeremiah began to mutter: 'Bastards ... Bastards ...' He was two from the end of the pew, but his anger gave him strength. He scrambled over his neighbours and propelled himself forwards, hands groping, his body horizontal, reaching for the nearest terrorist. He would pummel the life out of him. The gunman ducked, swung his gun up and let off a round. Jeremiah crumpled against the wall and lay still.

David was sitting as if dazed when the grenade landed in his lap, destroying his legs and one arm, shattering his ear drums, and blinding him.

Now the terrorists were running out of the church, and Emily, who had fumbled for the gun in her bag, her brain addled with grief, ran after them. 'Oh God, Oh God,' she panted as she fired. She saw one of them fall and clutch at his leg. His companion dragged him into the car which lurched forward with shrieking tyres and raced down the road, out of sight.

Then they were gone.

'Where's a telephone?' someone shouted over the groans and screams. 'Call the ambulance.'

The priest rushed to the presbytery. His housekeeper had let off the burglar alarm in the cottage next door and the siren merged with sobs and shouts. Those who were calmer began to comfort the distraught.

By the time the police arrived, the congregation had pulled itself together. First aid was being administered, people were being comforted. Rosemary was sitting on the floor cradling her son's corpse in her arms, waiting for someone to tend her shattered leg. Bob, who was shot through the top of his arm, was helping Pat, who was wounded in the thigh.

'You're going to be all right,' he said. 'I love you. I always loved you.'

'I love you, too,' she murmured and felt happy for the first time that year.

The dead, including Jeremiah, Biddy and Brian, were lying under altar cloths.

Afterwards all they could say to each other was: 'Why? Why us? Why?'

Tony was being driven to his office when he heard the news of the massacre on his car radio. Perhaps he should buy a hand gun, he thought, wondering what sort to choose. He was two blocks from his building when he heard the shouting. 'What the hell. . .?' he muttered. For a moment he felt scared. Then he pulled himself together. 'Go more slowly,' he told his driver.

Turning into Commissioner Street, he saw a massive crowd of blacks. They were shouting, singing, toyi-toying and leaping up and down like demented monkeys in the zoo. Some were waving placards. The noise was incredible.

He tried to read one, but the bloody fool wouldn't keep still. Then a man came running towards him and thrust a placard almost into the car. *Robber baron gets rich while our children starve*, he read. *Hands off MacGregor's Fruit Juice. Pay out the pensions. Robber baron robs the poor*.

There was nothing anyone could do about MacGregor's now. Tony's action had taken everyone by surprise. He had taken over the massive group over a month ago because he had realised that the equipment, buildings, land and farms were worth much more than the value shown on their balance sheet. The company canned fruit, vegetables and jam and owned huge farms, some of which were surrounded by built-up areas. All the assets had been privately sold before anyone even knew he'd bought the company. Then, at the final moment, his lawyers had dropped the bombshell and fired everyone. Three thousand, two hundred blacks and fifty whites had pocketed their notice pay and left, reeling with shock. The whites had seen their lawyers but Tony had not broken the law. Besides, how could anyone protest to a company that no longer existed?

With a sinking heart Tony realised that he was up against someone with brains. How the hell had they found out who had bought MacGregor's and exactly what else he owned? He'd acted through nominees throughout. But someone had decided to make a personal attack on him and carry their woes to his other holdings. Some smart-arsed lawyer. Who?

The police were attempting to maintain order and they had formed a chain of men and dogs to leave a path open to the main entrance. Tony parked and walked through the angry crowd. He felt vulnerable and afraid, but it would be suicide to show fear. His stomach knotted, his breath coming in short sharp gasps, he forced himself to walk naturally. It would take just one bullet fired from amongst those chanting savages to blow him into oblivion, or worse still into a living death.

Once inside the foyer he exploded with rage, all his pent-up fear and fury showering his staff. 'Where the hell is my secretary? My lawyer? Why is the security chief sitting at reception? What the hell is going on?' he ranted.

'The black staff have been intimidated into striking ... packers, despatch department, drivers, and some of the coloured typesetters. They're trying to intimidate the non-whites. Some of the girls went home. The demonstrators have been here since before dawn. It's not just here, Mr Cronjé. All your factories and holdings have similar pickets.'

'Get the police chief,' Tony said.

An hour later, Tony had learned that other than provoking another Sharpeville and bringing international condemnation around their necks, there wasn't much he could do, other than negotiate with their leader. Their leader, he discovered, was a Dan Tweneni. The name seemed familiar.

Later that day, the two men came face to face in Tony's board room. Dan Tweneni stood astride the carpet and refused to sit down.

'Look. What you've done is legal, man,' he said. 'I know that as well as you do, but it's morally wrong. You sacked a whole lot of older people who were within a few years of getting their pensions. Men who had worked twenty or thirty years with MacGregor's. I'm not just talking about blacks, I'm talking about whites, too. The way you did it was sneaky and underhand.

'First you merged the workers' pension fund, in which there was a huge surplus, with the executives' pension fund, which was basically just for the MacGregor family and other director-shareholders. As soon as the two funds were totally intermingled, you fired the work force, paying out only their own contributions plus a tiny rate of interest. All this is in accordance with the pension fund rules, of course, but these rules were drawn up long before we had 15% inflation.

'So then the whole surplus accrued to the remaining members – the MacGregor family, plus their lackeys. All of whom will no doubt be retiring soon. In other words you used our workers' pension fund to fund your takeover. This was how you paid off the MacGregor family. It also explains why you paid so little to take control of the company.'

'I wasn't aware of all these implications,' Tony said smoothly. 'My lawyers handled everything. I will look into it. Now call off your men.'

'Give me your word as an old colleague that you'll pay up and I'll call off the men.'

An old colleague? This time he was really floored. 'What the hell are you talking about?'

'We used to drive tractors together,' Dan said. 'And unless I'm very much mistaken I was beaten up for your crime. Of course it was a long time ago.'

Tony almost passed out with shock. His eyes became glazed, his face turned deathly white, and he felt dizzy. By the time he had recovered, Tweneni had left.

The effect of the Honeydew massacre was devastating for business and the stock market, Tony thought angrily as he skimmed through the financial news days later. He was sitting in his newspaper office, drinking coffee and smoking an expensive cigar. Everything about Tony was expensive nowadays: his suits, his signet ring, his haircut, his gold watch, and his women whom he flaunted at all the best clubs. His svelte Swedish secretary perched on the table beside him and ran her fingers through his hair.

'Buzz off,' he said irritably. 'I have to think.' He frowned as he read. Several proposed big overseas investments in South Africa had been cancelled. The stream of tourists had dried up. Hotels and the peripheral businesses that depended upon tourism were depressed, the property market had fallen to an all-time low, liquidations were at an unprecedented high, the stock market was down and the Rand was falling daily. Only two sectors had prospered from the disaster: gunsmiths and travel agents, as countless European families prepared to fly 'home'.

Most home-bred whites were prevented from leaving by economic circumstances, or South African passports, and they began to feel like rats trapped in a sinking ship. There was nowhere to swim to. Thousands of English families, who had been born and bred in Africa felt themselves to be white Africans and would never willingly leave. They had experienced the 'Africa run' – from Kenya, to Zambia, to Zimbabwe, to South Africa. There was nowhere else to go, for Africa was in their blood and their hearts. For most Afrikaners there had never been a choice and never would be. This was their home – their land – fought for and cultivated by their forefathers.

To Tony, the situation provided both challenges and advantages. He had never felt that he belonged to a specific group of people, perhaps because his mother had been English, his father Afrikaans. He did not feel a strong sense of patriotism, but most of his fortune was here. Sanctions had been making him rich, for he had been snapping up industries for next to nothing as American and British firms pulled out.

He sighed. Africa was dying. Somehow he must start shifting his fortune overseas. How? Getting money out was strictly illegal, but ways and means existed for those with the brains and guts to do it.

He had managed to buy an almost bankrupt mining company listed on the London Stock Exchange. It owned a failing chrome mine in Zimbabwe and several concessions in Mozambique where mining operations had been curtailed. That country had been crippled by nearly twenty years of civil war, but it would be opened up one day and there was a fortune to be grabbed. In particular he coveted the gold, uranium and emerald mines. The copper operation in Zaire was hazardous, too, which was why he had picked up the company for a song. He intended to add some profitable local gold mines to the assets and list more shares to the British public. Once he had a thriving London base it would be easy to transfer his wealth stealthily bit by bit.

His secretary popped her glossy head around the door again. 'Meester Cloete, he is here,' she sang, smiling provocatively.

Cloete looked worried. His blue eyes had lost their twinkle and his beard needed trimming.

'Internal security is at an all-time low,' he said. That was obvious, so why waste time, Tony wondered?

'Several arms caches have been found in the past month,' he told Tony. 'For every dump we find there are ten others hidden away. The boys on the borders are doing a fabulous job, over two hundred and fifty thousand rands worth of Russian-made arms have been picked up near Nelfontein in the past month alone.

'Thinking of what gets through undetected keeps me awake at night,' he went on. 'The security forces know the leaders of the various militant black movements, but proving their guilt is quite another matter. There's some very clever brains on their side.' He kept repeating that, looking worried to death, until Tony became impatient with him.

'Then do something about it,' he snapped. 'Must I think of everything?'

'If we move against them we'll have the press around our necks, that means more sanctions, more problems on a diplomatic level. Sometimes it seems as if every journalist is a fifth column agent pushing us towards extinction.'

Tony shrugged. They'd had this conversation before.

'Damn it, man, are you interested in our predicament at all, I sometimes wonder, or are you just in this to make money?'

'I'm interested in getting results,' Tony said. 'You people won't make the right moves. You haven't got the guts to do what is necessary. This is war. Unseen, undercover, undeclared, but war just the same. If you know who the leaders are, then deal with them.'

Cloete sighed. 'After a week in jail some fancy lawyer gets

them out, or they hold protest meetings overseas for their release. It's getting to be a nightmare. We seem to be fighting the world.'

'It's so simple. Kill them. End of story. Once they're dead, all the protests in the world can't help them.'

Cloete sat staring at his hands as if in shock. 'I could do with a drink,' he said at last.

Tony felt contemptuous. The whole government was like that. Do-gooders at heart. Not an ounce of spunk amongst them. That's why they had this problem in the first place. In Australia they'd hunted down their aborigines, in America they'd polished off most of the Native Indians. The British had put plague bacilli in blankets for the South American Indians, but here the problem kept on multiplying.

'Who do we order to do this? The army, the police? Don't be mad, man,' Cloete said, looking horrified.

'Create a special force,' Tony argued. 'Our MI is the best organised in the world. One of them must step outside the framework of the SADF and create his own team of men who have the experience and the right political views. I know the right man. Give me the list of targets and give me the funds. It will cost plenty. You can't allow this sort of thing to go through the SADF accounts system.'

'I've worked fast – a special fund has been set up,' Cloete told him the following day when they met. 'Here are the details of the bank and the bank number. It's quite outside and separate to all State accounting. You don't have to know the sources. You are accountable to me and if I should die, my successor would approach you. I don't want to know who your contact is. If you are sure he's high up in military intelligence, and that he can command the loyalty of the right type of men, then go for it. Here's the list of black leaders who must be "removed from society".'

Cloete left soon afterwards. Tony laughed at him. The two-faced old fool didn't have the courage of his convictions.

He studied the list thoughtfully. So they knew who had been responsible for the Honeydew massacre. Cloete had a point. They would get political amnesty after a year or so. Society could do without them. He picked up his pen and added Dan Tweneni to the list. As far as he was concerned, Dan was the most subversive man in Africa. The people worshipped him.

Single-handed he had united the tribes and brought trade unions, political parties and cultural groups into one massive group which he wielded like a tool to force home the reforms he wanted. Add to that his brains and his charisma and it was easy to see they'd all be better off with him dead.

He laughed and poured himself a drink. He'd just got rid of the biggest problem he'd had in years.

Chapter 42

Corporal Smit had been waiting for two hours at the Pretoria military airfield for an unscheduled flight that was bringing an unnamed officer back from God knows where. He was used to this type of assignment. As personal driver for Major Willis Groenewald he had spent more hours than he could count hanging around waiting for agents. He could almost sense a small aircraft when it was merely a pinprick in the sky and the sound no more than the murmur of a bee. He could hear it now, approaching from the east, probably a direct flight from Mozambique, a Kudu by the sound of things. They'd probably picked up the agent around 2 a.m.

As the Kudu droned closer, the first grey light of dawn was breaking. Soon the plane was a small flashing light against a backdrop of crimson and mauve so beautiful that it brought goosepimples to Smit's skin, while the veld was lit with a strange purple glow. This magic never lasted long. By the time the Kudu landed, the sky was oyster blue and the veld covered in white frost, for it was mid-winter.

Smit stood to attention as the steps were wheeled into place and the door opened. He tried not to look shocked as a tall, emaciated figure stooped to get through the doorway and stood on the top step gazing around him, with a happy grin on his face. He was a little over six foot, with a huge, bony frame, but he looked starved. He obviously hadn't shaved for months and his bushy black beard curled over his face and neck while his hair fell forward in a mass of curls to hide his forehead. His skin was burnt almost black, but his green eyes gave his race away. His nose had been broken. He was wearing a pair of khaki shorts that were torn, a khaki shirt, sandals and a gun belt. Smit noticed that his hand was never far away from his gun. He looked more like a hobo than a special agent.

Was he supposed to salute this apparition? Smit wondered. He must be freezing, Smit wished he'd thought to bring a blanket.

'I'm Corporal Smit, sir, Major Groenewald's driver. I have orders to take you to the canteen and feed you.'

'Ah. That sounds good.'

'After that you are requested to see the major and please do not shower or shave beforehand. Don't bother to change, either, he said, but I reckon you'll be cold.'

'I guessed as much,' he laughed. 'And you wouldn't believe how wonderful it is to be cold.' Suddenly Smit realised that the man was very young – hardly out of his twenties.

The agent glanced back over his shoulder and around him, grabbed his kit and bounded down the steps. There was that pause again. That almost imperceptible glance behind him, one hand free, hovering, never far from his holster. He was a mass of quick movements and his eyes were continually scanning the surroundings.

They were all alike when they came back from the bush. More like wild animals than people, Smit had noticed. He'd seen too many of them. This one had been operating in enemy territory for far too long by the look of things.

Smit had been a dog handler once. The defence force had experimented with Alsatians crossed with Siberian wolves, trying to exploit their incredible sense of smell and hearing and their intuitive sense of danger. The experiment had failed because the dogs were too nervous; the call of the wild was in them and they would never lose it. They watched, circled, slept with their eyes open, even eating was accomplished in quick snatches while they paced the area. This guy had had the wildness grafted on him, Smit decided.

'Was it a good flight, sir?'

'Unbelievable! It's hard to explain the joy of seeing hundreds of thousands of square miles of well-kept farms, safe little homes, dams, the trees planted for wind-breaks, the white-washed villages and churches. Everything as neat and clean and tidy as a man could ever wish for. It's good to get home from time to time,' he went on. 'It reminds you of what it's all about. What a beautiful morning it is.'

They were approaching headquarters. Pieter cringed in-wardly, but straightened his shoulders to disguise any tell-tale signs. Lately he had developed a dislike of being with people. He preferred to be alone in the bush.

Major Groenewald was glowing with health and vitality. His blue eyes blazed with the passion of a man with a mission. His beard, hair and moustache were still whiter than white, which contrasted strangely with his youthful complexion. Yet today something was different, a sense of secrecy about him, an opaqueness that Pieter had not seen before and it puzzled him. They shook hands and Pieter sat down and took the offered cigarette. Coffee arrived, although by now Pieter could hardly swallow another mouthful, he was so full of fried eggs, boerewors, fried tomatoes, toast and fresh butter, and real black coffee made the way he liked it.

The major's pretty secretary, Lieutenant Alicia de Jongh, brought the coffee in and hovered around. Pieter saw the flicker of surprise in the major's eyes, so presumably this was not one of her normal duties. He looked up and winked at her, and she flushed and smiled. A sudden painful longing for the delicate touch of her soft hand swept through him. As quickly, he switched off and saw the disappointment in her eyes. She hesitated and went out.

'Leave my secretary alone, captain,' the major growled. 'She's leaving at the end of the month.'

Pieter's eyes widened. She'd been here for as long as he'd been around.

'That surprises you, doesn't it? Things are changing, captain. You're out of touch. You have to be careful what you say, nowadays. The nation is split down the middle, traditionalists and liberals ... *verkramptes* and *verligtes*. It's come to a pretty pass when I can't trust my own secretary.

'That's what this meeting is all about, captain. We fear the power of the new liberals. They're very strong in the government. We have to look after our own now. The massacre in Honeydew prompted a new approach to security. The country can't afford this sort of thing, and neither could those wretched victims. We've kept the country safe for all these years and now ...' He shook himself like a dog emerging from the water. 'I have a special mission, but it's highly classified... I'm looking for volunteers. That's why I had you recalled.

'First things first,' he said in his slow, ponderous manner. 'My congratulations on your superb work. You're to receive the country's highest award. You're getting quite a collection of medals, man.'

Pieter shrugged. It meant nothing to him. Each job was done for its own sake. 'Sometimes I wonder if we're on the right track. All that destruction ... '

He closed his mouth firmly as he saw the major's eyes narrow speculatively. Besides, what was the point of moaning. Civic disobedience or mutiny against orders was as foreign to him as filth and disorder. If the government and the generals had seen the need for the destruction he had wrought, then that was that. He had not been sent there to think, but to act. He had a sudden memory of the tree. He hoped to God it had survived. Last night he had caught himself in the absurd act of praying for the tree. But then ... who else did he have to pray for? Liza was as lost to him as if she had died and he mourned her. Her colour had split them irrevocably.

The major was watching him through narrowed eyes, as if

seeing into his soul. Pieter pulled himself together with an obvious effort.

'You're tired. It's been rough on you, I can see that, man. Sometimes I feel we should take a gun to those fucking subversives. I'm talking about the journalists and some of our politicians and the businessmen. Yes, even those fucking wheelers and dealers thwart us at every turn. Some of them are meeting with terrorist leaders outside our borders, making deals, jockeying for power in the coming so-called 'new South Africa'. We can't do a bloody thing to stop them.'

Pieter tried to hide his shock, but did not succeed.

'Oh, it'll come, de Vries. Some of our MPs are more subversive than the opposition, but they think no one knows. They're waiting for the chance to get into the power seats and one of these days they will.

'We have to be prepared, captain. My forefathers came here over three hundred years ago and tilled the land with their bare hands. My father left my brother and me a thriving farm. He runs it, I help protect him and our families. What are we going to leave to our children? Turmoil? Violence? The land stolen away from us?

'Enough talk,' he said, pulling himself together. 'Take two days' leave. Don't shave, don't cut your hair. Your alibi as crazy Tomäs seems to have worked for you. Come to think of it, you do look a bit crazy with all that hair. Be at this address sharp at nine o'clock on Thursday night. Memorise the address and burn this. Until Thursday, captain.'

They shook hands and Pieter left.

It was Thursday night and Pieter had arrived early at the address he had been given in order to inspect the premises. The smallholding was called Honeysuckle Farm, but no one had attempted to farm the land. Instead the homestead had been converted into a conference hall and some offices and several good security systems had been recently installed. The situation was ideal, for while the building was screened from the road by thick scrub bushes, it was only three minutes from a major highway and ten kilometres from Pretoria.

He settled down in his car to see who came. First was the tall young Major Rousseau. Pieter recognised those eyes at once. They searched around the car park and scanned his face in passing, leaving Pieter feeling as if an X-ray machine had penetrated his innermost thoughts. Today he had a military moustache that was too large for his nervous, bony face. His eyes were deep set and almost hidden under prominent brows, his chin pointed. Despite his crewcut hair, Pieter recognised the 'hippie' who had supposedly died in a Maputo jail while serving a life sentence. Someone, somehow, had got him out. This made Pieter feel good.

René Coetze was another man he recognised although he didn't know him personally. He was a living legend in army circles, having led a squad into Angola against orders, stormed a jail and brought out five imprisoned pals. His brown eyes and square hard face spelled out strength and intelligence.

Fifteen more men arrived, parked and went into the conference centre. Most were either captains or lieutenants. By the look of their lined, sun-tanned faces they had all spent much of their adult lives in the bush. Pieter decided it was safe to join them.

Not long afterwards Major Groenewald walked in and held up one hand. 'At ease, men. This is the last time we'll meet in uniform. I just wanted you to see each other at least once this way, perhaps to inspire confidence in this force. You fifteen hand-picked men represent the cream of Military Intelligence. We are an independent, self-run, secret fighting force of top agents. This organisation has been set up to meet a major threat to the security of our country. . .'

While Groenewald was talking, Pieter was summing up the other members of the team. All were good men, the sort of guys you'd like to have at your back when things got rough. Presumably they were not going to be introduced to each other by name, but they were asked to stand up in turn and give their code-names.

'Together you will form a chain of intelligence from Maputo to our major cities, in constant radio communication, acting as one force. Now, gentlemen, let's get on with the task.'

He pulled down a screen from the ceiling and switched off most of the lights. The men leaned back and watched the aftermath of the Honeydew massacre, the bomb blast at a major park, a car blown up in a busy Pretoria thoroughfare and various mines laid in farms on border areas, ending with a film of David Ireland from Honeydew, blinded, deaf, minus three of his four limbs and his genitals, learning Braille with one hand. His wife Emily, they were told, had sold the family business and house and they were trying to exist on the interest on their capital, while she nursed him full time. The insurance company had not paid out because David had never thought of adding a riot cover clause to his accident policy, the major said in an unemotional voice.

'Now I'm not going to bother to show you shots of black on black violence in the townships. You all know it, and at one time or another, you've all been called in to help with black rioting and you know the score.

'Until recently, the blacks were afraid to turn against whites. They had us to contend with, as well as the police. But with the new *verligte* moves in government circles, I predict that this day will soon dawn. I also predict that the modern South African population is quite incapable of protecting itself, and the police force will be totally inadequate to cope.

'Now you men have been outside our borders destroying communist bases and preventing the terrorists from infiltrating South Africa or bringing in weapons. But alas, too many have got through and atrocities are happening on a daily basis. All the armaments used in the Honeydew massacre were Russian-made. The bomb that blew up at the park showgrounds was Czech-made, and so was the Pretoria car park explosion.

'We know the organisations responsible for planning these terrorist attacks, we know the names of most of the men involved although some of them called in trained assassins to do their dirty work. Our job is to see that these men are *permanently removed from society*. There's only one way to do that. Our prisons are overcrowded. Criminals get off after serving a fraction of their sentences if they are sentenced at all. In most cases it's impossible to prove their guilt. Furthermore, there's a new *verligte* movement that believes all political activists should be set free under some sort of amnesty. There's only one way to make sure these guys can never again kill or maim our people and that's *our* way. We'll start off with twenty-five highly dangerous men. Memorise the details please.'

A face flashed on to the projector screen. 'Nico Siselie,' the major said. 'Born in Bethlehem, 1968, lived on the streets of Johannesburg for several years, and joined the PAC in 1982. Three years ago he was arrested for stabbing a white. He was sentenced to five years, but he escaped and made his way to Tanzania for terrorist training. He returned a year later and formed his own group, called Youth for Revenge, the gang responsible for the Honeydew massacre. Right now he is holed up in Maputo waiting transport to Russia where he has been accepted for further military training.'

The meeting went on far into the night, while Pieter memorised the names and faces of the various wanted men and their last-known whereabouts.

The last person featured was a shock, for Pieter found himself gazing into Dan's face.

No! What the hell was Dan doing there? How did he get mixed up with this bunch of criminals? Something was terribly wrong.

'There's nothing clandestine about Tweneni's activities,' the major was saying. 'He's far too clever for that. Despite his youth he represents the greatest possible threat. He's a brilliant speaker with a magnetic personality and single-handedly has been the cause of countless industrial disputes and strikes. He's way up in the ANC with strong communist leanings. He has a genius for pulling the blacks together. Leave him at large for three years and he'll topple white rule.'

Pieter felt sick. With this one photograph his targets had become people. Was killing the only way? Was there no alternative? How many more would they have to murder? Was God still on their side? he wondered without much hope. But what was the alternative, the gradual debasement of all that was dear to them? Or becoming a suppressed minority amongst their enemies, with their land and their language lost forever? He knew now they had lost. Icy shivers ran down his spine. Finally it was the women who had won the battle for their men. Patient and sullen in their suffering, they had spawned a mammoth tide of black humanity that was sweeping away all opposition. They were the true mothers of the 'new South Africa.'

Chapter 43

Dan woke late from a night of uncanny dreams to find that his unquenchable passion was back. He caught hold of his throbbing member, clenched hard and painfully remembered Miriam and her own special perfume, those eyes, glittering with amused compassion, that beautiful body. He groaned, came into his hands and wept – for Miriam, for himself, for the emptiness of a future without her. As usual, the second-rate spasm brought physical release and mental anguish. Nowadays he tried to do without sex; with or without a partner, it opened him to sadness.

It was six a.m., but already as hot as hell. He lay sweating in the sheets and planned his day briefly: a full quota of morning lectures, a lunchtime trade union meeting, four hours of taxi work which would take care of immediate expenses and his afternoon, followed by two hours of soccer coaching starting at six. Later there was a party meeting and an essay to be written. Something would have to give.

The small attic room and the sounds of the wakening house were crowding in on him. Liza was running a bath. She'd got there first. Damn! He was late, but he'd only had four hours of sleep. At times Dan felt he was sweating his days away for nothing, that the future would never be attained. That all he worked for was merely an illusion.

Bad thoughts for a Monday morning. He jumped up, flinging back the damp sheet, wrapped a towel around his hips and hurried to the bathroom. 'Hi, Liza, try to hurry,' he called, his deep dark voice cracking with the effort of being gentle.

The door opened an inch. Part of Liza appeared, wrapped in a towel, her dark hair clinging to her, eyes open in surprise. 'You're the limit,' she scolded. 'Your time was six. It's half past.'

'Sorry, love.'

'You can have fifteen minutes,' she said. She swept past in a flurry of pink towels, sweet scents and friendly indignation.

Dan brooded about Liza as he showered. So much loveliness and sexuality hidden under her tough exterior. She never went out nights. Never dated. How could she? And then there was Pieter. She still loved him and that was the saddest part of her miserable fate. Dan reckoned her loss was harder than his.

Ten minutes later he went roaring off, his practical self firmly back in control as he worked out how to fit in all his appointments.

Finally it was the soccer coaching that was sacrificed. In the canteen later, Victor, the goalkeeper, volunteered to take his place and Dan went home to write his essay.

It was eight p.m. when Johannes, a colleague in the party, called to tell him that a bomb had exploded in his locker killing Victor outright. 'It was meant for you. Look out,' he said.

Filled with grief and guilt, Dan went by motorbike to the Commissioner Street police headquarters. It would save them coming here for him and disturbing Martha and Reg, he thought grimly.

'We've been looking for you, Tweneni,' the white corporal said. 'It's a fucking good day for us when you lot start killing off each other.'

With monumental willpower, Dan held back his retort and kept his face expressionless as he was driven to the state mortuary to identify what was left of Victor. Looking at that wrecked face, Dan was gripped with a sense of unreality. His mind seemed to have fled, leaving him as emotionless as a robot who could look at his dead colleague without sadness and contemplate his own narrow escape without fear or anger.

When he arrived back in the police station he was immediately detained for questioning. The interrogation lasted for eight hours, but he knew even less than the police did about the bomb. At the end of the interrogation he was taken to the cells.

'You are being detained for further questioning,' the sergeant told him.

'What's the charge?' he asked.

'Were you expecting a charge? You tell us. As far as we know there's no charge. As we said, detained for questioning in connection with the murder of Victor Bantu.'

Dan was put with four black activists. The food was adequate, there was plenty of water, toilet facilities were provided plus a short time for exercise in the prison yard. It was a luxury hotel compared with his last incarceration. Were they softening him up for the kill?

The following evening he was taken through to an interrogation room. He shuddered when he saw Captain Myers from Nelfontein. He had lost weight which made his features seem even more out of proportion, his ears more prominent and his eyes and nose excessively large.

'God, you've grown huge, Tweneni,' Myers said. 'Sit down. You intimidate me towering over my desk like that.'

'Why am I being detained?' Eyes smouldering, a slow anger starting up inside, his hands itching to get at Myers, Dan sat down and closed his eyes, fighting for self control.

'The plain truth is, I asked them to hold you until I could get down here. I was up north. Sorry. I believe that your close shave is part of a strange sequence of deaths that I am investigating.'

'It's pointless to hold me. I know nothing.' Dan was too big for the chair. He twisted his bony shoulders and placed one elbow on his knee.

'I know,' Myers said simply. 'You'll be free shortly.'

He looked up and smiled, but despite his genuine manner Dan felt only antagonism. On the whole he preferred the clearcut hatred of the Sergeant Smits of this world. Although Dan had never directly felt the frenzied enmity of racism he had learned to distrust whites through bitter experience.

'Cigarette?'

Dan shook his head, although he was dying for one.

'I've been following your career, Dan. You've been studying hard, recruiting hard, playing hard. You've kept your nose clean, too. You're a force to be reckoned with. You're going places, but I suppose you know that. You might easily head the Transvaal ANC within a year.'

Dan shrugged. It was a criminal offence to belong to the ANC and he had no intention of admitting anything. He had cramp in one leg. He stretched it cautiously, pressing down his heel until the pain went. He had to get out of there, he was longing to be back on the pitch.

'You could be in Mandela's shoes one day,' Myers was saying in a vain and tedious effort to establish a man-to-man rapport. 'If you stay alive that long. Now I want you to think back. Have you made any enemies along the way?'

Dan thought of Njoli and then discarded the idea. 'No,' he said.

'You've come a long way since Nelfontein, Dan. Strange that you never turned violent after the beating those farmers gave you.'

'If I ever see them alone on a dark night I'll turn violent soon enough,' Dan said. 'But if you're talking about indiscriminate violence against whites then I might surprise you by stating that racialism is an evil we are intent on stamping out. You see, many of us can see a little further than the end of our noses, although I realise that this might be difficult for you to grasp.'

'I can hold you indefinitely if you won't assist me. After all, you are a member of a banned organisation.'

'Oh, cut it out, man,' Dan said. 'You would need as many prisons as shops to lock up all of us. You'd lose your work force, the country would grind to a halt.'

'Over the past month,' Myers went on, ignoring his outburst, 'twenty-four black activist leaders have been killed or have died in suspicious circumstances. The evidence points to the Zulus. I have this theory that someone's put out a contract on the nation's top black leaders. You are on that list, Dan, make no mistake. That is, if I am right about this.'

'Why are you telling me?' Dan's eyes narrowed. Why should Myers give him classified information? After all, they were ancient enemies.

'I don't know. There could be many reasons. Perhaps because you are the sort of sane black leader this country needs. Perhaps because I owe you one. I should have guessed those small-time farmers would get hold of you. Perhaps because I sense an ally. You see, Dan, I've never been much taken up by racialism. Once upon a time my own kin would have called me a traitor. After all, I am a Boer. Now things are changing. My views might be in fashion one of these days. For my part I have a mission. It's plain and simple – I safeguard the law. I treasure it, Dan. I have only contempt for those who think they are upholding our civilisation by trampling on the law. Civilisation is the law. At least, that's how I see it.

'Now . . . I'll run through this list for you. Down in the Cape, Tom Muimbi went poaching crayfish at night and his boat capsized. His body was washed up later. His wife told me that he never went to sea because he got badly seasick. In Durban, Jon Sipoyo apparently committed suicide by hanging himself. Cebisa's car brakes failed and he crashed into a truck. Tshaba-lala was cleaning his gun – he had a licence – when it went off. Cele got dizzy and fell from the top of a twenty-four-storey building. Simon Nkosi got into a scrap with some Zulus and was knifed. Ben Thembisa was mugged and stabbed by Zulu criminals. Joe Muimbi, Tom's brother, became drunk in a Zulu hostel and was beaten to death, his body was flung outside the yard. Need I go on . . .?'

Real fear began to sink in at last. Dan stood up slowly. 'Who is behind this?'

'I was hoping you'd tell me.'

'Not Zulus. They don't have the organisation in the Transvaal. Can I go now?'

'Yes. There's just one thing more. Your detention was in the press. This morning several reporters were informed that you would be released in approximately half an hour's time. You might find a hot reception out there, but we won't be far behind. Look out and good luck.'

Myers held out his hand.

Dan's back was burning as he walked the hundred yards across the floodlit yard. He felt naked and vulnerable as he kick-started his bike and drove towards home.

Dan raced east. As he passed the Fordsburg warehouses, a cat, suddenly disturbed, raced across the road. Dan braked and swerved to avoid it. At that moment the road ahead was raked with rounds from a sub-machine gun. Dan made a quick U-turn, skidding badly. Twisting his head back, he saw a figure emerge from an alleyway and run after him. As he accelerated, red-hot pain shot through his calf and the bike's petrol tank exploded, bucking him into the air with the blast. He fell heavily against wrought-iron gates which burst open. Dan realised that he must get to the back of the building. Creeping amongst the shadows of piles of building materials he found a crevice between some pipes and stacked iron sheeting and squeezed himself into it.

He heard police sirens approaching. Then the yard was lit up in a blaze of lights. Running footsteps came from all directions. There were shots close by. Dan took advantage of the noise to yank some corrugated-iron sheets over his head. Then he lay low, squeezing his leg to staunch the flow of blood. He hoped he wouldn't bleed to death before morning.

Then he heard Myers calling. 'Dan Tweneni. Your attackers have fled. Please come out into the open. You are quite safe.'

Disbelieving the whole scene and not knowing whom he could trust, Dan remained where he was. He felt disorientated and lost. It was as if he was on an island in the middle of quicksands. The granite hard rock he'd been intent on destroying had dissolved. Now there were new enemies, but who were they? And who were his friends? In a war based on race you could recognise your allies and your enemies, he thought. Politics in the new South Africa was like playing blind man's buff in a minefield.

He reckoned he had better stay where he was until daylight. Then he would call Reg to fetch him.

Chapter 44

Liza was absolutely happy in Martha's rambling house. These years with the family would prove perhaps the happiest time of her life, but something drove her on. She would leave soon, she knew that, and the thought made her sad. Sunday mornings were the best. They were so free and easy. Martha prepared little treats for them, homemade croissants, honey and jam, lashings of cream, super black coffee. Her daughters went out and bought the newspapers and magazines and they all sprawled on cushions in front of the big roaring fire, for it was June and particularly cold this winter.

Martha was content, Liza could see. She had an amused half-smile on her face as she listened to Liza moaning about how the *Echo* exploited her and paid her next to nothing. Martha's eyes moved from one daughter to the next and back to Reg who was sitting on the couch beside her holding her hand. She was still an attractive woman and she dressed to please her husband in bright sexy clothes. The sunlight from the window behind reflected on them both and seemed to bond them in a halo of golden light. Their eyes met often with humour and caring. Then the spell was broken by the telephone ringing. Reg picked up the receiver.

Liza saw him turn pale. 'It's Dan. I'll be a while. I must get him to a doctor.' They heard his car racing off. An hour later he returned, half supporting Dan, who was covered in blood and grime, one trouser leg split down the side by the doctor who had stitched and bandaged his calf.

'It's nothing – believe me. Only a flesh wound,' Dan told them. 'It bled a lot last night. A few stitches, that's all, and I'm well dosed with antibiotics.' Dan limped off to shower and call headquarters. He returned half an hour later looking downcast. 'I'm leaving the country for a while. Orders from my superiors. I don't know how long I'll be gone. Damn! I'll have to leave my studies and I was doing so well.'

'Where will you go?' Reg asked, crinkling his brow with concern.

'Initially Mozambique. The party will pick me up at Ressano Garcia. After that – who knows? Right now I have to get to Nelfontein on my own. Once there it's easy enough to get across the border.'

'I'll drive you up. D'you want to take your combi? I could bus back,' Reg said. 'Or we can take my car.'

'They'd pick us up on the road. They're bound to know my combi registration, and possibly your car, too. They'll watch the routes to the border posts. Perhaps I should go by train, but there's always the risk they might search them. The same goes for the airports. Someone, or some organisation, are trying to kill me and they're well organised.' He told them about the attack and the bomb in the games room while sipping sweet black coffee laced with whisky.

'Don't worry, I'll borrow an *Echo* van from the pool,' Liza said. 'No one would suspect us. Yes, of course . . .' She leaped up, clicking her fingers. 'I can make you an employee's badge with someone else's name and your photograph. We do them in the darkroom, you see. The trouble is, I don't know how long it would take. It all depends on where Ed is and whether or not he'll help us. I'll call him now.'

The telephone rang for a long time, but at last she heard Ed's sleepy voice. 'I need help,' she began impatiently. 'For goodness sake wake up. I need transport to the border in an *Echo* van, and an *Echo* security badge. And I need you, Ed. Please don't ask why – just help me.'

The family watched her expression change from anxiety to joy. 'Ed will meet us at the studio in half an hour,' she said as she replaced the receiver.

'Quite honestly, I'm amazed and pleased to hear that you have any close friends, Liza,' Ed said jealously three hours later as they were speeding past Witbank on the way to the border. Dan was sleeping on a garden mattress, covered with Martha's best rug. 'At the same time, Dan is an unusual choice for someone like you who so obviously is not a philanthropist.'

'Stop prying, Ed,' she said. 'I'll explain later.'

'Just tell me one thing – so I know what to expect – are we fugitives from the police?'

'Tch! No. The police have warned Dan that someone is out to kill him. Now please don't ask any more questions.'

'You can be downright infuriating,' Ed said angrily.

After that they drove in silence. Then Dan woke and told Ed about his meeting with Captain Myers. 'I'm telling you all I can so you can investigate this team. All I know is that the one who shot me was white. I saw him clearly.'

Liza found herself nodding off. She looked round at Ed who smiled at her. 'Have a sleep, why don't you?'

'I haven't thanked you yet, have I?'

'No.'

'Why are you so kind to me?'

'If you had a better self-image, you'd know the answer to your question. Now go to sleep. It's making me sleepy watching you yawning.'

'It's so cold,' she moaned. She curled up on the seat and fell asleep.

They were approaching Nelfontein when Ed woke Liza and Dan. 'There's a roadblock ahead manned by camouflaged troops. Is this a problem?'

'They're not police,' Dan said. 'And they're not the defence force. Too old!'

'Put your *Echo* hat on and leave the talking to me. For God's sake look servile.'

Minutes later they were flagged down to the side of the road. Looking up into the soldier's eyes, Liza agreed with Dan. These were shrewd, clever men, well trained and well armed. The sort of men who organised recés into foreign lands, not roadblocks. She felt scared for Dan.

Ed was getting out of the car. 'What is it?' he asked.

'Routine search,' one of them said.

'Go ahead, but the van's full of cameras. Please be careful, it's not my property. I'd have to pay . . .'

'Would you please remove the cameras, sir?'

'Sure. If I can wake up our lazy *munt*,' he said. 'Hey, Cleo, get your arse out of there and look lively.'

Dan scrambled out. 'Sorry, baas,' he said, trying to disguise his limp as he removed the cameras and tripods.

'For fuck's sake. Be more careful, you fool.'

'Yes, baas, sorry, bass, sorry, baas . . .'

'Honestly,' Liza sniffed. 'We shouldn't have brought him. That boy goes back on the train, I insist. Either that or you buy some deodorant.'

'You people may proceed,' the soldier told them solemnly after only a cursory glance at Dan's *Echo* security card.

'Hurry up, and be more careful this time,' Ed snarled. Five minutes later they were laughing together as they drove on.

'Thanks,' Dan said briefly. 'I owe you, man. I won't forget this. You're from overseas, aren't you?'

Gazing out of the window, Liza sank into a somnambulant reverie. The veld was dazzling in the brilliant winter sunshine. The grass was dry and brown wherever you looked, neat haystacks stood at the side of fields and sheep gleaned amongst the stubble. There was no wind, and the trees planted for windbreaks stood tall and still. They moved in a straight line on the magnificent wide highway, passing neat little villages and whitewashed farmhouses. Was there another country in the world so tidy, so well ordered, so much loved and so brilliantly tended? There was not a verge or a bank or a hedge that was not cultivated by someone. And would it all be irrevocably changed? Treacherous thoughts! She fell into a restless sleep.

They were bumping over a grassy verge and then the van stopped. Liza sat up surprised to find that it was dusk.

'Nelfontein,' Ed said. 'Now where?'

They had stopped opposite the caravan park, near the river at the end of the town's main street. The familiar surroundings made her stomach lurch.

'This is fine,' Dan said. 'I have friends nearby. I can cope from here. I guess you guys will have to go back with some sort of an excuse for the mileage.'

'We'll cook up something,' Ed said. 'Don't worry about us.'

'Did you know that Minister Dennis Blum keeps a black mistress in KaNgwane and has a brood of kids by her?' Dan asked.

'You can't be serious,' Ed gasped.

'He used to spend every Sunday and Wednesday nights with her. He might have changed his schedule, but he's still around. I saw him last time I was here. Of course he gets a lot of protection around these parts, so watch out.'

'What a scoop,' Ed said grinning.

'Good luck, Dan,' Liza said. 'Thank you for everything. I'll miss you, but at least I'll get into the bathroom on time.' She grinned to show she was only joking and then clamped her mouth shut as Ed shot her a strange look. 'I hope I'll see you again soon.'

'Sooner than you think, Liza.' They shook hands. Dan limped across the road and disappeared into the park.

Now was not the time to poke into Liza's affairs. Ed felt that most strongly, but at the same time he was fired with a journalist's curiosity. There was a story here, but his affection for Liza prevented him from prying. 'I guess we'd better find accommodation for the night. I saw a hotel just up the road. We'll book in,' Ed said. 'How about Mr and Mrs? I need a bath and some food.'

Liza turned, eyes blazing, teeth gritted. Two crimson patches appeared on either cheek. 'How dare you,' she spluttered. When Liza was angry she was magnificent – a wild, wayward woman with flashing eyes, a tongue that stung like a whiplash and a temper like molten lava. It was then that Ed longed to photograph her, for she was superb. She was angry now. Silly girl! 'Why d'you feel insulted? It's not every girl who gets an offer from me.'

'I don't want to sleep in the hotel with or without you,' she snapped.

'Look here, Liza. I've just driven all day. I'm tired. You slept, remember? If we're to be in KaNgwane at dawn, we have to spend the night somewhere.'

'We can sleep in the back of the van. There's a park right over there,' she said sulkily.

Liza was being absurd. Perhaps she had no money, Ed thought. 'Why on earth should we sleep in the van?' he queried. 'Not that I object to passing the night on a small mattress with you, but if you're hell bent on a night of sin, let's do it in comfort. Besides, the *Echo* will pay.'

Oh, boy! What an explosion! 'I was teasing,' he said, knowing that he was going into a sulk, but unable to pull out of it. But I'm damned if I'll sit here all night. I'm staying right there.

He started the car and drove to the hotel's car park. 'Don't worry, I'll book separate rooms. I was only joking.'

He got out of the car, grabbed his equipment and set off, but Liza rushed past him murmuring, 'Oh God . . . Oh God . . .'

'Now what?' She reached the reception desk first, with Ed close behind her. He watched the young assistant manager's expression of welcome fade. 'Hey, wait a minute. Surely you're Liza . . .'

Liza turned pale. 'I'm Mrs Segal,' she lied. 'I've never

been to this dump before. Mrs Sarah Segal. This is my husband.' She glanced over her shoulder at him. He winked and she flushed.

Ed signed the register and followed the porter to their room. It was plain, clean, functional and little else, with twin beds covered with white bedspreads. He dumped his gear and tipped the porter.

'What was all that about?' he asked, trying to sound disinterested.

'Don't ask, Ed, but thank you.'

'What for?'

'For not letting on.'

'D'you think I'd turn down the chance of a night in the sack with you?' He couldn't help laughing at her annoyance.

Suddenly she calmed down. 'Ed,' she said, looking so sad and appealing he had difficulty in not grabbing her. 'There's someone else. Someone I love very dearly. There's nothing wrong with you. I think you are a most wonderful person and I'm so grateful to have you for my friend . . .' She burst into tears and collapsed on the bed.

He sighed. 'And where is this other person? You can't tell me. I thought not. Perhaps one day you'll trust me enough to tell me what's going on? Why you are like you are – well, prickly to say the least? And there's something else . . . why are you so afraid of being recognised here? Are you an escaped prisoner? Is my life in danger?'

'Oh, stop this inquisition, Ed.'

'Was it an inquisition?' He felt mildly hurt.

'I'm sorry, Ed. Forgive me. You do forgive me, don't you?'

Ed longed to gather her into his arms and comfort her, but that would be the very worst thing he could do, he sensed. After a while she got up and sat in the only chair looking aloof and sad and daring him to speak. The lamp shed a golden light around her. Silhouetted against it she looked so mysterious, her hair so black, her eyes lustrous and brimming with sadness. Ed knew that he loved her desperately and that he probably always would. He also knew that she had no such feelings for him. Then the moment of pathos was lost. She jumped up and stalked across the room, wringing her hands and tossing her hair over her shoulder. 'My name is not Liza. It is Sarah. Remember that, Ed.'

'Yes, dear, anything you say, my dear,' he said, aping a henpecked husband as he sprawled on the bed.

'That's not funny.'

'Isn't it? What a pity. Things are only bearable when they are funny.'

She sighed. All the world's sadness seemed to be in that sigh. He said: 'Whatever trouble you are in, I will help you, Liza. Is it politics? Are you in some banned organisation with Dan?'

She shook her head.

'Is it crime? Tell me the truth. I'm on your side.'

'It's nothing like that. Don't ask. I will tell you one thing, I hate this town. Hate it. D'you hear me? But there is a man who lives here and I love him more than I love my own life. I think of him as having died. To me he is dead. Do you understand?'

'No,' he said. 'Let's go down and get a drink.'

She would not. They had to order drinks and dinner from room service, and eat it in the suffocating room, which Ed hated. Eventually they spent the evening working on angles for new stories.

When bedtime came, Liza disappeared into the bathroom and emerged later scrubbed pink and smelling of soap and toothpaste. She scrambled into her bed and fell asleep almost immediately.

Ed knew he'd never sleep so he went down to the bar and soaked up the local gossip. When it closed he went to the milk bar across the road where he sat talking late with anyone who wanted company. By the time he walked back in the early hours he had at least twenty stories buzzing around in his head.

The next morning, Liza was apologetic and very contrite. They left before dawn and Ed tried to cheer her up as they drove towards KaNgwane.

'Listen to this,' he said. 'The only cinema here – which naturally is for whites only – is employing coloured girls as usherettes. I met the manager in the bar last night. He said . . .' He broke off chuckling to himself and then began again. 'I quote . . . "When we show a whites-only film, the girls are not allowed to look at the screen while they usher in patrons. They must look down at the floor." Evidently, the Department of Labour made this ruling at an urgent meeting called to discuss this serious lapse in apartheid regulations caused by lack of white manpower.'

Liza smiled faintly. That was better than crying.

'This patriotic hometown of yours has decided that when farm labourers attend church services they must not be allowed to say "*Our Father* which art in heaven". Since Jesus was white, it stands to reason that only whites can call him "*our father*". They must say "*the father*".'

Liza began to giggle and Ed felt proud of himself.

'Did you know that round these parts non-whites are officially debarred from making personal calls on party phone lines? This is to prevent interference and abusive language. I got that from the local post office lady. A certain prim Miss Johnston.'

'Amy Johnston! She's the embodiment of all that's evil here.' Liza sat pouting and trembling and looking as if she might burst into tears.

Oh heck! This was worse than snakes and ladders. 'Return to start . . . throw six to move,' he muttered. 'Here goes . . .

'Two Roman Catholic priests stopped at the drive-in road-house here last Thursday. They were en-route to KaNgwane, where the black Father Dominic Nxala was to take charge of the parish. They ordered toasted sandwiches and tea. Two teas arrived, one in a porcelain cup on a saucer and the other in a tin mug. Father Nxala drank out of the cup while Father Ludwig, from Austria, politely took the tin mug. The proprietor rushed out shouting: "That kafir can't drink out of my cups." He grabbed the cup out of the priest's hands and smashed it on the ground. This provoked the Austrian priest into flinging the tray at him. So the proprietor punched him through the window, giving Father Ludwig a black eye.

'I met the proprietor in the bar last night. He said: "I thought I was being kind serving a kafir with tea and naturally I used my garden boy's tin mug. Now I've been charged with assault. That's all the thanks I get for being kind-hearted."'

'I can picture it so vividly,' Liza said, rocking with laughter.

'Did you know that the "whites only" signs on the only town park have recently been removed?' he asked.

She nodded.

'Before taking this monumental step towards a new South Africa, they ripped up the grass and replaced it with paving stones, to prevent the blacks from lying in the park.'

She was giggling happily now.

'Guess what the local mayor said last week? "The coloured people need not be ashamed of being coloured. One is not responsible for one's birth."'

'That's enough now, Ed. Stop it! You're boring me,' she snarled.

'You don't have a sense of humour. That's your trouble,' Ed growled.

It was six o'clock when they arrived at the modest home of the Minister's mistress. Dan had been right, he fucked his black mistress every Sunday night. A coloured child ran out and heaved and puffed at the garage door until it opened. Moments later the Minister emerged to find an unwanted reception with flash bulbs popping from two cameras. Chaos erupted. The Minister pulled out a gun and let off several rounds into the trees, demanding that they hand over their cameras. His mistress raced out in a transparent négligé and hung around his neck screaming and distracting his aim, so that Ed managed to get another shot of them embracing. The children came roaring towards them brandishing sticks.

'Catch them,' the Minister roared.

'Run, Liza,' Ed yelled. They flung themselves into the van and moments later they were racing along the Homeland's only motorway towards Nelfontein.

'Fee ... fi ... fo ... fum ..., I smell the sacking of Minister Blum,' Ed said gleefully.

'That doesn't rhyme if you pronounce it properly. Just drive faster,' Liza grumbled.

Ed was driving and dictating while Liza scribbled in her notebook, a happy smile on her face. 'We'll be famous,' she crowed. 'What a waste to give this story to the *Echo*. I long to free-lance. I'd make much more money, but I don't have the courage or the cash.'

'How about going into partnership with me?'

'A partnership?' She gaped at him.

'I have the same problem you have, my salary is small, but my ambition limitless and my talent somewhere in the middle. I need to get capital before going it on my own. However, if we were to form our own news agency, we could sell a lot of our stuff abroad. If I kept my job, I could support you and our expenses until the cash started rolling in. Furthermore, we could do something I've always wanted to do – documentary films for TV. What do you say?'

'Yes,' she said quickly.

She sat in a daze and listened while Ed told her about the cottage in Auckland Park he had inherited from an aunt. It would make the perfect headquarters for them. If she wanted, she could live rent-free in the top half.

'Oh yes, yes, yes,' she sang. Then her conscience began nagging her.

'Ed, there's something I haven't told you ...' she began. She wanted so much to tell him about her forged ID and that they could not legally go into partnership, nor was she allowed to live in a white area, but the words would not come. She could not utter the hateful word 'coloured', and finally she ducked it.

They were both relieved to get back to Johannesburg.

Barbara was fuming. They had broken several company laws, including taking a company vehicle overnight without permission and being absent without leave, but all was forgiven when they produced the photographs.

Chapter 45

There was a chapel decorated in blue and white, with a choir of angels, dressed in white. The priest had a halo of white light shining on his white hair and Liza's wedding dress was of a silvery-white, lighter-than-air fabric. It flounced and bubbled around her. Pieter was waiting for her, his eyes shining with love, but everyone was staring at her in astonishment. Looking down, she saw that her skin was much darker, almost black. The aisle became a tunnel that was growing faster than she could run. She called: 'Pieter, wait for me,' but the bright little chapel became a twinkling star that zoomed into the heavens carrying away all that was dear to her.

She woke to find her cheeks wet with tears. She sighed and sat up blinking. How bright it was. Holy shit! It was nine o'clock. She bounded out of bed and shivered. Brr! Freezing! She closed the window with a bang. The sky was crystal blue. By ten the sun would have warmed the earth and by lunchtime it would be hot, but the nights were still cold. She grabbed her gown, thrust her feet into her slippers and stumbled into the kitchen, where she plugged in the coffee filter, before rushing back to the bathroom to clean her teeth and splash cold water on her face. She would shower after breakfast. Right now she badly needed a jolt of happiness. Damn Pieter!

Soon the smell of toast and coffee restored her good humour. She wandered from room to room, mug in hand, gloating over her fabulous apartment. Martha and Reg had come to dinner yesterday, and brought some yellow calendulas and they brightened the table. Wherever she looked was perfect and gave her a deep sense of satisfaction. Life was pretty good. Since she and Ed had formed their news agency, the money had rolled in and they were getting famous.

The newspaper was lying in the postbox. She took it out and spread it on the floor. She found four of her articles and three photos had been used. 'Tremendous,' she told herself. Her column was longer than usual, but they hadn't cut it, she noticed. Fantastic, she thought, snipping out the stories for her scrap book. Ed would be so pleased.

Then the phone rang and she answered it reluctantly. It was Sunday, *her* day. The woman's voice was unfamiliar and very English. She introduced herself as Julia Swift, wife of Michael Swift. *The* Michael Swift, head of the documentary division of English TV, Liza wondered? This was quickly confirmed and Liza listened in a daze as Julia invited her to lunch in the garden at their weekend hideaway near Hartbeespoortdam.

'Sorry it's such short notice, Liza,' Julia drawled, 'but Michael only picked up Jack – you know Jack Gilmore, the Australian comedian? – this morning. We thought he would want to sleep after his long flight, but evidently he's raring to go, so we've organised a little get-together in the garden – so lovely at this time of the year, don't you think? Try not to be later than one, please. Can you make it?' she added as an afterthought.

'Yes,' Liza gulped.

But could she? She replaced the receiver and sat trembling on her bed. She felt so unsure of herself. Why her? What on earth had they asked *her* for? She could cope with business, but when it came to a social event, she felt exactly as she had at school when the girls would not let her into the toilet. A pariah! So she avoided all social engagements.

Ed always popped round on Sunday mornings for coffee and he usually brought croissants. This morning he found her cowering under her duvet.

'I won't go,' she told him after she had explained about the call. 'They'll be rude to me,' she whispered. 'I'll never find my way there, and besides they won't miss me.'

'Of course they'd miss you.'

Ed watched her sadly. This was the Liza he remembered from Nelfontein, aggressive, insecure, a deprived child. He wondered what trauma had knocked the stuffing out of her.

'They wouldn't invite you if they didn't want you. I don't understand you, Liza. Day after day you amaze me with your courage and resilience. And then, without warning, you become a child.'

She tried to explain. 'Liza Frank, the journalist, can cope with almost anything, but she's not the real me. I don't like social arrangements. And anyway, I had a bad dream.'

Ed was remarkably astute in understanding. 'What a goose you are to imagine this is a social occasion,' he said. 'It *is* business. These sort of people live business. Have you sent in some scripts?'

'Some of yours and two of mine,' she said.

'I expect they'll put a proposition to you. If so, tell them you want time to consider. Don't sign anything until I see it. Okay?'

'Oh, yes,' she said, smiling happily. 'Business is a cinch. Now what shall I wear?' she called.

Ed watched her, smiling softly to himself. Liza was an enigma, but slowly he was beginning to understand her. She had the worst self-image he'd ever come across, but she'd managed to cope by creating Liza Frank, the well-known journalist, and that Liza Frank could do anything. Deep inside, she didn't relate to Liza Frank, he knew. She was afraid of people and deeply scarred. Ed loved her and he wished that he could do more for her. Helping Liza to become richer and more famous wasn't helping the lost girl inside.

'I'll drive you there,' he said. 'I have friends nearby. When you want to go, just call me. Will that make you feel better?'

She flung her arms around him and kissed him loudly on one cheek. There was no passion in the kiss. Just sisterly affection, but he'd already made the decision to take whatever relationship Liza could offer, for she was altogether special. He went into the kitchen to get some coffee.

'It's a braai,' he heard her calling. 'Well, something about lunch outdoors so it must be a braai. I have some new stretch jeans and a really jazzy sweat shirt. Maybe it's too way out. What d'you think?' It was black with some weird white writing on it. 'It says "peace" in every African dialect. Like it?' she asked, twirling round.

'Sure. Why not? It's only a braai.'

'Ed, I want to ask you something and you have to answer truthfully.'

'Fire away!' He was studying her scrapbook and not really listening.

'Do I look … dark?'

'No darker than usual.'

'I mean, dark as in *coloured*.' Ed looked up sharply as another piece of the jigsaw puzzle fell into place.

'I've always thought you look Jewish,' he said carefully. 'Or maybe Italian. I've often wondered about your roots. What are they – South American? Italian? Or possibly Spanish? Yes, I'd put my money on Spanish.'

'Maybe,' she said, looking happier.

'I've never been on a business braai, have you?' she asked anxiously, while gobbling toast and a boiled egg.

'Many times,' he lied.

The first thing she realised was her appalling mistake. It was a real English garden party. Amazing! Did people really do this in South Africa? Clearly they did. Ed dropped her at the gate and Liza forced her feet to move forward, and her face to assume a nonchalant expression. The women wore fussy, long floral dresses and picture hats, the men were in business suits and ties and they were all sweating and trying to look happy, for the day had turned exceptionally hot for May. She wanted to run, but they had seen her.

'Well, I see you prefer comfort to fashion. Who exactly are you?' Liza turned towards the voice. A short fat woman with a long Roman toga and a friendly face was panting towards her, looking ridiculous.

'Liza. Liza Frank.'

'I'm Andrea Jones, Michael's secretary,' she explained.

She had a friendly face with small features that were lost in her puddinglike flesh. She looked like a pet pig and Liza warmed to her. At least here was one woman who wouldn't intimidate her. 'Did no one tell you it's a garden party, as in the Queen and Buckingham Palace?'

'I wasn't sure,' Liza said, squaring her shoulders. Her chin jutted out. She was there, she looked absurd – a total scruff – and she would just have to endure it as best she could. 'I thought it was a braai.'

'In this house? God forbid! Well, come along, I'll introduce you to everyone.'

There were so many people and Liza was introduced to everyone at once. Most of their names and faces became jumbled, but one or two stuck in her mind. Hans Marais, for instance, programme producer. He whispered in her ear: 'I like your courage. Only the bloody English could organize a cock-up like this on such a hot day. Wish I'd worn my jeans.' She liked him, she decided. He was short, with a wide flat face, as if someone had rolled him out of pastry. His twinkling green eyes were elongated and set wide apart, his nose flattened, his lips quite thick and his hair blond and kinky, rising up like a bird's ruff from a pronounced widow's peak.

Mona Malherbe, programme director, stood out as someone to be avoided at all costs. She was dressed for a period play set in Victorian times, mainly in dusty pink, which was just as well, Liza thought, because the wind had got up, showering them all with dust from the driveway. Mona was a snob, Liza could sense that at once. She glanced at Liza, sneering at her face, her clothes, her skin, her hands, and turned away as quickly, finding nothing at all to interest her. She didn't even say 'Hi'.

Flushed and furious, Liza followed Andrea to find her hosts. 'Don't let Mona get you down,' Andrea said, looking amused. 'She's a perfectionist and always moaning. She's well named, don't you think? And she makes our lives hell.'

'Take my advice, dear,' Andrea murmured as they approached the house. 'Michael Swift is a terrible flirt. Swift by name and swift by nature, that's what I say, but just let his wife see you flirting with him and you'll be out before you're in, if you see what I mean. Oh, and another thing. If you agree with most everything he says, you'll find life easier around here.'

'Thank you, Andrea,' Liza said, sensing that she meant well. But what did she mean 'out before you're in'? Were they going to take one of her scripts? Had she ruined everything by wearing jeans?

'This is Liza Frank. She thought it was a braai.' Andrea sniffed and stood waiting. She was right about Michael. He pounced, holding her hands in his, then his hand was on her shoulders and touching her hair. She stepped away and took a long hard look at him. His grey hair was dyed reddish brown on top, he was wearing a bright paisley bow-tie over a striped grey and bottle-green shirt, and a dark green cummerband. She liked him, despite his wandering hands. He had such an engaging smile and beautiful white teeth, although the rest of him was nondescript. That's why he dressed up like this, Liza thought intuitively.

'Now for the prune,' Andrea whispered. Liza nearly burst out giggling, the name was so apt. Julia Swift's skin was deep red with a purplish glow, perhaps from drinking or bad circulation, Liza wondered. She had chosen purple eye shadow and eye-liner, the worst possible shade for her, perhaps because her eyes were large and a deep violet. Once she had been very lovely, Liza decided, but now she was haggard.

She looked briefly at Liza's jeans and said, 'Darling, how quaint. Have a good time,' and turned away leaving Liza flushed and miserable.

A man had come silently into the garden. He was tall and

bronzed and rather battered-looking except for his amazing eyes which were deep blue and full of humour. He was dressed in jeans and a vest and wearing tattered trainers. 'Bloody bitch!' he muttered.

'Oh dear! She's the hostess and it's my own fault. I didn't pay attention when she issued the invitation. I'm afraid you're equally out of place here. Who are you?'

'I'm the plumber,' he said, 'but I'm finished for the day. How about you and I having a drink? No one's got you one, I see.'

'Oh, yes, please,' Liza said. He took her arm and hugged her close and, glad of a friend, Liza smiled up at him.

'Maybe you shouldn't be seen with the plumber amongst all these toffs,' he said.

'Oh, who cares. You're the first human being I've met here.'

'We'll stick together, doll. What's your name?'

'Liza.'

'Follow me, Liza. I can sense a bar like a shark senses blood.'

Mona was there first. 'Are you two supposed to be here?' she said, raising her sunglasses and looking down her nose.

'Dunno, love. Maybe I got the wrong house.'

'What exactly is it that you do?'

'Plumbing, love. Got anything wrong with your waterworks? One year guarantee. That's me.'

She gasped and rushed off to find Julia.

Suddenly the day didn't seem so bad to Liza as arm-in-arm they inspected the rose garden, the pool and the bar. 'I don't care who he is,' she told herself. 'I like him. Yes, I really do.'

There was a sudden scream from the prune. 'Jack ... Jack Gilmore!' Moments later the plumber was wrested from Liza and clasped in Julia's skinny arms. 'I didn't even know you'd arrived, Jack,' she gasped.

Liza began to giggle. She couldn't stop. Suddenly the guests were clustered around them, shaking hands and clammering to be introduced.

'Here,' Jack said. 'I want to propose a toast to my old mate Liza here. Why didn't you folks tell us you'd organised a fancy dress party?' He turned and winked at Liza.

Suddenly she was popular. Bill Peters, the cockney camera-man, with a freckled face and crooked teeth, said: 'I want to do a camera test on you. You're a very unusual looker. Striking! Where d'you meet Jack?'

'I don't remember exactly,' Liza murmured.

Julia pulled her aside. 'I didn't realise you'd come with Jack. I just adore your sweatshirt,' she said. 'What exactly does it say?'

'Peace, and peace, and still more peace,' Liza replied.

'Really? Then I must get one,' she gushed.

Jack kept her laughing all afternoon, but left at four when jetlag and booze caught up with him.

Suddenly Michael Swift was at her side. 'Thanks for sticking with him, Liza. I can see you understand the Austr-eye-lian mind,' he said. 'Personally he drives me nuts. Come into my office. We must talk.'

An hour later, Liza was having difficulty keeping a grip on herself. She was in shock. Could good news have the same effect on you as bad news? she wondered. Was that why her hands were shaking, her head aching, her mouth dry and her knees had turned to rubber?

Michael Swift was sitting at his desk, with her two scripts in front of him.

'Darling, come here,' he called to Julia. 'And bring Andrea. Liza, stand over there and pretend this house is Nosisi's cottage. And over there,' he pointed to the rose garden, 'is the graveyard. You're live on TV . . . Got it?'

Liza gaped at him.

'Get on with it,' he said impatiently. 'Imagine you're presenting your own programme. Let's see how you do.'

Trembling with excitement, Liza pointed to a handsome crimson rose and said: 'Here lies Joshua Tweneni. Born 1890, died 1955. There's little here to indicate that Joshua Tweneni was a man with a dream. His dream was modest by white standards, but wellnigh impossible for a man born black. Quite simply he wanted to own a piece of land. He wanted to beget and rear his children on it, die on it, be buried on it, and he wanted to leave something real to his children.

'Driven by his dream, Joshua became an apprentice blacksmith and in 1915 he opened his own little workshop. He prospered, saved, went without, and we can only imagine the sacrifices he made, so that, in 1925, his dreams came true and he bought this land we are looking at now for five hundred pounds.

'Here are the deeds of sale,' she waved her hand towards the camera, 'and the receipt, duly registered at the Nelfontein Deeds office. It is for twenty acres in the Eastern Transvaal, near Nelfontein, and fifteen kilometres from the border of the KaNgwane Homeland.'

Suddenly Liza forgot where she was, her indignation and anger at the theft of Nosisi's land overcoming her shyness. She knitted her black brows and scowled ferociously at the camera, imagining those government officials trembling right in front of her as she poured out her indignation and presented her story, reaching her conclusion ten minutes later.

'Nosisi Tweneni is just one of three and a half million blacks who have been driven from their homes. The government has held the law in contempt by their theft of land legally owned and protected by the law. These enforced moves destroy the people, for they become impoverished, their communities shattered, livelihoods lost and hearts broken. I want to say this to you tonight,' she whispered. 'Will the day come when the whites' title deeds will be torn up? Shall we be driven off our farms and homes and dumped on barren ground or pavements? And if so, shall we remember that we taught them how?'

There was a long silence, and Liza came slowly back to her surroundings wondering if she had made herself look ridiculous.

'Wow!' Michael said.

'You've said it,' Andrea echoed.

'Who's going to dress her? Obviously she needs help,' Julia said crisply.

'Dynamite,' Michael mused. 'And she's so right for it.'

Andrea winked at her.

They settled down with a magnum of champagne and talked far into the evening, but the nitty-gritty was she would have her own regular TV programme, to be called *Quite Frankly*.

After she had drunk two glasses of champagne and was feeling quite dizzy with alcohol, happiness and success, she suddenly remembered Ed.

'Sign here,' Michael said pushing a contract towards her.

'I can't do that. Edward Segal ... well, Ed and I are in partnership in a news agency.'

'Well, I guess I can live with that,' Michael said. 'Get him round now. As long as it's you the cameras are focused on, I can't see how we can lose.'

Chapter 46

He'd been hanging around Beira's quays for months and no one knew for sure who he was or where he came from. He looked defeated as he walked in slow, jerky movements on stumbling feet, a dazed, crazy look in his eyes. His body was emaciated and burned almost black by the sun and he stank of sweat, dagga and booze. He could have been any junkie in any docks. He was a bum, that was all. Only his green eyes betrayed his origins. Rumour had it he'd once been a rich planter who stayed behind in the Portuguese exodus. Who cared? Nowadays he was a figure of fun to the locals as he scraped a livelihood of sorts from ships' garbage, tips, odd jobs, and occasional theft.

The three Russian army officers clustered at the rail of their ship looked down at him with detached, uncritical eyes. He was part of the malaise that was Africa. They had read about it and here it was spread out around them, the stench of garbage, sewage, polluted water and sweat, and worst of all, the muggy, steamy heat they had to breathe into their lungs.

'If this is winter,' one of them said, 'God help us when summer comes.'

'We should have brought bottled air with our bottled water, and bottled beer and tinned food. Every mouthful makes my gut crawl,' one of them grumbled.

They trooped down the gangway carrying a bag each and hesitated on the busy Beira quay. This was their first visit to Mozambique and they looked around curiously. The local harbour-master, middle-aged and of mixed blood, stood tall, beer-bellied and magnificent in his braided uniform. He owed his exalted position to his knowledge of Russian, learned in the heady, energetic pre-Revolution days when he'd been selected for terrorist training in the USSR. He saluted, then stepped forward and embraced them with an excessive heartiness that embarrassed the dour foreigners. By now they were red-faced and sweating from the heat and uncertain of just how friendly they should be.

'Welcome to Beira, comrades! I am the harbour-master, Antonio Da Silva, and your host for an hour or two.' He slapped their shoulders and breathed garlic over them. 'I have organised a welcome reception for you at my home, which is also my headquarters.' He pointed to a ramshackle building overlooking the harbour leading off the dock road.

'Hey, you,' he bellowed at the tramp. 'Bring these. Chop-chop, man.' The mumbling, shuffling figure, head bent to hide his burning green eyes, limped behind the Russians carrying their baggage on his shoulder and head, local fashion. This amused the Russians who kept peering over their shoulders on the walk to the road.

The harbour-master liked to eat well. It was not yet noon, but the mouth-watering aroma of peri-peri prawns, mussel soup and spiced rice was all around the house. His housekeeper, Suzanna, a pretty plump black girl with huge rolling eyes, giggled and swayed and rushed back and forth, wiping her sweaty forehead with her hand as she laid a large table on the balcony overlooking the road. Hot air reeking of spices and sour wine surged out each time the swing door opened. The Russians stood around unwillingly.

'Perhaps we should go straight to headquarters,' one of them protested. The tramp smiled to himself and began to polish the harbour-master's 1979 Lada. He saw the Russians turn pale as Da Silva explained they were his guests for lunch. Transport had been arranged for three p.m. Da Silva was not likely to lose a chance to entertain foreign visitors in full view of every passerby.

They sat around the table looking stern and forbidding. The wine was poured, the toasts were made, the back-slapping began and three bottles later the Russians were more jovial. One even pinched Suzanna's backside. Da Silva had a gargantuan appetite and he loved Portuguese green wine. To drink and eat in the shade of the overhanging roof and see passersby admiring him, and watch the down-and-out white bum suffer as he polished his car in the noon heat was exquisite pleasure and Da Silva was a connoisseur of pleasure.

'Hey, Tomäs, clean my boots, you stupid bum,' he bellowed. 'Use your vest. You want this?' He held up a hundred metical banknote. 'Or this?' He filled a glass of wine and pushed it to the edge of the table.

Pieter grinned oafishly, polished the shoes and pointed to the wine.

Da Silva winked at the Russians. 'This, my friends,' he said, extending one foot towards Pieter, 'is a white colonial fucked up to my total satisfaction. Now piss off back to the car,' he bellowed. He switched to Russian. 'He falls asleep every time he drinks and doesn't remember that I never tip him.'

Pieter returned to the car, switched on the long-range listening device hidden in his thick black hair behind his right ear and lay down in the shade. He heard the Russians explaining that they were in a hurry to reach the ANC headquarters. As the afternoon wore on they relaxed and answered the harbour-master's questions. Eventually Pieter learned that they had come to train twenty South African freedom fighters in the use of the latest Czech-made Commando mortars, grenade launchers, search radar and anti-aircraft guns. They had a new type of high-explosive mine which was ideal for use in border farms and villages – quick to lay, virtually undetectable, capable of inflicting maximum damage. They had to liaise with a man called Njani who would get the equipment through to South Africa.

'Don't trust Njani,' the harbour-master told the Reds. 'He's not on our side. He's a common criminal, motivated by greed, that's all.'

Pieter's interest quickened when he heard that name. The man had a finger in every pie, smuggling stolen goods and cars from South Africa to Mozambique, and trafficking arms back to South Africa. Even worse, he had a network from Maputo north to Palma, stealing aid from American and British distribution units and selling it in neighbouring territories. Pieter had been sickened by the dying children who could have been saved by antibiotics that had never reached their intended destination. Njani controlled a network engaged solely in this filthy business, quite apart from his other interests. Pieter had been after him for months, but he had never caught sight of him. Pieter had heard rumours of his ferocious cruelty and seen brave men cower at his name, yet state archives had no record of this name. Pieter had a hunch that he lived a double life under another, perfectly legal front.

'I have a youth staying with me,' Da Silva was saying, 'who's been waiting for transport for weeks.' By now he was slurring his words. 'I'm arranging his passage to Odessa for further training. He's one of the heroes who shot up the imperialists at the church near Johannesburg. Perhaps you read about it? Why don't you keep him with your group meantime? He's bored here.'

A dog sauntered over, nuzzled Pieter and pissed against a nearby tree. The sun moved from its zenith, the air became as warm as a turkish bath and nothing stirred. Only the flies were active, every other living creature had sunk into a torpor of sloth. Eventually the Russians recovered enough to ask when they were leaving. Da Silva explained that the damned locals were always late.

In the mid-afternoon, the tramp crawled to his feet and was seen to amble off towards the beach where he usually slept in a rough shack he'd made of palm leaves under a tree.

Later that evening, the freedom fighter, Nico, was found dead in his bed. The doctor was rushed over, but he was too late. The boy's heart had stopped for no apparent reason.

*

It was springtime, although this was hardly detectable in Mozambique, and Captain Pieter de Vries was nearing the end of his quest. From the window of a ramshackle, Portuguese-owned warehouse outside Marracuene, where he worked as a storeman, he could see the trees undulating in a mild breeze, leaves spiralling, and the grass rippling in the wind. The sight of some familiar spring flowers filled him with a longing to be far away, to wander over his own land, to hear the stream trickling, to watch the weaver birds building their nests, and the duikers frolicking through the long grass. He longed to create, to nourish the earth and protect all living creatures. When he got out of this he would never again kill anything or anyone, he promised himself daily. He heaved a deep sigh.

The Portuguese mafia boss, José Manuel, who owned the warehouse and the adjoining roadhouse, caught his mood and sighed, too.

'Oh to be young,' he said. 'When I was young and fit, a night like this would see me out on the tiles screwing every broad I saw, but now I can't even get it up.' He was a thin, pasty-faced fellow with an ulcer and putrid breath. Only his moustache was healthy and sleek. It was a glossy dark brown, contrasting with his grey hair and he was always touching it. He smoothed and twiddled the ends whenever he smiled. He was smiling now and that made Pieter shudder inwardly.

'Gotta reefer?' Pieter whined. To acknowledge understanding of the boss's statement would be to invite disaster. Only idiots were employed in this warehouse – they had to be Portuguese-speaking, too. The boss, who in these parts was as powerful as a Sicilian godfather, gathered his workers from the flotsam and jetsam of the beached ex-colonials – mainly junkies, although there was one crazy boy who'd been inside a Maputo prison for too long.

Manuel ruled the northern route in and out of Maputo. He knew each lorry and its load and he controlled two gangs of hoodlums who murdered anyone foolish enough to try trading in minerals or gemstones or oil without handing over a generous cut. Most lucrative of all of these consignments were Russian-made arms destined for South Africa.

Pieter guessed that Manuel and Njani were in league with each other. They had to be, so Pieter had worked his guts out here for the past four weeks hoping for a chance to photograph Njani, to find a clue to his other identity, or to kill him.

Unbelievably, Manuel was holding out a banknote in his white hand. 'Look here, Tomäs,' he said. 'You haven't yet had a night off. Why don't you get yourself a woman and screw the pants off her? I've given Nkosi time off, too. He'll give you a lift. You never know what you might find in Marracuene.'

A stiff dose of droopy-dick, Pieter thought, mumbling incomprehensibly and snatching at the note. He backed off, pocketing the cash, as if he thought the man might change his mind.

Manuel laughed cruelly and turned away.

Using his powerful night-sight binoculars Pieter watched the warehouse from the safety of the tallest branches of a convenient mahogany tree a few feet away from the back yard. It was up here in the rich foliage that he kept his gear and his radio receiver and transmitter, stowed in a box, wrapped in polythene and strapped to a branch. He was cramped and thirsty, but he knew he might have to sit out the night.

He had been waiting for six hours, but he knew Njani would come. All the signs said so. Manuel had not drunk wine with his supper, he had remained alert and not even smoked a joint. He was listening and tense, his hand never far from his jacket, under which he wore a handgun. From time to time he stood up and peered out of his office window.

At three a.m. Pieter heard the low rumble of a convoy of trucks and saw their headlights shining from some distance away. Manuel became agitated and started to pace his office, walking to the door and gazing out and walking back again. Eventually the trucks drew up in the yard. They were open trucks with Maputo registrations, the type used to transport road gangs, and they were packed with labourers.

The trucks waited in pitch darkness. Then one of them hooted. All at once all the lights were switched back on. Manuel walked outside, hands outstretched.

A man climbed down from the passenger's seat in the front compartment of the leading lorry and walked catlike towards Manuel's warehouse. He was very tall and black, and the whites of his eyes shone green in the nightscope. He had a dignified appearance, a long, bony face, heavy-lidded large eyes, and there was a solemn look about him. Something about him was familiar.

Manuel was dripping with friendliness. 'Sorry to keep you waiting. I must have dropped off,' he lied. 'Good to see you, Mr Njani, even though it is so late. Come inside and have some refreshments.' The two men walked back to the warehouse with linked arms, smiling falsely at each other.

Two deadly vipers, Pieter thought, shuddering. Tense with excitement, he put on his earphones and mentally recorded their lengthy conversation, while they shared a bottle of scotch and smoked cigars in Manuel's office. At last the two walked back to the lorry. Pieter slipped down from the tree and crept towards the house, moving slowly and cautiously. He could see nothing, but he could hear their voices nearby. He knew now that the weapons were going to be carried through the game reserve on the backs of the men in the trucks. Njani would drive through the border post legally and pick them up on the South African side. But how? What excuse could he give to have been in Mozambique?

The warehouse was deserted as Pieter moved in. He crept to the desk, wrapped Njani's glass and Manuel's silver cigarette case in plastic and pocketed them. Walking to the next room, which was dark, Pieter stared through the window at Njani. Once again he was struck by the familiarity of those solemn features. Who was he?

Suddenly Pieter felt Njani's eyes link with his. The man was psychic. Like a bird or a buck, he sensed when someone stared at him. Pieter cursed his stupidity and moved out fast. He was halfway across the yard towards the tree when the security light caught him in its beam. One of the gang raced towards him, arm raised to hurl a knife. It struck him in the arm. Pieter winced, caught hold of the hilt, yanking it out of his flesh. As the man dived at him, Pieter brought up the knife in a great sweep, ripping open his belly. He fell with a terrible groan and Pieter fled to the darkness of the trees.

There were thirty fit men after him, but Pieter knew the terrain intimately. He had a good chance, despite his wound. He began to run for his life.

He should have been smarter and quicker, Pieter thought ten days later as he sat at the computer console in the group's new headquarters on the sixth floor of a redbrick building in Pretoria, where they operated under the guise of a computer programming school.

Njani was none other than the so-called Reverend Ronald Sizani, founder and leader of his own religious movement. He was also a highly-paid police informer, who hobnobbed with government officials, lectured school children, gave talks on peace. The fingerprint was his. Sizani had been invited to attend a church seminar in Maputo where he had given a talk on the value of two-way dialogue. What an alibi! What a front! But that precious print had revealed him as a common criminal, dealing in stolen goods and stolen aid and making a fortune smuggling arms into South Africa.

Pieter reckoned it was a miracle the print had remained intact. He had run through the bush until the dawn and then hidden in a tree until nightfall. The glass had broken and cut through his clothes and into his flesh, but a piece large enough to contain one beautiful print had survived.

'You're as good as caught, you bastard, Njani,' he murmured. He glanced at his watch. He had a meeting with the major in ten minutes. He felt pretty pleased with himself.

*

'The whole point of the exercise is the *permanent removal from society* of these targets,' the major said in a firm, angry voice. Pieter wanted a public trial and they had argued the toss for some minutes.

'The public should know what's going on right under their noses,' Pieter snarled, knowing that he was overstepping the boundaries of military discipline.

'Can't you do it?' the major asked with a sudden change of tone. 'Have you lost your nerve? It happens sooner or later ... we all know that. When it's time to hang up your gun you have to say so.'

'Of course I can do it,' Pieter growled. 'But he wasn't on the list, this Njani. I found him. Can't you see what that makes me ... his prosecutor, judge, jury and executioner? I just thought ...'

'In this business it pays to do as you're ordered and think very little about it. A new government could see these terrorists free on the streets within weeks. Is that what you want? Besides, a trial would cause a hue and cry from those sons of bitches overseas who don't know what it's all about. Did you know that the Reverend Ronald Sizani organised a lecture tour of Africa on behalf of this so-called dialogue group of his. He collected fifty thousand dollars, all of which is in his numbered bank account in Switzerland. He'd get the best lawyers and he'd get off. One print on a glass – that's all we've got.'

'I saw him. I can identify him.'

'So it's your word against his. Come on, captain. The best place to see him is down the sights of your rifle. Let's get on with it.'

Chapter 47

The assassination of the Reverend Ronald Sizani made headline news, which Liza studied carefully. He had been gunned down at a mass funeral of fifteen Xhosa hostel dwellers. The victims had been hacked to pieces by angry Zulus in retribution for the death of several of their tribesmen who had been ambushed by Xhosas while returning from a wedding. The vendetta went back almost two years between rival hostel inmates and no one could remember how it all started.

Sizani had been invited to preach a sermon at the graveside and his words had been full of conciliatory statements. 'Love your enemies,' he had bellowed through the loudspeakers, according to the news report. When he had said: 'Let us learn to fight out our differences on a soccer pitch,' a shot had rung out and Sizani staggered headlong into the grave, dead before he landed.

No immediate reprisals followed his death for Sizani was a hybrid of a Zulu mother and a Xhosa father and he had no tribal affiliations. Liberal white church groups held mass meetings and nationwide prayer services. '*A martyr to peace*' was engraved on his tombstone.

Later the police revealed that the weapon used was a 7mm Remmington Magnum but it seemed that there was no motive for the crime. Interest flagged, but Liza wondered if it linked in with the spate of deaths Myers had revealed to Dan.

Days later, the PAC leaders in exile in Dar Es Salaam,

Tanzania, issued a statement that Sizani had been in liaison with their freedom fighters and that government forces were responsible for his death. This was vehemently denied by the Government and shortly afterwards a commission of inquiry was set up.

Liza began to tot up the deaths of black politicians. Who or what was involved? Two weeks after Sizani's murder, a gang of black youths terrorised the occupants of a train, killing a black teacher, who was also a militant political leader and who had instigated several school boycotts and riots. One of the youths was injured while leaving the train and he was taken into custody for interrogation. Hours later he revealed that white soldiers had recruited and trained him.

Liza thought about pulling all the deaths into one story. Was there an unknown organisation intent on killing off subversive black leaders? So far her research had drawn a blank, but the assassination of the Reverend Sizani gave her a chance to reopen her story. She decided to go right to the top.

Brigadier Manie Engelbrecht was extremely unhelpful. Liza and Ed had arrived with a full entourage of cameras, lighting assistants, programme director and herself. She was sitting in the boardroom of the police headquarters in Fordsburg and she was aware of how much trouble the police had taken to show their friendlier side. There were daffodils in vases and pretty young policewomen sitting in the background smiling at the cameras. Nowadays, her fame brought Liza red-carpet treatment wherever she went. She loved it, and the power she controlled. Engelbrecht would never have agreed to see her in her old freelancing days, but now she was a force to be reckoned with. Nevertheless, the interview wasn't working and she would have to admit defeat.

'Who is this Dan Tweneni?' Engelbrecht was saying. 'I've never heard of him. I am quite sure that a member of my staff would never have discussed classified information with him. I have no knowledge of a so-called Third Force. I don't believe that it exists. This unfortunate death was merely a continuation of the hostel feud. There's no stopping these people once they are pulled into a vendetta. You shouldn't take all these rumours you hear so seriously, my dear. Your viewers can rest assured that there is no sinister organisation at work.' He ended the interview with a patronising smile.

'Yet Dan Tweneni had to flee the country after two attempts on his life. A leading police officer warned him that he was in danger. How do you account for so many deaths of militant or powerful black leaders over the past three months?'

'Most of these are not in my area. I know nothing about them. You can't expect me to comment on something that has nothing to do with me.'

Liza motioned to Ed to turn off the camera and sound. She wanted to scream with frustration. 'I can't swim through the lies,' she snarled at the Brigadier. She left in a temper.

On the way out, she found herself face-to-face with Captain Myers. She flushed heavily, feeling shamed by the memory of their last meeting.

'Come this way, I want to talk to you,' he said, ushering her and Ed into a nearby office. He shut the door behind them. 'Miss Frank. You've come a long way since we last met. I can see your motivation and I sympathise. You want to hit back at society and you've done a good job. You want to hurt those who damaged you so badly and you have no regard for considerations of your own personal safety. That much is clear or you would never have embarked on this quest of yours.

'Now just think . . . Suppose you are right – just *suppose*,' he said, with heavy emphasis, 'that the Government, or another right-wing organisation, had set up a clandestine force to destroy those subversive elements the country has been unable to deal with through normal legal means. What sort of men would they have picked? Ruthless, would you say? Clever? Dedicated? Fanatical even? The sort of men who put ideals before lives. So what do you think they would do to you if you were to go on TV with real proof that they exist, and that they are, in fact, guilty of murder?'

For a moment Liza sat frozen into her chair. She could not speak. Her arms came out in goose-pimples as icy shudders ran up and down her spine.

'But . . . I . . .'

'You came here to get a scoop – something no one else knows – a death warrant perhaps. Don't be a fool, Miss Frank. Or do you have a death wish?'

She stood up slowly. 'My job is to find the truth and present it to my viewers. I won't be intimidated. I shall continue.' She would not admit to Myers that he had scared her.

'Nevertheless, I won't give in,' she told Ed in the car as they drove back to the cottage. 'Myers knows a great deal.'

Ed merely sighed. By now he knew that threatening Liza merely made her more determined. 'What did Myers mean about hitting back at those who destroyed you?'

'D'you know what I'm going to do, Ed?' she said, as if she hadn't heard his question. 'I'm going to interview every next of kin of every black leader who's died. We might get a new angle. We'll feature this news as part of next Thursday's programme. Perhaps we could ask viewers to send us their comments.'

Thursday's programme featured Liza wearing jeans and a blue angora sweater standing outside a fisherman's cottage by the sea at Langebaan in the Cape. A bitterly cold wind blew her hair wildly all over the place.

Tom Muimbi's wife was a heavy-set, ugly woman and her eyes were swollen with weeping. 'Why would he go fishing?' she asked. 'Poor Tom hated the sea. It caused a lot of trouble in his family because they're all fisherfolk, but he joined the PAC and he'd done well. Then, the night before he died, two white men came and spoke to him and he seemed very scared. Later that night he went out alone and wouldn't tell me where he was going, but I knew it was to meet "them". I never saw him alive again.'

The next shot was in Soweto, where Liza interviewed hostel

dwellers. She knew she looked divine in a pink slack suit with a black onyx necklace. The make-up artist had tried out a new eye make up and she looked quite different, like a startled teenager, she thought.

She smiled confidently into the cameras. 'This is where Ben Thembisa was supposedly mugged and stabbed by Zulu criminals,' she began, walking towards the hostel and trying not to trip over the stones and rubble. 'Yet rumours around these parts claim that Thembisa was seen drinking with whites an hour before he died. I have three hostel workers who want to tell you their views.' In turn the workers explained that they had been on nightshift, and they left Ben half-drunk and sleeping in the hostel and no party of Zulus could have got past the watchmen at the gates, for they took turns to stand guard.

'So there you have it,' she summed up after her eighth interview. 'It makes you think, doesn't it? If there is a Third Force, who is behind them? Perhaps you have heard rumours, or seen something strange. If you have any information, contact this number. We're hoping to shed some light on this very murky subject.'

Liza was out for the next two nights, covering business functions which might give her leads for TV or the newspaper stories. Sunday night, however, was her night home. She switched on her telephone answering machine and settled down for a happy evening of playing new jazz tapes she'd bought and doing her nails and giving herself a facial. She had never once missed her weekly skin-lightening programme.

It was midnight when she heard the telephone ring. Rather late she thought, frowning, and turned down the tape so she could hear the voice being recorded.

'Angel,' came a harsh whisper. 'Angel, switch off this damned machine and take this call. It's urgent!'

'Who is it?' she asked, grabbing the receiver.

'Angel! Listen to me carefully. Go to the telephone kiosk at the end of this road and call this number.' The voice rattled off a string of numbers. 'Got it?'

'Yes.' A click ended the call.

What a dark night. The street lights weren't working. That was strange. Was there no moon? She looked up anxiously and saw the Milky Way seeming brighter than usual. Damn! She should have brought a torch. When her eyes adjusted slightly, she felt her way to the telephone kiosk. She could not help asking herself why she was doing this? She could have called from her cosy home. But it could only be Ralph or Nico. Were they in trouble again?

At last she reached the kiosk and dialled the number. She got an out-of-order tone. After three attempts she called Inquiries and learned that there was no such number listed.

Suddenly she felt afraid. Why had the caller wanted to get her outside on a fool's errand? To murder her? To break into her home? That seemed the most likely answer. She began to run, but fell down the kerb, hurting her knee. Someone bent over her and a hand was clapped over her mouth.

'It's me, Ralph.' He took his hand away. 'Sh! I'm sorry you fell. Are you hurt?'

'Wow! You frightened me half to death.' She could hardly catch her breath and her heart was hammering against her ribs.

'Calm down, Angel. I'm sorry I dragged you out in the dark. I can't risk someone seeing me with you. I think I'm being followed. I want to tell you something,' he said. He hugged her close in his arms, rocking her backwards and forwards and she felt his wet cheeks against hers.

'You'll always be like my own little sister, Angel,' he muttered. 'I couldn't bear anything to happen to you. I watch your programme every Thursday. You get more and more beautiful, Angel, but I'm so scared for you.'

'You're so thin, Ralph,' she gasped, feeling his ribs as she hugged him. 'Come back with me, I'll cook you a meal.'

'No. It wouldn't be safe. You must never let on that you know me. Now listen carefully. I want to tell you a story. Remember the stories you used to tell us?'

'Yes, of course,' she whispered feeling suddenly afraid.

'Once upon a time . . .' He gave her another quick hug. 'There was a very cruel man. He was the most feared man in Africa and his name was Njani. He belonged to no particular party, but he made money out of everyone, gun-running, killing or maiming for a fee, handling stolen goods and cars, kidnapping. He had gangs of murderers in every centre and he controlled them through fear. He was ferocious. Hardly anyone saw him, but once Nico and I did. He sold us arms and we saw exactly what he looked like.'

'Why? What for? What are you involved in, Ralph?'

'Don't ask, Angel. Just listen. After a job we pulled he offered to get us out of the country. We knew he'd sell us as trainee soldiers to one or another group.'

He broke off at her cry. 'Sh! Don't interrupt. There isn't time. He offered us safe passages to Mozambique and from there on to Russia for training. Nico went, but I stayed.'

'What are you saying, Ralph. That you . . .?'

He put his arm around her waist.

She tried to swallow her sorrow for this new Ralph. 'So Nico's in Russia?'

'No. Nico died in Maputo. The doctor's report said he had a heart attack.'

She could feel Ralph's body shaking; with hatred or fear, she wondered? 'Believe me, Angel, there's someone around who will stop at nothing. Please don't get involved. That's why I'm here. To warn you.'

'But I'm not involved. I never heard of this Njani,' she argued.

'I went to the funeral of the Reverend Ronald Sizani,' Ralph went on. 'I couldn't believe my eyes when I walked past his coffin and recognised Njani. The Reverend Sizani was just his cover, but someone penetrated his front.'

'So?' she murmured.

'There is someone around who is even more cunning and ruthless than Njani. And you have set yourself up against these people. I've come here tonight to beg you to let it go. They are fanatics. D'you think they'd let *you* stand in the way of their mission?'

'What is their mission?' she whispered.

'Safeguarding the power and the survival of the whites. Whoever killed Njani will kill you if you become a threat. I'm sick with worry for you, Angel, that's why I came here tonight. They'll kill you. D'you believe me?'

'Yes,' she said shuddering. 'I learned long ago what happens to someone who threatens *their* way of life.'

'So you'll stop this programme of yours?'

'Surely you, of all people, must realise how much I want to hit back. I want to expose their every flaw and weakness.'

Ralph sighed and kissed her cheek. 'Remember this. Njani was a dangerous criminal, but he was gunned down probably because he was gun-running.'

'Thank you, Ralph. I shall use this in my programme,' she said.

He sighed, kissed her goodbye and disappeared into the darkness as silently as he had come, leaving her grieving for Nico. Poor, poor Nico. What chance had he ever had?

An emergency meeting was held at the Halfway House headquarters of the group. By the time Pieter arrived by a special helicopter flight from Nelfontein the others were already assembled. Pieter knew the score. They were all in shit. No whisper of a Third Force should ever have been mentioned. Now it was on everyone's tongue. As he'd thought, the major was furious. His blue eyes flashed contempt at them and his mouth was taut with tension.

The major swung down the screen and suddenly there was Liza, wearing an expensive pink suit and a very smug expression. Her thick black hair was pulled up on top of her head in a sort of roll, pearl earrings and necklace completed a picture of a really classy woman, a woman any guy would be proud to marry – brainy, beautiful and desirable. He wondered what her gran thought about the girl she had dumped so cruelly and whether or not she watched Liza's Thursday night programme as avidly as he did.

Liza was smiling as if she was at a picnic. This was the second time he'd seen this programme and each time it looked more like a fashion show than a dangerous exposé as she tripped backwards and forwards in one smart outfit after the next, interviewing the bereaved families, knitting her black eyebrows and accusing the government of setting up a Third Force. What the hell does she think she's doing? Pieter wondered. Has she no idea what she's letting herself in for? She looks like a silly teenager prancing around and offering herself as a live sacrifice.

Her third and latest programme, which he had not yet seen, was switched on. Pieter jumped with shock as he heard Liza say: 'Who was it who discovered that the Reverend Ronald Sizani and the criminal Njani were one and the same person? Somehow someone got past Njani's cover and gunned down one of the most feared and savage men in Africa known for his cruel reprisals. He was wanted for gun-running, smuggling terrorists, and a host of criminal activities all over Southern Africa. Someone out there was smarter than he was. Who? That's what this programme is all about.

'Have the beleaguered, right-wing whites, in a desperate last-ditch stand, set up a force to remove black leaders and their associates? Is that why the Reverend Ronald Sizani was murdered?'

The major switched off the programme in a swift jerk, as if he couldn't stand another moment of it.

Pieter swore silently. Now how the hell had Liza got hold of this information?'

'Our security has reached an all-time low,' the major was saying. His voice was so low it sounded like a growl. 'Some interfering female reporter, known as Liza Frank, has actually featured "us" on her talk show. Later in the programme, she asks viewers for information. So why don't we just go on her programme and tell her what she wants to know. You might as well, for all the attention you've paid to security.'

That was unfair, Pieter thought. Most of the deaths could never be proved to be anything other than accidental. The fact that Jon had employed young thugs for the train murder had been a stroke of idiocy. He should have foreseen that one of them might be interrogated.

He stood up slowly. 'Look here, sir,' he began. 'From the very outset we carried the seeds of our own destruction. The reason these deaths have come to the attention of the media is the fact that there have been so many of them in so short a time. In other words, it is our success that has made us visible. Basically that's all anyone has on us – simple statistics. There have been too many deaths featuring black leaders in too short a space of time. We did what we were ordered and set up to do. Perhaps the original planning was at fault.

'So now this Liza Frank has discovered that Sizani was Njani. Any hood could have told her, because hundreds of them saw his corpse at the public funeral. Come to think of it, they could have picked it up from newspaper photos of Sizani. There's been enough of them bandied around. Someone guessed the truth and called Miss Frank. Does it matter?'

'True,' the major said, calming down a bit. 'But we have to find out what else she knows. She's a potential danger ...' He left the threat hanging in the air.

'Put out her light,' someone growled.

'Then we'd really be in the shit,' Pieter retorted. 'What do we have at present – too many accidental deaths of subversive and militant black leaders? Add an innocent female reporter – a household name – and we'll have the entire legal structure of South Africa, to say nothing of local and foreign press, to contend with.'

'Aren't you going a little overboard in your efforts to protect this woman?' the major asked, giving him a steely look.

'With respect, sir, I've always been worried that we were

operating against the law, but because I'm under orders and because I know that it's the only way to eliminate dangerous elements I never queried what we were doing. Our job is to prevent massacres, such as the one at Honeydew. But when innocent people get in our way, or get on to us, there can be no possible justification in threatening *their* existence.'

The major had gone very white. 'Thank you for the sermon, captain. However, in times of war the innocent often suffer. And as you know, *we are at war*.'

Pieter sighed. 'Leave her to me. I'll take her to Mozambique … turn on the screws there. I'll find out exactly what she knows and what her motives are. If she's safe I'll bring her back, but if she's one of them …'

They all seemed to be relieved. None of them liked the killing, but it was a job that had to be done. They had all joined Special Services with stars in their eyes and dreams of heroism. How many of them saw themselves as heroes now, Pieter wondered? There's life as you dream it should be and life as it really is, he thought grimly. The two concepts seem to keep moving away from each other at a tangent. The trick of life was to keep on trying to pull them back together.

Chapter 48

———◆———

'Back me up before this lot eats me,' Liza hissed at Ed.

She dabbed her forehead. It was hot in the studio and tempers were flaring. Her new white linen dress was crumpled, her make-up was awash with sweat and her hairdo was drooping. 'Shit,' she muttered.

Liza had written a script lambasting the 'fatties' industry. Michael thought it was too contentious and he'd sent the prune to his lawyer with the script. Mona thought they could do without the humour. Hans, the programme producer, who was getting fat, thought it was insulting and even Ed was scared they'd annoy viewers. Everyone had a point of view and they were all shouting. Liza sighed. She'd need a stiff scotch to unwind enough to enjoy her evening jog.

'Oh, who cares,' she muttered to herself. 'I have a message, don't I?'

The programme opened with a shot of beggar children hanging around a supermarket as fat ladies emerged, wheeling trolleys laden with low-calorie food. Liza walked on-scene, holding her microphone, giving the statistics of the millions of rands invested into producing low-calorie soups, fruit juice, tinned fruit, bread, and even low-calorie dog biscuits for too-pampered pets, in a country where over a third of the nation's children suffered from malnutrition. Shot after shot posed the question: 'Is this an acceptable use of our country's limited resources?'

'Okay, Liza, get on the set. We'll wind it up,' Bill said gloomily half an hour later.

'There you have it, ladies,' Liza said, smiling sweetly into the camera. 'If you feel you need to shed a few kilos how about donating your housekeeping cash to "Operation Hunger" or the nearest kid's orphanage, or even hand out your food before it reaches your boot, or should I say your hips.'

'No, definitely no,' a new voice called out. Every head turned. It was the head of English TV, whom Hans had enlisted in a last-ditch stand. 'Tone it down or take it off. Your choice. And stop knocking our advertisers.'

'Oh shit!' Liza stormed off in a temper. 'I'll rewrite tomorrow,' she shouted over her shoulder. 'Enjoy supper,' she called to Hans.

Feeling furious, she hurried out of the building. Smash, smash, smash, went her heels on the brick paving. Shoulders squared, chin held high, eyes narrowed and mouth taut, she relived the squabble and her eventual humiliation.

'So that's how a successful career woman walks.' She heard a chuckle from behind and spun around.

'Pieter? Oh God! Oh, Pieter!'

'Only me.' He was laughing at her. 'Sorry to disappoint you.'

'Oh . . . You fool!' She flung herself in his arms. A small voice in her head was saying: Where's your pride, Liza? Shouldn't you play hard to get? But she couldn't stop hugging him.

'It's wonderful to see you.' She stepped back, resisting the temptation to nuzzle his beard and thrust her fingers through his thick black hair. The past four years of longing seemed to melt away as she gazed at him. It might have been yesterday they loved and parted. 'I've missed you so much,' she whispered.

His green eyes were full of laughter, his face was tanned almost black and his skin more lined than she remembered, but he looked terrific. She'd forgotten the impact of his size and strength and the sheer vitality and sex-appeal that surged out of him. Yet she had to admit that he looked a bit scruffy and sort of wild and tough. His battered running shoes had holes in them, his khaki shorts were grimy and torn and his T-shirt was washed-out. He looked like a bum.

'You sort of took me by surprise,' she said, smiling nervously.

He put his arm around her. 'I don't have a car,' he said. 'Do you?'

'Yes.'

'Let's go! Where is it?' She pointed to a white Alfa in the car park.

'You've come a long way, Liza,' Pieter said solemnly. 'Well done! You're a clever and resourceful woman, but I don't think I could trust you to drive me.' He held his hand out for the keys and after a moment's hesitation, she gave them to him. 'Where can we have coffee? I want to talk to you.'

'Want to come home and see my place?' she asked. 'It's near by.'

'I don't have time. Anywhere handy will do.'

Feeling disappointed, she directed him to a nearby restaurant patronised by the studio crowd. She caught a glimmer of unease in the manager's eyes when he saw Pieter. Then he recognised her and bowed. 'Good evening, Miss Frank. Any friend of yours is welcome here.'

Why shouldn't Pieter be welcome? She felt annoyed.

'Sorry if I don't match up to your new lifestyle,' Pieter said. 'I've been out of work for some time.'

'Oh! You should have told me. Couldn't you have written, or called, or any damn thing?'

'What's the point? Nowadays I'm a bum.'

'Oh no! Never. But why did you leave the army?'

'Long story.' He sighed. 'Finally I was sacked. They said I was mentally unstable – megalomania and paranoia – that's the standard term for bush-fucked. Most of us land up like that – I've been four years in the bush.'

So that was why he hadn't contacted her. Relief flooded through her. She couldn't think what to say in the long silence that followed. She longed to help him. Could she beg him to live with her until he found a job? Perhaps now was not the right time. Besides, his pride would be hurt.

'I didn't know where to find you,' he said, gulping his coffee, 'so I hung around the studio. I knew I'd see you eventually. I've watched some of your programmes.'

'So what did you want to talk about?' she asked, hoping he wanted her help.

'About Gran's farm.'

'Oh!' Disappointment flooded through her. Was that all?

'I merged my place with Tony's plantation to create a large game reserve right on the border of the Kruger Park. There's big money with foreign tourists nowadays. Gran has accepted Tony's offer to incorporate her farm into the game park.'

'I don't understand – Gran would never agree to part with her farm. It was her life.'

'She did it for you.'

Liza was too astonished to answer.

'By law, being coloured, you cannot own land in a white area . . .'

Liza flushed deep red. She felt burning hot all over. Glancing nervously around she saw with relief that no one had heard.

She whispered: 'No one knows . . . I've put all that behind me.' Damn Pieter! Why did he have to drag past humiliations into her new, successful world? The awful past was rushing up to engulf her again. She fought back an absurd desire to get up and run.

'Get off your high horse, Liza. You're allowed to own shares in a private company that owns land, so you now own ten per cent of our game park. Gran bargained for a very good deal for you. She held out – she was virtually walking through wild game every time she went shopping. Our one and only lion ate her last donkey, but she wouldn't budge – not until we upped your share to ten per cent of the whole lot. That includes the hotel, Tony's former house – they still live there, by the way– the various plantations and the game reserve.'

'You mean Gran's share?'

'No! It's going to be put in your name – when the company's formed, that is. Gran insists.'

Without warning tears came brimming out and rolled down her cheeks. She sat there stupidly trying to blink them away, wiping her cheeks with the back of her hand and then fumbling in her bag. 'Where're my sunglasses?' she spluttered. 'I know I had them. I've had a rough day. You've sort of taken me by surprise. I thought that Gran ...' her voice tailed off. She took out a tissue and blew her nose. 'Ten per cent? But how is that possible?' she queried.

'The place is a prime viewing site and the watering hole has good visibility all around it. Even more to the point, the borehole company found huge water reserves under her dam which is ideally situated to enlarge.'

'Good heavens!' She couldn't think of a single intelligent thing to say.

He laughed. 'You haven't been home for a long time, have you?'

'No. Not since ...' She broke off and bit her lip. 'I never forgave her for what she said when we were arrested.'

'I think she never forgave herself.' He sighed. 'The place is ready to be stocked – mainly with buck – although there's a baby rhino for sale – we might go for that. We have one old lion we bought from a zoo, the one that ate your donkey, but there's more on order. As for the big cats – well, who knows.'

'We?'

'I have a temporary job working for Tony. He wants me to stock the place cheaply. I'm planning to catch some buck in Mozambique and hop them over the border in an old, converted Dakota. It'll be exciting. I thought you might like to come along ...'

Suddenly her spirits soared. Sadness was forgotten.

'You could write a programme on private game farms,' he was saying. 'So you wouldn't be wasting your time. What d'you say?'

'Yes.'

He laughed. 'I like decisive women,' he teased her.

'There was no decision to be made. I still care, Pieter.'

He did not reply and the long silence that followed seemed to last an age.

It was dark and slightly chilly when she reached Nelfontein three days later, having driven through the night. Pieter was waiting at the airport gates.

'I'm glad you're early,' he said, kissing her briefly, 'because we're ready to go.' He parked her car in a large hangar and they walked over to the runway in pitch darkness.

Their pilot was introduced as Bob, an old friend of Pieter's, who strapped her into the co-pilot's seat. Pieter crouched on the floor behind them and minutes later they took off.

By the time they flew over the border the sun was already appearing over the horizon in a blinding golden glare. Below the virgin forest looked dark and impenetrable. She shivered, suddenly aware of the wildness of the territory they were flying over.

'No houses, no roads or farms – just nothing,' she whispered, feeling overawed.

'There's great winding rivers down there, and lakes like you've never seen in your life, and wild life and so many birds.'

After a while she became lulled into a trancelike state as they soared over forests and bushveld and rivers.

The next thing she knew Pieter was shaking her shoulder. 'We're going down. Swallow!'

They were following a river that cut into lush green summer grasslands dotted with trees.

'See that elephant,' Pieter said, bending over her.

She was aware of the musky scent of his body, and his strong hand gripping her. 'There!' he said, pointing impatiently.

Leaning forward, she saw a blob of grey near the water.

'Was that an elephant?' It might have been a rock, or any damn thing. She was far more interested in Pieter, who was so familiar yet so strangely changed that it unnerved her. There

was a new intentness about him that she did not remember
being there before. When he stared at her from under his thick
black brows, something about his narrowed eyes and savage
expression thrilled her. Was it fear? Or lust? Or a mixture of
both? She was not sure, but she sensed that here was a man who
would go to any extreme and who was driven by a deep
compulsive passion. The sight of those thick brown arms with
their tangle of black hairs, the long brown fingers gripping the
seat, his square shoulders, held with such military erectness
under his khaki shirt, his strong, muscled neck with sinews
rippling, and his curly black beard, was exciting and frustrating
all at the same time.

His green eyes swept over her with such intensity that her
stomach quivered. 'Later,' he murmured, his mouth nuzzling
her ear.

Jumping up, he snapped: 'Pull her up.'

'Yes, sir,' the pilot said.

A friend? she wondered silently as the plane made a steep,
upward curve. She had to push herself upright with all her
strength as her blood rushed to her feet. 'What's wrong?'

'The fools have planted mealies on the runway.'

He was bending over Bob barking instructions and the plane
swerved violently to the west. 'Try the old runway. I'll get this
one fixed once we're down.'

'Yes, *sir*.'

They hit the ground with a crash and reared up, racing
towards the river, and down again, thumping heavily over the
uneven surface. Liza hung on to her seat, convinced that the
tyres would burst, while the plane hopped forward at frightening speed and squealed to a halt on the edge of a riverbank.

As Pieter swung the door open the moist heat surged in. After
the dry, rarefied air of Johannesburg, it was like a soothing salve.
Liza loved the heat and the moisture. She stood up, stretched
and opened her door.

'Hang on. I'll do a recé.' Gripping his carbine, Pieter
disappeared into the bushes.

'What could be wrong?' she asked Bob.

'Most anything, ma'am,' he said politely.

Five minutes later Pieter returned. 'All clear,' he said. Bob and he unloaded several heavy steel boxes and some sacks of foodstuffs from the back and flung them down. Then their own gear was flung out, plus two rifles, two backpacks, and some ice boxes containing their food.

'I guess you'll make it,' he told Bob. 'I'll get the mealies pulled out before you return. See you.'

The plane moved forward with a massive surge, lifting clear after a short run. She watched it until it disappeared in the haze. With it went her last link with civilisation.

Chapter 49

Laden with packages, Pieter was striding towards a camp. Liza picked up two bags and staggered after him. The heat burned her skin through her T-shirt and scorched her shoulders, although it was still only nine.

Inside the barbed wire was a tall security fence enclosing what seemed to be only a grove of tall sausage trees, clustered around a baobab tree. Then she saw that a double-storey hut had been built around the baobab. It was perfectly camouflaged, the walls were circular and made of mud, with palm leaves laced around the plaster, under a thatched roof. The branches and leaves of the baobab hung over the hut concealing it from the air.

Pieter had unlocked the heavy bolts and disappeared inside. Following him she found herself in a large dark room with rough wooden benches and tables and a long bar in one corner, studded with half-husks of coconuts. There was an old paraffin refrigerator and Pieter was bent over it. 'First things first,' he said. Moments later the refrigerator thumped and shuddered into action and he sighed with relief. 'What a smell,' he grumbled. 'I'll open the windows. The last guys didn't clean up properly.' He swore as he looked around. She laughed at the explicit pin-ups around the walls. A flock of noisy starlings, of a deep, iridescent blue-green had followed her in and now they hopped and squabbled around her.

'They're so tame,' she called.

'Get them out of here. The boys used to feed them. They got spoiled and they mess up the place. Don't you feed them. It's kinder not to. They shouldn't hang around here, they might get trapped inside. There's plenty of food for them in the bush.'

She went outside and the birds followed, chirping greedily. Monkeys were chattering and leaping amongst long fronds of creepers hanging from the marula and wistaria trees along the river bank. They began to screech at a tribe of baboons in the baobab tree. She could hear the noise of a small waterfall below, and honking from two Egyptian geese as they flew low overhead. There was the noisy scream of a fish eagle as it plunged down to the river. A hoopoe dived overhead and a hornbill landed right beside her, putting its head on one side and staring up quizzically. Moments later a flock of guineafowls and their half-grown chicks darted through the enclosure.

'This is paradise,' she whispered to Pieter who had come outside.

'Mozambique is paradise most everywhere. One day I'm coming back to build and mend. I'll start a farm, or co-operative mining. I have so many dreams – for later.'

'Why not now since you're out of work?' she asked.

He gave her a strange, secretive look and turned away. She watched him go inside and shut the door, so she followed him. He was poised on a rickety ladder, trying to open a trap door in the ceiling. He was so full of grace, his legs long and supple, his arms strong and thick, buttocks straining in his jeans as he pushed upwards.

Eventually he managed to slam back the bolts and the door opened with a crash. Pieter disappeared through the hole. She followed him and found herself standing on a wooden platform under a thatched roof, but around was only mosquito wire nailed to wooden scaffolding. The wire hardly obscured her vision at all, it was so strange. 'It's like being a bird,' she called to Pieter. The monkeys were watching her curiously through the wire and the birds were hopping in the branches, twittering excitedly.

'I wish we could stay here forever.' She sighed with longing.

'We might not last too long. The camp's guarded by local villagers who support Renamo, but never forget we're in enemy territory without passports or permits, and we have about four days' grace, I should say, until the word spreads and Frelimo come to investigate. We'd best fetch our gear before something happens to it.'

The monkeys and baboons were already investigating. Pieter shooed them off and they made several trips to carry everything inside. Four days in this wonderful tree house with Pieter. What heaven, she was thinking as she trudged to and fro.

'Done,' he muttered. 'D'you want a shower?'

'Yes . . . wonderful . . . Where?'

'Come!'

Outside the fence, on a ridge overlooking a small natural dam in the river, was a cement platform under a shower nozzle rigged up from a large water tank. There was a tap and a large, wire-netting cage.

'What's that for?' she asked curiously.

'To put your clothes in while you shower. Those bastards pinch everything.' He glanced up at the baboons sitting in long solemn rows in the branches above them.

Climbing into the bottom branches of the wattle tree, he lifted a lid in the tank. 'Seems to be plenty of water,' he said. 'That's good. It's a hassle to pump it up.'

'Have you been here often?'

A sullen stare was all the answer she received. She mustn't pry into men's military matters, she realised.

Beside the shower was a row of latrines.

'What happens to . . .'

'Septic tank over there,' he said. 'It's well organised.'

'But no privacy.'

'Why bother?'

She would wait until he was busy somewhere else, she decided.

'Come on, you goose.' Pulling her to him, he kissed the top

of her nose and began to unfasten the buttons of her khaki blouse, which he flung in the cage. She gasped when he took off her bra. He smoothed his hands over her breasts and bent forward to run his tongue over her nipples. She could hardly breathe from pleasure. 'Mm, nice,' he said casually. 'You have the most beautiful breasts.' He took off her pants and her shoes and flung them in. Stripping off hurriedly, and removing the soap from his pocket, he slammed the cage door shut and switched on the water. How brown he was, only his buttocks and thighs were white. His penis stuck out like a clotheshanger. There's something ridiculous about a naked man with a long, bushy beard, she thought, but she wanted him badly all the same. The pain in her crotch was unendurable and she was slippery wet with longing. She was so greedy for sex. It had been so long.

He stood against her, looking into her eyes, smiling mockingly. 'I never guessed,' she gasped. 'It's such a sensual feeling – the water, your hands, oh, it's dreamy.'

The feel of his bare skin pressed against her body took her breath away. She put her arms around his neck, and stood on tiptoe, her mouth turned up, seeking his, but he jerked his head back out of reach and began to soap her all over, smoothing the water through her hair, using his fingers as a comb.

Crouching in front of her, he picked up her foot. 'Hang on to the tree,' he said as he lathered the soap around her toes and under her instep, smoothing his hands over her ankles and along her foot and her instep and reaching up to her thighs: stroking, caressing, exploring. It was shocking, but wonderfully intimate to feel his hands around her buttocks. She felt herself being picked up like a child and replaced back on her feet. She had lost her sense of balance, she wanted to fall flat on her back and feel his body impaling her. Now his tongue was probing her secret cleft, licking, smoothing, sucking . . . the pleasure was unendurable. She began to utter little sharp cries of agonised frustration.

Just as suddenly he stopped. 'We're wasting water,' he said.

He soaped her back and her stomach, using his fingers to probe her belly button and to wash in her ears, such strong fingers, intimate, demanding, controlling. She closed her eyes, dizzy with desire and groaned. . .

'Okay. Hop out.' She heard his brusque voice as if from far off. The water stopped running. Opening her eyes she saw that he was dressing.

'I hope it gets stuck in your zip,' she said sulkily. 'That would serve you right.'

'No chance of that. Look, no zip.' He pulled out his jeans and snapped the elastic back on his belly. He was laughing at her. He knew how she felt. Damn him! She would explode with frustration. 'Bastard,' she muttered under her breath.

'Why did you do that?' she asked a few minutes later, trying to hold back her anger.

'Sex is like food. I like to eat when I'm really hungry. Makes food taste better. Sex, too. I wait until I'm desperate and then it's great. Just great! I like my sex to be fantastic. When I come it has to be stupendous.'

'And me?'

'Go ahead,' he said. 'Make yourself come if you want to. I'll watch.'

'You are disgusting.'

'Nothing about sex is disgusting. Listen, Liza. You are a clever, decisive, hard-headed, intellectual woman while I am an out-of-work bum. Do you understand?'

'Understand what? That you're paying me back for my success?'

'No. But think – I'm a man. I must be able to dominate you in some way. If I can't dominate you with my brains – and I know I can't – then I must do it with my cock. A physical domination! For me it's essential that I dominate my woman.'

My woman! She thrilled to those two words.

'Do you understand?'

'Yes.'

'We'll make love when I say so and we'll do it my way.'

'Yes,' she whispered. She longed to be passive, to be dominated by this extraordinary man who was so brimful of sex appeal. Just looking at him made her pants wet with longing. That reminded her of something from long ago. She remembered and began giggling.

'What's so funny?' he said.

'D'you remember what you once said about Amy Johnston – that she trailed behind you with her fanny bubbling on the pavement?'

'Sure! All women are like that. All they think about is sex.'

Because of your looks and your maleness and your extraordinary appeal, she thought silently. If only Ed could have a fraction of your power over the female of the species, he wouldn't have to stick those silly pictures all over his walls and ceilings, and he wouldn't be so sad, or feel so alienated from women. And he would never have been so badly hurt . . .

'You're thinking of another man,' Pieter said, surprising her. 'Come on! I must start building a kraal.'

'I was thinking of Ed, my partner.' She trailed behind him, telling him about her past job on the *Echo* and the editorial team, and how they still used her column. She described the TV gang and her little flat over the studio in Ed's cottage. 'In a way I'm happy,' she said, her girlish voice giggling as she relived the jokes they played on each other. Then she became solemn as she described her mission in life. In between she passed the hammer, held the poles straight, fetched the nails. Was he listening? She wasn't sure, but she had an overwhelming urge to share her world with him.

At noon the cicadas were suddenly silenced, a dikkop screamed from the grass, a flock of doves rose in the air and the monkeys seemed to hold their breath. Then the guineafowls set up a warning din.

'Sh!' Pieter silenced her with a finger to his mouth and pushed her towards the tree house. 'Go up into the loft – be quick,' he muttered. 'Don't worry. It's the village men. I was expecting them, but stay out of sight until I call you.'

What am I doing here? she wondered as she peered through the leaves. She saw a file of black men moving along a track towards them, the whites of their eyes glittering in their coal black faces. They seemed so foreign to the blacks from home. Each one was wearing a brief loin cloth and holding a rifle. Behind them walked an older, fatter man, wearing a safari suit. He, too, was sooty black. At the sight of him, Pieter yelled: 'César.' Moments later César saluted and then they were clasped in each other's arms. When they spoke in Portuguese she could not understand, yet a recognition stirred from some distant memory buried deep within her. That was strange, she thought.

The tribesmen began to work in teams and Pieter strolled back with César and introduced her solemnly as his wife. The three of them sat in the shade and drank beer while the villagers sweated in the sun.

'César has been guarding our equipment,' Pieter told her. 'There's a couple of vehicles left behind here. We brought fuel. I hope I can get at least one to work.'

'Where are they?'

He gestured towards a distant grove of trees. 'Hidden over there under camouflage netting.'

While the tribesmen worked, Pieter tinkered with the engine of an armoured reconnaissance vehicle. It was a badly bashed and rusty Ratel, with the top half of the bodywork removed. When he was satisfied that it was running at optimum efficiency, he went racing off over the veld, twisting and turning, leaving a trail of dust rising into the moist heat. He roared back, yelling like a cowboy, and jumped out, wiping the sweat from his face, leaving khaki streaks on his cheeks. Even his beard and his hair were covered in dust. 'It's going to be fun,' he said, his eyes shining for once. 'We'll start at dawn. César will drive, you'll spot, I'll shoot the darts and we'll have a couple of guys to help out. The rest of them can finish the kraal and clear the runway.'

At dusk, the tribesmen left in a long file, each carrying a sack of meal or a box of tinned food, or medicines, with César behind them. They were singing and their deep voices lingered after they disappeared in the shadows.

'I want to shower alone,' Liza told Pieter that evening, remembering the morning's fiasco. 'Don't dare to come.' The torpid heat melted her inhibitions, leaving her on a slow boil, unable to switch off, mildly suffering from her lust. She tossed her hair, grabbed a towel and soap, her little box of toiletries and a mirror and stalked off to the shower.

She had been waiting a long time to visit the loo. With a sigh of relief she sat down overlooking the river, under a tall black wattle tree, facing west. The sky was rose-coloured and the huge crimson sun was sinking fast behind a massive baobab tree on the opposite bank.

How lovely it was, but the baboons bothered her. They sat in a straight row on a thick bough right overhead, rapt in their solemn curiosity. She heard the high-pitched screech of an owl and a distant call of a hyena emerging for the night's hunt. The last crescent of sun sank below the horizon and the shadows moved in fast. Suddenly it was night.

Stripping off nervously in the dark, she pushed her clothes into the cage and walked on to the platform. Turning on the tap, she gave herself up to the intense pleasure of being drenched in cool water. Through the splashing she heard Pieter's voice: 'That's enough. The water has to last four days.'

'I told you I wanted to be alone,' she scolded, unable to see him. 'How long have you been here?'

'As long as you've been here. You look like a lion's dream of supper – succulent, tasty . . .'

'You're just trying to frighten me.'

'The village lost a child to a lone lion three days ago. We'll probably see its tracks tomorrow. If I see it, I'll kill it. Once they strike humans they never stop.

'It's my turn,' Pieter said when she had pulled on her shorts and T-shirt. 'Hold the gun . . . if I call, or if you see anything, give it to me quickly, but try not to let it get wet.'

'I'm not a fool,' she said sulkily.

Watching Pieter cook supper was like old times. Liza was put to work peeling and chopping onions and tomatoes he'd brought along, while he built a braai. He fried the onions and tomatoes in a large iron pot, adding water from time to time and leaving it sizzling to make the sauce. The sweet potatoes were pushed into the fire and when the wood burned low, he put two rump steaks on the grid over the wood embers, spicing them with black pepper and turning them often. The succulent smell of braaing meat and onions reminded her of home and brought a lump to her throat.

He passed her a tin of coke. 'Cheers,' he said, holding up his. Liza had a strong longing for a glass of wine, but Pieter never drank so there was no point in wishing.

'I've been watching your TV programmes. You're pretty good. Particularly lately. What gave you the idea of featuring the death of Sizani?'

'A tip off,' she said briefly.

'From whom?'

'Does it matter?' She lay back, staring at the stars. Suddenly Pieter's head blocked the view. He pressed his lips over hers and she could feel his tongue caressing her mouth. His soft, full lips seemed to be all that was real in the world. She could feel her lust rising again. There was no escape. He had that effect on her.

Rolling on his side, he cupped her breasts with his hands. 'Nice,' he whispered. 'Bigger than I remember. I love your breasts.' His fingers fumbled with her nipples and she felt herself stiffening with longing.

'Make love to me,' she murmured.

He sat up. 'It's not safe. Out here I have to have my wits about me.' He bent over the meat leaving her feeling strangely empty. 'Fetch some water in the kettle, please. Would you?'

'From where?' She sat up reluctantly.

'The water tank by the shower.'

Me? she thought in silence. You want me to go down there in the dark? She wasn't going to show that she was scared. Taking the kettle, she wandered off into the dense darkness, stumbling over roots and walking into bushes. Damn him! What's got into him?

Then she tripped and fell headlong. Groping for the lost kettle, she heard hooves pounding close by. She could smell the buck and it was so close. Or was it a buffalo? She shrank against a tree and collided with the kettle. Well, that was something, she thought, grabbing hold of it. The baboons overhead set up a commotion of barking and screaming while sticks and stones fell around her. 'Bloody baboons,' she muttered, shaking her fist at them. Then she heard a growl. It was so close. She yelped, longing to run, but how could she? Pieter had lived alone in the bush for years. What sort of a fool would she look if she couldn't walk a hundred yards to fetch water? The strangest thought came – had Pieter deliberately sent her into danger?

Then real fear set in as she realised that something big was stalking her.

She could hear a soft, purring growl coming closer and the overpowering smell of a big cat was all about her. Was it the marauding lion? She wanted to call for help, but felt it was safer to keep quiet. She forced her feet to move faster, feeling her way in the darkness. When she reached the cage she would be safe. She'd just about made it. Suddenly a shot rang out and the beast charged off through the thicket. Liza's mouth opened to scream, but no sound came.

A split-second later Pieter flung her against the water tank. 'What's wrong with you, Liza?' he shouted, frightening her even more. 'You're out of your depths here, but this other jungle you've stumbled into is far more dangerous. You've set yourself up as a target. They're stalking you even now – your life is in danger. Now who put you on to Sizani? Who told you he was Njani? Who's tipping you off? Tell me – damn you!' His arm was forcing her head back against the tank and hurting her neck. As anger surged, her fear fled.

'Fuck you, Pieter,' she spat, trying to hide her trembling. 'You sent me down here to scare the living daylights out of me. I'm not one of Pavlov's dogs. Try your shock tactics on someone else.'

She pushed him violently, kicking out at the same time. Caught off balance, Pieter fell heavily and sprawled on the ground. She threw the kettle hard at him. 'Fetch your own damn water. I want to go home. You can call your so-called friend to fetch me – that friend who calls you "sir".'

He bounded back and caught her arm. 'No, wait.'

She spun round and punched his face hard. Moments later his hand was clapped over his mouth. 'You've cut my lip,' he said in astonishment. 'I can't believe this.'

'Good,' she said. 'It's your own fault. Your damned teeth stick out. They always have.' Heedless of danger and too angry to care, she rushed back to the camp.

Pieter's lip kept on bleeding. Sitting safely by the fire, with the camp's gate firmly locked, Liza felt a little bit sorry, but she wasn't going to let him know that. 'Serves you right,' she repeated as she turned the meat. 'You set me up for a nasty scare and followed me with those damned infra-red things. I'm not the fool you take me for.'

They ate in sulky silence. The food was delicious. What a shame to spoil it with a fight, she thought.

'Liza. I must insist that you tell me what you know.'

'Why must you know?'

'It's a long story.' He sighed.

'Start talking if you want to know anything.'

'I was in intelligence in the army. I was sure there was a Third Force at work and I was investigating this possibility. I suppose I got too close and I think that's why I was sacked. Someone high up wanted me out of the way.'

'I'll use that in my programme,' she said, her mouth full of sweet potato.

'No, you can't. You'd murder me. Besides. It's not for public consumption.'

'I beg to differ. The public deserves to know what's going on.'

'The public deserves to be kept safe, and that's all. I went off on a limb over these killings and I got axed. Doesn't that tell you something?'

She relaxed. So that was it. Relief flooded her like rain in a drought. 'Oh, Pieter, sweetie. Why didn't you tell me. I was so worried.' She swallowed the potato and leaned forward to kiss his cheek, rubbing her finger over his lip. 'You're not the only one investigating the Third Force. D'you remember Captain Myers of Nelfontein? He's heading the investigation on behalf of the police. You two should team up. He's stationed at police headquarters in Fordsburg, nowadays.'

'You must help me, Liza. If I could prove that I was on the right track I would get my career back on line, or at least force them to pay me a pension. I'm flat broke.'

All her womanly compassion surged. She looked away, not wanting him to see the tears in her eyes. The moon rose, lighting the veld with a strange ethereal glow. They heard the snarling of lions and the bellow of a beast in mortal pain. Then came the cry of hyenas and jackals. 'There's a kill not far off. We'll find it tomorrow,' he said.

Liza was lost in thought. She had misunderstood. He shouldn't have tried to bully her. 'Pieter, love,' she said, out of the blue. 'I'll do anything I can to help you.'

Now he was smiling happily. 'Let's go to bed,' he said. He kicked out the embers and covered them with earth. They closed the door of the hut and locked it, and climbed up the ladder into the roof, locking the trap door behind them. The moon was rising and moonlight was dancing on the leaves swaying and pulsating around them, while the baboons slept fitfully, clutched in each other's arms.

Pieter undressed her tenderly, taking his time, caressing her skin, stroking her hair, running his mouth over her cheeks and her hands.

'Turn over, I'll stroke your back.'

A million sparks of pleasure pulsated through her body. She lay in ecstasy, willing the night to last forever.

Then he said: 'Whatever possessed Myers to tell you about his investigation? That doesn't sound very professional. Not like him. He's a secretive bastard.'

'He didn't. He told Dan. It seems that Dan is on the list.' She felt Pieter stiffen and tense behind her. 'Well, a bomb went off in his locker and then he was shot up on his bike, but he was lucky ...' The story of Dan poured out while he stroked her back and her thighs and legs.

'So Dan told you that the Reverend Sizani was Njani and that he was killed by this so-called Third Force.'

'No! Not Dan. Can't we just make love? Must we talk?'

'Then who?'

'I can't tell you . . . and it wouldn't help you, anyway.'

Suddenly he was furious. He moved to the other side of the platform, sulking, and eventually he lay down and appeared to be asleep.

Liza got up and bent over him. 'Why do you keep probing and quarrelling? Isn't it enough that we're together?'

'I'm not interested in making love to someone who doesn't trust me. I was right about you. My career is smashed, but you don't care.'

'I *do* care.'

'Then tell me what you know about Njani. You must tell me this, otherwise it's all over between us.'

She sighed. Men were so damned childish however clever they were. But she wanted him to make love to her so she'd have to say something. Then she remembered that Nico had died in Maputo. She would tell him it was Nico.

She related what she could remember of the night she arrived in Johannesburg and how Nico had rescued her. Then, much later, she had stolen medicines for him from the clinic in Alexander Township. 'He called me one night after my second programme and begged me not to continue with this programme – just like you. He was so scared for me. So you see,' she said brightly, at the end of her story, 'that was how I found out.'

'You must have seen a ghost,' Pieter said gloomily. 'Nico died about a month before Njani. He was executed for killing and maiming members of the congregation at the Honeydew church. You knew he was dead, Liza. That's why you told me his name. You're covering up for someone. How the hell did you know? You must be on their side. You're working for the communists, aren't you?'

She sighed. 'Someone told me that Njani's killer was even more ruthless and cunning than Njani. It's you, isn't it, Pieter?'

He threw back his head and gave way to peals of mirth. It seemed so genuine.

There was a sudden commotion from the trees around them. She grabbed Pieter and clung to him. The baboons began barking in unison and the sound was terrifying, smashing at her eardrums like a bomb blast, while they pelted the ground with sticks. Then she saw the long sinuous shape of a leopard moving towards the tree. It paused, lashing its tail as it looked up. She saw green eyes flashing and she shuddered. It moved towards the tree trunk, teeth bared.

'Oh no ... oh no ...' she whimpered. She watched as if mesmerised until the leopard was only metres away, crawling along the bough towards her. The younger baboons had gathered against the netting and she could feel the vibrations as they gibbered and shook and cried. The old males shook the branches and barked, leaping up and down, but the leopard wanted a youngster.

She saw it steady itself for the final leap, its eyes burning into her. It was beautiful and it was deadly. Then, with a sudden mighty leap and a smash of paws, a baboon was snatched, screaming horribly. Moments later, the leopard bounded to the ground, the baboon dangling from its mouth and still crying pitifully.

Liza began to scream. She could not stop. 'Poor, poor little baby baboon,' she sobbed eventually.

Pieter's arms tightened around her. 'I will never let anything happen to you,' he said. 'I promise. Liza, get out of this jungle you're in. Promise me. Give up this crusade and you'll have nothing to fear,' he murmured. 'You're safe with me. I will never let anyone harm you. Sh! Calm down, Liza.'

Now he was comforting her, his mouth wandering over her body, his tongue creeping into every crevice. She was hardly able to move from the trauma of the killing and the force of her own lust, and her suspicions and fears. She loved him so desperately. But the awful question kept pounding in her head and would not go away. Was Pieter part of the Third Force?

'Come! Straddle me. Sit on my face.'

'I can't,' she whispered. 'I can't do that.'

'You must. In sex I'm in charge. Remember?'

It was too shocking to be borne, too sensual to withstand. She screamed and came . . . and came again. She no longer knew what he was doing, she was lost in frantic pleasure, screaming with lust and running out of control.

Later, she sat over him, pushing his penis into her, softly swaying her hips, watching him half close his eyes and give way to his own fulfilment. When, at last, they were both satiated, they fell into a light sleep, but Liza woke soon and lay listening to the scary sounds of the bush night. She was half awake and half asleep when she heard Pieter calling loudly: 'I must kill him. I can't leave him there.' Then came a long agonising scream. 'Koos, Koos, oh my God, Koos, what have they done to you?' he sobbed.

Then he switched to Russian – long rambling sentences she could not understand. Later he began to count: 'Ten . . . nine . . . eight . . .'

She woke him and he sat up, instantly alert. 'You've been having another nightmare. Won't they ever leave you alone?' she said.

Caught unaware, he nestled his head on her shoulder, still

shaking. She thought: Who are you, Pieter? Who are you really? But it did not matter. She loved him unconditionally. Whatever he stood for and no matter what he had done . . . he was the only man she would ever truly love.

She heard him whisper: 'I love you, Liza. I'll never let you be hurt.'

She lay with a smile on her lips, watching the sky lighten behind the leaves.

Liza felt sorry for the baboons. Each night was a torment as they waited for the leopard to come stalking them, but each day was a joy when their fears were forgotten and they romped in the trees and the tall grass and played together.

Am I like the baboons, she wondered? Her love for Pieter was all-encompassing; they seemed to have a deep emotional bond. The excitement and danger of catching the game each day seemed to have turned them into a team. They had learned to trust each other and they knew each other's strengths and weaknesses. Underlying their mutual bond was their passion and lust which could flare up at a touch, a glance, at any moment of the day or night. She adored each part of his body and knew all of him intimately.

After sex she would lie awake at night, worrying about Pieter and what he was really doing. During the daytime her fears seemed groundless and she decided to bury them for once and for all.

That morning they caught a zebra. When he was safely in the kraal, they made coffee and ate before going out again.

Then, out of the blue, Pieter said: 'Liza, did you know that old Mr Laubscher was murdered last week? D'you remember him? He sometimes gave us sweets when we came out of school. He lived down the bottom of Oosthuizen Street, and he used to walk up and down the main street with a stick. He was stabbed fourteen times in the chest last week. The robbers were after his old age pension, but there were only a hundred rands in the house. They didn't have to murder him. He could hardly stand up, let alone attack them. Then, last month, there was Mrs Streicher, who was seventy-nine. They tied her up and robbed her cottage and then strangled her for no reason. Mr Uys, eighty one. They bludgeoned him to death across the face with a metal pipe and took two blankets and some wine. They go for the weak, but when they are armed they will turn on everyone. I'll never forget what they did to my mother. You have to understand something, Liza. The government is losing control and there's a split coming. The situation couldn't be more dangerous. MI haven't succeeded in stemming the flow of arms into South Africa. South Africa is like an overheated boiler, waiting to blow up. All black leaders instigating violence are commies . . . commies are vermin and they must be destroyed. Surely you must see that?'

Liza realised with a jolt that Pieter had been rehearsing this. Why? Was he part of the killing machine? She sensed that he was trying to justify himself. Is that what this was all about? Had he brought her here to smooth his conscience, or to brainwash her? Or to silence her?

She thought long and hard before she answered. 'Pieter, I feel for the Afrikaner so deeply. Those are my roots, too, after all, and I can see how difficult it must be . . . I mean, if a man – I'm talking about a soldier – were ordered to kill black leaders then of course he must consider them vermin, otherwise he must accept himself as a mass-murderer. Just how far down the road of unreality he's prepared to go in order to live with his conscience is his private affair.

'You are the man I love most in all the world. I would protect you with my life, but my best friend is Dan and I have already done what little I could do to protect him. Dan is a man I admire. He has a fine intellect, he is fighting for democracy, he has no thoughts of revenge and I think he would rather die than kill someone. I love him, too, but in a different way. Dan is the head of the Witswatersrand ANC youth. To call someone like Dan vermin is to close one's eyes to the truth.'

'You've been brainwashed,' he said sullenly.

'And you?' She didn't say another word, but she noticed that Pieter was strangely quiet for the rest of the day.

It was their last morning and they were already packed and ready to leave the camp when they first caught sight of the massive black rhino. The moment Pieter saw it, he had to have it.

Pieter, she had discovered, liked to sit on the loo and contemplate, and there he was moodily gazing over the river towards the bushveld which he loved so much.

'I hate to leave,' he said, smiling at her. 'This has been the best holiday of my life and the best sex. You're terrific, Liza. The best ever.'

Then he tensed and grabbed his binoculars. 'There's something down there,' he said, frowning.

Liza was washing her feet in a bucket under the shower when Pieter beckoned to her. 'Look,' he said, pointing down.

The grass was rippling as a heavy body pushed through it. Suddenly a rhino broke cover. Head lowered and swaying from side to side, it trotted to the next tall clump.

'Fantastic,' he whispered. 'We've got to have her.'

'You said we were only going for buck. It's time to go. Besides, it looks so right where it is.'

'Poachers will get it – sooner or later – it doesn't stand a chance if it stays here. A reserve's the only safe place for it. They're practically extinct. You'll have to drive the Ratel. César's busy.'

'Me?' That was the last straw.

Why did he have to see it? They had enough, didn't they? Bob had been running a shuttle service backwards and forwards to move the game they had caught. So far there had been no casualties.

Liza reached for the binoculars. Watching the beast at close range did nothing to reassure her. It was massive and ferocious-looking. Its horn was over a foot long and there was nothing black about it, for it was a slate grey colour. Dangerous and mean-minded, she thought.

*

Pieter had decided that the open plain was where it would all happen. Liza shivered as she sat beside him in the open Ratel with four strong villagers squashed in the back. The rest of the men had been sent to beat the rhino out of the riverbed.

'Don't worry,' Pieter said. 'This vehicle can withstand anything. Just get alongside her.'

'How do you know it's a her?'

'I *know*, and she's a real beauty. Just look at her bristles. Like a moustache. I'm naming her Gertie.'

'Why Gertie?'

'Never you mind.'

Liza put her foot down nervously and they sped towards the rhino. Tossing her head, Gertie set off towards the nearest thicket.

'Go for it. For God's sake, put your foot down,' Pieter bellowed as he hung over the side watching the massive backside jump up and down as she fled. Liza accelerated and suddenly they were bouncing over the veld, just about taking off from each hump of earth, with the ground obscured by thick grass.

'I can't see where I'm going,' she called out.

'Get with it, Liza,' Pieter roared. 'You're doing thirty-five kilometres, she can do forty-five. It's like trying to catch a hare with a tortoise.'

Forty-five kilometres? In this terrain? Damn him! Why had she come? She put her foot down flat and the wheels screeched and skidded in a sandy patch as they lurched forward. The tread caught and then they were off again, bouncing and swaying and bumping, their ears ringing with the pounding of heavy hooves ahead of them.

'Closer! Get in closer,' Pieter yelled. She swung the wheel and skidded in a mass of sand, but the Ratel righted itself and rocketed towards the rhino. Now she could smell the beast's fear. Liza was within touching distance when she heard the whoosh of the gas gun. She saw the needle dangling loose from the beast's left shoulder.

'Damn!' Pieter swore.

The rhino suddenly skidded to a halt and stood there, head lowered, watching them, snorting with rage and panic, a mean and frantic look in her eyes. Then she charged.

Liza stalled the engine and pumped the accelerator in vain. She tried again, but the engine wouldn't catch.

'Get out of the driver's seat,' Pieter bawled, but she seemed to be frozen there.

A massive thump rocked them as two thousand kilos of enraged rhino slammed against the door. It caved in towards her. Pieter grabbed her shoulders and tossed her out of the driver's seat.

Another thump sent the Ratel toppling over. The tribesmen jumped, and Pieter caught hold of Liza and sent her sprawling over the veld. She scrambled to her feet in time to see that the rhino had trundled around the back and was charging straight at her, head lowered, razor-sharp horn aimed at her stomach. Where was everyone? Where was the rifle? Liza jumped for the Ratel and scrambled over it. The rifle lay on the ground just underneath. She grabbed it and aimed at the rhino.

'No!' Pieter's scream was long and agonised. 'Put that down!' He seemed to fly towards her, knocking the rifle out of her hand before his feet touched ground level.

Cowering against the side of the car, she watched Pieter dash towards Gertie, aiming the gas gun which he fired into her chest before dodging back again.

'I got her this time,' he yelled triumphantly.

The rhino rounded on him, but he jumped clear and ran behind the armoured car.

'Be quick!' Pieter told the tribesmen. 'We have to head her off. Rock it back.'

With Liza straining to help, they all pushed from the opposite side while the rhino pounded the steel with all her savage anger. Moments later the Ratel was toppled back on to its wheels, but the rhino circled the truck and came in fast, her head slamming the steel side, while Liza, panic giving her speed, leaped inside.

There was a strong smell of petrol. 'I hope to God we don't blow up,' Pieter said, clambering into the seat and watching the charging beast apprehensively. 'I wouldn't like her to be scorched.'

'And us?' Liza shrieked.

'Shut up, Liza.'

He turned the key and they held their breath as the engine caught. 'Okay, Liza, get in the driver's seat and don't fuck up again,' he said.

'I don't want to.'

'You have to. Otherwise I'll go after her on foot.'

I'll get him back, but later. Right now survival was her only priority. The pounding had stopped. Looking over her shoulder she saw that the rhino was running away.

'Okay, set off the flare.' Pieter watched the rhino as the tribesmen set off the flare to summon the truck with the pulley.

'Head her off, Liza. For God's sake. Get between her and the thicket. We can't get the truck into the thicket.'

Pieter was pointing towards a dense thicket of mopani trees. Gertie had seen it, too, and she was heading fast for it, doing a good forty ks. Looming in front of them was a steep grassy hillock. What was she supposed to do? She put her foot down flat and raced up one side, expecting to roll at the top, but the Ratel made it.

Miraculously, they got there before the rhino and headed her back towards the open plain. She seemed a bit laboured and dizzy. Minutes later she fell and Pieter bounded out of the truck and bent over her.

'Be careful,' Liza screamed. 'Maybe she's bluffing.'

He took no notice. He was too busy examining the beast's eyelids. 'Water,' he yelled. 'And bring the sponge. Start mopping her.'

'This M ninety-nine is good stuff,' he said beaming happily. 'It'll knock her out for a while and we'll keep topping it up. Where's the antibiotics?'

A villager passed him the medical kit and he jabbed the needle into the rhino's thigh.

'When we get her on the truck, drive the Ratel back and leave it near the camp,' Pieter said. 'I'll see you there.' He grabbed the gas gun and another syringe and stood waiting impatiently for the truck which was moving towards them.

Five minutes later the unconscious rhino had been roped and levered on to a platform and lifted by pulley on to the truck.

Liza relaxed enough to examine the damage. Her clothes were filthy and torn, every part of her body was badly bruised and her cheek was bleeding from a deep scratch. There was sand in her eyes and her mouth, her ankle was swelling up, she was dying of thirst and shaking like a leaf.

Pieter glanced over his shoulder and waved, grinning like a schoolboy. 'That wasn't so bad, was it?' he asked.

Liza resisted the temptation to punch him. After all, the villagers were watching.

Chapter 50

'*Why did you bring her here?*'

Eleanor had emerged from her suite which in itself was disturbing, and was about to invade the diningroom. She hesitated in the doorway, scowling like a vengeful phantom, haggard and white-faced in her ridiculous pale pink outfit, a vision of distress.

Tony watched her guardedly, hating her, knowing that hate could destroy and enjoying his sense of power. 'Hang on ... I'll fetch my crystal ball.' He looked at his plate, smugly smiling at his joke.

'You know who I mean. That Frank woman.'

Eleanor seemed to be both obsessed and terrified by Liza Frank, always surreptitiously cutting out her newspaper articles, but she tried to hide this from him.

'I didn't bring her ... Pieter de Vries did,' he answered nonchalantly. 'They've been trapping wild game in the bush. Perhaps he fancies her. Don't forget she's Grannie du Toit's only heir so one day she'll be our partner in the game reserve.'

'Oh God.' She wandered across the room, listlessly touching the objects, stroking a vase. 'Life never neglects its bitter lessons,' she said out of the blue. '"Vengeance is mine," saith the Lord. Oh but he's right, he's right. He's a past master at it too. Our ghosts return to mock us, make no mistake. If only ...'

Tony interrupted her. 'Are you having one of your turns again? I wish you'd stay in your quarters and take your sedatives. You can't afford to make a scene. You know how the staff gossip. Go back to bed, Eleanor.' He rang for her nurse. Passively she allowed herself to be put to bed and drugged.

'Put my special programme on, nurse,' she pleaded. 'I'll fall asleep watching it.' The nurse put on the video and Eleanor sat with a silly, proud smile on her face watching Liza's latest exposé.

'*I will not be intimidated. Not even if my life is threatened,*' Liza was saying. 'If there is a Third Force, it must be exposed.'

And what was it Emile had said? '*I will not be intimidated by the authorities.*' His genes! His courage! Liza was a living replica of Emile. Eleanor could hear his voice as clearly as if he were in the room. 'Oh God, how it hurts,' she whispered. Her guilt was tormenting her.

Even in childhood, guilt had dogged her days, for she had been privileged. She had never been without enough cash, servants, space, time for herself, and a sense of being special, but guilt was the price she had paid even when she was very young.

One of her earliest memories was of their black cook. Each January he took his annual three-week leave, travelling for two days and nights on a bus to reach his mudhut, and each October his wife gave birth to another baby. That was their lives, for he was a migrant worker, as most blacks were, and his wife could never legally visit his workplace. Then there was Zola, their Nanny, who had nursed them devotedly for years. She, too, saw her own children for only three weeks a year, but she sent home every penny she earned. It was the only way she had to show her love, since her children could not live in a white area.

Separated from their various families, the workers lived in a compound and ate lungs, offal and chuck with huge mounds of mealie pap. Their lives were so different from her own, they might have been beings from outer space. Yet sometimes she would see them cry and then she would wonder uneasily – did they feel hurt and pain just like white people?

Much later, at university, she had joined a democratic students' group and it was there that she heard a young half-Indian,

Portuguese student, called Emile de Novrega, giving a talk. By the time his speech ended she was half in love with him.

Soon she was working with Emile on leaflets, speeches, plans and dreams. Heady days . . . How they had loved. Five months later Emile left to run the family plantations and mines in Northern Mozambique, leaving her to head the group with Shireen Desai, Emile's second cousin, and several Africans whom she didn't much like. From then on she was ostracised by white students and drawn increasingly into the company of non-white students who never accepted her.

One day, after a bitter fight with her father, she dropped out of university and set off after Emile, driving to Maputo, taking the train north through forest and scrub veld, until she reached Gilé. The de Novregas lived on their plantations 300 kms from the nearest station, she learned, so she hitched a lift on a company plane and arrived at sunset, stepping into a tropical downpour that left her breathless. Grubby, dishevelled, sweaty and scared, she had stumbled up the wide marble staircase into her future.

It was like a moment frozen in time and it would be with her for always. The house was huge and graceful with a vast entrance hall of inlaid quartz tiles. Inside were large rooms with antique furniture, and Persian and Chinese carpets scattered around. Someone was playing the piano quite beautifully. The sound drifted from a room whose doorway was hidden by an alabaster pot full of ferns.

A black servant, dressed in white uniform, with a red fez and cummerband, stepped up to her from the shadows. He spoke in Portuguese, which she could hardly understand.

'Is Emile de Novrega here?' she asked. 'I called to see him.' Absurd, really! She wanted to giggle out loud. Perhaps she should leave her calling card and trek back to Johannesburg.

'You can wait there,' he said in broken English, indicating a monk's bench of carved ebony by the door. She waited, then heard a soft rustle of silk and smelled sweet musky perfume. An Indian woman approached silently, wearing moccasin embroidered slippers and a traditional robe of blue silk embroidered with golden thread, with beautiful gold jewellery inset with emeralds and rubies. Her hair fell straight and black. She was so enchanting Eleanor could only gulp and stare. She felt so grimy. She looked down at her dirty jeans, her crumpled T-shirt, the manly boots, covered in mud and her backpack which lay on the floor beside her. The contrast between her and this woman was hurtful.

She stood up and held out her hand which the woman touched too briefly.

'I am Eleanor Christie, a friend of Emile's,' she said hoarsely. 'We met at university. I came . . .' She broke off, bit her lip and tried to fight back her tears. 'Perhaps I have been foolish,' she said.

The woman gasped slightly. She turned as they heard heavy footsteps approaching.

The man coming out of the shadows was quite dark, but she guessed at once he was Emile's Portuguese father. He looked tough and strong and something about him made her tremble. He was a stocky, thickset man with a hooked nose, shrewd brown, heavy-lidded eyes, with a deeply-lined brown skin. He had a shock of grey hair cut short, and every movement showed his massive strength. He spoke to the woman in Portuguese and she answered in a soft, caressing voice. From the way they stood together she knew they were married. Were they Emile's parents? She felt intimidated by his strength and she remembered Emile's nervousness when he spoke of his father and told her how he had forged an empire single-handed.

The man turned to her and smiled courteously, but she sensed the unaccustomed effort.

'Leave us,' he said to his wife in English. Taking her arm, he led her to another room. It was lined with books and rich with carpets and antique furniture. Protecting these treasures in this damp heat must be a nightmare, she thought.

'So you love my son and you have come a long way looking for him.'

'Yes,' she said.

'You are a headstrong, self-willed, tough woman. You see, I know that much about you already. My son is lucky. What do you drink? You look exhausted and I'm not surprised. I am Emile's father. My name is Manuel de Novrega, but you will call me Papa.'

'Yes,' she whispered, feeling as if she had entered an enchanted world where nothing was real.

She waited while 'Papa' ordered fruit juice with a dash of wine and plenty of ice, and some sandwiches.

She had not realised how hungry she was until she munched the sandwiches and drained the juice.

He plagued her with questions about her home and her parents. 'I hope you don't mind me asking,' he repeated often. 'I like to know about my son's life in South Africa. He doesn't talk much about it. Did he get on well with your parents?'

She stumbled through some explanation of how busy they had been, and how far away her parents' farm was, but he seemed to understand. 'Do your parents know you are here?'

'Yes. I told them I was going to find Emile.'

'And did they approve?'

'Well . . . actually, no.'

'It must have been difficult for you loving my son when he is of mixed blood – he would be classified coloured in your country. Isn't that so?'

Without planning to, her story poured out; how she had been ostracised by the other students, her parents' wrath, her love of Emile which was more important than her friends, and her loneliness after he left.

'I understand my dear,' he said, putting one hand over hers. 'Your troubles are over.'

'Now, let's call Emile.' He rang the bell and after a while sent a servant to fetch his son. Abruptly the piano playing stopped and she realised with a jolt that it had been Emile who had been playing so beautifully. How little she knew about him.

Emile walked in, saw her and reared back in shock. There was no pleasure on his face. He looked betrayed. It was as if she had damaged him.

'I missed you so much,' she stammered. 'So I came. Just for a quick visit, you understand.'

'Well now, Emile,' his father said in English. 'You want to be married – didn't you say so? Well, so you shall be, and here is your bride. She loves you, she tells me, and you have loved her too. So we shall arrange the wedding without any further waste of time.'

Eleanor was in shock. Her wildest dreams were coming true, but Emile's face was a picture of anguish.

The next few days were a whirl of activity. She was taken to Beira by Madam de Novrega where manicurists, dressmakers, hairdressers, beauticians and jewellers set to work on her. Papa lavished jewels on her. A beautiful diamond ring so heavy that it kept twisting round on her finger, a necklace of emeralds from their own mine, ruby bracelets, and beautiful gifts from Cartiers. Emile was strangely quiet, but he was kind to her and they were married in the garden by a visiting priest a week later.

Two months after her marriage, Emile went missing for three weeks. It was then that his mother told her how he had longed to marry a young Indian girl whom he had loved since childhood, but that his father had been totally against the marriage. Rather than be disinherited, he had set her up in a home at Beira, intending to marry one day when his father died. Eleanor had felt so sorry for him, almost sorry enough to leave him, but she was pregnant.

Her daughter, whom she named Elisabete Maria de Novrega, was born exactly nine months after the wedding, but by then her parents-in-law had been killed in the aircrash of one of their own company planes and Emile was spending most of his time with his Indian mistress.

Oh God! The anguish of her days still hurt. She burst into tears at her remembered grief and sobbed herself to sleep.

*

Tony had to wait for days to get the story out of Eleanor. On the following Thursday he switched on the TV to find himself looking at Liza Frank's image. As usual she was tackling a highly emotive subject.

'Apartheid has been murdered,' she was saying in her usual direct style, glaring at the cameras.

'Here in Zululand is where the first mortal blow was struck.'

Tony stood up and switched off the TV. Now might be a very good time to get the story out of Eleanor, he thought. She was doubtless watching the programme.

As he had thought, she was sitting up in bed nursing a glass of hot milk with a yellowish tinge, which he guessed was from whisky. As usual, she was crying and looking distressed.

'Don't you think it's time you told me what's going on?' he said, switching off her set.

Eleanor wasn't listening. She was gazing out of the window in a world of her own. The dam was particularly lovely in mid-summer, the willow fronds were gently stroking the smooth water. Egyptian geese were shepherding their young amongst the safety of roots and creepers and overhanging branches as they chirped and foraged for food.

'I wish I had her courage,' she said, gazing wistfully at the blank screen. 'You see, Elisabete takes after her grandfather.'

After some prompting, Tony managed to extract most of her story. It was one of sadness and immense wealth, both in Africa and Portugal, but the family had been isolated from their Portuguese roots by de Novrega's marriage to an Indian woman. He intended that his son should not make the same mistake.

Then came the threat of revolution, when Emile sent his child to his divorced wife for safety until the political situation quietened down.

'My parents turned me out,' Eleanor sobbed. 'They could not stand the scandal of having a coloured grandchild. I took Elisabete, who was four years old, to Johannesburg. I managed to find a job, hire a room and get a maid, but I couldn't exist on my earnings and I couldn't leave her alone. I hated the small room we had to live in and the miserable maid who guarded Elisabete until I got home at night.

'I really tried,' her face was screwed up with self pity, 'but it was so hard. I had no friends, of course. Who would befriend a young white girl with a coloured child? Then came the news that Emile had been executed and his plantations nationalised. My mother persuaded me to book Elisabete into a coloured orphanage, but I thought she stood a chance of being accepted as a white, so I tied a note to her saying: "My name is Liza, I need a home, please could someone look after me?" I left her at the Nelfontein police station.'

'Why Nelfontein?'

'I wanted to know she would be near — just in case,' she said vaguely.

'Just in case what?'

'I thought . . . I hoped . . . maybe one day I'd be able to look after her. I thought that if I married a kind man, an older man, someone powerful enough to defy the gossip. And I did. Oh God! You can't believe how cruel Marius was when I told him about Elisabete. He said the girl would become more coloured-looking as she grew older and that I would ruin his political career. He said he couldn't have it known that his wife had fucked and then married an Indian. He said he would have the marriage annulled because he'd married me under false pretences, he said I was lower than a prostitute, that even they fuck whites only, and that I would be ostracised by everyone . . .' She broke off, bit her lip and smeared the tears from her cheeks leaving sooty streaks. 'Later, when I found out about his black mistress, I just wanted him dead.'

'So you gave up your plan to take her back . . . just like that?'

'Yes.' She looked down at her hands. 'Oh God! Try to understand what it was like. Here I was, rich, accepted, part of the community. Someone to be looked up to, but divorced and with a coloured child I was untouchable. Have you any idea how much I've suffered since I lost my little girl? It wasn't so bad when she was with Mrs du Toit, but when she ran away . . .'

Tony did not answer. 'So where exactly were their mines?' he asked.

'Outside Gilé.'

'Have you ever heard the names: Maria One, Maria Two . . .?'

'Maria Three and Four. Of course,' she interrupted him. 'They were our mines, but Frelimo took everything.'

But now Frelimo are giving back the land and mines to the former owners if they have the cash and the will to develop them and provide jobs, Tony thought, deciding not to tell Eleanor that there were vast deposits of rare minerals there.

'So didn't the Portuguese side of the family leave her anything.'

'She has a large inheritance in Portugal, I believe, but the lawyers don't know what happened to her and I never told them.'

'And you just dumped her and never thought about letting her know who she was, or what she owned.'

'Tony! Stop it!' She jumped up, threw her arms around his neck, and tried to force him to hug her. She was longing for forgiveness and understanding.

Tony pushed her aside. 'I'm going to help you to regain your sordid little soul,' he said. 'But I'm warning you, not to interfere. Leave it to me. I have to do some research first. It's a very delicate situation and you could be in a great deal of trouble. It's a crime to abandon your child, so I suggest you keep your mouth zipped up while I sort things out.'

Now she was sobbing in a tumult of relief, her head in her hands. 'Thank you . . . Oh, thank you. You'll never believe how I've suffered. You see, I loved Emile, but he . . .'

Tony went out, closing the door softly behind him.

Chapter 51

———◆———

It was 2 a.m., but Liza could not sleep. When she had returned home the previous evening, she had taken a long, hard look at herself in the mirror and noticed with horror how suntanned she had become, almost as dark as Nosisi. Happiness had made her reckless. Now she would pay the price by looking coloured. What would they say at the studio? Perhaps she could pretend to be sick and stay home, but it would be weeks before her skin lightened. No, not weeks, months! 'Oh God! What have I done?' she whispered to herself.

It was then that she heard the sound of a snap, like glass cracking. It was very slight and for a moment she thought she might have imagined it. She held her breath while her hand fumbled under the pillow for her handgun. There was no mistake, someone was in the house. Her body reacted with pangs of fear. Someone was creeping up the stairs. The passage floor creaked and the soft scraping sound moved towards her room.

She slipped her revolver out of its holster and aimed at the door, watching as if mesmerised as it swung open. Then she fired. The report crashed in her head leaving her ears singing, but she heard a cry. Then someone bounded downstairs. A door slammed.

Moments later Liza found the courage to switch on the lights. When she tried to call the police, she found that her telephone was dead. Feeling frantic, she remembered the panic button of her alarm, but that was cut off, too. She heard footsteps in the garden and a car's engine starting followed by the sound of squealing tyres.

Had he gone? She would have to go down there and call the neighbours. It took every ounce of willpower she could summon to force herself to walk outside into the dark. Her neighbour had heard the shots and was leaning out of the window. 'Call the police,' Liza shouted.

By the time she reached the studio later that morning, she was suffering badly from tension, but she tried not to show this. She had dressed carefully, choosing a navy linen suit with a dark blouse and her hair was piled up on her head in a discreet roll. This would make her dark skin less obvious.

'Wow! What a tan, you lucky thing,' Andrea greeted her.

'You look terrific,' Ed added with a wry smile. 'Holidays suit you.'

At midday they took a break from their latest programme and Liza showed the TV team shots of the game being set free into the game park. Watching Gertie amble off made her feel lonesome. Pieter had left at once, but she had stayed on for a few days with Gran. She had no idea where Pieter was. She had expected him to contact her, but he seemed to have opted out of her life as suddenly as he had appeared. She was missing him badly.

'So where's the shots of the boyfriend?' Ed asked, looking jealous.

'He read me the riot act. Most insistent ... seems to be camera shy. Perhaps it's his beard.'

'What d'you expect? After all, he's a recé scout. Military Intelligence agents are not allowed to be photographed. Didn't you know that?'

She spun around at the voice behind her and found herself face to face with a tall blond man. She had not seen Tony for years, but she recognised him from the many press photographs. She smiled warmly.

'Do you remember me, Tony Cronjé? I missed you at the farm, so I came here to find you. I hope you don't mind, but I've been watching from back there.' He gestured towards the shadows. 'I really love your latest programme. Congratulations!' He shook her hand and then kissed her cheek in the manner of very old friends.

I suppose we are in a way, she thought.

'We're business partners,' Tony reminded her, 'as you probably know, so I thought we ought to get together. The last time I saw you, you were wandering around my home in a daze, smothered in talcum powder. Now you own ten per cent of it. So hi, partner. How about coming to lunch? Do you have time?'

'Wow!' she said, taking a good look at him. 'What a speech.'

Obviously he'd rehearsed it, but why was he so intent on creating a good impression? Tony was attractive with his innocent blue eyes, turned-up nose and golden hair. Even Mona was eyeing him up, she noticed, and Andrea was clearly taken by his charm. Was that how he got onto the set? Tony hung around pestering her and eventually she agreed to go to lunch.

The proprietor of the local restaurant recognised a good client when he saw one. He led them to the best table and hovered over them, taking their order himself. Liza felt annoyed. He had been so rude to Pieter.

Being rich suited Tony. He had become worldly and charming, she discovered over lunch. He was also remarkably well-informed. She listened avidly while he told her the latest inside information behind the parliamentary scenes, hoping to pick up something she could use. Tony liked talking, she discovered.

'When Frederik Willem de Klerk was elected head of the National Party in February we all thought he would carry on the old right-wing party line, but it's rumoured that he's about to do an about-face. He's scaring some of the Nats with some very liberal sentiments. President Botha is a sick man. If de Klerk takes over as President we could have a government that's even more liberal than the English opposition.'

'I can't believe what I'm hearing,' she said, laughingly. 'The Nats could never be liberal.'

'Believe me, Liza, there's a dramatic switch coming. My guess is we could reach a situation where a rightwinger would be synonymous with "traitor" – at least in government circles.'

'Come on, Tony. You're exaggerating. By the way,' she steered the conversation towards the real reason that she had accepted his invitation to lunch. 'You mentioned that Pieter was still in the army. Well, he isn't. He was sacked. After all, that's why you gave him a job, isn't it?'

'No,' he said guardedly. 'He isn't and I didn't. We decided to stock our mutually-owned farm and I provided the cash, but we couldn't afford what we wanted, so Pieter hit on the bright idea of stealing the game from Frelimo. We rationalised that we're saving these animals from poachers, so it didn't seem such a crime. With his influence he managed to get permission to use the old military camp over there, plus a few days leave. Right now he's back on duty.'

Liza sat in a daze, hardly listening to what Tony was saying. Memories and doubts were whirling through her mind. If Pieter was still in the army then his story about being dumped because he was investigating the Third Force, was a lie. All her instincts had told her that he was part of this force. She should have listened to her intuition. It had been so obvious that Bob was not his friend. Then there were his nightmares. And he'd deliberately sent her down to the tap to send her into shock, in order to question her. Why? The answer was all too obvious.

She felt depressed and very alone. One thing she knew for sure, it wasn't Pieter who had broken into her home. She would never have heard a sound, nor known anything about it. If Pieter wanted her dead, she would have been dead long ago. So who was the intruder?

'What's the matter. You're shivering. You look so frightened.'

'I was just thinking. Sorry, Tony. Someone broke into my cottage in the night and I was up half the night with the police.

I'm suddenly terribly tired. I don't feel too well.'

'Do the police have any idea who it was?'

'They think it might be connected with one of my pro-grammes. You see, the intruder came in a car. My neighbour caught sight of a white Mercedes. Not the normal house-breaker.'

'Look Liza, there's something I want to ask you. Back at the ranch, we'll soon be well enough organised to hold the official opening. I'll organise a party if you'll come and be hostess. We've decided to call the park *Jacana Lodge*. Of course, that's if you approve,' he added hastily.

She smiled. 'I like the name, but I couldn't possibly . . .' she said quickly.

Tony reached out and touched her hand, but she pulled it away. 'Please reconsider. After all, you're part of the manage-ment. It would please Mrs du Toit, I know. She fought long and hard for you. Besides, I can't tell you how much I admire you, Liza. You and I had to pull ourselves up by our bootstraps. No one helped us. We're go-getters Liza, and we have a lot in common. Sorry to be so blunt, but I want to be your friend. I can be a good friend, I promise you.'

'You see . . .' She hesitated, trying to find the right words to explain her fears. 'You can't have forgotten how I was flung out of school. They were going to send me to live with a coloured family, that's why I ran away. Everyone in that one-horse, narrow-minded little dorp knows about it. I simply couldn't face them.'

'Not even with me at your side? They practically lick the floor every time they see me. Money counts around those parts. Put your past behind you, Liza. I never thought you were coloured. Look at your beautiful straight hair.' He ran his fingers lightly over her head. 'You might be Spanish, or Portuguese. I've always thought of you as a very beautiful gypsy. I don't think you realised how much I wanted to be friends with you.' He smiled so appeal-ingly she almost burst out laughing. If he weren't so damned rich they could use him in a programme.

'Why not come back to Nelfontein to spite them,' he was saying. 'Wouldn't you love to see them fighting to be friends with you. Besides, back home everyone knows at least five families who have colour in them. It's hushed up because they're so powerful. But you were so alone. I think you need a friend, Liza, and it might as well be me.'

His hand slid across the table and gripped hers. It felt strong and cool and this time she let her hand lie there, feeling that at least there was one man who was normal, dependable and straightforward.

'You see, there's Pieter,' she stammered. 'I love him still.'

'I know.' There was a long pause. 'He's the reason why you need a friend so badly. I won't take no for an answer, Liza, and I'm going to send a bodyguard to look after you until this business has died down.'

Over the next few months Liza found it so easy to give in to Tony. He made no demands on her, other than that she should enjoy herself. Her friendship with him tossed her into a whole new lifestyle. Some people sneered at Tony's opulent lifestyle. Come to think of it, it definitely took a certain amount of chutzpah·to enjoy a four course meal – pâté de foie gras, smoked salmon, wild boar, and fresh strawberries – with ice cold champagne, on a tiny island in the middle of the Okavango Delta. But then again, nothing was too much trouble for Tony, she discovered as their friendship grew and the weeks flew past. Plunged into a whirlpool of activity, she enjoyed a jet-set life she would never have dreamed existed. Tony indulged her every whim. No matter where they went it was first class all the way. Travelling Concorde from London to New York became a frequent experience each time they went overseas. With Tony, fastest was always best.

Together they'd been skiing in Cortina D'Ampezzo and Gstaad, and scuba diving in Mauritius and the Caribbean – where they hired a yacht and crew and sailed round the islands. They jumped on a plane at the drop of a hat. It meant nothing to Tony to fly to the French Riviera for the Cannes Film Festival or the World Music Awards in Monte Carlo, or to London to see Pavarotti at Covent Garden. Liza had only just realised how much she loved theatre. She particularly enjoyed seeing Mikhail Baryshnikov's 'Metamorphosis' on Broadway, and she was thrilled at the chance of an interview for her programme.

Oh, it was such a joy to be very, very rich! And it wasn't *just* the money. No, there was much, much more. It was the glamour and power that went with it, the way people bowed down before you. Revenge was sweet. Remembering her street days she felt that this new lifestyle fitted her like a glove.

It was February 2, 1990. Acting on a tip from Tony, Ed and Liza had flown to the Cape from Jan Smuts to hear the newly appointed State President, Frederik Willem de Klerk give his inaugural speech.

It was when they were stuck in the traffic jam on the way to Parliament, that they suddenly found themselves embroiled in a bitter argument. 'I don't like Tony,' Ed said. 'He's false. You're only attracted by his money and his power. I don't like what I'm seeing. Why are you associating with him?'

'You make Tony sound like a criminal. He's one of the most admired businessmen in Johannesburg. The trouble is, you're jealous.'

'Liza, listen to me, please. Tony is unscrupulous, neurotic and unable to love. He uses people. Can't you see that? In addition, he's power mad, unstable and disloyal. He's as smooth as those damned polished shoes of his. Can't you see what a bloody con he is?'

'Those are all insinuations. You don't have a scrap of evidence to back your accusations.' She was almost crying with rage. She clenched her fists so hard the nails cut into her hand and made her palms bleed.

'For one thing, his business reputation is getting a bit tarnished. People are beginning to wonder if he's quite what he seems. He's had too much government backing, particularly with his newspaper.' Ed snapped his fingers. 'He's like a rocket. He's gone up fast enough, but what next?'

'He's so rich, the newspaper doesn't matter to him.'

'Liza, believe me, I've seen too many of these so-called whizz kids come and go. It's not real wealth, it's all show-wealth. Look at the way you two have been carrying on these past six months. It's just crazy. Normal people don't live like this.'

'Well, he's not normal. Oh Ed. What does it matter? I'm not a gold-digger.'

'I'm glad to hear that. I was beginning to wonder. If it's not his gold, then what is it? What's the fatal attraction that gets you out with him night after night, and away on all these holidays. I've hardly seen you for the past six months and your work is suffering badly. I've had to carry most of your share.'

Liza swallowed guiltily. Ed was right. She barely had time to write her articles.

'You see, Ed, it's the chance to hit back at all those people . . .' She broke off. Ed must never know about her past. Tony knew and he didn't care and that was the hold he had over her – her gratitude.

'I really can't explain,' she said. 'Even though you are my very best friend, Ed, why should I explain?'

After this Ed sulked until they parked in the press car-park outside parliament.

Sitting amongst the huge contingent of local and foreign journalists, Liza began to wonder if the entire trip had been a mistake. De Klerk began his address by toting the same dreary reformist line. When he said: 'Only a negotiated understanding among the representative leaders of the entire population will ensure lasting peace,' she yawned and winked at Ed. To her relief, he winked back. These same words had been trotted out by every government spokesman since sanctions began.

Then de Klerk said: 'Today I am able to announce far-reaching decisions in this connection.'

To gasps of astonishment from his audience, De Klerk announced the lifting of the ban on the exiled organisations, the ANC, the PAC and the SA Communist Party. 'All political prisoners will be released shortly,' he added to the astonished press. Liza could hardly catch her breath before she heard that major changes would be made to security regulations, chief of which would be the lifting of media and education emergency regulations. Adding: 'I wish to put it plainly that the government has taken a firm decision to release Mr Mandela unconditionally. I am serious about bringing this matter to finality without delay.'

'He's taken my breath away,' Liza whispered to Ed. 'So Tony was right after all.'

'The right-wing Afrikaners won't take this lying down,' Liza said to Ed over drinks at the airport later. 'They'll be threatening civil war. I don't understand why he's done this about-face.'

'Perhaps because the economy is in deep water.'

'But didn't we always think that the Afrikaners would live on sticks and stones before they'd give up power. This is their homeland, a country they've suffered and died for, and they have nowhere else to go?'

'At times you revert back to that little Boer maiden, despite your sophistication,' Ed said laughing. 'Change had to come and it's going to hurt a lot of people. It's clear that De Klerk is moving fast. I guess he knows he has to. Mandela is to be released in nine days time.'

'And our so-called "Third Force?"' Liza asked.

'Officially it never existed. My guess is it's being disbanded right now.'

Back in his office, Tony's bland expression changed to thoughtfulness after he locked his office door. He sat doodling with a pencil and pad, which was his best way of concentrating. He could see only trouble ahead. His hand flew over the calculator as he totted up his wealth. He had managed to salt away a small fortune overseas, but small was the operative word. It was not enough to establish him as a person of substance over there, or to maintain his present lifestyle which he thoroughly enjoyed.

The coming multi-racial government would affect all his assets and particularly his newspaper which needed heavy government subsidies to break even.

He took out the file and went through Liza's wealth, which he had researched. It appeared that once she had proved her identity in Portugal she would inherit several industrial buildings, some large wine estates, an old country house in the Douro district and some extensive overseas holdings including a defunct mine in Zaire which could be resurrected. All this was quite apart from the family's wealth in Mozambique which might never be hers, but with the communists out, who knew what might happen. The sooner she was safely married to him, the better.

Tony glanced at his watch impatiently. His next visitor was late for his appointment. That was a sign of the times and it could only get worse.

Tony went through last night's meeting with Cloete. The man had looked haggard and distraught as he had told Tony about the closure of most of the country's clandestine security movements. 'The government's moving fast,' he'd said. 'De Klerk faces a huge job of weeding out the right-wing security chiefs who have taken plum jobs. It's over,' Cloete went on, looking sick. 'Burn all your files. There's a massive bonfire in Pretoria right now. You see, a black government will poke into everything. I foresee endless ramifications.'

His visitor arrived two hours late without any apologies. He was unusually tall for an African with a mass of white hair that stuck up like a fez. He had large, solemn features and heavy-lidded eyes, and a saintly expression which contrasted with his reputation for ruthlessness in pushing home his demands. Tony was not sure exactly what he wanted. He only knew that his name was Norman Mkosi and that he was a powerful man in trade union circles, and the communist party and that privately he had initiated the first black-owned insurance company of which he was now chairman.

'Please sit down, Mr Mkosi,' Tony said. 'I want to congratulate you on the launch of your insurance company and I have a proposition to put to you. Would you like coffee, or a drink?'

Mr Mkosi chose neat scotch and black coffee and he drank liberally of both far into the night as Tony outlined his proposal. He wanted his newspaper to receive clandestine backing in return for editorial aimed at pulling the different black political parties and tribes together, gradually moving towards a news slant that would prepare white readers for eventual all-African unity. He knew this was a goal that was close to Mkosi's heart.

When they got down to the bare facts of how much and when, Tony knew he was halfway there. Mkosi, however, wanted much more than the use of Tony's editorial columns; he wanted details of all the secret business and political coups that Cloete and he had put together and especially the list of names of the agents in the Third Force.

After some hard bargaining, Tony realised that he could compromise and keep his own deals secret, since it was the names Mkosi wanted most of all. It was around 3 a.m. when he handed over the list of Groenewald's special force.

The future of his newspaper was secure and he felt that he could look forward to extensive government backing in the future. The colour of the backers was of very little interest to Tony.

Chapter 52

He was operating alone along the northern Mozambique coastline, moving from Beira to Quelimane, and north to Pemba and occasionally right up to Palma on the Tanzanian border, a place of white sand, coral reefs and impenetrable bushveld of incredible beauty. While he moved on, he was gathering scraps of information and hoarding them as intently as he gleaned crayfish and squid from amongst the rocks. Each morsel was a gift of infinite value.

In the beginning, Major Robert Rousseau had been with him and they had built up a bond based on trust, respect and affection. Rob, whom he had once known as the hippie on the Maputo bus, was a great guy, brave, resourceful and clever.

They had used the aliases of two visiting Portuguese shippers touting new business. Together they had researched details of all the shipping lines plying the East African coast, finding out which shipowners worked with the communists and transported 'live' cargo, and where the terrorists would disembark. Fifty insurgents had been pin-pointed and either destroyed or traced to their final entry point into South Africa where local MI agents took over.

Then their bank account had unexpectedly dried up. When their cash dwindled, their aliases crumpled. They moved down to Maputo, booked into a seedy rooming house and hung around the central bank for six weeks, but no funds came. Eventually the bank closed their account. It became impossible to maintain their lifestyle or their cover. Lately, too, their chain of contacts from Nelfontein to Pretoria had simply disintegrated. One by one, the agents had dropped out. They decided that one of them must fly back, using the last of their cash, and contact the major at headquarters. They had to find out what was happening. After Rob left, Pieter let his beard and hair grow long and unkempt and he reverted to Tomäs.

The alias soon become all too real. He had no money to pay for a room so he made a shack on the beach and slept there. Without cash in his pocket he had no means of buying information or food. He existed from scraps he gleaned and tips from the docks and everyone said: 'Tomäs is back. I wonder where he's been?' He began to move from one major harbour to the next, doing the work of two men, wondering where the hell Rob was?

By July, 1990, Pieter found himself facing a tough choice. He could finish the job he had been sent to do, or return to South Africa to find Rob and discover what had happened to their funds. The fact that Rob had not returned was an on-going source of grief to Pieter. Something bad had happened. If Rob had survived he would never have left him out in the cold.

Pieter had heard the news and knew that De Klerk had promised to free all political prisoners. Was someone over there going crazy? He knew he must work fast. Terrorists and arms were coming through in ever-increasing numbers from Russia, Tanzania and Libya.

What if I'm no longer under orders? That was another nightmare that plagued him. If he were to carry on without orders what did that make him – a murderer? And was the subtle difference enough to save his soul? Had it ever been? He held fast to one belief – *terrorism was wrong*. Killing innocent civilians was wrong, and the criminals had to be eradicated for the protection of the people. So he pushed himself to carry on.

Then he received a message from Quanto, an old friend, and a former Renamo general who now lived in Moma, in the

Zambezia province. 'Come at once. One of the men on your list fled to Kenya. He is expected here shortly. I will try to hold him until you arrive.'

Pieter hitched north again towards Quelimane, existing on a diet of cassava and the occasional fish or shellfish gleaned from the sea. His body began to eat itself, consuming every ounce of fat and then the muscle, until he was emaciated. Everything about him looked defeated except his eyes. He was like the Mozambique countryside, destroyed and depleted, abused and stripped of its assets and now abandoned.

Pieter longed to go home. Mozambique was rotten to the core and he was tired of the corruption, filth and waste of resources. He was tired, too, of human misery and ignorance. Law and order was non-existent. In each village, the men had regressed to their old tribal ways. The settlements had become armed fortresses, guarded by squads of soldiers under a war-lord, who dispensed justice as he felt fit and who controlled the area's resources. Local soldiers went out on frequent raids against neighbouring villages. There was no reason for the fighting and no one was safe. It was just as the tribes had been hundreds of years ago, but now they brandished AK-47s instead of traditional spears, thanks to the Russians.

From Quelimane, Pieter hitched a lift on a trader's lorry, but when they reached the bridge over the Luala River, they ran into a fight. After twenty-four hours of hiding, the lorry was discovered and confiscated by bandits, its driver beheaded with a panga. Pieter escaped into the bush and made his way north by foot. He saw no one for two days and nights until he arrived at the outskirts of Moma, just before noon. The first indication of humanity was an unbelievably fetid stench. Next came a gang of small children who poked fun at him and begged and tried to pick his pockets.

Quanto was standing in the middle of the main street, inspecting a bulldozer that had been stripped down to the bare frame. When he saw Pieter he let out a roar of welcome and clasped him in his arms. Then he stepped back and stared at him in dismay.

'My friend. You have fallen upon hard times,' he said.

'No,' Pieter lied. 'It's my cover. I'm supposed to be a hobo. I can't even approach the bank to draw cash. I would immediately be suspect.'

Quanto frowned. His black eyes narrowed with suspicion. Then he shrugged. 'Things are changing. We listen to the news here. Without help, Frelimo will never be defeated, but who will help us now? Look at this bulldozer, Pieter. Those bloody Arabs did this,' he said. 'It's the only one left and I was hoping one day someone might make it work. You, for instance. They've taken everything usable. They give me electricity from their generator, but they pay nothing for all they take. Well, next to nothing. It's not good enough.'

Quanto lived in a beautiful old villa perched on a hill overlooking the bay. Once it had belonged to a Portuguese planter. High ornate ceilings, spacious rooms, revolving punkahs in the ceiling and heavy slatted wooden shutters were all reminiscent of colonial times. Quanto had done all right for himself, Pieter noticed.

He was taken in to meet Quanto's wife. 'My new wife,' he explained with a smirk. Pieter dimly remembered an older, fat lady who used to feed him well. This one was young, and nubile, with long eyelashes that fluttered over peach-coloured cheeks. Presumably his stomach was not one of Quanto's main preoccupations. Clinging to her skirt was a toddler who looked aggressive and thug-like, just like Quanto.

'About your message . . .' Pieter began.

'Later . . . much later, my friend. We have plenty of time. You need feeding up. We have a day or two to spare. You see, I don't know exactly when the boat will arrive. I know you'd like a bath. I remember how you boys were always washing. Wherever you went, the first necessity was a shower. Well, I have hot and cold running water. That surprises you? I can read your face like a book. I always could. Perhaps we're not as savage as you thought.' He clapped Pieter on the back and laughed heartily, but there was an edge to his voice.

Pieter pulled himself together fast. 'I thought the water mains were broken.'

'True, but the *Arabs* connected my house to their water supply.'

Pieter nodded, thinking silence was his best bet, for despite the famine in Mozambique, Quanto looked aggressively healthy. He was a short, stocky man with skin the colour of soot, and slightly oriental eyes that were large and would have been striking if the whites had not been yellow. He was permanently wet with sweat, wiping his face with a handkerchief. He was wearing a pair of black shorts which kept slipping down from his fat belly and his black T-shirt read: 'I love Africa'. Pieter had only ever seen him in a braided uniform covered in stars and decorations. Despite his casual clothes, it was obvious that Quanto was the local war-lord and that he had become very rich. He had a fleet of ramshackle diesel trucks including a Caball, a couple of Leylands, a Toyota, a 5-ton Sisu and a 1979 Landcruiser, which he kept for his personal use. Tied to the wharf near the harbour was a ski-boat and a couple of motor launches which, Quanto explained, he used to bring emeralds and aquamarines from his heavily fortified depot, twenty kilometres up the Ligonha River, to the quay.

Quanto's major preoccupation was the Arabs. Pieter learned that a Middle-Eastern consortium had 'persuaded' Quanto to give them a mining concession. They had 50 hectares in one of the best areas. They had set up an armed camp with guards and they flew the stones and minerals out of the camp and across the border into Zaire, en-route to the Middle East. They flew in all their requirements, including food, and did nothing for the local population. They were removing the minerals in bulk, leaving the country and its people the poorer. They looted whatever they found lying around, such as the bulldozer, and kept Quanto quiet with bribes: so he had hot and cold running water, a septic tank, television and a satellite aerial. Quanto could not live without the Arabs, but he felt he should get more.

Pieter had nothing to do but mooch around the town during the next few days of waiting. How did these people keep alive? They were too scared to go into the bush and they lived in a state of siege, depending on fish and cassava. The town was in a bad state of disrepair and although the water reservoir was full, no one had connected the pipes. Sewers, taps and electricity were non-existent. The refuse lay uncollected, the place was infested with flies and the townsfolk sat around oblivious to them as they crawled in and out of thelr eyes and ears and noses.

It was clear that all the aid sent to this province had disappeared, a recurring pattern throughout Africa. In the town's one filthy hospital, children were dying for the want of antibiotics. Most of the men had 'droopy dick' and there was no penicillin to cure them. The children were emaciated and the dogs lay in the roads too weak to get out of the way. Life was cheap and people were murdered for next to nothing, which was why Quanto lived inside a high-wire enclosure and employed four armed guards who worked round the clock.

'Your ship has arrived at last,' Quanto told him. They were playing poker on the terrace, an occupation which Pieter detested, but which he had not been able to avoid.

'D'you see that old tramp steamer flying the Union Jack? It loaded at Southampton and came through the Suez Canal, stopping at Dar Es Salaam and Mombasa. It is here to unload a cargo of penicillin, flour, skim-milk powder, disinfectants and pain killers. It has contraband cargo too – a certain terrorist. He is the reason why I sent for you. He is a wanted man. He is also in league with those who steal the aid and sell it overseas. There are massive profits in this filthy business.'

'The terrorist boarded the ship in Kenya and has remained hidden ever since. He is here to liaise with the men who sell the aid. He is a dangerous and clever man, but he is also a fool for he imagines that he is still undetected,' Quanto said. 'Be careful,

Pieter, I've been told that he is a very slippery customer. The ship's leaving tomorrow so you have tonight . . .'

It was two a.m. The ship was dark and stank of rotten fish. There were lights in the crew's quarters. They shed a soft glow on to the deck as Pieter hauled himself over the rail and crept towards the hatch leading to the hold. A solitary sentry stood smoking by the gangway, softly humming to himself and gazing towards the beach. Pieter paused and listened. Oily water splashed against the hull, there was the plaintive cry of a seagull and the sound of a man snoring heavily near by. Good, the hatch had been left open. From the moment he entered the hold, instinct took over. From Quanto's description, Pieter had a rough idea of where the stowaway was holed up, but he waited, listening, sensing the atmosphere, before moving forward. Like a predator he was sure-footed in the darkness.

Someone was there . . . close . . . too close . . .He could feel the body heat . . . but no sound. Whoever was there was holding his breath. Danger . . . He sensed movement and heard the snap of a knife flicked open. He ducked. There was a rush of air and a thwack as metal hit wood.

Crouching, his hand closed over an object and he flung it into the darkness. As it fell, a dark shape spun towards the clatter. Now he had him. He cocked his gun. 'Get your hands up. Go up on deck now.'

There was something about him . . . some memory stirred as Pieter climbed up close behind the stowaway. Catching his breath he said: 'Move to the rail and turn round.'

His finger trembled on the trigger. Then shock hit him. 'Dan!' In that split-second of hesitation Dan Tweneni dived over the side. Pieter leaned over the rail and aimed at the water. Dan had to break surface. Could he pull the trigger? 'Jesus! I'm getting past it,' he muttered.

A few seconds later he heard a roar coming from behind the boat. The motor launch! Goddammit! He was getting away.

Pieter raced down the gangway and along the quay, but the

launch raced off up-river. Ignoring the shouts of the guard, he leaped into the ski-boat and set off in pursuit.

I could have got him. I could have killed him down there in the hold. Why didn't I? It would have been so easy. One shot! His corpse would have bothered no one. There's only one law here and that's Quanto's. Why was it so necessary for me to see his face? Did I sense that it was Dan? Goddammit, I knew – and I hesitated. I'm going soft. I must be bush-fucked!

Where the hell was Dan? Moments ago he had realised that the roar of the engines had stopped and he had quickly cut off his own and sat gently rocking, listening. The moon had risen and the river glittered like a silvery ribbon stretching ahead into the dark heart of Africa. Dense trees and bushes lined the banks. The forest seemed to be holding its breath. An African owl hooted from a bushwillow tree, bats were flitting over the water, and the air was soft and balmy. Nights like this soothed his soul.

A strange idea came welling up out of his sub-conscious. He must come back here and help to repair the damage that seventeen years of civil war had wrought. This beautiful country deserved guarding and pampering and its people needed help.

With a jolt he brought himself back to the job on hand. 'You're a fucking fool if you expect a future,' he growled to himself. Further away a hyena found a kill and called its clan to the feast. The sound depressed Pieter. He, too, longed to be a part of a clan. He was sick to death of being a loner. A nearby plop sent him slithering to the bottom of the boat, but it was only a river bass breaking surface.

Then he heard Dan start his engine again and roar up-river, trying to keep his boat off the mud flats and shake the ski boat off his tail, but he didn't stand a chance.

'I've got you this time, Dan. You're in foreign territory.' With the throttle turned to full blast, the ski boat leaped over the river in a series of crashes, sending the birdlife winging away. Still he was losing ground, but not losing Dan, for the launch left a dark trail in the green fetid water, where it cut through slime and algae. He would follow the trail to wherever Dan dumped the launch and track him through the bush and then he would kill him. *He was a soldier and this was what he had been trained and ordered to do.*

At the same time, it would be better to catch him on the river and avoid tracking him through dense bush, for Dan was one of the best trackers he'd ever come across. How many times had Dan warned them of lions or bushpigs, or found them their quarry when they were out there hunting as kids. His mind went back to their many expeditions.

A bad time to think of the past. Pieter pulled himself together. This is the time to think of only one thing – that for which I was trained – killing. Was I ever anything more than a killer? All those medals and parades and pep talks. It was all a load of bull.

The moon was rising and the river widening. He could not see the river banks at all, but the treetops glistened in the moonlight and Dan's trail shimmered with phosphorescence.

Suddenly the trail ended. Pieter cut his engine quickly and sat drifting in the gurgling river, listening to the sounds of the night. Why had Dan stopped? Was he waiting for him to go back? Would he take a pot shot at him from the bulrushes? Pieter glanced round intently, listening. For a while there were no clues to his whereabouts. He lay low in the boat, gripping his gun, for Dan might be foolish enough to swim out to get him. All at once, from the north bank, he heard a commotion which he recognised as crocodiles leaping for the safety of the water and disappearing under with a flurry of beating tails. So that's where Dan was. In the distance he could see a broad sandy ledge under an overhanging nyala tree. A perfect place for crocs to lie waiting for game. Then he realised with a shock that it was almost dawn. The first shy bucks or bushpigs would be coming for a drink soon.

Still he waited, crouched low in the swaying ski boat, listening for more signs. He could always count on the guinea-fowls. Their sentinels missed nothing. As he had hoped, a few minutes later they set up their cacophonous, shrill complaints from their treetop vantage points where they could see all intruders. Dan was doubling back, but moving away from the river in a north-easterly direction.

Leaving the ski-boat hidden in the rushes, he set off after him, hurrying to get close behind so he could learn from the noisy clues put out by the wild creatures – the warlike barks of the baboons in the trees, the sudden shrill cry of a disturbed owl, a hyena running with its tail between its legs. Man, the most feared of all creatures, was penetrating their territory.

Half an hour later, he stopped, realising that he had lost his quarry. He leaned against a tree, listening, watching the sky turn pearly grey and then a mystical rose colour in the east. He had to have a pee. He was splashing the trunk of a wild fig tree, hidden in the black pool of the dense foliage, when he heard a voice that brought his skin out in prickles.

'Hands on your head, Piet. Right up!' The voice came from the branches above him. 'You've fucked up, man. Lean against the trunk fast.' He heard Dan leap on to the ground. Now he was feeling in his pockets for his gun, which he took. Perhaps he was bluffing. Pieter swung round, but the muzzle of a handgun hit his temple with a sharp crack. 'Next time I'll pull the trigger. Now stretch your hands behind your back.'

Handcuffs! How the hell did Dan get hold of handcuffs?

'You were never much good at tracking, Piet, although I tried to teach you.'

Pieter stared hard at Dan, his eyes revealing his contempt. Dan represented all that he detested: a trumped-up black commie who was threatening the civilised world. A world he'd given his life to protect. Well, this time he'd failed. He was about to be killed. The thought was strangely welcoming. He was tired. He'd seen too much action. Sometimes it seemed that he was lost in a maze and the more he destroyed the more lost he became.

'If you're going to shoot me, get on with it,' he muttered.

'Of course I'm going to shoot you. It's kill or be killed in your world, isn't it? I'm going to have you stuffed and mounted. Jesus, you'll look good stuck on a wooden block and mounted in my livingroom. "*The last of the great white racists.*" I'll have that put on a plaque. Your species is almost extinct. Don't you know that? Men like you are an embarrassment to your new liberal government. They want you out of the way. They sold the list of your names to us and we sold it to the PAC and they gave it to God knows who. So just about everyone in the country is putting you guys out, including your own people. Nobody wants an embarrassing reminder of the bad old days walking around.'

'You're lying,' Pieter grunted.

'Am I? What d'you think you're doing here, you poor bush-fucked sod? Did you get paid lately? What are you living on?'

'Screw you, Dan. Get on with it.'

'Not yet. I want to swop some information.'

'You should know better than that.'

'I think I might be able to tempt you.'

'Try.' Pieter said. There was the smallest hope that if he kept Dan talking long enough some Renamo soldiers might come by.

'I'll start the ball rolling,' Dan said. 'I left the country because your gang had me on the list to be "*permanently removed from society*". Many of our leaders were put on that list, together with a bunch of criminals, but you guys wouldn't care about the difference. A clever kafir should be dead, isn't that so? You personally took care of quite a few of them. D'you remember when you guys sat in your Honeysuckle smallholding, watching the mug shots of the so-called "vermin" you had to kill, Piet?'

Pieter shrugged. 'I don't know what you're talking about,' he said.

'Yes you do. One of your guys – one very near the top, the one who created your gang, and who gave you the list of black leaders to be destroyed, also handed the list of every member of your gang to one of our leaders. I think it might be Major Groenewald, but I'm not sure. He's hiding out on his brother's farm in Namibia, pretending to be a sheep farmer. Because of him, most of your buddies are dead. Major Rob Rousseau is dead. Yeah! That hurts, doesn't it? He was thrown out of a ten-storey building and they said it was suicide. It might have been whites who did it. As I said, no one wants this sort of evidence walking around alive. Do you think Major Groenewald would sell you out?'

'This is crap,' Pieter said. 'I've never heard of him. Did you kill Rob?' he asked in a quiet voice. He was slowly working on pulling his hand free. He could feel the blood running down his hands, but he had switched his mind off the pain. He had always had thin hands. . .

'No, Piet. Sorry to disappoint you. The last time I killed, it was a tiny buffalo calf, bleating by the side of its dead mother. You'd had to shoot its mother to save my life, because of my stupid blunder. I've never killed since. For the past four years I've been a vegetarian.'

Pieter stared at him in amazement, sensing that he was telling the truth.

'After I fled South Africa,' Dan went on, 'I was sent to a camp in Uganda. I tell you, Piet, that was hell on earth. Beatings, torture, filth, sadistic swines in charge, they had no concept of the sanctity of life. I had a tiff with the guy in charge of the camp and I was put into solitary, but I escaped. I made my way to the nearest ANC headquarters and laid a charge. I forced them to start an independent inquiry. After that I was offered a job to keep me busy until it was deemed safe to return to South Africa. The job took me round Africa and what I saw there made me think. I'm finished with communism. I'm going to take the best of what the West can offer and improve on it by adding some of our own simple rules, rules Nosisi taught me when I was a kid, things like *Ubuntu*, group caring for those who can't care for themselves, group loving. We've got a few things to teach your people, too. I can't wait to get home, but first I have a job to finish.

'Believe it or not, Pieter, I'm being paid for being here right now, which is more than you are. I am working for the United Nations Children's Fund, investigating the theft of medicines and skim-milk powder and maize, which is sent into Mozambique almost weekly. Have you seen the hospital here? Have you seen the state of the children? Have you seen what people look like when they are deprived of any medical supplies? You and your kind wrecked this country.

'Now I have a question for you. Do you know where it is going? I won't insult you by asking if you are involved. You look like a man who is rapidly starving to death, so I guess you aren't getting any handouts. At the same time, you are a guest in the house of a criminal who is getting very rich on stolen aid. Quanto has a Swiss bank account, a house in Italy, etcetera etcetera. It's only a matter of time before he opts out of Africa with his new wife. Strange friends you have, Piet. I remember what an idealist you were. Funny how people change.'

Pieter sat in silence gazing at Dan. Watching those earnest, clever eyes and that candid open expression he wished like hell that he and Dan were on the same side. His hands were going numb and the cramp in his arms was terrible, but the pain in his heart was even worse. Quanto had somehow got wind that an agent was investigating him. He'd brought him up to kill Dan, not because he was on the list, but because his criminal activities were about to be stopped by Dan. Strange how their positions were suddenly reversed. Dan was on the side of the angels – so what did that make him?

'Now get up slowly and walk up to that ridge and sit there and keep quiet. I'll be right behind you,' Dan said.

The sun rose, the bush hummed noisily around them, it became very hot and Pieter was so thirsty he could hardly swallow.

'People are corrupt by nature,' Dan went on. 'A good society is one with good laws and a government that lives by those laws. Once the authorities start taking the law into their own hands, for whatever reason, you're on a path down to corruption. You and I are only pawns, Pieter. We were fed so much shit we came to believe it. Me with communism and you with racialism. Don't you understand, man?

'Look at that dung beetle,' he said, pointing to one of the glistening black beetles, which was pushing a ball of manure far bigger than itself over a sandy ridge. 'Why are we any different? We gather our shit and we spend our lives pushing it, practically killing ourselves to do it. My dream has crashed and so has yours. It's time to shed our self-imposed loads. We were close once, Piet. As close as brothers could be. We played together and hunted together, but this system we lived under pulled us apart, taught us to despise each other, later to hate each other, and finally to kill each other. I used to love you, man.'

He broke off. For a moment they both sat listening to a distant roar. Then, up the river, came a string of barges laden with all the aid that had been unloaded from the West.

'So I was right,' Dan said. 'The loot gets stored in the Arabs' so-called mining camp and sent off by plane to God knows where. The Middle East I assume. I shall inform Frelimo and no doubt they'll bomb this place to bits. The bastards will start up again somewhere else, together with Quanto, but we'll get them again.

'Now,' Dan said standing up. 'I'm going to make one more killing, which I resent since I'm hellbent on going to heaven.

'Turn and face the tree. I don't want to see your face. I'm giving you five minutes to say your prayers. I'm even going to unlock your hands.' He flicked the lock open. 'I wouldn't like you to die in handcuffs. Jesus, what a mess you've made of your wrists. Kneel down, Pieter, like you do in church. Put your hands together in front of your face. Now pray, because it's your last chance. You've got five minutes. If you move, you're dead.'

Pieter peered around for possible cover. He would have to make a dash for it. There was a ditch on the left . . . some thick scrub bushes on his right and before him the ground fell away in a sheer drop to some rocks and the river. If he could leap over the ridge, he might make it, even if he was shot or wounded. He didn't stand much of a chance, but it was better than no chance at all. It was difficult to kill a man falling through space. Where exactly was Dan standing? He had to know. Besides, he had a strong impulse to say something meaningful before he died.

'I always loved you, Dan, but I put duty first, just like you. If the position were reversed, I'd kill you. I came after you to kill you. If I got another chance, I would. Do you blame me?'

There was no answer. 'Well, do you . . . ?'

Still there was no reply. Cautiously he turned his head to find that he was quite alone.

Chapter 53

Dan was standing at the back of the queue at Jan Smuts Airport, Johannesburg, waiting to go through immigration and wondering if there would be complications, for he had left the country illegally and his passport had not been stamped. An earnest young airport official in a grey peaked cap, with a pale complexion and grey eyes, tapped him on the shoulder. 'Excuse me, sir. Are you Dan Tweneni?'

Strange, Dan thought as he nodded. It was the first time anyone white had called him sir. From '*boy*' to '*sir*' in two years of exile – not bad, he thought. But why did they want him?

'Would you come this way please, sir.'

He was led into a crowded, noisy room. There was a sudden silence. 'Dan,' roared Joshua Bene, his mentor and superior in the party. Glasses were raised and someone began to sing the ANC anthem. Nosisi hurried forward looking magnificent in a green silk suit and golden turban. When she smiled at him he knew that everything was all right. Liza was there, too. How smart and sophisticated she looked. Martha was hanging on to Reg's arm – *in public*! That was amazing. Surely things couldn't have changed that much? There were several of his buddies from the ANC, the trade union and the soccer club. Crazy to see them out in the open, shaking hands and slapping backs with those white officials trying to smile through their tight lips and pretending they were enjoying the occasion.

'Hi, everyone,' Dan said, shaking hands in a daze. When he

reached Nosisi he whispered: 'What the hell's going on?'

'We're here to meet you. That's what's going on.'

The airport manager came up to him and made a show of shaking hands and congratulating him on his return. 'Sir,' he said. 'Just give me your passport for stamping, I'd like to hurry you through. Your luggage is here.'

Dan grabbed his backpack and grinned. 'Thanks,' he said, still feeling puzzled. 'But why?'

'A large crowd came to meet you and they are disrupting airport routine, so we want to get you out quickly.'

Dan frowned and went to the window. A sea of faces were looking up expectantly, waving gold, green and black flags. There were thousands of people out there. 'Why so much fuss?' he asked.

'You are your father's son,' Nosisi said looking smug. 'The people expect a great deal from you.'

The pale young airport official tapped him on the shoulder. 'Could I have your autograph, please, sir?' he asked. A book and a pen were thrust towards him.

Dan dropped his backpack and put his hand on the boy's shoulder again. 'Sure thing, buddy,' he said. 'What do you want me to say?'

For Dan, apartheid died at that precise moment.

Weeks later, after the speeches and press conferences, the crowds, the cheering, the toyi-toying women and the riots at his first soccer match, came the soul-searching task of planning his future. He was terrified that he would not be equal to the awesome task of living up to the people's expectations.

Reg had kept his taxi in good order, but Bene had asked him to keep out of that business. 'It's too contentious – too much violence, you can't afford to taint your image, Dan,' he said. 'You're being groomed for higher things.'

The party offered him the position of Transvaal leader and Dan accepted. He felt that this would enable him to sway the ANC and its members towards private enterprise.

Liza begged him to appear on her TV show. A panel of young political leaders were talking about the country's growing violence. Dan arrived to find that the others were wearing white collars and ties and Liza was looking pretty good in an expensive black suit with a white lace blouse and her hair in a chignon. Dan felt out of place in his khaki jeans and shirt, but no one had asked him to dress up. He was so scared he could hardly speak.

'I have here Dan Tweneni, ex-youth leader of the ANC. Dan has just returned to this country after two years in Africa, working for the United Nations Children's Fund. Dan, has your trip in Africa altered your political affiliations in any way?' Liza asked with an encouraging smile.

Dan gulped. At first he was nervous, but after a few minutes he relaxed and tried to tell the viewers of the horror of civil war, and the resulting anarchy.

'Here in South Africa we have the law – that's what civilisation is all about,' he said. 'Long before the white man came to South Africa our tribes had a highly developed legal system with local courts for minor infringements, going right up to the Chief's court. In some tribes, there was even a court of appeal above the Chief. The black man has always loved the law.

'We stand now on the brink of civil war, but we can emerge from this maelstrom of violence and change if we hang on to the law. The law is our lifeline. Lately we have had a Third Force operating outside the law. Several of these men are still at large. The ANC is in a position to reveal the names of these so-called vigilantes,' he said sternly. 'I am calling on the authorities to show their sincerity by bringing these agents to trial without further delay.'

He tried to ignore Liza's startled expression and her wide eyes willing him to change the subject. 'I am warning you now, unless we impose a just system that applies to everyone, we shall not be able to trust each other sufficiently to go forward. What I saw in Mozambique and Angola and further north, too, frightened me. We must make sure that this never happens here.'

'Well, you've set yourself up as a target for the Third Force, or what's left of them,' Tony said. 'I wouldn't like to be your insurers. Don't you ever think before you speak? All that could have been said to the proper authorities in a confidential meeting.'

Dan shrugged contemptuously. They were sitting in what Liza had promised was the most exclusive restaurant in Johannesburg. La Rôtisserie Ladurée was huge and spacious with a high ceiling, chandeliers, beautiful carpets, gold brocade on the walls, gentle classical music playing in the background and a hushed, peaceful atmosphere. From the moment the *Maître d'* greeted them it had been clear that he was the only black man in the restaurant. Not that it bothered him.

Liza was wearing a dress that took Dan's breath away. The beautiful, black silk creation was held up with shoe-string straps over her shoulders, there was no back and it clung to her in all the right places, covering only the bare minimum. Her long hair was loose, almost the same colour and texture as the silk. The white flower she'd put behind one ear made her look very young and vulnerable, and Dan couldn't help wondering if she really knew what she was doing in this ultra-sophisticated world she had gatecrashed.

'This place is so chic. Do you like it?' she asked, fingering her diamond-drop earrings, a present from Tony presumably.

'No,' he said. 'Not really.'

She giggled. 'Anyway, the food is heavenly. Just you wait.'

What a kid she still was. If this was just a growing-up phase he hoped she'd soon get over it.

'Let me order for you,' Tony said patronisingly as he watched Dan eyeing the menu blankly.

'That's fine by me,' Dan muttered.

Tony ordered. 'Oh, and bring us a bottle of *Dom Perignon*,' he added as the waiter took his order.

The food was put before them reverently. If you could call it food, Dan thought as he glanced at his plate. A mess that looked like frog's eggs was nestling on the crystal plate. Tiny spoons of mother of pearl lay beside the goo, so presumably he was supposed to eat it. *Yuch!* The waiter was filling their glasses with champagne – Dan gulped his, hoping it would soften the horror of the fishy black mess.

'Sip it,' Liza hissed in his ear.

God, what a horrible night this promised to be.

'I was talking to Nelson yesterday,' Tony said confidentially. 'He asked me what I thought about the ANC's idea of nationalising the mines.'

Nelson? Dan frowned.

Tony smirked at him. 'I told him it would be national suicide. It seems that Cyril has recommended a certain amount of nationalisation. I wonder if you guys realise the repercussions this would have overseas?'

Dan stared across the table, mesmerised by a tiny, black egg stuck between Tony's teeth. He glanced at Liza. How could she bear Tony's obvious name-dropping? He doubted if Tony had ever spoken to 'Nelson' or 'Cyril'.

'You shocked me, Dan. I don't mind telling you that, with your ideas on abandoning communism and going hellbent for private enterprise. It takes a great man to admit he's been wrong.'

'But with definite built-in social benefits,' Dan added quickly.

'Why don't you list your ideas? Let's see if we're on the same wavelength. . .'

Dan's barely touched caviar was whipped away and replaced with some minty-flavoured sorbet which was so cold it hurt his teeth. It tasted like frozen toothpaste. Well, at least supper's over, he thought, polishing off the ice-cold dessert. But he was wrong, he found, for next came a watery liquid that tasted like nothing.

'If you think their *Consommé Célestine* is good, just wait until you taste their *Homard á la Parisien*,' Liza enthused.

Silence would be a good answer. The champagne, which he'd enjoyed, was whipped away and Chablis took its place.

Dan began to talk, unwillingly at first, but Tony was a good listener and he wanted to hear Dan's views on combining private enterprise with certain social safeguards.

When a large lobster was set before him, Dan cheered up. He forked a large mouthful and almost gagged on the sweetish mayonnaise. He hated mayonnaise. 'Where's the lobster gone?' He poked at the horrid mess. 'This joint is a rip-off. I bet you pay a fortune for having diced veg put in crayfish shells.'

Liza flushed and bent her head over her plate, so Dan got off the subject of food.

After this the fillet was almost raw. Dan pushed it around with his fork, too embarrassed to tell them that he'd never enjoyed meat since his hunting days. Once again his wine was snatched away and now he had a glass full of red wine.

'It's a 1971 *Château Margaux*, darling. They keep it just for me,' Tony told Liza with a triumphant leer.

By the time they reached the cheese, which stank and a rich sweet wine that made him dizzy, Dan was talking too loudly and too much. He sensed this, but he could not stop. He told Tony of his dreams of creating a model workforce, with bonus incentives for productivity, pensions, co-operative insurance schemes, educational funds jointly contributed by management and workers, subsidised housing, and frequent get-togethers between management and workers. There was more, much more and he kept on talking, amazed that Tony would want to listen.

'What would you say if I offered you a job, Dan?' Tony said over coffee. 'I'd like to make your dreams come true in my outfit. I employ something like ten thousand workers overall. I would push all the cash I could towards your welfare ideas, but of course I would expect the Government and the ANC to back me all the way.'

Dan leaned back feeling that he was going into shock. He

wished he hadn't drunk so much. He had to concentrate.

'Excuse me for saying this, Tony, but the last time you and I clashed, you didn't strike me as being even slightly philanthropic. As for caring for workers' job security, it was as far from your list of priorities as that moth you've just crushed without a second's hesitation.'

'We're not talking about moths, we're talking about the future security of the country. Just think,' Tony went on. 'For you it would be like playing God. Why don't you come on board as personnel director and work out how to set your plans into action.'

'I have a job,' Dan said slowly, 'but I think my superiors would lend me to you on a part-time basis – just for a few months. If we could succeed in getting a model outfit set up at your plants, other industrialists would follow your example.' He was starting to get excited.

'Will he put his money where his mouth is?' Dan asked Liza when Tony went to the loo.

Liza's eyes were sparkling. 'Tony's word is his bond,' she said happily.

It seemed a shame to spoil her evening by telling her that Tony was as reliable as a boa constrictor, and as greedy. He's got self-interest at heart, Dan thought, but if the workers benefit then what the hell. When the bill came, Dan peeped and almost gasped. They could feed Soweto's lost kids for a year on that much cash.

'Does it make you feel good – I mean, eating at places like this?' he asked Liza.

'Yes,' she hissed. 'It makes me realise how far I've come.'

'In terms of what – morals, spiritual values, learning, or simply showing off?'

'Oh, get off your high horse,' she said, glowering at him.

Tony was moving from table to table laughing and chatting as he slowly made his way back to them. He's overdoing it. Even I can see that, Dan thought to himself. He wants to be accepted here, but the truth is, he isn't.

'I'll be at your head office first thing in the morning,' Dan said, standing up and shaking Tony's hand. He sensed that he had supped with the devil.

Chapter 54

It was early morning and temperatures were close to freezing when Pieter arrived at his home after days spent hitching and busing from Moma. He was deeply tired and defeat showed in his eyes and the slope of his shoulders and the way his feet hesitated as if he were teetering on the very edge of the world.

He paused at the roadside, shivering and wondering if he had lost his way home. There was nothing here he could recognise. An automatic barrier had replaced the old neglected gate and on either side stretched a heavily fortified high-wire fence. Pieter could see a zebra grazing just inside and this cheered him. He pressed a bell and a guard in a smart green safari suit and a peaked hat with the words *Jacana Lodge welcomes you* rushed out and let him in.

'Have you booked, sir?' he said, scowling as his eyes scanned Pieter's torn khaki shorts and shirt, his beard and long hair and beat-up sandals. 'Reception is closed.'

'I live here,' Pieter said wearily. Then he recognised Tony's farm foreman. 'No more tractor driving, eh?' He clapped him on the shoulder. 'You look good, man.'

He walked the two hundred metres to his house, encountering three bushpigs, an ardvaark and a herd of young antelopes. The place seemed to be booming.

His home, he discovered, had become the admittance office. The front wall had been knocked out to make one huge plate-glass window and looking through he could see a counter with stacks of permits and brochures. Posters of wild game covered the walls. A sign read: 'Ring here for night service.'

He rang, and a sleepy old man tottered out from a room behind the counter, tucking his shirt into his pants.

'Sam!' Pieter roared.

'Young baas? Is that the young baasie?' he said blinking as he opened the door. 'Welcome home, baas. Oh, but you're too thin. You've been starving.' He pinched Pieter on the arm and stepped back, the tears streaming down his eyes. 'You've suffered,' he said simply.

'Sam, you look great,' Pieter laughed, shrugging off the old man's concern. 'No more lazy donkeys. D'you like the changes?'

Sam nodded. Watching him closely, Pieter noticed that his eyes were no longer so swollen, or his face so blotchy. He guessed Sam had reduced his drinking.

'I run this admittance office,' Sam said, with quiet dignity. 'Some days it's really humming. You wouldn't believe how many guests we've had. Mister Tony is talking about building extra rondavels.'

'Where did they put my clothes, Sam?' Pieter asked. 'In my life I never felt so cold.' He was so hoarse his voice was cracking.

'I put them in the loft. I hope that's all right. Mister Tony wanted to give you an apartment up at the house, but I thought you'd rather stay here. Your Pa came and collected some of the furniture and the rest is up there. Here's the key. I'll bring you something to eat.'

Like all old Dutch farm houses, the way to the loft was via an outside staircase fixed to the wall. Pieter walked up slowly, hoping something was left. When he swung open the door, he frowned and shook his head wonderingly. The thatch had been cleaned and treated and it gleamed like gold in the dim electric light and so did the polished yellow-wood floor. He recognised the mohair rugs that used to be in the sitting room, an occasional lamp, bookcases and his bed and wardrobe. His radio and tapedeck stood on a table beside an easy chair.

'Ma would have loved to see this,' he said aloud. He heard footsteps behind him. 'Who did this, Sam?' he asked.

'I did, baas. I felt you needed a place to come home to.'

Pieter was too confused and exhausted to express his thanks. He flung himself on the bed and lay with his face buried in the pillow, dimly aware that someone was covering him with rugs.

A knock woke him in the morning. It was Sam with a tray of real breakfast: bacon, boerewors, toast, fried tomato, onions and eggs, with orange juice, melon and strong black coffee. Food had never tasted so good and Pieter blessed every mouthful. He dressed and drove to the village for a haircut and shave. How odd he looked with ashen cheeks and chin and the rest of his face tanned brown. When he put on his uniform Sam had pressed he realised how thin he was, for it hung loose around him. He packed a bag, borrowed a jeep and left for Pretoria.

The group's headquarters were situated in a redbrick building in downtown Pretoria. Pieter arrived and parked his car, but when he entered the foyer the guard at reception barred his way to the lift. 'You have to sign the visitor's book,' he said. 'Who do you want to see?'

Pieter looked around warily. 'I have an appointment with the manager of *Centratech*, on the sixth floor.'

The guard laughed. 'What's your name – Rip van Winkle? The place was raided by police months ago. They took the files and tapes and closed everything down. There's an inquiry taking place. It was in all the newspapers. The truth is they were right-wing military agents of some sort, or so I read. Hey! Are you one of them?'

Pieter paled with shock. 'I'm looking for a friend.'

'They haven't been here since they were closed down and that doesn't surprise me much. There's a wholesale shoe company up there now.'

Pieter drove out to the conference hall Groenewald had built on his Honeysuckle smallholding. The gate was closed and locked with a chain and padlock. Pieter parked, climbed over the gate and walked up the driveway. The place looked neglected, leaves and weeds choked the driveway and a guard was standing at the locked and barred front door. He could see that it hadn't been opened for some time for a swift was making its nest above.

'You're trespassing on private property,' the guard said fingering his gun, a standard police Baretta 92F.

'No, I'm not,' Pieter said. 'This farm belongs to a friend of mine, a Major Groenewald. He asked me to look around and see if it's been broken into.'

'I've never heard of him and you're still trespassing.' The policeman watched him warily while pretending to study a bird.

Peering through the glass windows behind the bars, Pieter saw that the rooms were empty. 'Why are you guarding an empty house?' he asked. 'Isn't this a job for security guards, not the police?'

The young man shrugged and looked awkward. 'I am a security guard.' He flushed. Lying seemed to upset him.

As Pieter climbed back over the gate he saw the young man calling someone on his walkie-talkie.

Pieter decided to wait. Fifteen minutes later a police vehicle approached, sirens blaring, tyres screeching. A plain-clothed policeman jumped out and raced towards the gate, his gun in his hand.

'I'm over here,' Pieter called. He would have liked to have disarmed him, just to show him how *not* to chase a suspect. Instead he allowed himself to be disarmed and 'detained for questioning', and driven to a tall building in the centre of the city.

There were several detectives in civvies. One of them flashed a badge at him, which was odd, since he hadn't asked for their identification. No one would tell him why he was being detained.

Pieter gave them details of his name, rank and number, and asked for transport to military headquarters to see his superior officer. Instead they put him into a clean cell and served a very good lunch which he ate hungrily. An hour later a police officer arrived and told him politely that they were sorry he had to wait. They could supply some books or magazines. Would he like coffee?

'Why are you holding me?' he asked.

The man shrugged. 'Why ask me? It's nothing to do with me. I just have to make sure you're comfortable.'

In the afternoon, Major Myers arrived.

'Congratulations on your promotion,' Pieter said. The major looked fitter and happier than Pieter remembered. From his trim stomach, bulging muscles and out-of-season tan, Pieter deduced he was spending time in a gym. 'Not many police officers can find the time or the cash to attend a private gym, Myers. You're looking good. The police force seems to have changed a lot lately.'

'You've been out in the cold, captain,' Myers said. 'You look like you've had a rough time. I want you to make a full statement and I'll try to look after you. We have enough evidence on you to arrest you for the murder of ten citizens, including the Reverend Ronald Sizani. However, I'm aware that you thought you were obeying orders. Those orders were cancelled on February 2, 1990, if indeed they ever existed. Strictly speaking you are a common murderer and you will be tried and sentenced for murder. However, you were a recé scout and you've seen a lot of action. In your own, misguided way, you devoted your life to the protection of your country. That will go a long way to help you.

'We're offering you a chance to protect yourself permanently by becoming a state witness,' he went on. 'You'll get full immunity guaranteed by the State Prosecutor. Furthermore, we'll offer you twenty-four-hour protection and if necessary an alternative name and ID number. We could even make the army find your backpay and pension. How about that? There's hardly any of you boys left.'

Pieter listened in total disbelief. When Myers formally asked him for a statement he stood to attention, stared at the wall and gave his name, rank and number. From then on he stood in silence while questions were fired at him.

'Who gave you your orders? Who paid your salaries? How many of you are there? What were you called?'

An hour later, Myers leaned back. 'Would you like some coffee? I have the impression that you won't talk even if I hold you for a month. I think I got off on the wrong foot. You're so out of touch, captain. Everything has been disbanded. Those of you who are still alive have gone into hiding. Some have fled overseas. You walked in here like Daniel into the lions' den.'

'And what happened to Daniel, sir?' he asked quietly.

'True. But if you walk out of here, you'll be lucky to be alive at the end of the week. You see, captain, your crowd have become an embarrassment to the authorities and that includes the military. You're being eliminated one by one. Yes, I can see you're shocked. You can't hide that. I'm shocked, too. I don't know who's responsible, but I do know all about the list you guys were given of people to be *permanently removed from society*. D'you remember how those blacks were "removed" as you put it? Oh, for God's sake sit down and have a cigarette.'

Pieter kept his face blank, determined to give nothing away.

'Now, let's see,' Myers said, paging through his folder. 'You lot are getting the same sort of treatment, it seems. Major Groenewald has gone into hiding, Major Rob Rousseau accidentally fell off the top of a building. René Coetze slipped on a bar of soap and drowned in his bath. Someone called "Slim" drowned in a foot of water at Germiston Lake, mainly because his knees and elbows had been smashed with a hammer. It must have been a relief to die. *Etcetera* ... savage reprisals – makes you sick to read them.

'I haven't been able to discover who is responsible. We suspect that someone high up in your outfit sold you out, but to whom? The ANC – the PAC – the Azanian People's

Liberation Organisation? Or perhaps the communists, or some right-wing group created especially to get rid of you.

'As far as I can ascertain, captain, there are only three men left alive out of your original group. Anything can happen in a country where those at the top break the law. One day all that is going to stop and I'm doing my bit to make sure that it does. Now why don't you help me clean up this mess?'

'I don't know what you're talking about, sir. I have never heard of any such group. Major Groenewald is a bona fide member of MI and he is my immediate superior. I have been liaising with Renamo in Northern Mozambique. I was trapped there by the enemy. Eventually I escaped and here I am.'

'It's a good story, but it won't help you, because we know better.'

'Off the record,' Pieter said, watching Myers' eyes flicker with interest. 'You're an Afrikaner. Your family has owned land here for generations. You know the score. How come you're prepared to turn against your own kind?'

'I'm not,' Myers said. 'I have enlarged my concept of "my kind" to include all South Africans. I'm for the goodies – against the baddies. I don't even notice the colour of a man's skin.'

'What are you going to do when a black government expropriates your land? What makes you feel that our bunch are any better than those further north? Why are you so damned naive? Don't you care about the Afrikaner nation? We want to survive as a nation, don't we? We want our language to survive?'

Myers did not reply.

'If you don't care about that, then what about law and order? This country is becoming ungovernable, giving in is not a solution. When we've signed away control of our security forces what will happen to whites in future revolutions? D'you think the Zulus, the Xhosas, the ANC and the PAC are going to live happily ever after? D'you believe in fairies, Myers?'

Myers shrugged. 'You make me sick,' he said. 'You people think you have a God-given right to hog this country's resources.'

'You'll see,' Pieter said bitterly. 'You despise me, but history will prove you wrong. I am a Boer, never forget that. I and my kind refuse to be subjected to a black government. We shall stand back and bide our time and wait until you liberals and blacks have brought the country to its knees and then we'll sweep in.

'You've seen what's happening further north. Countries that were once paradise can no longer feed their populations. They're infested with cholera, malaria and soil erosion. There are 450 million people starving in Africa in countries that once exported foodstuffs. Right now it's costing sixty-five million rands a year just to send illegal immigrants back where they came from. Soon Africa's chaos will be inside our own borders, that's if people like you hand over power to those whose motto is *Kill the Boer, kill the farmer*. You make me sick, Myers. Now let me out of here.'

'I told you, you're detained until you come to your senses.'

'Suck my arse,' Pieter said. He flung himself across the desk and gripped Myers by the throat. 'You're not a policeman's backside, not any more. Did you think I was fooled? This is not a police station. Who are you and who pays your fancy salary?'

Myers managed to reach a bell and two colleagues rushed in and grabbed Pieter. One of them was a woman and she looked frightened.

'I have no intention of hurting you,' Pieter said, shrugging her off. 'I've been out in the bush for years protecting people like you, but I seem to have come back to the wrong century.'

Why was he pleading to her? He felt a fool. He was relieved when she smiled sympathetically.

'We are part of the Goldstone Commission,' she told him, 'which was set up by the Government to inquire into the existence of a Third Force and other illegal activities. We want to know who was responsible for creating such a force.'

'Surely the government should know?'

She looked towards Myers who nodded imperceptibly. 'It's not so simple,' she went on nervously. 'There's a deep split in the Afrikaner establishment. No one really knows exactly who wants what or who did what. Some right-wing elements in the government and the army were responsible for certain acts which the others knew nothing about. It was all in the name of security, of course. We need someone who will testify.'

'I'm not your man. Find someone else. Can I go now?' he asked wearily.

'Be careful,' Myers said bitterly. 'We don't want to lose you.'

'Then give me back my gun.'

'You've got to be joking. It's government property,' Myers told him.

Shattered and furious Pieter raced to military headquarters, but he could not fnd anyone he knew. By evening he was still being sent from one department head to the next as he struggled to prove that he was an officer in military intelligence.

'Too many files have been destroyed,' Colonel André Potgieter, head of personnel told him. 'Come back tomorrow morning. I'll do what I can.'

The next morning, Potgieter informed Pieter that there was no trace of Pieter ever having been in the army.

Pieter leaned back in his chair and took a deep breath. 'What the hell is going on?' he asked quietly, fighting to remain calm.

'Come down to the canteen and I'll tell you unofficially what mlght have happened, without in anyway involving the SADF.

'On February 2, 1990,' Potgieter began over coffee, 'the unbanning of the formerly banned organisations had the immediate effect that all ideological offences and activities became totally irrelevant. Consequently, information about them became irrelevant, too. Security police and the MI destroyed all files relating to these matters. Masses of documents were destroyed ... records, pay cheques, all details of peripheral intelligence cells. I don't mind telling you that we worked day and night to carry out these orders. All those millions of files, compiled with teutonic thoroughness ... '

The word *teutonic* stuck in Pieter's gullet. Were the generals shifting the right-wingers out of the army and putting 'pink' guys in positions of authority? And where had *they* been all these years? Drawing their pay with their mouths zipped?

He brought his mind back to what Potgieter was saying. 'All details of surveillance, and the monitoring of anti-apartheid activists, as well as the "dirty tricks" brigade, were totally destroyed. Were you one of them I wonder? In any event your records, if indeed they ever existed, went at this time I assume.' He put down his cup and stood up. 'I can't help you any further, *Mister* de Vries,' he said pointedly.

'You guys are not going to get away with this. My pay cheque was paid into my building society up until nine months ago. I can trace the deposits back to the force. If I go to the press with that, plus the work I was *ordered* to do, I think it might raise quite a storm. Someone had better be able to find my back pay, and my pension and reinstate me. The army is my life. It always has been.'

The colonel's face became frozen into a mask of disapproval. 'Not a very patriotic stance, my boy. Very well, come back tomorrow morning.'

'I want to see Major Groenewald.'

'Groenewald?' the colonel queried. 'I don't think I've heard of him. I'll make a note of your unusual case and I'll try for compensation – on medical grounds.'

'Damn you,' Pieter swore. He got up and left.

Two days later he drove across the border into Namibia. It became oven-hot and every breath seared his lungs as he drove through the baking, sparsely populated Kalahari scrubland to the one-horse town of Rooikop and then two hundred kilometres further north until he reached his destination.

It took Pieter half an hour to drive from the farm gate to the main buildings. He found the major in a long low shed surrounded by karakul sheep. About twelve black workers were shoving the sheep this way and that way. It was noisy, chaotic, stinking and very hot.

When the major saw him, he ducked fast and leaped behind a lorry. 'I've got you covered. Drop your gun,' he bellowed above the cries of the sheep.

'I don't have a gun,' Pieter shouted.

'Turn around, put your hands on your head and go back the way you came, captain,' he heard, 'or I'll blow your head off.'

Pieter sat on a stone. 'You can't run forever, major,' he called out. 'You might as well come out of there. If I wanted to kill you, sooner or later I would. You should know. You trained me.'

Grim-faced and ashen the major emerged, pushing his gun into his trouser pocket. 'Don't try anything, de Vries. I'm still very fit for my age. So they got at you, did they? It was only a matter of time before someone turned State Evidence.'

Pieter glanced anxiously at the farm workers.

'Don't worry about these guys. They don't speak a word of English. Am I under arrest? Are you with the Goldstone Commission now? Who told you where to find me?'

'Relax man,' Pieter muttered.

Groenewald had aged twenty years since Pieter last saw him. He was dressed in corduroy trousers and a khaki shirt, but he still looked like a soldier. It was something to do with his bearing and his stern, alert eyes. After a while he stood up and began to inoculate the black woolly sheep. Each time he plunged the syringe in, the sheep was pushed through a gate to the outside field. There were two gangs of helpers, but the job seemed endless. Another sheep kept appearing before him and he kept jabbing in the needle.

'You reckon you'll ever get done here, major?' Pieter asked, gazing at hundreds of black blobs milling around them.

'Don't call me major.' Groenewald looked over his shoulder. 'That's a word this lot can understand. My story is that my sugar plantation went phut in the drought, so I'm helping my brother with his karakul farm. Come on, de Vries. What the hell are you doing here, and how did you find me?' he repeated quietly.

'First I want to tell you what's happened to me in the past twelve months. I'm hoping you can shed some light on this nightmare.'

While he talked he was watching the major intently. There was no guilt on his face, only sadness.

'Most of the gang are dead because we were sold out to the terrorists. What could be worth so much to you, that you would sell out your own men?'

'Oh, for God's sake. Get off my back, de Vries. You know, some days I fear death and on others I welcome it. I can't take the tension of hiding out here waiting for some fucking terrorist to blow my brains out, or worse. It's only a matter of time before they find me.'

Pieter came to a quick decision – it wasn't Groenewald who had sold them out. So who was it?

'But Groenewald, it was the ANC who told me where to find you.'

Groenewald turned even whiter and his hands started to shake. His eyes were watering badly. He took out a handkerchief and mopped them. 'Bloody sheep give me hayfever,' he said. 'Try to save yourself. That's my advice. Leave the country. If you're looking for a private vendetta that's your own business. I'm out of all that. I served my country well for forty years and this is all the thanks I get, I eat, sleep and dream bloody black sheep.

'I'll tell you all I know – for what it's worth. I was ordered to set up a group of top agents. I chose the best men, naturally, and you were one of them. I liaised with Tony Cronjé. He's a civilian, but he's also – or rather he was – the government's front man for propaganda and so-called information. He passed all the info on to me together with the cash for running our secret agents. I know for a fact that his immediate superior was Doctor Cloete, a backbencher from a very old family. I expect you've heard of him. It was only six months ago when I learned that we were ex-SADF, working on funds provided by right-wing supporters. Without my knowledge we were all wiped off MI records. The truth is, we never even existed.

'Cronjé's newspaper, the *Sunday Echo*, was our mouthpiece, although hardly anyone knew that. The strange thing is that same newspaper now has clandestine *commie* backing. Dan Tweneni has joined him. They're setting up some sort of a model workforce. That could be where the leak occurred. Makes you think, doesn't it?'

'It's you who should think about leaving the country,' Pieter told him. 'You're an easy target here and they know where you are.'

'Africa is my home. I'll never leave. But you're young. You can adapt. You should go.'

Pieter had plenty to think as he drove back to Nelfontein. Someone wanted them out of the way and had plotted their deaths, just as they had plotted the deaths of the black leaders. '*But the killing is not yet over,*' he muttered aloud.

He was tired when he reached home in the early hours two nights later. Sam's kindness bewildered him. He brought him sandwiches and hot milk and a bag full of Liquorice Allsorts, which had been Pieter's favourite when he was a kid. Sam must have sent to the village for them. When he'd eaten them all he flung himself on to his bed and fell asleep. And dreamed . . .

He was stalking the enemy through a grove of mopani trees – all his senses on full alert, as he strained to see in the dim moonlight. There was a sound in the distance that set his skin crawling with fear – a savage, inhuman cry. He began to run faster towards the sound, racing headlong through the trees.

He found himself on the edge of a small village. The houses were white-washed, the gardens neat and colourful, the road empty. There was a blonde woman clutching a baby, and she was huddled in the doorway of a house. Her mouth was open, but no sound came.

He ran to her and shook her, but she was immobilised with terror.

'I'll look after you,' he shouted, above the savage roar that seemed to rock the foundations of the house. He blundered in, longing for a gun. He saw a figure lying on the floor covered in sacks and the groaning was coming from it.

Instinctively he knew that this was the enemy and he must destroy it, but when he rolled the figure on to its back, he saw that its face had been sliced off clean, leaving the bare bone, but its eyes gleamed with hatred. Was it black or white? The figure rose up, towering over him, laughing crazily. All the evil in the world was shining in those terrible eyes.

He saw a pile of weapons on the ground. Grabbing a rifle he tried to shoot the apparition, but the gun jammed. And so did the next one. The thing laughed and fled. Pieter followed, but he could not keep up. He ran until he was dropping with exhaustion. Then panic surged as he remembered the woman he had left alone and unprotected. He began to run back, using every ounce of strength he had left, but he arrived too late. She was dead and so was her baby and there was no one left alive in the village.

He knew then that the Volk were in mortal danger, and that only he was left to kill the enemy. He was unarmed and alone and he no longer knew who the enemy was. He began to scream.

He woke to find Sam bending over him, wiping his face with a damp cloth.

Chapter 55

———◆———

Tony had one sure-fire method of dealing with opposition, Dan discovered. If it resists, buy it. Whatever he needed was gobbled up and became part of the group, adding more and still more workers to the list of men and women under Dan's care.

Dan became very uneasy. He sensed that something was horribly wrong, but what? Why was Tony in such a rush to grab everything? Or was this how tycoons operated? All the workers were paying part of their wages into the pension, insurance, health and educational funds, but so far the only real concrete evidence of new benefits were the sports fields under construction. Early days he told himself. Tony had some crazy ideas about what he could do for the workers. Many of them were totally unrealistic. 'We can't make promises if we're not sure we can deliver the goods,' Dan told Tony time and again. Sometimes they fought bitterly. In particular, they fought over the car Tony gave Dan for his exclusive use. It was a long, sleek, stretch limousine, but at least it was owned by the company and that was some small comfort. Next they fought about the house Tony offered him. It was a graceful old mansion with a pool and several old oak trees set amongst spacious lawns in Parktown. 'It's totally unsuitable,' Dan had exploded. 'Besides, blacks are not allowed to live around these parts – or had you forgotten?'

'Not yet, but the laws are changing and this one will change very soon. Meantime, I've got special dispensation for you. No problem!'

'Well, it's a problem for me. I feel like a sell-out.'

'But it's available and it's empty, and I need one of my managers to live in it,' Tony had argued. 'I need you to be near the office and I have no other accommodation available.'

Dan went back to his mentor in the party to ask his advice.

'Perhaps it's a good idea to show our people the fruits of success and start breaking down residential segregation,' he said after some thought. 'Yes, it makes sense.'

Dan was on-site in Soweto, with a team of architects and builders, discussing plans for low-cost, two-roomed homes when a policeman raced up on a motorbike and paused long enough to tell him that two of their buses had been trapped in Soweto and set alight. The drivers had been stabbed several times and a queue of pedestrians waiting at the bus stop had been machine gunned by one of the gangsters, no doubt to discourage them from catching buses instead of taxis.

It was like something out of a war movie, Dan saw when he arrived at the scene. He felt a surge of murderous fury as he saw kids lying groaning on the ground. The police were trying to get statements from witnesses, but no one would talk. It was always the same, Dan thought gritting his teeth. He was sure it was Njoli's outfit. He had the men and the arms and enough muscle to ensure that no one split on him. He could sense the crowd's frustration. They were looking for a scapegoat and they began to pelt stones at four passing Zulu youths.

'Hey, stop that! It's nothing to do with them,' he heard a girl shout. He saw the back of a white coat and black hair tumbling forward. It was Judy Turner, the American doctor, and she was bent over the wounded giving them first aid. The Zulus and the Sothos were turning on each other, emotions flaring, reason fleeing. Out came the sticks and stones and moments later a mob of fighting people was threatening to trample the casualties underfoot.

'Somebody help me!' she yelled, as she struggled to drag a man to the shelter of a wall.

At that moment, riot police and the ambulances raced round the corner. The rioters took to their heels and Judy supervised the victims' transfer on to stretchers.

'Don't ever do that again,' Dan said, grabbing her arm. 'You're lucky to be alive. In future, if they start fighting get out of the way.'

'And leave these poor people to be murdered? Are you crazy or something?'

'No, I just have my priorities in order,' he said.

She looked at him contemptuously. 'Self-survival?' she sneered.

He felt like laughing at her, or crying – he wasn't sure which. She was so beautiful and so brave, so fired with the American dream of honour and helping the underdog. She was not cowed, or sullen, or afraid to speak her mind, and she stuck out in Soweto like a lily in a bog. She was vulnerable, too, for she had never seen pointless cruelty, she had never been made to feel second-class, she'd never been beaten up, no one had ever scared her badly, and she knew next to nothing about evil. She was naive and vulnerable and he loved her for this. She badly needed protecting. There and then he voted himself the best person to do it on a permanent basis. The strength of his determination surprised him, for he knew that he was going to marry her, and soon, too. As for Judy, he'd have to break it to her gently.

'*Your* survival, you goose,' he laughed. 'You're far too pretty to get lost in a riot. It's lucky for me I bumped into you. I need help. You see, I'm trying to set a guideline for minimum working benefits on a long-term basis. I know what men need, but when it comes to womenpower I'm quite lost. Can you spare me a few evenings?'

'If it's serious I guess I'll have to,' she said.

He almost felt sorry for her. She never stood a chance. A month later they were married at the St Saviour's church in Soweto. The reception was held at their Parktown home.

*

'Why are you so on edge?' Judy asked him a few weeks later. 'I've never known anyone sleep so lightly, and why the gun? Are you expecting something specific or have you always been this nervous?'

'I told you before we married that someone might be after me.'

She sighed. 'Is it for real, or is this what Soweto does to people? Perhaps you've seen too much horror, experienced too much. If you were an aircraft I'd say you had metal fatigue.'

She didn't believe him. Perhaps that was a good thing. Later that night, Dan heard a sound in the garden and he walked on to the balcony, his hand-gun in his dressing-gown pocket. What a lovely night. An African owl was hooting from a larch tree, the full moon was shining over the garden, there was a scent of jasmine and new-mown grass. He might as well be on another planet, Soweto seemed so far away. Yet it was only a short drive to get there. Dan sat outside enjoying the ambience from the gracious old house and the trees that seemed to be telling him something, and the cat he saw gliding stealthily across the lawn. Maybe one day he and Judy would have a place like this that wasn't on loan from Tony.

Judy got up at five and found him leaning over the balustrade gazing at the dawn.

'Same dawn,' he said with an awkward grin. 'Everything else is much improved. Will it hurt badly when we leave here? Could you go back to a Soweto shack after this?'

'As long as I'm with you I won't even notice,' she said staunchly. She put her arms around his neck and hugged him close, pushing her open mouth on his, caressing his lips with her tongue. 'Come back to bed,' she said.

'I have a soccer match this afternoon. Besides, I want to talk. I know there's something wrong. My instinct is always right. I should have listened to it long ago. Something stinks at head office, but I'm not clued up enough to work it out. That bastard Tony is up to something. I feel it and I sense it. All this,' he gestured at the house and the garden, 'is to anchor me. I don't know what he wants, but he wants something.'

'You'll find out,' she murmured. She moved her hips against his, and tightened her grip around his neck. To hell with soccer, he thought as he carried her back to their bed. Later, Judy told him that she was pregnant.

The following Monday, Dan was invited to coffee in the boardroom at ten. After a minimum of small talk, Tony came to the point. That was his style.

'The City Hypermarket chain would make a most welcome addition to our group,' he said.

'Haven't we got enough companies to worry about?'

'That's not the point.'

'So what is the point?'

Tony looked at him speculatively. 'Their pension fund. It controls millions because it grew out of the old Transvaal Trading and Supply Company, established almost a century ago. If we got hold of that pension fund we could immediately provide better benefits. Besides, the company has a huge cash base, no debts, it owns warehouses situated on prime land. The warehouses could be moved out of town, and the sites sold for a fortune.'

'So why doesn't their management do that?'

'Their management consists of a board of old fuddy-duddies who don't want any hassles. The company makes profits and performs a service – so why should they worry? I made them an offer and they laughed at me.'

'So that's it then.'

'That's not *it* at all. You, with your union contacts, will bring their workers and managers out on strike while our workers boycott the stores.'

Dan gasped. 'That's not only immoral, it's illegal. I'm amazed you have the gall to suggest such a campaign.'

'Why? What's the matter with you? You wanted to get into private enterprise. Well, learn how it goes. It's a jungle out there. You should know all about the jungle. Let me explain . . . capital is a management tool and so is labour. This is just a slightly more imaginative way of using our tools.'

'It's crooked and I'll have nothing to do with it.'

'But, Dan, just think. The soccer fields are almost ready, the workers are thrilled with their new benefits. Their homes are being built, their pensions are ensured, their kids' educations catered for. If we don't initiate a new welfare deal, do you think anyone else ever will?'

'So what's to stop us?' Dan asked carefully.

'Only your pompous attitude. If you don't go along with me, I'll stop everything right now. I'll just announce that the whole idea was untenable because of the attitude of a certain man. That won't do your career any good.'

'That's a lie.'

'Well, who are businessmen going to believe? You or me?'

Dan seemed to be trapped. What had his mentor said? 'You can't afford to taint your image, Dan. Your political career would be finished.'

After a few nights of indecision, Dan decided to go along with Tony. Far more was at stake than his group and his labour. Once the scheme was seen to be working, all overseas companies wishing to invest in South Africa would be required to initiate similar welfare schemes. Just for once in his life, Dan decided, he would fight dirty. Later, when he'd won, he could clean up his act.

The resulting strikes and unrest persuaded City's management to take the easy route to retirement and sell out. The massive pension fund that Tony coveted was merged with their own. Only Dan suffered. He wasn't sure whether or not he'd broken any laws, but he'd fallen in his own estimation. Tony had caught him out and used him and he felt dirty and apprehensive. That bastard would stop at nothing.

Midnight in Parktown. The garden by moonlight was a wonder

of delicate fragrances and flowers of frail beauty. The trees were so stately and so still. There was a deep pond where frogs croaked under the hanging fronds of a willow tree. Dan loved this spot and had moved a bench there. A laughing dove had made a precarious nest in the branches overhead and he'd put some wire round the trunk to stop the neighbours' cat from climbing up. Dan was sitting there listening to the comforting cooing of the dove sitting on her nest. She was doing her best to keep her young safe, but an African owl was also keeping a careful eye on the nest. Dan had seen it quite a few times. Since learning that Judy was pregnant, Dan had become neurotic about protection and security, not only for himself, but for all the workers in his group.

Tonight he could not sleep. He sat on the bench, leaning against the tree, listening to the dikkops and the nightjars and the African owl that was sneaking up for the baby doves under cover of darkness. Something was bugging the hell out of him, but he wasn't sure what it was. A sort of frenzied fear was forming in his guts rather than his head. What was it? How come Tony had spent most of the past two months overseas? His business was here, wasn't it? How come he'd been so determined to grab a defunct offshore mining operation in Namibia? Perhaps he should take his problems to the ANC. But what if he were wrong?

He heard a voice and his skin crawled. 'Put your hands up. Right up. Over the branch. That's right.' Dazed with surprise and fearing that Judy might come outside, Dan stood with his hands raised and felt his gun being removed from his pocket.

'Before I kill you, I want to tell you a few things you should know, Dan. The man you're working for, Tony Cronjé, put your name on the list of those to be "removed". It was back at the time when you were opposing him over the closure of MacGregor's. He helped to create the force that was supposed to remove you – and others. Later, when our so-called government opted out, Tony sold this force out to you lot. So here we are, programmed to kill each other. I have you on my list and you have me on your list.

'I've been having some very interesting talks with Doctor Cloete. It seems that Tony was a front for certain wealthy, far-right individuals. He himself is not all that rich, but he spends lavishly. He's been putting the cash from the various pension funds into his company to keep going. The cash that should have been generated by his own group has been transferred overseas, bit by bit, through African mining companies and the London Stock Exchange. It would take me all night to explain the scams he's been up to.

'The point is, there will be no pensions left or funding for houses if someone doesn't stop Tony. Did you know he's marrying Liza next week? Everyone knew except me.'

'Yes.'

'Then they're leaving. Your precious workers can kiss goodbye to their security, so don't expect a hero's funeral.'

Dan frowned and shivered. There was a burning place in the middle of his shoulder blades right where he was expecting to be shot.

Pieter chuckled. ''Bye, Dan. You should have killed me when you had the chance. But you just couldn't do it, could you?'

Dan waited a split second. Jesus! Piet was stringing it out. Holding his breath, he made a sudden swift soccer dive into the pond. There were no shots. Feeling puzzled, he surfaced cautiously amongst the lily leaves and black slime and waited. No one was there.

Chapter 56

———————————◆———————————

At last she had made it . . . just as she had planned all those years ago when she was foraging in Johannesburg's refuse bins for something to eat – or sell. But only Liza knew the real cost of her success – nights of despair and poignant dreams of Pieter. 'Damn him,' she whispered under her breath.

She stood in front of her open wardrobe, fingering the beautiful lace of her wedding gown, with hundreds of tiny pearls sewn into it. The morning sunbeams shone lustrously around her face, playing with glints in her dark hair and lighting her wideset, wistful eyes. She was young and very beautiful, but the success she had fought for so bitterly was bitter-sweet and she felt unfulfilled.

Feeling restless and dissatisfied, she flung open her safe and examined the fabulous diamond necklace Tony had given her. A scent of honeysuckle came through the open door and suddenly she was transported back to the army camp in Mozambique. Tears began to trickle down her cheeks. She flung the necklace back and locked the safe.

There was a buzz on the portable telephone. It was Tony's housekeeper. Would she come and check the chapel and the final wedding arrangements? Liza sighed with relief – leisure time was danger time.

'I'll be ten minutes,' she said. She walked on to the front stoep that ran the length of the newly built lodge. It stood on a ridge overlooking the dam where once Gran's cottage had stood. The old chimney was still sticking out of the water and a heron had made its nest there. Beyond the dam, the hills and valleys of the game farm stretched to the horizon. How beautiful it was this morning with a hazy violet glow in the valleys and the sunlight sparkling on the dew-drenched grass. Scores of weaver birds twittered around the dam and a herd of newly acquired nyala buck were grazing by the calm water where flamingos and ibis waded in the shallows. They had bought thousands of tiny minnows from the State hatcheries to attract the birdlife to the dam.

Her guests, making up the bride's group, were staying with her at Nyala Lodge and they would be arriving soon. Tony was flying them up in relays. Most of the TV crew would be coming as well as the staff of the *Echo*. Ed would be there, too, and Gran.

Sauntering along the stoep to the dining room, she stood blinking for a few seconds, unable to see into the shadowy room after the blinding sunlight. A buffet lunch would be served from a central stone table which was already massed with flowers. Tonight her guests would be transported to the old boma which had been rebuilt to accommodate at least a hundred people. She had planned a cocktail party in the bush, with caviar and smoked salmon and ice-cold champagne. They would be entertained by Zulu dancers and singers and who knew what wild creatures might pass by. It would be madly different and very exciting.

Liza gazed at herself in the mirror. Nowadays her hair fell straight to her shoulders and she was slimmer than ever. She knew that she looked striking in her new safari outfit of olive green T-shirt and khaki shorts – *but who cared anyway?* Melancholy was settling in. She smoothed her hair behind her ears and fingered her new drop-emerald earrings. 'Get moving, Liza,' she whispered. The helicopter pad was right behind the lodge, and the pilot was waiting for her. She climbed into the bubble-like craft and they soared over the veld.

Their pilot flew her low over the bush so they could see the elephant herd moving through the mopani trees towards the marula grove near the boma. The herd would get drunk on the alcoholic marula fruit tonight. Liza had a moment of misgiving wondering if the game warden should have allowed the herd to move so close to the homestead with so many guests wandering around. She would speak to him about it. She could see their pride of lions stalking a buck. Tony was so proud of those lions which he had purchased at great cost from a Zimbabwe game farm. The buck were looking sleek, the grass was dry, but not badly so, and everything was just perfect.

Well, almost everything. At moments like this love seemed a small price to pay for her marvellous lifestyle, and the fawning of the locals, who had once cast her out so cruelly. They had all begged her for invitations to the wedding, but there was no room for them. Dozens of far more important people were being flown up from Johannesburg. Fifty of Tony's friends were staying at the *Jacana Lodge* tonight, the remainder would arrive tomorrow in time for the wedding. She would marry Tony in the morning in Impala Lodge which had been converted into a chapel. The reception would last for most of the afternoon, and they would fly to Johannesburg in Tony's private jet to spend a night at the penthouse suite of the Mayfair hotel in Johannesburg, an important part of her triumph, then on to the Seychelles to join a chartered yacht, anchored off Mahé, for their scuba-diving honeymoon.

The old homestead had been redecorated, except for the wing where Tony's crazy step-mother was incarcerated with her sedatives and her grim-faced nurses. Everything was gleaming – the yellow-wood tables, huge copper bowls full of strelitzias and roses, the beautiful old tiles, for she had flung out all the carpets. There was space and lightness and several beautiful old paintings hung on the plain white walls. The Zulu staff lined up for inspection and Liza made some last-minute changes to the flowers. Five minutes later she was driving her jeep towards the boma by the river.

She heard shouts in the distance as she passed the latrines in the new camping site. Strange! She braked, reversed and drove into the camp which had been constructed around a baobab tree overlooking a river. A female warthog, surrounded by six young, was standing guard outside a latrine door. She parked and ran towards the angry beast. 'Shoo,' she yelled, but the warthog bared its teeth and charged the door with its tusk.

Liza picked up a stone and hurled it at the warthog and it turned towards her, grunting and bewildered. Then the latrine door crashed open and Ed rushed between her and the angry mother, brandishing a stick. The warthog ran off, its squealing young in a straight row behind, tails curled over their backs.

'I'm touched by your bravery, Ed,' Liza said when she could stop laughing. 'As it happens she's quite tame. You must have frightened her with your flashgun. Nevertheless, I'm impressed. I didn't know you'd arrived.'

'Sometimes you amaze me, Liza,' Ed said, straightening his clothes and trying to recover his dignity.

What a kind face he had, Liza thought. What a shame he's so lonely. She'd often seen girls flirting with him, but he was so wary of the female sex. He put them off with his dour manner. Yet he was good-looking with his deep-set blue eyes, his stern roman nose, clearcut features, and his short wiry black hair. He was tall and manly and highly intelligent, with a tremendous sense of humour. Talented, too. Recently, a London publishing house had accepted his half-written manuscript for a novel. Ed deserves the best, she thought. One day some lovely girl will realise what a treasure she has.

'What a tough little Boer maiden you are,' he was saying. 'You should be marrying a pioneer, or a farmer, not that creep, Tony. You're made for the bush, despite your sophistication.'

That was the last straw. All Liza's defences crumbled. 'Oh, how I wish I was,' she wailed. 'Pieter and I grew up together on this very farm,' she said. 'He taught me all I know about the bush.' She broke off. This was not the time to think about Pieter. 'What are you doing in the camping site?'

'First I was looking for you,' Ed said. 'Then I tried to

photograph that damn pig and it chased me here ... Oh God, Liza. You don't look like a happy bride should. Call the damn thing off.'

'It's not a pig, it's a warthog.'

'Okay, warthog.'

'Did you let off a flash gun in her face?'

'Yes.' He glared at her defiantly. 'The shot was so right, but the shadows were so wrong.'

'Then it serves you right. She was frightened for her babies. Shame on you!'

'Liza, listen to me. I don't usually bore you, but there's something I want you to know. I love you. I know you don't feel much more than friendship for me, but I'll always be around should you need me. I don't think I could ever express exactly how I feel for you, it would sound so sloppy.'

Liza turned her back on Ed and blinked hard. She was so fond of him, but her love was reserved for Pieter. Tony represented material success and the destruction of her miserable self-image. So where did fondness figure? 'You are my very best friend,' she whispered. 'You always will be. Oh, Ed.' Blinded by tears she groped towards him, winding her arms tightly round his neck. 'It's too late. I can't cancel now. All these people ... all this expense ... and anyway, the priest is flying all the way from Johannesburg.'

'I've heard better reasons for getting married. Silly Liza. He can fly all the way back again. Pretend you're ill. You can call it off later when the guests have left. Rather a day of embarrassment than a lifetime stuck with Tony.'

'He's not so bad,' she whispered, wiping her tears on her T-shirt. 'You don't understand him.'

'The trouble is, *I* do, but *you* don't,' Ed said morosely.

Liza drove Ed to Nyala Lodge and on impulse turned towards the village. She would go and see Gran, she decided. Ed had unnerved her.

Half an hour later, she found Gran staring at herself in the mirror, a look of nervousness about her that Liza had never seen before. Her hair had been blued and waved and she was trying on her new dress for the wedding.

'There's something wrong here,' Gran said, hitching the skirt this way and that way.

'It's too long, I think.' Liza knelt down, groped for the pin cushion and began to pin up the hem. The dress was of brown silk. It was too severe for Gran, for it heightened the pallor of her skin and the scantiness of her white hair. She's like a little sparrow, Liza thought with a surge of love.

'I wish I were your real granddaughter, but I feel as if I am,' she said.

Gran flushed. 'So do I, Liza. We should try to put the past behind us. You've had a bad start – I think I said this to you before – you don't have to compound the error.'

'Several bad starts,' Liza said.

'That's no reason to shut love out of your life as you are doing, my girl. You're fooling no one but yourself. Even I have had my share of happiness. My goodness, when I met my husband, I thought he was the most handsome man anyone could wish for. We were picking apples . . .'

Liza sighed. When Gran got that faraway look in her eyes you could sit and listen for hours and she always told the same stories. She'd heard them so often. Feeling strangely protective and loving, she sat on the floor with her legs crossed and listened to Gran reliving her past. Then Gran said out of the blue:

'There's only one man I've ever seen who could hold the candle to my husband and that's young Pieter de Vries. I saw him in the village yesterday and I thought to myself . . .' But by this time Liza was halfway down to the gate.

'Oh, I hate you. How I hate you,' Liza muttered under her breath as she raced up the staircase to the loft and flung open Pieter's door.

A bulge in the bed rocked out of it. Suddenly Pieter was

crouched behind a chair and his gun was pointing straight at her.

He straightened up looking pale and taut. 'I nearly shot you.'

'You lied to me, you bastard!' she snarled, ignoring the gun. 'You said you'd been sacked, but you were still in Military Intelligence. You pretended to love me because you wanted to spy on me, and question me, and afterwards you sent your thugs to kill me.' The anger was fading from her tone and she struggled to maintain it. 'Did you think I was dead? *Did you?* Sorry to disappoint you. Loving you is the worst thing that could ever have happened to me, you lousy bastard!'

Now her anger was seeping away. She had been longing for a fight, but his eyes were so full of misery. She hesitated, standing just inside the doorway, wondering where to go from here. Pieter flung himself on the bed and lay with his back turned staring at the wall.

She shut the door and walked to the bedside and stood there peering at him. 'You never loved me. You never wrote, or bothered to come and see how I was. Look at you. You can't even face me. You won't even look at me. Well, you shall, you shall.' She flung herself on him and began to punch his shoulder and his back.

'Hey ... Hey ...' He twisted, lithe and fast as a snake, gripped her wrists too hard and held them over her head. 'Just what do you think you're doing?'

'Making you notice me ...' she gasped. 'I will not be ignored by you ...'

She lunged out with her foot, catching him on the shin. Pieter swore and pushed her back on to the bed. Moments later his heavy body was pinning hers down. When she looked up into his eyes she saw that he was crying. It was the most shattering experience. Her Pieter, the toughest, calmest, strongest guy in the world was crying.

'Of course I love you,' he told her, 'but don't let that ruin your life. The truth is, I never stopped loving you. Not ever, but it took me a long time to come to terms with that. I never tried to kill you and neither did anyone else in our outfit. If they had tried you would be dead – believe me.'

'Someone tried.'

'Come on, Liza! Look at you – you are helpless, yet you're alive. No one tried, but perhaps someone wanted to frighten you, or make you think that I would harm you. Yes, I can see that makes sense to you. I told you before, you're such a child. Why did you come here? What's the point, since you're about to marry Cronjé? You belong to him, don't you? From what I hear, he's bought you lock, stock and barrel. Does he fuck well? Does he make you cry out? Do you come? Is it as good as what we had?'

Suddenly his fingers were boring into her shoulder and she cried out with pain. She slapped him hard. 'Don't hurt me.'

'Answer me,' he said, thrusting his hand into her crotch. 'Does he know you're here?'

Anger and lust were equally balanced. She squirmed and pulled his face down on hers, trying to kiss him, but he pushed his head back.

'I'm not kissing Tony's girl.'

'It's not like that,' she admitted reluctantly. 'He respects me too much,' she muttered. 'We're waiting until we're married.'

'Oh!' He burst out laughing, but it was a cruel laugh. 'Good God. Am I supposed to believe that?' He pushed his tongue into his cheek and wiggled it up and down – a vulgar gesture which she had always hated.

Pushing him aside, she sat up and rubbed her wrists. 'You've changed. You're like a skeleton. To answer your question, I'm sure I'll come when I'm married to Tony. It will be thrilling and I'll be able to put you behind me forever.'

His eyes were questioning, his face twisted with jealousy. Suddenly he changed. Like a light being switched off, his passion and anger were gone.

'I was going to kill that bastard, but if you want him you can have him. Let's see your ring. Hm,' he said examining the huge diamond. 'It's ugly, pretentious, and too heavy for your finger.'

She took it off slowly and put it in her pocket. 'I'm not going to marry Tony,' she said. 'I've been worrying about it for days, but now I know I can't. You see, I still love you. I've been waiting for you for years. I should have more pride.' There was fear and resignation in her voice. She crumpled into a chair and buried her head in her hands. She tried to speak, but could not. After a while she cleared her throat.

'Don't be upset. I don't like it when you're upset,' he said. 'But I'm not on the list of available bridegrooms. I see my life as being over, or almost over.'

'That's ridiculous.' She began to shudder. She felt shivery cold all over. 'Pieter,' she said softly, trying to calm him. 'Don't talk like that.'

'Think of it this way – the person that you loved no longer exists. There's only an empty husk left. The juice … the essence of life … that's all gone.'

Something about his tone of voice frightened her. She had never heard him talk like this. She stiffened, longing to scream, but fighting for her self control. 'Where have you been all this year?'

He looked so lost and hurt and she longed to comfort him, but how could she?

'Sorry – it's classified.'

'Everything's always bloody classified. You use that to pull the wool over my eyes.'

'No, I don't.'

How gaunt he looked. His green eyes were bleak, his face might have been sculpted out of stone. All her anger was sliding away. *He is the sun of my life and he is leaving me.* The thought was like ice crystals settling around her. 'I love you,' she blurted out. 'Don't throw me away.'

'Oh God, Liza. What a fucking mess.' He grabbed hold of her and buried his head on her shoulder. 'I love you, too. It's so much more than that. You are the only good thing that ever happened to me. You're special.'

She ran her fingers through his hair, feeling the strong neck she loved so much, and smelling the familiar smell of him, and the feeling of his beard against her cheeks. She closed her eyes and hung on tightly, trying to banish the strangest sensation that this might be the last time they loved, that it might have to last a lifetime.

She stood up and took off her clothes. His eyes had always glowed with passion, but now it was as if they were turned inwards to some hell he carried inside him. Leaning over him she unbuttoned his shirt and lay beside him, pushing her body hard against his, feeling his strong, hairy chest against her bare breasts. He pushed his arms around her and held her close.

At last his passion surged. She leaned over him and kissed his lips tenderly, moving her mouth over his neck and his chest and stroking his smooth white belly. She felt him quiver and relax when her mouth enclosed his penis. She could feel it quivering and stirring, softly growing. He closed his eyes and his mouth half opened as he sighed. 'I love you,' he whispered.

She sat over him, gently lowering herself on to him, feeling his penis rearing and pulsating inside her, swaying her hips languidly, urging him on . . . and on . . .

Suddenly his arms were pulling her down on to him until she lay over him. 'Kiss me,' he murmured. His hands were pressing down on her buttocks, as he swayed his hips and pulled her harder on to him, moving her backwards and forwards while his tongue caressed her mouth. Pleasure rose and became unbearable ecstasy as they made love with an intensity of feeling she had never before known.

After they came they lay silent and close for a long time. She could feel him shuddering . . . great waves of shudders that moved through him, convulsing him, and flowing out again.

'That was good stuff,' he murmured eventually. 'Good stuff. Whoever gets you, Liza, will be a very lucky man. Don't let it be Tony.'

'What a cruel thing to say. You were always cruel. You – it's you who will get me. Listen to me, damn you. You are the only man for me.'

He sighed. 'No, Liza. Something happened in Mozambique. Something . . . I don't know how to explain.'

She waited, but he turned away towards the wall. 'Please tell me,' she whispered.

He shuddered. Then he said. 'I was walking through the bush. It was noon. Hot . . . Jesus, it was hot. I was feeling pretty good and I was unarmed. The rest of them were back there . . . on a hill . . . having a rest. Then this smell came . . . suddenly . . . I suppose the wind changed. I went on and what I saw then made me feel so low. I wanted to dig a hole and crawl into it and never come out. I knew then that I wasn't on God's side. And with that knowledge I felt utterly lost. At that moment I realised then that I had based my life on a faulty premise. I mean, I'd got to think of blacks as vermin – better off dead.'

'So what was it? Please tell me. I must understand you.'

'Every child in the village had been brought there and put to death. They were not shot, you understand. I can't tell you . . .'

She wrapped her arms around him, longing to heal him.

'I can't live with myself.'

'No . . . Don't say that. We were at war. Undeclared, but real just the same. You only did what you were ordered to do.'

Now she was frightened – truly frightened. Something made her realise that Pieter had been dealt a mortal blow.

'Liza, I can't cope with this thing – it's too heavy for me. There's something I must do, but I can't find the courage to do it.

'You know something, Liza. There's only three ways someone like me can end up: in an asylum, or prison, or picking up odd jobs around the docks. I don't fancy any of those fates.'

'Please don't talk like this! You're just depressed. I'm going to break off the engagement tonight. I'll tell the guests I'm ill. We'll go away together. We'll start again, perhaps in Mozambique. You'd like that wouldn't you? Do you remember telling me you'd go back there one day and rebuild part of what was destroyed. That's a fine dream. We'll do it together.' She babbled on, trying to fill him with her courage, trying to reach him.

'Did you mean what you said – about you and Tony – that you've never . . .'

'Yes, I swear it.'

Pieter laughed cruelly. 'That's because he's still having it off with his Swedish secretary. That's why she's there – didn't you know? In Tony's world people perform certain functions for him and they're all dispensable. I wonder what he wants out of you?'

Moving stiffly, like an old man, he moved to the cupboard at the end of the room and took out an envelope. 'Perhaps this has something to do with it,' he said, tossing it on the bed.

The envelope was addressed to her, as if Pieter had intended to post it. She opened it curiously.

'I've been in Mozambique,' Pieter was saying. 'There's a hell of a scam going on with aid from Britain and the States. I wanted to clean up a part of it.

'I had heard through my intelligence sources that an ex-Mozambique Portuguese, a de Novrega, was moving a lot of the stolen aid into the neighbouring territory. On a routine check I found local police had a very detailed file on an Emile de Novrega, a Portuguese from Mozambique, who was a student activist at one of our student universities more than twenty years ago. De Novrega is not a common name, and I went to the family's old plantations in Mozambique to see if I could gain any information that would help me. As it turned out Emile was not the man I was looking for, but to cap a long story short, I got hold of these certificates . . . a marriage certificate between a certain Eleanor Christie, and Emile de Novrega. Then the birth certificate of their daughter, Elisabete Maria, their divorce papers and later Emile's death certificate. This must be Tony's stepmother. There can't be two women named Eleanor Maria Christie, born in Nelfontein in 1948.

'The locals who were still at the plantation told me that Emile had been married and had sent his little daughter, Elisabete to his divorced wife for safety about a year before the revolution. That child would have been the same age as you, and I know for a fact that Eleanor hoards all the news clippings of your articles and stories about you and constantly watches video tapes of your TV programmes. Take these and confront Eleanor. Force her to tell you the truth. I'll see you later.'

'Promise?'

'Promise!'

Liza felt so shocked she could hardly think or stand. She was shaking violently and it was difficult to put on her clothes. Her mind seemed blurred and out of focus, like a camera after a hard knock. She hesitated in the doorway wanting to express her thanks, but not knowing how to begin.

Chapter 57

———◆———

Could Eleanor be her mother? The thought was shocking and abhorrent to her. She kept trying to make sense out of it as she sped across the game park to the Lodge.

She had never been into Eleanor's private wing, but the passage door was unlocked. As she walked through the antiseptic corridors she noted the lack of any comfort. She would change that, she decided.

Eleanor was sitting on a divan in her sitting room, her eyes fixed on the TV screen. She did not look up as Liza entered. For a few moments Liza stood staring longingly at her. Was this woman her very own mother? Oh, how she had longed for this moment.

Eleanor was dressed in a mini skirt of pale pink and a pink silk blouse with a deep V-neckline. Her hair had turned completely white and the pink bow on her head looked absurd. She was so thin, almost emaciated, like a stick insect. Her blue eyes were sunk into her head and there were deep shadows under them.

'Go away! I don't want a sedative, nurse,' she said crossly. 'I want to watch the video. This is my Liza, isn't she lovely, and so brave . . . You see, she takes after her father.'

'I'm not your nurse. I'm Liza, your daughter.'

Eleanor dropped the remote controller and half turned. She looked afraid. 'Liza?' she queried. 'I knew you'd come. I've been waiting for you for such a long time.' She began to shake badly as tears zig-zagged down her eroded cheeks.

'You could have told me who I was.' Liza clasped Eleanor's cold hands in hers. "Please don't be afraid. From now on I'm going to look after you.' She put her hand on Eleanor's shoulder. She was just skin and bone. Liza felt cheated. The moment seemed to have no meaning, there was no instantaneous bonding, only a strong feeling of pity and incredulity.

'I have been afraid for a very long time, but I've decided to borrow some of your courage. I'm not going to be a coward any longer.'

She looked up laughing craftily and Liza went cold with fright. Was Tony really evil? Or was Eleanor crazy?

'I've been tricking them,' she whispered, pointing towards the nurses' room. 'They're not real nurses, they're Tony's guards. He keeps me locked up and fuddled with tranquillisers because he's afraid of what I might say. A few words from me can destroy Tony. I've told him that we will go to the gallows together before I'll let him marry you. He has destroyed me, but he will never harm you.'

Oh God! Help this woman, Liza prayed. I'll get her the best psychiatrists. She won't stay locked up here by herself. Somehow I'll get her better. 'Perhaps you'd feel better if you took that sedative,' Liza said gently. 'Don't upset yourself.'

'Why not? I have a right to be upset. I have a great deal to tell you, but it will wait a few days longer. I'll come to your dinner tonight, but what shall I wear? It has to be something very striking. Now let me see . . .?' She stood up and rifled through her wardrobe.

Liza felt very sad. 'I must go now, Eleanor,' she said. 'You and I are going to become very close, I promise. I shall look after you. There's just one thing I must know now – does Tony know who I am?'

'Of course he does. He's after your fortune. After all, you are an heiress, my dear. Your father's family were very wealthy in Portugal as well as Mozambique. You didn't think he was after you, did you? He only likes blondes. As for you looking after me, I think it's time someone cared for *you*. I intend to expose

Tony for what he is and I shall do it tonight at dinner.'

Liza crept out feeling totally confused.

'I must pull myself together,' Liza whispered. She could hear cars driving into the car park outside. 'God help me, I have so many problems I don't know which one to tackle first.' Uppermost in her mind was Pieter. Everything else seemed trivial in the face of his terrible trauma. 'I must go to him,' she told herself.

But then Liza saw Dan arrive. She knew how much Dan hated the stretch limousine Tony had forced on him, so she was not surprised to see him and Judy climb out of an old jeep. He stood frowning at her, as if undecided. He looked so sad – why? – and his eyes were brimming with compassion. She waved and called out: 'You're in the wrong camp. Follow me,' as she ran to her jeep.

Liza liked Judy, but today something was wrong. Icy silence prevailed despite her efforts at small talk as she showed them around the Nyala camp and settled them into their cabin overlooking the dam.

'I thought . . . well, never mind, but I want you to know that I kept you the best chalet,' she said.

Dan pressed his lips together. 'Stay here, Judy,' he said. 'I'll have a word with Liza.'

Dan plunged straight into his problem. 'Liza, I'm sorry to do this to you,' he said, putting his arm around her and hugging her close, 'but I want you to know that I've applied for a court order to prevent Tony from leaving the country. Despite my feelings for you, I can't allow him to get away with what he's done.'

I can take it, Liza thought. This and whatever else the day has in store for me. I'm tough, aren't I? If only my damned headache would go away.

'Come to my room, Dan. We can talk there. Look! It's there where the curtains are blowing out. Bring Judy. She does know, doesn't she? I felt her anger.'

Dan hesitated. 'Okay. I'll be right over.'

She just had time to swallow two headache pills and order tea before they arrived.

Judy was a quiet woman, but it seemed that she had elected to do the talking. She kept straightening her shoulders and pushing herself erect, as if her heavy burden was too much for her. It was very still in the room, even the birds were drugged by the afternoon torpor. Judy looked away from her, gazing steadfastly through the open door towards the dam. 'Tony is a criminal,' she said. 'He should be behind bars where we intend to put him.'

'I think I should tell you that I have decided not to marry Tony. This might put you more at ease. I'll make the announcement tonight and beg your forgiveness for wasting your time. One of the reasons is that I've discovered I still love Pieter. Another is that Eleanor is my mother. I've just found out.'

Dan hugged her tightly. 'You can count on our support, Liza.'

'Let's get this over and done with.' Judy's voice had acquired a new firmness, Liza noticed.

'He has used Dan. This could mean the end of Dan's career. Dan persuaded Tony's workers – all ten thousand of them to part with a considerable part of their wages – for pensions, insurance, housing pools, education . . . well, you probably know what for. But Tony's had his hands in the piggy bank . . . I want to kill the bastard.' She broke off with a sob.

Dan took over. 'My career is not as important as their savings. Tony has used the pension fund to buy assets which have not been transferred to the fund's accounts. There's so much more. Somehow Pieter discovered this and many other scams and he let me know. I contacted the fraud squad, but they are totally snowed under. They are working through a backlog of corruption on a grand scale. It's part of our lives. D'you know what Myers told me: there are 22,800 allegations of economic crime involving some R5 billion which the police can't begin to clear up. Everyone's trying to move assets out of the country. Even the bureaucracy has become corrupt – and why? Because the original system was corrupt. It will take a decade to clean up this economic sewer. Once Tony skips the country it's too late to save the funds. I'm going to stop him from leaving if I have to kill him with my bare hands, Liza.' He stood up and took Judy's hand. 'Let's go,' he said to Judy.

'I just wanted to warn you,' he called over his shoulder. 'For old time's sake.'

'I've got to get away. I must go back to Pieter. He needs me.' She drove to the gatehouse, but the loft was deserted. Feeling strangely apprehensive and let down Liza returned to the homestead.

She decided to see Eleanor again. Maybe one day she would be able to call her Mother, but right now she was Eleanor.

When she entered the east wing, the nurse barred her way. 'She can't be disturbed,' the nurse said. 'She's resting.'

Liza tried to push her aside, but the nurse proved to be surprisingly strong. 'I'm her daughter and I must see her.'

The woman looked menacing, but Liza managed to get past her. Eleanor was out for the count.

'Why did you drug her?' Liza called out.

'Mr Cronjé's orders. He had reason to believe that Mrs Cronjé was not taking her tranquillisers.'

Good heavens, was the place bugged? Liza looked around apprehensively. Yes, Eleanor was right, she decided. These women were guards not nurses. I'll get her away from here soon.

A hundred guests were gathered around trestle tables which had been assembled on the ridge overlooking the sandy beach and the river, near the boma. Liza felt that she had wandered into a world of make-believe – it was so strange to sip ice-cold champagne and gobble smoked salmon and caviare with that other world crowding in on them – the savage roar of lions hunting near by, elephants moving past, watched cautiously by the game rangers. She looked down to where guests were pointing and saw Gertie, their rhino, moving amongst the bulrushes on the opposite shore.

Fortunately there were only a few foreigners present. She knew from experience they were inclined to treat the reserve like a glorified zoo. Only last week they had rescued an Italian about to offer a bun to an elephant. Thankfully they had been in time. The locals kept well within the enclosure lit by flaming torches.

Liza had been longing to see Pieter, but there was no sign of him. She moved from group to group, greeting her friends, trying to appear calm. When she saw Martha and Reg she almost broke down. She felt like a fraud. There would be no wedding and she wanted to tell them this, but she had to tell Tony first and she could not find him.

Glancing at her watch, Liza saw that it was half past nine. It would soon be time for the braai, which was to be held in the boma. She could see the flickering fires where the buck were roasting, but first they were to be entertained.

A long line of Zulu maidens holding flaming torches and wearing bright red robes were moving towards them from the bush, singing a traditional wedding song, their voices blending with the sounds of a bush night. An elephant squealed, too loud and too close, momentarily drowning the song. Liza turned to the game ranger who nodded reassuringly, but fingered his gun. Next a dance team of Zulu warriors leaped amongst them tossing their plumes, kicking up their feet and slapping them hard in split-second timing to the sound of drums and singing. They looked so fierce in the flickering torches.

Dan was beside her. 'You can do it,' he whispered. Father Shepstone put one hand on her shoulder. He had flown up that afternoon and he looked harassed and out of place. It had taken Tony weeks to persuade him to perform the marriage at the game farm and she shuddered to think what he would say when he learned that there would be no ceremony.

'I don't like the bush,' the priest whispered.

Liza took his arm. 'Let's lead the way to the boma,' she suggested.

Soon the guests were sitting around a large circular table under the boma's thatch roof. The food was being heaped on to a large table: spit-roasted wild boar and antelope, mealie pap traditionally cooked with masses of onion and tomato sauce, pumpkin, peas, salads . . . their chef had excelled himself.

Tony was to sit on one side and she on the other. Then she heard his voice as he hurried in, calling out to everyone, cracking jokes and laughing. He lifted his glass. 'To my lovely bride,' he said. Glasses were lifted, someone began to clap, Tony was looking smug and the waiters were placing the plates before the guests. But then there was a sudden hush.

Looking up, Liza saw Eleanor weaving her way unsteadily towards the table wearing a white nightdress.

Tony jumped up and grabbed hold of her. She seemed to be resisting him while he tried to push her out vainly trying not to create too much of a commotion.

Liza hurried towards them and took Eleanor's hand.

'Help me,' Tony whispered. 'She's crazy. We've got to get her out of here. You're not invited,' he told Eleanor, scowling ferociously. 'Go back to your quarters.'

'I should have been invited,' Eleanor said in a loud voice, her mouth stretched into a macabre grimace as she gazed towards the table. 'As the bride's mother I have a right ... but never mind, there will be no marriage. You see,' she turned to Tony and shot him a brief, triumphant smile. 'I have an announcement to make.' She turned towards the table and Liza could see how badly she was shaking. 'Seven years ago,' she said hoarsely. 'Right here in this boma, I shot my husband, Marius. Tony, my lover, helped me to conceal the crime.' She hesitated and turned back to Liza. 'I'm sorry,' she whispered. 'I have lived in hell since then . . . he has used this . . . controlled me . . .' she faltered and looked back towards their guests. 'I just don't want my daughter . . . Liza here is my daughter, you see.' She paused. 'I have served a long sentence,' she said. 'I can't let her . . .'

As Liza wrapped her arms around her mother, Tony wrenched her away. 'She's crazy. She always has been. Don't listen to her.' He gazed around the room, ashen-faced and shaking visibly. 'I must apologise to our guests. My step-mother has been insane for years. She's normally kept under sedation. I don't know what happened. I must take her back to her room. Call the nurses,' Tony snarled at the waiters.

'No, listen to her,' Dan called sharply. 'I was arrested, interrogated and beaten for Cronjé's murder. I have the rifle she used and you hid in the reeds by the river. With this testimony, you'll both be put out of harm's way. I'm going to fetch the police.'

He went outside and they heard the sound of a vehicle's engine roaring off over the veld. After a moment of stunned incredulity, Tony raced after him.

'Gran, help me. Look after Eleanor,' Liza said, thrusting the dazed woman into her grandmother's arms.

As she ran for her Landrover, Pieter came towards her.

'It's madness to let the elephants roam around here. They're drunk on the marula fruit. We've got to drive them off,' he shouted.

'No, no. We've got to save Dan. For God's sake, help me. Dan's fetching the police.'

Pieter drove flat out while Liza tried to explain, panting with the effort. The old causeway was underwater, but they just made it over the river. Then they cut across the bush, trying to head off the vehicles. When they skidded over a steep ridge they saw two sets of headlights behind the next hump. Then the shots began.

Pieter swore. They lurched forward to skid down the steep slope, twisting and turning in a series of bumps, reaching the valley with a sickening impact and swerving through the trees, as they raced up the next rocky ridge.

As they rounded the crest Pieter braked suddenly. Tony was firing wildly at the vehicle ahead of him which was zig-zagging across the road. A shot hit Dan's petrol tank and a second later the jeep exploded. Flaming debris fell around. Liza screamed, but Pieter hung onto her wrist.

'He got out,' he muttered. 'I saw him jump moments before the explosion. He's all right. If he can make it, he'll climb up here.' He flicked his lights on and off.

The bush was blazing around the jeep. Tony braked violently and let off a round of shots in the direction where he had seen Dan run. Then he started the engine again, but it stalled. The flames were racing towards him.

Grabbing his gun, Tony leaped out and ran towards the ridge, firing crazily. He did not notice the elephants flapping their ears and trumpeting with panic as they fled from the fire. One had a baby by her side. She heard the shots and moved in fast. Before Tony could move, her tusk tore through him, with several tons of savage force behind it. It pierced through his flesh and tossed him into the air as if he were a broken twig.

Tony lay on the ground screaming in agony, but his screams of pain changed to cries of terror as he saw through swirls of dust the stampeding herd bearing down on him.

Then there was silence as the elephants melted into the bush as quickly as they had appeared.

Dan emerged from the smoke and collapsed on the ground beside Liza. The three of them sat in shock, gazing after the herd. The ground was damp from recent rains and the fire soon fizzled out. Five minutes later there was only smoke.

'I used to sleep up here in a sack,' Dan said. 'For me, this is where it all began. I used to hang out under that thorn tree there and play my whistle and plan how I would change the world. Funny how things work out. I never dreamed . . .' He broke off and gazed back at the burned out scene.

'Is there nothing left?' Liza whispered, swinging her Land-rover's searchlight over the grass. Two flattened shoes lay amongst some bloody debris.

'I'd better go. Stay here,' Pieter said. He took a tarpaulin from the back of the vehicle and climbed down the ridge, to wrap what was left of the mangled body in this makeshift shroud.

'Please don't look,' Dan said. He got up to go, but Liza clung to his hand.

'Stay with me.'

He nodded. 'Not much anyone can do,' he muttered. He gripped her hand and pressed it hard. 'I wanted to kill Tony, but he destroyed himself.'

'I feel so strange, sort of dreamlike. Nothing seems real.'

Dan put his arm around her. 'It will pass.'

The moon rose bringing an ethereal, tranquil glow that seemed to light the bush with an inner radiance.

Pieter emerged from the shadows looking grim. 'I'll call the police.'

Dan gestured over his shoulder. 'There's someone on the way. I saw the dust trail leaving the house. I must warn you, I called Myers. You see, I knew you were here, but you have a while. They don't know exactly where we are.' Dan got up and switched off the searchlight.

'I'm not running,' Pieter said.

As the implication of his words sank in, Liza's skin crawled. 'What's it all about? You must tell me what's going on.'

'Piet will probably be arrested for murder.'

'No! They can't … How can this be?' She gazed at them imploringly, but there was no comfort in their eyes. She crumpled on the ground and sat hunched up, her cheek rested on her knees. 'What choice did you ever have?' she said in a muffled voice. 'This is horribly wrong.'

'It has been very wrong, but now we're coming right,' Dan said.

A soft breeze wafted over them bringing the scent of moist earth and flowering herbs. A hadeda ibis cried out, and a flock of whistling ducks passed along the river. Then came the mournful cries of scavengers drawn by the scent of blood. A vulture circled overhead and landed heavily on the branches in the thorn tree beside them and then took off again with a heavy beating of wings.

'I feel cheated. I wanted to bring that bastard to trial,' Dan muttered. 'And you, too, Pieter ... or so I thought, but now ... Listen, I can get you across the border – we have an escape route and I'll get you on to it. You'll be able to return in a couple of years. Let's go. Liza can hang on here.'

'The day I let your guys save my life is the day I'd rather be dead,' Pieter said, his voice thick with self-loathing.

Liza gasped. 'Don't say that! Please, Pieter. I love you and I need you. I always will.'

'I'm sorry, Liza. I can't go along with it.'

She swallowed her pleas, understanding that he had to take the lonely road to self-forgiveness, yet suffering for him. She longed to scream and beg and hang on to him, but what good would that do? Instead, she sat shuddering, her stomach quivering with fear, her mind in a turmoil. 'Oh God,' she whispered. 'Help Pieter.'

A searchlight caught them in its beam. The vehicle came straight towards them, bumping over the rough ground until the scavengers stopped sniffing and scratching over the bloody sand and slunk towards the cover of the bush.

The van parked, and three policemen began to search around, shining their torches. Then they shone their beams into the thorn tree where Pieter had hung the remains wrapped in the tarpaulin. They lifted down the bundle and Major Myers climbed up towards them.

'So that's the end of Tony Cronjé?'

'Yes,' Dan muttered.

Myers fumbled for a cigarette.

'Not a pleasant sight. Elephants?' he asked.

'Yes,' Pieter said.

Myers sighed. 'I'd been after the Cronjés for a long time, but when I left the force someone else took over.' He ground out his cigarette. He straightened up and turned to Pieter.

'Captain de Vries. I have a warrant for your arrest for the

murder of the Reverend Ronald Sizani. Are you armed?'

'No.' Pieter stood up shivering.

'Here, take my windcheater,' Dan said, handing it to him. Pieter pulled it over his head.

'Pieter, I love you,' Liza cried out, flinging herself at him.

'Of course you do,' he said. 'You have all my love, too. You've always had it.' He ran his fingers gently down her cheek.

'I'll wait in the van,' Myers said.

'Listen, Liza. We each have to cut our path through the thicket of life. You are on one path, I am on another, and I must keep going on mine. That doesn't stop us from loving each other, and perhaps in some subtle way, our love will keep growing even though we're far apart. Goodbye, my love.'

He turned to Dan and clapped him on the shoulder before climbing down to join Myers.

Liza sat gazing at the car while the headlights slowly faded. Gradually the jackals slunk back and the bush came alive again.

'They can't get away with this,' Liza said. 'I'll get the best lawyers ... the best brains in the country.'

Dan laughed cynically. 'Of course you will,' he said gently. 'But he'll probably be freed quite soon. It's not that justice must be done, only that it must be seen to be done. Don't cry too hard,' he said, hugging her close. 'He can take whatever they deal out to him. He's one tough bastard.'

Chapter 58

The studio never ceased to fascinate Liza however often she went there – the tangle of electric cables, cameras, lights and sound-recording equipment, the hyped-up emotions, the sheer intensity of creative power. Today the tension was tangible – the air hissed and crackled with it. Hans was chain-smoking, Mona was in a piss because her best sound technician was sick, Bill Peters was swearing at his camera as if it could hear him and Ed was so tense he could not keep still. He was scared stiff because he wasn't sure what she was up to.

As usual, most of the programme had been filmed on location, but Liza was to round it off live this afternoon with a short talk which she had kept secret, hence Ed's fears.

She had just been made up by the beautician and she knew she looked good in her dark green linen suit with a shimmering bottle green camisole underneath and a double strand of choker pearls around her throat. She felt good, too, for she had just learned that the government was going to grant amnesty to all political prisoners. Pieter would soon be free.

Michael hurried over. 'You look superb, Liza.' He fussed around, fixing the microphone under the lapel of her suit. 'We'll start running the shots now – thirty seconds to go . . .'

She nodded, unable to banish a sudden shaft of fear. Suddenly her mouth was dry and her palms sweating.

The programme began and she watched herself introducing her theme for the week. 'Yesterday, on June 28, 1991, a law which was passed over forty years ago, came to an end with the repeal of the Population Registration Act. There were no fanfares or trumpets or triumphant marches through the city, although there should have been, because it signalled the end of an evil system that victimised us all. Suddenly we were no longer classified according to the colour of our skins.

'Apartheid was conceived in order to protect our white-dominated parliament from the danger of black voting power. The plan required massive social restructuring and over the past forty years more than three and a half million people were uprooted from their homes and moved around like so many herds of cattle. Entire tribes were exiled from ancestral lands and banished to new areas in order to tidy up the new borders. In urban areas, countless coloured families were deprived of homes they had owned for three or more generations and shifted to "coloured" villages. This master-plan sent people scurrying to their new quarters and firmly labelled them first, second and third class citizens – not different, but inferior.

'But some people defied the system – they would not give in. I call them the shadow people.'

She leaned back and smiled sadly. 'This is death row.' The camera zoomed into a cell where Ralph sat crouched on his bunk. 'Ralph graduated from the toughest school imaginable,' she heard her voice say . . . 'Johannesburg's streets.' The camera focused on a group of skinny boys begging around cars. 'He fled here after continual beatings from his step-father. This is Ralph's story . . .'

The camera switched to a pleasant white suburb in the Orange Free State. 'Meet Ethel de Wet,' she said. 'Here amongst the brawny Free State farmers, Mrs de Wet – blue-eyed, blonde-haired – gave birth to a child of a darker hue, so dark in fact that her husband Willem left her a month later accusing her of infidelity.'

The tear-streaked face of Ethel gazed towards viewers. 'I don't know how it happened,' she sniffed. 'They say Ralph was a throwback to God knows what, but who's to tell which side he came from. I've had six kids since then, all of them white.' She tossed her head defiantly. 'I reckon it was *his* side.'

'So Ralph was beaten until he learned that he didn't belong, for his family could not cope with the trauma of a non-white child,' Liza said.

'Today, Mrs de Wet is a victim of chronic depression resulting in frequent hospitalisation. Ralph turned against society and joined a militant group that aimed to smash apartheid. Later he was convicted of taking part in the shooting at the Honeydew church. We call him a terrorist. He calls himself a Freedom Fighter, and he is hoping for political amnesty.

'This is Martha and Reg Jessop. They have a real and lasting love story and they hung on to it, even though Reg was imprisoned for sleeping with Martha. When he was released they travelled to Swaziland to be married and returned to South Africa where they lived together illegally for twenty-five years, jointly rearing their children – illegally – and even sitting down to eat and sleeping together – illegally. Imagine that – twenty-five years of wondering when they would be caught out just for loving each other.'

As the camera swung to Martha's neat home, with separate entrances into coloured and white areas, the ludicrous double exit seemed to highlight the absurdity of a system based on the colour of a person's skin.

The camera flicked to a new scene, and another, but Liza saw none of this, she was remembering Eleanor who had been let out on bail earlier that morning. Eleanor seemed to welcome her coming trial and their lawyers were confident that she would be committed to an asylum. With good care Liza was sure that her mother would soon be cured and free. Perhaps they would start a new life in Portugal. Liza was flying there next month to sort out her inheritance.

Liza was brought back to the present with a jolt when Mona beckoned to her. A moment of blind panic dried her mouth and set her heart hammering. She hadn't felt this scared since her first programme. She walked on to the set, sat down and rearranged her clothes, tucking the microphone out of sight, and waited for the red light.

She forced a smile. 'Just a few instances of the shadow people around you,' she said. 'They kept out of sight, living a lie. What will they do now? The law is defunct, but what about the racism we carry in our hearts? Is that truly over?

'I want to tell you one last story. It's about a little girl who lived happily with her foster gran until she turned darker than norm, whereupon she was flung out of her school and her home. Knowing that she was to be reclassified and sent to live with the colour-eds she ran away. For a while she became just one of the thousands of homeless children who roam our cities' streets. Luckier than most, she was taken in by a catholic convent, where she was reared and educated. She managed, with skin-lightening creams and a forged ID book, to find a precarious niche amongst the whites of Johannesburg and she fought her way up through freelance jour-nalism until she found the power to hit back at society – to expose the flaws . . . to shame the bigots . . . and to humiliate those bas-tions of a society that she hated so much. But all the time she was so afraid that someone would expose her for what she was – second-class, unworthy, an imposter.

'That little girl was Liza Frank – yes me!

'My power to expose was my weapon and I used it because I hated . . . I hated the village that threw me out . . . I hated having to lie and cheat and feel second-class, I hated having to act a role and keep people apart from me in case they asked questions. But most of all I hated myself.

'Now it's all over, but the wounds are deep and it might take decades to heal them.

'Unless . . .'

The image of Dan Tweneni flashed on to the screen.

'This is Dan Tweneni, who has been a guest on my programme before,' she said. 'He is the Transvaal leader of the ANC and the son of Victor Tweneni, the famous human rights activist who died on Robben Island. He has a message for all of us.'

Dan was pictured standing in front of Nosisi's shack in KaNgwane.

'I want to tell you about an African concept,' he began haltingly. 'It's called *Ubuntu* and it means togetherness and mutual caring for each other – in a family, or a tribe, or a nation. It could even mean loving each other. *Ubuntu* is one of our oldest traditions. It's something we live by. But I believe that *Ubuntu* exists between our different cultures here and that it always has done. For instance, take a child's love for its black nanny, or an old family retainer for his employers, or the patient for his nurse. It has been taboo to feel for each other, so we pushed our feelings out of sight.

'You whites have no word for such a concept as *Ubuntu*, but I offer ours to you. It is one of the few things you can learn from us, for we have learned so much from you. Take the word and live out *Ubuntu*, as we must, for this is our only hope of survival.'

The programme was over. Liza stood up. She wanted to get out into the fresh air. She heard her signature tune and then the screen was switched off. The lights were dimmed and there was a long silence.

'Okay, folks,' she said. 'I guess I'll get off home.'

She grabbed her bag and picked her way towards the end of the set. Michael began clapping, and Andrea, too. Mona and Bill stood in front of her barring her way. They, too, began to clap, solemnly and slowly, their eyes locked with hers. She felt her throat close with emotion and tears pricked her eyes.

'Don't,' she whispered. 'Don't be kind.'

'It's not kindness,' Mona said. 'Admiration, perhaps, and affection. Congratulations, Liza. You are the bravest girl I ever met.'

Ed produced a magnum of champagne. How had he ever guessed? 'Oh, Ed,' she whispered. She felt such a strong surge of affection for him.

'The switchboard is jammed,' Andrea called out. 'Amazing reaction. Just about every viewer wants to congratulate you.'

Liza smiled and sipped her champagne, feeling calm and at peace with herself, knowing that by accepting herself at last she had won a personal triumph against her own self-imposed prejudices.

Epilogue

On August 5, 1991, the cell door swung open and Pieter found himself staring at the prison governor. 'You are free to go,' he said. 'The government has granted amnesty for all political prisoners serving sentences or awaiting trial. You have been unconditionally released as from now.

'There's a Major Myers waiting in my office. He wishes to speak to you. Will you need the assistance of a welfare officer?'

'No, thanks.'

Pieter went through the rigmarole of being handed his clothes and watch. He had been arrested wearing a sweater and shorts and he stalked into the governor's office barefooted and shivering with cold.

'Justice was done, but it was tempered with mercy,' he said. 'Everyone is satisfied and you're free to start your life again. Do you need any assistance – cash? Or transport?'

Pieter frowned at him, trying to pull himself together sufficiently to make his plans. He didn't have much time.

'I'd like a lift to the nearest bank. There are some details ... A personal matter.' He broke off.

He resisted Myers' attempts to get him to talk about his future. Half an hour later he was dropped on the pavement in Pretoria outside the main branch of his bank.

Myers attempted to shake his hand, but Pieter avoided this. 'I want you to know,' Myers began, 'that you hit home with your gibe about my feelings for my own kind. You see, in my opinion . . .'

Pieter put one hand on his shoulder. 'Save your breath. Your opinion is of no interest to me whatsoever, major,' he said. 'It seems that I must be my own judge, jury and executioner after all.' He disappeared into the crowd.

It was midnight that night when Sam heard the shot and rushed upstairs to the loft. Pieter was lying on the floor in a pool of blood, a bible on his chest. Despite the shattered right side of his head he was muttering: 'God forgive me, God forgive me,' over and over. He died before the ambulance arrived.

Long after his body had been taken away, Sam sat crying on his bed. 'He never stood a chance,' Sam muttered. 'Just as my Victor never stood a chance. The hatred destroyed them both.'

So who must God forgive? Sam wondered later that night as he sat huddled in Pieter's room. The young baas? Or the fifty thousand young men like him who had been turned into killers? Or the military who trained him? Or the system that moulded them? Or the beast that God created in the heart of every man?

Tears streaming down his cheeks, he decided to pray, but he got on to his knees with difficulty for he was old now.

'*Cast no blame,*' he muttered to God. '*Pieter was the finest boy I ever knew.*'

SUMMER HARVEST

Madge Swindells

Set between 1938 and 1968 in a land where gruelling poverty rubs shoulders with remarkable opulence, and moving from the Cape to London and the West Coast of America, *Summer Harvest* is a family saga in the finest tradition.

At the heart of the story is Anna, a woman as strong and passionate as she is ambitious, who fights her way up from near destitution to become one of the Cape's most prominent and powerful businesswomen. Only love eludes her. For Simon – a poor farmer when they marry – has too much masculine pride to stand on the sidelines while Anna plunders her way to a success that threatens tragedy and loss.

'A spellbinding read' Sarah Harrison

SONG OF THE WIND

Madge Swindells

Marika Magos is a woman whose heart has been turned to stone by the ravages of war-torn Europe and whose passions burn with a bitter desire for revenge. Even the sweet promise of a love affair with a handsome Swiss immigrant turns to ashes when she learns that his name and papers are false, used only to protect his German identity in the final days of World War II.

In a journey that takes Marika from the diamond-rich canyons of South Africa and the glittering high-fashion world of London to the glamorous playgrounds of Switzerland and a drama-filled courtroom in Paris, *Song of the Wind* tells a powerful tale of romance, adventure and intrigue . . .

'Irresistible . . . keeps your emotions trembling over hundreds of pages'
Mail on Sunday

'Just right!'
Woman's World

SHADOWS ON THE SNOW

Madge Swindells

The Winter Olympics are a prestigious display of glamour, courage and public splendour. They are also, though discreetly, a huge merchandising operation involving talent, technique – and flesh and blood.

MEGAN CARROLL is the ultimate agent to the sparkling stars, a whiz kid who knows just what she wants.

NIKKI PETROVA, exquisite and ice-cool, a Russian whose figure-skating audacity captivates audiences everywhere.

JACQUI DOUGLAS, headstrong American downhill skier, whose recklessness is such that her racing seems like suicide postponed.

Megan can take them both to fame and fortune – at a price.

But there is a dangerous distraction – an enigmatic Scots scriptwriter of magnetic personality. Megan cannot afford to get involved. But will she care, when the chips are down?

0 7515 0707 5

THE CORSICAN
WOMAN
Madge Swindells

Sybilia turned as if sleepwalking and, trancelike, walked down the stone steps to the living room. She shuddered as she took the rifle from the peg on the wall, but after only a moment's hesitation, she loaded it and went outside.

Sybilia Rocca is beautiful, gentle and intelligent. But she is also Corsican and in her blood run the intense passions of her race – the passions that drive her to shoot her father-in-law before stunned witnesses in the small square of a sea-swept town set high on a Corsican cliffside.

What is the terrible secret – the dark act of treachery twenty years before – that compels Sybilia to carry out her vendetta? Virtually everyone in the village knows, yet the unwritten law of their culture keeps them silenced. And now Sybilia is fighting for her life, gripped by a passion strong enough to destroy . . .

'Madge Swindells captures beautifully the flavour of Corsica and its turbulent inhabitants'
Evening Standard

☐	Summer Harvest	Madge Swindells	£5.99
☐	Song of the Wind	Madge Swindells	£5.99
☐	Shadows on the Snow	Madge Swindells	£5.99
☐	The Corsican Woman	Madge Swindells	£5.99
☐	Edelweiss	Madge Swindells	£4.99

Warner Books now offer an exciting range of quality titles by both established and new authors which can be ordered from the following address:

Little, Brown and Company (UK),
P.O. Box 11,
Falmouth,
Cornwall TR10 9EN.

Alternatively you may fax your order to the above address.
Fax No. 01326 317444.

Payments can be made as follows: cheque, postal order (payable to Little, Brown and Company) or by credit cards, Visa/Access. Do not send cash or currency. UK customers and B.F.P.O. please allow £1.00 for postage and packing for the first book, plus 50p for the second book, plus 30p for each additional book up to a maximum charge of £3.00 (7 books plus).

Overseas customers including Ireland, please allow £2.00 for the first book plus £1.00 for the second book, plus 50p for each additional book.

NAME (Block Letters) ....

....

ADDRESS ....

....

....

☐ I enclose my remittance for ....

☐ I wish to pay by Access/Visa Card

Number ☐☐☐☐☐☐☐☐☐☐☐☐☐☐☐☐

Card Expiry Date ☐☐☐☐